DONALD NEWLOVE has been a reporter, a book reviewer, and has written short stories for *Esquire, New York*, and *Evergreen Review*. He is the author of the widely acclaimed novel THE PAINTER GABRIEL, which *Time* has called, "One of the best fictional studies of madness, descent, and purification that any American has written since Ken Kesey's ONE FLEW OVER THE CUCKOO'S NEST." He lives in New York City where he is a contributing editor of *Esquire*. He recently completed a novel entitled ETERNAL LIFE, which will be published by Avon in 1979.

SWEET ADVERSITY

DONALD NEWLOVE

Embodying the author's
final revisions for
Leo & Theodore and *The Drunks.*

A BARD BOOK/PUBLISHED BY AVON BOOKS

AVON BOOKS
A division of
The Hearst Corporation
959 Eighth Avenue
New York, New York 10019

Published by arrangement with E. P. Dutton & Co., Inc.
Library of Congress Catalog Card Number:
ISBN: 0-380-38364-0

First Bard Printing, August, 1978

Printed in the U.S.A.

AUTHOR'S NOTE

THIS one-volume edition of *Sweet Adversity,* a new title, embodies my final revisions for my Siamese twin novels *Leo & Theodore* and *The Drunks.* Should a new hardcover edition appear someday, or other paperback editions, the book now in hand is the text I wish kept alive. Avon's *Sweet Adversity* fulfills my hopes for my story about Leo-Teddy, and may the original Saturday Review Press hardcover editions (never reprinted) of *Leo & Theodore* and *The Drunks* now be laid to rest. I hope that these two volumes will never again be printed separately, by Saturday Review Press/Dutton, by Avon or by any other reprint house. The story loses scope and force when halved into two books. Should Saturday Review Press/ Dutton, my original publisher, ever be moved to reissue my novel in hardcover (and may that happen!), I trust they will set type afresh from this Avon paperback. And should my old publisher someday resell my Siamese twins novel to another reprint house, after the Avon edition goes out of print, may that reprint be set from this Avon edition. My original texts, as published by Saturday Review Press in 1972 and 1974, are now forever CANCELLED and do not represent my final thoughts about my twins.

Many readers ask me if I plan to write another book about the twins. I keep mulling over something I call *The Higher Power,* which may or may not appear someday. For now, let my twinless novel *Eternal Life* (1978) stand in place of the as yet unwritten book, since some of my friends in *Sweet Adversity* reappear in *Eternal Life.*

My thanks to Robert Wyatt of Avon for setting type anew (instead of photographing the original editions) and giving me a fresh chance to clear away the deadwood and more mindless make-believe of the early editions.

Reader, this is a readable book! Go the distance and you'll be happy you stayed—the ending is worth it.

My especial thanks to Byron Dobell, my editor during his various captaincies at *Esquire,* Saturday Review Press (then McCall), *Book Week* and *New York* magazine. His style suggestions add greatly to the clearness and reader-welcoming openness I hope *Sweet Adversity* now has. Entering the privacy of Siamese twins does not require a private language. His encouragement, as well as that of Susan Stanwood, my former Saturday Review Press editor, is the stuff that books are made on.

And to all my friends in the Fellowship of the Sun, from whom I have received a second life, where would I be without you?

Donald Newlove
August 5, 1977
Cape Cod

LEO & THEODORE

To Dr. Nathaniel David Mttron Hirsch

One's-Self I Sing—a simple, separate Person.

—Walt Whitman

Is there no exit from the dream boy's jail?

—Jack McManis,
Autobiography of Narcissus

LEO-Teddy under gas-blue Lake Erie sky where Daddy rows past the nightline searching for sturgeon. Gray waves and white glow on skyburning wave. Daddy, a whale! Teddy cries and the twins scream down at a sturgeon circling the rowboat. The long fish hovers by the oarlock while Durwood stands with the gaff. Quickly he drives pole under snout and hooks up through mouthroof and then five-foot whale beats in the boat white belly up and Durwood drives knife into heart and splits the fish in a stroke from throat to vent. Leo and Teddy gape at bowels slipping overboard and there in the wide cavity spills gleaming gray caviar. Daddy grins blissfully, rinsing his bloody blade in waves, and sheathes it. Stars rise on the watergardens. They row home, a red railroad lamp burning on the bow in the night.

They spend a summer at Great-great-grandfather Alford's farm on the lake. Great-skulled and shrunken, he is ninety-two and all day long rocks by his window, clear blue eyes in the Erie *Times.* An old man in a golden oak rocker, old rag rugs on living-room floor and by doorways. A blue granite cistern by kitchen sink-pump, crazy-quilt beds and each bedstand with a pitted blue granite washbowl. Their father's father's father's father, whose spine still carries their being.

Such fields to run, orchards to search. Blacksnake sunning on tree trunk. They play so hard they forget mother and city. Through fallen pears to stony lake shore. Vast morning lawns by the Danner mansion, stone walls to walk, waves to crawl. They swim the first time they light on a wave. They go out too far and rest in the rough waters. Stumble home blue at supper, drained and waterlogged.

Daddy cooks for railroad gangs on the Nickel Plate

line, when he works. Free days he earns spare cash catching sturgeon. He drinks in bars and plays pool. In a Ripley bar he shows them a magic trick. He dips a lighted kitchen match deep into whiskey and lifts the blue flame out of the shot-glass unquenched. Marvel at the blue-dancing spirit on the glass!

They lived only one summer with Durwood—Daddy and Mother kept apart. Sometimes he plays "Chinatown, My Chinatown" on the saxophone. Hocked, the horn's never seen again.

Daddy's flat wooden rifle, given him as a boy, thrills them. They fill with the rifle's power and play from sunrise until sunset. No toy matches this cutout. Daddy is careful they don't lose it and every evening he stores it downcellar. He reveres his rifle. It was once his great-grandfather's and is still straight as the old man's spine.

Running, their flesh is heaven. Forgotten goddess arriving in a Franklin touring car driven by Spike and Red, Mother comes from the city to take them to her new apartment. Red is a plumber and Spike wears derby and cigarette. Daddy says good-bye and, eyes strained, takes their rifle downcellar guiltily. The twins fill the backseat and read pictures in Red's comicbooks. Spike's green velvet upholstery puffs with dust. They never live with Daddy again. His bad cough carries him into the county hospital.

They live in their new apartment with Mother and Red's girlfriend, Carrie. First morning home, they are given bowls of buttered toast and warm milk and sent to school by themselves to start first grade. As they leave the porch, morning sunlight burns their great chestnut tree. Mother and Carrie wave hope from an open window of their upstairs flat. The twins enroll and find their way home alone.

"We're boys now," Leo says.

"We can cross the street!" Teddy says.

They smash open spiky green chestnuts, sometimes surprised by two or three glossy fruits in the bur. Caterpillars spin in bark crevices. Orange ladybirds creep polkadotted on palm, fly away home.

On Saturday morning they are given twenty cents and sent up Parade Street to find the Regent moviehouse by themselves. Out front, a long line of kids buys tickets.

Strange. As they go in they hear a sea of screaming kids and see . . . a magic picture. Burn 'em up Barnes, a speedway racer burns rubber. They sit front row. Suddenly Barnes's racer twists hurtling upsidedown off track—and the picture ends. Two more movies shown, kids get up to leave, *Burn 'em up Barnes* is back! The twins sit waiting and again his racer catches fire and hurtles off track—and the picture ends. They marvel. Going home they reason that movies are dreams. Above nature.

"What happened?" Teddy asks.

"He must have died," Leo says.

Next Saturday they return and Barnes now leaps from the racer before it bursts wheels leaping and the house erupts with whistles screams cheers stamping victory.

"I knew he'd get out of it," Teddy says.

"Well, I didn't know how," Leo says.

"He just jumped out!"

Going home they glow, shouting plot into each other's face.

"The hero's always saved," Teddy says. They nod knowingly.

Columbus Day holiday they run to school and find it closed. And wander through Erie, down to the docks. They find an odd yellowbrown lake, flat and marshy. Go wading, shoes on. Water not deep enough to swim in. They get home late, legs filthy.

"Where have you been?" Stella asks. "My heavens! never go there again, my sons. You've been wading in what goes down the toilet!"

Mother works as hatcheck girl at the City Club, and late evenings they have Smiling Alice for babysitter. Fat Smiling Alice, bucktoothed and feebleminded, leaves as soon as they fake sleep. Then they sleep. One night Smiling Alice takes them out into the bluepeople to a giant bingo hall filled with hundreds of players at picnic tables. Each twin has a card and Alice tells them how to play. First game, Leo gulps and cries bingo to Alice, who shrieks. They win groceries. Now Leo and Teddy burn to play and soon Teddy cries bingo. *Ohhh!* the hall groans hugely, wounded under layered blue smoke. Night's end, Leo wins again. They leave, plunged under groceries, confirmed as born winners.

One free day, wandering past smashed factory windows, they cut through a stony lot and find great packing crates with bums sleeping inside. Bay rum bottles litter the gravel. A Lucky Tiger label shows a barber dousing a man's head.

"Red and Spike drink rum," Teddy says.

"But this is for hair," Leo says.

Sunlight bares loss, ruin, filth and flies in the hard lot. They sense deep mystery in these shameful scummed bottles.

The twins come to a great stone drinking fountain with a stone trough for horses. Warned not to drink!

"Dog germs cause humpback," Teddy says. Knowing nods.

They watch a little old ragdealer halt his horse and cart and drink from the impure fountain, back hunched, neck hooked like a vulture's.

Bums, humpbacks, warnings.

Still in first grade, stricken with scarlet fever. Mumps. Tonsillitis. A week at Hamot Hospital, one morning they are given ether. Greengolden lawns of the Danner manse fill them—tonsils plucked out. Before leaving, their band is pricked, response measured. The cartilage joining their thighs also joins their blood. Stella tells them in their bed at home, "You will always be together, my sons, for the rest of your lives. But keep hope and stick in there so I can be proud of you. I'll be right behind you." They fail first grade.

In school the twins walk with an arm about each other's shoulder, their band in a khaki sleeve. They ignore stares. Share one desk. Stella asks very little about school and only signs their report cards.

Teddy tells her, "We answer more questions than anyone else."

"We run twice as fast," Leo says.

"That's because you're sure-footed, my sons."

"We feel like a horse when we run," Leo says.

But left behind in first grade! Lining up with their friends going into second, then turned back to the first grade room. They breathe heavily, hearts scorched. Lofty first graders now, they hurl out the alphabet backwards.

"ZYXWVUTSRQPONMLKJIHGFEDCBA!"

They move to a flat over the Mayflower Bar, a block from the City Club, without Carrie and Smiling Alice. They forget their sister Millie's face. She lives with Anna, Durwood's mother. One day Stella sends them crosstown for a visit. Millie's out back burning trash in a barrel—four years older than the twins, straight brown hair, wire-frame glasses. She eyes them coming up the cinder path.

"Mother sent us," Leo says. "We're your brothers."

"Oh. Hi." She stares. "You here for the day?"

"Sure," Leo says. "Hear about us moving?"

"We moved from Jones School up across State Street!" Teddy says.

"You did? Maybe we'll see more of you now. Come in and say hello to Anna. Remember her? She's your Grandmother Alford."

"Oh, merciful heavens!" Anna cries seeing them. Thin and elderly, nerves tearing her heart. She wears a green eyeshade, rests in bed with crossword puzzles under a lightbulb. Rooms not as picked up as Stella's. Anna drinks Coke and aspirin, her eyes pinpointed, scolds Millie, slaps her, but laughs with love for the twins.

"Mark my words, if you boys hadn't been born the very day the stock market crashed, you'd be the most famous kids in this godforsaken outhouse of the Roosevelts." The twins shake as if trapped with a wasp. "You'd be on the stage by now and we'd all be on Easy Street! By God, can you dance yet? *No!*—well, it's not too late yet. I'd have you on that stage faster than you can sing 'God Damn the King.' You kids have never had the advantages of publicity. Let me see your hands. I pray you'll be surgeons someday. I was a nurse for twenty years and believe me you have surgeons' fingers. And I can see you have *heads* on your shoulders. Dear God, it's a crime what you're missing! Have you ever heard of Mr. Robert Ripley? He runs a traveling 'Believe It or Not' and he'd pay *thousands* just to show you off. Thousands! That bastard would pay through the nose. Did you hear what happened to the Dionne quints? Canada made them wards of the country. Those little shits won't have to lift a finger the rest of their lives! Hah, we'd be on Easy Street! Well, you'll go into the professions. You're not cut out to be carnival bozos. Remember that! You rascals are bright little whipper-snappers. Maybe that sonofabitch Ripley can use you in his daily cartoon—and we'll *damned* well see that he pays for the rights!"

No play during Anna's harangues. Millie bites her lips in the corner.

* * *

They live in the heart of town, just turncorner to the endless party on the City Club's matchbooks. Stella's male visitors. Some are cops. She's chased by a trim-mustached married man, Jim Deal, who kisses her and is sometimes found kneeling at the couch, clasping her palm. The twins see Stella for breakfast and supper and before she goes to work. Famous among visitors for their movie news, given dimes, running off to the Shea's. Still six, they pester Stella for more movie money, learn to sneak in exits. Fallasleep quickly before Mother leaves, then up and dress, out the halldoor. Streetmeteors with small plans working through crowds to the yellowbulb palaces. Sometimes they steal dimes from Mother's change purse while she dresses. Or milk a visitor. They beg with great heart on the street. Racing scholars, rarely home before twelve.

Great event!—Thurston the Magician opens with Sally Rand the Fan Dancer. Leo-Teddy knows nothing of Sally Rand, the white angel billed with the dark forces of Thurston.

Outside the theater for the first evening show, begging corner to corner. Stills of Sally with white ostrich feathers. *Bitten!*—what white deep dream hides beneath those feathers? Slouching in first row of the vast vaudeville house, their band past the armrest. During Laurel and Hardy a man asks if they'd like to help Thurston. He takes them backstage and stuffs colored silks down their backs. They go back to their seats in wonder. After the acrobats and hornplaying bicyclist, Thurston rises through flashpowder in black cape and tails. And pulls a longeared white rabbit from his hat! They hope this is real magic. Surprised hearts beating, they are called as volunteers. We're finally *on,* Anna! They glide so smoothly no one sees they are joined. Thurston pulls scarves from their shirts, the twins quicken to stone. They'd forgotten the silks in their hope of magic. Now Thurston charms their eyes with his long fingers, turns the 'sleeping' twins to the audience and stands with his back to them. Calls out questions, casts the twins their answers under his breath. They descend to their seats to great applause, flushed.

Sally Rand dances in red and blue limelights, full-length white ostrich fans quivering.

"I don't like dancing," Teddy whispers.

"But this is all right," Leo says. They nod.

They sit stunned by her last Statue of Liberty pose,

silver G-string, naked bosom, blue-sparkling eyes fixed above waves of whistling. They sit through the whole show twice and leave without faith in Thurston.

Tales of the nightowls are carried back to Stella and soon Smiling Alice is back. But bucktooth, chinless, bingo-loving Alice is outwitted by their openmouth fakery of sleep and takes to leaving at nine-thirty. One night she leaves at nine. They're dressed and at the door before finding it locked. They open a back window and see a garage roof across the cement walk.

"That's not far," Leo says.

"We can make it," Teddy says.

They poise on the black windowsill, then leap, landing on a dark roof and hurt their band. Lie quietly, wait for the throb to dim out—then hang from garage roof and drop. Like wind to the Warner!—but the box office is closed. Small fingers worm open the back exit. Four-footed shadow gliding backstage past moonglaring screen and drapes by front row. Crawling on carpet to nearest seats. Slumping up onto movie spines, even their heads not seen. Bad luck, a musical, oh mush. *Nerves.* A big dance number bursts and Eleanor Powell taps in sequin top hat and black pelvis-cut satin, kicks head-high, tattoos on jet black like a lovemad cricket.

"Maybe I like dancing," Teddy says.

"Oh, I'd like to sit through this again," Leo says.

Lights up. Leave nervously through redcarpet lobby. No one speaks to them though it's after eleven. Dawdle home, only two blocks, eying plastic sundaes in Woolworth's window. Stills and posters of coming movies at the Strand. Circle past Shea's and back by still another theater, where *Frankenstein* opens. Saturday they'll catch it. Past Mayflower Bar and up hallway steps . . . door locked.

"We *forgot!*" Teddy cries.

"Let's see the back window."

Black window over darkshadowed garage. They pile boxes and garbage cans against the garage, climb up to the roof. Face the window across deep pavement. Suck a lungful of hope, count together, and leap. Their arms lock over the sill. The great crab-shadow hauls itself over, falls on its heads. Undressing, strongly uplifted by their room, straight to sleep. Saved!

Next morning to the Regent for Clyde Beatty's jungle serial, then home to supper and strike Stella's purse for late *Frankenstein*. Smiling Alice watches Mother make up at her vanity, twins abed. Stella's face heartshaped in the powdery oval mirror, she leans into light and draws thin black hoops over bare brows. Cupid's bow on upper lip. The twins see her, torch aloft and toga in folds, her chaste, lungfilling, deathless beauty, the trademark for Columbia Pictures.

"Stella," says Smiling Alice, "can you lend me a dollar till Monday?"

Mother searches her change purse, usually bulging with tips. "Hm!—I thought I had more than this."

Alice sits on the bed. Their eyes closed quickly. "Why, they're asleep already," she says. Breathing deeply, blank angels.

She leaves at nine and again they leap onto the dark garage roof. One block and down to front row. Surprisingly, *Bride of Frankenstein* comes on. Lord Byron and Percy and Mary Shelley sit around a Swiss chalet on a stormy night telling horror stories. Mary starts. The monster's cracked skull rises from slime under a burnt windmill. Lipless mouth, black eyes lidded with slaughter. A mad doctor keeps a tiny king and queen under belljars. He talks casually with the monster in a webbed cellar tomb, shares his meat and wine. The happy monster slobbers from the bottle, gurgling, *Good, good!*

"This is the best story I ever saw," Leo says.

"I love it," Teddy says.

The wounded monster is consoled by a blind hermit who gives him bread, and fiddles sad music. The monster weeps at the beautiful song, moving the twins. Soon he strangles Dr. Frankenstein into making a mate for him. Her wrapped body lifted to tower roof, awakened by lightning, unbandaged upright. Electric queen, hair powered upward! The twins pinned to their seats, blissful, nodding. She sees the monster. *Screams!*

"She doesn't *like* him!" Teddy whispers. Leo sighs.

Dr. Frankenstein escapes as the monster blows up his bride and tower. *"We—belong—dead."*

Lights up. They sit stunned with sadness. Get up to leave—but the theater's still full. They sit again in wonder. *Dracula!* What luck—although they've never heard of him.

After the vampire movie, they rise again and still the audience keeps seated. One-twenty by the theater clock.

What's happening now? Teddy mugs. Leo mugs being punchdrunk.

Frankenstein, the original! They freeze to their seats. How the monster first got sewn together!

They leave at two-thirty as the monster burns in a windmill they know he escapes from. Streets empty. Drained, they walk home slowly, making up dangers. By a bank a police car with two of Stella's pals pulls up. Cops walk them home and one goes into the City Club for the door key. A cop puts them to bed, they pass out. Next morning they confess their escape route to Stella the Lawgiver.

Within a week Mother breaks off with her married boyfriend and marries a fat German twice her age who manages a vast German beerhouse and club uptown. Stella, Millie and Leo-Teddy all move into their first house together . . . with Hermann Fuehrer.

STELLA thinks Leo and Teddy are a wonder like the stars. She makes secret visits twice yearly to an elder spiritualist now living in a lakeshore cottage. She never mentions these to Hermann, who is violent.

Since Leo and Teddy first crawled, she has turned them away from each other to stretch their band. The band is now about four inches long, quite thick, gristly on top, and bends. Left-handed, his heart on the right, Leo mirrors Teddy, who is right-handed (and left-hearted), though the twins breathe as one with single heartbeats, hungers, energies, sleepings. Asleep they have one skin. Both feel. But awake, should a twin burn or cut himself, as when Teddy split his thumb-cushion on a hunting knife in Woolworth's, his brother feels no pain. They focus as one being, their inner eyes weaker than the outer, their inner legs more favored in walking than their unjoined legs. They never trip when running, though they fell once when hurrying down the back stairs, screaming as they fell, *Help! Murder! Police!* One falls, the other catches. Running, they hold earth like a horse, rarely look down. They juggle balls, stones—on their way home from the grocery a can of beans once balanced on a tree limb, rolled, then dropped, gashing Leo's scalp. Leo an inch shorter, wears thick soles to keep height with Teddy. When Stella watches their four hands at building blocks or domino castles, hears them sing backward alphabet in waltz time for visitors, backroll room by room all over the apartment, her faith in their future takes strength. Leo and Teddy move with magnetic likeness, climbing furniture, falling onto bed or couch (standing on the foot of their bed they cry, *The Last Days of* POMPEII-I-I-I! and crash like statues into the dust), and forsee each other so nimbly that they join every move with sweet balance and feel finished and whole.

Stella, a country girl whose mother died in her thirties, took her mother's place as cook and housekeeper for their vigorous family. Her father is hard as God, fully as hard as he's been taught. Raped by Durwood, she marries him and shares her farmgirl's strength with her children. Thin Durwood gives his shrewdness. Durwood's country health fails in the city. Diabetes. Tuberculosis. A county ward, he drinks whenever out of the hospital, rooms with his sick mother, Anna, kills time on corners and in pool halls. He gives Stella nothing, without fail, and beats her, without fail. One day while she suckles the twins, his kick to her chin leaves a scar. Kept black and blue, she always stays in on holidays. All his radiance goes into fishing. He combs his dark devil's peak over piercing green eyes in pale-tan highcheekbones. The twins throb loyally, see him but little. Very little. Millie inherits his nerves, and deepest love. The twins are heart-property of Stella. She is not bitter despite giant despair.

Millie sees her schoolwork outshone and learns with a jolt that they are not to be beaten at anything. Aside from their fudgemaking, Millie avoids Leo and Teddy. The twins see few movies. They visit the library and natural history museum, play outdoors, and trade comics. Millie loves Anthony Adverse, whose father owns a shoe repair store, and sometimes comes home weeping and wails on her bed for hours.

"What happened?" Teddy asks.

"An accident?" Leo asks.

"It was *Janet G-G-Gaynor!*" Millie wails.

The twins harden.

"What was it about?" Leo asks.

"Ohh!" Millie sobs into her pillow. "J-J-Janet Gaynor becomes a big movie star and her husband's a BIG DRUNK and he finally walks into the ocean and drowns!"

"Why's he do that?" Teddy asks.

"Because he isn't *good enough* for her!"

Leo groans at Teddy, who smiles wistfully.

"Why doesn't he just stop drinking instead of walk into the ocean?" Teddy asks.

"I don't know—he *tries!*—but can't help himself! Oh leave me alone, you're too young to understand!"

"What a measly movie," Leo says.

Millie jumps up, pushes them out, slams the bedroom door. The twins ta-ta the fanfare to Paramount News at her door.

"Someday you'll both know what it's all about!" Millie rages from her bed. *"But I'm not going to be the one to tell you!"*

Stung by her passion, they go out after supper for a walk. "Your turn," Teddy says.

"Let's go up the hill," Leo says.

Teddy sighs under rocks. "You're hopeless," he says.

They cut crosslots wordlessly. Leo loves Patricia Van Allen, the richest girl in second grade, who wears a legbrace, and he's drawn to her windows. On the hill they creep up Patty's drive to peer into her dark bedroom.

"She's not in bed yet," Leo whispers. They tiptoe backyard and around house. Slowly Leo creeps onto the front porch and stares through the doorwindow while Teddy keeps lookout and holds Leo's hand. "Gosh, they've taken her brace off," Leo whispers. "She'll fall!"

Patty talks with her father. Leo's eyes sting with her brown spitcurls.

Back on the walk, he throws gravel lightly onto the porch. And again. Mr. Van Allen scuffs onto the porch, cleaning it. Twins behind tree. He goes back in.

"She still doesn't know we're here!" Leo says. They go back up the bedroom drive. "Pa-atty!" Leo whispers while Teddy claps his own mouth in embarrassment. Leo fingers the screen softly. "She's not here or she's not answering," he says.

They go off. Moonlit backyard. Cross the fence into another backyard chalkblue with lilies.

"I'll write her a note!" Leo cries.

Teddy groans.

"Maybe take her to the Regent on Saturday."

"What if I don't want to go with her?" Teddy says.

"I'll pay you back."

"Heck," Teddy says. "What am I worried about? You don't dare write a lovenote."

"Don't I! We'll just see about that, young man," Leo says.

"Look, the Regent's a bad neighborhood. Invite her to our birthday party."

"Would you rather kiss Shirley Temple or Patty?" Leo asks. "Seriously."

"Shirley Temple!" Teddy says.

They comet home, arguing by starlight.

Leo gives Patty a note at recess and later tags her home. She pivots on her brace at the pipe-iron rail to her house. Leo runs by. "Hi! Can you come?"

"I'll have to ask my mother." Patty glows at them.

Teddy prickles with Leo.

The birthday party. Blue suits, bow ties. Millie with Anthony. Stella sits aside while Millie leads spin-the-bottle. The twins tremble.

A dark closet for post office. Millie chooses Patty as first postmistress and Patty goes into the closet. Millie hands a letter to Teddy. He blazes. "I've got a letter!" Teddy cries.

Leo wants to pound Teddy for having the letter.

"Who's it for?" Patty asks in the dark.

"Not yet, Patty," Millie coaches.

"Oh," Patty says. "Do you have a *stamp* on it?"

"Yes I have!" Teddy sings as Leo burns.

Stella's eyes raygun their blood to bubbles.

"What's your name?" Patty asks.

"Guess!" Teddy cries.

"Leo!" Patty cries.

The children roar. Stella whoops.

"Guess again!" Teddy cries falsetto.

"Teddy!" Patty cries.

"And it's for you-hoo!" he singsongs and goes into the

closet with Patty, Leo closing the door. Teddy kisses Patty.

"Might as well have mine now too," Leo says. He kisses Patty.

The twins go out of the closet, Teddy grinning, Leo veiled. They sit, and Teddy hands Leo the letter. "I've got a letter!" Leo croaks.

"Go to it, young man!" Stella laughs.

"Do you have a stamp on it?" Patty asks in the dark.

"Yes I have!" Leo says.

"Who's it for?" Patty asks.

"It's for *you-hoo!*" Leo singsongs and goes into the closet, closing the door.

Teddy stands waiting in shame as if slapped. Leo the thief steals his extra kiss while Teddy prickles and prickles. They stand still. Leo leaves. Teddy looks back at Patty's hurt eyes. He has passed her by without stealing a second kiss as Leo did. Leo can't swallow his roaring grin.

Stella watches her spirit and matter at play in a four-legged dream.

Let there be dirges for Hermann the Two-fisted Sudsbelter, let walrus-fat brewmasters dirge Guzzler! Hunter! Puncher! Thumper! Grunter!

Balding bear-lump with arched broken nose, shining lidded brown eyes hungry and drained, purple mouth slit to the ears. Dirge barrelbelly dirge beerpisser dirge wurstglutton dirge krautgas dirge kicktable dirge swatpalm dirge punchfist. A hamhanded killer at home, beloved in office.

Saturday night and Sunday afternoon and evening spent at Hermann's three-story family beerbarn, a good racecourse for twins. Great top floor for meals, cards, dominos, ground floor a sixty-foot bar, slot machines, cardtables, meal hall, basement bowling alleys, duckpin lanes, and small bar. The club serves Erie's Germans, the office door reads HERMANN FUEHRER, Director. (*Honored in office!*) Dancing *Gemütlichkeit* to violin, accordion, and piano, pinochle tourneys, slow-motion cribbage battles for the aged. Old checker players cannot beat either twin. Leo and Teddy can't play each other, they rehash too many moves, take back jumps, play only for pure skill. In the basement they become duckpin masters, famous throughout the membership. Hermann shines them up with ankle shoes, poppy-red silk bowling shirts. They are a show. Lets them behind the bar to uncap their own Cokes. The whole family, but Millie, has bowling uniforms and balls. A deep-red sheen lights the air as the twins toe their mark, sweep into a rolling glide, dip to the lane and with confident howls blitz the kingpin. Wheeling, flushed, flaming in silk.

Sunday mornings Hermann likes to take the family onto dirt roads in his huge Lincoln and shoot far woodchucks from the road, *Cr-rack! crack!* He belongs to a gun club, has a trunk full of rifles, shotguns, pistols. One Sunday morning he shoots a bear, then hires a truck to bring the body back to the club. Later, at the crest of his joy, smiling through blood, photographed with hanging bear, he belts Stella's eyes. Millie screams and wails, Stella drinks and sobs, Carrie strengthens her.

"Hang onto your bowling ball," Teddy says.

"Sure will!" Leo says. "One more step and we bean him and start kicking." They nod.

Hermann sweats and rails over his stein of beer, drains a doubleshot, popped brown eyebulbs like ballbearings rolling to stillness in his sockets. "You wanna know what I think of you and your damned children? I wouldn't trade this bear for the four of you!" And other dirges.

Christmas Sunday Hermann grows red at Millie's screech and rams her through the living room's glass cocktail table, bestrews Stella over the couch, uproots the tree and its lighted houses, heaves Christmas off the front porch, then drives off to his gun club, sucking a scratched finger. Millie patched, Stella packs, the family stays overnight with Carrie and Red. Next day Stella looks for a new apartment. She finds a back flat in a tiny gingerbread house on a broad street where great tractor-trailers grind and hump and lay clouds of oil.

The police raid Hermann's slot machines, the 20th Century-Fox newsreel shows a boatload of Hermann's slots being axed and then dumped from a scow into bottomless Lake Erie, and within a week Hermann dies in Hamot Hospital of ruptured spleen. His family hires lawyers to flummox Stella out of the will—common-law marriage. Millie goes back with Anna, who thinks badly of Germans. Daddy is in county hospital. Mother has no job.

They are poor.

BUSHY streetkids, skip school, steal Woolworth's penny toys, hang out by piers where rats and orangepeel corrupt under freighters. Fire-escape foxes in empty buildings. A vacant hotel, break into cellar. Climb marble flights. Room-echoes twanging distant coughs. Top floor, staring down on sleeting State Street where a trolley drips blue sparks in twilight. By stairs they find a huge Egyptian cigarette urn filled with sand, roll it down a flight. The egg cracks, spilling. A heavy fire extinguisher draws them, its careful copper legend: Do Not Turn Upside Down Except in Case of Fire. Upside down, its hose spurts wildly. They scream at the snake and race to the stairs. Above, the mad hose raves and whips, yellow foam falls step by marble step, hissing through sand. White-faced, they dash to basement and, gasping, shake their tails down alley and up a lamplit passage, tracking through pure white slush, flooded prints fleeing.

Up a night fire escape. On a sill sit a pineapple and two bottles of ale. Down twins go with their loot, uncap bottles at a pop stand, sneak into Shea's through fire exit. Alone in front row, drink their first ale, gnaw the pineapple, mouths raw with acid. On screen, Gary Cooper as Marco Polo masses gunpowder up the gates of a Chinese fort, blows them open. Leo gets a toothache. Gallop home through Chinese hordes; Stella leaves for the City Club. Leo sleeps poorly. Stella home, he wakes up crying with toothache. "Bear up," she says, "aren't you my son?" Sunday, no dentist to be found. Teddy jokes about Leo's pain, Leo hits Teddy's forehead, they have their first fistfight, stopped by Stella. Leo says his toothache's gone, so they can go out, but she sends them to bed to memorize the Lord's Prayer. Rattle off the prayer after three minutes. Stella stunned, lets them go. Fly to Wallace Johnson's great house skidding corners on their heels, crow to him about Marco Polo's gunpowder. Wallace's father is keeper of Shriners' circus gear, and in the storehouse next door rest a field cannon and gallons of gray gunpowder in sunlight. Steal a gallon, circle to an empty lot, where the three boys build a fat pile of loose powder, then dribble a trail from the mound.

"Is it safe?" Wally asks.

"Oh, it burns slow," Leo says.

Teddy lights the trail, the trail and mound burst, the boys blow backward in a vast flash, land on their shoulders screaming. Leo and Teddy sit up stinging and red. Run home bawling, shorts filled with lumps. Stella bathes them, smears on salve. Bald eyebrows in the mirror and boiled outlines of flyers' helmet flaps around their cheeks. She puts her red spirits to bed, starts them on the Twenty-third Psalm.

"How's your toothache?" Teddy asks.

"Gone."

"Good. I hate that darn dentist chair. *You* jerk too much."

"I'm afraid you're gonna jerk," Leo says.

"Let's stay away from Wally's for a while."

"And his father," Leo says. "It's just too bad, Ollie."

"I know, Stan," Teddy says. "Now we'll never get to play with the rifles and cartridges."

Going to bed, Leo lets his clothes lie where they fall. He seeks Stella's order that he get up and put things away.

"You just do this to get my goat," Teddy groans.

Naked for their turning-away exercise, the band stretches.

"You boss me too much." Leo says.

"Shrimp."

"Big cheese."

Dressing, they help each other, Leo tucks while Teddy ties, a binding rite of tuckings, crossings, tyings until they stand bound to the last button and greenglop their hair for cardboard hardness.

They answer, turn their heads, wave good-bye, and say hello as one. Dislike and fear having their sight divided—too many sights dizzy them, they forget, and may jerk their band painfully. Fear drives them to deepest harmony. When either dreams of separation, the dream deepens to sad horror.

"I had to learn to walk all over again," Teddy tells Leo. "I kept lurching off sideways!"

"What happened to me in your dream?" Leo asks.

"You learned to fly and went off in an airplane, that's all," Teddy says.

"Where did I go?"

"How do I know!" Teddy says. "I was left in the dark. And when I knew I couldn't get out of it before I woke up, I woke up. Was I happy to find you here!"

"I'm always here." They squeeze hands. *Thumbs up!*

One weekend Stella takes the twins and Millie, who is still with Anna, out to the country to visit Stella's father and new stepmother. Millie runs off with older cousins. Leo and Teddy find them beating a six-foot blacksnake wrapped around an apple tree in the hot sunlight.

"Blacksnakes are harmless," Leo echoes Granddad Kerris.

"Why did they kill it?" Teddy asks Millie.

"Oh, it was an *evil* snake." Millie shakes. *"Ugh!* Just ask Mother."

The twins hurtle down a hot stone path by the henhouse. A rattlesnake coils before them. In a terrified bound they lift birdarmed over the rattler, bare legs tingling with fright. Turn and look back. Go closer without sticks. The snake bolts away from the henhouse. Fear burns their legs. Follow slowly. The snake goes into the back clearing and swims hot stones to the stream.

They report the snake to Stella, giving her the exact passage of the snake through the grass. She watches her reborn and grinning father with his hallelujah wife, remembering his blacksnake whip, its blossoms on her criminal body.

One black night the lights go on. Stella lightly touches Leo in bed, but Teddy awakes.

"I want you to get up and at last meet Mr. George Fox in the flesh," she says. "You'll like him! He's brought you a sailboat."

Up in pajamas. A bright-eyed whitehaired man in a black tuxedo smokes by the couch, gives them a storebought sailboat with yard-high mast, racing sails, lead keel.

They thank Mr. Fox, who gives each a dollar for next day. "And there's more where that came from!" he says, Irish eyes blueglittering.

By morning they forget Mr. Fox and pace themselves to a great concrete pool downtown where kids sail boats. Push the boat out into still water, where it hangs windless in hot sunshine.

"I'm sick of this boat," Leo says.

"Maybe we can trade it for something. Maybe Ray Cunning will trade his tommy gun!"

But they trade Wally Johnson for his box of lead soldiers and horsemen. Race up to the Nickel Plate tracks, stand a soldier on a rail, wait for a train. An engine passes —the soldier shakes off before getting crushed. They find and set up a dressmaker's dummy on the tracks, then hide happily, waiting with cat-smiles. THUMP! the model bounds from the cowcatcher.

"Dummy!" Teddy says. Leo nods.

"Where's your boat!" Stella cries.

All march down to Wally's, where Mother waits on the walk, and the twins go up to the great house. The sailboat anchors between their mattress and footboard before Mr. Fox shows up that evening. He leaves a box of cherry chocolates for them and gives Stella twenty bucks to buy them new clothes.

"He's sixty or seventy, isn't he?" Leo asks.

"Mr. Fox is thirty-eight," Stella says. "He has prematurely white hair, it turned white when he was a young man. And he's *very* friendly to us, so you two boys promise you'll be on your good behavior when he's here. Don't eat all that candy at one gulp! Save some for tomorrow, where's your horse sense?"

That night she brings home a Fourth of July bag of caps and capguns, warns them not to shoot them off early in the morning. Twins awaken at seven, find the caps, scream to the empty lot across the street, firing four guns steadily into the blue.

Stella calls to them in her kimono. "You get in here!"

"What'd we do now?" Teddy asks.

"I dunno," Leo says.

"I told you *not* to wake up all creation shooting those capguns," she says. She reads their wonder. "You only remember what you want to remember!"

"We just found them on the table," Leo says.

"You didn't tell us anything." Teddy says.

"I know you're not stupid," she says. "Hereafter listen when I speak."

They feel guilt for a crime they were unwarned against.

George visits Stella nightly from King James, a town sixty miles away. The twins look forward to sailing their boat on Lake Erie on their next visit to Great-great-grandfather Alford's farm.

"When are we going to the farm again?" Leo asks.

"Perhaps we'll all be going somewhere else," Stella says during the nightly hour at her oval mirror.

"Where's that?" Teddy asks. "Grandfather Kerris's?"

"You just forget that slipped out and keep your fingers crossed. Time for your bed."

The twins plop onto the couch with *Huckleberry Finn*. A green bill flutters out of the book. "Fifty bucks!" they cry together. *"Fifty bucks!"*

"What are you talking about?" Stella asks. The twins walk in dazed. "Oh, my *heavens!*" Stella cries, taking the bill. "Where did you young men get this?" She thumbs their book. *"Well!*—will miracles never cease, my sons?"

The twins eye the bill, charmed by power engraved into bulging numbers, the firm steel face of U. S. Grant.

"When we woke up last night!" Leo says. *"He* was in the living room."

"Reading this book," Teddy says. "We fell asleep."

"I like Mr. Fox," Leo says. Teddy nods.

One morning Stella says they are moving—with Millie—to a house of their own in King James to live in Mr. Fox's saving hands. Furniture left behind, their few belongings packed into the high trunk of Mr. Fox's tall forest-green Oldsmobile, off they start with Millie for King James, inner threads snapping with a pang. Docks of State Street, the flat over the Mayflower, the Parade Street circus animals' parade, the house with Hermann Fuehrer, the city parks, Jones School, the Shea's, the Warner, and the Regent, even the German beerbarn where they were duckpin masters, Patty's porch, Wally Johnson's field cannon, Ray Cunning's sick mother who calls them pisspots as a joke—all fall behind as they leave the industrial streets, Nickel Plate underpasses, crackling heavy electric streetcar cables, and cinder-strewn factory yards of Erie. Their Olds is struck by sweeping rain, wind buffets the tall car, the highway bursts with drops, and panes steam up.

"Mr. Fox says you may call him George," Stella says.

"Georgie Porgie, pudding pie," the twins duet, "kissed the girls and made them cry!"

"It's ungentlemanly to tease," Stella warns.

Lake Erie swells, rainbeaten. They pass white-raging grape orchards and, cresting the last Pennsylvania hill, drop down into Southwestern New York while panes dry and sun burns over blue thunderheads behind them.

Their spirits rise over greenrolling hills by a long lake whose waters are smoothly bound by fields, blue pastures, and hamlets. Water glitters. They pull into a lakeshore cottage and are home.

HEAVEN banking blueblack heaven, dirty white clapboard cottage.

"Gonna rain," Teddy says on the screen porch.

"Sure is," Leo says.

"We'll finally have some excitement around here."

Violet cools the hills. Fast black clouds deepen the air ghostgreen under near firs. Grass glows. Night dims the lake, lights on the far shore blink on in cottages.

"Let's swim in the rain!" Leo cries. Lightning whitens their faces.

"We might get fried," Teddy says.

"Idiot," Leo says. "Let's put our trunks on."

"Oh hell," Millie says, "It's so dark you could swim bareassed."

Changing in cramped bedroom. Storm cracks its first hard wild drops. The window chatters, turns white as pearl. The steep roof slanting overhead thrums as they hop afire. Their giant fir rushes the clapboard, the gutter spills by their screen, rainpipe beaten hard. Twins race carefully downstairs, straight across porch, out screen-door. Leap on the grass. Roll on soaked lawn, for Millie's eyes, jump and land on their rears. Dirt runs down their tanned white spines. They glide on hands and knees, an eight-footed beast, then rise like things out of the earth and scratch to be let in the screendoor, their lips mashed on the screening. Millie shoves the screendoor open, they fall back, scream at her in horror, crawl off in play fright. They rise and rush off, barking. The shore heaves at them. Wind bends the rain, whips into squalls.

They crawl waist-deep through radium. Running gravel sucks their ankles. Waves pit and blister. Lightning breaks above, the dark air cracks, and splitting bolts palsy the trees and shore. White-eyed twins turn back. The undertow runs lead against their striving ankles. Cannot step forward. Each lifted foot drives backward as force drags them foot by foot and sobbing into the lake. They hope to ride waves in, but each foot set into the gravel sucks them out. Leo slips and Teddy lifts him. The flow tugs their legs to the powerful god of the lake bottom. Leo screams as Teddy cries for help. Clutch each other's shoulders, straining to move. Millie goes indoors, hearing nothing, lamplight floods the living-room window as Teddy shouts, Leo screams. The giant fir whales the shingles loose. No one sees the swimmers. Teddy shakes Leo, they shout alone in the waters. Stiffened, they look up. The sky boils black, a bright beard stabs from the the clouds, bolts dance on water, whiting the hills. Leo panics from Teddy, tearing and hoping to be saved alone. Teddy screams in darkness and bends over their band. Leo pushes away, yanking and hopping. Teddy clamps him under pounding fists. Leo shoves Teddy's head under, but Teddy falls back as his legs rise. The twins sink. Undertow rakes their backs over gravel. Deep current grips as they tumble, necks thumped on the bottom. Teddy fears a broken neck. They rise from their backs, strangling, and kick up. Hang past the docks, waves lifting their blood.

"Let's try for Sundeens' raft!" Teddy cries, shocked by Leo's blue face.

"I'm afraid of the lightning!" Leo cries. They tread as one.

"Well, you drown while I go over to the raft!" Teddy says and tugs Leo with him.

They lie flat on the heaving raft until rain hardens to drizzle. Swim to Sundeens' dock, drag home in the pour. Straggle into the living room, moaning.

Millie looks over her magazine, biting her lip. "I've got an idea! Let's make popcorn."

"Thought we'd never see popcorn again!" Teddy gasps.

"Good old popcorn," Leo gasps. "Let's have some good old popcorn."

"We'll have popcorn supper," Millie says firmly.

"Lots of butter and salt," Teddy says.

They go up to clothe their spirits.

By eleven Stella and George arrive arguing and leave fuming for George's club in King James. Leo and Teddy lie reading abed. House silent, ceilingbulb clotting with bugs. Crickets spasm in grass and shrubs. A thump sounds on the bedroom stairway. Twins eye each other. A second thump sounds the stairs. Someone laughs on the landing, *cackles*. Twins turn to rock, popeyed. The laugh loosens and rises, Millie's head—hair flying snakes!—rises wide-eyed up the stairs. She wears a white nightshift, her eyes roll back, teeth bared. Lips swabbed with iodine, chin blood-dappled, laugh freezing. She thumps toward them blindly, arms out. Twins scream and hide undercovers.

"I DRANK IODINE! *Whoo ah ha ha ha ha ha ha ha!"*

"AGHH, go away, Millie!" Teddy shrieks.

Leo shrieks without stopping.

They gibber and hold each other under the sheet as Millie laughs above. She claws into them. Squealing Leo falls out with Teddy on top. They lie on their backs, white, shaking. Millie kneels on the bed.

"You all right?" she asks.

"Tell us you didn't drink iodine!" Teddy cries.

"Good Lord, of course I didn't," she says. "What babies!"

The twins pull out their mouths, make Mongolian eyelids, crossing eyes, tongues down.

"Stop that!" Millie cries. "I can't bear to look at you. You look like *IDIOTS* when you make those disgusting faces. *Oh!"* She stamps out, arms crawling.

* * *

Very late they hear two cars drive up. Voices fill the kitchen.

"Let's play sick and get a Coke," Leo says. They limp downstairs.

"And what are you young men doing out of bed?" Stella asks.

"Oh, we had an accident," Teddy says. They drop their pajamas to show Stella great bruises around their band.

"Merciful heaven! What happened to you?" Stella asks.

"We went swimming in the rain," Leo says.

"We couldn't get back to shore," Teddy says.

"Where was that sister of yours?" Stella cries. "She let you nearly d*r*rown in a storm?"

"Mother!" Millie cries from the top steps. "I didn't know a thing about them drowning. They never *mentioned* it once!"

"You march down here and look at these boys," Stella orders.

Millie comes to the livingroom, looks at their bruises. "Why you little liars," she says, stinging them, "you got those falling out of bed. Mother, we were playing and they fell. You tell Mother the truth!"

"She scared us with iodine," Leo says.

"Stella," George calls from the kitchen. "We have guests!"

"I'll get to the bottom of this in the morning," Stella says. "You three march upstairs and get your stories straight."

"I didn't do anything!" Millie insists. "I was just playing, they're not made of glass!"

"We want a Coke," Teddy says.

Twins follow Stella into the summer kitchen. Millie stomps upstairs. George's drinking staffs Arnold Sundberg and Fred Johnson stand at the kitchen sink awaiting icecubes for scotch. Smoke drifts out the kitchen screens.

"Well, look at these two soldiers!" Fred says, a dapper furniture salesman with pencil mustache. He parts his slicked hair like Dad's. "How are you guys? Arnold, if you wanna know *any*thing about movies, ask these crackerjacks."

"Show Arnold how you say the alphabet," Stella says proudly. The twins grumble. *"Speak!"*

"Zyxwvut srqponm lkjihgf edcba!"

"What!" Arnold cries, portly and grinning.

"ZYXWVUTSRQPONMLKJIHGFEDCBA!"

"Why that's incredible," Arnold says. Secretary of the telephone company, a bachelor like Fred. "What's to eat, Stella?"

Millie marches into the kitchen. *"I* want a Coke too."

"You children get up to bed," George says, tipping back his straw skimmer. He lights a long cigarette, right forefinger stumped, eyes sly through smoke.

"I'm out," Arnold says. "Let me have a Pall Mall, Fox."

"Pell Mell," George corrects. Arnold says nothing, accepting a flame from George's hammeredsilver lighter.

"Holy Toledo, toots, I think you've grown this month," Fred says, tucking Millie's waist. "When you moving to town so I can take you out? We'll paint this burg red, hah?"

'September first," Millie says. "Don't think I won't take you up on that!"

"We haven't been to King James yet," Teddy says. "Only to Lakewood and Bemus Point."

"We're moving next week," Leo says.

Fred wipes off his carefree grin, raises his glass in wonder. "Stella, these kids are a great credit to you, believe me."

"Thank you, Fred. It hasn't been easy—but I give them all the wind that's in me!"

"You guys are aces with me, hear that?" Fred says. "Let's hear Paramount News!"

"We are the Eyes and Ears of Paramount—ta-ta ta-TA ta-ta TA TAA!"

"You only rent this shack, Fox?" Arnold asks.

"Arnold, George is renting a mansion on Lakeview, he's none of yer shanty Irish," Fred says, a fist defending George.

"And for what I pay, this is no shack," George says, pouring scotch over their glasses.

"In the glass!" Stella cries.

"I'm gonna belt you," George says, missing Fred's glass.

"Oh, don't act like an old fogy," Stella says. "Give me that bottle."

"Stella, where's the jakes?" Fred asks, rising sly-eyed. He follows Millie, outlining her hips for Arnold. "What a twist!" he croaks.

"Fox," Arnold says, tapping George. "Catch that degenerate couch merchant."

"Degenerate? Degenerate?—which way'd he go?" Fred asks, thumping back on his knees. The room roars. The twins see a light come on next door.

"It's that degenerate hunchback Quasimodo!" George sniggers.

Fred knee-thumps to the twins, pulls dark hair over his eye, sticks comb under nose, and stiff-arms *Heil!*

"Heil!" twins salute.

"Marsch!" Fred calls. *"Ein! Zwei! Drei! Veir!"*

Leo and Teddy goosestep the kitchen, kicking waist-high.

"My God," Arnold says, "they're better than real Nazis."

"Nay-zis," George corrects.

"Oh, *ta-mah-to,"* Fred says.

"Your British is lousy, Fox," Arnold says. "For your information, Bainbridge Colby says Nazi."

"He does not, he says Nay-zi!" George shouts, blue eyes cloudwhite.

"Who's Bainbridge Colby?" Millie asks.

"The one man on earth I respect!" George says.

"Present company excepted, Fox?" Arnold asks.

"You kids want a history lesson? Then listen to this!" George says, rapping the table. "Bainbridge Colby was Secretary of State under Woodrow Wilson and he is *from* King James—"

"So's Robert Jackson of the Supreme Court," Millie says firmly.

"I know that very well, young lady," George says. "He's a personal friend of mine. He and Bainbridge Colby eat at my club. And yesterday, Arnold, I heard Colby say Nay-zi!"

"Maybe because he's eighty and can't hear the radio?" Arnold asks Fred.

"He's seventy-one!" George beats his knee. "I know for a fact."

"No, he's eighty-one, Fox," Arnold says. "He's older than Birthington's washday. Herr Schicklgruber, do you call yourself Nazi or Nay-zi?"

Fred simpers on his knees, sucks his comb. "I call myself Adolf."

The twins scream delight.

"Down!" Fred orders. The twins fall. Fred rises over them, comb in knifegrip. "Thumbs up or thumbs down, Stella?" he cries.

"Thumbs up!" Arnold and Stella cry.

Fred presses their breastbones and the twins squirm like goats.

After the bottle, Fred and Arnold drive off singing. George and Stella fight in the kitchen. The twins tremble in bed and watch dawn flood their fir.

"We near died," Leo whispers.

"Or fried," Teddy says. "Think we were goners?"

"Sure did. We might not have come up for a week."

"Nuts," Teddy says. "We're gonna live to be as old as Great-great-grandfather Alford."

"Maybe."

"Sure we are," Teddy says. "We swim too good to drown."

AWAKING quarter to seven, rise and dress by iced windows. Without eating, scuff into freshfallen snow of Lakeview, under still-lighted streetlamps' pulsing webs. Sky brightens luster of snowclouds. Blue-eyed twins, arms on each other's shoulder, wade the virgin street. Pure yards, no traffic, cars plastered under. High elm branches shelter Lakeview, tufts shaken by small breezes down the cavern. Cresting Eighth Street hill, they lie side by side on the flexible racers and push off. Runners lose rust, sleds fall faster, boots trail lightly. Danger of losing the greenlight burning midhill, heartbeats rising. *Straight through!* Teddy shouts. *We better pray!* Leo says. Lift toes and shoot the redlight, hill dropping steeply as sleds rocket from crest and slam to ice. Burn through the bottom lamp blinking yellow, and coast past Samuel Love grade school to Five

Point's white intersection where Friday's comics arrive even earlier. A fresher, colder snowfall begins.

As streetlights die, loss fills them and Five Point lies deserted and gray in its whipping, snowdeviled streets. They pull their sleds up North Main to their candy and magazine store. The tiny store is closed, its semiweekly magazine bundle bound with wire at the door. Look about keenly, kneel to bundle, check titles, slip out six bright comics and head home with magazines under jackets. Halfway up Eighth Street hill, they stop to breathe and glance at covers. Yellowredblue inks glimmer with demons and lift their hope for monsters in weird artwork. Reading as they climb. Steam into the kitchen like a great woolly dog in four wet galoshes. Sink into bed and read until breakfast.

At eight, their door cracks and Stella whispers, "Breakfast will be on the table in five minutes. Please don't make me call twice." Millie groans awake and into the bathroom.

"Let's," Leo says.

Tap softly on bathroom door. "I'm in here," Millie warns.

"Just wanna brush our teeth," Leo whispers.

"Oh come on," Millie sighs. Sitting upright in her shift, she feigns sleep while the twins brush teeth, wetcomb hair, close door. Tiptoe downstairs, giggling at Millie's pain and at sleeping George. They know each musical nerve in the steps.

Drown in comics at kitchen table. Oatmeal gasps in the pan. "You young men be home by five tonight," Stella warns, "we're eating at the Club." Millie races to table with her math book. "Don't talk to me, anyone," she says, then looks up crying, *"Mother!*—what happened to you?" Stella turns from the stove, a bruise on her eye. "I walked into a door. Keep quiet and eat your breakfasts."

Breakfast with Mama with a purple eye, pouring white milk on oatmeal and red strawberries. Veined bruise.

"George," Stella says over black coffee—"and *I* got *drunk.* I *walked* into a door. It will not happen again in the near future, I assure you."

"Where was the door?" Leo asks. "Was it left open?"

"This conversation is ended," Stella says.

"Why?" Leo asks.

"Don't be dippy!" Millie cries. "If Mother doesn't want

to tell us, she's not going to. She walked into a door, Leo, *ahem!*" Millie looks up and, pierced by Stella's blackened dignity, cries, "Oh, Mother," and weeps into her hands, then braces Stella's shoulder, and wails again.

"Stop that this instant," Stella says. "Do you want that man to come down?"

"What about him!" Millie cries, fleeing to Teddy. The children are wide-eyed at Stella. Sighing high annoyance she falls into a blank stare at the snowing drive. Winds rip, howl, lift in huge hoops in neighbors' yards. "I sure hope this dies down," Stella says. The twins glance at their stolen comics and eat their oatmeal. Millie blows her nose. "Well, you two are cool in the face of this!" she cries.

"What did we do?" Teddy asks.

"You stuff your faces while Mother—"

"Let them be," Stella says.

"Well, this is too much for me," Millie says, bent over the table and staring at each. Sweeps book from table and dresses to leave. "You come back here, young lady," Stella says. Millie sits at the table in her snowsuit and eats by law. "You're in no rush," Stella says. "I have *not* done my algebra!" Millie scatters guilt to all and eats. "I'm finished," she says, rising, taking books. Slams storm door. "That girl gives me gray hair," Stella says.

"What's all that goddamned racket?" George rages above. "You'd better teach that girl how to close doors when people are sleeping! And show those boys how to piss more quietly!"

He comes down in his faded brown bathrobe, the twins' spines stiffening straight up, and belts a shot in the pantry. "I sleep poor enough without this anvil chorus every morning. And I'm not kidding!"

The twins sit whitefaced at their bowls, shaking.

"*Don't* you shout at my sons like that!" Stella says, rising. "You let them alone, Mr. George Fox, unless you have some real complaint."

"I'm giving fair warning," George says and goes up. "There are going to be some asses kicked and goddamn soon! *You're driving me to hell!*"

Crossing backyards, they pass the sidewindow of Grandma Fox's house. She waves from her rocker. George visits weekly, a half hour or less. Irish immigrant, she's seventy-two and lives with her spinster sister. Her husband, a drinker, died in Gowanda, the local madhouse. He's never spoken of when George is at hand. Like George, his hair turned white in his twenties. George brings him up only when urging the twins, "I never had your advantages, my father had me into a foundry at your ages, right down on Steel Street—and we lived in the midst of famine!—so you little buggers thank God for the sweet deal you've got." Once, out riding, George points out his house of birth. Leo and Teddy see a tall, sooty house flaking to ash and cinders.

Grandma Fox watches them raid McIntyre's tiny grocery and candy store, come out with a root beer half-gallon, walk off to school sucking the jug. They've borrowed a dollar on the bill. Warned not to bring sleds to school, they slide down Eighth Street hill sitting up and passing the jug as they coast with feet on crossbars, Russian dancers with arms folded. Stand their sleds across from school on their friend Dick Grey's side porch, hiding their jug in his hall.

Into school for their white patrol-boy belts, then stand by the corner grocery. Their curb is icy slick. "Why don't we pour salt on it?" Teddy asks. They buy four boxes of table salt, try melting their corner. "It doesn't really work," Leo says. They buy three more boxes, showing off. Paul Clark and Ham Knudsen gibe at wasted money, mock their folly. Aloof, the twins relish the fable of their salt losses, born Siberians.

In home room they have one desk. Miss Rice, their elderly teacher, wears long black skirts. A very wide cat-grin under her pince-nez as she greets her children for the day. Her face hangs in a bold horse loop under flag-blue eyes and wavy skullcap. The twins go dry as their salt tale reaches Miss Rice. She smiles at them, asking, "Where did you get the money?"

"It was some old birthday money we'd saved," Teddy says.

"Since last October?" she asks. "Oh, you boys are quite thrifty, aren't you? Perhaps you'd better ask me before you buy salt again. Will I see your mother at tonight's PTA meeting?"

"No!" Teddy croaks. "She's going to Buffalo." Leo nods hard.

"She won't come, d'you think?" Leo whispers.

"Never has yet," Teddy says. "And we won't remind her!"

Leo smooths comicbooks under his sweater, palms and fingers pink with ink. He pens "Fap! Fap!" in his palm, shows Teddy. Teddy pens in his palm, "Great Caesar's ghost!"

Stand for flag-salute. Leo drones, "I pledge allegiance to this fap and to Great Caesar's ghost upon which it stands, one nation, indivisible, with fap fap and fap for all."

Sit. Teddy pens a whale on his shirtcuff. "What's that?" he asks Leo.

"Sturgeon," Leo whispers.

"Oh, you're *not* an idiot!" Teddy says.

At lunch they find spines of ice in their root beer and give the jug to Dick Grey. Pace glaring snow three blocks uphill to Lakeview, pulling sleds. Noon burns blue over frozen elms. A three-story flagstone house binds their eyes with its fantasy of dry vines and thatched Tudor roof, and only the caretaker lives in Sheldon mansion with its great red-brick walls and half-acre snow garden. Their own house, two fronts down, is the same King James brick as Sheldon mansion and King James's old brick streets. Their house has two floors, attic, and liquor cellar, music room with small club piano, gas-fireplace living room, small play room, four bedrooms upstairs, one unused, and pink tile bathroom with walled pink bathtub and mirror faucets and mirrored medicine chest so polished it makes their eyes shine.

In the kitchen for lunch Leo and Teddy gnaw three-decker toasted chicken, bacon, lettuce and tomato sandwiches, leaking butter and mayonnaise. Stella copies the King James Club George owns and runs. Chins drip grease at the sunlit table.

"I like it here," Teddy says. "King James has more trees than Erie."

"Believe you me it's better than Erie," Stella says. Black coffee strong with whiskey, bruise dark, spine erect. Sun barbs the window ice. "It seems to have cleared up out there," she says.

"I wonder whatever happened to Jim Deal?" Teddy says.

"I've no idea," she says, "but you keep him to yourself

around George. He was handsome but married, and that's all he offered."

"You didn't want to marry him?" Leo asks.

"If I did it's none of your beeswax," Stella says.

"Well, would you rather have married him than George?" Leo asks. "I always liked Jim Deal."

"You just thank your stars you have this roof and sandwich," Stella says.

The twins drink milk, arms in rhyme. "I'm sorry about your eye," Leo says.

"And I," Teddy says.

"You don't have to pull that with me," she says. "You're very clever young men. I know what all this eye-shine's for—and you're not getting another word out of me." Her five-diamond wedding ring sparkles. "But you two listen to me. Anything I may have done I've done for you two boys and your sister, and don't ever mistake that. I've thought only of you. So please don't add to the confusion with useless questions. Good lord, he's back again!"

George parks his new Cadillac by the kitchen door, comes in on a surging draft. Shucks soft stretch boots. "Hi," twins breathe. George ignores them. Takes off his long yellow cashmere coat, shined yellow gloves, wide pearl broad brim, and cold silver scarf. "Don't let me sleep past two," he says, "and we'll go down together." "I surely will," Stella says. He hangs his coat in the foyer and with a fine, quaking intentness lies on the living-room couch.

"Where you going?" Teddy whispers.

"We're buying me a sealskin fur coat," Stella whispers with a hard glance. "But keep that under your bonnets until we see it. I want you both home at five tonight. And try not to tell your sister about his harping on you this morning—let's just buck up and *every*body do better."

Leo slices his throat to Teddy. "Let's go, Jack!"

"Ripping," Teddy says.

Big woolly dog, a half-hour early for school. They sled downhill on their way to Ham Knudsen's, the only boy in their room who gets better grades. Coast into Isabella Avenue, tramp onto Ham's back porch. Goat-plaint of Kreisler's "Frasquita" on a violin. "Vy, look who iss here!" Mrs. Knudsen cries in delight. "Hamilton, de tvins are here! Come in, come in."

Ham comes to the doorway of his older brother's tiny

study, holding a violin and bow, says shyly, "Come into the study."

They follow while Mrs. Knudsen tries to force more lunch down them. "Keep playing," Teddy says on Ham's brother's divan.

"I can't play when anyone's listening," Ham says, facing his music.

"Vy, vat do you mean, Hamilton!" his mother cries from the sink. "I listen to every note you play, *eyah* I do!"

"Well, you're not very critical." Ham sighs agedly. "Okay, I have ten more minutes to practice, do you mind?"

The twins sit charged as Ham bows C-scale off-pitch. *"Drat that string!"* Ham cries, king of fiddlers. "Fap! fap!" Leo says. "Play that song you were playing," Teddy says, "you sound good."

Ham scrapes "Frasquita" flatly and weakly. "I haven't got to vibrato yet," he says, sheepblank. "What's vibrato?" Teddy asks. Quickly Ham's violin sings and pulses on a pressed string. "Wow," Teddy says, "why don't you always play like that?"

"I'm not allowed to yet," Ham says. "I have to avoid bad habits." He looks down. "I have to force myself to be bad and sound dull." Actor!

Ham stands back from his stand and bows strongly, blue eyes piercing the page. Fiddlesqueaks search for pitch. Leo and Teddy hang eagerly while bits croak from the strings. Ham winces, goes on, tones drawn cruelly. "It's a real struggle to sound this bad," he says sharply.

The twins fall back howling and Ham slips to the floor leaking happy tears. "Well, maybe I have too much rosin on my bow," he says, bowing on his two great hare's teeth. Again tears swim, the twins gasping on the floor too.

Gentle, strong blond, Ham's father worked in one of King James's world-famous furniture factories as lumber inspector until he died on Thanksgiving.

"The heavens are merciful," Stella says as the twins pant into the kitchen at five-ten. "Get up to the tub!"

Fagged, laughing, they rush upstairs and undress. Millie sings Rachmaninoff in the bathtub. Blackwindowed night. Naked tiptoe giggle to linen closet, wrap waists in downy bath towels. *Hurry up,* Leo knocks on the bathroom door. "Do you wanta wash my back?" Millie drawls. Twins gulp in the steaming pink room strewn with towels like the toilet of Venus. Millie sits in a low wash of suds, washcloth pressed to bosom. She covers herself with a hand and gives the washcloth to Leo, who starts scrubbing. "Easy!" she cries. Leo sees a wave of fat under Millie's fingers, feels strong craving as Teddy strains to see a nipple in the steamed mirror-faucet. "Close your eyes," Millie says, and sinks back underwater as twins watch whiteness through their lashes. Teddy's spine shakes, eyes ashine, head trembling. Leo grunts a bowel cramp, sits naked on the bowl as Teddy sits on their corktopped stool. "Agh!" Teddy says, friendly cramp. Leo sits, eyes half-closed, croaking to Millie about her makeup kit on sink. "I'm covered," she says under her crossed arm and maidenly hand, "you can open your eyes." Leo flushes the bowl and sits on the tub in his towel while Teddy slips onto the bowl. Leo stares into Millie's eyes, jabbering, his round eyes seizing pink and hair. Twins brush teeth unusually long, cracking open the chest mirror. Millie rises to dry and twists not to notice their mirror view.

"Wash the tub!" Leo cries as they run to bedroom and peel boners.

"You'd better save George and Mother some hot water," Millie says at their return. "Get in, I won't look."

Drop towels, Leo sinks in. The twins never bathe, together—Teddy likes hot, Leo, lukewarm. Teddy sits on the tub, palm over twig, Leo's back to the faucet. Millie stands brain in towel at the medicine chest, bobby pins cleaving her lip. "Crap!" she says through the pins, paring away the towel, and retucking. She leaves as Leo cries, "Shut the door!" No answer. *"Shut the door!"* they duet. "I'm coming back!" she sighs from the bedroom loudly. Leo winks, waving his twig, and Teddy hides his in his thighs and swanwings his arms, borne as a girl.

"Where does the bone come from?" Leo asks.

"Must be up inside," Teddy says, "and comes down when it needs to."

Millie in her slip closes the door and unwraps her head as the twins see a fine bush prickle her slip. Teddy and Leo wash Leo. Leo says, "Don't look," and gets up. Teddy stands foot in tub rinsing Leo's legs as Leo waits with twig up. They both get out of the tub while Teddy runs it hot. "I can't put my foot in!" Leo cries as Teddy lowers himself by shivers into wreathing heat. Teddy slips into the tub saddle, facing the faucets, shuddering, eyes boiling. "Good God," Millie gleams at Leo's fear, "why do you have it so hot, Teddy!"

"I like it!" Teddy cries, but Leo screams off balance, slips wailing onto Teddy. He jerks and screams as Millie rushes to haul him out. She grabs a leg and yanks but his shoulders slip deeper. "What's going on up there!" Stella cries below. "Take *hold* of me," Millie says, pulling as Teddy pushes. Leo lies along the rim, breast heaving, then turns and beats Teddy's head. "You *did* that!" he cries. "Stop it!" Millie orders, grabbing Leo's wrists, and, wounded, he strikes her collarbone. "Oh, you little bug!" she cries and pushes him back in. Leo screams and pulls out, bawling, trying to crawl after Millie as Teddy hangs onto the tub. "I'll get you!" Leo shouts, pounding the bowl seat. "I've never seen such madness in my life!" Millie screeches. Teddy sits weeping on the bathmat and holds their throbbing band. Both strangely on tears. George rages below.

"Out, Cadillac!" Stella says to the garage.

Fat snowbanks taller than porches. Roof ice hangs to the footwalk. Frost sparkles dark beds, yards glowing. High hard stars. Silence sharpens the twins' anger.

In the backseat Millie ignores them and talks only to Stella, when speaking. George fountains whiskey and talcum. Stella wrapped in her sealskin, sucking a stinging clove in her front teeth. Leo and Teddy, unable to move in overcoats, tight bottoms burning.

"You have *not* seen your mother this week," Stella says, "and she's already sent three pies."

"Goddamn it, I'm busy," George says. The Club's little Italian janitor, a crooklegged hunchback who waxes a marvel, died Wednesday, and now George weaves the waxer, hauls garbage after labors rigging slot machines, rolling coins, counting the till. He will bribe the janitor from Gandy's Oyster House to switch work, even as he stole the chef. "Tell her I haven't got home before five in the morning this week—and it's the God's honest truth!"

"Dead drunk," Millie says to herself.

The car skids braked into a snowbank as George turns white-eyed on Millie. *"Bitch! Bitch! Little bitch!"* he cries, swatting her face. Millie screams. All press into corners in terror of his flying palm, Leo's tongue sticks to his roof. Stella grabs George's arm, crying, "You stop that, mister!"

"She's been *asking!*" George howls. "I'll teach that little pest!"

"Get out of this car, you old fool!" Stella cries, pushing George against the door.

George whitens. "Don't ever tell me what to do!"

"I will and you'll listen," Stella says.

"Christ almighty!" George shouts, near tears, punching Stella's shoulder. Stella barks with pain. "Mother! Mother!" Millie cries, pounding George's face. Twins scream.

"Stop that," Stella cries, grabbing Millie's wrists.

"He was *beating* you!" Millie cries.

"And I'll teach those two pisspots too!" George says, leaning into the twins. The twins beat George's arms, shaken by his white eyes.

"You *stop* that!" Stella cries, battering his head with her purse. Millie screams, boots beating upward. Stella grabs his hat and pulls it over his face. George's shined yellow glove rams by, striking the door frame, grabs car keys, opens door, and he plunges onto the frost-sparkling avenue under the streetlamp. He crosses through the headlights like an Arctic monster and walks toward town along the snowbank.

"Mother, are *you* all right?" Millie weeps.

"I can take care of myself," Stella says. "Are you boys in one piece? Well, thank heaven for little favors."

"What're we going to do?" Millie asks.

"We'll sit right here until *I* decide, young lady." She watches George's far yellow figure.

"Boy, we showed him," Teddy says.

"Shut your trap," Stella says.

"Well, he started it!" Teddy says.

"Not another peep out of you, Theodore, my son," Stella says.

"She started it," Leo says.

"What!" Millie cries.

"Kindly keep your traps closed one and all, and give me some peace!" Stella says. "Oh my God, I could . . . Well, I'm *not* giving in. Nor will I cook tonight! We shall proceed to the Club as planned and let the devil take the hindmost."

"I want to stay home," Millie says.

Stella digs out her car keys, takes the wheel. Cadillac burns stuck. Millie gets out and stands in the headlights signaling. "I'll feel more confident when I have my license," Stella says.

Cadillac pulls out. Millie says, "I'll walk home. If you have any sanity, Mother, you'll drive home."

"Get in this car, young lady."

"Mother, I'm *going home*. Do *you* want another fight tonight with that—that *bastard?"*

"Lower your voice, you'll bring the police down on us. Oh, my God, the neighbors are out."

Down Lakeview. "Why don't we go home?" Leo asks.

"I am not cooking, nor do I trust myself going up that icy drive. I'd appreciate your silence."

"Look, there's that big pot," Teddy says.

"Big cheese," Leo says. "Hey, let's drive right by!"

Stella pulls up by George, his faded blue eyes fierce under his pearl stetson. He waves her on. "Get in here!" she shouts, braking Cadillac. Gets out, argues in headlights. "I will not get in with those monsters"—they hear George clearly. Warning stabs them. George mutters about Millie. "She's walking home," Stella says. George takes the driver's seat, slamming the door. "And you make damned sure she understands that," he says, yellow-fingered. "I shall give her a talking to," Stella says. The twins swallow fear into prickling spirits.

"That girl's getting her comeuppance shortly and I won't be held accountable," George says.

"Accountable for what?" Stella asks.

"Just mark my words."

They drive to the Club in plush silence, the twins suffering under their many crimes. They hope family madness is blown away.

"And I want these two out earning their spending money," George says. "No more allowance. You two hear that?"

"Yes," the twins say, eased by the law's loopholes.

"I don't care what you do, shovel snow or sell pencils, you two will stand on your own four feet starting now. At your age I was earning ten dollars a week!—and giving every penny to my mother. You've had it too easy. No more movies till you have a job. You're old enough now to pitch in and get your eyes out of those brain-slop comics. Hear that?"

"Yes!"

"And I'll arrange with Father Tobin for catechism."

Spite rises as he finds his parking space behind the Club taken. "I don't care how deep this snow is, that bastard's being towed away!" He drives around front and lets them out under the curb-to-door awning lettered The King James Club. In ties and suits, the twins wait royally, high flakes longfalling, deep darkness piling silence below on factory roofs.

Glass lusters glitter over the waiting lounge. George's aged pet, Duchess, a stub-legged Pekingese he loves, splits with barking. Buttles, the English bartender, says, "Why, good evening, Stella—and Masters Leo and Teddy!" Buttles buries his chin under his pouchy downcast eyes. "What's this old rag we're wearing, Stella?" he asks.

"Like it?" she asks. "A little pixie brought it early for Christmas. And before you ask, I walked into a door last night, *that* door," pouting at the closed door to the cellar. "Came out here in the dark and didn't see it was open."

"Lucky you didn't fall downcellar," Buttles says.

"Well, I'll be greatly relieved when we get someone to take Tony's place," Stella says, slipping strongly into her story. "Hauling tables around at 3 A.M. is too gruesome for me! Why, I get dizzy just shoving and pushing!"

George sits at his rolltop, Duchess beside him, checks the night's held tables, phones the police about the car in his parking space, skims bills in his work-mask of hornrims. Leo and Teddy follow Stella's queen's gait with sealskin and black eye through barroom diners. John McCormack, the Irish bartender, waves warmly. Sit at George's round corner table. George walks up, quickly pale with work. "Order me a shrimp cocktail and porterhouse. Put on your glasses."

Stella slips on rimless reading glasses, clears her throat loftily, and says, *Sit up* to the slumped twins. Erect on chair edges, reading the menu. Fred Johnson and Arnold Sundberg wave from the bar. *"Achtung!"* Fred calls. The twins heil. Arnold's chins lift with a turned-down irony.

Teddy opens a novelties catalog under the table to plastic ice cubes, cigar caps, hollow coins, stink bombs. Fred angles for dinner at Fox's table. "Watch' reading, ace? Hey, that's great, I want one of these catalogs. Where's the twist tonight?"

"She got all dressed up and decided to stay home," Leo says.

Fred looks at Stella's eye and clucks. "You hotshots bring me luck. Why don't you invest this buck for me in the nickel bandits?"

They cash the dollar with Buttles and glide into the slot room. Teddy hits eighteen nickels for three plums first pull. Hopes rise. Leo hits lemon after lemon, then three bars. Ogles last dancing bar, stunned. Cough spills jackpot, nickels on floor as Leo cries, "Great Caesar's ghost!"

Wet with winning, hurry to table with swaggering pockets. Fred earnest with Stella. "What, flat already?"—"We won, won!" Leo cries, digging out nickels. "Did you shysters take off the winner?" Fred asks. "You gotta take off the winner! Nobody'll play a slot that's still showing a jackpot's just been won. Then divvy this between you."—"Come here," Stella says, "let me whisper something." She tells them, "Keep this money under your hats, *ahem!* Now take off your winner and get right back, dinner's on the dumbwaiter."

Leo and Teddy find Fred back at the bar with Arnold. George favors Joe Printz at their table. Clothier Printz, fashion setter, graying waves, high sunken cheeks, shrewd brown eyes. George orders all his suits months early from Joe. Tonight George wears the first box plaid ever seen in King James. The twins' shrimp cocktails served on goblets of crushed ice. George watches them unfold napkins, says, "No, like this," and sweeps his napkin across lap by one corner carelessly. They sweep napkins, Joe Printz smiles his blessing. They reach for lemon wedges. George says, "No, like this—fork your lemon and squeeze it over the sauce, not over the shrimp. Squeezing all over your shrimps is for big Swedes, remember that." They watch George disdain his butter knife and break off butter chunks with his saltine. "They've never had shrimp," Stella tells Joe. Joe Printz mixes horseradish and Tabasco with his sauce. The twins watch his slow, rich chewing of jumbo shrimp, long relish of chilled flavors, under tongue, in cheeks, his grave jaw crunching.

"Beautiful texture, George. Beautifully firm."

Esquire and *Fortune* lie in leather sleeves under the

table lamp by George's redleather chair at the round table. He drinks very old scotch with his steak.

George allows the twins to stay to move tables and polish floors. He hits the high-stakes poker game upstairs. The twins give time to cellar stores, the world's drinking treasures, stacked dainties, tins of English and Dutch biscuits, the kitchen with its huge walk-in box of meats and sauces, and under a hanging bulb among whiskey cases they pore through George's tall *Esquire* piles, cartoon showgirls, playboys, old goats carried over to real life as George's joke bible, each copy tasted, saved, the way seen. The twins fill until their heads sag with girls. Surely newness and Tabasco and horseradish shall follow them all the days of their magic in the King James Club and they shall have cedar woodwork and panels, redleather chairs and brass studs, black onyx tables drenched with linens, tall oak chairs and the bar's glossy redwood smooth as red syrup forever, praise Fox, his slots, his hills of coin. Past closing hour, they find boxes of key-rings and ashtrays with seals balancing black and white Carstairs circus balls, swizzlesticks with white horses, plastic Black and White Scotties, busts of Old Grand-Dad with his doped pinpoint eyes drooping and white face smilewrinkled, sighful, grim. In the rear dining room paintings of spotted white bird dogs and snowy creeks freshen the cedar, stir desire for steak, chop, shrimp, with plastic fireplace birch logs wrapped in red stagefire under dust-rot sails of Spanish ships in a show of high dining.

George and Stella tally slots and bag bills for his nightly bank drop. All slot coin is gain, aside from George's payoff whiskey cases to cops. George lost two forefinger joints in a factory, but the twins think of his stub as a war wound, so deeply do they fix on George as a doughboy. They watch John McCormack fill orders for poker players. George, pickled, savors standing behind the bar and singing trench songs and Irish tearjerkers with John McCormack and Buttles, heads together, John McCormack deathless tenor, George baring his black-sheep heart, Buttles' pouches flooding—*Oh, God bless you and keep you, Mother Machree*eeeee!—George never closer to the auld sod than a Guinness, Stella says, and rarely crossing the backyard to his mother's.

Leo-Teddy shoves tables and chairs with Stella.

George dons coveralls from his hard proud days as a press operator before bootlegging led to the King James Club, which was built on loans and opened fully stocked on Repeal Day. He fades from sight—soon the twins follow Stella up to the card room where he sits at stud with his cronies. Dark walls hung with drawings of dogs playing cards, George's nickname being The Fox, green-baize table burning under green lamp. George drunk, Stella tight-lipped beside him. He draws to a pair of queens, doubles the raise of Dr. Sweets Gogarty, a huge curlyheaded surgeon who drinks two fifths a day. Sweets has aces over kings and says, "Since you opened on queens or better, Foxy, you better have a third lady or your ass'll need hot and cold towels. I bump fifty." George raises fifty too, straightfaced. All chill. "I *know* you don't have it, Fox, so I'll just call and save you blood. Where's that lady?" Sly George sucks his thumb and shows the queen of spades, the queen of diamonds, two threes and tickled, the queen of hearts, roaring with a wet snigger, *"Her did!"*

Sweets smiles, grateful that he wasn't bluffed, players howl, and George's favored punchline, Her did, its lewdness from anal baby jokes, pins high his skinning skill as brayed by players. "This is your last hand, mister," Stella says, "until we finish waxing." "Don't nag me," George says, Stella grim beside him. "We'll not start without you. And you can take the starch out of it, sir," she says, misreading a fold in his pants. "My God, did Stella say that?" Bel asks, George's close friend who owns Gandy's and will soon lose his janitor. *"Her did! Her did!"* George cries.

George wins on, Stella drinks. At last she and the twins haul the heavy waxer up from cellar to barroom. Tables pushed aside, chairs on top. They tip the waxer and clip in its heavy bristle wheel. Stella's corset and garters wheeze as she kneels. "Oh, my heavens," she says, "that's heavy," takes off her dress jacket. The twins gasp, her arms are blue. "Don't think I don't feel this, my sons, and don't forget these if you should *ever* feel like judging me someday." She goes behind the bar for a straight scotch, then takes Waxer's handles and switches on. Waxer hums. "You pour wax and I'll follow," she says but when she tightens her grip Waxer spins off, tractors into tables, spilling chairs, and chews through tables and chairs in a rockslide. Duchess howls through the lounge and barks upstairs.

Leo-Teddy chases Waxer, switches it off, helps Stella from the floor. "Pick up those chairs," she orders. Twins in rhyme set up tables and chairs as George comes down. "What in God's name's going on down here!"—his eyes white. "A minor accident, little man, go back to your game," Stella says. Leo-Teddy trembles beside her. "Give me that," George says, switching on. He wheels wax swaths of gloss. Leo and Teddy sit on the footrail as George in coveralls polishes tiles that Eleanor Powell might tap on. Stella drinks. "All right," George says, flushed and moist, "move everything back and I'll do the rest."

"You come back here, mister," Stella calls. "We'll be ready in two shakes of a lamb's tail!" George goes upstairs to his game. "All right, we'll show him," Stella says. "*Hop!*"

Tables skate with chairs. "Now go up and tell him," she says. The twins, in the dumbwaiter, hoist themselves up through darkness. "George, we're all ready," Teddy says nervously. "I'll be right down," George says, dealing. "He'll be a few minutes," Leo tells Stella, the dumbwaiter in the barroom. After a few minutes, she mutters behind the bar, fixing Leo and Teddy on a glare. "We'll see about that," she says, marching to the stairs. "George, you get down here!" Duchess barks above. "And *you* shut your yap," she says. "George Fox, get down here!"

George comes in a quaking white cloud to the top stair. "I'll come down, goddamn it!" he cries.

"Then do it!"

"When I'm goddamn good and ready! Now leave me alone!" He goes back to his game.

Quickly Stella charges upstairs. "You've asked for it, my fine feathered friend." Listening at the dumbwaiter, Leo-Teddy hears glasses break and George's shouts fill the airshaft. "I'll kill the bitch! I'll kill her, I'll kill her!" Sweets cries, "Stella, get out of here!" *"I will not!"* "I'll kill her, lemme at her! What do you mean tipping over my table!" Duchess barks down the stairs.

Stella screams pain. "Let go of me!" Sweets comes down, leading her to the bar. "Put your coats on, boys," he says, "I'm taking you and Stella home." Stella soothes a dangling blue arm and weeps. "You'll be all right in the morning, Stella," he says, his tall three hundred pounds lending strength.

Leo and Teddy and Sweets and Stella leave by the front door. George foams from the middle landing, "Don't come back or you'll get worse!"

They wait under the Chinese black and gold canopy in falling snow as Sweets brings his Lincoln uphill. The twins tremble. Stella hangs on their shoulders, her fur soft as butter whiteflaked. "Keep this all from your sister." She looks up at the highfalling flakes. *"Ohh!"* she weeps, "what will the Lord bring next, my sons?"

WINTERSWEET Lakeview brick porch, ice casing stone railings, morningblue branches. Church bells.

Twins spuming breath, they are a horse on the porch, in white shirts, creased Sunday pants, pomped manes freezing. They hear calling rooms of the mystery house across the street. Such floors to read! No holding them, they cross the street without jackets, go up the deserted house's drive. Try back door, opening to another door, locked. Empty rooms beyond stir them. Back to their front porch, dress shoes wet. Snorting into rich handkerchiefs, packed into haunch pockets.

"King James doesn't have slums like Erie," Leo says.

"Has a cathouse," Teddy says. "We should go down to Metallic Avenue and look for it. Pretend we're watching for trains, hah!"

Church. Stella sucks Dentyne. George, a sinner, prays with white eyes clouded. Leo and Teddy kneel, wrecked by the city's virgins—no remedy. Millie aflame, eyes full and torn, nails nipped.

Pancake contests follow, tinned maple syrup from Cold Springs, the last cold sausage to be forced down. Comics flood the music parlor. George plays the radio. Furry black voices, "For Thine is the KINGdom, and the POWer, and the GLORy, for EVer and *EVER* . . ." Atomic liners and death rays in the rotogravure. Atlantis sinking.

George makes a rare visit to his mother. "Pick up these papers before I get back," he tells the twins. Millie vamps the piano without stop, without lesson. Stella cries from the kitchen, "Cease and desist!"

"You've made my head soggy," Teddy says to Millie.

"And mine," Leo mumbles on the rug.

"Stop pestering, I'm almost through."

Black memories of Rachmaninoff surge with harping and swamp the bass.

"Play Chopsticks," Leo says. Death-thumps in the music room.

Millie sits back drymouthed and charged, clutching her legs. Twins lie on the living-room rug. Leaded cutglass fractures the music room red. Day fades, the house darkens. God rides away into the maroon sunset.

Millie dances upstairs in a gypsy bedspread and nothing else.

The twins go downcellar and piss on red-hot coals. Ventilators flood with burnt urine.

"What in heaven!" Stella cries. "What's that *stink?"*

She fixes the twins on prongs. "Open the doors and get that smell out of here!" Looks out the backwindow for George, now visiting mother in earnest. Penance. Leo-Teddy is stabled in silence in the kitchen corner, sniffing mucus.

Nothing said. Later, drying supper dishes, begging, sulking.

"For God's sake, yes, I'll give you movie money," she sighs. "But I want your solemn promises—you know for what!"

The twins face bottomless sin and agree to goodness—anything for *Son of Frankenstein* and *Cleopatra.*

"I want to be proud of you gentlemen. And I want you home like jackrabbits afterward. Don't get George on my neck for letting you go."

The moon in bare limbs. Nancy Ruleburner's starry house. Leo says, "I love her in spite of her money."

He loves her porch, her back bedroom too high for scratching.

"D'ya think those high school guys feel her up?" Teddy asks.

"Don't say that to me!" Leo cries.

"What bumpers," Teddy says. "That's a compliment."

At Washington Junior High Christmas assembly, Nancy hulaed in a grass skirt and bare feet. Leo still smarts over a small candy heart, lettered "I Love You," he planted in her desk between classes at Love School. She left the nameless gift with Miss Rice. "I don't want *that,*" Nancy said to Miss Rice. Leo burned. Teddy prickled.

Waiting for Boris, they soak in De Mille's *Cleopatra* with Claudette Colbert in a milk bath. "Boy, she looks like Mama," Teddy says. Reborn, the monster, shepherded by little Ygor, "dies" in a sulfur pit.

Walk home by the library, sit in the park. White moonstream on star-bed snow under star-bed deep and brilliant. Moonlit firs slope with snow and shadow. Leo says, "I feel like I've never lived before. *Or else forever!* We should sit here more often."

"It's terrific," Teddy says. Hands Leo sour-apple Life Savers, sucks bitter cold fire, waits for sugar to flush his jawpain. Works hinges.

"What if we couldn't leave the park?" Leo says. "We're prisoners here. Reborn every night on this bench—moon-prisoners!"

"Who'd want that? Besides, the moon's not out every night."

"No," Leo says, "we'd sit here forever at this moment like the monster until Dr. Frankenstein gives us a blast."

Sit quietly seeing a four-armed Siamese monster in Nancy Ruleburner's rainlightninged back garden, climbing into her high bedroom—Arrhh! Arrhh! *Love me!*—Nancy turning her nose from his body odor.

"Hey," Teddy says, "I had the weirdest dream last night. My head was floating in front of me—and it didn't have any face!"

"How could you tell it was you?"

"I felt it. No eyes or nose or mouth, just a pink face looking at me real hard," Teddy says. "I could see it was very tender, like the head of my dingleberry. Was I surprised!"

"I dreamed I was over a river and a car was sinking in it and I saved a little black pig in the backseat," Leo says.

"Then I saw a hawkman trying to get through a revolving door, but his wings were stuck. You ever fly?"

"All the time," Teddy says. "Sometimes I jump so high I'm afraid."

Orange stormcoat, dark hair flooding kerchief, body flooding wasp waist, dark eyes boiling white, stops and points. "You're Leo and Teddy, the *S*iamese twins. You don't know me, do you? You've never *s*een me before, have you? I'm Geraldine Palmer, four times in *s*eventh grade. You've never noti*c*ed me on*c*e, have you? *Ei*ther of you?"

"Washington Junior High?" Leo asks.

"Yes," she stresses. "You haven't, have you?"

"I don't know, we must have seen you. Hey, sit down." Leo shoves Teddy over. Geraldine sits, breath moonwhite, flesh scent pouring. "You don't know me, do you, Leo?"

"I'm Teddy," Leo says.

"Hi," Teddy says.

"I thought all *s*eme*s*ter *you* were Leo!"

"Did you ask me?"

"But everybody knows you're Leo. I *s*aw your picture in the *Evening Journal!*"

"That was taken in a mirror," Leo says.

"Stop kidding, I'm Teddy."

"Well! I don't think that'*s* very con*s*iderate," she lisps.

"You're right, I'm a snake," Leo says and kneels, taking her gloved hand. "Geraldine Palmer, forgive me."

"And me." Teddy kneels with her other hand.

"I do. Please, get up!"

"Boy, your orange coat's beautiful," Leo says. "May I walk you home?"

"Where do you live?" Teddy asks quickly.

"I'll bet you're the kind of per*s*ons who think everything's a game. That'*s* terrible! You are, aren't you?"

Leo raps his knees to find his life story. "I don't know. Do we think it's all a game, Teddy? Are we that revolting?"

"I don't think so. We're not monstrous."

Leo-Teddy eyes the hungry gnaw of stars, lust filling his chests, tongues dry, eyes rilling. "How about it?" Leo croaks. "Can we walk you home?"

"You may, but right now. I live below the Boatlanding."

Leo beside her, Teddy clomping through drifts, Geraldine mincing swiftly. “What are you gonna be?” Leo asks her.

“Why, I’m a *s*inger. I *s*ang with Paul Whiteman’s band!”

“Who’s Paul Whiteman?” Teddy asks.

“He’s a great orche*s*tra leader,” Geraldine says. “You must have heard of him. I want to sing in an orchestra. I’ve done it already.”

“Paul Whiteman?” Leo asks. “What did you sing?”

“I sang—! I don’t remember the *s*ongs.”

“How can you be four years in seventh grade after singing with Paul Whiteman?” Teddy asks.

“If you don’t mind telling us,” Leo says.

“They won’t let me go into eighth grade. Maybe I’m too *s*mart for eighth grade and they’re waiting to put me into ninth in*s*tead. *I* don’t know!”

“Weird!” Teddy says.

“What are you doing tomorrow?” Leo asks.

“I’m staying home.” Fleshbreath. “To practi*c*e my guitar.”

“Oh, too bad,” Leo says. “I’d hoped we might take you on a winter picnic.”

“A winter picnic! What’*s* that?” she asks.

“Like a summer picnic,” Leo says. “You take all the food and pop and stuff. Indian blankets. We have a bow and real arrows.”

“And Omar Khayyám,” Teddy says. “It’s beautiful out past Lakeview Cemetery. Perfect for winter picnics.”

“Woods are wonderful in winter,” Leo says, drawing woods in the air.

“Hm,” Geraldine says. “I *could* play my guitar. All right, I’ll come—if you’re *s*erious. When shall we meet?”

“Early,” Leo says. “We’ll be at your back door at eight.”

Scooped white snowroad, white iceflats stretching, Chadakoin marshes, Geraldine’s icicled house.

“Thank you for walking me home,” she says at her buried porch. “*S*ee you at eight.”

Leo touches his cheek. “A kiss!” he whispers.

“Oh, I can’t do that yet.”

“Well, then I’ll bury myself in a drift and freeze to death,” Leo says. “Just one?—I’ll split it with Teddy.”

Geraldine kisses both their cheeks. The twins tramp home, French legionnaires singing “The Desert Song” to the sharp stars.

Tiptoeing into kitchen. George snores above. Creak up

to their bedroom, undress. Stella opens their door in her nightgown and whispers, "I'll speak to you wanderers in the morning."

"We're going tobogganing at seven!" Leo says.

"With Ham Knudsen and Paul Clark." Teddy coughs.

"Where are you going tobogganing?"

"Up Swede Hill," Leo says.

"When will you be home?" *Sigh.*

"At supper," Teddy says. "If we're late, don't worry about us."

"Believe me, my sons, I do nothing else. You be home for supper."

"Can you let us have two bucks?" Leo asks.

"Two dollars! You may have one and make do."

Tiptoe down in pajamas, make sandwiches, pack hamper with pickles, tins of shrimp from the cellar. Stella, two dollars in hand. She kisses their lips. "You give me gray hairs but you are my sons!"

Kitchen still dark at seven. Teddy thumbs his pocketbook Omar drawing of a slim-breasted nymph he loves. Pack sleds with blankets, hamper, bow, and steeltipped arrows, set off. Lamps die as streets lighten. Sky firm blue before sunrise, roofs and treetops scribbled with halo. The sun rises over Geraldine's back step as they tap the lighted pane. She pulls a kitchen lightstring, and comes out with a blanket and orange-flamed black guitar.

"Have everything?" she asks "Are we taking *s*leds into the woods?"

"We bury them by the road," Teddy says.

Rosewhite skin, cleft nosetip, browndark eyes. *"Boy!"* Leo says, "how did we miss you up at Washington?"

"I don't like to be *s*een, I'm very shy. Is it far?"

"No—but it's deep," Teddy says. "Good you wore leggings, Snow Maiden."

Past Lakeview Cemetery, frozen fields open with pale blaze skimming the crust. They bury their sleds at the field's stiff edge. Carrying blankets and hamper, strike out through eggwhite snowworks. Midway to the birches, stop waist-deep in roaring sweat. Leo points, strings bow, lofts an arrow rattling into stripped branches. "We'll get it back!" A centaur, he teaches Geraldine archery, his steaming arms around her orange sleeves, but her arrows snake feebly over the snowcrust.

In the birches they find a great drumhead clearing and strip their coats. Tramp a circle, sit with greased bread pans and butter knives, pack bricks for an igloo. Faint noon whistles rise from furniture factories. Breathless, the igloo only half-built, pack bricks far off in deeper snow. Leo begs Geraldine to play her guitar.

"Oh, the *s*un shines bright on my old Kentucky home," she singtalks out of tune.

Teddy strums an unseen guitar and shakes his head.

"Lucky for Stephen Foster he's dead," Leo whispers.

"Are you laughing at me?" Geraldine cries, muting her strings.

"No, no!" the twins cry. "Play on, play more!"

"I'm very *s*erious about my music. It'*s* all I dream about."

Day darkens weirdly. Pack and chisel the last brick of the open dome, then blanket the floor around stacked kindling from home. Out gathering branches. Birches icy, fallen branches shelled with ice. Top the woodpile with twigs as flakes twirl through the vent.

"Is it ready? I'm dying!" She faints over the orange flame she strums.

"Not yet!" Leo says. "First we waltz you around it."

"It's the Eskimo ceremony," Teddy says. "Hop on."

Arms saddled, they swing Geraldine around the igloo, singing:

> Skaters fly on
> Light as the swan
> Skate till the pale
> Winter sun is gone

—a rollerskating act that won a five-dollar first prize at the Palace's Saturday morning Popeye Club.

"It'*s* too *s*mall," Geraldine says inside.

"Better to gobble you down, my dear," Teddy says.

"This is tragic," Leo says as twigs smoke.

Geraldine clutches her bosom. "I have a knife in here!"

The twins gape. "What for?" Leo asks.

"Why, for protection."

"Expecting an elk?" Teddy asks.

Twins check for elk. "A hoof! I see a hoof!" Leo cries.

Geraldine squeaks, fierce with her unseen knife, and glares at Leo. "Are you making fun of me?"

Leo thinks twice. "I thought I saw a hoof."

"Go out and look," she says palely. Twins crawl out and search for tracks. Stare at each other about the knife. Back in, strip jackets.

"Nothing!" Teddy says.

"It might only have been a cow," Leo says.

"What kind of cow!" she says.

"In this weather, Leo?" Teddy asks.

"Well, I'm not afraid," she says. White fist at orange bosom, eyelids shuttering, lying.

"Let's eat," Teddy says.

"It'*s* too *s*moky in here," she says, her black scarf off and hair falling as she thumbs buttons.

"And hot," Leo says. "These twigs are waterlogged, let's throw some out."

"You wouldn't kill a bird," she says.

"Kill a bird?" Teddy asks.

"Isn't that why you brought your bow and arrows? To kill *s*omething? If I'd known you were going to do that, I'd've never come! Oh, I can't *s*tand it in here. It'*s* too smoky."

"Let's get rid of the fire," Leo says.

"I want the fire!" Teddy says.

"Well, do you want all this *putrid s*moke?" Geraldine asks.

Twins rake out twigs and kindling, blanket the floor and cover the roof vent with Leo's plaid lumberjacket.

Geraldine comes out in a red cardigan. "Cover those filthy ashes and *s*ticks," she says, feebly kicking snow. "Don't you hate a dirty doorway?"

Chinese bow, palms together, throw smoking sticks aside, scoop snow over ash with breadpans, speaking, "Velly velly chop chop, Missy, *ming ting hwang chao sing wu!*" She turns her back.

White birches pierce upward, black branches rooting down.

"Want to climb?" Leo asks.

"I want to eat!" she says.

"We'll eat, just a minute," Teddy says.

Climb wishbone birches over her head. She stamps, hand on hip.

"Hey," Leo says. "We should have all our friends out here and build igloos."

"I'm hungry!"

"Igloos all over the whole woods," Teddy says.

"And the field," Leo says. "Igloo City!"

"Terrific," Teddy says. White braille curls under fingertips.

Geraldine's fist in her cardigan, face white. Swing out and fall at her feet. She points to the hole. They creep into the igloo's sour icelight. Geraldine, dim red dragon, snorts on hands and knees, cheeks flushed. Sit up within, open the hamper.

"You sing pretty, Gerry," Leo says. "Have an olive."

Teddy hands her the uncapped jar of pimiento-stuffed olives. "I like to be fed," he says, turning, and drops his head onto her calves, mouth open. Leo smiles up from her lap, then grabs Teddy's hand.

"I fear I have brain fever, Lucien, and may die! Brother, be brave."

"Louis, you can't die," Teddy says, "Corsica will not be the same without you!" He eyes Geraldine. "We are the Corsican brothers who, though separated by a thousand miles, feel each other's heartbeat."

Dark eyes roll above baby bow lips and her deep red sweater mouth, fixing twins in her glitter. Her chin rises, sinks, her breath heaves, she weaves two olives between nipping mouths. Dandles fruit at their lips. Her tongue snakes from his cave, binding their heartbeats, sways, asks more and more hunger from them. Their eyes please her. Her fast sighs steam in their ears. Gingery flesh floods their noses and breasts. So much! still she's not full. And more she asks, hair falling, nostrils cupping, her eyes like hot brown eggs sucking up their wriggling heads. Her teeth clip sharply at the drop of each olive. Peace flushes the chewing twins, their heads afloat, severed, joyously parted. She bunches her sweater mouth, swelling up, swallowing them.

"Everybody I know thinks you're very conceited, Leo," she says.

"What about Teddy?" he asks, redfaced.

"Teddy's *sin*cere," Geraldine says. "Aren't you?"

"Just more mature," Teddy says nervously.

"That's that sappy look you get reading Omar," Leo says.

"Who's he?" she asks, and leans forward as Leo whispers, "*A big drunk! . . .*"

Teddy's head rolls on her calf and speaks to the vent above—

A Book of Verses underneath the Bough,
A Jug of Wine, a Loaf of Bread, and Thou
    Beside me singing in the Wilderness—
Ah, Wilderness were Paradise enow!

"See?" Leo says.

Geraldine, pale and moist, raves, *"Oh, more!"*

Teddy digs in the hamper, opens the *Rubáiyát*. Geraldine opens her cardigan. "Oh, pictures!' she says. "Let's move, I want to see them."

She climbs over Leo, a tiny purple pad bumping his nose as he stares down her Mexican blouse. Teddy sees her moist throat above him. She sits with Teddy's head in her lap. He opens to slim-breasted Spring flinging aside her Winter Garment of Repentance.

Teddy sniffs. "What's that smell?"

"My sachet," she says. Lifts it from her blouse. Teddy's eyes flutter, his jaw drops for the pad at his nose. Cool fumes open him. "Read," she says.

"Root beer!" Teddy whispers.

She holds the jug for each. Teddy reads through peanut butter and jelly. Day darkens nymph-dancing pages.

"Ohh!" Geraldine says. "Let's dance in the woods."

"I'm asleep," Teddy says.

"Let's stay all night and finish the book!" she says.

"It's not that long," Teddy says.

"We don't have enough food," Leo says.

"We have blankets," Geraldine says. "And we'll have candles and napkins!"

'From where?' Leo asks.

"We'll have to send someone back," Geraldine says.

"Who?" Leo asks.

"Oh, I'll go," Teddy says. "I'll be Gerry's genie."

"You'll go back for candles and napkins?" she asks.

"I'm your slave," Teddy says.

"Go!" she says. Her cheeks are dark rhubarb. "We'll watch the *moon* come up."

"Go where?" Leo asks.

"For napkins and candles," she says, "don't be so silly all the time!"

"It's snowing out!" Leo says. "Really snowing, Gerry."

"I'm going," Teddy says. "Come on."

"I'm staying," Leo says.

"We're going to Anderson's grocery on Durant," Teddy tells Gerry.

"Is that far?" she asks, stroking Leo's cheek.

"We'll be back in twenty minutes," Teddy says. "Come on, they sell jelly doughnuts."

Leo quiet. "Oh, all right, let's go."

Geraldine opens the hamper. "I'll fix what's in here."

Cross the flakeflooding field's late-in-the-day trance, heaven falling everywhere.

"What do you say about her knife?" Leo asks.

"What knife?"

"I wanted to go ice-skating."

"We'll leave early!" Teddy says. "And stop for our skates on the way."

"She's strange," Leo says.

"Don't think I know what I'm doing, huh? Wait till you see her dance," Teddy says, his hair feathering. Neither twin wears a hat—they like to *freeze* their pampered forelocks.

"Just so she don't play. She's worse than Millie. Left my darn jacket on the smokehole."

"Let's cut over there," Teddy says, and they break from their path.

Steamwindowed grocery. Only birthday candles. Get ten boxes, fancy napkins, pound of jellyroll.

Go back on their new path. Wind-carved snowbanks.

"Igloo City should have tunnels everywhere," Teddy says.

"It's really getting dark," Leo says. "Dibs on her lap, *okay?*"

"And we could have bonfires everywhere," Teddy says.

Crawl in with their groceries.

"Where've you been?" Geraldine asks under a blanket. "I had a good mind to leave."

"We weren't long!" Teddy says.

"She's only kidding, aren't you, Gerry?" Leo says. "Where's supper?"

"I almost left, don't you forget it," she says, handing the napkins to Teddy. "Serve me."

Teddy sets places. "How do you like the candles?"

"They're too small. Light a whole box."

"I obey," Teddy says. Sticks candles in orange cupcakes

and jellyroll, sets out pickles, last sandwiches, and tiny shrimps. "Get rid of those awful things," Geraldine says, choking at shrimps.

"An acquired taste," Teddy quotes Joe Printz. "Hey, the snow stopped."

Leo lights a match for the candles.

"Wait," Teddy says. "Let's see if the moon's out."

"*S*plendid," Geraldine quotes Mrs. Matthews, her homeroom teacher.

Dusk. Teddy trembles beside her at field's edge. Chill yellow bulbs in farmwindows. Moonrags glowing. Eveblooming Venus.

"Not even five o'clock," Leo says. "I guess we'll miss supper."

"Let'*s* read more," she says.

She crawls in and sits on Teddy's side, but Leo forces himself around beside her.

"You *bent* the candles," Geraldine says. Leo sets up the candles and lights a match, his heart near her, then lights the candles, her hair spidery beside him. She glows, eyes orange. Palm-shaped candleflames. "Can't eat without a kiss," Teddy says.

"How can you talk like that with *Leo s*itting right here?" she asks.

"Do you want me to leave?" Leo laughs.

"That isn't funny Leo," she says. "Don't you know that Teddy and I can never be alone?"

"Neither can I," Leo says.

"I think I love you," Teddy says. She stares away. "I know I do," he says.

"She's too shy," Leo says.

"I am not! I do like Teddy."

Leo smiles slyly. "Like a sister or as a brother?"

She closes up. Her fist at bosom. "Don't forget what I have in here—and I'll use it too, Leo. I want to go home."

"We have jellyroll and cupcakes!" Leo says. "We can't go home without eating."

"Not *yet,*" Teddy says, kissing her fingers, sighing, "That'll have to do!"

"It'*s* more than you deserve," Geraldine says. "Lie on my lap, I'll feed you."

"It's my—" Leo begins, shuts up.

"Sit over here," Teddy says, kissing her fingers again. She crosses over the candles. He sweeps her hair from the flames, her strong, sickly violet sachet swinging. A caul rips, his heart pounds nakedly in its butcher shop. Head into her lap, prickling cheeks, tongue stinging as birch.

"Did you dance for Paul Whiteman?" he asks far away, feeling his heart pump.

"I *s*ang. But I do dan*c*e."

"Great," Teddy says. "You gonna dance for us?"

"For *you*."

"I won't watch," Leo says.

"I didn't *s*ay you couldn't watch," she says. "But I'll dan*c*e for Teddy." Fingers feed a peanut-butter sandwich into Teddy's mouth.

"Let's take about fifty candles outdoors," Teddy says, "that's the way I feel, and stick them in a circle when Gerry dances."

"We don't have any music," Geraldine says.

"We'll sing," Leo says.

"I haven't practi*c*ed anything."

"We don't care," Teddy says.

"We just want to see you dance," Leo says.

"Oh, you think I can't dan*c*e!"

"You dance beautiful, I betcha," Teddy says.

"I can't just dan*c*e any dan*c*e!"

"Dance a war dance," Leo says. "You ever see Nancy Ruleburner hula?"

"I *s*ee her in the halls," Geraldine says. "She's too con*c*eited. And she has no per*s*onality. I'm sure she can't dan*c*e."

"She's been asked to try out for the junior ice-capades," Leo says.

"That's not dan*c*ing, that'*s* *s*kating," she says, fixing Leo. "Does Leo have a crush on Nan*c*y Ruleburner?"

"You'll have to ask him," Teddy says.

"Shut up," Leo says. "These candles are dying. Let's go out."

"I can't move," Teddy says, sniffing violet. "I'm *drugged!*" Her face is pointed and bright as a mouse's above him. Teddy's candled in her eyes, her eyes returning ginger currents, spices. Flames waver in wax, die. Pale darkness, half-asleep, her breath tart on their spirits.

"Let'*s* go out," Geraldine says.

They crawl out with boxes of candles. Teddy apecalls, beating his chest. They make a circle of candled snowballs in the birch clearing. Leo wears his cold jacket from the smokehole. "Ready!" he cries. "Hey, where'd she go? We're ready to light the candles."

"Come on out," Teddy cries into the igloo. Lights the first snowball.

"I'm too shy," she says, backed against the wall within.

"You can't back down now!" Leo says.

Teddy shushes him. They kneel at the hole. *"Salaam,"* Leo says, palm on forehead.

"Carry me," she says. Twins cross arms. She lifts a lighted snowball. Carry her into the circle. She stands with snowball burning as they light candles in a wide ring around her.

"Don't come into my *c*ircle!" she warns.

Flames ghost ringed trees, white moon riding white birches. The twins kneel. Orange-eyed Geraldine eyes them, then steps forth in baggy leggings and V-necked sweater, raises her red-spluttering snowball, turns about tunelessly, freely, twists and loops about her fires. Brainless, mincing, stammering steps. A candle dies, then two. Her handheld candle gutters redly. Teddy holds her a fresher snowball candle. "Put that down!" She stamps, glaring, then looks about and takes the longest candle still burning. Again she dips and loops about her waning flames, then her eyes fix on Leo and she dances up to Teddy. "Get me my bow and arrow!" The twins jump up and bring them. Leo jabs the bow and arrow upright within the circle. Geraldine runs at him. "I told you never to break my magic *c*ircle!"

A few candles burning. Leo and Teddy sit again, forced down by her eyes. Now she lofts mock arrows above trees, into the woods, at the moon. Standing by the last three candles, she stamps an order. "*S*tep into the ring." Leo and Teddy rise and cross dead candles. "Wait there!" she says. "Now, Leo, I am going to kill you."

Leo swallows a smile, turning his face, but Geraldine strings her arrow and points it at him. "*S*ay good-bye to Teddy," she says.

"If I go, Teddy goes," Leo says brightly.

But the bow snaps and the arrow thuds into his lumberjacket, bouncing. Leo-Teddy stiffens to ice.

"That's dangerous!" Leo cries.

"*Geraldin*e!" Teddy cries.

"I *missed,"* Geraldine says. "Give me my arrow back."

"And let you put my *eye* out?"

The last candle dies.

"Bring it to me!" she orders.

"I want to go home, Gerry," Leo says.

"Bring me my arrow!"

"No, I want to live to go ice-skating tonight," Leo says.

"With Nancy Ruleburner?" she asks.

"No," Leo says. "Give me the bow. Let's pack up." She clutches the bow. "All right," Leo says, "carry it!"

She hands Teddy the bow. "That really was very dangerous, Gerry," Teddy says.

"I wanted to kill him," she says. "And I may."

Twins fold blankets in the dark dome, look out the overhead vent. Through the navel, stars pinhole a brightness beyond the night. The twins stick their last candles into the igloo roof. Crossing through the field with blankets and hamper, they look back. A birthday house burns in the birches.

The glazed field blazes nightblue.

"Let's write a story about Igloo City," Teddy says.

Look up, their focus wide-angled, every fiery star hurtling at them. "Can't write about it," Leo says.

"Why'd you want to kill Leo?" Teddy asks.

"I don't have to say," Geraldine says. "He knows why."

"Hurt your feelings?" Leo asks.

"Yes," she says. "Deeply."

"What'd I say?"

"You should know," she says. "I never want to see you again."

"Me, too?" Teddy asks.

"I *may* want to see you, Teddy," she says. "I haven't decided."

Stop at the road, a fenceless blue sea of light.

"Where's our sleds!" Teddy cries.

"You buried them, for heaven's sake."

"I know we did, but where?"

Blue smoothness. The twins stomp about.

"I have to get home!" Geraldine says.

"Maybe we'll have to come back tomorrow," Teddy says.

"I touched something!" Leo cries. Kneel and dig. No sleds.

"Please take me home, Teddy. *I'm falling!* Oh, here are your stupid sleds, I slipped on them!"

Teddy pulls Geraldine on his sled, Leo the blankets and

hamper. Past moonwastes and milky granite of Lakeview Cemetery, on one side, and past bay windows speckled with red, blue and amber bulbs. The Carlsons' brick wall vined with hot-hearted bulbs. On the steep peak of the Swanson manse, a floodlit Santa with reindeer. Desire for marriage, vined house, floodlit Christmas fills each twin, certainty flooding his fingertips.

Starry trees. A plow scrapes before them down Lakeview. Horsebreath and fresh manure fumes, heavy, rich, bitter, and blood-stinging.

A nightlight, their house dark, the twins grateful for bricks and silence. Bring Gerry into the kitchen and find a note and two dollars under a salt shaker. Take her into the music room to show her Stella's Christmas tree village, small mica-coated pasteboard houses, each with a colored bulb within—green-dyed hedges, nooks, gables, porches, a chapel's stained windows, heaven glistering on rolls of cotton.

"Oh, it'*s* *s*o nice, Teddy!" Geraldine says overzestfully.

"Agh!" Leo cries, a blot of blood on his thumbcushion. "Stuck myself on a wire."

"Put iodine on it right away," Geraldine says. Go to the downstairs closet medicine chest. Leo rinses his hand. "It's just a puncture," he says.

"Oh no, you can get lockjaw," Geraldine says, pouring iodine over his whole palm.

"Christ, stop!" Leo cries.

Geraldine stares in shock, turning red. Drops the bottle bouncing into the sink, heads for the kitchen, and slams the back door. Teddy pulls at Leo, crying, *"Why'd* you swear?"

"Well, that moron should have used the glass stick! Let's let her go, for God's sake." Washes his purple hand, caps the empty bottle. Teddy half drags him to the kitchen. They hang their skates on their necks, lock the door, and race after Geraldine, sleds in tow.

"Apologize," Teddy mutters.

"Gerry," Leo says, catching up in lamplight, "I didn't mean to swear. I'm sorry."

"I'm never *s*peaking to you again!"

"Well, *s*peak to me," Teddy says, lisping unwittingly—he bites his lip with remorse. Casts his voice low and careful: "Leo's real sorry he's such a big mouth."

At Eighth Street hill, Teddy talks her onto his sled. They

sit, push off together, his mittens gripping the frame, his heels around her on the steering bar.

"Hold me," she says, breath streaming. Puts his arms under hers.

Sachet violets soak him and, sleds bumping on sleek ice, he moans into her steamed cheek, "You're so beautiful!"

She raises her chin. "And you're too *fast*, Teddy. I am *s*everal month*s* older than you!"

"I don't care!" Teddy cries, hugging her orange waist. She turns and kisses him, their teeth striking. Teddy turns to sparks in his fork. His back stiffens, sweet bloodsalt filling his gums.

"Watch the light!" Leo shouts. Shoot through and over the hump down the deep dip to Love School. Past Five Point coast to the Boatlanding. Webbed lampshine in back-o'-town silence, heels crushing crystal, high winter moon riding white. Teddy fills with powerless strength. He holds Geraldine's mitten as they follow her deep-filled road. Iced air rivers from the marsh. Leo gapes at the drifts, pulls back, but Teddy bumps him silently and Geraldine follows They stand their sleds in a bank, hang skates from steering grips. Kick a path to her dark porch. The porch sits askew, the ceilinglamp smashed.

"May I see you again this week?" Teddy asks.

"I'll con*s*ider that *s*eriously, Teddy. It depends on the future!" She looks at Leo.

"And Paul Whiteman?" Leo asks.

Her glove clutches her hidden knife. "Ye*s*!"

"Maybe we can go skating some night this week?" Teddy says. "May I stop by and see you?"

"I don't *s*kate," she says. Gives Teddy a peck on the lips. "Good night, and thank you for a wonderful winter picnic." She turns.

"Will you give me your sachet, Gerry?" Teddy asks. "I'll keep it forever."

Her gaze weighs this gift; she pulls the pad over her head silently. Teddy sees a blazing bare ceilingbulb within.

"Won't you say goodnight to me?" Leo asks.

"Your ears are too big!" she says and stamps indoors.

A shout goes up within and a man howls drunkenly, "Where the hell've you been all night? Make my supper —*and no eggs on toast!*"

Teddy says, "Let's go around back."

"I wanna go skating!" Leo whispers. "All right, it's your

night. Her pa must be some stewbum. Sounds like all he needs is a tail and horns to be just like George."

Get their sleds and go down to the next road. No path past the frozen streetsign. Plow to the house behind Geraldine's, stand up their sleds and skates, wade quietly through dim waist-high drifts beside the strange house and through a mountainous drift-shelf in the back. "Boy, are you crazy," Leo says. Geraldine's backyard, windscooped, glistening. Her father slouches past the kitchen window in smoke. Another lighted window, shade up. They slide by inches up a creaking iceshelf. Raise heads slowly over sill, a squat two-headed monster at the yellow pane. Geraldine's bedroom. Strips of plasterboard gape from a smashed wall, the very boards of her floor warped and apart. Geraldine's guitar lies abed where Teddy drinks its blackness and orange flame. "Let's go!" Leo says. The ice cracks, sinking. They turn to stone. The ice splits and falls with a great crack and puff. They drop two feet, freeze under the window. Listening for footsteps. Slowly, they raise up. A baby mouse bolts through the molten living room, stops, runs under a bedroom floorboard.

Back through roof-high drift and lamplit ice to their sleds. Strike upward for Lincoln in downwhirling cold. Thick-shingled white marsh, too weak for skaters—sink into darkness!

"Bodies come up in the spring," Leo says. Teddy nods. "Nancy Ruleburner's been away from Washington for two nights, so she might be at Lincoln."

"In this cold you're crazy," Teddy says. "And the short way's the hardest."

"You mean down Steel Street, then straight up that crazy hill?" Leo says.

"Straight up Armory hill," Teddy groans.

"Let's not fall asleep halfway."

Race down Steel to Armory hill with its high lamps in the stars. The hill saps them, steeper than thought. White moon, brick armory, slope coiling windflakes.

"Hey, we're halfway," Leo says, leaning on his sled.

"Boy, I'm tired," Teddy says.

"I want to rest," Leo says. "Look at the stars. They're like pinholes," he yawns. "As if it's daylight behind them. *Tired!*"

"Look at me," Teddy says. Leo looks at Teddy and Teddy blazes into Leo's eyes.

They trudge to the lamps and rest.

Light uppours Lincoln rink, blotting out stars. Change shoes in the skaters' hut. "*There* she is!" Leo cries gratefully.

Nancy Ruleburner drilling in a black costume, twirling a black walkingstick. Leo sucks air. *Eleanor Powell!*

"Let's keep an eye on our sleds," Teddy says.

Watch the half-strange rink nervously. Girls skating lazily. "Ain't bad!" Leo says.

"We gotta come more often," Teddy says under his breath—as a longhaired blonde keeps her steelblue eyes to herself. "That's a Lois," he says. "Pure-bred."

They touch ice and glide off like fish.

"I'm gonna neck with her tonight if it has to be over her dead body," Leo says.

"It may be Nancy loves me, Leo. Secretly, of course."

"You're only half-kidding," Leo says.

On a bench Nancy slips into her black, scarlet-lined hooded cape as Leo sits beside her.

"Well, how are you," Nancy drawls, relacing her skates.

"Spinning," Leo says, holding his head.

"What brings this on?" Nancy asks.

"Not seeing you at Washington for two nights," Leo says. "I got dizzy looking."

"Hell," Nancy says, brown eyes dawdling on the twins.

"Oh, searched like a beaver," Teddy says.

"Whatever for?" she asks.

"Saw a star," Leo says. "Discovered it myself. A new star in the heavens! You can see it off Armory hill. Really beautiful. Come and look."

"Right now?" Nancy asks.

Leo stands, hand out. "I'll write to Washington and have it named after you."

"Well!" Nancy says. "You really think it's a new star?"

"Come, come!" Leo says. "See for yourself. It'll only take a minute."

"All right, one minute," she says.

Leo swallows like a country glutton. She stops, measures his boorish gulping.

"This street is bad for our skates," she says, her blades gritting on ash.

"We're almost there," Leo says. "Down the hill a little."

"You can only see the stars when you get out of the lights," Teddy says.

Nancy goes downhill silently. Leo's hands rise in prayer to Teddy. "Where is it?" she asks.

"This is it," Leo says, taking her shoulders.

Nancy smolders, then melts.

"Don't move," Leo says. "Your eyes kill me."

Teddy's skin burns with Leo's.

"Let me kiss you again," Leo husks. Hugs her heavily. All three fall back on the hill. Nancy beside him, Leo stoned with his luck.

"Where'd you learn it all?" Nancy asks. Leo sinks onto her lips, moves his hand up her caped costume. She moves it down. "Show me that star," she says.

Breathes deeply, his bare hand on her. Blood rising, she tongues him. Leo sucks a deep breath through their spittle. "Maybe we should get back," she says. "It's getting awfully damp out here."

"Let's not get too cold," Leo says. She moves against him, they kiss soulfully, bones braced. Without warning, his spine spurts with fire. Teddy's skin sucks Leo's burn. She lies back, eyes slitted at Leo, far off.

"Thinking about your high school guys?" Leo whispers away, away.

"That's my business," she says. "My father should be here now."

Back. Nancy's father waits, owlish in white evening scarf. "It's too cold to walk," Mr. Ruleburner says. "How're George and Stella?"

Driven home, sleds in trunk, twins alone in backseat. Out on Lakeview. She gives Leo no real look. Forgotten already! Leo cries in his heart. The Ruleburners drive off. Moonlit ice driveway. House still dark.

"I think I peed my pants while we were necking," Leo says.

"Oh, I did that on Eighth Street hill," Teddy touches himself with bare fingers and smells. "Stale peanuts," he says.

"Well, once in a lifetime," Leo says. "Anyway, I bet I can get a boner whenever I want to."

Millie reads in bed, the house to herself. "Thank God you're home, I was frightened stiff. The whole house is croaking."

Sit on her bed, drained, in smelly shorts.

"Boys, are your eyes red," Millie says. Nipples under silk. She reads, grinding her lips. Nipples around *Jane*

Eyre, dumb dogs slumbering. "This is the most beautiful book ever written!" Millie thumps.

"Better than *Gone With the Wind?"* Leo asks. Selfless gaze into gown.

"Oh, this is on a much higher plane," Millie says, fingers on ribs for a scratch. A thought vexes her. She lowers a strap, half-draping a redbrown nipple. "Do you think this mole might be a lump?"

"It's a mole," Teddy husks. "Does it feel like a lump?"

She takes his fingers and presses them against her sickbed lump. "It's a lump or a swollen gland," Teddy says. She presses his fingers gravely about. "I can't tell," Teddy says. She takes Leo's fingers and presses the tips to her breast. "What do you think?" she asks.

Leo feels the breast sternly. "I don't know," he says, eying the half-shown everlasting mystery. "Is there one on the other side?" Millie drops her other strap and Leo presses about. "There's something, but I think it's a gland. I really don't know."

"Well, let's hope it isn't cancer," Millie says. "How are *your* glands?"

"What!" the twins cry.

"Oh," Millie says, pulling up straps. "You know what I mean, don't fib me." She turns to her stomach and drops her straps again, cupping herself. "Hop to it," she says. The twins scratch her back. She moans. "I have the only brother with four hands in the whole universe. Harder so it really hurts." Red welts. "I asked about your glands because I'd *like to know* in case I'm ever called upon by science."

"Which glands do you mean?" Teddy says.

"Ye gods! I mean *gonads.* If you don't want to tell me, don't."

"We don't know what to tell!" Leo says.

"We get boners," Teddy croaks.

"What are they?"

"Oh, you know," Leo says. "You've see one."

"I've never seen such a thing in my life!" Millie swears on *Jane Eyre.* They stand with poled shorts.

"You saw Toughie Kopeck's that time in Erie he got us all into that shack with those tough kids," Teddy says.

"I don't remember that far back! That's disgraceful—*leave!* And I *didn't look,* you may recall, I covered my face! You'd both better take a very hot shower, you smell like a barnyard!"

The twins shower, spurting through suds.

"What's this stuff?" Leo says.

"I don't know," Teddy says, pulling off a fingerstrand.

Teddy awakens, smelling the sachet on his neck. Leo grinding his teeth. He shakes Leo but cannot wake him, though Leo's eyes are half-open in the bedlight. Teddy trembles. Leo alone can bring himself out of it. Leo stiffens in his fit, mind awake, dark walls swelling, body sliding soles forward into star spaces. Fear of fire, fear of drowning grip him. He cannot save himself. Fear of heart thud stopping. Teddy waits, praying. Leo's stiffness weakens. Toes and fingertips open, eyes blink. He fills with loss for soft blue bliss.

"Okay now?" Teddy whispers.

"I was floating. There was a blue angel. Then I came back. It was awful, I was afraid of everything. Even of flies choking me."

"What was the angel doing?"

"Blowing a big yellow seashell. This beautiful sound blew me right out of the sky. I was damn scared, Teddy —wide awake and I couldn't move. The house coulda been burning down!"

"I tried shaking you," Teddy says.

They grip hands and climb straight up Armory hill to the lampwebs.

FLUSHED red-eyed bull smashes the chimes, beats Stella on the stairwell. Stella hangs over the banister. Millie screams from her room. The twins rush burning-haired to the stairs.

Coming home from school, Leo and Teddy note Cadillac parked out back. They cross the kitchen quietly, dreading to find George quaking on the sofa. He kneels instead, weeping where Stella lies with yesterday's bruises. His pale eyes drip as he begs. Last night at three a rage of beating, screaming, howling. Now he's bawling, his locked fingers begging her deepest atom of forgiveness. Stella listens mercifully above the great blue bloodflowers on her arms. The twins tiptoe up to their bedroom.

Finish homework. Stella stops by in her dressing gown, sits on their bed, abashed. "He has promised to switch to beer forever. And he means it, my sons. I know we'll see some change in him." Hammering rises from the cellar. "Go down and thank him, he's bought you a present."

"An electric chair?" Leo asks.

"Oh, that's for himself," Teddy says.

"Now don't be that way," Stella says. "I know it isn't easy for you boys. But life isn't easy! Thank your stars this isn't the madhouse I grew up in. My rear end was paddled from the day I was born. My father whaled me until I couldn't rise! And there's more I'm not telling. Well, you boys thank him, and make peace."

"Grandfather Kerris used to *drink?*" Leo asks. "Gee, he's so happy and smiling and religious!"

"Do you doubt me?" Stella asks from her throne. "He beat the life out of me!"

"Well, you can't judge a book by its cover, Stan," Teddy says.

"You certainly can't, Ollie," Leo says.

"That's right, chins up! Pretend nothing's happened," Stella says. "We only live once on *this* earth and you're both at the easy part." She walks them to the stairs. "My sons, I see you aging before my eyes, and that's *good* for me at this moment. Go now."

George calls from the cellar. "Come down here, boys."

Down winterdim cellar, mold fumes from damp dirt and stones. Cool racks of peaches, strawberries, pears in clove syrup.

George straps an oxblood punching bag to a frame screwed into the rafters. "Let's hope you learn something from this," he grunts.

"Thanks, George." Leo-Teddy smiles through dust and ashes.

"I want you two boys able to take care of yourselves," George says. "These bags aren't as easy as you may think." He drums the thudding bag amid whiskey fumes, king cigarette aslant. "Like that, try it."

"Shoulda bought it for himself," Teddy whispers.

Twins turn to, fumbling. "Well, you first," Leo says. Teddy shifts to fast drumming. "Stars fell on Alabama," he sings. Stops bag. "Go ahead."

Leo steps up. Wobbling blows. "Show me again."

Teddy drums. Stops. "Alphonse?"

Leo pounds balanced blows.

"That's all you needed," Teddy says.

"Balance."

George flushes the cellar toilet. "It doesn't rinse! I'll fix that in a jiffy." Gets his great tool box from foundry days. Now he's a plumber in his box plaid suit. Taps highdusted pipe. "Where's this pipe lead?" Unscrews a joint. Gets rust in his eyes, dust, sludge.

"How's it going?" Teddy asks.

"Just looking for a match," George says, pinching a cough in his nose, blue eyes watering. Digs out black packet King James Club pearl matches, lights a silk tip, hunching bullwinged shoulderpads. Pockets fag deep into stubbed forefinger, palms his face when dragging. "Crap!" he says at a screeching joint. "You don't stick on me!—not on George C. Fox." Looks at his swan-necked oil can, too big, then his pint cup oil can, then takes up his smallest puckered beaker. *Cluck tuck tuck. . . .*

Twins pound a fourfisted drumroll. Cellar window bright skyblue over ice, afternoon fading in the rafters. George flushes the toilet. *Hello,* it croaks. He turns a spigot, water hisses into rusty bowl, sprays from the high tank. He jumps out, grunts, closes spigot. "Needs a goddamn washer." Watches them at the bag. "I didn't expect this. Keep punching. Stella! Come down her."

"I'm coming, hold your horses!"

Stella combed, the day's first housedress. "Well, upon my word. You boys are no surprise to me! *Go to it.*" She laughs. The cellar drums. George, forgiven, unlocks the liquor cellar, the Club's dearest stores. "My heavens it's cold in here!" she shudders, rubbing her blue arms. "Why, here's that fancy scotch we were looking for last month! Twenty-five years old—that's too rich for my blood. But let's tote it upstairs so we'll know where it's hiding."

"Maybe we should put it back," George says over the twins' drumroll.

"Well, if you want me to."

"The idea of leaving a bottle like this upstairs, woman! We can't afford to serve this."

"Not even to Bel and Mildred?" Stella asks. "Then who's it for?"

"Oh, I suppose we could serve it to them."

"And who, sir, is to say when to serve it?"

"Why, that's your privilege!" George says chastely.

"I couldn't drink this varnish myself," Stella says, climbing ahead of George. George giggles. *"Oh!* don't think *you're* getting any of this, Mr. Fox!"

"I just want to open it for you, my God. There'll be terrible corkage on a bottle this ancient. It should be opened with care."

"I might let you use you expert powers on that and that alone, sir. I for one don't need a drink."

"Oh, I'm not drinking anything," George says.

"Then why do I have this bottle up here, may I ask? If you have misled yourself that it's for me, take it back." She holds the bottle out sternly for eternal cellarage. "Our friends can do without."

"Stella, it *is* for our friends," George says. "We already agreed."

"Just so you understand."

"But it'd be good to open the cork and let the bitter off."

"What makes you think it's bitter?"

"It gets a dark head in the light."

Stare up the dark neck together.

"I can't see in this light," Stella says. "Oh yes! the glass gets darker."

"That's what I said."

"No, the glass gets dark, not the scotch, Mr. Fox."

"Sure it's the scotch, Stella." Wide blue amaze.

"Open it," she orders. "But don't think you're fooling me. We both know what's going on."

"I wouldn't know!" George says. "Heaven strike me if I know what you mean."

"This is a complicity," Stella says.

"Between whom?"

"Between you and I, Mr. Fox. Don't think we're hoodwinking *me*."

The cork pops oilily. "Here, try this."

"Very professional. And I'll try one drop of the dark to see if it's bitter, as you say."

"It's very bitter," George says. "Honestly."

Stella smells her shot. Scotch beads silkenly, fuming. She drinks, turns aghast with dragonflame, runs cold water hard. *"Ohhh!"* She shakes, face shriveling at the bitterness she's drunk. "If you can drink that, go to it, sir. That sting has no bottom to it."

"Oh, I don't want any."

"You may have *one* for the road."

"Pour it," he says, washing hands, dousing face. Dries himself on paper towels, slips on his cashmere coat, pearl stetson. Sniffs his shot, then raps it against his palate. His face is brick-red with eagerness. Swelches the bitter scotch burning his mouth, swallows it, then snaps down his own fumes deeply. He sees heavenly cedars. Feels marrowburning fatherlessness. Eyes sharp-pointed, his mouth draws poisonously, he says, "I know there's *one* small part of you for me alone." Stella turns to stone.

"Don't be too sure," she says.

"There has to be!" He pounds her new aluminum sink and grinder.

"When I can summon it up," she says.

George holds her. "That's all I want—just one atom for me!"

"Stop that whining!"

"That's all I need!"

"And you have it. Now pull yourself together, the cellar door's open. Have another drink."

"Not tonight!" he says.

"Ho! I *know* you have a thousand bottles downtown."

"Call me when you want to come down. On my word, Stella, I'll be sober as a judge."

"I'll think about it. But I'm not promising anything."

His three-fingered kiss speeds on the cold draft.

"Don't think you're getting out of this so easily, dear man," Stella says, queen of scotch. "I want to see some improvements around here."

"I meant every word I said. But don't kick me when I'm on my knees to you! Trust me."

"I don't trust anything but my horsesense. I only know that we're drinking people and there's hell to pay for it. But what can we do? Maybe we'll both just have to try harder. Now pluck up."

Faded blue eyes crinkle from prison, Irish, apart. He gapes, pleading. "I think only of you, Stella. God bless you."

Stella goes up to bed with a belt of bitter scotch and ice, followed by her twins. "If I still have enough left in this glass when he phones, I'll stay home," she tells herself.

Twins work at their bedroom desk. She lies amid twelve magazines she takes for stories and advice. On the far bedstand is stored a freshly cracked five-pound box of chocolates George brought home for his whiskey famine. Stella's greenvelvet wallpaper, her heavy Grand Rapids bureau, her long dresser, her vanity of King James's finest blond mahogany panel. Her full closet and George's twenty-odd suits here and mothballed in the attic. Deep under shoebags hides her greensteel Erie strong-box for jewels and birth certificates, insurance policies, squirreled cash.

Leo and Teddy spy the chocolates.

"Those are George's, you may have two apiece. By the way, for our future comfort, George is having a walk-in shower built into the bathroom this week."

"What!" Then face to face: *"Well, isn't that something?"*

"He saw it in a magazine. With a frosted glass door, no less."

"You never had a shower, did you, Stan?" Teddy says.

"Yes, I never did," Leo says.

"And since you'll have to be in there together with the door closed, I hope and pray that you'll both come to your senses about water temperature. You *can* find some heat you both like."

"I can't stand his boiling water!" Leo says.

Stella turns aside. "Ohh, not that old song! Hasn't anything I've said today made a dent in either of you?"

"Well, why can't he have it under boiling?" Leo asks.

"Can you give up your boiling showers?"

"I love 'em!" Teddy says. *"He* still stinks like an Eskimo when he gets out of the tub. It's embarrassing."

"Be serious!" Stella cries. "I'll thank you on bended knee if you work something out. And if you don't, I'll set the taps myself. So don't try to bedevil me, it won't work."

Stella's bruises. "We'll figure it out," Teddy says. "Where are we going Sunday?"

"Why do you want to know?"

"We haven't been to Erie in years," Teddy says.

"Well, I think we're going out to Olean. Biff and Fanny have opened a new bar and they have a *set* of skiball bowling machines just for you boys." Stella's letters net faithfully every friend she's had since girlhood. "And we'll have no horsing around in the shower." The twins knock foreheads. "You may fritter and play today, but when the time comes you will toe the mark. *Don't smile at me like that!* Go to your room! Shine all your shoes. *March.* But me no buts, get in there. You are both staying in this afternoon."

Leo-Teddy howls but soon sits at his bedroom desk, the hawkmen having decided earlier to work on their Flash Rogers chapter for Ham Knudsen and Paul Clark. They pencil twenty thunderbolt pages before supper, their lights traveling in a single eye. Flash Rogers's mighty body, hellish helmet, his steel shield starred and striped. A glowing red trident gripped in his heatproof glove. He chases Herlit the Goth Magician through star-strewn Tartarus, which upholds galaxy Hades. Flash ripening his trident on the anvil, forging new weapons against Herlit's fancies. Herlit steals Flash's torchgun and builds a mile-wide wall of fire about his grisly gates where Wilma Deer starves in the dark. Flash races from his workshop to Dr. Einstein's stardome. . . .

Stella calls them down as Millie hurtles indoors, blood-red with frost. Twins bolt dinner to hear the radio. "Slow down!" Stella orders. Family skits and mysteries at seven. Lying by their cedarwood Zenith, a green eye for correct tuning. Millie's oil of a Swiss lake and Byronic chalet hangs by a framed three-year-old girl hearing "The First Robin of Spring." Stella's showcabinet, the world's liqueurs in two hundred small bottles. Stella's wax fruit is disneyed in a glass bowl mirrored through lace on the mahogany dining-room table rising over George's chi-chi red broadloom. After dishes Millie goes downcellar to work at her easel. Chick Johnson taps at the cellar door. She lets in a short thin boy with wavy chestnut hair, spaniel eyes. They sit on the steps. Twins light on upper steps to eavesdrop.

"Maybe you can help me," Chick says.

"Well, I will if I can," Millie says.

"Have you read *The Turmoil?*"

"No, I'm doing *Jane Eyre.*"

"How's that?" Clearing throat.

"Oh, it's tragic. I love it."

"Well, I'm doing *The Turmoil.* It has me terribly upset."

"How?" Millie asks.

"Well, this fellow Bibbs is faced with the choice of going into industry or staying home sick to become a poet. His whole life's joy hangs in the balance."

"What's turmoil?" Leo whispers. Teddy shrugs.

"Well, isn't that awful?" Chick asks.

Leo peeks around the corner. Chick sits knotting his elbow and biting his knuckles. "It's the story of my life, Booth Tarkington's writing about *me.* My dad's put his life into industrial management down at King James Veneer and Plywood. And I know he thinks I should go into the factory with him when I graduate. But I just can't go into the factory! I sure can't. When he comes home he smells of baked glue—all his suits in the closet smell of it. I can't look forward to a life of baked glue!"

"Of course not!" Millie agrees. Chick grips her hand, his eyes saucered with sadness. "Have you talked it over with your mom and dad?"

"That'd only upset them. Let me ask you a hypothetical question. Your honest opinion, don't spare my feelings."

"I'll be as honest as I can," Millie says. "I'm swept off my feet that you're asking me."

Leo and Teddy, hangnecked vultures, eyes slitted.

"Do you think I should risk failure in life?"

"I'd do it in your place!" Millie says, biting her lip white.

Leo jeers. Teddy whispers, "She *might!*"

"I want to be a fly-by-night foreign correspondent."

"What's that!" Millie asks.

"That's a reporter who travels around the world for newspapers," Chick says, boiling, blinking at the floor. "That's better than poet-essayist like Bibbs. I don't want my family upset by any announcements yet, you understand? But you know what King James salaries are like—lowest-income city in the North. Swedes work for nothing! It's lovely in King James, but there's no money."

"And money's important, believe me," Millie says, her chin a white bump.

"There isn't any here!" Chick cries. "Oh I shouldn't be bothering you."

"Why, I'm honored that you ask my opinion. But I've

never faced a problem this big before. It all goes off in too many directions." Millie sits back gravely. "I think you should let the money go to blazes and do what you like."

"She just said money was important," Leo whispers.

"She's covering both directions. Very shrewd!"

Chick cries suddenly at the furnace, "O my God, who wants to live in King James forever!"

Millie sits thrilled, stricken by his fire. "Are you depressed, Chick? Or just awfully restless?"

"Restless? *Restless!* I gotta do something with my life, Millie! Ye gods, I'm in such a—"

"Turmoil?" Millie asks.

Chick raises her cheek. They kiss as the coal shifts, falling.

Twin's eyes roll in pain. Lightly close cellar door, go back to programs. Leo gibbers on the rug. "You understand me! Oh, Bibbs!"

At ten-thirty Stella comes down with her sealskin to wait for a cab. "When that program's over, get your arms and legs together and get up to bed."

George in winter daylight.

"Can't go home, it's still daylight," George tells Stella in the Cadillac. "Drive to Mayville."

"How can you get so tight so early?" Stella asks.

"I'm not tight. Take me to Hotel Holland."

"It's only two in the afternoon!"

"I want to go to the road just outside of Mayville," George says. "Just drive there. Can't go home—neighbors might see me!"

Leo-Teddy, wary and trembling, sit with his magazines in the sunlit backseat. Stella drives twenty-six miles to Mayville, uphill, downhill along the sunglaring frozen lake. George sits sweating, drooping, twins fearing his fists. Warm winter afternoon.

"Is this the road you mean, sir?" Stella asks.

"Pull into that picnic area," George orders. "I want to get out."

Stella parks and George gets out clutching his hammeredsilver pint flask. Opens trunk, lifts out horsehair blanket. Crawls down the top of a picnic table, pulling the blanket over him. "Wake me up at four," he says, pearl stetson slipping onto bright snow. Eyes close. Gone.

"Go down to the creek for a while," Stella tells the twins. "We have a long wait—again. I don't know why we have to come so far out of town for this!"

Stella watches the twins skid down to their bluesky creek. She thinks of George in his lights, the full glory of his sins, with the pat pert waitresses down at the Club, the apartments he keeps. George ablaze, fist on her cheek, Stella the scapegoat for his whitehot anger at himself, but giving her even less than Durwood gave to live on. Beating her head in with a snowshovel in the garage, leaving her stranded with the twins in Erie and Buffalo, George at the drying-out farm, George with $47,000 bulging his coat pocket not a penny for her, his Catholic soul eaten from head to toe by endless error but on his feet every bursting moment, spending, gadgets, clothes, new vanities to keep himself erect, distracted, smiling, fearing every customer he greets at the Club's front door, beating Stella before two lawyers in the Club lobby, kicking her on the Club's floor in front of his mistress, losing $5,000 until the twins find a wet wad of his New Year's Eve boodle from the Club in his tuxedo pocket in a camphorated attic box when Leo tries on the tux, Stella peeling loose the liquorsoaked bills and drying them until the whole attic floor turns green with damp fives tens and twenties, George again not giving her a penny when the lost cash is handed over. George who doesn't know who he is, sunrise to sunset, cheating, smiling, gladhanded, suave, but a monster when his pure Napoleon booze energy and money has to stop for a few hours and see itself naked. George on the picnic table, or in some hidden sleeping nook, every afternoon.

Whitehaired. Silver flask at hand. Every cell athirst.

George peerlessly suited, shaved, long head balding, seated for a salon photo in the Club's lobby. Whiskey-proud, his eyes, his lush red eyes, brimming!

Split a two-ounce bootle of banana liqueur while Teddy writes Geraldine at their desk. Eyes glossy, he asks her to go with him to the winter prom. Leo sighs, fiddling a ghost fiddle, *Ya da dahh da da dahh!*

"I wanna see the Christmas decorations on Third Street," Leo says.

"We'll hit the post office after I write my letter."

"I wanna try that Cherry Heering Danish stuff," Leo says.

Taking a second bottle from Stella's liquor cabinet, shuffle bottles to mask the theft.

Teddy writes on. "Gimme a drink of that stuff."

"'S all gone."

"Hey! Now would I drink a whole bottle on you?"

"Oh, come off it. There's more."

"But would I?" Teddy asks.

"Not likely, hah! D'ya wanta bottle? Let's go down and get one—try that Lemon Hart Jamaica rum."

Steal rum, shuffle the shrinkage.

Teddy stamps envelope, off to the post office. Icy night. Star-locked bright chasm, teasing breath from innermost deeps. Downtown cloud glow.

"Don't stand so stiff," Leo says.

Teddy bends a bit.

Into post office crowd. Leo says, "Gerry's gonna call you up and say, What do you *mean* sending me a letter like that? My stewbum daddy has read it to me and explained every word! I'll never speak to you again."

"She'll understand."

"Hope on, Omar."

Into Bigelow's to see the toys. Nancy Ruleburner and Joan Erlandson coming out. "Hey, I wanna see you!" Leo says.

"What about?" Nancy asks. Dark curls over fox collar.

"Not here. Let's go to Fulmer's Dairy."

"What's so important?" Nancy asks.

"I'm learning to dance." Leo winks.

"That's too bad." She shrugs at Joan, whose sigh smells of salmon loaf. "Okay, Wolf Man," Nancy says. "Joan?"

"Sure. But *dutch,"* Joan says. She lives with her mother in a plain two-family house. Teddy walks her home at times.

Wait for a booth inside Fulmer's steamed windows. Paul Clark rises from a round rear booth with Loretta Mirabile. "*Teddy's* all right," the twins hear Paul tell Loretta, "but that *Leo* has a dirty mind. Really crude. Oh, hello, fellas, Leo, didn't see you standing there, ha ha!"

Leo slips the Cherry Heering bottle into Paul's jacket. "Take this home for your bureau."

"But it's empty," Paul says. "Although I detect a lingering odor somewhere, Watson. Hey, how'd you beat out the high school rats?" he asks, clucking toward Nancy.

Leo leers at his fingernails.

Twins slide into the round booth, Nancy by Leo and Joan by Teddy. As Loretta and Paul leave, she nudges Teddy and whispers, "We gotta dig into your living-room rug again, big boy!"

"Isn't this choice," Nancy says. "Now what's so important?"

"Let's order first," Leo says.

Helene the blonde whips up. "Okay, make it snappy." She sees Leo redden. "Holding your breath? What'll it be, squirts?"

Nancy looks about to leave. "Well," she asks, "is your whipped cream real or canned?"

"Canned?" Helene's pure Swedish beauty outshines Nancy. "In Fulmer's *Dairy?* Ha!—yeah, it's canned."

All order hot chocolate with whipped cream. Teddy groans quietly as Helene walks away, tendons balling. "Boy, I'd like to work here," he whispers to Leo. They eye the waitress goddesses and counterboy gods.

Nancy takes a cigarette from her deep alligator purse.

"Nancy!" Joan cries, covering her mouth.

Nancy leans archly at Leo. "Gee, I haven't a match," Leo says. She takes a pack from her purse, lays it on the table. Teddy snatches it, lights her cigarette, and is shocked by the lung-deep cloud spouting out of her.

"What have you been drinking?" she asks Leo.

"Nothing you'd know about," Leo says.

"Get it at home?"

Leo nods. "Four bottles."

"Four bottles!" Joan says. "I never heard of such a thing. What'd you do with 'em?"

"Drank 'em," Leo says.

"What were they?" Nancy asks.

"How'd you know if I told you?" Leo asks.

"My father drinks scotch and my mother brandy," Nancy says. "What's your poison?"

"Pernod," Teddy says.

"And Lemon Hart Jamaica rum and Cherry Heering," Leo says.

"Here she comes," Nancy says. "She better not ask me how old I am."

Helene serves four chocolates. "Hey, does your daughter know you started smoking?"

Nancy drags slowly. "May we have some water, please?" She throws her head back and swallows smoke. The twins have never seen such beauty. Her sockets darken into Egyptian starlight. Joan is fisheyed. Nancy drops her head into shadowy fingers, tragically. Well, her eyes say, we'll all lie dead someday, won't we . . .

"Ahem," Leo croaks. "You been asked to the winter prom?"

"I don't even know if I'll go. Why should I?"

"I'd like to take you."

"Whom are *you* going with?" she asks Teddy.

"Gerry Palmer," Teddy says.

Nancy drags in scorn. "That top-heavy flirt with her itsy-bitsy lisp."

"Whattaya mean?" Teddy asks.

"That creep. The only way she's gonna get out of seventh grade is by marrying. She's feebleminded."

Teddy blushes.

"Oh, she's a lot of fun," Leo says.

"I don't like laughing at idiots," Nancy says. "Four years in seventh grade, my God!

Teddy tonguetied, betrayed before Joan.

"I like her," Leo says. "She's unpredictable. Don't laugh!"

Nancy smiles. "She say yes?—Cat got your tongue, Teddy?"

"He wrote her a love letter," Leo says.

Teddy thrills with anger.

Nancy bursts into her fingers.

"Why didn't she say yes?" Joan asks.

"I just mailed the letter," Teddy husks. Stares at the table's carved initials, hearts. Harry James blows "Sleepy Lagoon."

"She's very nice," Leo says. "I really like her."

"Well, I'm not bats enough to be stuck with her for a whole night," Nancy says. "We've nothing in common. Besides, she's too old for you, Teddy. How old is she, fifteen, sixteen? Ye gods, those tacky blouses—I'll bet every guy in school has seen her development."

"Well, she's not responsible for that," Leo says.

"She could wear better covering," Nancy says.

"She's not immodest," Teddy says hoarsely. "She's so shy she can barely talk. Staring at her feet, pigeon-toed because—"

"Because she's ashamed of her headlamps," Leo says.

Joan hides her face while Nancy guffaws. Teddy's eyes burn.

"Oh God, let's get off this subject," Nancy says. "Teddy's purple."

"So am I!" Joan cries.

"Besides, Chuck Goodell's already asked me, Leo," Nancy says. "But I may go to Yale instead. And Ed Simpson wants me at Lincoln."

"Well put me down for fourths," Leo says. Pulsing jealousy.

"I'm not promising anything," Nancy says. "Who could stand Gerry Palmer all night anyway? Joan, ready?"

"Like me to carry your packages?" Teddy, still pink, asks Joan.

"Not tonight, Teddy."

Nancy stands, raising her arms for her coat.

"That's against the Pure Food Law," Wayne Coon says behind the soda taps.

"What is?" Nancy asks coldly.

"Letting all that babyfat sit outside the refrigerator," Wayne says.

"Yeah? Well, that's where you belong. On ice."

"Hey, I close this joint up at eleven-thirty. Why don't you and I go for a midnight skate up at Lincoln?"

"No, thanks."

"I guess I'm too old for you," Wayne says, setting up water.

"Too old, ha!"

"But I'm a sucker for babyfat. Think it over. Eleven-thirty."

"Come on, Joan."

"Bring your skates. Hey, one thing. Is all that for real?"

Nancy tilts her head and smolders. Reaches for a waterglass and belts Wayne's chest.

"Some of that missed me," Wayne says. "Try again. Then I'll try."

"If Old Man Fulmer were here, I'd have you fired." Nancy smiles through flame.

"You want his number?" Wayne asks. He rings No

Sale. "Here's a nickel. Number's right over the phone. Be my guest."

Helene drapes over the counter, howling, *"You finally got it, Coon!"*

"Be my guest," Wayne says shoving a glass at her.

Helene splashes Wayne and runs to the back room.

"Now it's my turn," Wayne says and runs after her, calling at Nancy, "Don't go away!" Catches Helene at the washroom, lifts her screaming, and drops her kicking into a half-full soapbarrel.

"Wayne Coon, get me outta here!" she cries.

Twins gleam through window of swinging door. Wayne comes out. Leo asks, "Hey, d'ya think Old Man Fulmer'd hire us?"

"Why not?" Wayne asks. "Ask him. Gunny Nelson's leaving for Parris Island next week. You two together might be able to do half as much work as he does alone—and he works like ten men. I'll be joining the Marines myself as soon as I get rid of this pimple on my nose. I gotta get me some Japs before Gunny ends the war."

"Help!" Helene screams from the kitchen.

"You both wanna work here or just Leo?" Wayne asks. "Just kidding. Tell you what. Get the Swede outta the soapbarrel for a trial flight. But don't let her out unless she gives you a kiss—or you've broken the code."

Nancy and Joan gone. Twins watch Helene burn in the soapbarrel. "Whatta you two morons want?"

"Wayne sent us to get you out," Teddy says.

"If I've got a runner, that pimpled moron's goin' off the Third Street bridge. Get me outta here."

"We're not allowed to break the code," Leo says.

"What's that mean?" Helene asks.

"She's not up on the code," Leo tells Teddy.

"Maybe we better ask Wayne," Teddy says.

"Get me the hell outta here! Come on, put your half wits together and lift!"

Twins bend over her blue fox eyes. She lifts herself on their shoulders just as Leo pecks her cheek. Soft perfume. She glares, dusting herself. Teddy backs away, but she grabs his shirt, kisses him. "And that, mister, is something you'll never get," she sneers at Leo, leaving, murder on her breath.

Wayne sees her coming and runs out the front door. An elderly couple waits at the ice cream counter. Helene dashes to the door—but he's gone. Soon the twins hear Wayne behind them, tapping down the garage backsteps. He stands at the bottom, eying Teddy's lipsticked red mouth.

"Tell Old Man Fulmer I said you do good work," Wayne says thoughtfully.

George splurges on gas stamps for a Sunday drive to Erie. Skyblue snoworchards. Villages rotting slush. White grapevines, far brown and red farms, the Nickel Plate freight flat out for Erie, blue steam vomiting on crystal air. Deep seat jouncing, rocksalt hard-ons, Millie's jiggle. Erie. Longforgotten factories. Cinders and parks in burning daylight, and then the Warner, the Shea's, and out past Hermann Fuehrer's beerhall (duckpin kings!) to a scooping road to the county lung hospital. Park.

Large ward, germ-killers shrinking the breath. Durwood yellow, surprised, puts in teeth. Wears a green eyeshade, dopes horses, writes the ward's weekly tout sheet and mimeographed newspaper. Millie swallows him, glowing nervously. He asks the twins what they're going to be.

"I'm gonna be a trumpet player," Leo says, "and Teddy's gonna be a comedian."

"Or I can always be a cartoonist," Teddy says.

George snorts.

"Have you been studying music?" Durwood asks.

"Not really," Leo says. "We play the piano a bit."

"Oh, you play quite well together," Millie says.

"You couldn't call that playing," Leo says.

"That's for sure," George agrees.

Durwood takes the twins aside and shows them a snapshot of a dancer with navelheavy breasts. Their inner eye pricks with sin. Durwood gets back in bed. Shock at his thin legs, stale yellow soles.

"We can play 'Chinatown, My Chinatown,'" Teddy says.

"You used to play that on your saxophone," Leo says.

"Did I?" Durwood says. "That's a long time ago, boys."

"Oh, it wasn't that long, Dad!" Millie says, patting him.

"Ha!" Cheerful, shrewd under green eyeshade. He gives the twins a green hempbound copy of *Leaves of Grass* his father gave him.

"You take good care of that," Millie says.

Going home, George stops at the choicest roadhouses to breathe and reckon their business magic. He enters taverns like a saint, sampling plastic leather and bar fumes. He is The Fox.

Dew Drop Inn. "Nice bar you got here," George tells the bartender. He and Stella hit the bar while twins play pinball and the jukebox. Sunday evening, the dance hall dark, Millie dancing with twins or alone, winding her heart into orange and blue trellis bulbs.

"I'm George Fox, I run the King James Club."

Shoptalk, then off to the next club in the dark where George knows the owner or spies a light.

"Oh, there's a pretty light," he says.

"They're all pretty to you, mister," Stella says.

"How you talk. One last one won't hurt. Shall we?"

"I'm not lettin' you go in there alone. Lead on, Macduff."

"I'll open the door for you, there may be ice," George says, getting out.

But George walks straight into the bar.

"Oh! did my ears deceive me?" Stella asks. "You kids hold down on the noise in this bistro."

"We're not children, Mother," Millie says, biting her lip.

George steps out of the roadhouse again, *opens* Stella's door. "They'll stay open till ten," he says.

"I thought your thirst had gotten the better of you," Stella says.

"I'll wait in the car," Millie says. Stale yellow soles.

"You'd better cut back to ale," Stella tells George as they go in. "And *I* will too."

"Don't tell me what to drink. Let's sit at the bar."

"Closer to the bottles," Stella says.

Dwarf bartender, owlface with tufted brows, wafting eyes. Leo and Teddy recall him playing saxophone at the Fairmount Grill.

"Black Horse ale," George says.

"Blackout ale," Stella says. "How can you drink that heavy Canadian ale? Make mine Genessee beer."

"Drink a premium beer," George says.

Stella huffs, fists on hips. "Scotch and soda, if you please."

"Where'd you leave your saxophone?" Teddy asks.

"Oh, I'm only an *artiste* on Fridays. What's your poison, boys?"

"I'll have a grenadine cocktail," Leo says.

"That's like a Horse's Neck," Stella says. Fake cocktail.

"Same," Teddy says. "How long'd you study the sax?"

"Started when I was eighteen. Played in a band my first year."

"I think you play good," Teddy says.

"Sure do," Leo says.

"I put my heart into it."

"Leo's thinking of starting trumpet lessons," Teddy says.

"You should both play," the dwarf says. "Then you could play duets."

"Oh, my God," Stella says. "That's all I'd need, two trumpets around the house!"

"Oh, they weren't serious," George says. "Any news about the Nayzis?"

"Never heard of 'em," the dwarf says. "Out for a Sunday drive?"

"Glide," Stella says.

Headlamps glimmer like silver searchlights, no way to dim them. George clings hopefully to his side of the road, boozes through the rising glare. The twins sigh as the air cushion from the passing car rocks them and all goes black but for the endless flakes crashing into lamp beams and flat windshield.

"AND I want to see the dust fly!" Stella says. Twins set to sweeping the basement. Seven mean days for theft. Days slip by, painful only within.

Stealing money before the alarm rings, Stella still, numbed George snoring. Twins tiptoe from bathroom sidedoor. George's pants hang on a closet hook, wallet bulging. Trembling creak. Minutes. Drawn shade orange with early fire. Soft gulps of silence, flyquiet along the wall as Leo's fingers cop the wallet. Slowly two twenties peel out. Teddy bugs. Too much! he cries. Leo slips back a bill, takes a ten. Counts three hundred dollars in the wallet, gives up. Bright nerves, silent boys in Stella's vanity mirror past the sleepers.

Their own bedroom a prison. Sky chokes the window. Must get out.

Hot bodies skidding Eighth Street ice on galoshes. Sunbright blue winter.

Cut up Prendergast. Throats burning and peeling. Sky red. Houses give bronze beams into the dim street.

"We did it," Teddy says. "It's too late to go back. Let's trust our luck. How often've we got caught?"

"Let's get some hot chocolate."

"We'll have to break a ten," Teddy says.

"So? Are we criminals?"

Nervous friends, they sit as if not joined at the Hotel King James coffee counter. Leo fumbles his menu onto the floor. Their bond strains as he scratches at the floor and Teddy bends a bit, then steeply—still not joined. Pain mounts as Leo hangs below. At last Teddy lifts Leo and the menu.

"Lets have toasted English with our chocolate," Teddy says, flexing his thigh.

"Okay. I want two."

"Oh me too.—I was just thinking of that green riding crop."

"He wouldn't use it on us."

"We saw Millie," Teddy says.

Leo's bun drips. "Grease on your chin," Teddy says. Wipes Leo's chin, urging him higher with his own chin. Leo eyes Teddy. They are as one jaw raised—eaters watching. Twins lower buns, outstare a man and woman. Leo and Teddy scorn being watched eat, although they eat helplessly in rhyme.

Teddy breaks the ten and they go out stuffed. Too early for Bigelow's, walk down to the train station. Sunrise brick smokestacks orange over the town powerhouse on the Chadakoin.

"Boy, that's something for Charles Chickens," Leo says.

"Should he ever write again," Teddy says.

"Sketches by Chickens," their column in the school paper, nears deadline.

Valleyfilling snowfall, roomy, wide, falls afar on house and hill of coldsoaked sycamores. White sun a hard pearl point. Rough snowflakes, slowfalling, the Chadakoin a cold-moving mirror as the twins lean on a pipe-iron rail above it, flakes melting silver.

Into Bigelow's. Countergirls yawning. The store's dim crime of empty aisles. A jewelry girl's face, hard green beetle, the dawn.

Twins ride up to the sixth floor. A $14 remote-control indoor plane they've come to buy. Must have this secret of flight as their own. Teddy pays. A can with their bill and money, piped by vacuum to cashier. Twins wait. Ringing fear as the can pops back into the basket with the change. Does a note bare their theft? Saleslady counts their change to them, goes on wrapping the clumsy package.

"That's really w-w-wrapped well enough!" Teddy says.

"Just give it to us," Leo says.

Skip down slate stairs. Women's hats, windowblinds, curtains. Lending library. Corsets, brassieres with fake flesh. Over snowing Third to the Humidor. Fast-check the comicbooks—"The Claw"—a moondrenched Chinese peril looming over skyscrapers! Their eyes race under green woolen caps.

"Let's get one of those zombie pipes," Leo says. "Okay, Ted?"

"Good idea," Ted says. Mr. Lofgren holds up a zombie pipe. "What'll we smoke, Rum and Maple? London Dock?"

"Sir Walter's not bad," Leo says. Mr. Lofgren's hand passes from London Dock to Sir Walter.

"I like sweet and aromatic," Ted says. Mr. Lofgren skips back to more costly London Dock. "But I like Rum and Maple flavor too."

"Let's take all three," Leo says. Ted nods.

"A wise decision, boys," Mr. Lofgren says.

"Where'll we take the plane?" Leo asks going up Spring. Friends' houses pass through their future. "Let's hide it upstairs in our garage," Teddy says. Walk around rear of their block, cut backyard, climb a fence, sneak into their own garage unseen. Icy car stinks. Let down the steps and climb upstairs.

"Well, we can't fly it till George leaves," Teddy says. Hide plane, pipe and tobacco, go down, tie up ladder behind them. In the kitchen, $12.45 is left in Teddy's pocket. "D'ya think it's safe to have it on us?" Leo whispers. Teddy shrugs. They open the dining-room bureau where George's whitebound copy of James Joyce's *Ulysses* hides under doilies with its dirty words. Twins carry the book up to their room by the back stairs, read a *Time* clipping in the book, look for dirty words. George snores in paradise across the hall. Back downstairs, hide book again. Stand in thought at back door. Where to wait out George's leaving? Out on porch, pull on galoshes. "Where the hell shall we go?"

"Let's read in the cellar," Teddy says. "It's warm."

"Maybe too warm—if George counts his money."

"That's just the take on the slots. He can't miss thirty dollars, you heard him stagger upstairs. *Sheist!* We've come out without our money."

"Let's knock up the store bill for some root beer and cream puffs."

"My very plan, Holmes. Let's bring our skates."

McIntyre's grocery. Charge a half-gallon of root beer, four sugardusted cream puffs. One-armed Mr. McIntyre takes pencil from plaid cap, wets it, and runs up the week's bill: $19.28. Clears his throat, not looking at the boys, then puts the bill pad away and sits smoking in his rocker by the potbelly stove. His wall-eyed wife, Josie, uses a cane to move her black-gowned heap about painfully, says hello, fills the candy case. Twins' eyes rove over candy bars. They charge six Mallo Cups and leave. "Come again, boys," Mr. McIntyre calls, his pencil out again and point wet on the pad. George's mother, watching from her window, waves as they pass on their way to the rink with their marshmallow cups, cream puffs, skates, the root beer barrel passing between them.

"Stella will turn purple," Leo groans.

"When she sees the bill," Teddy says. "Maybe she won't pay it today."

"Let's hope George doesn't pay it himself," Leo says. "Or we better head for Zanzibar."

Powdered sugar, banana cream filling in flaky pastry, running sugar under the tongue, numbing sweetness, and belches.

* * *

Red and yellow mapleleaf electric plane circles hums dips its arm as Leo gooses and dims the power. Sitting on George's workbench, Teddy stuffs the zombie with Rum and Maple, lights it. Looks down on the kitchen's ruffled muslin.

"Not bad!" he says, spuming pearlblue in harsh windowshine. He holds the pipe to Leo's mouth. *Whoof!* Leo coughs. "It burns!"

"Ya shouldn't swallow so much, dummkopf. Trying to kill us?"

"No, just me." Hands Teddy the powerbox, empties the zombie into a coffee can, fills the bowl with Sir Walter. Teddy lands the plane, starts slow takeoff around floorboards. Red and yellow plastic slants up a ramp of power. "Ah," he sighs. "How's the power make it go up and down, *mein Führer?"*

"By sheer imachination, my boy," Leo says in pipesmoke. "This is easier to swallow." He holds the pipe for Teddy, who swallows slowly. Teddy's eyes water, he waves clouds from his twisting head. Smoke pierces his crotch. Worry courses his arms, killing his lift. The power buzzes in his lap. "I got a terrible boner," he says.

"Great idea," Leo says, unbuttoning. They hold the power-box to Leo's lap and watch blood flood Leo's tail. "Boy, that's tremendous!" Leo says. "But let's not come or we'll be tired all day." His eyes close. He waves away a rising blue light. "Ahhh, I'm feeling up Nancy."

"I'm undressing Gerry in the igloo," Teddy says. His balls tighten on blind cords, then fall slowly like balancing pans.

"I'm so big!" Leo says. "What if we're too big for girls?"

"It's possible," Teddy says.

Desire in spine and limbs, breasts urging, breath cleaving the single wave gathering, three billion lives pressing cell by cell to be burned on the breath, germ-blasts spasming, flooding, red maple treesweet nerves alight.

"Cut that fucking airplane!" Teddy cries.

Plane lands through blue smokebanks. Millie's out back in her snowsuit. "We gotta hide this!" Leo says.

"Shit, you know George hasn't even left yet," Teddy says. "We must be *fools!"*

Grind sperm into boards, hide the plane in a doorless closet. "What smells up here?" Millie asks, coming up.

"*What* have you been smoking?" Sniffs tobaccos and pipe. "Where'd you get these?"

"We bought 'em," Leo says, standing on his wet spot.

"Want to try some?" Teddy asks, roots burning.

"No, thank you," Millie says.

"Well, if you don't try, you'll never know," Teddy says.

"I don't ever plan to take up smoking," Millie says. "Let me watch."

Teddy stuffs the zombie full of London Dock and puffs at Millie. "Smell that!" He slips the pipe to Leo with an alerting rap on the leg. Leo puffs, hands the pipe back. "Watch," Teddy says. Takes a long deep pull, then puts more smoke on top, puffs his cheeks at Millie while smoke pl*uu*mes out of Leo.

"Oh, you make me seasick, "Millie says. "Look outside. Here comes George. You'd better watch yourselves."

George slides the rollerdoor up. "Are you boys up there?"

"Yes," they say. "We're just coming down," Teddy says.

Hurry down with Millie, pull up hinged ladder as George rolls down his window, warms motor. "How about doing some shoveling out here?"

"Sure," they say. Cologne prickles George's air. Yellow cashmere coat, pearl stetson back out the drive, face crisp for business, blue eye fearless with money.

"Will he ever change?" Teddy asks.

"Never!" Millie cries, hanging skates about her neck. "Have a nice morning shoveling, boys, if you haven't lost your *wind,* ahem."

Half the drive shoveled. Leo says, "I'm tired! Look, we can't play with the plane in the garage all the time. We gotta say we borrowed it."

Windriver ice. Snowtails whip and sigh over the porch-roof. Leo slips and Teddy grabs him, they thump onto their spines, lie quietly, band pulsing in its sleeve. Stella opens the front door.

"Are you in your right senses? Get up!" she calls shivering.

"We're resting," Teddy says.

"Wake us in half an hour," Leo says, closing his eyes.

"You young men do a good job and I'll thank you for it!"

They jump up and begin picking ice fourhandedly with a crowbar.

"Will wonders never cease?" Stella asks and goes in.

Her eye hoping to give thanks lingers in Leo, worry saps him. Flakefall dense and steady, the drive fuzzing over. "Let's say we borrowed the plane from Paul Clark," he says.

"Sure!" Teddy says. "Let's go down to Paul's, then pretend we brought the plane back." Teddy stands gasping at the empty Sheldon mansion. He and Leo dumped over half the magazines from their magazine route into a basement windowwell of the mansion, having filched from George's wallet and become too careless to walk their route. Somehow the magazines were found, and a week later a man showed up at the house. Sitting in the living room with Stella and the magazine man, they split with guilt. Another time, with Jason Barnes, they lifted the skirt of a three-year-old on her back porch, and next afternoon a pair of city detectives came on a charge by the mother. Sitting with Stella and the detectives, the twins burn hoarsely. No charges. No George. Only angry sadness, unable to bear each other in the bathroom mirror.

"Don't look at me, Teddy, I can't bear to look at you."

"I can't bear to look at *you!*"

"Big cheese."

"Shrimp."

Sliding down Eighth Street hill in cutting wind, over to Paul Clark's on Lafayette. Passing his music parlor, they see Paul on the rug with Loretta Mirabile. Twins rap, teeth bared, the hopping hunchbacks Quasimodo and Ygor. Paul waves them in. Stomp up back porch, pull off each other's galoshes, peel jackets in empty kitchen. The twins feel awe in the kitchen of Paul's father, who is running for mayor on the Socialist ticket. They have listened to Mr. Clark's flat palm make plain the printers' union strike against the *King James Evening Journal*—a strike of which he is a leader—right in this kitchen, face red, hair red, eyes pale as a righteous angel's.

Late afternoon. Plane circling music parlor, cutglass sunstains on wall and piano.

"Where'd that come from?" Stella asks.

"We borrowed it from Paul," Leo says.

Stella gives mock country surprise. "It looks expensive!"

"Nah," Teddy croaks. Plane landing on rainbow blots.

"Don't tell me it isn't. Why'd he let you borrow it?"

"We're friends," Leo says.

"Young men, look at me.—Are you lying to me?"

"Why should we lie!" they say.

"You tell me why."

"We got no reason to lie," Teddy says straight into her.

"You're both foolish to think you can pull the wool over my eyes."

Ringing pain. Scarlet flame blinds their eyes. They fear to their deeps.

Stella's sternness pours. "Do I have to call Paul's mother?"

"Call her for what!" Leo cries.

"Don't call her," Teddy says.

"I'll call her if I don't hear some straight talk mighty quick."

"Well, you haven't proved anything!" Teddy cries.

"We're guilty without doing anything!" Leo says.

"You've earned it, believe me!" Stella says. "Now what I want to know is where you got the money to buy this and when did you buy it?"

"We didn't buy it!" they cry.

"Oh yes you did. Now where'd the money come from?"

"What money!"

"Why are you lying to me? I can see deep inside the both of you."

"We're *not* lying!"

"No," Teddy says. "You don't have to call Mrs. Clark, Mother."

"Don't sweettalk me, Theodore, my son." She snorts at heaven, then with a deep cry of loss stares at them wretchedly. "You boys have no conception of the misery you cause me. Have you finished lying? Where'd you get the money? Did you take it from me?"

"No," Teddy says.

"We wouldn't," Leo says.

"Don't say that, because you have—and many times! Now let your shame be your guide. I wish you *had* taken it from me. Now I'm ashamed."

Teddy, hellsick, says, "We took it from George."

Leo's heart races. "This morning," he says.

"How'd you manage that?" she asks.

"From his wallet. We sneaked in from the bathroom this morning," Teddy says. "Forty dollars. . ."

"Thirty!" Leo sobs.

"Which was it, thirty or forty?"

"We put ten back," Teddy bawls.

"And now we're sorry," Leo says.

"And well you should be," Stella says. "My dear sons, what am I going to do with you? Where could we ever go and live like this? Why did you have to have this toy so badly?"

Leo stares at the resting secret of flight, pale rainbow fading. "I don't know," he says, his tongue still white-swollen from pipesmoke.

Teddy crosslegged, heavyheaded. "We don't like to steal," he says.

"When are you ever going to learn that?" Stella asks. Her eye bears a far glint of forgiveness.

Next day Durwood's mother, Anna, comes on her Christmas visit. George likes her acid tongue.

Alone with the twins, wearing Stella's purple robe, she calls them up from their cellar cleaning. Crosslegged on gray music-room rug while Anna hooks a square lace doily for her great table spread for Stella. Fingers blue and fine-boned, violet arteries. Lace, tough as chain-mail, hooked and noosed into everlasting knots. Green eyeshade, gray hair waved for her visit, withered cheek-bones, shrewd eye under rimless glasses barred with daylight.

"Your day will come, mark my words, your day will come with bells on. Who *cares* about the 'Quints' any-more? And look how Shirley Temple's faded, that little pot.

"Your mother's very upset, but *thank* God she saw that plane before George got home. She went down to Bigelow's this morning and they've given her a due-bill for fourteen dollars. Now answer me, you naughty devils, why'd you need that toy so badly?"

"We don't know," Leo says.

"Can't you explain why?" she asks. "I know you're not insane—the world hasn't driven you to that, at least not yet." She smiles.

"We liked to fly the plane," Teddy says.

"And watch it," Leo says.

"Well, when you're going to steal George's money—"

"We aren't gonna anymore!" Leo says.

"—do your minds sort of cloud over?" she asks. "Could you stop right at that moment if you had to?"

"We don't have to steal," Teddy says.

"Some people can't resist stealing," Anna says. "Kleptomaniacs. Do you feel neglected? Do you feel stopped at every turn when you try to do things?"

"No," Teddy says.

"Do you feel your mother doesn't love you?"

"Of course not!"

"Is it exciting to steal?" she asks. "Well, it beats me. Maybe you like being caught."

Twins laugh painfully.

"Did you want to hurt your mother?"

"No!"

"Sometimes people steal to get caught," Anna says again.

"We don't!" Teddy says.

"We didn't think we'd get caught," Leo says.

"But you knew you'd break your mother's heart if you got caught," she says.

"Well, we thought *we'd* get punished, not Mother," Leo says. "Didn't we?" Teddy nods.

"But you laid yourselves wide open bringing the plane home."

"We thought we could *lie* better," Teddy says.

Stare out at the healing snow. Anna holds back her smile.

Leo-Teddy in the cellar. Durwood lives there with his family. The twins are joyous, but Durwood fails to see them. He walks gravely apart. The cellar is a cabin with warped boards the breeze blows through. Trash slopes out front. A sun-blue day in the backwoods.

Durwood looks fearful, shaken. He walks by dry white ashes bordering the trash slide. His family lives as outcasts. He wears a frock coat and vest, smiles with cold warmth, walks stiffly. His face has a black fungus shingle covering his nose and cheekbones.

Ten members in the family, all younger than Durwood, each with a curse. Leo and Teddy first meet two little old ladies, dwarfish daughters who look even older than Durwood, their father. One tiny daughter has reddish coloring and bulbous wet eyes like a drunken Pekingese, a finished lady floating on splintered nerves, mingling notions. Each time she tries to speak with Leo and Teddy, her mind clouds, she falls into tiny barks and wailings. The other little old dwarf sister has a small bloated body and no flesh on her legs, just skin and bone. She's carried everywhere by hand for each family occasion, for she can't walk and is muddled speechless.

Durwood has three blond sons in their teens, each impaired, bent sidelong with worries. A balding older son seems fit and powerful. A ready smile flicks under a self-willed glint, his friendliness broken by gasps, his breath held above a wound, a gap in thought freezing him helplessly until breath sucks in. His smile breaks with passion, an embrace of his illness.

The four are sons of the dwarf daughters and Durwood. The sons age their mothers by daily incest. Durwood's wife, nearby but unseen, has a hidden scourge so overflowing that she breathes with wounds. Durwood's pity is the family. Each soothes the others, as he has been taught by Durwood with his hard spongy shingle and grave temper. All their sex is pity. Each gives all to the family, the twins see.

For repentance, the family keeps in a corner a great brown crock in place of an outhouse. Wooden cover. Monthly, all join in a sacred shit-throwing custom that is feared with awe. The ceremony starts, and shit and piss wash through the air like matter of gold. A light binds the room.

Turning over the crock, Durwood goes slowly to the door, rips the black fungus shingle from his nose and cheeks, and throws it into the trash slide. Leo and Teddy thrill with pain.

Two wounded birds rustle in the trash, skittering. A cat . . .

The twins jolt up in bed, currents in their nerves.

Parolees go carelessly into the train station, rest with bags of potato chips among servicemen on Christmas leave. Watch a plainclothesman sit cuffed to a prisoner. "Wonder what *he* did?" Leo whispers. The prisoner a blond bony kid about twenty, with cool blue heart-chilling eyes. Plainclothesman seems a rookie. "Think he might escape?" Teddy whispers. "Cuffs burn," Leo says. The idea of a pained wrist in a scuffle spreads a twinge in their band. They sit back burning.

Finish chips on the street, creak through snow up to the stores on Third. Third is not strung with Christmas bulbs this year because of the Nayzi air-raid hazard. They think of the twenty-seven-pound turkey home in the oven. "He couldn't get away," Teddy says, "the detective has a gun."

"Hey, maybe the other guy is the prisoner," Leo says.

"Are you mad, Holmes?"

Shun Bigelow's (scene of the Electric Airplane Fiasco) and go up past the post office, clerks laboring at long tables of holiday mail. Past the pillared gloom of the *Post-Journal,* a building bleak as the Lindbergh kidnap. Past the YMCA where, not as members, they had their hands burned on dry ice in a black room during a Halloween party—a spiteful hurt, they felt—palms red for three days.

"I don't want to leave King James," Teddy says.

"Oh, I like it here. It's a helluva lot nicer than Erie."

"And the trees are so beautiful, every street!" Teddy says.

"It's very nice. Where'd we go if we did leave?"

"I dunno. I mean I'd like to live in King James when we grow up," Teddy says.

"Oh, this is the best. How many towns have we seen, twenty, thirty, forty? King James is the most beautiful town I ever saw," Leo says.

Stop at Prendergast and Fourth and view the Christmas bulbs of the Scottish Rites Temple, the Elks manor, the Eagles manor, the blue-neon funeral manor, and the private manors across the street, a broad lane of wealth and elms and vast blue lawns of snow.

"How could we ever think of leaving?" Teddy whispers.

Leo's silence chimes.

Walk uphill to feathery lamplit snow of Lakeview and turn onto their home walk. Hushed snow glitters under high goblin branches in a yellow cavern. Lakeview starts here and goes an unwavering mile of candlelit houses to the winds of Lakeview Cemetery, which is unlighted. Here are barn-sized houses, steeply roofed, brimming with music parlors. Here lies Yvonne the doctor's daughter, their fair love who has sleeping sickness. Here's an empty manor whose rooms they have entered in moonlight, curiosity echoing through musical rooms, and a menace of bay rum bottles. Whose windows are these, this tall white house with Greek porch and dining room aglow, as bitter chill pierces the scarves at their mouths? Here's the Tudor manor whose huge cozy shape warms them with thoughts of dwarves. And now Eighth Street hill falls away like decks of the *Titanic* sliding under, amazed with falling snow and blinking red and green at the bottom.

Stomp into the outer hall. Arnold Sundberg cracks nuts while Fred Johnson marvels at Stella's tree village. George in needleworked midnightblue smoking jacket. Wheels his mahogany and mirror-aluminum whiskey wagon with cocktail shaker, ice bucket, bubbling siphon. Hot rooms reek with baking turkey. The boys groan with hunger, Fred and Arnold laugh.

"Hereafter don't track snow into the hall," George says. "Go around back."

Stella waves from the kitchen in all her stones, purple dress, upswept hair, country girl perk. "If I asked two young gentlemen to put on their good suits, would they do that for me?"

"Hey, Toots," Fred calls upstairs. "Come down and put some music on.—How's the market in Amalgamated Doorknobs, Fox, old snake?"

"I'll be right down," Millie calls.

"Come here and kiss me, you dickenses," Anna says, gowned and waving a glass. "I'm having my medicine! You believe that and I'll tell you another."

The bird cools on the oven, the dining room shines with dishware and linen. The glass door is open to Stella's whiskey shelves and small bottles. Twins go up to change, find Millie in makeup, trying to hook her bra. "Let's watch that wandering eye trouble," she says.

Change into blue suits, douse their hair. Hard-ons. Close the door, shoot into sink.

"We're crazy," Teddy says. "That wasn't worth the effort."

Leo breaks into tears. "I'm so hungry!" he cries.

"I know how you feel. Don't make me cry too."

"We may never have a girl in bed for our whole lives!" Leo sobs.

"Yeah, well, maybe so. Buck up. You're getting me sad too."

"Don't you cry, Teddy."

Teddy bursts into Leo's beautiful smelling hair. Go into their room, close door, cry abed. Millie goes downstairs to Anna and Stella. "My God, they're having a nervous breakdown up there, the both of them!"

Anna and Stella go up to the twins but get nothing from them. At last, they're put to bed weeping. Cry in bed all through supper.

Dr. Gogarty's called across town. He comes into their room, closes out Anna and Stella.

"Boy, that kitchen smells fit for a king," he says dead drunk. "Well, what's been so demoralizing, boys?"

Twins speechless. Dr. Gogarty's three hundred pounds sag the bed, redwaffle brow dripping.

"This's an interesting condition you describe, boys. I need rest. Would you like t' sleep?"

Shake their heads no.

"What brought this on?" he asks.

"We're alone!" Teddy cries.

"Alone!" Leo cries.

"Right now and forever," Dr. Gogarty says. "Now you can get up, 'cause I know Stella's got a great spread for you. Millie's down there eating all the dumplings, I gotta go." Slumps across them, snoring, bed creaking like a freighter. Twins pull out from under, get up for late dinner. George drinks below with Fred and Arnold in the kitchen.

"Aw, we know it's tough on you kids," Fred says as they open the icebox. Smile wordlessly, take out bird and stuffing. Eat in the dining room, hollow-eyed, robed. "You're the champs!" Fred calls out. "Whatta ya think, Toots?"

"I think they're my brothers!" Millie trumps. "That's what I think, buster!"

"Cut 'er off!" Arnold cries.

"No, she hasn't had enough yet," Fred says.

"Oh you—!" Millie shrieks, pouring apricot brandy at the sink.

"What do you think you're doing, young lady?" Stella asks. "That isn't wine."

"Oh, I don't want to get naughty!" Millie says.

George roars.

"Fox! Fox!" Arnold cries. "When're you gonna knock off the beeswax and break out that 151-year-old scotch you're hiding?"

George snickers, bursts into braying. "It's only fifty years old. And I'm never gonna open it!"

"Yes, you will, by God," Anna says, queening downstairs. "I'm not gonna live forever. If that's the finest liquor in the world, I want a shot of it, you old skinflint. I can taste it now—that's a flavor I'll remember till my dying day, *ha ha!* By heavens, do you know that rapscallion Gogarty is asleep on the twins' bed? It's the funniest thing I ever saw. They've put the doctor to bed."

Leo-Teddy is very silent. "All they need is a laxative," she says. "George, you old scoundrel, where's that scotch?"

"Millie," Stella says, "fetch the bottle from my cabinet."

"Are you sure it's in here?" Millie calls out. Twins freeze. "I can't find it."

"Oh, it must be there," Stella says. She weaves into the dining room and with great peering inspects her shelves. "Well, my word, where could it have gone?" Turns, a surprised general. "Mr. George Fox, what have you done with that bottle?"

"Stella's lost a bottle, Foxie," Arnold says, ducking his neat throat scar.

"What are you accusing me of?" George asks blue-eyed.

"Where's that bottle gone, sir? I want a straight answer."

"I swear to God, I don't know, Stella."

"I can tell when you're lying, sir."

"Lying? About my own bottle in my own house? There's a doctor upstairs, if you can wake him."

"And he'll be there if I need him!" Stella says, arms crossed. "We have guests I'd like to serve that scotch to."

"Now don't you two go getting rambunctious over me," Anna says. "Forget the damned scotch. I'll taste it next year."

"I will not forget that bottle," Stella says into George's face. "I'd like to know where that bottle has gotten up and walked off to."

"Well, I don't know!" George shouts strangling. "And I don't have to answer to you! So shut your mouth about that bottle!"

"I'll not shut my mouth, sir! Not until I get an answer that I can say I like." Chin thrust over folded arms. "Just what do you think you're getting away with, little man?"

He rises above her, whitefaced.

"Watch it, Foxie," Arnold says.

"Hey, Stella, baby, forget the bottle," Fred says, rising between her and George. "Who cares about the frigging bottle anyway?"

"Fred Johnson, mend your language in my kitchen," Stella says.

"Hey, sweetheart, I was just talking among the boys, you know."

"Well, I'd appreciate the discontinuance of such talk."

"I'll beat your face in!" George shouts.

"There speaks the jawbone of an ass," Teddy whispers at the dining-room table.

Stella bounces from the icebox as Fred and Arnold hold George back. Stella sits holding her jaw on the linoleum.

"Boys! Boys!" Anna shrieks in tears.

"I'll get my gun!" George shouts.

"Hold him, Arnold!"

"You boys get out of here!" Anna shouts at the twins.

Twins race to the stairs, shaking, go back for Stella. "Well, that took the lights out of me," she says, moving her jaw slowly. She reaches out. "Now you two sons of mine get me onto my feet and we'll show this—"

"I will not eat your shit!" George shouts.

Stella looks away in pain. "Oh! keep your foul mouth to yourself."

Feet pound as George struggles. Anna knocked, turkey platter cracking in the sink.

"Oh my God, it's Christmas Eve!" Anna wails, holding the sink.

"And I'm the one who's crucified!" George shrieks at Stella.

"Come on, Foxie, that's Easter, not Christmas," Arnold says. "Jesus Christ, don't you know your own religion?"

"Not a word about my religion!" George cries at Arnold.

"You know me, Fox." Arnold winks. "How could I go talking about anybody's religion? I don't even know what it is. I'm just out here on the same earth as you and Roosevelt, George."

"And now, sir, where'd that bottle go?" Stella asks.

Face redblotched, George bursts free, goes trembling and swearing into the living room, bellowing at the ceiling. Twins stand thrilled as white anger comes at them with fists upraised. Teddy pulls out a fistful of George's white hair to keep him from Stella. She lunges at George.

Millie screams at George, "I'm standing up for my mother!"

"Oh you're gonna get yours," scalped George says hard at Millie.

"Are you threatening my daughter?" Stella asks. "I want you to know there are people listening to every word you say, mister."

"Hey, Foxie, you're really murder when the sauce hits you," Arnold says.

George's eyes burn with a full breath and he lurches outdoors in his smoking jacket.

"Hey, Fox, whereya goin'?" Fred calls. "Get back in here."

"Let the bastard *freeze!*" Anna cries. "Close the door, we're better off."

George under dashboard of his car, getting gun. He sometimes fires his .45 into bushel baskets in the Club cellar Sunday nights, unbothered by police. Looks about wildly in deep backyard snow, goes off cross-lots to Steel Street in his smoking jacket, gripping the gun.

Dr. Gogarty comes down carrying an empty scotch bottle. "Fox, you got any more of this old shellac? What's this disaster?"

"Oh, my God," Anna cries, "what we've seen tonight, Doctor, would drive a sane man crazy!"

"Where's George?" he asks.

"Gone to the Races!" Anna cries. "And good riddance! Doctor, this has been the most painful night of my life."

"Thank you for telling me."

"I want you to know that. The torments I have passed through this night are indescribable. Don't laugh at an old woman. I mean *indescribable!*"

"Hey, Stella, put some ice on that eye," he says, opening the icebox.

"Well, hand us the ice tray!" Anna says.

"Stella, where's that piccalilli you make?" Gogarty asks.

"For God's sake, it's on the *shelf,* Doctor!" Millie yells.

"Where's George?"

"He's raving around in the damned blizzard," Anna says. "And just where he belongs! You boys get your mother upstairs and get into bed, and you too, Millie, my poor darling."

"I think we better get dressed and look for Foxie," Arnold tells Fred.

"Don't you dare bring that bastard back here tonight," Anna says.

As the twins help Stella upstairs, she moans, "Oh, what have I done to deserve all this? Oh, what have I done? O my God, let me drop here, I can't go another step. *Just bury me!"*

"Oh my God in heaven," Anna says, following, "get a grip on yourself, Stella, you poor darling. You're all done in by that monster. *God damn him*! He'll not harm one hair on your head as long as I can stand up to him with these two boys. But you've got to help. I'll clean the kitchen."

"What for? Oh, what for," Stella sobs on the stairs in her purple dress and diamonds.

"Stella, is this any way for your sons to see you?"

"It's all that's left."

"Stella Marie, you stand on your feet!" Anna says.

"By God I will," Stella says and mounts the stairs.

"Maybe we should listen on short wave for the cops," Leo says.

"Are you out of your minds?" Millie asks loudly. She stands crucified in her bedroom doorway. "Oh, what you have been through for us, Mother."

"Don't remind me! But I've always stood up for my children!"

"He wants to drive these boys from the house," Anna says beside her. "That's what the sonofabitch wants."

"Well, I'm ready to go," Millie says. "Except for *Mother."*

"Save yourself, my daughter," Stella says. "If you want to go, I'm not stopping you."

"Mother!" Millie screams.

"Mother my foot, young lady," Stella says, weaving

in charge. "You get into your room and stay there. I want to hear your radios and that's all I want to hear. At least I don't want to hear that man in my house again tonight. Turn them on, loud and clear."

"Mother, I will not turn my radio on," Millie says and slams her door. "Goodnight to everyone!—and a happy new year to all," under her breath.

"If she wasn't my own daughter, Anna, I couldn't live with her. I don't know how you managed. How did she— I'll remember that slam, young lady, and I have a long remembrancer."

"Stella, lie down," Anna says.

"Thank God you've spoken!"

Anna turns to Leo and Teddy. "You know the world is there, you poor innocents, but you just haven't been touched by it yet. God preserve you both."

"You're going to need preserving," Stella says. "Is the back door locked?"

Twins go down. Dr. Gogarty hangs over the kitchen sink, fumbling into the bombed nave of the turkey carcass.

In a barren lot on Steel Street, George fires six bullets into the forsaken house he was born in.

RACING *with the moon!* the jukebox boomscratches. Fulmer's splits with smoke after King James cracks tiny Lakewood on the Friday night gridiron. Car herds roar Third. Fevered twins set up orders, spirits pitchforked. White-eyed Helene and Joyce wait table in a blue burn of uniforms. Wayne yawns in the back kitchen roasting peanuts, steps out into the squeeze for tables, cries in the jukeblare, *"Swill, you swine!"* and goes back to his roasting oil.

"This is the last ball game I work!" Helene growls. Twins behind in their orders.

"Ravishing," Teddy says.

"Oh, are you two sick! Gimme some setups."

Teddy sets up glasses while Leo taps water, lines up sundae dishes. Teddy cleaves into frozen cream. "It's hard as rock!" he says, knuckles sun-red.

Helene hits the kitchen door. "Coon, get out here!"

Wayne turns from boiling grease, spreads salt over cooling pecans. "Oh, hi. Need me?"

"All the real men are in the movies killing Japs!" she says.

"And all the dead Japs get up at five and go home for supper," Wayne says. "All right, clear the decks!"

Bursts from kitchen, a Greek at Marathon, clears the dish-stacked counter, plunges glassware through suds, takes counter orders, moves in on Leo and Teddy. "The Marines are landing," he says, "go down and wait on the old folks and cripples." Racks up sundaes, whips shakes, needles sodas. "Swill's up, girls!" he calls.

Twins, abashed, pack bulk butterscotch for an elderly couple being jostled by rough fans near the door. Watch nervously, packing. The lady turns to a short boisterous noise and says, "Would you mind!"

"Sorry!" a dim Kid simpers, lids moron-fluttering.

Leo prickles and Teddy feels it in the freezer.

"You could have better manners," Leo says.

The Kid eyes Leo lovingly. Teddy's heart pounds with Leo's. He rises from the freezer, their four hands cleaver-mashing ice cream, folding box closed, squares his shoulders. Leo's lip slowly convulses against his teeth. The twins are the fastest ropeclimbers in Lincoln Junior High, their new school closer to work. They belong to the deathless brotherhood of Fulmer counter-boys, baying stags all. The short Kid shakes his head, amazed that Leo finds his manners twisted.

Teddy makes change.

"Are you in this too?" he asks Teddy.

"What? Leo doesn't need me."

"You need a purple heart, huh?" the Kid asks Leo.

"Well," Leo says, "I'll ask you to leave. Get out."

"Wonderful," the Kid says. "I can't believe my ears. See you outside, how's that?"

"It's unfair of me to take advantage of you," Leo says.

"Don't give it a thought!" the Kid goes out front, twins follow. Mill on the neon walk. Up the hilly dim boardinghouse lawn. Scorched weeds an evil wonder. Shadows swim. A ragged circle grows. Moontide lifts their hearts.

"You're welcome to join in," the Kid tells Teddy.

"I'll stand aside," Teddy says. "But don't hit me or I'll be forced to hit back."

"No promises! I don't like you any more'n I like him."

"You brought this on yourself," Leo says and almost taps the Kid's shoulder. His cheek bursts.

"Give it to him," Teddy says. "Leo?"

Leo grunts, hit again. Face burns numbly while turning lights settle. "I can't believe it," he tells Teddy. "I'll plow him."

Step forward, Leo ready to fight, Teddy ablaze. Teddy moves with Leo's striking twice at the ducking Kid, who hits Leo's ear and nose. Leo's nose bleeds. Teddy moves faithfully with Leo, whose fists lag. "Keep 'em up!" Teddy cries. "*I'll purge you!*" Leo cries, swinging hard missing blows between blows landing hard, Teddy his silent mighty fortress. The Kid raps Leo's eye, asks, "More?"

Teddy steps back, cold warning turning back heavy rage. Leo glares at him. "We'll cut this short," Teddy says. Sees himself leaping in while Leo faints pulling them down, himself writhing to get up.

"Another day," the Kid says.

Wayne walks up. "What's going on, gang?"

"We're settling differences," Leo says. Blazed face.

"Are they settled?" Wayne asks.

"Yesh," Leo says.

"Can you work?" Wayne asks.

"Maybe we better not," Teddy says.

"Whatta you talkin' about?" Leo says. "I'm workin'. Let's go."

"Go around back and wash up," Wayne says. "And save that apron for the butcher shop. A clean pelt will do wonders for you."

The Kid stands in the crowd before the store as Leo-Teddy passes through to the alley. Climbs the brick road to the garage, goes in. Joyce opens the door, tawny, startled. "Are you both all right?"

"Yeah," Leo says. "Be on the counter in a second."

"You don't have to work for my sake," Teddy tells Leo.

"Here's a clean apron," she says.

"Thanks. Wow, I lost in the first round."

"You did better'n that," Teddy says. They go down the back steps to the kitchen.

"Ha!" Leo cries.

"You'll feel better," Teddy says. "Come on, we'll clobber that guy together. If that's the fair way."

"I'll smash you."

"Don't get me going," Teddy says. "We're down at the store."

They crowd into the one-man restroom.

"Lean over," Teddy says. "Lemme wash thy offending image."

"Thank you, Grandfather Kerris, I'll wash myself."

Leo looks at his bloody face. "Why'd you step back?" he asks.

"We mighta killed him. I was turning into Karloff. But you were getting awful dizzy. What if you'd gone down? —How would I fight?"

Leo stiffens. "I didn't even land one hit, Teddy!"

"I saw some. You did, think back."

"Maybe I must have. Yeah, I hit his hip."

"We only lost the first round. We'll have another."

Both scrub the bloody sink, borne under by unbearable desire. One bodysoul.

Leo looks at his face. Staring, pinkbutchered pig, eye blackening, cheek cut.

"Let'a put on a Band-aid," Teddy says.

"Oh, shit!"

"Think of the customers, Tarzan."

"Well, you get a clean apron too. We'll be the Gold Dust Twins."

"I don't feel like an *act,* Leo."

"Yeah, you do. Get a fresh apron. We'll look better."

Into the kitchen. Helene falls through the doorway laughing. "Don't stop me!" she cries. "I can't stop laughing. You shoulda seen him!"

"Seen who?" Teddy asks.

"Wayne in the doorway. Right out of Alan Ladd! Those guys tried to come in and Wayne says, 'I'm afraid you gents aren't allowed. We have a special case here and I'm store manager. Go home and kick your dog.' *The Kid starts to boil!* Wayne says, 'I'm *tellin'* you. I've watched you in the gym and you got a very flowery left hand about four inches shorter than mine from me to you. Wanna see it?'

" 'Another day!' the Kid says.

" 'You're gonna be a great fighter,' Wayne says. 'But you're lucky you're alive. Don't mix with those twins again or you won't come out of it.' I was right behind him with the bulk ice cream cleaver," she says.

Zealous, watching Wayne set up orders, they tie each other's apron. Push through the kitchen swingingdoor. They flush. The dairy's packed.

"So watch it," Teddy warns. "No act."

"Reinforcements to the sink," Wayne calls. "Gentlemen, will you?"

Twins dig into syrupy sundae dishes in clean aprons and, pulsebright, raise a fountain of water in fire-shovel haste, sudsing, rinsing. A sprinkled girl screams in a booth. "Pep it up a bit," Wayne says. "But keep the rinsings in the sink."

Leo burns. "Now watch yourself," Teddy says, "you'll break a glass."

Leo reckless. Eye swelling. Cocks his head to work with his outer eye. "We're suffering for nothing," Teddy says. "We should go home."

"I'm not goin' home!" Leo shouts.

"Well, screw you," Teddy says. *"Big* wheel."

Washing dishes, foreheads steamed. Breast-hunger in smoothswelling Coke glasses, booths of sweatered bed-ready smokewrapped virgins sipping sugar, spooning syrup, rooting, snuffling, snorting through gossip. Twins' muffled heat-heaviness deep and hot, simmering the marrow. Leo ready to bite his own forearm with anger, or sweltering earthly happiness, fingers white in germkiller rinsewater.

The twins are in deep silence for the weekend, washing, eating, reading. Every move is by habit alone. On Monday Stella says they need new suits, sends them down to Joe Printz's men's shop. Joe out, they choose for themselves. Tangled minds at racks, they hate being watched by clerks. Step into three-way mirror, Leo in collarless yellow Woody Herman bandjacket and holding smooth powderblue trousers to his waist, Teddy in banker's charcoal pinstripe suitcoat and black homburg, draping pants from his waist: Leo leans forward for a sideview past Teddy, Teddy straight, then Teddy leans; Leo straight; lean back, tops new, old bottoms baggy, shinyrumped, shameful. The ashen khaki snap-on sleeve on their band is Stella's handiwork—"We don't want your band naked on the street! And keep your pants buttoned up too," she warns, "until you get married. You *wait* so I can be proud of you." Teddy's heavily wisped upper lip mirrored endlessly, Leo's new knee-length gold keychain gleaming on lucky blue. Purple carbuncle tripled, tripled, tripled on Leo's neck.

"Gotta cut down," Leo says.

Hole cut and pants side-zippered for their band, they walk to the dairy in new skins. "One of us is ridiculous," Teddy says, homburg raked.

"I hope you don't take up bookkeeping," Leo says. "Belong in a bank!"

"Well, I hope you don't take up clarinet, Woody."

"I'd rather sit in a band than a bank," Leo rasps.

Sit in a back booth with Helene, their smoking gear out.

"Finished for the day and rarin' to go!" she says. "Where ya takin' me, Zoot?"

Dream Boy Leo smiles down a fag while Teddy crams his zombie.

"Where'd ya like to go, Scarlett?" Leo asks.

"Why, to the King James Club, where else?"

"I'm game," Leo says. Teddy's heart leaps.

"Cashed in your life insurance today?" she asks. "Aw, I don't want to go there, it's too fancy." She goggles at Leo's rainbow-pineapple silk tie. "Hey, give me a souvenir," he says. "Go ahead!" She bites rouge lips onto his pineapple. "I'll never have it cleaned," Leo says. Beaming.

"How about Gandy's?" Teddy asks.

"You *both* really wanna take me out to dinner?"

"Oh, indeed," Leo says.

"Oh, yes," Teddy says. "Very much." *Nudge.*

Leo holds his fag to his outer ear, inhaling through nose: Teddy turns his own outer ear like a spigot, slowly lip-plumes upward.

"Goes right through, huh?" she asks.

Leo keeps Teddy curbside on the evening street, Helene on Leo's arm. Six years older than the twins, her fiancé a sailor at Pearl Harbor. Lively, blue-eyed chiseled blonde, pure Swedish blood. The twins' hearts race, grip hope like a thief.

Leo sits by Helene on a couch-bench at Gandy's new seafood house. Dim linen, fine wood. Bel's working wife, Mildred, strews menus. "Hi, boys. How's your mother?"

Parisians stand for Mildred, show Helene. As they lift their menus, Helene eyes the waitresses. An army flight captain comes in, his hat a fifty-mission crush. Ahoy from two salts on stools. Leo kisses Helene's fingers over his ginger ale. "You're svelte tonight!" he says.

"There's Kenny at Pearl Harbor," she says over her martini. "And here have I languished, buster, for the two finest years of my life. Me, with an unblemished reputation, how've I done it! Are you two talking tonight? How about posting a truce?"

"Happily," Teddy says.

Watch Dr. Gogarty heave in.

"We should all go out dancing some night," Helene says.

"All around the lake, hit every spot," Leo says.

"We only fox-trot," Teddy says.

"Well, we could learn," Leo says.

"Heck, yes, I'll teachya!" Helene says. "And we'll get Myrtle."

"Great idea," Leo says. "You go with Myrtle," he tells Teddy.

"What's it matter who goes with who?" Teddy asks. "It's my day."

"Maybe you two shouldn't talk," Helene says. "Hey, let's hit the band tonight! Whoo, I'm hittin' already, ha ha."

"Wanna hit Celeron?" Leo asks.

"Heck, yes! Let's call Myrtle, she's got her brother's car."

Helene phones Myrtle, Leo and Teddy say nothing. Dr. Gogarty downs a double brandy, walks over.

"You two look better in matching suits, frankly. How's Stella? I know how George is. He's gonna lay off that sauce or I'll kill him."

"Kill him," Leo says.

"He's been drinking in bed for two weeks," Teddy says.

"Yeah? Why hasn't Stella called me?"

"Well, he's not sick, you know," Leo says.

"Just drinking," Teddy says.

"Can't she get him up?"

"He just lays there and says What's the use," Teddy says.

"Says he's taking a three-week vacation," Leo says.

"Does he know which week it is?" Gogarty asks. "I'll stop up tonight and help him count bottles."

"He won't be going anywhere," Leo says.

Gogarty hits the bar for his evening blackout as Helene returns glowing. "We meet Myrt at eight at the store and we'll be in the ballroom by the time the band comes on." Leo takes her hand. "Let's cut the mustard, Wolf Man," she says.

After dinner buy flowers for the girls, meet Myrtle. Myrtle's a Fulmer girl who married a sailor. "Get in," she says, "I brought some *glögg*."

"Oh, my God, I'll get pie-eyed!" Helene says.

"Real *glögg?*" Leo asks from the backseat.

"Yeah, half a bottle. Dat's all ve had left from Christmas," Myrtle says. "Wait'll we get outta town, you guys."

"How're you tonight, Myrt?" Teddy asks.

"Hey, I'm great!"

"Then have a carnation, lover," he says.

"Hey, I'll start thinking there's something between you two!" Helene cries. Myrtle pushes her while driving. Very hardy girl with broad shoulders, brown hair, brown eyes stamped with faith. Teddy once loved her sister Grace from afar. "Who's playing tonight?" she asks.

"Stu Snyder the trumpet-player," Leo says. "He plays dance trumpet."

Pass the City of King James riverboat at the Boatlanding.

"But he's not Harry James!" Helene says.

"I think you're lovelier than Betty Grable," Leo says.

"Shut up!" Helene cries.

"Heck, ya know it's true!" Myrtle says.

"Whatta ya want me to sign?" Helene asks.

Park at the Pier Ballroom, drain Myrtle's *glögg*.

"Well, I'll be the goat," Myrtle says. "*Oof,* it's got sediment. Let's dump the bottle."

"I'm ready to lose my reputation," Helene cries. "Whoop de do!"

"Let's not whoop till we pass the ticket-taker," Myrtle says.

"Well, I'm just gettin' ready," Helene says, taking Leo's arm.

Ballroom in a snowcovered fun park. Look for a trash basket, walking through blind arcades toward the rollercoaster. Great white dripping skytrellis, rolling into dead night. World's fourth largest Ferris wheel, still. Empty waves under airplaneless Airplane Island, its tower turning flakes.

The ballroom fills with girls and servicemen as Myrtle claims a table near the dance floor, brown eyes braving the crowd.

"Monday night's a tough date to play," Leo says, watching musicians find their stands.

"Hell, it's Live Today!" Helene says. "Let's powder before the band starts."

Homburg Teddy, stroking his mustache, tags a rushed waitress for four rum cokes.

"Let's make the bar for a fast one," Leo says.

"Sit down and constrain yourself," Teddy says. "We should be here when the girls get back. Anyway, we'll be recognized."

"Look, I'll take a chance if I want to."

"I don't think ya should. But it's your day."

They stand apart at the marine bar, banker and bandleader. Leo belts a rum. Winding back to their table, strangers.

Teddy pays the waitress.

"Hey, ya got away with it," Myrtle says, nudging him.

"As I expected to," Teddy says, hat off at last.

Stu blows "You Made Me Love You." "That's the James solo," Leo says. "Hey, not bad."

"What're we waitin' for?" Myrtle asks.

"Hell, yes!" Leo says.

Dance with small steps to the beat. "Boy, you're feeling your oats, aren'tcha?" Helene asks Leo.

"I love you," Leo whispers.

"You shouldn't," she whispers, but he holds her close. "Stop this moment or I can't dance with you."

"Je vous aime parler d'amour!" Leo whispers. Dance, dance.

"Where's your brother George?" Teddy asks.

"Treasure Island," Myrtle says. "Hey, you're good!"

"He was a great counterboy. Wish I'd worked with him, he'd have taught me a lot. Will he be coming back to the store after the war?"

"Not if he has any brains." Myrtle laughs.

"God, I'd like to be a trumpet-player," Leo whispers to yellowhair. Kisses her neck.

"Not on the dance floor!" she gasps. "I'm wearing my ring."

"Wayne's great to work for too," Teddy says. "Terrific counterboy."

"You roast peanuts yet?" Myrtle asks.

"That's coming up," Teddy says. "Wes's breaking me in on the sandwich board first. Boy, he's fast—and really paperthin slices of ham. Takes skill to cut ham like that."

"Instead of your thumb," she says. "Hey, I'm getting a crush on Teddy," she tells Helene. "We'll have to change partners. Some people think a married woman should stay home, you know?"

"Hell, I forgot you're hitched," Teddy says.

"Ya think these rings are from Woolworth's?" Myrtle asks.

"No, Cracker Jacks," Teddy says.

Change partners. A lumbering alto leads off on "My Blue Heaven." Fox-trotting to the bounce, Leo and

Myrtle clinch silently while Teddy holds Helene at picture distance. "I rarely get a chance to look at you," he says.

"Who dya think I am—Frankenstein?"

"You're no monster." Presses her. "You're a viking flower."

"Comes on mighty strong, don't he?" Helene asks.

"This is a standard tune," Leo says. "Oh, pardon."

"I walk on 'em all the time," Myrtle says.

A throttled trombone follows the clarinet's cracked ornaments. Above the dancers a burning ball twists, rainbow-mirroring. Change partners. Stu blows "Silver Wings in the Moonlight." "We may try to invent something to help the war effort," Leo whispers to Helene. "I mean, if the war keeps up, we may devote ourselves to scientific research." They fox-trot their box step, then pivot on Leo, box-step again, and pivot on Teddy, Leo sweeping Helene, dusting her ear with sweet-talk. Rum.

Crosstalk at table, twins ignoring each other, kings mountaintops apart.

"Ever hear of Louis Armstrong?" Leo asks Helene.

"How long ago'd George work at the store?" Teddy asks Myrtle.

The band boogies, shakes hoarsely, the girls jump up, jitterbug together. Twins sit, drink, careless lords beating the table-edge. Leo hails the waitress. "Great crisis," he says, "we needa refill."

By night's end Leo is queasy. Twins to the men's room. Rinsing faces, wetcombing hair. Leo suddenly heaves.

"Oh, God," Teddy says, holding down his own sinking sourness. Rinses bowl while Leo drools. "Let's get outta here before we're recognized!"

"Hold your horses," Leo says. Bloodred eyes. "Need a quickie at the bar."

Myrtle drops Helene off first, twins wrangling all the way. Leo-Teddy walks Helene to her snowdrift porch.

"Shh, don't step on the porch, you two'll wake everyone. Well, I ain't *pie-eyed* but I'm happy. It's been a swell night, boys." Pecks them both, Leo first. He holds her hand. "And I've still got to write Kenny tonight!" Leo squeezes her gloved hand, quickly kisses her lips. "Enough of that! See you tomorrow."

"Goodnight, loveboat," Leo sighs. She bares a long half-wounded farewell in lamplight, creaks indoors on crushed snow. He stares at the Christmas wreath, envious of Swedish customs although his own house has a door wreath.

Leo silent beside Myrtle. She drives miles uphill to Lakeview. Snow falling, Teddy and Myrt whistle "Dixie." As she drives off with kiss and carnation, Teddy says, "The cellar lights are on."

"George's up," Leo says. "We can't sneak in."

"Le's wash our mouths with snow."

"Good idea," Leo says. "When we get in, head straight for the root beer."

"Merciful heavens, *what* are you wearing!" Stella cries in her robe in the kitchen. Covers her eyes. "Get upstairs before George sees you—you *comedians.* I'll talk with you later."

George crawls up cellar steps, bearing a fifth of Chivas Regal. His graybrown robe from bachelor days. White hair ruffs its devil's peak, spikes prickle his chin. "Get outta my way," he says, deeply hoarse.

"Changed your brand, have you?" Stella asks. "I'll not move mister, you'll crawl by me."

Twins glimpse blue eyes faded red on the kitchen floor, race upstairs—they always avoid three on a stairway. Close door, undress. George lurches below against the chimes.

"You'll get up there on your own power, my fine feathered friend," Stella says loudly. "You're waking the dead!"

George falls back, mangling the chimes again. "*Oh, Christ, will you let me die in peace!*" he cries, belljambled.

"He belongs on the Chinese Broadcasting System," Leo says.

"We may have to take that bastard tonight," Teddy says. Knocks Leo's shoulder, holds Leo's robe for him. "We gotta stick together about these clothes," he says.

"Wanna make up?"

"Well, it's the only way to live together," Teddy says. "I wouldn't wanna have to knock you downstairs to teach you a lesson, Einstein."

"Boy, are you crazy!" Leo laughs.

"So you shouldn't provoke me."

"I'll never shout at you again," Leo says.

"Maybe you should listen to me sometimes. You fought a good fight—I couldn't have done better. The Kid's out for the Golden Gloves, after all."

Cuff links into tray. Lift Millie's cast-off satin memento box from dresser. Sit on bed, smell Nancy Ruleburner's lipstick stub, magnolia sweetscent curdling the lungs, Gerry's sachet and ten-cent Woolworth perfume bottle, Joyce's lavender sachet, heartdeep valentines, Helene's napkin liprouge smudged, Pier Ballroom ticket stubs, a banjo bracelet charm, notes signed, and a matchbook cover green-inked by Louis Armstrong.

"Now that *he's* locked up, you two come downstairs," Stella whispers. Millie haggard in her doorway. "Go back to your bed."

"I'm going to the *bathroom,* Mother," Millie says.

"March," Stella says. Twins down to kitchen. Stella's green-iron strongbox on the table. "We'll have to *scrimp,* my friends," she states.

"Scrimp on what?" Teddy asks.

"Scrimp! If that man doesn't get out of his bed. Why, Father Tobin was here tonight and couldn't raise him! And if the father tells him he's going *straight to hell*—as he *did* tonight—and that man just goes downcellar for more, then I say it's time for the rats to think. If we're still here after the ship goes down!" Bursts into tears.

"Don't cry, Mama," Leo says. "It doesn't help."

She falls against them, weeping fumes. Straightens up. "No, I will not give in!"

Straightens herself against the sink, chin up. She rays an infrared stare. "You twins are all I've ever have. God hasn't give me much in this life—but when He gave me *you,* He made up for everything. Now what's this horseplay? What're those clothes? Is Joe Printz out of his mind! I did not send you down to come back like comedians. Was Joe there?"

"No," Teddy says. "I like my suit."

"In ten years perhaps," Stella says. "And a *homburg.* Are you going hoity-toity? And *you* in technicolor—I mean you *look* like a pansy! Where'd you get that pineapple tie?"

"It's silk," Leo says.

"You don't like homburgs?" Teddy says.

"My likes and dislikes aren't the question," Stella says.

"My pants and jacket are very good material," Leo says.

"My *foot!*" Stella softly slams the table, braking her palm. "Well, you take my breath away, the both of you."

"We're not worried about appearances," Teddy says.

"That's right," Leo says. Bright, tired, pupils doped. "We don't worry." Worry? Wha-a-a? . . .

"Do you mean to stand there and say you're going to disgrace me in those clothes? I won't be able to leave this house for a month! Oh my heavens, can't you give in just this once? For your aging mother? I'm so tired of dying!" she sobs. "Don't you two know I think you're both something special? That you're my gift from heaven?—not like your sister and *not* a pair of clowns!"

"Come on, Mama," Teddy says. "I got my heart set on a homburg. I like to wear it."

"To junior high school?"

"What's going on down here?" Millie huffs. "Haven't we enough crazy people in this house without the three of you trying to wake him up? What're you looking in there for?"

Stella clamps her strongbox lid. "I was counting how much we have to live on."

"Can't that wait until morning? It's gettin' late, Maw," Millie says.

"My dear, our every possession is in this box."

"And it'll be there in the morning," Millie says.

"Don't be too sure of yourself. Now go to bed, all of you. I'm giving up for today. We'll talk about those clothes tomorrow. Goodnight, one and all. Just think of me as something the cat dragged in." Marches into the pantry for a nightcap.

"Oh, good heavens, go to bed, Mother!" Millie rages. Races upstairs, sobbing.

Leo and Teddy in pantry, kiss Stella goodnight through fumes. "Thank you, my sons. What have I done to deserve this? I can bear your sister and I can bear George, but your *clowning* takes the wind right out of me."

"Let's go upstairs," Teddy says.

"Will you gentlemen go down and close the liquor cellar door for me?"

In the cellar they slam the lock they've learned to pick. "Thank heaven there's no blackout tonight," Leo says. "Let's hope the black market feds don't check in here."

"Just a little sugar, a little coffee," Teddy says. "Shall we open some of that dark rum and hide the bottle?"

"Let's just hit the pantry for a snort. How about sneaking up a five-pound bag of sugar to Gerry at Washington tomorrow? Show her our clothes."

Next afternoon Geraldine stabs at Teddy's hand with a linoleum cutter in art class. The cutter sticks in the table. Teddy's stoned. Geraldine walks out of the class, leaving Teddy blushing rash-red in his old art class, Leo thirsty. Wrap up the sugar with artpaper, leave it as a five-pound present inside the rear stormdoor at Loretta Mirabile's with a mash note sighed by King Kong.

Lenten midwinter, earthfrost and sun. Blue glare on Saturday morning lawns and roofs. Blind day squeezes from burning alley, ditch, and gravel. The twins shake in their blood as Leo leads Teddy down to Abie Present's shadowy hockshop by First Street Rescue Mission's great red metal sign:

C
H
R
I
S
T
GOD IS LOVE
S
A
V
I
O
U
R

"Show me the horn in the window," Leo says. Short Mr. Present, soft hands, thick glasses, sweet blue business eyes.

Nervous wonder as he goes to his window. Crimefingered cornershadows. Pawned watches, rings, twins' dim fingers in pockets. Touch no germ in this sunless underworld the Nickel Plate engines shake from the overpass.

Leo cradles the horn. "How d'ya hold it?"

"Put your fourth finger through the ring," Mr. Present says.

"Oh," Leo says. "Sticky valves, hm."

"Sure it's sticky, been in the window a year. Needs a little valve oil, that's all. Blow it."

"Can't get anything out of it," Leo says. "Is it stuffed up?"

"Lemme try," Teddy says. Blasts. Jumps.

"That's it!" Mr. Present says. Takes chammyshiner, burnishes the bell to chrism. Rim dents, large crook crumpled partly, lacquer-eaten valves. Sundeep redgold hole.

The twins pay $36, Leo into Teddy for $16. Mr. Present pens his sales slip. Leo's wind bounds, nose flaring, smoke-blue eyes hardpointed. Mr. Present smiles from his sacred gulf, master of seabottoms of King James, guarding this horn for the coming lover. The twins course with fresh purpose.

Walk upvalley to Third, cross granite quarter-mile span of Third Street bridge. Great trainyards, radium tracks. Bright Chadakoin three hundred yards below. Over the river Leo lifts his horn, hoots waveringly. Sapphire daylight on hills. His spirit struggles at the mouthpiece.

"Blow reveille," Teddy says.

Leo blows wake-up. "Hey, do you feel the song of nature? Let's go to the gravel pit and blow."

"Beautiful day, let's go, gate," Teddy says. "And drop in on Chuck Campbell."

Whip to the tail of Livingston Avenue, cut to the abandoned gravel pit. Climb old mill up to the hopper where stones go in, stand on the great blue rollingtrough, now still. Eye its deep turn down yawning raintrenched cliffs. Farmland beyond, soon to be April loam, now strawgold in lenten sunlight.

"I get a lift up here," Teddy says.

"Look at that toy coupe."

A beetle crawls Jones and Gifford Avenue. Twins watch from wings. Coupe putters into trees.

"Best friends?" Teddy says, redoubling peace.

"All right." Leo shakes. Hands gripped, shoulders clasped, nerves joined in a rush. "I didn't mean what I said after the fight," Leo says.

"Aw, you meant some of it," Teddy says. "I feel that way too at times but keep my trap shut. Forgive and forget?"

"We're fools. We think we can lead separate lives."

"We do," Teddy says. "Quite a bit. I help you on your days and you help me extra. I know you do."

"That's not what I mean."

"Well, learn trumpet. We got to try."

"Try what!"

"To save ourselves." Teddy squints. Bending blue light above.

Leo sees hazegolden farmland, a house he knows quickly he will never enter. Its life draws him into it. He sees a table he will never sit at with a family that may not be. "What'll we do when one of us wants to get married?" he asks.

"We'll face that when it comes."

"But what'll we do?" Leo sighs. Rubs a shrunken railing, sees a double coffin.

"Well, someday we'll look back and say, 'That's what we did.' We'll do something."

"Just take it as it comes," Leo says.

"That's it," Teddy says. "Now let's go down and blow the horn."

They search the blue going back to Eden.

"Thumbs up!"

Warped narrow stairladder, slats missing. Go down carefully, their weight on joints. The pit gapes steeply beneath. Flooringboards lost. Hop over skinny boards, missing holes.

"Terrible way to go," Leo says.

"Let's not theorize," Teddy says.

Cliff's edge, dropping stones down raingullies into pools and brush. Leo lifts his horn, puckers crabbily, bleats long and high. "What's that?" he asks, listening closely. From a faraway barn a cow screams.

Teddy watches Leo's lips, urging. "Punch it out like a bugle," he says.

"Needs spit!"

Takes out rusted valves. Spits. Third valve sticks.

"I had an *awful* dream just now!" Teddy says. "You dropped this valve and we went down the gully after it. We're fourfooted."

Leo looks down the sheer gully. "That's *far!*'

"That's what makes it so awful."

"No more like that, please. Pull down your homburg, Muggsy." Leo tightens third valve, lifts his horn. "I'm Christopher Princeton." He strangles "Stardust." Teddy fixes on the woodsmoke farm, calls back a dream and dreams it afresh. He sees an old man in a coffin with a huge summer sausage hard-on springing from his breast, his lungs giant testicles.

"Let me ask you something," Teddy says.

"Wait'll I finish practicing."

"Oh! I thought you were really blowing. Tell me when to listen."

"I'll tell you. Look who's coming."

Chuck Campbell, his old frame house overlooking the gravel pit. He raps drumsticks, chasing a ghost drum. Brown hair; brown eyes that try to split the twins. Staggering wild surprise.

"What is this vast talent? I asked myself," Chuck says. "I *just* sit down to my bones in my bedroom when suddenly I hear Bix blowing 'Stardust'! Well, the first three notes. Right outside my window! I tell myself, *This is history*. It must be recorded. Mr. Beiderbecke, would you be so kind as to step into my, *ahem,* recording studio? Mr. Petrillo is waiting."

Wend up a stony path through brush. Chuck's bedroom windows burn blue and cloudy.

"My dad lost a leg in the trainyards. He's pensioned," Chuck says. Past sodajerk, Chuck sometimes puts in weekends at the dairy with the twins. His father sits on the back porch breathing the light. Soapsmelling sheets breeze on the clotheslines.

"Who's Mr. Petrillo?" Leo asks.

"You don't know Mr. Petrillo?" Chuck asks. "Mr. Petrillo, dear boy, is our president. James Caesar Petrillo, American Federation of Musicians, now striking. You haven't heard about the strike? My, my, you are behind."

"We heard about the goddamn strike," Teddy says.

Mr. Campbell says hello. Pudgy, smiling, thinskinned cheeks brightveined. "You the boys killin' that cow down there?" he asks.

"Ha ha, Dad, that was music," Chuck says. "You weren't listening. You wouldn't offend our guests, would you?"

"Naw, I wouldn't do that." Spits brownjuice, sits back an angel.

"All right, lads," Chuck says. "A little easy on the profanity, if you will. We try to keep a square cover on our otherwise illegal games."

"What games and when should we be here?" Teddy asks.

"Gents, a few of us, *ahem,* older Fulmer jocks are having a poker shindig here from ten-thirty until I take everyone's money," Chuck says. "If you'd like to chip in a buck-fifty apiece there'll be all the beer you can drink. And sandwiches! But bring cash or you'll find it dull. Wayne'll drop by after he closes the store. Don Johnston on leave from Texas, a Fulmer *giant*. Donnie Knowlquist, our mascot, Joyce's younger brother. You haven't met him."

"We see him around," Leo says. "He's twelve or thirteen."

"Just a fawn," Teddy says.

"Yes, but he loses like an adult," Chuck says. "And Alan Ladd Rishell, who's going back to base in the morning, and I hope he goes penniless. He won't need cash in the South Pacific—highly unlikely."

"Hello, boys," Mrs. Campbell calls from the kitchen.

"We're about to rehearse an impromptu cut," Chuck tells her. "So I'm not taking any calls, unless feminine in character or concerning business. Oh, forget the girls! We'd like not to be disturbed. Get my drift?"

"Disturb you!" Mrs. Campbell says. "Well, that isn't likely. Pound away, you don't bother me."

"Practice, Mother, not pound," Chuck says. "Follow me, gents."

"Does your dad play too?" Teddy asks Chuck. Up to Chuck's bedroom. Pearl-rimmed drums, cymbals, highhat.

"Poker? No. He'll have a beer with us, not much. He's not very active yet. I don't know how badly he misses his leg, because he never mentions it, but I think he's happy to be alive after the accident. It seems to have wakened him. Now here, gents, is my new record cutter. And here are two brand-new uncut disks. We just put the mike over here, close the door, turn on my extra record player. 'Cherokee' by Charlie Barnet, no relation," Chuck says. "Then we set the cutting needle down, I leap to the phonograph, start music, sit at my drums and . . ."

Twins jump at the loud drumfare.

"That's my ad lib," Chuck whispers over his rimtaps. "Not in the original, I'm afraid. Blow away, gents."

Leo cups his bell and wah-wahs "Cherokee."

"You'll have to build up your embouchure a bit," Chuck says. "Your *lip,* dear boy. I'll tell you later."

Leo splits ears. Teddy chills. Chuck shakes his head,

saying, "Calm down and try to play. You are too fortissimo, maestro."

Leo catches a phrase. "*Bunny!*" Chuck cries, hunched, drumming. "Oh, hand me down my walkingstick!" Twirls a stick, catching it egglike. The twins shout praise. Record ends.

"The song is ended," Chuck sighs, "but the melody lingers on. You amaze me, Harry. You just picked up a trumpet and already you can play it."

"Gimme time," Leo says.

"Now hear what we sound like," Chuck says. Blows black ribbons fron the new-cut disk, plays music. "Sounds like the gravel pit when I was a kid," Chuck says. Recorded room-sounds boom. Leo and Teddy laugh down a long tunnel. "Cherokee" faroff wah-wah. Leo screams, echoes crazed static, blurts pain. The record ends.

"You might try to learn the fingering," Chuck says. "Now, gents, this is the stark truth of the matter. One of you needs lessons. Let's try 'Sing Sing Sing,' Bix."

Mrs. Campbell bears a cookie tray, her country eyes bluebells in the din. "Here are some maple sugar stars I made for Ralph! Why don't you try them for me? They have walnuts. I'm leaving, I'm sorry I disturbed you."

"Mother, you can always disturb us for your maple stars. Dive in, gents."

Leo's scream. Eardrums needled.

"Is that what you just recorded?" Mrs. Campbell asks.

"Yes, Mother, but it's just warm-up stuff. It's not perfected. If you close the door behind you, it might not seem so loud."

The music fades, winding down a conch into the past. "You sound great!" Teddy says.

"Please, I'm modest," Chuck says. "Now I have the perfect viper's platter for the flip side of our debut disk. The fabulous Chuck Campbell Stardust Trio will now blow 'Let Me Off Uptown' with the Gene Krupa Grass Jockeys and 'Little Jazz' Eldridge, former boy marvel and trumpet wonder, with Teddy on comb and tissue. Unfortunately we have no grass for that extra zip. You haven't heard of grass, the musician's medicine? My, my, your education's in sad shape. It's a mild stimulant many sidemen smoke, sometimes called marijuana."

"Oh, that must be loco weed," Teddy says. "You remember that Tim McCoy movie at the Regent where the rustler smoked loco weed?"

"Sure. What does it do?" Leo asks.

"I've never had it!" Chuck says. "*What* do you accuse me of?"

"Does Stu Snyder smoke it?" Leo asks.

"Very unlikely. Grass is rarely found this far from the big apple."

"How about Harry James?" Leo asks, heart sinking.

"I'm telling you," Chuck says, "the frontmen don't smoke, just the sidemen. Have you ever heard musicians talk? They're worse than Marines, you never heard such foulness. Sometimes I despair for my art." Throws his sticks up. "But I go on!"

"Well, you don't *have* to swear," Teddy says. Breathes deep, comb and tissue up, virginal blood awaiting the downbeat.

"I try like hell not to but it slips out! Are we ready, gents? Enough education for now. Wait a minute, would you like to know which valves are which? Give me the horn. Now down here, this is low C, then you press the first and third valves and go up to D. There's a half-step, but we'll skip that difficulty for now, I can see you're being overburdened. Watch my fingers, I'll start again. Watching? This is C-scale, ahem. Just a little something I picked up." Blows a C-scale. "A bit leaky, Charles," he tells himself. "You try it."

Leo copies Chuck. "Hey, it works!"

"Yes," Chuck says, "it often does when you know what you're doing. Are we ready to record? Ted—you understand the fundamentals on the comb and tissue? *Ah,* change my cutting needle first. And these are fifty cents apiece! This's an expensive hobby. Are you set for the downbeat? We are about to cut, so swing out, gates."

"Let Me Off Uptown," which the twins have never heard, starts with a bounce, Chuck beating with Krupa. Leo joins with the C-scale.

"You're playing half-time!" Chuck shouts.

"What's *that?*" Leo asks.

"Play twice as fast and *keep* to my beat! You have to work even in heaven."

Leo soars to his torture.

Chuck holds his forehead in rapture, beating rim-shots. Blows dust from his sticks, not missing a measure. The twins gape. "And I'm working on my *tripple*-paradiddle!" he cries." But it's not quite perfected yet."

"Dya think they hear us down the block?" Teddy asks, clapping.

"Down to the bridge!" Chuck says.

"Woo hoo!" Teddy shouts. "Gotta have some woo hoo!"

Leo screams, screams, screams. The music stops. Soaring knife of sunglance horn, seeking a heart.

"You have a very modern style," Chuck says. "Nobody knows what you're playing."

Leo's lips swelling. "Who's the greatest? Harry James?"

"He's not bad on instrumentals," Chuck says, "when he's rid of those violins. In fact, he's very good. But then there's Randy, Bobby, Bunny, Sonny, and Bix, who all have great tones. On tone I can't really say Harry's best. Who do you think is?"

"Louis Armstrong," Leo says. Teddy husks, *"Satchelmouth, gate!"*

"You agree to his folly?" Chuck asks Teddy. "Well, this is too much. Gentlemen, Dixieland is *kaput*."

"What?" the twins cry.

"It is *très très passé.*"

"Dixieland'll never die!" Teddy cries.

"Ah, sanity. Where are you flown to?" Chuck asks, snare whispering. "Aren't you aware that Dixieland's turned into Swing and gone through vast technical changes too progressive for most listeners? And that there are players seriously reaching for Louis's crown? Besides, he's an old man."

"He's only in his forties!" Leo says.

"That's old in this business," Chuck says. "That's very old."

Leo searches for Louis on the C-scale. Lips swelling primrose.

Teddy beside himself, clapping. "Blow it, Hans!"

"Yah, Fritz!"

"Enough," Chuck says. "Shall we dig the playback? I hope you're both picking up on my viper's jive, gates, you can't swing without it or your fellow hep cats will think you're ricky-ticky-too—from Hicksville, if I must be plain. Ted, I think you'll have to double on valve trombone. Two trumpets in a combo our size is too Wagnerian for our purposes, not to say monotonous."

"What's valve trombone?" Teddy asks.

"It has three valves like a trumpet and no slide to bother with. And it plays in B-flat and uses the same fingering I just showed Leo. So whatever Leo learns, you'll learn too, and all together we'll have a very mellow sound, gents. You'll have to take lessons from Carl. He runs the one-man trumpet college under the viaduct down in Brooklyn Square. You have to blow louder than the trains overhead, but you'll learn your rudiments. You *are* interested in learning? Just making sure. Carl's a very great musician, he knows more than Harry James and Ziggy Elman put together, but he only plays classical. But believe me, there's no bottom to what you can learn about music. Sometimes even the rudiments take a lifetime and aren't mastered even then—but you two are cleverer than that, I'm sure. Now, gents, *ahem,* a buck-fifty apiece. I'll do the shopping and sandwiches between sets while Leo rests his new embouchure."

"You're getting one," Teddy says. "Looks like pink bubblegum. Does it burn?" Leo nods deeply, confirmed.

"I declare intermission," Chuck says. "Let's hit the store and you two strongmen help me carry back the beer and cold cuts. Beer should *chill.*"

At the store Chuck chooses cold cuts. Twins carry back two cases of beer between themselves. Chuck lays out white bread on the kitchen table, spreads mustard and baloney. "Nothing fancy, gents, but you'll eat every one of 'em. Be*lieve* me!"

After the next set, cutting "Well, Git It!" the twins stride home for supper. Spines charged with musical futures, four lungs hoping.

Stella mocks surprise in the kitchen. "Why, what's that instrument?"

"We bought it down at Present's. I'm learning trumpet," Leo says. *"Oh boy, chili!"* He and Teddy at the pot like magnets.

"You're what? What got that into your head? Does that dern thing make a loud noise?"

"He won't play it when George's home," Teddy says. "Chuck Campbell says I should double on valve trombone so we can play duets."

"Oh, heavens! That man lying up there next to death and you two want to bring home trumpets and—*trombones?* Where's your horse sense?"

"I forgot about George," Leo says.

"But we gotta live too," Teddy says. "We just won't play while George is, ahem, on vacation."

"Then make sure you play far away."

"Far, far away," Teddy says.

"The Swanee," Leo says, singing with Teddy. *"Far from the old folks at home."* Stella frosty.

Go up to their bedroom, sit at their cramped thinwood desk. White-lettered iron sign LINDSEY AVENUE faces them, stolen. George sleeps. They smell saucy chili, Stella stirring George's ashheap.

"*Emancipator* deadline's tomorrow," Teddy whispers. "Charles Chickens'd better get cooking."

"How about a fifteen-year-old kid goes into the Tennessee hills to visit a 110-year-old whiteheaded trumpet-player?" Leo asks.

"Sounds good. Why Tennessee? We know more about New Orleans."

"Well, we don't want the old guy confused with Louis. He plays like Louis but at 110."

"Well, it's appealing," Teddy says. "What happens?"

"The kid comes from a small town in Southwestern New York and wants the old man to teach him 'What a Friend I Have in Jesus.' "

"You mean 'The Carnival of Venice,' " Teddy says. "They'll think we're kidding."

"No, no, this old guy has *tone* and that's what the kid wants. Hell, he can already play 'What a Friend.' What he wants is the refinements. He's searching for the lost tone."

"What lost tone?" Teddy asks.

"The tone this old guy had that made him the world's greatest trumpet-player," Leo says. "The kid wants it and he goes to plead with the old man to teach him. So the kid comes up the hill. There's the old man blowing his cornet."

"How's his tone?" Teddy asks.

"Incredible. Like you can feel the wind in it."

"Sort of lazy? Let's write this down."

"Okay, now what happens?" Leo asks. Stares out at backyards rising uphill, shacks, and apple trees.

"Oh!" Teddy says. "Uh, the old guy is on his rocker in the burning sunset, blowing a hymn. He's given up jazz, except for funerals. The kid sits listening. The hills fill with the soft sweet tone. He's the Tennessee Sibelius."

"Too bad he's not W. C. Handy," Leo says. "So what's the kid learn?"

"We'll find out when we write it. He learns that the tone is in being subdued by nature and yearning for the land, like Stephen Foster," Teddy says. "Or *Finlandia*. 'Above thy hills with dignity and beauty—' "

"He *mutes* the tone!" Leo says.

"Right," Teddy says. "Tone's everything. To end it, Bix discovers he has to find the tone in himself. That's enough."

"Does he ever play 'What a Friend'?" Leo asks.

"Well, the old man teaches him, but the kid doesn't play hymns anymore because he's in Paul Whiteman's jazz band playing the blues."

"Terrific," Leo says. "But when he feels real sick of everything, he goes up on his Manhattan hotel roof and blows 'What a Friend' to the night heavens. Soft as the wind. How's that?"

Teddy nods. "Let's get it down before supper. God, that chili could raise the dead. So we open on a Tabasco sunset."

Chimes. Stella talks with Dr. Gogarty. Stairs groan, vast Gogarty goes alone into George and Stella's bedroom. Twins crack their door, listening. "He's the one man on earth," Teddy whispers, "who could meet the Frankenstein monster face to face and not flinch. Just take his pulse!"

"Get that horrible midget out of my room," George whispers hoarsely.

"What midget, Fox?" Gogarty asks. "Breathe deep. Deeper."

"I'm not talking," George squawks, *"unless you get that midget out!"*

"Let's check your eyes."

"Get him out!"

"Shut up."

"You're no doctor, you cheap phony fraud."

"Hey buddy, what am I gonna think at your funeral?" Gogarty asks. "The other eye."

"No real doctor'd allow that filthy bleeding thing in here."

"Am I the midget?" Gogarty asks, spidery chair creaking.

George snorts. "Are you crazy? How could you be a midget?"

"What's he look like?"

"Look for yourself," George says. "He's waiting to shave me at the mirror."

"I can't make him out."

"The top of his head's cut off," George whimpers.

"He lost his crown?" Gogarty asks.

"Sliced off like a pineapple!"

"Why don't we move you instead?" Gogarty asks. "That's solving the problem, don't you think, Fox?"

"No, I'm not going anywhere. I'm *not* sick! Who called you?—Not that I don't want you here."

"Your Filipino midget called me."

Twins watch George's door open. See themselves in Stella's vanity mirror past the bed. George white-bearded, teary-eyed, red.

"What's this varnish?" Gogarty asks. "Is this glass dirty? Let's have a belt for the days gone by. Ah, Chivas! Want one?"

"I'll have it if I want it. And keep your stoolie in the corner. *That fiend wants to kill me and doesn't even know why.*"

"How long since you held some medicine down?" Gogarty asks. "I mean scotch, Fox."

"Why, two hours."

"Stella says twenty. But I'm not calling you a liar. Not to your face."

"I should know! It was night—I mean daylight. Toward evening."

"Fox, Stella might think of committing you. We don't want that, do we? We gotta get you back on the bottle, Paddy. You need B_{12}, I guess, but I think something's eating you no pill can reach. Great slosh, this Chivas, *ahh!*"

"Have another," George says. "It's only vitamin deficiency, I know that. You know it too. Have a drink."

"Not alone, I gotta watch my habits. So phone me if you feel like it. I gotta get home t'bed. Good-bye, pineapplehead," he tells the mirror.

"Don't you have a kind word for me?" George asks. "You're my tower of strength, you sonofabitch!"

"Fox, all your strength comes in fifths, just like mine."

George's speechless bones.

"How can you talk to me that way, Sweets?" he asks. "Maybe I'm sick. Maybe I'm really sick."

"I'm not made of miracles, Fox. Would you like some morphine?"

"What're you suggesting? You can't give me morphine. I'm a sick man!"

"You're not sick, you're just resting between drinks. You got any more of that fifty-year-old varnish? I tellya the one Bel told me last week? This little old lady looks in her icebox one morning and sees a little man sitting in there on the oranges with an old-fashioned. She asks, 'What are you doing in there?' And he says, 'Is this a Westinghouse?' She says, 'Yes.' He says, 'I'm westing.' "

"I gotta get up!" George cries. "I've gotta get out of this house!"

"Wonderful. Where ya goin'?"

"I wanna get up!" George sobs.

"You don't think it's too late?"

"I gotta get well!"

"You're not sick, Fox." Gogarty empties the Chivas into two waterglasses. His brims. Holds the empty bottle over George's full glass. "Let's catch those last drops," he says.

"Get that filthy bottle out of here!" George cried.

"It's no good to switch to beer, you bloat right up—I know! You want my advice, pal? Drink hearty, you got years left."

"You big lout! I'll be at your funeral," George screams, getting up with a stomp.

"Don't step on the Filipino," Gogarty says. "Where ya goin'?"

"To the *bathroom.*"

"You *need* a shave," Gogarty says. "Look, I wanna confess. Remember Christmas? I'm the one who drank your fifty-year-old hooch. Hear you missed it later." He drinks half his glass. "Goes down like Mother's," he says, winking.

"There's more in the cellar."

"If I ever go down there, I'll never get out again," Gogarty says, coughing spray. "You go down. Oh, would you like some B_{12}? I have an ampul."

"Yes!"

George marches downhall. Gogarty drinks, takes out needle and syringe, starts to screw them together, missing. Moves to the bed for better light, fails the screw, sips the top off George's scotch. Slowly toppling back. "No, thank you," he says aloud, "I can't stay the night. Jus' westing. . . . *Somebody!*—pick me up in your arms, carry me home, and take care of me. . . ."

Paperwinged maple seeds peel from high, spiral to yeasty evening-showered beds.

Blue-green twilight over Davis's Drugstore, three green stars rising through branches above a Flying Red Horse. Meet the Redfield twins, Wilma and Wanda, five years younger. The auburn girls tilt their pale faces, steelrimmed vixens grinning. Eight hands crossing, elbows nudging.

"The Johnson twins moved to Busti," Teddy says.

"Now how many are we?" Wilma asks.

"I don't keep track anymore," Teddy says. "What was it last count?"

"Nine," Leo says. "No, ten. The Lasser twins on Spruce, they're new."

"What's your average?" Wanda asks. "We had 98."

"We're not working quite that hard," Leo says.

"We're running for vice-president of ninth grade," Teddy says. "We formed the Paratrooper ticket with Phyllis Cass."

"We'll call you to find out who won," Wilma says. "Still on Lakeview?"

"Yep," Leo says. "How're your folks? We hear 'The Gypsy Hour' whenever we're home Friday evening. Does their show carry to Buffalo?"

"No," Wilma says. "Just old WNKJ."

"And it's only fifteen minutes, not an hour," Wanda says.

"They still play nights at the Baghdad Lounge?" Leo asks. "Terrific. Like my new horn?" Toots at Flying Red Horse. "Ahem, we never thought they were spies."

"*Spies!*" Wilma cries. "We're Jews, not Germans."

"*Émigrés,*" Wanda says.

Leo claps his brow. "And all this time I thought you mighta been Nazis!"

"That's not even funny," Wilma says.

"Don't you hate the Germans?" Wanda asks.

"I hate Hitler," Leo says. Teddy simpers Adolf.

"Well, we hate Nazis, not Germans," Wilma says. "Don't we?" Wanda nods. "Let's cross the street, Wanda. Good-bye and good luck."

"Be sure to call when you feel like it," Leo says.

"Be sure to," Teddy says. Up Livingston to Lovall. "They're gonna be ripe someday. Big goon, you were pretty dumb there."

Wormsmelling streetbricks, greenseeded glow.

Shoot up Chuck's porch, knock under the dark ceiling-globe. Mrs. Campbell calls upstairs for Chuck, who floats down bone by bone, fingersnapping.. "You're early, gents. I was going out for a romp in my chariot, *ta ta!* Care to join me?"

"Thought I'd blow in the gravel pit," Leo says.

"Practice never hurts," Chuck says. "Not even a giant talent like yours."

Mr. Campbell snorts on the couch.

"Now, Dad," Chuck says. "You never know where musicians will spring from. There are remote possibilities we should not overlook, *ahem.*"

"I've heard steamwhistles sing better," Mr. Campbell says.

"He's Steamboat and I'm Dreamboat," Teddy says. "I'm gonna play trombone."

Slide into Chuck's peeling brown Ford. Canvas top back, creep out slowly.

"Driving a little carefully, aren't you?" Teddy asks.

"I try to keep blood off the fenders," Chuck says. "Where to gents?"

"Let's take a pizza up to Reservoir hill," Leo says. "I'd like to blow."

"I just ate," Chuck says. "Let's save your lunchmoney for the game tonight."

"We just ate too," Teddy says.

Open coupe gliding redbrick street under budding yellow-green bowerlimbs.

Leo by Chuck toots over the windshield. "Getting a callous inside my upper lip," he tells Chuck.

Cut over Third Street bridge, nightgreen valley beneath; star-hanging moon; stop at Fulmer's burning window. Store empty but for Wayne and Joyce. Leo blows the opening bar to "Stardust" in the tonebouncing dairy. Back to car with two pounds of hot salted mixed nuts filched for the party. Drive over Third, wait for the light at Main. The Salvation Army on the corner hymns "What a Friend"—the twins wave to Little Boona the cornetist.

"You gotta begin somewhere!" Chuck says.

Up North Main, Leo blows over the windshield, bangs his lip painfully.

Park on Thirteenth. Chuck goes to a porch and knocks. Johnny Rishell comes out in blues and swabbie hat, climbs in back, gripping hands.

"You 4-Fs remember I gotta leave for Sampson at 6 A.M.," John says. "Just in case I'm too tired to remember."

"We're 8-F," Teddy says. "Maybe worse."

"We'll get you on that bus, old salt," Chuck says. "We're only drinking beer tonight."

"I don't want no whiskey," John says. Highbrushed curl, faint lisp, tough lip. "Okay, where you 8-F slackers takin' me?"

"We're buying you a farewell piece down on Metallic," Teddy says.

"Start thinking about it now, John." Chuck says.

"Oh, I never go down there!" John says. "I don't go for dark meat. I'll sit out here while you minute men go in. I'm happy."

"We're not wasting precious lucre on Metallic Avenue tonight," Chuck warns Teddy.

"You're saving it all for my goin'-away present," John says. "I'm due for a winning night. Boy, it's spring. Let's hit Lakewood beach after the game, dya mind? I wanna see the lake."

Out of town to the Apple Inn for beers. Twins stand a round of blended whiskey. Back over dipping lakehills to Chuck's.

"Oh, man, do I hate to leave!" John cries, Ladd foreknot breezing. Under charged stars, passing Ashville turnoff's heavenhigh poplar lanes toptwisting in nightwinds down to the lake's harsh moonblast. "Damn those Japs!—draggin' me away from Mom's apple pie. I'll kill 'em!"

"Maybe we'll join the USO," Leo says. "Take up tapdancing."

"And tour with a band," Teddy says. "Maybe we'll see you out there, John."

"John, does the USO have 8-F and slacker patches?" Chuck asks.

At ten-thirty Don Johnston, a tall, bony, darkeyed Scot, shows up at Chuck's in his air cadet dogsuit, clapping, "Ready for the slaughter? You guys are lookin' at a winner! I warn you fair and square, tonight I *win!* You'll be registered aliens before I finish with you."

"It's Black Death tonight, fellas." Chuck shudders.

"He looks a little wild to me," Mrs. Campbell says from her rocker.

"Lemme count the cards," Johnston says. "Oh, hell, I trust you, Campbell."

"You may trust me," Chuck says, "but I'm not sure I trust these two. How d'we know you twins don't have a secret waveband or 'strange powers'?"

"We're honest!" Leo cries. Teddy grins.

"Oh, you can't believe a guy who says that," John says. "And especially not *two* guys! Not if they steal street-signs."

"They *lifted* Helene's streetsign," Chuck tells Johnston.

"That's not what I'd . . ." Johnston starts. "Well, who's dealing!" Johnston deals first hand. Chuck wins his last hand.

"In the midst of life, we are cut down," Chuck says, raking in the pot. *"And* I win the deal!"

"Show your openers and shut up," Johnston says.

Chuck turns a blind ace. "Ah, how'd that sneak in there?"

"Well, God," Johnston says, "I hope I'm not getting the message I think I'm getting."

Wayne comes with Donnie Knowlquist. "Okay, move over, the Marines are landing! Let's hold down on the variations tonight, gents," Wayne says, "no whores, fours, and one-eyed jacks wild, or those sissy kid games, huh?"

One-legged Mr. Campbell goes upstairs to bed backward, sitting steps. "Get a house cut, Chuck," he calls. Mrs. Campbell waits above.

"Oh no he doesn't!" Johnston cries.

"We paid for this beer," Wayne says.

"You've got your nerve," John says to Chuck.

"Nice try, Dad," Chuck calls. "Now, gentlemen, to work. I shall come by my winnings honestly."

"Are you sometimes known as Fresh Deck Campbell?" Johnston asks.

"Honest Deck Campbell," Chuck says.

"He's saying he's *honest!"* John says. "Do you steal streetsigns?"

"I'll give you an even break, John," Chuck says, shuffling. "Or I would, but I need this bread tonight. I've a car payment due at Shine's."

"But I'm not paying for your car," Wayne says.

"Maybe you better go to bed, Campbell," Johnston says.

"What!" Chuck cries. "Before I'm wiped out by you giants?"

"Now that's talk I like to hear," Johnston says.

"Can I get in?" Donnie Knowlquist asks. Fawn-faced, thirteen. "Can seven play?"

"Hell, yes," Johnston says. "And give this kid all the beer he can drink. How much money ya got? You might be wise to bank some—*friend.*"

"Ten cents, gentlemen," Teddy says. "Who's staying?"

By 2 A.M. down to a half case of Genessee. Donnie Knowlquist leaves, owing Chuck. Nightwalk home.

"Leo, shall we get down to the money in our shoes?" Wayne asks.

"Just gettin' my second wind," Leo says. "Happens every game."

"Well, don't breathe on me, I might pass out," Teddy says.

The twins get into a bet with each other. Chuck stays. Leo raises, then taps Teddy's foot. Teddy raises rather than fold. Chuck grips his forehead, gives a quarter to the pot. Leo wins. Teddy sits back red and gives Leo a hard look.

"What's wrong?" Leo asks him.

"I don't mind losing," Teddy says.

"I'll keep that in mind," Leo says.

"Do that."

"You got to be sly, slick and wicked to beat me, kid," Leo says. Teddy kicks his ankle. Leo straightfaced, shuffling. "Everybody in," Leo says, "showdown for a quarter opener."

"Last hand," Chuck says. "Let's hope the house recoups from a disastrous evening."

"Somethin's gotta change," John says. "I got a sick horse to feed."

"Taking him with you on the bus?" Wayne asks.

"Sure am. Name's John and he *loves* steak and french fries."

Teddy nicks Leo for a quarter. Dealt jack of diamonds. Leo gets the joker up first card, bumps a big green dollar.

John gets three of clubs. "I paid a whole dollar for this card!" he moans.

"My God, we're all in for one-fifty already," Chuck says. "I feel degenerate at such stakes. But I stay."

"Think of these as real tears," Johnston says.

Leo deals himself no help, high with joker-nine. Teddy eyes jack-queen high, Wayne spade queen high, John jack of spades.

"I'm plucked, Campbell!" Johnston cries. "I fold."

Chuck folds. "Gents, the house crumbles. Devastated! Can anybody tell me what this deep pain is I feel choking me?"

Shinyeyed, Leo bumps a dollar, deals last card. Teddy gets ace of spades. Leo says, "No help but mighty impressive!"

"Now don't be hasty," Chuck warns. "Cards are fickle."

Leo flips. Wayne sits back with the two of hearts and says, "Good morning, Pearl Harbor, I read you loud and clear."

John waits. "Be there, Jackson!"

"John, try pearldiving," Johnston says.

John's fists in prayer, tight mouth to heaven. Leo leers, deals him jack of hearts. Leo's heart drops. "Thank you, Lord!" John cries.

"Watch his fingers carefully," Wayne warns John about Leo.

"You watch for me," John says. "I can't look."

Leo deals himself hard a ten, elbow clipping Teddy. *"I win, I win!"* John cries. "I hate these long-drawn-out nights where you only win two pots!"

"Teddy, you look very tired," Chuck says. "Are you sure you want to go to Lakewood?"

"Sure, I love Lakewood," Teddy says, broke, owing. "How about you?" Wayne asks.

"Sure, I wanna go," Leo says. "John's las' night."

Drive downtown, gas up, cruise to the dairy. Wayne unlocks. Sundaes for the beach in glopbuckets. Pat the cop raps the half-lighted door, comes in for a maple mexican.

Ride up the lake, drooling syrup.

"Sloppy car you have here, Campbell," Wayne says in back, John on his lap beside the twins.

Open top, windbitten hair, limbs bracing salt stars.

Forsaken night streets of Lakewood, tires over cornflakes. Park at beach. Dusky, cricketing. Moonhills waterbright. Waves lapping, barely. Blue crown, deep peacedazzle.

Chuck breaks out the beercase. Shadowed by boathouse, the twins pumpship into weeds.

"There used to be fireflies out here," John says, sitting on the dock. His face matchflames.

"I don't see any fireflies, Johnston," Wayne says. "Do you see any fireflies?"

"I don't see any fireflies," Johnston says, "and I'm an aerial expert."

"Hey, what's that red dot on all the Zeros?" Wayne asks.

"What red dot?" Johnston asks.

"Look closely next time," Wayne says. "It's a big red dot."

"Does it go on and off?" Johnston asks.

"Good idea. I'll write to the emperor about that," Wayne says. "When are you getting your wings?"

"Why, after I solo," Johnston says. "Up with the birds."

"Fasten that safety belt," Wayne says. "They'll let you fly at night? They're not afraid you won't bump into a tower? Tell me, what does a flying red horse mean to you?"

"Medical discharge," Johnston says.

"Waiting for the fireflies?" Leo asks John.

"I meant last summer when we first came here," John says, clouded with moonfumes. Coughs, barking helplessly, flicks his red butt into the limp lazing waves.

"It's too early for fireflies," Teddy says. Claps John's back. "I pine to go with you, John," he says.

Move back to the beach and army blankets. Twins' starched shirts white aglow. An ell-top streetlamp hangs a yellowbulb needleblaze down the shore road. High but dimming out, they talk of old times.

Rise before dawn. Dock and lake befogged. Out Townline Road to the creamery. Drive home, valleys toweled, pastures fresh white, milkquarts bouncing at their mouths.

Tallwindowed rainblasts. Lightning! Houses blistered and thumped yellow across the playing field. Miss Swift's Mask & Wig Club watches a skit by the twins. Endless lightning crashes.

"Drink, Jekyll, drink!" Teddy cries, forcing a test tube on Leo.

"Nay, Hyde, never!" Leo says.

"I'll *die* if you don't!" Hyde cries.

"Then die," Leo says. "I'll never drink this again!"

"Then I shall," Hyde gargles, shakes the root beer tube, swallows its foam-swell. Gasps back against couch. Jekyll and Hyde fall over the back out of sight. On the floor their four hands stick Teddy's makeup fast. Swiftly they curl from the couch, Edward Hyde clutching his hidden face.

"We need a light, Hyde," Leo says.

"No light, Jekyll!" Hyde cries.

The club giggles in yellowbright light, the sky awash, green.

"Hey, we don't have a match for the candle," Leo tells Teddy.

"Oh, Christ," Miss Swift says, chin raised in back of class. "Somebody give him a goddamn match." The club howls. "You pipsqueaks forget you heard that," she says. "Will the Barrymores please get this tragedy over with so I can get home for a whole cigarette?"

Leo fakes lighting the candle. *"Henry!* I mean *HYDE!"*

Hyde shows his soremarked rotting face and eggshell eyes.

Deep surprise at the quickchange.

Waspgown and flowered hat, Marie McBride, Jekyll's promised, hops from a dressingscreen. *"Henry!"*

Hyde grabs her, snorting lungdeep, his veined eyebulbs fearful. Hit the couch. All three go over the back.

"How'd I ever get inta this?" Marie mutters under them.

Twins rise at each other's neck. Hyde breaks free and leaps into clenched onlookers, Jekyll coasting beside. The twins howl, half-facing in a three-legged waltz of neck-choking. Kids bristle. Hyde lifts over Jekyll, then Jekyll over Hyde, choking. Hyde fades gasping, but surges again. Chokes Jekyll against rainbattered panes. Miss Swift sags on her palm. KRRTHMMPP! claps the black schoolyard, shaken yellow. Marie faints behatted over the couch. Leo strangles Hyde. Hyde falls back, step by tango step, stiffens dead, wolftongue over chin, eggshells glaring.

Leo sits up. "Thank heaven I didn't *drink* that stuff!"

Marie wakes by Leo. The skit ends. The room sits shocked by Marie's back-leaning clinch, cheek to cheek, fish-flat.

"Curtain," says Miss Swift. "It's too slow. Play faster or cut something out. And sit up for the smooch! I don't care who's dead."

*"No*body likes me in this role," Marie cries. Unpins her hat, snarls at the floor. "I'm not well liked, you'll notice. Maybe I'm too wise-Irish!"

"Our stepdad's a big shamrock," Jekyll says. "We know what's wrong with you."

"What?" she asks. "Is my hair too short for this role? Do they think I'm a tomboy—at my age! Those drips. Oh ho, I'm not gonna win as treasurer. That's *for sure."*

"Hey, we're all winning," Hyde whispers bloodyfaced. "Look at the other candidates, angel."

"But I'll never beat Paul Clark!" she says.

"We'll win on your legs," Jekyll whispers.

"I don't have good legs!" Marie says. "Do *you* think so? Oh don't tell me, I'm not interested. Just bury me when it's over."

The twins kiss Marie in a supermarket parking lot, first on her hands, bowing like headwaiters, then on her lips, passionately, twisting twin-to-twin.

Morning assembly. Candidates glittering, starched, brushed.

Teddy glints can't-lose. "Thank you, Mr. Donley, fellow candidates, voters of Lincoln, and also you custodians out in the hall."

Laughter brims into clapping. Leo and Teddy, a brace of smiles, fourfooted, glory without effort. Mr. Donley scratches his temple, hand one-fingered.

"Let's have it for Phyllis!" Teddy cries.

Phyllis Cass at crosspurposes listens.

"Stand up," Teddy says.

Teddy's clapping builds for Phyllis. "Thanks, Phyllis," Teddy says. *"I'm* not giving a speech! I'm saying my brother and I'll work twice as hard as any other candidate —if elected. Thank you!"

"Geronimo!" Leo shouts. "That's four times as hard!"

The twins win, Marie loses to Paul Clark, Phyllis carries the Paratroopers. Leo drinks a small Pernod in the washroom before algebra. Miss Hollister numbers the blackboard beside Teddy. Leo sucks Spearmint, algebra book swimming. Teddy letters as Leo doodles.

After the shower that afternoon they prod their body.

"We're turning in," Leo says doormirrored. "We're not pulling away hard enough. We have to pull away or we'll face each other."

"Our band isn't growing," Teddy says. "I feel a bind across the shoulders, don't you? Does this look like an ice cream boil to you?" Teddy breaks thigh pushead, dabs blood with toilet paper. "Hurts," he says.

"Maybe we should cut down on ice cream," Leo says. "Be trim and maybe a little underweight?"

"We'll turn away three times a day until we feel free," Teddy says.

"Yes," Leo says. Hair soaked with beautiful tree smells.

Turn away for five minutes.

"Well, there's my dangle," Leo says, sinkbeating. Teddy's jack flies past the toilet bowl. Clean the black tile floor.

"Vice-presidents!" Leo says doormirror.

Teddy nods. Hanging ball, bag of hope. Heartworks burning.

"WHAT WAS THAT?" Carl shouts. An Erie-Lackawanna passes over his one-man trumpet college in Brooklyn Square.

" 'Robin Adair'!" Teddy shouts. Leo rests his trumpet as the floor shakes.

"What?" Carl cries.

" 'ROBIN ADAIR'!" they shout.

"Oh!" Carl grins, wincing. "The engine was overhead! Play it again!"

Leo droops, raises his horn. Deepflaps blood into lips. Comes down hard on "Robin Adair," eyes poppingblue.

"Dolce!" Carl points into Leo's Arban book. *"Sweetly!"*

"You can't hear it over the train!" Leo cries redlipped.

"I *can* hear you! *Dolce, dolce!"*

Leo fluffs, fist vowing to play better, shaking.

"I have patience," Carl says. "Blow on your lips like this." Carl shortbarreled, fifty-five, screws up his hair-penciled lip into a learned face, blows flapping, stretches his lips flat as velvet on his teeth. "That makes the blood go. But take your time."

He waits. Leo motors his lips, sweeps a breath, lifts his horn. Slurs G to A, tongues D.

"From the stomach!" Carl cries. "Not the chest!"

Leo sings the first notes, then blows them. His lip mushes.

"I am patient," Carl says. "Warm up, Teddy."

Teddy blows whole tones on his rented valve trombone. Leo blows "Robin Adair." Carl sits listening to both horns.

A train passes.

Saturday afternoon at the dairy, sunny blue summer clouds. The twins working indoors till five. Teddy's day. Roasting popcorn by sunbeaten window. Salesman Joe Sinatra, plaidsuited jokester, asks, "Did you boys go to the wedding?"

"What wedding?" Teddy asks.

"Helene's!" Joe says, head raked. "I had a previous engagement, you tell her that."

Dairy turns to an echoing grotto, weirdly sunlit. "When was it?" Leo asks.

"Two o'clock. You didn't know about it?" Joe asks.

"We had to work," Teddy says hoarsely. Joe leaves singing, *La donna è mobile!* "So Kenny came home," Teddy says, "and they got married. And nobody told us—it was a secret from us through the whole store!"

Leo boils. Smashes a barrel waterglass on an ice cream cabinet. Teddy shocked. Booths quiet. Leo rings, cloven with bodyshame. Teddy walks him back to the kitchen. "I'm getting drunk," Leo says. "Let's go home." Hand under tapwater, he pulls warped glass from his thumbcushion, blood leaking watercolor. "I can't even see what I'm doing!" he cries. "Let's get outta here!"

Teddy sees Joyce making orders, serving. He ties a white dishtowel around Leo's cuts and unties their aprons. They climb to the garage, sneak up-alley to Fourth. Sky so bright Leo can't breathe. Gulps at high clouds, gripping himself.

"Breathe deep," Teddy says.

"I want Southern Comfort."

"We don't have any in the liquor cellar," Teddy says. "Do we dare buy it?"

"This store," Leo says. Go into Cherry Street liquor store. The owner's grayhaired wife alone. Teddy tips his homburg. "Pint of Southern Comfort, please," he says. Leo masters his gritting teeth, smiles hoopeyed.

"It's like June out," she says, bagging a pint. "What a beautiful day for a wedding!"

Leo grips the towel in his pocket. Teddy pays. Walk home panting. Wordlessly, Teddy gives Leo his day. "Does it hurt?" he asks.

"Where?" Leo asks.

House after hillhigh house down Lakeview. Eighth Street houses fall away in a landslide of bodydeath into the pit of Five Point. Blue day, groaning breath.

Leo uncorks the bottle on the dining-room table, hands it to Teddy. "Get it while it's here," he says.

Teddy drinks. Leo gulps, whiskey showering his stomach. His scalp floods, eyes leak. They play Harry James's "I Cried for You" torch special. Leo lifts his horn, sobs, then shrieks on the trumpet. It sounds as never before, wildly strong, tuneless, screaming, bloodytowel hand gripping the valves. Teddy bellows on his trombone. Saxthumped walls shake with wailing, twin hearts rise into horns they cannot play. Din of bleats and grief. Leo bends over, pounding on the table, drinks, plays again. Teddy stutters noise, beside himself, on bruise-red lips, eyes dripping with Leo's.

"We're fucking monsters is what we are," Leo husks.

"You don't have to tell me," Teddy says.

"I don't know why we take it. Have another."

"Thanks. You can have the day today." Drinks, empties his spit-valve. Leo shakes his spitdrooling horn. Play "West End Blues." Satchmo unknots a showpiece passage. Leo listens with blind love. Slow blues, sure and strong. Leo fluffs along in three flats.

"I'm playing three flats," he says.

"Are *they?*"

"I'm just explaining, if you want to harmonize. Three flats is blues."

"So are one and two flats," Teddy says.

"So just play flat! Play D-flat."

Teddy blows D-flat.

"What're ya doin'?" Leo asks. "It's two-and-three."

"*Two*-and-three is E-flat," Teddy says.

"Oh. Well, that's what I meant. What, are you getting

tight? Now go up to the next two-and-three. Now B-flat. Play all those notes flat and that's the blues. That's all there is to it."

"But there are more flats," Teddy says.

"When ya have more flats it goes into the minor," Leo says. "It's not blues, it's symphonic or something. Just listen to Louis, knucklehead."

Play, Leo wavering above, Teddy blatting.

"Maybe we lost our jobs," Teddy says.

"Who gives a fuck?" Leo asks. Glares at the wax fruit bowl, their long-ago Christmas gift to Stella.

"We should phone. We open the store tomorrow morning."

"I'm not goin' back," Leo says. Drinks, passes bottle. "I'm not going anywhere ever. How can we live this way?" Coughs, sobbing, knots a fist, lifts his horn.

"I could stand it if they'd told us!" Teddy cries.

"Well, they didn't!"

Their horns sweep and writhe.

"I can't get out another note," Leo says lips bulging.

Split bottle's last drop, look for beer. Beside the pink icebox sits Stella's pink power stove, first in King James, George's gift, whose coils turn bright red on high charge. Go out back. Teddy slides the empty bottle down the trash can. In the kitchen he swigs his beer, then shouts, *"I wanna die!"* Falls across stainless steel sink, beating it. Leo hugs Teddy, gasps at his ear, "Let's do it!"

Teddy cocks back thoughtfully, eyes showering. "How?"

"Iodine," Leo says. "It's poison."

They light upstairs to the bathroom, take the iodine bottle to their desk.

Do Not Drink

POISON!

"It looks old," Teddy says, sniffing. "Smells good."

Leo smells, then painfully unwraps his sticking bandage, swabs iodine on his cuts.

"Why bother?" Teddy asks.

"I'm seeing if it's strong." Jumps, catching the bottle. "It's *strong*. I just hope there's enough."

"That's quite a bit," Teddy says.

"To do the job right? No accidents, please. Let's not have you dying and me sitting here."

Weave carefully down to pantry. Tall frosted zombie glasses stickered with Haitian witch doctors casting spells.

"We'll make our own zombies," Teddy says. "Beer should cut iodine."

"That sounds bitter. I want apricot liqueur."

Pick into Stella's small bottles.

"No apricot," Leo says. "I'll settle for peach."

Go up to their desk. Teddy halves the iodine finely, fills his glass with beer, watches blooddark bubbles foam. Sniffs violet. Looks deeply at his frosted rim, then at Leo. "Your health, Jekyll," he says.

Leo pours beer into peach iodine. "They're gonna miss us."

"Let's not think about any of them."

Look out their window. Star-green evening over rubber dusk. "But they'll miss us!" Teddy says, chest heaving. "Shall we write one note or two?" Gets out paper, tears wetting their green inkpad. "Maybe we should write it together."

"I don't really want to write anything!" Leo bursts. *"You write!"* Lifts his glass and Teddy his, swallowing the heads. "*Ughh!*' they cry.

"Awful!" Teddy says.

"Just write," Leo says, sipping more.

LINDSEY AVENUE

Teddy sips. Dips his straight pen, scratches date in bluemidnight ink. "I wish they wouldn't call ink black if it's blue," he says, waving pen. "Who'm I writing to? Why're we killing ourselves?—this is my first suicide note."

"Don't ask me to write your note, goddamn it!"

Teddy writes *Dear* . . . "Dear who?"

"If ya can't thinka someone, shut up!"

Teddy stares at his paper. "Wha' will our folks say?"

"They shouldna brought us inta this horrible place!"

"You can't have anything you really want!" Teddy cries. "Oh, my God!"

"Thank heaven I had you for a brother," Leo sobs. "It woulda been *hell* without you! You were the best brother I could hope to have!"

"So were you," Teddy says. "I honestly even liked your horn-playing today. You were carried away. I could hear."

Their eyes give love through the haze of flesh.

Leo reaches for his glass.

"I can't write," Teddy says. "Do you feel anything yet?"

"You're not chickening?"

"I'm only thinking there's a lot to live for."

"Like what?" Leo belches, eyes crossing.

"Well, I'm curious t'know what'll happen to us if we don't die."

"Well," Leo says, sitting back. "My curiosity's very strong too."

"Maybe we coulda been great musicians."

"I'm more innarested can we be more happy than unhappy? Can't make the worl' happy, but maybe we can make *us* happy?" Leo's hair hangs into his glass. "We could be famous if we wanted."

"For our music?" Teddy asks.

"Sure. We can do anything." Grits his jaw. "All right, bottoms up."

Clink. Zombies up, the last deep drop. Lips stained purple.

"I'm gettin' sick," Leo says.

"So'm I. 'S comin' up!"

Stagger to bathroom holding their bellies. Leo gushes into the pink sink, Teddy belts the pink toilet purple. Fingers down throats. Rise reeling, faint onto their backs, lie panting.

"We might still be poisoned," Teddy says, fluorescent blue.

Back to the iodine bottle. Read the cure. *In case of internal consumption, induce vomiting with mixture of flour and water. Call physician.*

"We gotta vomit some more!" Teddy says.

Hurry with heavy care to the pantry flour bin. Dip in glasses, carry flour to the tap. Leo pulls the silverware drawer wildly out. Spoons dance over the floor. Flour pastes the bottoms of their glasses, stir and drink.

"Not enough!" Leo says. "I can't puke!"

"Raw eggs!" Teddy cries.

Get six eggs, crack them into their glasses. Drink the unstirred eggs whole-yolked. Heave into sink, fingers rammed down throats.

"Again?" Teddy asks.

"We're empty. Let's hope it's not in our bloodstreams."

Look about palely. "Let's clean up," Teddy says, "and go to bed."

Pick up spilled silver, clean sink, grind shells, turn off record player. They watch the dining-room light die on their horns into burning darkness.

Clean the candypink bathroom. Undress, piss, turn out lights. Leo lights a fag in the dark, hands it to Teddy. "Boy, I'm rolling on top of a mast!"

"And can't get down," Teddy says. "I haven't felt off-balance like this since we were six years old and fell down the back stairs in Erie. Maybe we shouldn't smoke, we need energy to fight back."

"Condemned man's last smoke," Leo groans. Drained, tense. "I'm *buzzing*."

"I'm wobbling like a ship," Teddy says. "I can see the sun in the dark."

"So can I. I can make it go on and off."

"We gotta get a girl. Why don't we go down on Metallic?"

"We don't know which house it is," Leo says.

"Somebody must know! Iceberg'll take us."

"I wish the bed would stop. Let's throw up again."

Go back to bathroom, painfully throw up water. Rinse with cinnamon mouthwash, back to bed.

"Let's never do this again," Teddy says. "I'm too dizzy to sleep."

They phone the Redfield twins on Stella's bedroom phone.

"Hello, beautiful," Teddy says to Wanda.

"Teddy? Hi. Why're you calling?"

"You're talking with half of a vice-president," Teddy says.

"Oh, wow!" Wanda cries. "*Wilma!*"

"I'm right here," Wilma says. "What are you talking about?"

"How about a concert?" Leo asks.

"A concert?" Wilma asks. "What kind of concert?"

"Wait and hear," Leo says. "Hold on," Teddy says.

Twins go down naked in the dark of fifteen watts from the pink stove, get their horns, lay the downstairs phone on the Persian throwrug. Stand on stairs, horns facing the phone. Striving and mooing. No wind, no lips. Lower their horns, shot. "We finished," Teddy says.

"You need practice!" Wilma says.

Phone Wayne that they'll open in the morning. "Did anyone tell Wes we left early?" Teddy asks, trembling.

"*Did* you?" Wayne asks. "Didn't know about it. Had to go to Buffalo for my physical today. I'm being sworn into the Marines Monday. I'm having a blast tonight. Come by later—but bring money. Hey, I just found a mouse in my Coke bottle."

"In your Coke!" the twins howl.

"America crumbles, eh?" Wayne asks.

Throats raw, the twins dress in sport clothes, walk downtown. Simmering night, streets lamplit, heels echoing on redbrick paving. Pass Nancy Ruleburner's high white house, yearning. Drinking with a sailor, Nancy lost an eye and was scarred in a wreck up the lake. The sailor died. "Well, I'd still marry her," Leo says. "Sure would," Teddy says.

Third Street Saturday night, servicemen cramming bars and singing on the walks, secret Albanian brown sauce smells flooding from hot dog stands. Stop into Elias's Lunch for four dogs with chopped onions and sauce, chatting with bald old Louie at his griddle. In the alley by the dairy drink small bottles of blackberry and cherry brandy, then go into the dim store. Older counterboys roll in from rival fountains for Wayne's poker blast.

Sunday morning waking alone in the back booth, counter chores before latching the door open, battling giant headaches with Bromos and milkshakes. Cheat the jukebox and roast pecans until homebound churchgoers stop by for bulk ice cream packed to order. The twins pack bulk fast as Wayne, even with Leo's bandaged hand.

Stuffing down a half-burned tray of hot salted crisp pecans, stomachs awash with milk like tom-toms.

NIGHTBILLOWING cannons deafen the North African desert. Twins smoke in Shea's empty balcony, two girls behind them.

"They smoke together, turn their heads together, everything," the blond whispers above shellfire. "Hey, are you really Siamese?"

Twins prickle. "We're Americans," Teddy says. "Want company?"

The straightback smiling girl moves over and the twins sit between them, skin charged, hopes boiling. The blonde by Teddy smiles worriedly, slouching, watching the screen, twining a lock at her ear as he drops his homburg on the seat past her, brushing her sweater. He lifts her near hand, sniffs it for a ring, holds it on her thin skirt.

"Don't lose any time, do you?" the dark one drawls at Teddy across Leo. "Are you Leo or Teddy?"

"I'm Leo," Leo says. "Boy, you have hair like a mermaid. Really luscious. Smells like cider! You use apple soap?"

"Lemon!" she says. "Hey, d'you drive? Well, does he?"

"Naw," Teddy says. "I'm waiting to get an English car."

"Why English?" the blonde asks, her homeliness fading quickly.

"Right-hand steering," Teddy says. "Why?"

"We'd rather be out riding," the stiffback dark one says. "Why, this whole movie's just *news!*"

"Where you from?" Leo asks her.

"Gainesville, Florida. But Clara was raised in Albuquerque. We're sisters."

"What's your name?" Leo asks.

"Mary Poe," she drawls.

"Ever had a *po'* little lamb?" Leo asks. Mary clucks.

"Where d'ya live?" Teddy asks Clara.

"Our folks got a cottage up in Driftwood, Clara says.

"Driftwood!" Teddy says. "Above Greenhurst on the lake?" Clara smiles. His stomach dries. "You need attention, not a movie," he quotes Wayne.

"Well, we have to catch the last trolley," Clara says. "We don't have a car."

"Let's hit the trail," Teddy says. "We'll take you home."

"How'll you get back?" Clara asks.

"We'll hitch," Leo says. "Let's vamoose."

Mary and Clara glare at the shellfire and rise. Twins follow them down, eying Mary's slender back, Clara's legs. In the Moorish lobby pass Mr. Gilhula, who asked after George and Stella when the twins came in but now is silent as they leave midfeature with the country girls.

"How about Kliney's for a beer and beef on kummelwick?" Teddy asks, amazed by their bright pagan faces under the marquee.

"We don't drink," Clara says.

"You Moslem?" Teddy asks.

"No!" Mary says. "We drink very little, that's all."

"Well, you're underage anyway, aren't you?" Leo asks.

"Naw, I'm eighteen!" Mary says. "And Clara's twenty."

"I have a boyfriend in Germany," Clara says guiltily.

Hit Fulmer's for sundaes, then amble to the Boatlanding trolley stop. Large warm charged night, elms preaching in the high breezes of Baker Park. Squeeze onto a dark bench by tall bushes. Leo finds a brace under Mary's sweater. Teddy pulls Clara's hand over his pants.

"I broke my back in a car accident last year," Mary says. "I got six more months in this brace."

"Gee, I'm sorry," Leo says.

"I should lie down more than I do," Mary says.

"We'll have to get you right home," Teddy says.

"I'll be all right," she says. Leo smells vanilla behind her ear.

"I was driving the dern car," Clara says, looking down as the messenger of bad news, then up to be forgiven by Teddy. He decides that homeliness can be set aside for a night. "That was hard luck," he tells her, feeling insightful.

Walk down breezing Fairmount to the trolley. Moonpearl sky. Twins slip into the Lake House for a bag of beer, then buy four rides in the ticket office. Twenty-minute wait. Walk by the outlet where the dark City of King James steamer sits bonewhite on the marsh. They lie back, open beers, and share them. Cinnamongiving night, soothing, sapfilled, stars teasing the deeps.

The trolley pulls in, twin poles crackling, cable blurting-blue.

Spring on after the girls, sit back in lone car, away from conductor. Older lake folk get on, then the trolley bell dings. Glide into nightwoods of the Chadakoin, low trees ghostblue in dripping sparks. The car strippings shine, yellow bulbs screened, wheels beneath pulled by liquid magic. Teddy hoping, grips Clara's hand. Victim smile, faintly returns squeeze, something passive but energy-sucking in her slow glance, fearing to be moved—yet hungry!

More Lakers at Fluvanna. Thirsty boys keep their beer in its bag. Soon Sheldon Hall, passing flats of Greenhurst. Blackgap trestle, lakesilver breaking below. Moonshadow shores lift a cold aura from the water, glittering, speechless.

"That's really tragic," Leo says. "Your accident."

Mary shrugs. Blue trees shadowleap the window, hissing.

Driftwood. Ramble down the hard blue road to the lake. Bullfrogs bellow close to foot. Thick grass cricket-singing to tiny cottage, back bulb with wings aburn.

Stop in shadow. Teddy asks, "Should we bring the beer in?"

"Sure," Clara says.

"Do they imbibe?" Leo asks.

"Shucks, no," Mary says.

Teddy turns Clara. "Give me something," he says and gives her the hand as she kisses him. Leo holds Mary's cheeks, presses her lips—they hardly kiss. Her sweetness warns him as it did in the park. "You smile easy," he says. They look up. Blue atoms.

Cross the backyard's dim burn.

Two people bend over the kitchen table, spent, and rise back slowly as Mary leads in Leo by his yellow orchestra jacket. Homburg in hand, Teddy and Clara. The two at the table wipe sleep from their eyes, or tears, or wonder.

"Hi, folks!" Mary says. "Meet Leo and Teddy."

"Them joined twins from King James?" Mr. Poe asks.

The twins grin, runaway slaves in shadeless ceiling light.

"You look a lot alike!" Mr. Poe says, wide-eyed at their win over nature.

"How are you, boys?" Mrs. Poe asks.

"Great!" Leo says. Teddy all teeth, steel ego.

"Sit down," Mr. Poe beckons, waving at their offered hands.

Twins rack two chairs, sit with the Poes. Clara ices the beer. Mary plunders a huge cardboard steamer trunk swamping the living room. Twin smiles at Mrs. Poe, Mr. Poe. Drained demons, the Poes, worn, empty faces fading. Mr. Poe's hand trembles at his milk straw. Mrs. Poe pushes away a curled stiff baloney sandwich, braces her forehead.

"You from out West?" Teddy asks.

"Tulsa," she says. *He* moans. Eyes dust flats, cheeks seamed.

"How d'ya like Chautauqua County?" Leo asks Mr. Poe.

"Hope our girls make some money," he says. His straw wild as he sips. "Baloney sure needs some corn relish, Ada."

Mrs. Poe gives him eye support from world's end. Teddy smells rank kitchen must.

"We're country people too," Leo lies, Teddy nodding. "We're from the Lake Erie grape region."

Mrs. Poe's silent eye doesn't dote on Lake Erie.

"You don't like Lake Erie?" Teddy chimes on Leo's tale.

"We had bad times on Lake Erie," she says.

"They stood for two days in a snowstorm on Route 20," downcast Clara says as if herself a hardhearted driver. "Nobody'd pick 'em up with that *dern* steamer trunk."

"That's how Daddy got sick in the nerves," Mary says.

" 'Bout that time," Mr. Poe says to his wife.

Mrs. Poe faces bedtime, a death sentence. Mr. Poe shuffles to the front stairs. She follows, frail, tiny, powerful. Nobody says goodnight.

Leo nudges Teddy. "*Goodnight!*"

"Anytime, boys," Mr. Poe says.

"Always welcome," Mrs. Poe says grimly.

Footsteps on the ceiling. Teddy slaps Paramount News on his knees. "Let's have some beer, chillun!"

Ringing numbness seizes Teddy as Clara opens beers and rinses four grapelabel jellyglasses without soap, a crazed fantasy, his breath swimming above water, held beneath, rising and sinking before the face of death. Twins look over the front room's great clothes box, split couch. No room for four. Eye the rindy kitchen linoleum and waterbugs. The Karloff monster is horny.

Teddy pours for Clara. "Why don't we take a walk down to the lake?" he asks her bitten fingers, beer bitter on his tongue. "Drink up."

"I like your mustache," Clara tells Teddy. "Why doesn't he have one?"

"Does he look like Gable?" Teddy asks.

"Hoo! Do *you?*" Leo asks down his nose, spine up.

"No!" Teddy laughs, sinks spraddled, swigs upward.

"Shucks, the toilet don't work," Mary says. "Nobody use it."

"We'd like a walk," Leo says, handing her a jellyglass.

Out front, no porch. Squishy path overgrown. Shore marshy, bugs whining. . . . Go back to house.

"Let's use the bushes," Leo says.

"We'll bring out blankets," Clara says. "Okay?"

"Great," Teddy says. Off to a bush. "Gee, we shoulda brought our rubbers. Why didn't we think of it?"

"Why, Mary's a cripple. I wouldn't chance knocking her up."

"That's what rubbers are for," Teddy says. "I'm so hard I can't piss."

The girls come out with blankets the twins help spread. All lie down face up. Dim kitchenshine tunnels the dark living room.

"Pa and Ada sleep in the back," Clara says.

"I love swimming," Teddy sighs.

"I can't go in the water," Mary says.

"And we don't have suits," Clara says.

"Who does?" Teddy says. "Shorts do the same job."

Twins turn from each other. Teddy holds Clara, on the make.

"Do you have a boyfriend in Germany?" Leo asks Mary.

"Nope. Don't want one neither."

"Why not?"

"I'm no mossback old turtle!" Mary says.

"Clara is *not* a turtle," Teddy says.

"Just waitin' to get outta that harness, huh?" Leo asks. "I wish I could help. You sure have good spirits. It's not painful?"

"Nope." She searches his face, lovehanging hair.

"Oh, God," he whispers. His eyes close. Lights whorl back to birth. "Oh, you could be paradise," Leo says.

"I'm turnin' out the light," she says. "It's too bright out here."

"Open another beer," Teddy calls.

Leo stares above. The heavens brace hope and loss. Mary sits again, lowering slowly back.

Teddy grips a warm bottle from the iceless icebox. "Horsefeathers, I really wanna swim." Swigs, hands beer to Clara. Her eye begs for help. "You go in first," he urges, "and we'll follow. Go ahead." She lies still. "Take everything off," he whispers, nerves flooded. "For me." Squeezes her hand steadfastly. "Whistle when you're ready."

"We're going in," Clara says. "No sharks in this lake?"

"Not too many," Teddy croaks. "We'll keep an eye peeled for fins."

Clara goes into the dark. Twins and Mary silent. Mary pulls up a spare blanket.

"Lemme do that," Leo says. She lies back. He covers her, Teddy unbuttoning himself.

"Sure hope Sis can find some place that's not all guck." Leo holds her hand. Clara whistles afar. "Enjoy yourselves," Mary says, "bring me back a mudpuppy."

"Yipes," Leo says. "We'll be right back."

Downshore. Clara's pale shadow waves from the water. Twins strip to their shorts, step into muck and harsh rocks. Wade painfully out to Clara, ankledeep in sharp ooze. She says nothing. "Water's beautiful!" Leo says as they tread for a while.

Water covers her shoulders. Teddy arms her waist, Leo aside. They swim until Teddy leads her more shoreward.

"First time I been in this lake," Clara says. "Gettin' chilly. Let's swim some more."

Teddy pulls her close. "Thank you."

"You'll have to get suits," Leo says.

"They only been here three days," Teddy says. Deep surprise at her softfloating breasts. Can this be? he wonders.

"Maybe we better go back," Clara says.

"Wait." Teddy turns her.

"We better go in," she says, trembling in the water.

Teddy kisses her wet slippery lips, guiding her hand into his shorts. First touch, he bursts. Gulps, still up. "Have you ever done it?" he asks.

"Only with my boyfriend."

"I never have. What do you do? Will you do it?"

"For you," she nods. "But I'm bashful."

Leo sings to himself as Teddy strips, and double-tongues "The Carnival of Venice," his fist a mouthpiece.

"You're supposed to lie down," she says.

"Can't you do it floating?" Teddy asks. "If you put your legs around my waist? He won't watch."

Leo tongues, hums louder.

She raises a mucky foot, lays it over their band. "Ready?" she asks.

"Yes." He slides her arms about his neck, closes his eyes on the moon. "Now!"

She crosses her ankles on his back, hanging from his neck. Breasts float up as he sinks in muck. *"Oh, I . . . I . . . I"* he says. Can't fit himself into her. "Maybe you better do it." She reaches under, guides him. Teddy straightens, pulls out spurting. Leo hums, da-dahing "Dance of the Hours" for Mary, loudly. *"I didn't . . . I didn't . . . want to give you a baby!"* Teddy whispers shamed. She gets down slowly, undone, bearing up.

"I'm cold," Teddy says.

"Let's go in," Leo says.

"Give me a minute to dress," Clara says.

They watch her bright back hungrily, then the moon. Leo asks, "How was it?"

"I didn't get all the way in."

"Why not?"

"It doesn't work that easy. I was too excited—but I did get my head in. I never came twice in five minutes before. Did you come?"

"I'm *trying* not to feel that way," Leo says.

"I wish I didn't feel like I do."

"You feel bad?" Leo asks. *"Really?"*

"I feel awful. I never felt this bad in my life."

"Jesus, I'll wait till I get married."

Teddy glares at the moon. "That's my last time. I'm sorry I didn't wait." He starts sobbing.

"Hey, they'll hear you," Leo says.

Teddy ducks underwater and groans hard as he can. A hill from his grandfather's farm comes to his mind and full desire to be there. Looks out of water at the lamb-white moon, then ducks again, howling underwater. "I could die right now," he sobs, rising, muscles convulsing.

Leo silent.

"I wanna go home," Teddy says.

"But I *want* to see Mary," Leo says.

"See her your day."

"What's got into you?"

"I don't know!" Teddy cries. "I'd give my arm not to have done it!"

"Well, it's gonna be *my* day in two hours. What if I wanna turn around and come back?"

"They'll be in bed. Can't we just go without arguing?"

"No," Leo says. *"Be fair!* Mary is—*I only have pure feelings for her."*

"Must you remind me!" Teddy groans.

"Oh, God, buck up. Look, we have to go in and dry off. Let's, huh? For an hour? Get warm."

"Half an hour."

"It's gotta be an hour, for Christ's sake. I can't say everything I gotta say in a half hour. Besides, you don't want Clara thinking you hate her."

"I don't hate Clara," Teddy says. "I hate life. And I wish to God I'd never seen this whole family."

"Well, ya don't feel that way about Mary. Let's just dry off and see what happens."

"What *could* happen? Only that it gets to be three or four before we start walking back, Got an idea how many miles it is?"

"We'll hitch," Leo says.

"I don't want to ride, I wanna walk."

"What for?"

"I *need* the punishment!" Teddy wails. "Just hope you don't find out what it's all about. I'm freezing."

They go in and Teddy dresses.

"You're gonna be soaked all night," Leo says.

"Wonderful," Teddy mutters.

Leo in shorts, they go back to the blanket. "This nut didn't even dry off before getting dressed," he says.

"I'm cold," Teddy says.

"Get under," Clara says, moving over. Bra straps.

"You don't mind?" Leo asks Mary.

"Oh, I seen shorts before."

On their backs, Teddy silent, stars bitter. "I can't get warm," Teddy says. Clara takes his hand. "Just what I always wanted," he thinks and drops shaking onto her breast. She grips his hand hard.

"What's wrong with Teddy?" Mary asks.

"He's overwrought," Leo says.

"I'm crying because I'm a fool!" Teddy says, returning her grip. The farm—a smallhorned white baby ram stares at Teddy with wide-apart human eyes. Stella's father walks in his blossoming cherry orchard, cheerful, wise, loving. Teddy bursts within, his spirit washed. He hears Clara's heart spasming in darkness, blindly leading her. An orange blaze fills his closed eyes.

Leo speaks bottomlessly to Mary's ear. He wants to get her a job at Fulmer's. He wants to fight Hitler. His feelings will last until the end of time, without lessening, without stain—*starbright!*

Walk home at one, in their kitchen by three-fifteen. Turn out the stovelight, creep noiselessly upstairs. Stella clears her throat while George snores. The twins freeze in the darkness, Teddy shivering, jerking like a beheaded lamb.

DR. Sweets Gogarty checks the twins at his desk. Teddy stands on Gray's *Anatomy,* Leo the scale.

"How's the goldfish bowl?" Gogarty asks.

"Doesn't bother us," Leo says. "We're musicians."

"We're sure not going into any carnival," Teddy says.

"You wouldn't like carnie life," Gogarty says. "Here, take these into the bathroom."

Twins bring back stale samples. "There may be some sperm in mine," Teddy says nervously, "I had a wet dream last night."

"Mine too," Leo says.

"You have wet dreams together?" Gogarty asks.

"Not really together," Teddy croaks.

"If one of you reaches climax, does the other feel it?" Twins speechless. "No!" Leo says dismally.

"Yes," Teddy rasps.

"Well, sometimes," Leo says. "It depends."

"It doesn't happen very often," Teddy claims.

"That's too bad," Gogarty says, touching both their chests at once. "Do you know you have the same pulse?" Twins nod. "How's your digestion? No constipation, either of you? I'd like to try a little test. Put this disc under your tongue, Ted."

"What ish it?"

"Zinc," Gogarty says. "Ever hear of Galvani? He invented this test. Only not for Siamese twins." Sweets slips a silver baby spoon under Leo's tongue.

"Shour!" Teddy cries.

"Shour!" Leo cries.

"That's galvanism," Gogarty says and offers his nickel-box of pink wintergreen candy. "Shows electricity can be made chemically. Zinc and silver taste sour together—but not separately. It also shows that your nervous systems connect. I suppose you boys would like to be separated?"

"We think about it," Leo says.

"Quite often," Teddy says.

"But we don't mind, do we?" Leo asks Teddy.

"We mind," Teddy says. "But what can we do?"

"Not much," Gogarty says. "As yet there's no operation for severing conjoined twins—I've studied the cases. When you were four or five, it might've been possible. But at this age, it's very dangerous."

"Dangerous?" Teddy asks.

"A very great shock to both your systems. Feel that?" he asks pressing the joints of their band. "How deep does this cartilage go? How many arteries are in there? Is it mostly cartilage or flesh? I can't answer and I'm sure not gonna touch it with a knife."

Stomachs sink.

"But!—I'm not the last word on this by a long shot. Just because this operation's never been done doesn't mean it can't be. I'm speaking to you as men, though. You may be bound together for the rest of your lives. Now look out the window."

"Getting dark," Leo says.

"Teddy, look out the other window," Gogarty says.

The twins arch back. "I can't," Teddy says.

"Why not?"

"I get dizzy," Teddy says.

"We'll fall," Leo says.

"You can't look out two different windows at once?" Gogarty asks.

"Oh no!" Teddy says. "We lose our balance."

"Well, just try it," Gogarty asks.

"It's—*too horrible,"* Leo says.

Teddy says, "My head swims to think about it."

"Okay," Gogarty says pinktongued with candy. "I think you'll live another six months—but remember to call me in case . . ."

"In case we don't know?" Leo asks.

"Know what?" Gogarty asks.

"Which window to jump out of," Teddy says.

"In case of fire," Leo says.

"In case something *horrible* happens," Gogarty says. Twins eye cloudy urine for telltale seed.

Leo and Teddy walk with Jack Zimmerman past the great rough stones of Prendergast Free Library. High fortress, eveningyellow windows. They stop out front, marking Saints Peter and Paul rectory's dim porch.

"It's only quarter to seven," Jack says, fag palmcupped. Slim blond, a year younger than the twins, no home phone. "The fathers won't be finished eating yet," he says. Tobaccocroak.

"Let's wait in the library," Leo says.

"Wow," Jack says, "what am I doing with you guys!"

"Look," Teddy says, "you don't believe in the church either, so what's the harm?"

"I don't know if I believe or not!" Jack says. "Don't forget, I went to Catholic school since I was five."

"So?" Leo asks. "We took catechism. We know what it's all about even if we weren't baptized."

"You mean confirmed," Jack says. "Everybody's baptized."

"I mean baptized," Leo says. "The day we were supposed to be baptized, something came up and our mother never got us to the church. We don't even have souls, Jack. Save me the butt, there's a war on."

"Don't you feel sorta queer, never being baptized?" Jack asks.

"Hell, Jack, we don't exist," Evileye Teddy says, dragging smoke.

"We're very interested in God," Leo says, "but who wants to be brainwashed?"

"That's why we wrote this," Teddy says, "*this*—"

"—document," Leo says. "Let's see what the priests have to say about it."

Grind lipburning butt into step, go in. Yawning ceilings, ringing footsteps. Twins lead Jack straight to the stacks, scan the date-stamped borrowers' card at the back of Wylie's *Generation of Vipers*. "It's being *read,*" Leo says.

"Well, three of these stamps are ours," Teddy says. "This is strong stuff, Jack."

"Should I read it?" Jack asks. "What's it about?"

"Well, it took *us* three weeks with the dictionary," Leo says.

"It's hard to say what it's about," Teddy says. "It's about, uh, subjectivity, Jack."

"There's a whole world in here," Leo says tapping his skull, "that you'll never know about unless you read this book. Nobody else says these things."

"It's about the total annihilation of American culture," Teddy says.

"I don't know," Jack says, "that sounds pretty deep."

"Well," Leo sighs, shelving *Vipers*. "Let's go back and look at the paintings."

"What paintings?" Jack asks.

Bid him follow, go into the stone silence of the reading room, the twins' footsteps cadenced, old men crisping newspapers on wooden spines, and into the back showroom. Nineteenth-century canvases in weddingcake frames in a small tall room. Jack stops at a large still-life of spilling great green and blue grapes, fuzzy peaches and fruits, with a peach torn open to the pit, a tear lighting its flesh.

Look at that teardrop," Teddy says. "It never fails to amaze me."

"Sta-a-ah!" Jack shakes his hand, body dancing with a half-spoken Italian obscenity.

"You can practically see yourself in that drop," Leo tells Jack. Jack laughs nervously, looks harder.

Leaving, the Easter-week bells of Saints Peter and Paul chime late vespers in the green dusk. Teddy rings the rectory bell.

"You talk, Jack," Teddy says, "you're the Catholic."

"Sure," Jack says, quickly serious. "Uh, who should I ask for?"

"Why not Father Tobin?" Leo smiles. "Let's take him on."

Teddy agrees, jaw set, fist ready to split rails in debate.

Father Tobin himself cracks wide the door. A tall bald man with scalp moles, glasses, a tired fringe. "Yes?" he asks.

"Good evening, Father." Jack grins, suddenly wheels and hangs hacking and croaking over the porchrail.

"Yes, Jack?"

"Oh, my friends and I were having a problem, sort of, uh . . ."

"Intellectual," Teddy says, flushing.

". . . Uh, debate," Jack says. "And, uh, we were wondering if we could talk with you about it for a few minutes, ha ha."

"Is it urgent?"

"Just to us." Leo smiles. "It's subjective."

"If you're busy . . ." Jack says.

"Well, come into the parlor a minute."

The parlor: dark-green curtains down like bulletproof steel.

"We're George Fox's stepsons," Teddy says, hand out.

"How's George? I haven't seen him lately," Father Tobin says, touching their hands and seating the twins on a couch. Sits on a chair and Jack across the room. Sounds of dinnerware beyond.

"He's, uh, back on his feet," Teddy says.

"What's the problem?"

"Well," Jack says, "I think I better let Ted and Leo do the talking."

Leo says, "We came across some questions we can't answer, Father."

"Where'd you come across them?" Tall Father Tobin hunches toward Leo, hands bridged, moled.

Priestgreen eyes staring at him in lamplight, Leo sits tonguetied.

"Uh, in books, Father," Teddy says.

"Well! What are the ideas?"

"Well," Leo says, "we wrote them out." As decided, he hands the handwritten questions to the priest.

Father Tobin reads swiftly. "Well, these aren't questions, they're statements."

"They're, uh, lucid?" Teddy asks.

"What are the *questions?"* Father Tobin asks.

"Well, what we've written," Teddy says.

"God is too private to become a church; He is subjective, not something social," Father Tobin reads aloud.

Twins creep with unease. Both cross their ankles.

"You're asking about charities?" Father Tobin asks.

"Sodalities," Jack says to the twins.

"No, we—it means in the larger sense," Teddy says.

"Larger than what?" the priest asks.

"Of all society," Leo says.

"No, not all society," Teddy says to Leo.

"What do we mean?" Leo asks.

"We mean religious groups, not society," Teddy says.

"Oh, of course," Leo says.

"What about religious groups?" the priest asks.

"They're not subjective." Teddy flushes.

"What's—what's this *subjective?"* the priest asks.

"Well, that's difficult," Teddy says. "It means, uh, well, let's say it means the inward life, Father."

"Is that right? I'll remember that. Now what's the question?"

"Well." Leo tells Teddy, "let's skip this question. It's not that big."

Teddy takes the list, hands it back to Father Tobin. "The second question, uh, intrigues us, Father."

" 'Christ blasted the fig tree because he had a Death Wish,' " the priest reads. Twins catch Jack turning his head aside. "What's this 'death wish'?" Father Tobin asks.

"Well, it's something psychological," Leo says. "And hard to believe! But it seems to be true."

"What seems to be true?" the priest asks.

"That everyone has a death wish," Leo says. "Well, I don't know, that's not so hard to believe."

"You know, on the other question," Teddy says, *"harrumph,* we meant that by socializing God He becomes a lot of rituals and no longer private."

"That happens all too often," Father Tobin says. Cabbage broth curing corned beef mustard odorously.

"Yes," Leo agrees. Teddy seconds firmly. Jack scowls. Hear priests go up the near staircase, talking, fed.

"What does the death wish have to do with the fig tree?" Father Tobin asks.

Teddy silent. Leo clears his throat. At last, trembling, Teddy says, "Well, wasn't that rather infantile?"

"It was just a green fig tree," Leo says.

"Yes, what's it all about?" Teddy asks.

"It's about faith in yourself," Father Tobin says.

"I don't understand that," Leo says.

"Faith in your heart can work miracles and move mountains or wither a fig tree. I'd say that's what it means."

"But why should Jesus want to wither a fig tree?" Leo asks. "To show off his faith in himself?"

"I think there's more to it," the priest says. "I think Our Lord means that heaven's earned in your heart."

Twins sit back. "That may be it," Teddy says. "But I'm not sure I understand it."

The priest reads, " 'What Hath God Rot?' " and says, "That's beyond me. Have I helped you enough? My supper's getting hard."

Twins rise with Jack, thank the priest, shake his hand. He closes the door after them. They walk into the park smoking and shaking, look back at the bulletproof shades.

"Well, he wasn't ready for the death wish!" Teddy says.

"Oh, we could *never* get it across to him," Leo says. "Much too complex."

"He didn't even know what subjectivity was!" Teddy cries for joy.

"I can't believe we did it!" Jack says.

"Well, it took guts," Leo says.

Teddy stops Leo. "It's something we'll always remember."

"Sure is," Leo says, quick fierce squint. "Well, ignorance is oblivion, Jack."

"But I still think 'What Hath God Rot?' was too strong," Teddy says.

"Much too subtle," Leo says.

Graduation Day. Blue suits, Leo and Teddy downstage among ninth grade officers. Mr. Donley reads honors and grades of those passing into King James High School.

Twins writhe, fingers crossed. These Fulmer giants have dropped biology, failed algebra.

"He *might* read our names," Leo mutters. "It's just possible."

"Sure," Teddy says, "they can't fail us. They'll send us down on probation."

Faintly grin at Phyllis Cass and Paul Clark. Phyllis gets up for her handshake from Mr. Donley, returns glassyeyed through whistles and clapping. Soon Paul walks red to Mr. Donley, comes back wet with pride. Leo and Teddy wait, blood rising, spines abristle. Mr. Donley reads on, somehow skipping their alphabetical listing. Graduation goes on and on.

"We're sitting here for no frigging reason at all," Teddy whispers. Leo yeses blindly. "Remember," Teddy says, "when we won Best Camper award at Camp Turner? This is just the reverse. I can't breathe!"

"Let's go home," Leo quavers.

Sit choked as Mr. Donley softly but firmly parts wheat from chaff. More than once they've sat in his waiting room for punishment, though not this year. They've not been around school very much this term—even English sagged to B+ while cigarettes sapped the goatboys' vigor.

After the school song, they invite Paul home for a farewell drink.

"Farewell drink?" Paul asks. "This sounds suspicious. What kind of a drink?"

Pass the Armory amid diploma bearers, watch tall Bob Burns dancing. "How'd that damn dumb bastard make it?" Teddy asks. "Even *he* thought he'd flunked."

Burns knots his dress tie about his forehead, whoops, somersaults on armory grass, leaps up kissing parchment.

"Am I right that my ear failed to register a certain pair of familiar names?" Paul asks. "Well, I suppose this farce doesn't really matter. Hm. How's *George* these days? Still raking in on the slots and paying off in the alley?"

"He'd never do a thing like that," Leo says.

"No, of course not," Paul says. "Don't know what I was thinking!"

"He pays off up at the house," Teddy says.

"Not in the alley," Leo says.

"I see," Paul says. "I suppose it wouldn't be cricket to ask *whom* he pays off?"

"There are hints," Teddy says. "Beautiful day for a hatchet slaying."

"Discretion forever!" Paul cries. "You're, uh, expecting a little friction in that department?"

"He will faint with rage," Teddy says.

"We'll make up at summer school and not tell him about it," Leo says. Teddy makes a papal cross forgiving Leo.

"That's the spirit," Paul says. Walk sunlit Third Street bridge, the Chadakoin bending far below. Paul chortles. "Remember when Leo blew up the Trojan and it floated over the light plant?"

"It was a Sheik," Leo says.

"Oh, we *must* keep the chronicle accurate," Paul says. "There it was! floating right up over the whole town." He chortles. "Ah, that was a triumph!—Oh, sorry."

Wait in Paul's house on Lafayette while he changes clothes. Paul's father dead, the house silent. In the kitchen his mother cracks walnuts for a cake.

"How'd it go?" Mrs. Clark asks. Small country woman with hooded, bulbous hazel eyes.

"Well, all right," Teddy says, "if you go in for those things."

"Oh! You hate to leave Lincoln?" she asks, voice farm-flat.

"We'll remember it fondly," Leo says.

"Though, I really don't feel like we've left," Teddy tells Leo. *"Ahem!"*

She cracks a walnut hard, looks about unseeingly, then says, "Oh! I'm baking a cake. Getting set for college?"

"We don't know," Teddy says.

"College isn't too appealing," Leo says. "We're going into music."

Paul wears a new summer jacket, blue duck. "Well, am I peachy-keen? That means presentable, Mother. Or I might say, personable!"

"You're over my head," she says.

"I'll be at Leo and Teddy's this afternoon," Paul says. "Should the President phone."

"Reading wicked books," Leo says, smile strained.

"That's uncalled for," Paul says. "I brush my sleeve of such suggestions."

Stride up Eighth Street hill. "Where'll you take summer school?" Paul asks.

"We might go up to Chautauqua," Teddy says.

"Ah," Paul says. "Getting away from those microcephalic buddies of yours down at Fulmer's? Admit it—that rabble of goons has been your downfall. Oh, well, how's Millie these days?" he clucks lewdly.

"We're supposedly going over to Erie Sunday to see her graduate from Villa Marie," Leo says. "She's turned into a good Catholic."

"I imagine that'll cut into her gypsy routine around the house?" Paul says. "The old blanket tango? This is at George's suggestion?"

"He just sent her there to get rid of her," Leo says.

"Well, he can send her over to my house anytime," Paul says. "Tell him that. How is she, fellas?"

"What're you suggesting?" Teddy says.

Empty house, they go straight to the silver drawer for two butter knives and hit the liquor cellar lock.

"Close your eyes," Leo tells Paul. "This is slightly Japanese." Jimmies the Yale lock. Go into the liquor cellar with its hoarded bags of hardened sugar and cases of coffee.

"I don't see that sugar," Paul says. "Scout's honor, I *never* saw it, your Honor."

"That's good," Teddy says. "Now I think Graduation Day deserves *select* hard stuff."

"Right," Leo says. "Let's not kid around."

"You see, we're taking it from the cellar," Teddy tells Paul, "so that nothing will be missed from the pantry. Get it?"

"You mean George isn't clever enough to see a bottle's missing from the cellar?" Paul asks.

"You're dreaming," Leo says. "This stuff isn't here. It doesn't exist. Let's take a few of these havanas too."

"How long've you been coming down here, may I ask?" Paul asks.

Go up to sink counting bottles stolen. Get out three shot glasses, Leo uncorks the gin. Pours.

"You say this is *gin?*" Paul asks.

"We drink it neat," Teddy says. "Would you like Coke?"

"Do you sip it? Show me properly!" Paul says, knocks Nazi heels. Nazi shoulders back.

Twins breathe deep, belt their shots. Paul watches Leo bellow and shake his head. Teddy snorts. "Well, that deserves another!" Teddy takes the bottle.

"I see. Just like that, eh?" Paul says.

"Just open up and throw it down," Leo says.

"Okay," Paul says. "Cheers."

"Sure you wouldn't like Coke?" Teddy asks.

"No, no! Maybe afterwards. Well, here goes. Doesn't smell too bad—doesn't smell too good, either."

Belts his shot, turns blue, grabs his neck. His throat opens with a loud suck and he cries hoarsely, *"It was like a lump in my throat!"* He starts coughing, Teddy pounds his back as he hangs off the sink, face red, eyes watering. "Okay—cease!—I'm all right now! That stuff sure has a *sock* to it." He runs water as Teddy pours again.

"Sure you wouldn't like Coke?" Teddy asks.

"No, no, water's just fine. Now I'm better. Or am I? I seem to be sweating all of a sudden. Maybe Coke's a good idea. Is it my imagination or is it getting dark in here?"

"That's just a cloud passing over the sun," Leo says.

"Oh! Well, I thought for a minute . . ." Paul laughs uncertainly. Slaps the sink firmly. "Yes, still here!" he cries triumphantly.

"Down the hatch," Leo says.

"Here's to Harry Truman," Teddy says, "may he be a better vice-president than we ever were."

Leo chokes, guffawing as Paul cries over the sink.

"No more like that, please," Paul says, "or I won't be able to get this one down. Hey, how am I going to get home?"

"Feeling something?" Teddy asks.

"I pretty sure am," Paul says.

"Hey," Leo asks, "did we tell you about when we were in Crozier's office and he left our personality reports on his desk? Well, Mrs. Matthews sends us down to Donley's office for breaking egg in study hall—"

"—for an ass-chewing," Teddy says.

"More of that Fulmer language!" Paul cries.

The twins drink. Paul lifts his, closes his eyes, belts it. "Agh," he says. "You were *breaking egg* in study hall?"

Teddy holds an egg fist on Paul's crown, Leo smashes it lightly, then their four hands mock an egg slowly seeping, creeping down Paul's hair, ears, forehead, cheeks, neck, very slowly. Paul shivers. "Boy, that's realistic!" he cries.

"Donley's not in, so we go to Crozier's," Leo says, putting a cigar into Paul's mouth. "And Crozier opens our files, when he's called to the main office. So we sneak a look at our reports."

"I'm really sweating," Paul says, puffing. "My forehead's burning up."

"It'll go away." Leo puffs. "So what's it say but that we're quick-tempered."

"That's—*unjust!*" Paul says. "You guys are—lump in my throat . . ."

"Such an exagger*a*tion," Teddy says. "Maybe *Leo's* quick-tempered, but not me!"

Paul's face sucks in, disgust stiffens him like a robot. Turns, bursts into downstairs toilet closet, falls to his knees, and heaves.

Twins have another, waiting. Paul flushes the toilet, comes out buttoning his jacket. "I gotta go home," he says.

"Sorry you're sick," Leo says.

"I couldn't help it," Paul says, chopping cigar smoke. "Let's hope it's the last time. Oh, my throat's raw. Boy, I just couldn't hold it. Believe me, I'm sorry."

"Could happen to anyone," Teddy says. "Maybe it's gin."

"And I want to thank you fellas for a peachy-keen graduation," Paul says, pale and blue.

They clean kitchen, leave a false note about sleeping at Paul's, pack their horns, gin and cigars. Pad the grocery bill for three dollars. Walk Paul home on their way to the gravel pit to blow some blues. Later, a long evening walk down Steel Street along the Chadakoin, trains recoupling in the Erie nightyards. Carry a boxed pizza up Reservoir hill, eat, drink and smoke, try to play with handkerchiefs muting their bells. Their lips are blubber. King James lies fast asleep, its valleys dark and great bridge pearled under starlace. They sink back and sleep until dawn in their graduation suits.

AFTER Gershwin concert evening, the twins ramble from the amphitheater, among cane-leaning ladies and elderly gentlemen, back to their porch at the Ashland Hotel. Saddled with moonlight, ragged porches rise on whitefading porches—Ashland at Chautauqua, fenced-in summer home for Methodists, Baptists, and all wandering Protestants. Twins perch on unlighted porchsteps, cuckoos gawking at ladies in flowered hats and girls in shorts.

"Shorts are shorter," Teddy says to Omar Krauss. Short, frail redheaded clarinet student from Cleveland. Omar turns on the steps, peers sharply at the street over colorless glasses, says, "You're right! I'm happy you bring this to my attention. I believe there's an Institutional stricture against shorts after 6 P.M. It's *not* being enforced, gentlemen."

Omar bows as a couple on the walk comes up and sits on the dark porchswing. Leaves hide the streetlamp. The short man on the porchswing holds his deer-eyed young wife's hand and says nothing in the darkness.

"Well, what'd you think of the concert?" Omar asks, tapping a butt.

"Ridiculous," Teddy says.

"Oh?" Omar says. "What about the *Rhapsody?*"

"Terrible," Teddy says.

"Oh? How's that?" Omar asks.

"The clarinet, for heaven's sake!" Teddy says. "You know that opening warble—"

"Obbligato?" Omar says.

"I mean did you hear it?" Teddy asks. Leo snorts.

"He cracked on the glissando?" Omar suggests.

"I didn't mind that so much," Teddy says. "He's just too restrained, no rhythm, no bounce—no—"

"Schmaltz," Leo says. "No schmaltz at all."

"What," Omar asks, "may I ask is schmaltz?"

"I'd like to know too," the man on the porchswing says to his wife.

"Oomph!" Leo says. "Ya know, I play trumpet and Teddy blows the gutbucket. But bluesy! Not boring and classical."

"I was just wondering," Omar says. "Care to come up for a nightcap? After a few more shorts pass so I can complete my ornithological research?"

"Well, who's the greatest schmaltz clarinetist?" the wife asks.

"Sidney Bechet's the all-around top reed man," Leo says.

"Well, survey's over," Omar says. "Let's go up."

Follow Omar into the parlor while Mrs. Milligan, the landlady, squints from her diningtable. Up the cramped stairway to Omar's room on the fourth landing. Tiny den, double bed, hand sink. Omar flops gasping onto his bed as twins perch on edge. Snakes a pint of cognac from under his pillow, kissing it, eyes wet. "That's my clarinet teacher," he says.

"The guy on the porch?" Leo asks. Omar nods, sighing bliss.

"Who's he play with?" Teddy asks.

"The Chautauqua Symphony," Omar says. "First chair."

"He played the Gershwin concert!" Leo says.

Omar nods. Twins clap foreheads, fall back on the bed.

"Oh, that was satisfying." Omar sighs deeply shaking himself.

"We said he didn't have any schmaltz!" Teddy cries.

"Yes, yes, yes," Omar cries. "And he hasn't!"

"Why didn't you stop us?" Leo wails.

"He deserves every bit of it," Omar says. "He spends more time reading the *Wall Street Journal* than I do practicing. Gentlemen, this orgasm calls for a drink. I don't think anything more satisfying will happen to me all summer—and I'm playing the Mozart quintet for a student concert next month. When did you artistes arrive at the graveyard? Shall we dispense with glasses since I have only one?"

Teddy drinks. "We started summer school last week."

"God," Leo groans, "algebra and biology. We flunked algebra—even cheating."

"It was Greek," Teddy says. "And we weren't in our best minds."

"We were pie-eyed," Leo says.

"Are you taking horn lessons?" Omar asks.

"Not for the summer," Leo says. "Schoolwork's enough—we're behind already. It's cigarettes, I think."

"Hey," Teddy says, "we smuggled in a gallon of purple nectar. Let's go upstairs and hear some music."

"We have Tchaikovsky's Sixth Symphony and Brahms' First," Leo says. "D'ya like those?"

"Not since childhood," Omar says. "But I'll listen to the Brahms orgasm."

Top floor to the twins' room. "No basin," Omar says. "Well," Leo says, "we only pay five a week." He digs the closet gallon out. Omar glances within. "I see getting rid of the empties is something of a problem in this bastion of temperance," he says. "Where's the nearest grog shop?"

"Bar—about a mile up the road," Teddy says. "You have to thumb up to Mayville for bottled goods. Wow, when we hit class at eight in the morning, our brains are solid rock. Can't get a thought in."

"Even if we could stay awake," Leo says. "What headaches!"

"Correction," Omar says, "hangovers." Fondles jug, scans label. "Not a bad bouquet," he says and drinks long. Lowers the burgundy, thinks, drinks again. "Not a bit brackish!" he cries.

"No music after eleven," Teddy says, searching for Brahms. "What a ridiculous rule. Ya know they really do have a WCTU temple here?"

"Ah, Temperance!" Omar says. "We must pay it a visit when the moon is high. Sprinkle a few spirits on the holy pillars. It has pillars?"

"Sure does," Leo says.

"I must inspect this edifice this evening," Omar says. "After the Brahms. And why not deposit your departed friends to be prayed over?"

"Great!" the twins agree. Teddy starts Brahms' First. A loud held throbbing fills them. Omar falls, clutching his crotch. "O my God, can't you hear it?" He laughs. "Isn't that the closest thing to female orgasm you've ever heard? Start it over! Is that Szell?"

"Just says Hamburg Symphony Orchestra," Teddy says.

Omar reads the jacket. "Just as I thought. Amazing. Nobody's conducting! Ha, they couldn't fool me. They hit that downbeat like a herd of camels."

"Who's Szell?" Leo asks.

"He conducts the Cleveland," Omar says. "And does it with one finger, like this." Omar leads the Brahms with his forefinger, then, inspired, gives them his hands to hold, his smile swelling with a secret. Teddy turns a palm. "Remarkable, isn't it?" Omar says. "The other one's just like it. Look. See these two tiny scars by my little fingers? These are the hands of a man who was robbed at birth of being the world's greatest clarinetist." Takes off his shoes and socks. "What do you see?" he asks, feet up.

"Two feet," Teddy laughs.

Twins stare at strange feet. "Twelve toes!" Teddy shouts.

"Right," Omar sighs. "A little piggy extra on each foot. And I was born with twelve fingers also, but they cut the two little ones off because they didn't have bones. You see, gentlemen, I am a monster too! You have nothing on me."

Shaking his hands heavily, Leo lifts the jug and Teddy hallows it, bestowing it again on Omar. Omar rubs up a purple bottleshine, drinks again. *"Ahem!* tell me," he asks, "do you think you're from a double egg, a single egg—or a two-headed sperm? Oh, you hadn't thought of a two-headed sperm?"

Twins laugh heartily with pain. Omar jerks his head, a redheaded woodpecker eying them curiously. "I'm a blockhead to have wounded you," he sighs.

After Brahms they fill their laundrybag with empties, creep downstairs through the breathing house. Squeak out screen door. Whisper under the pulsing streetlamp.

"You haven't met Bob Harvey yet?" Leo asks. "He lives in our basement with Bob Burns, who's from King James. Harvey's a student with the Cleveland Repertory players here. So last night Burns is sawing wood when Harvey comes in drunk about one o'clock and—Burns feels something *damp* in his dreams!"

"But it's not what he hopes it is!" Teddy whispers.

"Sure ain't," Leo says. "Harvey's standing on his own cot stark naked in the dark when Burns *hears* him. Harvey's reciting his PukeSpeech from *Winterset* and pissing in circles all over the basement. He doesn't even know Burns is there."

"Did they fight?" Omar asks.

"No," Leo says. "Burns just hung his mattress outdoors and slept down at the belltower."

Short gold-spending lamps, the deserted plaza harsh-green as billiard cloth. Cross to a gingerbread street and go into the dark, cobbles echoing on carless, noiseless streets without sidewalks. Pass the dark pit of the amphitheater, the Athenaeum's great rambling well-to-do porches, and go down to the lake front. Sparsewhite the WCTU temple rises two-and-a-half stories with arched gables, tall windows, a Babylon of bushes with spreading bays and lawn moonflood to the starlit lake.

Creep up the lawn, space their empties up the porch-steps. Omar uncorks his cognac, blesses the steps, speaks to the temple in song—

> Morally we roll along!
> Roll along! Roll along!
> Morally we roll along
> Through the darkest night!

"To bad we don't have our instruments," he says. "Well, tomorrow night!"

Cross to rocky belltower point. "We read *Faust* down here every night," Teddy says. The stars bake in rising heat, a seething, mellow sky, waves lapping slimed rock.

The twins loom over a dim body on the grass and jump back. The body sits up. *"How now, brown cow?"* it voices at the fourfooted twins.

"Harvey?" Teddy asks.

"What have you in that bag?" Harvey asks. "Something alcoholic?"

Teddy gives Harvey the wine. "This is Omar, a fellow Ashlander," he says.

"Can you stand me some food?" Harvey asks from the grass. "Canned tuna, any food at all. . . ."

Strike out for the diner outside the gate. Ghostly houses camped on the hill. Harvey, crossing grass and baring the heavens, pukes out, *"Bwahh!* Here lies the true American empire, asleep on its ass!"

As they climb the hill, a passing guard says, "Let's keep that down, boys."

Ashland shadowporches. Cross the green plaza, hike to the gate. Harvey goes down-fence and climbs over while the twins and Omar show passes to the guard. Harvey waits ahead at the diner. Go in and order at a table.

"That's the short cut?" Omar asks Harvey.

"You don't need a pass," Harvey says. Slim, husky, pasty sly. "What's the movie Friday night?"

"The Stone Flower," Teddy says. "Something from Russia."

Harvey sneers at the diner. "A film at last! The Russians are the greatest moviemakers. Eisenstein's *Ten Days That Shook the World, Potemkin, Alexander Nevsky, Ivan the Terrible*—since Stanislavski, Chekhov, Dostoi*effs*ki and Tol*stoi,* the Russians have led the world. It will be a Russian century."

"You mean Communist?" Omar asks from newsmagazine heights.

"I mean everything. It doesn't matter—none of us will be here. What can you say of an institution that only plays one film a week for one performance?" Harvey nabs the first cheeseburger from the waitress, orders another. "Look at that puke-sniveling girl," he says.

A girl alone at the counter. Cotton blouse, small paperboard suitcase. Harvey flashes his Irish movieface, asks, "What's your name?"

"Beverly." Not a terrifically interesting blouse, the twins decide.

"Hi, I'm Bob Harvey, the actor. Waiting for hotels to open?"

"How'd ya guess," Beverly asks. Tiny strong blonde with slowbrown eyes.

"Need a room?" Harvey asks.

"I need a job," she says. "Do the hotels still need girls?"

"I heard you ask the counterman," Harvey says. "Sit down, we'll all put our heads together. This diner attracts a lot of riffraff—you better sit with us."

Omar gives up his seat, gets a chair. "May I ask," he says, "how old you are?"

"Seventeen." Stirring white coffee. Her lips uncleft.

"Really?" Omar asks. He nosedrags a Benzedrine inhaler.

"I look young for my age because I'm short," Beverly says.

"I'm Leo, this is Teddy—he's Omar."

"Krauss," Omar says, sniffing. Smiles sweetly precise.

"Cheeseburger?" Harvey asks Beverly through ketchup and onions. "One or two? Onions?"

The waitress brings his second cheeseburger and Harvey says, "Two more with onions. You men want another?"

"I'm not sure how much we have," Teddy says, counting bills in his pocket. "Four bucks. Our rent's due tomorrow."

"I have eight-sixty," Leo says. "We have two-sixty for the bill."

"There's always more," Teddy says. "We'll get by."

"Okay, spendthrift, blow our rent."

"So I'm a spendthrift! You benefit," Teddy says.

"Where are you from?" Omar asks Beverly.

"I just hitched in from Cleveland to get a waitress job. My friend worked here last summer and made good. She says you can get a job for all summer if you get here early."

"You're late," Harvey says, "but there'll be openings. Stay at the Ashland until you're taken on."

"That's where we stay," Leo says. Slowburning mischief in her brown eyes.

"There's a room on our floor for five bucks a week," Teddy says. "You can move in tonight and see Mrs. Milligan in the morning."

"She won't mind my moving in without asking?" Beverly asks.

"We'll speak to her," Omar says, unscrewing his inhaler. Takes out the tab, rips it up, stirs the bits into black coffee.

"What's that?" Beverly asks.

"Cleveland champagne," Omar says.

"What is it?" Leo reads the inhaler.

"Benny," Omar says. Lowers his glasses. "It wakes you all the way up for an hour or two."

"Zap?" Harvey asks.

"A lift," Omar says.

"You feel good?" Leo asks.

"A very gentle lift," Omar says, "that clears your mind."

"Is there enough for all of us?" Teddy asks.

"There's enough for an elephant," Omar says. Sips.

"Just a sip?" Leo asks. He and Teddy sip, then Beverly. Harvey drains half the cup. "How long's it take?" he asks.

"Oh, I feel it already," Omar says.

Harvey falls back against the seat. "Look at me," he says to Beverly. He glitters at her. Your face is a chalice in my palms. . . ."

"Go on," Omar says.

"O rose," Harvey says—

"... thou art sick!
The invisible worm
That flies in the night,
In the howling storm,

"Has found out thy bed
Of crimson joy,
And his dark secret love
Does thy life destroy."

Beverly stares at her coffee. The twins clap. Harvey, puffing, sneers boyishly and bangs his head against the window. The diner quiet; a car passes. Harvey turns to the counterman and says, "Sorry." Silence.

"Was that Poe?" Teddy asks.

"William Blake," Harvey says, *"the greatest living poet."*

"He's been dead two hundred years," Leo says.

"Don't be an idiot," Harvey says.

"Who's your favorite actor?" Teddy asks.

Harvey's eyes hood. "Olivier."

"Did you ever hear of biological time?" Leo asks.

"What is it?" Harvey asks.

"We see time differently than we did as children," Leo says.

"The older I get the faster it goes," Beverly says.

"That's right," Teddy says. Twins sit back. "We read here nights."

"Time's on the wing," Omar says. "Shall we go?"

Harvey waits outside. Split the bills with Omar. He rolls his eyes about Harvey and goes out. "You won't need a pass," Harvey says to Beverly, "come with me."

"Where are you taking her?" Leo asks.

"There's a hole by the piano shacks."

"Can *we* both get through it?" Teddy asks.

"No," Harvey says.

"How much is a pass?" Beverly asks.

"You won't need one," Harvey insists, gripping her bag.

A car shineblasts by.

"We'll meet you within," Omar says at the gate. Harvey and Beverly cross the road, go off into darkness. Inside, the twins and Omar follow a dim road to the piano shacks. Cutting across grass in leafshaded darkness. Search the black shacks, find the fence hole. Whisperings unanswered. Cross dark back lots of cottages rich with grass.

"I keep hoping I'll find a body," Omar says. "Harvey's."

"They must've gone to the Ashland," Teddy says. "Bet they're waiting for us on the porch swing."

"Isn't it pretty to think so?" Omar says.

In the plaza they see Harvey and Beverly bombed on a bench by a lamp. "We missed you," Teddy says.

"We chose to wait down here," Harvey says.

"Are you all right?" Leo asks Beverly.

"Yes," she says, clearing her throat.

White wreck of the Ashland. Climb hardcreaking stairs to fifth floor. Teddy twists the empty room's knob. "It's locked!" he whispers.

"Try our key," Leo says. Teddy opens her door. A bare bulb lights a narrow single. Beverly steps into her new cage, turns about half hurt, smiles with hard labor. "It's clean," she says.

"This one's *four* dollars," Teddy says. "Put your bag in the closet and let's go to our room."

Into the twins' room. Twins pour Beverly burgundy and pass the gallon. Teddy rasps the record needle for power. "What're you drinking, old sport?" Harvey asks Omar.

"Oh, would anyone like cognac?" Omar asks, bows thriftily.

Harvey drains half the pint. Omar measures the remains. "Had enough?" he asks.

"Wine chaser," Harvey says and hooks the burgundy, guzzles juice, hands Leo the jug. "There," he says, "is the snotgreen sea." Harvey's peeved green undersea eyes.

Omar fills a glass with wine. "I'll take this down to my room."

"Getting up early for your scales?" Teddy asks.

"I keep banker's hours with my instrument, because I have a very wise teacher," Omar says. "What's this?"

"Tchaikovsky's Sixth," Leo says. "Stay and hear some music."

"It's too *pathétique,"* Omar says—"but I'll break training and stay up five more minutes."

"Start that over," Harvey says, rising. Leo stands the needle back. Harvey closes his eyes, guiding the music. Cueing instruments like Stowkowski. Twins impressed. Teddy starts the next wax record. Harvey says, "Louder."

"It's loud," Teddy says in benny glare.

"Not enough," Harvey says, the music aroused. Harvey bends, sweeps, falls with the fiddles. Omar grins wine-red teeth, glistens and says, "You skipped that clarinet!"

"Louder," Harvey says.

"It's too loud," Beverly says.

"Not enough," Harvey says.

"Ah, Peter Ilyich," Omar sighs. "Homosexual melancholy—so self-pitying, don't you think?"

Feet on the stairs. *"Quiet!"* A rap. "It's Ann," a voice whispers.

"A girl!" Omar says, opening the door. Ann, a weary-slim browneyed girl, ambles in. "I heard the music from outdoors," she drawls. "Hi, gang," she says to the twins.

"Won't you have some wine?" Omar says. "I'm Omar, may I sell you a tent?"

"Say, I'll take the wine and think about the tent. I'm Ann, I sack up here."

"Beverly's taken the empty room," Omar tells Ann. *"I* moved in tonight on the fourth floor."

"Hey, great," Ann twangs softly. Droops to the bed with Omar's glass. "You'll like it here, Beverly. Where ya from?"

"Cleveland. Hear of any waitress jobs open?"

"Gee, no," Ann says. "I'm a musician. But I'll ask around for you."

"She plays the carillon in the belltower," Leo says.

"Louder!" Harvey says.

"Do you know Bob Harvey?" Omar asks. "He raises the dead."

"Louder!" Harvey bends, twists sound up full as violins build and the walls burn with the theme. The twins ripple.

"Peter Ilyich is ravishing his mother," Omar says. "I'm going to bed."

"I'm going too," Ann says. "Gotta play the seven o'clock bells. Do you want this?" She hands Omar's glass to Beverly, who has downed her own. Omar fills the empty glass, shakes hands, and says to the twins, *"No conductor!"* He leaves with Ann, a finger in his ear. Twins watch Harvey, their hearts beating. Leo cuts the sound. Harvey looks up at the lightbulb and says, "Put out the light, and then put out the light. . . ."

Harvey clicks the light off and grabs at Beverly, who snaps the wallswitch back on.

"Did you know," he asks stiffly, "that if you want a female to stick to you like tape, all you do is tell her you love her—when she's coming? Isn't that true?" he asks Beverly.

She shrugs, redfaced.

"Stand up," Harvey says to her.

She stands holding her glass, face open.

"You can make any woman love you—except a slut," Harvey says. Swats the wine out of her hand. Twins sit up dumbfounded.

"Aren't you afraid?" Harvey asks her.

"No," Beverly says, her blouse stained.

"Because I'm going to slap you," Harvey says.

"I'm not afraid, though."

"This will help," Harvey says and slaps her cheek. Beverly gasps. Teddy catches Harvey's other hand, but it rakes her.

"What the hell are you doing?" Leo cries, grabbing Harvey's shoulders.

"You damned fool!" Teddy says, striking Harvey's arm down.

Harvey's green eyes coil and he punches Teddy's cheek. Leo raps Harvey's skull and Harvey beats both twins with the back of his fist. They fall against the bedstead, thud to the linoleum. The needle rasps from the record. Beverly stands crying. Harvey hovers over her. "I puke on you, slut!" he bursts, her temples in the heels of his palms. *"I could squash your brains out."* Her eyelids buckle.

Nerves white, band throbbing, the twins rise and rush Harvey against the door. He heaves on their breasts and again they fall, their band jerking. Leap up, hurl at Harvey again. He grabs Teddy's throat in both hands, swinging Teddy against the wall so that Leo hops off-balance. Harvey rams Teddy's head on the doorframe, strangling him. Leo pounds Harvey's head and side while Teddy hits his chest and stomach. The twins swim, dizzily apart. Teddy sinks, fading. Light dies from his eyes. But Harvey lifts him back up by the neck and Teddy's shoulder clicks the lightswitch back on. Light floods Teddy and the room. Beverly stands rooted, bluewhite. Harvey steps back, glaring at them. "Keep your stinking wine," he says and leaves. Thumps downstairs.

Beverly sobs on the chair. "You all right?" Leo gasps.

Teddy sucks his breath. "He was *crazy!*"

"I'll pull through," Beverly says. "How are you?"

"Alive," Teddy says. "I thought I was dying—everything went black!"

Footsteps. Ann in the door in her wrapper. "My God, what happened?"

Footsteps on the stairs. Quickly twins pick up bottles, glasses, close them into closet. Mrs. Milligan looks in, wide-eyed as an addict, gray hair flying. "My heavens, she says in her robe, "*what's* all this racket?"

Twins look at each other, Stan and Ollie. "Bob Harvey went berserk!" Leo says pleading, near tears.

"I *think* he was drunk, ma'am," Teddy adds thoughtfully.

"Who's this girl?" Mrs. Milligan asks.

"Well, Harvey attacked her," Leo says. "We brought her over because she wants to rent your empty room."

"Are you all right now?" she asks. "I can not run a disorderly house!"

"Mrs. Milligan," Teddy says, "we'd like to offer to paint your front porches for a few weeks' rent."

"Yes, we would," Leo says.

"We'll talk about that in the morning." She leads Beverly into her room. "Another disturbance like this and you'll have to leave," she tells the twins. "My heavens, that music!" Beverly closes her door, wiping her eyes.

"I'm sure it's Bob Harvey's fault," Ann tells the landlady. "He was corked."

"*Un*corked," Mrs. Milligan says. "I know there's been drinking up here, I can smell it. That girl had wine on her blouse. If I smell one more drop up here, you boys are going out." She floats downstairs, hardly a stair creaking.

Leo sighs. "She really didn't understand, Teddy."

Omar knocks, glass aloft. "I believe I heard you rehearsing the 1812 Overture," he whispers. "More Tchaikovsky!—May I?" he asks, hooking the wine from closet.

"That's the loudest noise ever heard at Chautauqua," Leo says. "It felt like the floor was going through."

"I *really* thought I was dying," Teddy tells Leo. "I was worried for you."

Twins sit on the bed, drained, drink wearily, a hand gripping each other's knee. Get up, Teddy's eye swelling purple in the tiny calendar mirror. Bruises on his throat. "Well, Hyde," Leo sighs, "fall off the roof?"

"I'd've come up to help but my shoes were off," Omar says.

"Oh, you mighta got a bust lip," Leo says. "He was wild!"

"He won't come back and piss on you?" Omar asks.

"There are two of us," Teddy says.

Omar goes down to his room. Beverly knocks on their door. "Can you come in and sit with me for a while? I'm scared he might come back."

"He's gone," Teddy says. "Harvey's only crazy, he's not insane. How's your face? You don't want bruises, looking for work."

"I'm all right," she says. "Your eye's swollen."

Twins sit on her bed while she eyes her bare room. "Maybe some wine would help you sleep," Leo says.

"It might," she says. "Where's the bathroom?"

Show her the bathroom beside their room, get gallon and glass. Flop onto their bed, waiting, throbbing.

Beverly stands in the door. "Let's stay here awhile, it's nicer," she says, locking the door. Twins sit up, pour her a glass, drop their shoes. She sits crosslegged on the bed, twins facing her, bottle midway. Leo pulls the lightstring and they talk in the shadows of the streetlamp.

"You were wonderful," she says, her face milky darkness. "I saw you limping. Are you sure you're all right?"

"Maybe we should look," Leo says.

Strip off their pants, stand by the window. "I can't tell anything in this light," Teddy says. "But it feels awful."

"Put on the light," Beverly says. "Oh my lord, doesn't that hurt?"

Their joined thighs, bluerotten. "That's the worst we've ever had," Leo says. "We'll feel this for a while."

"Oh, it looks horrible," Beverly says. "You better go to bed."

Teddy pulls the lightstring. Beverly against the wall by Leo. "You're trembling," she says. "Boy, you guys were great. Are you in pain?"

"We'll live," Teddy says.

"We been hurt before," Leo rasps.

"I won't forget how you protected me. When he knocked you down, it hurt me worse than it did you, believe me."

Leo takes her hand. "We're here with you. That makes up for everything, doesn't it?"

"Sure does," Teddy says.

Twins ambushed by nerves, the bed spidery with silence.

"How'd you like to go swimming in the morning?" Leo asks.

"Great," Beverly says. "Where? I brought my suit."

"There are some private beaches past the fence," Leo says. "Sleep here."

"This blouse stinks," she says.

"Take it off," Leo says.

Teddy takes Beverly's hand. "Make love with us," he says.

"Well"—she sighs—"it may as well be you twins as anyone else."

"You're a virgin?" Leo husks.

"Yep," she says.

"So'm I," Leo says.

"Me too," Teddy says. "Technically." She throws her blouse on the chair. "Oh, stand up on the bed," he begs. "We've never really seen a girl with nothing on."

"You haven't even kissed me," Beverly says.

"Oh come here!" Leo says.

Leo kisses her, then strokes her back and unhooks her bra as she slips fully into Teddy's arms. "Stand up," Teddy whispers, sighing.

She stands, strips her panties, hands on hips. Small-breasted, plump. "Not so great, huh?" she asks. "I never thought it would be like this! I mean, *Si*amese twins, holy Christmas."

"You're beautiful," Leo says.

"Oh, lovely," Teddy says.

Twins rise, undress. Peel rubbers. "I'll go first," Teddy says, "since I know a little bit about it."

"I don't think it's gonna work," Beverly says under Teddy.

"Put your leg over our band," Teddy says.

Beverly gasps.

"Does it hurt?" Teddy asks.

"No. Forget about me."

Teddy begs strength in the golden sluice. A cellar door opens on wheatfields. "Oh," he says. "Oh. *Heaven!*"

She changes legs, Leo mounts. "Help me," he says.

Teddy rides the wall, eyes closed on sunmemories.

"Lovely," Leo says.

"I never felt anything like this before!" she cries.

An angel dies, dropping through Leo's earth.

Twins wash their privates in the bathroom, check droopy rubbers for wholeness.

"Let's go swimming now and make love on the beach," Leo asks Beverly.

"Rest one minute," she begs. "My heart just beat a million beats!"

Dress, take blankets and bottle, tiptoe downstairs. The screen door croaks. Follow the lake drive to the fence. Heaven charged in the mild night air. Teddy throws blankets over the barbed stormfence. Twins climb up, leap carefully. Beverly climbs over, loosens the blankets, and the twins lower her gently. Moving shadowsilent over private grounds. Beverly seated on their crossed arms, they wade out through rocks to a cove in the woods, spread their blankets. They swim and play. Dry off. Lovemaker Teddy sees himself weaving boondoggles in Camp Turner's hobby shop, then burning a brownsmoking heart with a hot poker on white birch bark.

Lie awake on the lightening shore. Beverly starts crying. She loves them both, but she's blasted with thoughts about her parents and her trombonist brother. She makes the twins bury their waste rubbers. Her father works in the Trojan rubber factory in Akron.

"Look!" Teddy whispers, throat blue with Harvey's fingerprints.

A strayed, bright rosepink flamingo steps out of rushes ten yards away, wades into still-misted water, stands on one leg searching the lake bottom, yellow iris pulsing, and then lifts droopnecked into the pearl sky, crooked legs trailing.

All three feel waking wonder as the great bird fades with a part of their spirits.

ALARM. Wake with aching spines at 6 A.M. Wretched muscles, scratchy eyes. Rise in fog, weak, agape, dress each other in dungarees and clodhoppers, wash muck from inflamed eyelids, go down to kitchen. Not even sugar-heavy coffee with thick cream stirs their zombie blood. Make heavy meat and mustard sandwiches, pack thermoses into lunchbuckets, go to Harding and Hall to await their bus. Lids fall in leaden birdsong. Not a word spoken. Eyeball-burning skyglare.

Bus pulling out, watch their new home on Harding vanish with a pang. Good-bye, bed.

Out at Third and Main. Walk downhill to Brooklyn Square's breezeless stone trance, pass Carl's one-man trumpet academy. No wind today. Teddy's rented valve trombone is back in Besh-ge-toor's music house and Leo's trumpet gathers rust at Abie Present's hock shop.

"Let's get our horns back next paycheck," Leo says.

"I couldn't blow if my life depended on it," Teddy says. "And what about Thelma's budget?"

"Let 'er weep," Leo says, "we gotta manage our own money. Anyway, she won't marry us, for Christ's sake. We never even finished ninth grade and she's a freshman in college."

"Well, I can't believe it happened," Teddy says. "To us!"

"She should know," Leo says. "Look, I think we're lucky. We might never have found a girl who'd even consider marrying us."

"Not me, she's marrying *you,*" Teddy says.

"Nobody's gettin' married, buster. We're not even engaged. Oh shit, who can think at quarter to seven?"

"Wish these fucking bars would open," Teddy says.

"I wish my eyes could stay open."

"You can say that again," Teddy says darkly. *"Eyah!"*

"She won't *have* me!"

"That's lucky."

"Your immaturity amazes me," Leo says.

Walk over Steel to King James Veneer and Plywood, get in line at timeclock. Old Swedes joking. Air thick and blue, sapped dry with sawdust, baking glue. Twins pass down aisles of saws, veneer facings and bake-presses to the freightyard, where great boxcars with fourteen-foot planks wait to be unlumbered. Waiting in the yardworkers' shack for the whistle, sitting drained, after three weeks still uneasy with the old yardhands, thickfingered, hard-browed Swedes. Steamwhistle pain. Twins grind out butts, leave the shack's sparse strength, creak out to their boxcar. Climb inside while Olaf and Ragnar wait on a lumber pile. Twins run out a thick plank, glovefingers frazzled. "My back's on fire," Teddy groans. Leo quiet, muscles burning. Old Olaf handles the plank like balsawood.

"D'ya think we could still go back to school?" Leo asks.

"Who wants it? We're better off," Teddy says. "Education ruins jazz musicians. Look at Louis. Devotion is everything. Of course, we'd be the oldest guys in our classes, aside from the vets. And some girls like older guys but are shy of exservicemen."

"My head feels like hard shit," Leo says. "I don't think I can study anymore. All that stuff really doesn't interest me."

"Aw, we'd shape up," Teddy says.

"Yeah? What've we got but a lot of show, Teddy? Just good clothes and a couple of dozen white shirts. I gotta get some kind of profession for Thelma's sake!"

"Well, *without* school," Teddy says. "We can start practicing again, maybe get in with Stu Snyder for a start. Not that we'll spend our lives in King James—ha! talk about premature burials. Do you realize we've never heard a live Dixie combo? Even Louis has an orchestra now, terrific as *he* is."

Hot work loosening muscles as the inspector grades planks beside them. Breakfast fire fades. Pace starved bodies and empty brains for the long sweat to lunch. Mouths dry, heart beached. "I can only think of beer and sex," Teddy says asweat. The last half hour to noon, sawdust Sahara.

A Cadillac parks in the yard. Chauffeur opens trunk, takes out a wheelchair. Opens it beside a front door, helps a heavy old man into it. Wheels the old man toward the factory, but the old man points to the boxcar and the chauffeur wheels him over. The inspector greets the old man. "How's this shipment?" the old man asks. "Oh, about forty percent first grade, Mr. Summerfield," the inspector says.

"Ha! That day'll never come again, my boy," the old man says. "These the twins, Kenny?"

"Sure look like twins, boss," Kenny the chauffeur says.

"Hi, boys." Mr. Summerfield waves. Hand trembling.

Leo grins through hunger. "Hi, Mr. Summerfield," Teddy says.

"Getting thirsty?" Mr. Summerfield smiles. Twins wipe their foreheads. "I wish I was up there with you," he says, "I like handling wood. These boys do good work, Ragnar?"

Ragnar, his hair straight back and sticking out splinteredly, purses his lips above his great fist of chinbone. "Eyah, yoost about!"

"But not as goot as de last poy!" gray Olaf says anointedly.

"Oh?" Mr. Summerfield asks. "But they sent *him* up to Gowanda."

"Eyah," Olaf admits seriously. "He vas not goot in de mind."

"But he vas a goot *vorker.*" Ragnar squints above.

"They want us to work ourselves into Gowanda," Teddy says. "Let's pop over to Town Hall for a few drafts."

Steamwhistle mocking blue skies. Lunchhour burning.

"Thelma may come," Leo says.

"Louis preserve us."

"My day," Leo says. "Let's keep an eye out on Hospital Hill."

Mr. Summerfield waves good-bye as they climb high grass looking down on the factory.

Teddy sips from his thermos. *"Mmm!*—black lead."

Thelma waves from the sunburning street. Climbs hill, grinning. Their blood opens. Leo wets his lips, standing. Sleeveless blouse lace-yoked, schoolbooks, paper bag.

Sheltering breasts. Strong blue eyes, nose straight and thin, jut teeth, eaglebrow busy. Boy, are you guys losing width!" she says, eying their rumps"—maybe *I* should get a job here. I come bearing gifts."

"Svenska flicka," Leo says. He puckers.

"Not in public," she says, "how many times do I have to tell you? This is for Teddy, and this is for you, Leo Nikolaevich. My grandmother Sundberg made it, so it must be good."

Teddy unwraps a small bottle. "Wine!"

"Glögg," she tells Leo. "Just what you begged for." He holds his half pint to the sun. "Maybe you shouldn't drink it now," she says, watching Teddy uncap. "I don't want you two falling out of your boxcars! Oh well, this is a celebration. Ahem!"

"What're we celebrating?" Leo asks.

"It came."

Twins sit dazed, fall back in pollen-splotched sunlight. *"Ohh,"* Teddy moans happily.

"I thought that would get to you, Feodor Mikhailovich!" she says.

"Oh, it does," Teddy says.

"Keerist," Leo says. "I guess we won't be getting married."

"You're complaining!" Thelma groans. *"Oi-yoi-yoi,* back to ninth grade for you, my boy."

"Now we *can* go back," Leo says. "If we take extra courses and summer school, we'll breeze through in two years. Now that we don't have to work."

"You *really* are disappointed," she says. "Aren't you?"

"Yes I'm disappointed!"

She laughs. "Breathe deep, it'll go away."

"Well, I'm happy," Teddy says. "No disrespect intended, Thelma Axelovna."

"Ho!" she says. "I know all about you, Teddy."

"I didn't want it to be like this!" Leo cries.

Thelma stares fiercely. "I can't believe my ears!" Blue eyes search his strength. Teddy feels the power of her beauty, the hollows and kisses given to Leo. "I don't love you," she tells Leo, "you're too frank and I can never tell what you're thinking. I've told you many times. *Oh!* I can't be with you twenty minutes but you depress me by tearing my church apart or calling me custard-brained."

"I was quoting Philip Wylie. I didn't mean you!"

"Let's eat," Teddy says, sniffing his bottle.

Thelma says, "You take away my God and put nothing in his place."

"This is the Swedish sulks," Leo says. "And you know why." She pulls away. "Well," he says, "as long as there's no more budget, let's blow ourselves to the Peacock Saturday and come back Sunday. You like the Peacock."

"Oh no!" Thelma says. "Out of the frying pan into the frying pan, huh? No, thank you."

"We'll say we're going to Chautauqua," Leo entreats. "Will you think about it? There's gotta be more to life than all this biological arguing!"

"Here, these are for you," Thelma says. "Blueberry cupcakes. I made brandied applecake for the dinner tonight. Oh boy. Do you know I've lost fifteen pounds since I met you two guys? I was seduced by your white shirts—pairs of them, fresh every day, and twice a day! I was *dazzled*."

"Well, we're not wearing white shirts now," Leo says.

"No, you're not, I'll say that for you."

"Will you think about the Peacock? Don't you remember Winsor hill last night, how green the leaves were in the streetlights? We weren't cynical about anything. Why can't we be like that all the time? Life's not worth living if you're cynical."

"He can charm a bird out of a bush," Thelma tells Teddy.

"Oh, I agree with him," Teddy says.

"I gotta go up to the Prendergast and study my Russian," she says.

"What time's dinner?" Teddy asks, warming her up for Leo. "When should we be there?"

"Seven. But be early," she says, "this dinner's an engineering feat. *And* there'll be plenty to drink, believe me. You might bring flowers. And wear your best, it's their twenty-fifth anniversary, after all."

Wine speckles Teddy's sight. Heartfilled tiredness. Desire.

"Maybe you could give me my first driving lesson Saturday," Leo asks Thelma.

"That'll be certain to break us up," she says. "Well, I'm off."

Leo takes her books. "We'll walk you to the corner. Ah, what gams!"

"Oh, the *huit* is flying," she says.

Watch Thelma churn around the corner, their carcass bereaved.

"Let's make this our last day," Teddy says.

"Last hour, you mean," Leo says drinking at last, cars passing.

"Great! I'd rather be a bum than a robot, that's for fucking sure."

"Town Hall sounds dull," Leo says. "Let's hit Kliney's for a beef on kummelwick. But we gotta punch out."

"What's wrong with us? Diarrhea? How do we outwit these morons?"

"Terrible spinal pains," Leo says. "Gotta see a doctor."

"Glorious! We absolutely quit right now—agreed? We could even run up to Lakewood beach, if we hurry."

Downhill to the freightyard. "We'll come back Friday for our paychecks," Teddy says. "Boy, a perfect day for Lakewood quail. Hey, maybe the Cassidy sisters'll be there!"

Threelegged drag into the yard shack, Teddy limping, chin up, Leo hopping on one foot. Ragnar and Olaf smoke on the floor, watching. Twins sit carefully, Leo shucks clodhopper, rubs his ankle.

"Can you *stand* on it for long?" Teddy asks.

"Well, it's swelling pretty damn bad," Leo says.

"Vass wrong vid your foot?" Ragnar asks, cigarette perched between his two complete fingers.

"Took a spill on Hospital Hill," Leo says.

Ragnar wrinkles his brow at the foot question, bites his breath heavily.

*"Lee*na*ment,"* Olaf says.

"What?" Leo asks.

*"Lee*na*ment!"* Olaf says fixedly.

"Linament," Leo says. "Yeah, I guess so."

"Eyah, Ragnar," Olaf says. "Dat is vat de doctor orders."

"Eyah," Ragnar says. *"Lee*na*ment* and Epsom salts."

"We'll have to get some," Teddy says.

"Eyah," Olaf says. "Ven you get home tonight, soak his foot for an hour in hot water."

"Vid Epsom salts," Ragnar says. "And den rub vid *lee*na*ment."*

"And py morning you vill be goot in de foot," Olaf says.

"Like new," Ragnar says. "*Vork* is de best medicine. Don't vorry a bit."

Steamwhistle pain. Ragnar and Olaf's fierce eyes give manhood.

They all go out to the boxcar, twins limping.

Climbing Winsor hill in twilight, the steep redbrick street still smutty with winter cinders. Twins pace themselves upward without a breather. Birds fall quiet in squat shade trees. Late news echoes from screendoors, cramped porches.

"Thelma's the first girl I've ever seen as a real person," Leo says.

"You don't understand her," Teddy says. "Not that *I* grasp her eaglemind entirely, Leo Nikolaevich."

"Well, girls don't think like men," Leo says. "D'ya suppose we're the reason she gets depressed all the time? Right in the middle of a sunny day you shouldn't get depressed, for God's sake. Maybe it's morals, though."

"It's biological," Teddy says. "That long Swedish twilight—all Swedes have black cycles, right in their genes! But maybe it's her ten cups of black coffee a day. *That's* unhealthy!—I wonder what they'll have for booze. That *glögg* has a kick I like."

"Hit me right off," Leo says. "You'd think both of us together would be at least as keen as Thelma. But when we sat up by the belltower reading *Hamlet,* we didn't understand half the lines and she caught everything."

"And without footnotes," Teddy says. "A sobering experience. Philip Wylie is not enough."

"That's why we have the twenty-two volumes of Leo Stovepipevsky on order at Boorady's. We do *read* more than she does. I mean, *she* hasn't read *Warren Piss.*"

"It's a case," Teddy says, "of the hare and the herd of turtles."

Thelma's house, cloven into Orchard Street's rising banks. Short stony side street thinly paved, overlooking Chadakoin valley's leafy treetops. Panting twins shoot the half-porch steps, rap the screendoor. A hound howls within.

"Julia, answer the door!" Thelma's mother, Karen, cries from the kitchen.

"Oh, Mama, it's just those twins, for heaven's sake," Julia wails from the couch. "I know their feet already."

"We're in!" Leo says waving at Julia. Tall, sweettoothed twelve-year-old, she barely nods, watching Hopalong Cassidy on fuzzy TV. Struck by living-room darkness and drawn shades, Leo asks, "Why so dim?"

"Helps the picture," Julia groans.

"Julia! Set the table."

"Mother! Nobody's here yet!"

Twins shake their heads about the living room. "Scandinavian melancholy!" Teddy whispers.

A shortlegged basset mongrel growls from her rug by the study gas heater. "Oh shut up, Suzie," Julia says.

Into kitchen. "Well, here we are," Leo says.

"In our native costume," Teddy says.

"Hi, boys! Hey, don't you look spiffy," Karen says from the sink. "Thelma's not home from de library yet. Help yourselfs to a drink. There's beer on the side porch."

"We brought our own," Teddy says, tabling the bag like gold dust.

"Well, it's a present." Leo nudges Teddy.

"Oh you din't have to do that," she says. "Vat you bring?"

Leo holds up a fresh bottle crisply cellophaned. *"Akvavit!"* she cries. Strong, bosomy, eyes sparked deep-blue. "Where you get that? D'you know, I never had it? Nossir. I vas too young when I left de old country an' too poor to afford it here. Yah, it's de truth, I wouldn't lie."

"Well, *happy anniversary,"* Teddy says forcefully, longing for a drink to put him at ease.

"Say, I alvays say you boys have goot hearts," Karen says. "Vy don't we have a little snert right now?"

"Oh, we like a drink now and then," Leo says.

"Hey, don't ve all! De glasses are in de cupboard. You like *lutfisk?"*

"Never had it," Leo says. "Straight or with water?"

"Make mine a short snifter," Karen says. "Julia! set de table. Dat kid, I'm telling you, I need a truck to move her!"

A piercing whistle asks *where-are-you* from the porch and Thelma cries, "I'm home!" Leo beams, Teddy reddens.

"Don't let de dog out!" Karen cries.

"I got her," Thelma says, throwing books on study desk. "Julia, you finished with the bathroom? I'm taking a fast bath—get up there pronto if you don't wanta be last after Ma."

"Pick, pick, pick, all day long!" Julia cries. Heaves into kitchen, smears butter on stale skorper, stomps upstairs chewing.

"We don't have to worry about *her* appetite," Thelma says. "Where's the mail? So you got here early *and* in your blue suits—a double miracle! Where's the flowers?"

"What flowers?" Leo asks.

"We brought a bottle instead." Teddy smiles, trembling.

"I *might* have known, *ha ha.*"

"Akvavit," Karen says. "Okay boys, *skoal!"*

"Want some?" Leo asks.

"None for me," Thelma says, "I haven't eaten breakfast yet. Coffee hot, Ma? I want it strong and black."

Pours herself a scalding cup, sips without pain, goes to to the study. *"I-yi-yi!* it's from Albany!"—she comes out reading a letter. *"I've been accepted!"* she shrieks, dancing. "I'm going to Albany State Teachers College in September!"

Twins smile over shots, hearts sinking. *"Skoal,"* Teddy tells Leo.

"Now isn't dat de best present I could have?" Karen asks. "Of course I knew dey vould *haff* to take you vid your marks!" She hugs Thelma and even the twins get Thelma's cracking cheek smooch.

"Well, enough sentiment," Thelma says, "before I turn into custard."

As she pounds upstairs, Leo eyes legs rounded by a lifetime on Winsor hill, his breath leaden. "Well, darn it, that calls for another!" he says.

"I'll drink to that," Teddy mutters.

"Yah, it does!" Karen says, stove steaming. Deep twilight brightens the kitchen. "Now what vill you boys do?" she asks slyly.

"Where there's hope—" Leo says, pouring.

"Dat's right," Karen says. "Never say die! How's work?"

"Murder," Leo says.

"Yah, you boys are too good for dat hunky work. You should go back to school and get your education, I think."

"We're just vacationing," Teddy says.

"Some vacation!" she cries. "How many years now?"

"We're getting serious about our music," Leo says, a bonds salesman.

"Boys, you want my advice? Musicians don't do too good. Dey drink too much."

Twins watch TV on the dark couch. "Suffering Jesus—*Albany!*" Leo groans. "That's all the way across state!"

"We'll figure something out," Teddy says. "Don't we always? Buck up."

"I can't bear this. Let's go out on the porch."

As they drink on the porch, streetlamps suddenly prickle the valley deeps. Blue twilight filling their lungs.

A small truck glares into Orchard and parks. Janice, Thelma's sister heavy with child, and her husband, Stanley, get out.

"How's the construction businesss" Leo asks, grinning hard.

"Coming along," Stanley says, shaking hands. Bony, dark, muscled veteran. "How's the music business?"

"In King James?" Leo asks. "A recession—except for Stu Snyder."

"Dead on its ass, huh?" Stanley asks.

"Oh, the Redfields are boffo at the Baghdad Lounge," Leo says.

"We hope to cop a gig at Thule Lodge, if we're lucky," Teddy says.

They go in. "We're here, Ma!" Janice cries, *"where's the grub?* That dern Julia hasn't even set the table yet. Happy anniversary!"

"Hey, I t'ink dat lilla fallar growed since Sunday!" Karen says, seizing and sifting her daughter's spirit.

Twins freshen their glasses, pour for Stanley. Karen sees Suzie licking herself in the dining room. *"Su-uzie,"* she says sternly. The bitch droops low, creeps to her rug, settles browbeaten. "I swear dat hound understands everyting I say," Karen says. "Sure does!" Leo laughs.

Thelma's father, Axel, leads his mother through the back entry. "Well, I see everyone's here for chow," he says and tables a full fifth of whiskey. "Hey, Karen, look what the boys down at the firehouse gave us for a present." He unwraps a haunch of meat. "Venison!" Karen cries over bloodystiff paper. "Put it in de freezer, Axel."

"You mean we can't have it tonight?" he asks, then groans boyishly. Strong tight dark suit, diet-bright piercing blue eyes. "You know I can't eat no *bruna bönor* or *rotmos,*" he says.

His mother stares at him as at a rare peacock. "Den you can haff *limpa* or *Knackebröd* and go to bed hungry!"

"No, Ma, I can't eat that either," Axel says. "I can only eat meat."

Grandmother Sundberg sniffs at her son's diet, her dark hair tightly netted, round steel glasses on sparkblue eyes. "Py yiminy, you are cr-razy in de belly, Axel!"

Karen's laugh rings from the sink. Twins glow hollowly through family roar. Thelma starched and pressed comes downstairs and growls for work, grabbing an apron. Soon, all sit. The table steams. Meatballs, herring and onion rings, whitefish and creamed potatoes, turnip-whipped potatoes, stuffed cabbage, Swedish sausage, roast chicken with gravied dumplings, lingonberry sauce, sweet rye, and hardtack.

"Yah, I vas born in de old country," Karen answers Leo. "I remember de countryside and streams where I grew up, jus' a lilla shaver. Ay come to King Yames when I vas only fifteen—and *so* young and pretty you wouldn't believe it!"

"But you bane hard verker ever since, Karen," Grandmother Sundberg says, "not only home but down at de vorsted mill."

"Vell, I don't mind dat, if it helps," Karen says. "Thelma, she has my piss and vinegar too."

"I guess that dried up when Julia came along," Axel says.

"No, Yulia iss pretty girl!" Grandmother Sundberg says. "Big and strong as goot Svedish country girl."

"She is my peewee," Karen says.

Julia drops her fork. "You're drivin' me away from the table!"

Karen asks Grandmother Sundberg, "How about a drink, Ma?"

"Ay got plenty, t'ank you. Ay yust sip Axel's *glögg* if I get t'irsty."

"He's not drinking *glögg,"* Janice says, "it's Seagram's."

"I don't like no vhiskey," she says. "Iss all bellyvash."

"Hey, Ma," Stanley asks her, "did you hear about Ole in the liquor store asking for squirrel whiskey? Store owner says, 'We don't have any squirrel whiskey, but we have some Old Crow, which is just about the same.' 'Oh no,' says Ole, 'I don't vant to fly, I yust vant to hop around a bit!' "

Grandmother Sundberg smiles slightly. "Dat vas not funny, Stanley. Dey are yust like peas in a pod."

The twins eat, lightly flushed, knowing they are eating in rhyme.

"Vy don't dey get separate?" she asks.

"Ask them," Thelma says.

"We're too old," Leo says. "Some babies were separated last year in Stockholm, but their band was still soft. We'd wind up with canes or crutches if we were separated now."

"Oof!" Karen says.

"Not during dinner, please," Thelma says.

"Ya, Sveden has de best doctors in de vorld," Grandmother Sundberg says. "You should go dere, maybe. You are such nice-looking boys. Iss pity."

Thelma serves applecake and cherry brandy, sails into mountainous dishwashing. At ten-thirty the twins walk home, bar by bar, looking for Venus in the traps and joints.

Levandoski's looks dull. Go in anyway.

Sweating ale. Surrender. Ah.

Four elbows resting, thumbs at lip. Surrender. Foam-cool tongue.

A wide swing to Kliney's, first hitting the dull cedar panel Malta Grill. Noiseless cadavers at their drafts. Then Shanahan's, quite empty. Back to Stoney's and Ted's. For Christ's sake, let's see what's at the Haymarket. They go on to Town Hall, a palace of boredom. Let's try the Brown Derby and Otto's. At last, they swim into Kliney's. Mustard assails the mourners.

"Ya know," Leo says, gripping beer firmly as a judge, "we haven't been to the Colored Elks all week." Bites hot crisp rocksalt juicesoaked beef and hot mustard, sighs as fumes split his nose. "We *might* pick up a girl down there. Some of 'em sell it."

"I'm stuffed," Teddy belches. "But okay."

Hike four blocks uphill without rest, backs aching. Pass the library, cut through the long park, follow Seventh to Washington, head out for the Colored Elks, running sweat, pores like hydrants.

Knock first. Cellar club, lavenderlighted. Hit the bar amid greetings. Two bowties, soaked.

Sniff full waterglasses of whiskey, sip the cream off. No girls. Oh.

Racing hopes, stalled. Long, long fogwalk home uphill, a hard full moon whitening their veins with hunger.

HERMITS, awake! Caretakers, on an artist's farm, twenty miles outside Albany.

Sherry hangover firstlight strikes bedroom wall. Groaning twins arise. Sunburnt yard mist. Shave two-week calico silk beards. Armorweight flesh waddling flatfooted. Set kettle to boil, go out back, molars grinding sliced cheese-plastic slaverlessly.

Deep bushes, woods rushing in. The barn they broomed and trimmed. The posing stand on which they modeled bare for middleaged lady painters. Fold up their steel music stand, carry horns back to kitchen. Leaving for good, once their eyes open.

Icebox harps bare but for sherry gallon and can of pimientos. Bolt down cold wine, eyes closed, split a last pimiento, tongues' metallic ash. Bathmat stomach spasms, rubber burps. Sunbeams fade and bloom in the kitchen.

Pack in upstairs bedroom, suitcases on bed. "Christ, we didn't write Mother once all summer," Leo says.

"We were breaking our backs."

"*What?* We cut those weeds in three days," Leo says.

Bedroom dimming, blooming. Heavy darkness falls, light sucked down a floor drain. Breath weighted, brains solid fuzz.

"Okay, we didn't write," Teddy says. "What'd we have written about? Mowing? Painting the barn? We were too dull to write. Snap on the light. Oh, that's depressing—turn it off. Besides, not writing keeps us from asking for money. We'll see her tomorrow. And you want this trip with Mr. Summerfield as much as I do. You knew what he was like after we nursebuggied him to South Carolina. Now California, Colorado, Texas—and getting paid for it! What in hell d'ya want?"

Leo snaps his suitcase, Teddy his.

"*Well!*" Teddy asks.

"Sure—I'm tempted!"

"Tempted? Ha! You've accepted. You're as eager as me."

Breastcarry their suitcases down narrow stairs to kitchen. Coldshocking breath of sherry. "And maybe we'll meet some cunt," Teddy says, lips flapping fumes. "Maybe we can 'borrow' the Caddie and hit those Tijuana cathouses."

"For some syph," Leo says. "You get it, I get it—that's for sure."

"Don't tell me you won't jump anything that spreads," Teddy says.

"Maybe. But I *hope* to be faithful."

"To Thelma!"

"She's faithful to me."

"Noodlehead," Teddy says, "she just studies too hard. Ohh, you simp, two years chasing this— Let's have a drink. Still buddies? Y'know, as depressing and insensitively cheerful as Thelma is, to me, I envy you. You really must have something I don't have."

"Don't run yourself down," Leo says. "Her IQ's higher than both of us together."

"Oh, hell, we were bombed for that IQ test, I remember it clearly. Half the morning at the Brown Bear—or was it Wisteria Grill?"

"No, the vets bar at Second and Prendergast."

"Well, it's no wonder. See?" Teddy says.

Sit on the back stoop, waiting. Leo digs out Durwood's Whitman, reads their underlinings—

I hear the key'd cornet, it glides quickly through my
ears,
It shakes mad-sweet pangs through my belly and
breast.
I hear the chorus, it is a grand opera,
Ah this indeed is music—this suits me.

"Let's walk around the house," Leo says. "We may never see it again."

Walk out front. Blue thunderheads, bottlegreen sky awash. Blowing shrubs, saplings bending. An elephant lurches unseen through leaves, lazy, lashing.

"A cunt is a bag with an elastic band," Teddy says. "It don't make sense that all life revolves around a little bag."

"What the hell are we reading Whitman for if you think like that? Where's that body poem?"

This is the female form,
A divine nimbus exhales from it from head to foot,
It attracts with fierce undeniable attraction,
I am drawn by its breath as if I were no more than a
helpless vapor, all falls aside but myself and it—

"Now that's not cunt," Leo says, "that's some other feeling and not any damned elastic band."

Watch windlicked saplings, the milky palates of leaves.

"If I get married," Leo says, "I don't ever want to be unfaithful."

"We don't ever write Dad either," Teddy says, drinking. "We spend all our time trying to keep cheerful. We do like the family reunions out at Lake Erie, though. Felt awful grown up at the last one."

"Whale of a lot of rain coming."

"Sure hope Dad's diabetes isn't hereditary," Teddy says.

"Don't know."

". . . It must be sort of dangerous to be two-footed—like you're always gonna fall over. I don't know that I'd like that. Boy, I hate gray thoughts."

"I don't want to be unfaithful."

"Oh you'll get carried away," Teddy sighs.

"Well, I don't wanna give in to the impulse. And I'm sick and tired of jacking off. More impulses! Remind me. *Hard.*"

"I don't think it'll work," Teddy says.

"That's what I say! Somebody's gotta *remind* you! Look at our advantage over those other poor bastards. Christ, d'ya think I don't know about impulses?"

"I could give in to a few right now," Teddy says. "South Carolina's a long time gone."

"Don't remind me of South Carolina. *Il pleut,* let's go in. Our eyes have changed. Noticed? There used to be a little extra energy or light in them, and it's gone. Something's died and I don't know what."

"Look into my eyes," Teddy says.

"It was a light," Leo says.

"Well, we're hungover. We didn't even make it upstairs last night."

"You haven't noticed?"

"Quiet," Teddy says.

Standing against front windowpour. Faces, eyes silver.

"You *look* hungover," Teddy says.

"Look harder."

Swiftly, an urgent gleam fills Leo, his spirit's waters rise filling and eager. Leo's eyes break bare, he aches for all his injuries to Teddy and himself. Fright runs up Teddy's spine at what Leo asks from him. They lock brows, Teddy plunges into Leo's eyes. Their fused spirit breathes with four lungs.

Bolts crack into saplings, yellow curtains shake the house. Rooms fill with smoke, kitchen blueboiling.

"I thought it was just water!" Leo wails. Race to stove carefully. Coffeepot sootblack, fluming.

"I left the grounds in," Teddy groans.

Throw the pot into the roaring yard, air the house with wet doorblasts.

Wait soaked at the front window. The road floods in green air. Pale saplings, breasting darkness, wash in the down-pouring green.

"When this trip's over, buster," Teddy says, "we start lessons."

"Let's practice now," Leo says. "Oh God, I'm zonked."

Set up music stand in livingroom. Warm up.

"My mouthpiece's too cold," Leo says. They warm their mouth-pieces at the tap, fill with restless strength. Warm up, spirits sticking.

"Let's have a drink," Teddy says.

"For energy."

Chugalug shower for dry cells. *"Aghh!"*

"Rrrff! that did it," Teddy shakes himself.

Sherry lips slippery on mouthpieces, suck dry.

"You wanna play that allegretto?" Teddy asks.

"Let's warm up first. Do our long tones."

"Well, not for five whole minutes," Teddy says.

Pipe C octave long tones, five seconds each.

"I feel positively virtuous," Leo says. "How's your lip? Mine's got a rasp."

"I could be better, but I get good tone. What'll we heat up? 'Cornet Chop Suey'?"

"Nah, we'd blow our lips for the allegretto," Leo says.

"No, we won't. It'll warm us up."

"But the allegretto's more like practice."

"D'ya *want* to play the allegretto?" Teddy asks.

"No, no, I can wait."

Dig out *Louis Satchmo Armstrong's Dixieland Trumpet Solos,* clip its tatters open.

"Remember to sock the stop chorus," Leo says.

"Yeah, but we don't get the first shake right on the F."

"It's too hard to lip down from the shake to the rising triplet. We're scared we're not gonna hit the E," Leo says. Glisses two octaves to high C. "Hey, let's memorize something for the party tonight. We don't know anything note-perfect, Leopold. Something easy, 'Body and Soul.' "

"That has four flats in the bridge!" Leo cries. "I'll never remember that fingering."

"That's it, we *have* to memorize. We'll just help each other. Boy, how long's it been?"

"Clip it up," Leo says. "Ah, crap, are we memorizing the intro*duc*tion? That's a hell of a long intro. We might as well memorize the allegretto."

"Nobody wants to hear musical exercises!" Teddy says.

"But the allegretto's beautiful."

"To us! But those damn dotted notes and sixteenths are too hard to remember. Let's do something simple like 'My Blue Heaven.' "

"Too hard," Leo says. " 'My Blue Heaven' is that Harry James book. Let's figure out 'Blue Skies.' Skip the intro. How's the bridge go? Well, hell, how's the *chorus* go?"

"Come on, let's just bash on down the lane," Teddy says.

Rain batters the window. They blow "Blue Skies" heavily. Leo fumbles the bridge, screams above it. Teddy boots Leo with stumbling harmonies.

"Well, that's not long enough," Teddy says, "and you don't know the bridge. Must be chromatics or something. Let's work out the fingering."

"Let's have a drink. All we play good is 'What a Friend We Have in Jesus,' " Leo says. "We get real tone on that. Ha, that should be played at our funeral."

"But not at a costume party, Stan. We should play something like 'Sleepy Time Down South'—but we don't have the music."

"Let's play 'Cornet Chop Suey' and forget about it. But let's try to save our lips for tonight."

They blow "Cornet Chop Suey" 's opening flourish and stop.

"That's too slow and swingy," Leo says. "Too smooth. Ya know, the Hot Five run out like jazz babies into paradise. Really childish!"

"Try to pretend you don't know the notes, like Louis does."

"Louis knows the notes!" Leo says. "Christ, he *wrote* the piece."

"Are you crazy? He doesn't know what he's blowing half the time. He never plays the same twice. Let's blow."

Leo flubs the dotted F shake. Teddy socks the stop chorus. They get lost in the Solo.

"How can this part be solo?" Teddy asks.

"There's a *piano* too," Leo says.

"Oh. Let's save our lips," Teddy says.

"And not play the allegretto!"

"You *want* to play the allegretto?" Teddy asks.

"It's our prettiest music. And that polka rhythm in the middle, now that's *beautiful!*"

"Let's save that for real practice when we get home tomorrow," Teddy says.

Drink. Shake spit from their instruments.

"How about 'What a Friend' for tone?" Leo asks. "*Molto lento.*"

"And *dolce,*" Teddy says.

They blow "What a Friend" with long tones, full feelings.

"Boy," Leo says slowly.

"Coupla born winners here!" Teddy says. "We'll be horn players yet. Too bad we can't transpose up a step into our right key. We should write that transposition out someday. How's your lip?"

"Oh, I could play all day, Big Tea!"

"Big Tea is fading," Teddy says.

"Well, we don't rest properly. Course we get tired. We should play and read, play and read, we'd last longer. Is your outer ear buckling?"

"No, but I think my left ear's getting weak."

"Maybe we'll get over this damn cold someday," Leo says"—two *years* we've had it! Hey, here they come."

A stationwagon parks on the back flood. Georgia Jones and Stu Armstrong stomp into the kitchen.

"Ready to go!" she pleads. A painter, bantam, practical.

"No more food, booze and free cigarettes for this summer! I'm firing you."

"Free?" Teddy says. "We broke our backs—three hours, every morning—almost."

Her fiancé, Stu, runs to the sink, rinses his mouth. "Hi," he says softly to the twins, "how do my gums look? Swollen? I can't go onstage with swollen gums."

"Do you know what this idiot did this morning?" Georgia says. "He brushed his teeth with Ajax cleanser. I can't express what an idiot he is!"

"No, I'm not," he whispers.

"But that's for sinks and toilets!" she says.

"I thought it would work and I didn't have any toothpowder," he says mildly. Tall, balding actor, wiving in alimony.

Twins bag their sherry, pack the stationwagon. Georgia slides their portrait in. The twins happy to ride again. Stu turns, ever reading the twins' depths, and says softly, "Boy, did you hear that lightning?" His green eyes dance. "We should all get out and run in the fields."

"Stark naked," Georgia says. "I wouldn't have it any other way."

"As I came out of the playhouse," Stu says, "the whole sky lighted up and a green wave hit me in the parking lot. Did you see it?"

"We thought it hit Chatham," Teddy says.

"Yeah! So did I!" Stu breathes, smile bared. "Right on the playhouse!"

"You won't have a show tonight," Teddy says. "What're you playing?"

"*Dunnigan's Daughter* by Behrman," Stu says. "I'm Dunnigan."

"Can you play it as you want?" Leo asks.

"Oh, no. I'd be out of key. You can't have somebody up there feeling his way through his lines while everyone else is playing technically. That's grotesque."

"How many parts did you learn this summer?" Teddy asks.

"About sixty," Stu says. "Just for reference."

The wagon edges by a fallen branch, everyone leaning uphill.

"Do you think we should call off the party?" Georgia asks.

"Why?" Stu says. "I love a storm for a party."

"Do you know *Lear?*" Teddy asks.

"Whisperingly," Stu whispers.

"Do you *think* we should call off the party!" Georgia says.

"Not at all," Stu says. "We can turn out the lights and find each other with grunts and fingers."

"Is Ruth Drummond coming?" Leo asks.

"She's my territory," Teddy says. "And I bet I bounce her bubbies before the night's out."

"Yeah, she's a kind of exotic *sensuelliste,* isn't she?" Stu says. "Have you ever read one of her stories?"

"Just her eyes," Teddy says. "But that's very perceptive of you about her—*sensuelliste.*"

"Oh my God," Georgia says, "you've certainly made a conquest in these boys."

Stu rubs away window steam, smiling silence.

"Hey, what'd DeWitt Forsythe say in the *Sun* about your Hamlet?" Teddy asks, drinking.

"I don't remember," Stu says.

"Oh, you do too," Georgia says. "He said you were inspiring and that the play was the Little Theatre's greatest triumph in King James."

"Did you read Ray Finch's review?" Teddy asks Georgia. "He said we played Rosencrantz and Guildenstern like a pair of Graustarkian streetcar conductors! What'd you think of your Hamlet?"

"Didn't like it," Stu says. "Too technical. How do my gums look now?"

"My God," Georgia cries, "those are blisters!"

"I couldn't keep George Gordon down in the dueling scene." Stu says. "He kept getting carried away and one night he rapped my pate just as I was supposed to spin his foil away—knocked me dizzy."

"Can you come back from your triumph for half a second?" Georgia asks. "*Ser*iously, should I call off the party?"

"No!" the twins cry.

Pull into a rivering lane and park by a dim-bowered house where the Chatham summer troupe boards. "What do you think of Brando?" Teddy asks.

"He's better onstage," Stu says.

"Boy, there's a guy *no*body can imitate," Leo says firmly.

"Pearls! Ropes of them!" Stu cries. "What is this sister

of yours, a deepsea diver? Bracelets of solid gold, too! Where are your pearls and gold bracelets, Stella? And when are we gonna get them colored lights going again?"

"Brando! He did it!" Leo cries. Out in gurgling downpour, gallop through cheesy mud.

Thelma's chopping salad in a great screened kitchen overhung with fir limbs, one bulb burning in forest gloom. The twins' Brando hiproll fades as she pins them, smiling, blackly. "Get out of my kitchen or get out of my way," she says, "I've got twenty people to feed lunch. Keep your fingers out of those strawberries, they're *counted*. Well, good to see you," she says at the sink, tearing lettuce. "What brings you out this way for the fifth time on my eight weeks of drudgery that you talked me into when my mother needed me home this summer? Hm, cat got your tongue?"

Leo coughs. "I should have been around more."

"Ha," she says.

"Like some sherry?" Leo asks.

"Is that all you've got to offer after two weeks without a word? I mean you're only staying ten miles away or is it too much for you to hitch over here? You walk like the wind, you could have been here in two hours *on foot*."

"Yes, well—there's no excuse," Leo says. "I can't excuse myself. We *have* been working *very hard* at our music. But I really didn't think you'd taken this job for me. I mean I *really didn't!*"

"Oh? When I could be in King James studying and living at home? You must have a very funny idea about me. Tell me more—it's good to hear anything from you. You think I enjoy making three meals a day, seven days a week, for twenty people—and more on Sunday?"

"Yes, well—we were practicing and had the barn to fix—"

"—mornings," she says. She fixes Teddy's silence.

"He's no good," Teddy says.

"Were you drunk all summer?"

"Oh no," Leo lies. "Ask Georgia."

"You're half drunk now."

"No I'm not," Leo says.

"I can smell it from the sink!"

"We had some sherry this morning, that's all," Leo says.

"Nothing we can't handle gracefully," Teddy says.

"Gee, and we just had such a great ride over!" Leo says. Rain whales the firs.

"Don't let me dampen your day. Ha!" Thelma says. "Oh, it must be nice to take a ride. Are you packed? When are you supposed to see Mr. Summerfield?"

"Monday morning," Leo says.

"Then on to California, huh?" she says.

"I'm beginning to feel very bad," Leo sighs.

"If it's hunger, suffer," Thelma says.

"It's a place food doesn't get to," Leo says. "Are you getting the night off?"

"Yes, my *first* this summer—only because the show's rained out."

"Have you thought of a costume?" Teddy asks.

"Yeah, *Cinderella!* Ho, all I've thought of are grocery lists!"

Twins glide slowly near. Leo touches her shoulder. "You're so beautiful. I don't know why I didn't get over more often."

"You didn't think of it," she says. "Speak the truth!"

"I-yi-yi," Leo groans. "Thelma, we'll get those colored lights goin' again. Honey, believe me."

"Neither of you thought to come over—with two heads!" she says.

"I certainly did," Teddy says. "But I didn't think it was my place to come without Leo."

"Oi! Smerdyakov."

"I was very lonely, sweetheart," Leo says.

"Don't speak to me about loneliness," Thelma says. "I've lost ten pounds and you've gained ten. You're getting *fat!"*

"Baby fat," Teddy says. "It'll go like a virgin's first kiss."

"You can skip that subject too," she says. "I've never been the victim of a con before."

"Unh!" Leo says. "I wish I had a headache or something simple. My sins are bottomless. Honey, don't you want those colored—"

"I don't know what you're talking about! I didn't even love you *before this!* Oh, you shysters are something to behold. *For heaven's sake!* Get off your knees before somebody sees you!—*And don't think I'm finished."*

* * *

Rainbitten skylight above shaved gray shadows in Georgia's North Pearl Street studio in Albany.

"Don't turn on the light," Stu says. "Let's just stand here a minute."

Twins put down their bags and horn cases. "We're getting a room at the Ten Eyck," Leo says.

"Peace, break thee off," Stu whispers. "Look where it comes again!"

Stu hovers above them, gloomsilver eye unsettling. Turns under skylight to twins and Thelma.

"In the same figure, like the King that's dead," he whispers. Eye spinetingling. "We need some *ghastly* costumes tonight. Something frightening."

"Why don't *we* take care of that?" Teddy says. "I know just the thing, and it's cheap. We'll be ghastly for you, Stu."

"Real-l-ly ghastly," Stu whispers.

"You won't want to look at us," Teddy says. "We'll be right back, we're going over to register at the hotel."

"Why don't I come along with you?" Thelma asks. "Oh, I don't want to get my hair wet."

"Honey, your hair'll be beautiful," Leo says.

Down to the stormwhipping entrance, dash into wind. Gnashing rain.

"In here!" Leo shouts turning Thelma into a flower store.

"What *is* this?" she asks.

"You need a flower for tonight, don'tcha—for your hair?"

"For my hair? *Sure!* I'm coming in a sarong."

"Of course you need an orchid." He pats her.

"What are you coming as?" she asks.

"A multiple auto fatality," Teddy says. "Ask no more, my *blini.*"

"Where's your sarong?" Leo asks.

She holds up her knitting bag.

Into a candy store. Leo buys Thelma a tin of glazed chestnuts. Liquor store for pink champagne. Check into Ten Eyck, drink the champagne, Thelma models her sarong and orchid. Off to Farnham's, a wooden pub with Old King Cole on the wall.

"Roast beef," Teddy tells Thelma, his eyes pink.

"Hey, there's Clif," Thelma says, waving at the bar.

A thin dark hangoverhaggard rake comes from the bar,

devil's neat mustache and black homburg, ups his brandy and milk at them, sits.

"Nothing for me!" Clif tells the waitress, "I'll pull through on this toddy." Smoke swaddles brown eyes, tired devil. "My eyes feel like brandied oysters," he says. "Ghastly day, isn't it? What Picasso might call *corpsepenis blue*. Breakfast." He sips. "I'd put an egg in, but I can't take the energy jolt. Did a sveltelooking dish just come in and sit at the bar? She looking at me? Take a look out that window, Ted. See a long black limousine down the street? No? She must be around the corner with the motor running. I think I'm getting pneumonia again. This tall dish in a long limousine is tailing me—wants to know what I'm doing every minute!"

"Who is she?" Thelma asks.

"Well, she's not the Governor's wife," Clif says. "She has a black Rolls, that's all I know about her. And I'm perfectly sober. I'm more sober than you may ever see me again."

"Wow, what's your great secret with women?" Thelma asks.

"Just press 'em on the boobs, Thelma, and look hungry."

"Whoops!" she cries. "I discourage such attentions."

"I pretend I didn't hear that," Clif says and drinks up. "See you at the party."

Watch him stiffen into the wind.

"An inspiring drinker," Teddy says.

Thelma blooms mightily in Leo's eyes. "Are we three agreed I have a clear head?" he asks. "Honey, I want you to marry me."

"You've asked that before," she says.

"I want to live with you for the rest of my life," he says.

"Or lives," Thelma says. "Something I don't think about."

Twinspines whitening.

"We think about it," Leo says. "Teddy and I have a solemn agreement about separate marriages when either of us wants to marry. Now—"

"I don't want to think about this now," Thelma says. "I want to go to Georgia's party and *laugh*."

"I've a lot to offer you—so much to give," Leo says. "I

feel I have to marry you or miss the most profound experience of my life. I was a goddamned louse this summer, I admit it. But I am crazy about you."

"And I," Teddy says. "God knows I am!"

"Every day with you is the richest of my life," Leo says. "Now I *will* be a trumpet-player. That I put before everything. I've no control over being a musician—"

"Nor I," Teddy says.

"No matter how long it takes," Leo says. "That's gotta be clear, if you marry me. Now the day may come when Teddy marries—God, I hope so—and this is what we figure. Teddy'll spend three days at our house with us, and I'll spend three with them. Should he marry. This is terrible, but it's the fairest we can manage. Separate marriages and living at home three days in a row. You don't just marry me, you marry this arrangement. But you'll have a say—"

"—very great," Teddy says.

"—over the girl Teddy marries, believe me."

"I swear it," Teddy says.

"But you're going on your trip," she says.

"Just for marriage money, sweetie!" Leo says. "We'll come back with nearly a thousand dollars saved. Now I leave myself open to you."

She falls against him, sobbing. "I should hate you for doing this to me!"

"Don't have misgivings," Leo says into her hair. "Just give me all the heaven that's in you."

"Oh, Leo, you stinker!" Thelma says.

They hug over the table corner. She goes around the table and kisses Teddy with sisterly vows.

Two full bottles of ketchupblood oozing down their skulls and shirts, the multiple auto fatalities watch Ruth Drummond arrive in green parrot-feather bra, sapphire navel, and silverspangled eyeshadow.

"My dears you both look ravishing as a pizza," Ruth says. Shakes both their hands at once. "Don't kiss me." Teddy cups a handful of feathers, not lightly. "That's very alluring," he says.

She stamps Cossack. "I've already danced on one bar and who knows what'll happen by midnight!"

"Are you Rima the bird girl?" Leo asks.

"Sorry, kiddo, I don't get my kicks standing in trees."

"What kind of kicks?" Teddy asks, blinking tomato.

"You think of it, I've got it," Ruth says. "What a cute outfit, Thelma—song of Tahiti!"

"She's just looking forward to her honeymoon," Teddy says.

"Oh, are you two finally tying up?" Ruth asks Thelma. "Kid, I envy the hell out of you. This kind of decision takes guts."

"Well, keep it under your turban," Thelma says. "It's a secret engagement."

"How absolutely thrilling," Ruth says. "Which pizza are you marrying?"

"The responsible one," Thelma says.

"I'm still free, Ruth," Teddy says. "Hey, Stu, are we ghastly enough?"

"Maybe you've overdone it," Stu says.

"We must have," Leo says. "Nobody'll come near us."

"Maybe we are too ghastly," Teddy says. "Let's go back and shower."

"Hell, just go up on the roof!" Phil Drapkin says. Short painter-druggist, now a black pirate in hornrims. "Let the *RAIN* wash off all your bloody heads! And I'll guard your clothes."

Up to roof, undress by firedoor, hop onto pouring roof in shorts.

"Fabulous coordination!" Phil cries from the doorway. "I could watch you hop forever!"

"How's it coming?" Leo asks.

"Slowly," Phil says, "but I can almost see your faces. Pick off those scabs. Oh I gotta get out there, *I can't resist! THIS IS A HAPPY RAIN!*" Dances around skylight, runs back to door. "I'm a coward, gang, but I was out there for a while. Hey, somebody's playing the vio-in!"

Twins wash each other, looking over the roofs of Albany. Grinding rain.

"Hey, gang, now we can all go back as drowned rats," Phil calls.

Dress, comb hair, go down shaking.

"Our shirts reek," Leo says.

"That's not ketchup, it's glory!" Phil says.

Lights out. Esmerelda the Gypsy fiddles Brahms' "Rain Sonata" in pure nightshadow, skylight beating, whistling silver. Twins stretch out by Thelma, listening. Esmerelda fiddles tirelessly. Twins keep waiting for the end.

"How can she remember it all?" Leo whispers.

"I don't know, I can't even follow it," Teddy says. "Maybe she makes it all up." Ah, clap.

"Did she finish?" Phil asks. "Oh, that was glorious—*and* divine, I mustn't leave that out. ANOTHER *WORLD!*"

"Should we play?" Leo asks.

"Why not?" Teddy says. "I bet we're better than we know."

"Do it," Phil says, lighting a candle, "play all night! What instruments do you play?"

Twins get out their horns.

"Now quiet, quiet, everyone!" Phil calls. "The twins are gonna play their trumpets and tubas. Now *quiet,* all you Bohemians!"

Twins sit on chairs in candlelight, raise their horns, hair soaked, breasts scabbed. " 'Body and Soul,' " Leo whispers, "for Thelma."

Strength fills them. They begin together, slowbeating, smearing phrases. Too early, Leo falls into variations. At last they slip into the bridge—four flats, or six sharps, and Leo fires a stream of notes searching for melody. Teddy moos and sobs while Leo circles.

"What are they playing?" Phil asks Esmerelda.

"I can't follow it," the violinist says.

"It used to be 'Body and Soul,' " Thelma says. "They read better than they improvise."

Twins end in misery.

"No more, no more!" Georgia cries over Phil's cheer.

"We'll have the law on us," Clif rasps.

"The rarest night of my life!" Phil says. "My God, what I would have missed had I not been here! You both play with *VERY* deep feeling. I don't care what the others think. That's what *I* say."

"I forgot the bridge," Leo says.

"Didn't we both!" Teddy says. "I lost you a long time before the bridge."

"I couldn't remember that bridge to save my life," Leo says.

"Well, you shouldn't play variations before we even get to the bridge," Teddy says. "I know we get carried away, but you ad libbed too goddamn much."

"Ad libbing? I was *lost!*"

"I'm too restless," Teddy whispers. "Stopped raining. I wanna go out for a walk."

Teddy's day since midnight. Dress in darkness, Thelma inert, slip from hotel room. Leo half-asleep, spent. Glide deepdown to Greene Street, passing a lamplit hot sausage cart, on their way to Rabbit's speakeasy for collards. Whores in their doorways, walks steaming. "Just like South Carolina," Teddy says, "only paved." They follow a young lightskinned girl up to her crib.

Livingroom into bedroom. Pan of soapy water. Her both palms out.

"Oh, I'm to remind you," Teddy tells Leo. "You're not getting any."

"Ain't no free rides here, John," she says.

BRANDY sunrise over Ashville. Teddy's day off from work.

He wakes charged. A crested red cardinal darts to a limb by Teddy's window. What-cheer cheer cheer. Hard hope for the day fills him.

Driving from Leo's cottage in Ashville to Teddy's pad with Salome. "Hey, I forgot Thelma's overdue books!"

"It's five miles!" Teddy cries. "And today's my day back in real life—away from Thelma."

"If ya don't mind," Leo says.

"All right, I love Thelma too. Wonderful. To *my* house. And let's hope her husband's still on Staten Island, wherever the hell that is."

Ashville turnoff. Breathing poplars flame to the lake.

"I'm hungry," Teddy says. "Pretend I'm driving—we'd be to Lakewood by now."

"Let's take Lakewood turnoff and see if our old cottage's still there," Leo says. No response. "Try to keep your hands still or put 'em under your arms," he says. "I'm afraid you're gonna grab the wheel."

Teddy watches the road as carefully as Leo, leaning with each shift of gears, leg muscles braking quietly. "I need a drink," Teddy says.

King James over Fairmount, up Lakeview, turn over to Liberty. Park before a violet house set back from the street. Out, stretch, seven A.M. Orange streets deserted.

"I'm damp already," Leo says, plucking his shirt. Blue thinlayered sky.

"Let's make Stella's lemonade," Teddy says. "A dozen lemons, two cups of sugar. Make burgundy mixers."

"Hey, brilliant," Leo says. "But I have a yen for some gin. Christ, it's a perfect day for spiked lemonade."

Camp outside the liquor store until it opens. Into Chautauqua Dairy, home with gin, wine, lemons, sugar, pretzels, chips, popcorn. Upstairs into Teddy's kitchen, where Salome sits nursing Raphael, brown hair bunched past her waist, brown eyes bulging in sallow worry hoops. Blue loincloth and nursing bra. Toys everywhere, the living room-bedroom a ragyard of colored clothes. Three-year-old Fayaway runs up bareskinned and hugs Leo's leg. Teddy gives Leo the flakiest little smile.

"Who are you?" Leo asks.

"I'm Josephine," Fayaway says. "Play with me!"

"She's Josephine today," Salome says, "and I'm Josephine's Daddy. You're early! Whatcha got there?—come on, tell me."

She hugs Teddy, kisses Leo on the mouth. Fayaway parts them.

"Lemonade for breakfast!" Teddy tells Salome.

She opens and closes ragged nursing snaps, shifts Raphael to her runny nipple. "Sometimes he conks out while I'm still full, then it's painful."

"Can't you empty some into the sink?" Teddy asks.

"I don't believe in that," Salome says. "Oh, I missed you so much!" Her arm winds about Teddy's neck over the baby. "How long are you here for?" she asks, gypsy eyes hopeful.

"Play with me!" Fayaway cries.

"Leo and I can't play with Josephine today," Teddy says, "because we're playing with Fayaway and Josephine's Daddy. Tomorrow midnight," he tells Salome. "Ah, dishes! You wash, I'll dry," he tells Leo. "No word from Superman?"

"He calls my parents six times a day," Salome says. "But even they don't know my address down here."

"You don't have to worry about Superman," Teddy says. "We're pretty hard to get around."

"Nobody's ever given himself to me the way you have," she says. "You make me feel worth having."

"Save everything for me," Teddy says. "This is gonna be a glorious day."

"Oh, the beach!" Salome asks.

"We'll run up to Stow and catch the ferry to Bemus," Teddy says. "Start packing."

"Oh, I was gonna make earrings this morning!" Sighs at a dozen cups of chalkcolored beads on the table. "I thought I'd pick up some extra money selling them through a friend in the city."

"Earrings!" Teddy cries. "Earrings on the happiest day of my life? Pack, pack!"

The twins cupboard dishes, sip gin, start lemonade.

"How's Stuart?" Salome asks.

"Terrific," Leo says. "I'll have to bring him over to play with Fayaway, I don't think he's seen a bare nymph before."

"Last night," Teddy says, "we got up twice to see if Stuart was breathing."

"He sleeps so quiet!" Leo says.

"He checks the pulse," Teddy says. Swirls lemonade sugar. "Boy, you painted this floor a deep blue. Hurts my eyes."

"Well, I can't stand a black kitchen floor," Salome says in her big-city tonelessness. "And the cats got in while the paint was drying. There are fucking blue prints all over the icebox and living-room table and bedspread."

"You can't handle two cats and four kittens," Teddy says. "Give one to Leo for his house." Salome parts a front curtain. "Looking for detectives?" Teddy asks.

"He told my mother he had two different agencies after me," Salome says. "Somebody out there's earning money looking for me."

"Hey, you gotta meet Thelma," Leo jollies her.

"A terrific idea!" Teddy says, coughing. "Too bad she's teaching today. She'll miss the beach."

"Oh, that's a shame," Salome says.

"Well," Leo says, "we can practice the cavatina on the beach."

"That might make me nervous," Salome says, already uncovering detectives in the sand. "Or I could go sit in the casino while you play. Hiding outdoors with a pair of hornplaying Siamese twins—that's not cool. I'd be happy if nobody knows you're stowing me away. Does Thelma know?"

"Well—not yet," Leo says. "She might actually get jealous."

"And she's not too happy with my habits anyway," Teddy says, halving the lemonade with burgundy mixer. "Okay, no horns on the beach." He gins the purple lemonade stiffly; stiffens it more. "Hey, we haven't had breakfast! What's this brown stuff on the burner?"

"Brown rice," she says. "Eat it like it is."

"I like it with butter, sugar, milk and cinnamon," Teddy says. "Or soy sauce—but not for breakfast."

"Play the twumpet," Fayaway says.

"Too early," Leo says, "neighbors aren't up yet."

"I want the rent," she says.

Twins sing, tap toes and heels, pattacake knees—

> Reuben Rastus Johnson Brown
> Whatcha gonna do when the rent comes round!

"I want a banana."

Salome stops combing her bunch at the kitchen mirror and peels a banana. "Some days she'll eat five in a row," she says.

Fayaway takes white bananafruit out front. Sits naked on wide windowsill, looks out, legs drawn up, early light bathing white curtains, a velvet flesh plant bare. "D'ya think she should sit in the window like that?" Leo asks, spying two rather well-to-do houses on hills across the street.

"Let 'er," Teddy says. "No law against it."

"I'm so miserably afraid to take them out for a walk,"

Salome says. "And they get tired of being indoors." Screws dangling gypsy earrings through her lobes. "There! What about these?"

"Lovely," Teddy says. *"Marlene!"* Leo sighs, cupping his liver.

"Made 'em myself!"

"All gypsies are metalworkers," Teddy says. "Boy, maybe it's this blue floor, Salome—but I swear I've seen you at that mirror a thousand times screwing in earrings." She spoons brown rice into a bowl, cracks an egg, dandles the yolk onto brown rice. Fayaway comes in to watch Raphael being fed, climbs on Teddy's leg. "I'm hungry."

"Do you want another banana, Fay?" Salome asks.

"No," Fayaway says tearfully.

"Do you have to go to the bathroom?"

"Yes."

"Will you go to the bathroom without your duck?"

"No!"

"Go find your duck, then I'll take you to the bathroom."

"No! I can't find my duck!"

"Look, Fay," Salome says, "it's too early in the morning for this bullshit. Do you want some rice?"

"Yes."

"Do you have to go to the bathroom?"

"No."

Leo pours purpleade. Fayaway takes a jar of strained peaches, dollops yellow peach onto her rice in place of eggyolk. "Imitating Raphael's something new," Salome says.

"She's a raging beauty," Leo says.

"Oh, the devil has sure put a sweet taste in my mouth!" Teddy glows over his drink. Hands his glass to Salome. She sips twice. "Hey, it's spiked. But too sweet! Put a glass in the refrigerator, I'll have it when we get back. Boy, I've drunk more with you guys than I have all my life."

Teddy takes her hand across the table. "I been alone a long time," he says. "I been the Frankenstein monster for years."

"And I," Leo sighs, drinking.

"Doesn't Thelma comfort you?" Salome asks Teddy.

"She's married to Leo!" Teddy says. "Or I'll put it this way—Leo scrubs her back in the tub, but *Stuart* treats me very much like his own daddyo. But I'm happier to live with her than without her, believe me. And she's a marvelous cook. Speaks Russian, French and Swedish—though I don't, and though she wasn't Phi Beta Kappa like someone at this table." He pets Salome's hand.

"Ahh!" Salome smiles, petted. "Did I tell you I made $5,000 last year substitute teaching? That's what gave me the incentive to leave Ray. I saw I could support myself better alone."

"Apart from Herr Übermensch," Teddy says. "D'ya realize," he asks Leo, "I went Seventy-two Weeks without a piece of ass after Mexico? The sheer hunger that builds up is insane."

"My God!" Salome says. "What'd you do?"

"I'd rather forget it. We do have a cathouse in King James—well, just a colored man selling beer and whiskey afterhours and a fat woman turning tricks for him—but I can't drag Dmitri Tolstoievski down there. Not with Thelma a schoolteacher."

"She'd be jealous?" Salome asks Leo.

"The scandal!" Leo says. "That little foray'd stay about as secret as Washcloth crossing the Delaware. Hey, *thar's George!"* Leo grins purple.

"Five grand last year?" Teddy says. "And this year it's earrings. What kind of anarchist are you?"

"I'll start teaching again in January," Salome says, "but right now I need expense money. Go easy with Yin, Fay."

Fayaway walks about bearing a fullgrown black and white cat by its neck.

"Isn't it rather early for the beach?" Salome asks. "Lemme pick up a bit first."

Shifts baby to Teddy, gives him babyspoon, gravely starts picking up diapers, dresses, rompers. Stores old piles in new places, new piles in old places. Suddenly Teddy sits back groaning with the baby.

"You all right?" Salome asks.

Teddy can't speak, kissing Raphael's head. At last he says, "We can't go on like this, Leo, we gotta get back to our lessons!" Leans over the table, groaning again. "Oh, I don't know what's wrong with me." Sits up, gripping the table. "Hey, honey, show us that dance again!"

"What're you crying about?" she asks.

"Happiness!"

Kicking over her head, longlegged Salome hops about on arched bare feet, loincloth flapping, bra jouncing, eyes alight through kitchen and living room, tall bones willowy, smile begging.

"That's better than Millie," Leo says.

"Than Eleanor Powell," Teddy says. "Boy—felt like I had a big tumor in my chest."

"That's enough dancing," Salome says. "I'm not firm enough since having Raphael."

"What a great day it is," Teddy says. *"Rnnh!—I could carry the world—RRNNHH!* That we can sit here at eight-thirty in the morning watching Salome dance. I think I been holding everything back since Charlie died," he tells her. "Our sister Millie's son."

"Oh how awful," Salome says. "How'd it happen?"

"In his blankets," Leo says. Blue floor.

"It snowed at the funeral," Teddy says. "Frozen weeds and snow blowing through 'em. You couldn't believe anybody'd lay a baby into such cold earth." Sits back drained, then slaps the table. "Honey, tonight'll be sex and caviar! No more tragedy."

Salome hugs him. "Nobody's ever thought about me the way you do!"

Teddy lifts a squat bottle on the table. "Hey, you didn't drink any of this Spanish sherry."

"I saved it for you two," Salome says.

"Feel free!" Teddy says, amazed.

"I don't dare to—but you're making me. Kiss me. Oh, I want you so. You're the first Wasp I ever loved."

"My gypsy Jewess," Teddy says, nuzzling her bosom.

Fayaway starts crying.

"What's wrong, Fay?" Salome asks.

"You were cocking."

"No, we're just kissing."

"No! You're mad at each other."

Teddy kisses Salome's hand. "We're not mad a bit."

"Tell us a story," Leo says to her. "Come on."

"Once a time," Fayaway says, "there were three bears and they ate her up and lived happily ever after. I don't want you to cock."

"Why don't you?" Salome asks.

"I want you to be with Daddy."

"Don't you like Teddy? And all your games together?"

"Yes."

"Well, Mommy doesn't cock with Daddy anymore. Daddy cocks with Marie, remember?"

"I want you to cock with Daddy."

"Mommy likes Teddy," Salome says.

"Do you like Daddy?"

"Of course I like Daddy. And *Marie* likes Daddy. But right now I like Teddy more than anyone. I've *got* to get her out of this erotic atmosphere. We brought her up to be natural about sex. But this isn't the South Seas, she's gotta learn to live in this culture."

Fayaway walks about the living room, a crayon cocked between her legs.

"We gotta quit Summerfield and get a better job," Teddy tells Leo.

"Sure," Leo says. "Doin' what?"

"Real work," Teddy says. "We can't chauffeur and nurse forever."

"You don't have to get a new job for me," Salome says.

"I wanna support you," Teddy says. Salome starts crying on his shoulder. "Hey, honey, I only said I was gonna get a better job."

"You really do love me, don't you!" Salome says.

Fayaway starts crying.

"Don't cry, Fay, Mommy's happy," Salome says. "See, I'm all right!"

Leo spreads his legs, arms out to Fayaway. "Let's play house," he tells her. "Josephine and Dmitri!"

Teddy looks at Raphael and Fayaway and Salome and feels a cold nail in his bowels. Sure loss fills him as he smiles, sips deep.

Late afternoon, leaving the beach, looping over to Ashville for the phonograph and records. Black asphalt foams at the car, earth breasting gin energy. Across from a country cemetery, Leo's tiny white cottage. Thelma typing lesson plans on the only table. "Hi, sweetie!" Leo greets her.

"Well, hello, stranger," Thelma says. "I see my library books are still here."

"I'll take 'em now. Where's Stuart?"

"Still at my mother's. What are you doing home? I can see you've been having a good time with Teddy."

"Just enjoying a day off," Teddy says, clapping her shoulder. "Thelma, this is my gypsy beauty, Salome.

Fayaway, Raphael." Thinking aloud: "I hope to render them in bronze someday."

Thelma rises grinning, admires the children, falls in with Salome about teaching.

"Lesson plans are a lot of crap," Salome says. "Kids need anarchy."

"Oh ho! not in King James they don't," Thelma says. "You gotta bear down on 'em here or they won't learn anything."

"I think they learn best through curiosity," Salome says. "And anarchy encourages curiosity and they learn twice as fast—but what they naturally want and need to learn, not what we think they need."

"Well, you can only learn math by discipline," Thelma says. "And languages."

"Bull," Salome says. "You can always find a table in a book. What's important is to be curious about math as math. The more you learn it on your own, the more fascinated you become and the faster and farther you go."

"Wow, that'll *never* work here!" Thelma laughs nervously. "We have regents, you know?"

Fayaway climbs on Leo's knee, rides his leg like a hobbyhorse.

"Shit on regents," Salome says. "Regents are total fucking insanity. Let the kids come *when* they want and study *what* they want. If they want to run around town, let 'em run—they're learning. Same with sex education."

"What about that?" Thelma asks.

"Have free contraceptives and let the ones who want it go to it. Clean out the bugs their parents gave 'em. Wipe out sex neuroses. We gotta de-structure the system and start over. Our greatest social injustice is child conformity. Kids are dead by the time they're seven—seven's too late."

"Have you ever heard anything like this!" Teddy asks Thelma. Salome suckles Raphael, long bluejeans spread wide, tight in the joint.

"But children want system and discipline whether they know it or not," Thelma says. "Even ninth graders, *ahem,* whether their mother thinks they're the gift of God or not."

"Bullshit. Only prisoners are afraid of anarchy," Salome says.

"Well, I'll think about this when next I see my noble savages," Thelma says.

"We gotta treat 'em like equals," Salome says. "We bring 'em into this fucked-up country—let's give 'em half a chance against the fucking capitalist credit structure. Let's get the bombs down to the common man, give everybody a vote. I mean fuck civics, we need high school courses in how to make a Molotov cocktail. *Dig me?"*

Horn cases, phonograph and records into the car. Leo kisses Thelma's pure frost.

"Leo's cocking," Fayaway says.

"Kissing, Fay," Teddy laughs, boiling pink. "Well, let's go."

"Have a good time," Thelma says. "When'll I see you again?"

"Tomorrow, honey." Leo red. *"We'll be ho-ome for supper!"* he sings, the homesick soldier bound to his brother.

"I'll look forward to it. Where are you staying?" she asks Salome.

"At my place," Teddy says.

"How'd that come about?" Thelma asks.

"Well, Salome was staying with a guy down on Washington Street who was some kind of drug addict," Teddy says. "And she got tired of him being bombed all the time."

"Frank wasn't a drug addict," Salome says, "he was a pothead."

"What's pot?" Thelma asks.

"Marijuana," Teddy says. "It's smoked in little cigarettes—though not around here."

"Tried it yet?" Thelma asks.

"Hell no!" Teddy says. "Can't get it outside New York."

"Where'd Frank get it?" Thelma asks.

"He brought half a kilo with him from New York," Salome says.

"He did?" Leo cries.

Silent Thelma numbs him to the bone. "Raphael is Frank's child?" she asks.

"Salome's married," Teddy says. "She's an anarchist and fleeing her husband."

"I have a lot to learn about anarchy," Thelma says.

At Ashville turnoff, Leo turns off into the poplar lane, parks. Break out their horns, test their wobbling tones on the trees. Yellow and red poplars spire above, breathe high breezes, leaves falling. Flaming floor. Twins on car roof, blowing their Ellington songbook. "Mood Indigo" . . . *baby said goodbye. . . .*

"She *hated* me," Salome says on the ride downtown.

"Oh, she liked you," Teddy says over the seat, nudging Leo, who grunts. "And it was about time she knew about us. I mean, let's not hide anything."

"She's jealous a mile deep," Salome says. "Like ice, I mean."

"Didn't notice," Leo says. "But Teddy's gotta have his own life."

"Boy, I love to blow in the country," Teddy sighs, drinking, holding up a thermos cup of gin for Leo, watching the road.

Carry phonograph upstairs to Teddy's. From a living-room window they watch a long barnlike tractor-trailor park out front.

"That must be twenty tons," Teddy says.

Salome looks out. "My God, it's Ray and Marie!"

"Daddy! Daddy!" Fayaway cries.

"Hush, Fay, please hush, yes, it's Daddy, but I don't want him coming up here right now. Oh, Christ, one of Frank's friends must have told him I'm here."

"Daddy! Daddy!" Fayaway screams at the front window.

Salome pulls her back. Little Ray leaps to the walk, calling, "I hear my little darling up there! Yes, it's Daddy, sweetheart!" Sinks straight to his knees on hard sidewalk, shooting up kisses with his palms.

Salome hustles Fay to the kitchen, locks the door. "Don't let him in!"

"Why should I?—it's my house," Teddy says at the window. "A girl's coming up."

"That's Marie," Salome says. "I'll talk with her. What's Ray doing?"

"Just looking up," Teddy says. "Superman style. I thought he'd shattered his kneecaps."

The kitchen door rattles. "Let *her* in," Salome says. Teddy opens the door on a dark blond spinster and forcefully bored eyes.

"Marie!" Fayaway runs to her.

"Hello, Marie," Salome says with hard tonelessness. "What do you want?"

"Hello, Fayaway," Marie says.

"I'm Josephine," Fayaway says.

"Have a seat," Teddy says, pulling out a table chair. Blood burning and dancing, he holds Salome's waist lightly feeling his winesweated white shirt stick shamefully.

"Hello, Salomé," Marie says, sitting. "I have a message from Raymondo." Fayaway crawls onto her lap, hugging her.

"What is it?" Salome asks.

"He'd like to have Fay for the weekend. We're gonna visit his uncle in Buffalo."

"Well. All right," Salome says. Behind her, Teddy unsticks his wet shirt, smelling yeast.

"Well, he really wants her for a week," Marie says. "He thinks she's getting all fucked up living with you and your weird friends. She doesn't even know who she is anymore, as far as I can see."

"I can't let her go for a whole week," Salome says.

"Well, actually it's two weeks he wants her for."

"Two weeks!"

"Well, he may be able to get her back to normal in two weeks. There's a lot of work to be done—Raymondo really doesn't like her playing with other children, you know. She gets too many divided loyalties and confused. One thing, Raymondo and I've been making it, so we'll be good for her." Marie hands Salome an envelope. "Here's a letter explaining Raymondo's plan. Read it, Salomé."

"I'll read it later."

"It's a schedule explaining how each of you can have Fayaway for alternating two-month periods."

Salome's eyes pop, then hood. "I'll think about it. When's he want her?"

"Well, the sooner the better. How about this evening?"

"But my mother's phoning her tonight."

"Well, you know what Raymondo thinks of your mother," Marie says.

"Yeah. But she wants to hear Fay."

"Well, you'll have Raphael," Marie says wearily. "I'm sure you'll get by. *Raymondo* hasn't seen a wink of sleep in six weeks and I've missed *all* my singing lessons. You obviously don't know how deeply devoted he is to his children or you wouldn't have deprived him of them so cruelly. Tomorrow belongs to Raymondo, don't you think?"

"I'll think about it," Salome says. "Have him call me here—5070. After nine o'clock so I'll have time to give him a straight answer."

She walks Marie coolly to the door. Fayaway starts crying.

"You'll see me later, Fay," Marie says.

"I'm Josephine!"

Marie shakes her head going downstairs. *"Josephine!"* she says. *"Unh!"*

Teddy locks the door. "Whatta stormtrooper!"

"Sings too," Leo says. "Nazi folk songs."

Salome reads the letter. "Ray says they're beginning to make it. With grass."

"You can't let her browbeat you," Teddy says.

"I never listen to her. His rights!—that's all he ever writes about. His bullshit rights. And she parrots it."

"Maybe I should have said *some*thing," Teddy says.

"Well, you know. You kept quiet," she says. "Fay, stop crying—would you like a banana?" She peels a banana, taking in the blueburning kitchen as if for the last time. "Well, I'm standing up to him finally. But I can't talk with Ray, he twists everything to fit his ego. Can I make a long-distance call?"

"Call Paris if it'll help," Teddy says.

Salome starts crying. *"You've been so good to me!"*

Teddy holds her. Fayaway starts crying, banana-mouthed.

"We're not fighting, Fay," Salome says.

"No, not fighting," Teddy says, hugging Salome with might.

"Oh!" Salome wails. "He won't let us get away again! *I haven't gotten anywhere!"* Fayaway cries again. "Salome's all right, Fay," Salome says, wiping her eyes. "Come to the phone and we'll talk to Uncle Max together." Sunburnt Teddy painfully stripes pale skin from his hairy red arm as Salome phones the Bronx. "I'm sorry to ask you, Uncle Max, but can you lend me $500? I don't know when I can get it back to you either. . . . Well, can you wire it in the morning? You're saving my life, Uncle Max." She mumbles an address in Quimby, Ohio. "Then burn that address and forget it." Teddy shakes, pounds the couch arm with Brando-awakened heart.

"Say hello to Uncle Max."

"Hello. I have a banana."

"Are they still out there?" Salome asks.

"They're talking in the truck," Leo says.

She phones the airport for the next flight to Cleveland. "Can we get to the airport in forty-five minutes?" she asks Teddy. She reserves two seats, starts heaving clothes into suitcases. "Get away from the window, Fay."

"We *both* lay into him if he tries anything," Leo assures Teddy. "How do we get into the car without 'em seeing us?"

"We have to phone a cab to pick us up on Lincoln and Eighth," Teddy says hoarsely, "and go down the back way and crosslots. What about the diaper pail?"

"Throw them away. I'll have to leave the toys, I'm sorry."

"I'll save 'em," Teddy says. "I'll save the pail too." He phones for a cab while Salome changes Raphael's diaper.

"Are we going with Daddy?" Fayaway asks.

"We're going to Quimby," Salome says. "Let me dress you." Fayaway starts crying. "Now knock off the bullshit, Fay. I need a map. Do you have an atlas? Soon as I cash that money order tomorrow, we're gonna hide wherever my finger falls on the map." She looks through the curtain, sees Ray searching the windows. "Why doesn't he go away?" she whimpers. "He doesn't even move!" She pulls Fay back.

Ray covers his face with both hands. His shoulders heave. Shakes a fist at the violet house as Marie pulls him to the mud-caked cab. Ray climbs in, winds up the engine with a blue roar.

"He's going!" Salome cries. "But he might just park around the corner. We can't move your car or he'll get suspicious. You have to stay here and make a lot of noise as if we're all still here."

"Blow our horns," Leo says, jaw set. Teddy's eyes are wet.

Fayaway's scream mushrooms at the window, her nails digging at the screen. Salome carries her to the bathroom, closes the door. Teddy and Leo watch Ray. He sobs into the steering wheel, beating the dashboard. Marie shakes her fist out the window. Ray gets out, engine running, stands with bold fists ready to break Teddy's door down. Fayaway howls in the bathroom. Marie pulls Ray back in again. The truck snorts thunderously, growls a blue cloud over Liberty.

Salome comes out of the bathroom: black dress, stockings, heels. Rakes her hair at sink mirror. "Is he gone? I thought he'd never go."

"He looked pretty miserable," Teddy says.

"Am I doing right?" Salome cries. "He looked so sad. And I'm hurting *you!*"

"Daddy, Daddy!"

"Yes, Fay, Daddy's all right," Salome says without feeling.

"Daddy's going to take me!" Fayaway cries, nodding, pulling toward the window.

"No, I won't let him take you, sweetheart." Salome holds Fayaway on the couch, tries to rise, but turns blind with tears. Fayaway screams. Salome falls with her arms over Fayaway. "I have to hide!" she sobs. "I h-h-have to build a new character so he can't take them away from me! I don't want to leave you!"

"Well, don't leave, for Christ's sake!" Teddy cries.

"I have to become a new person and I don't want to," she says. "Or don't I?"

Teddy grips her. "Nobody ever— Honey, you *can't* become a new person."

"Yes I can, and I have to," she growls.

Teddy. Fixed hopes breaking. *"Life!"* he screams.

"Teddy," Salome says, "you'll find a nice unmarried girl with no kids."

"Shit! I don't even know where you'll be!"

"I've told you everything I can tell," Salome says. "I don't know if I'm going to Seattle or Texas or Mexico, I'm just going far."

"All I know is you'll be out there somewhere screwing with somebody else!" Teddy cries. "And after *I* 'wakened you,' as you say!"

"I will."

"Well, fuck you! Fuck you! Fuck you!" Teddy kicks Fay's duck looping onto the kitchen table from the living room. Cups full of chalkcolored beads spill from the table, dance and hop on the blue floor. A wounded cry rises from Fay, her eyes panic white.

"Teddy, the cops will come," Leo beseeches, holding him against the doorframe. "Get a hold of yourself!"

"I don't care about the cops!" Teddy roars.

"You'll find a girl just as good as I've been," Salome pleads.

"Fuck *good* girls!" Teddy howls. Fay screams against Salome, her cheeks pouring. Teddy sees the child's face, turns from Fay in shame. He grabs the kitchen doorway lintel suddenly, pulling himself upward with frantic force. Leo screams, hanging by their band. Teddy's eyes swell like golfballs, his jawmuscles cinched with strain. Leo hangs blue with fear of death. The lintel splinters from the doorway, twins falling hard. Teddy climbs up, beats the wall with flat palms, then drives his fist through flowered-wallpaper plasterboard. Kicks a hole in the side of the couch as Leo again holds him. "Lemme go! What am I, a monster?" He beats his forehead. "How can you leave me!" Black Yin screams from the living room, races under the bathtub.

"O my God, we'll be arrested before I can get away," Salome says. "Oh, Teddy, please! Wash your face and help me get to the cab. I'll phone you as soon as I get to Quimby tonight, I promise you."

"I'll come to you wherever you are," Teddy says, face stove-red.

"Even my parents won't know where I am," Salome pleads. "I can't let anyone know. Ray served me with a subpoena on Staten Island, I can't face the court as I am —he has my diary. I *gotta* change my character or I'll lose custody of my children. And I've got to do it alone or the court won't recognize it."

Quiet Fayaway, carry bags down back stairs, cut backyard to bowering red maples of Eighth and Lincoln. Orange leaves clot the lawns. The cabbie puts her bags in the trunk. Teddy grips her waist, black dress binding. Quick good-byes. Salome gets into the cab, grins a little-girl simper, and is gone. Leo-Teddy goes back upstairs and starts noisemaking with his horns.

Next day two cops on Teddy's porch slap each twin with a writ charging adultery. That evening the *Post-Journal* boxes the writs in heavy type on the city page. Thelma moves in with her mother. Black Leo moves in with Teddy, Ashville fading, Salome flown.

Fayaway, milk-smelling Raphael.

Nursing bra hung over tub.

Blue floor.

APRIL showers the red-brick house and worm-heavy leaves. "T-take me to the windows," Dale stutters in a whisper.

Twins hoist the palsied ox from his reading chair, wheel him down his long dark living room to the french windows. Rain. Lightning. Heaven's freightyards rumbling. Cracking, clanking.

"I guess they're switching cars," Dale says.

Down Lakeview Avenue, an iron spear fence—April's pining fury in the cemetery.

"Betcha . . ." Dale forgets.

Porcelain cupids chime.

"Nurse? Where are you, boys?"

"Right here, sir," Teddy says—his day as nurse—and leans into the old man's face. "Get you something?"

"Lemonade, boy."

Into dim kitchen, squeeze lemons.

"You drink too much," Dale says. "Wh-wh-where you been?"

"Lemonade."

"Oh." Sucks glass tube Teddy holds for him.

Green rain, deep living room. Dale and the twins at the french windows. Time.

"Wh-wh-where's the evening paper?" Dale asks.

"Want your reading stand down here?" Teddy asks.

Dale says nothing. Twins vacuum deep-red carpet before the cook-and-housekeeper arrives.

"You still here, eh?" Dale asks.

"Right here, sir," Teddy says.

"Where's . . ." Forgets.

"Like to read? No?"

Dim. An icecube turns.

"Wa-water."

"It's lemonade," Teddy says. Holds tube to the old man's spasming lips.

"Thank you very much," Dale says.

Teddy places the glass on a cork coaster, blots a drop off the table with a napkin, folds the napkin beside the glass. Dale looks up with a sneer, or snort.

Phone rings. Leo answers. Dale brings his bell. "Who's on the phone?"

"Your sister, Ethel," Leo says. "Just inquiring."

"Tell her I'm very fine."

The housekeeper arrives. "Hello, Mr. Summerfield, and how're you today!"

"Fine. Very fine."

"Did you clean the carpet?" she asks Teddy. "Well, that's good. Is the bed made? Did you clean the bathroom? Did you *clean* the bathroom?"

"Martha, this boy won't . . ." Dale points at lemonade.

"What's that, Mr. Summerfield?"

"Do you want lemonade?" Teddy asks, lifting the glass, but Dale turns away.

"You do what Mr. Summerfield says," Martha clucks, and goes humming into the kitchen.

"Where are you taking me?" Dale asks wide-eyed.

"To the bathroom," Teddy says.

"I'll let you know when I have to go. *Aghh!"*

"Want to lie down on the couch?" Teddy asks. "Or read?"

"Can't you leave me—"

Wheel Dale to redleather easy chair, pick him up, swing him in. Twin smiles.

"You boys're going a long way," Dale says and swings a fist.

"Here's your reading stand, sir."

"If I'd hit you, you wouldn't be smiling like that," Dale says.

Twins glide to far shadowy end of the living room.

"Think you're pretty smart, don'tcha?" Dale says. "Get me a candy, please."

Teddy puts a butterscotch Life Saver on Dale's tongue. "Thank you very much, my boy. But *he's* fired," he adds, pointing at Leo. "T-t-tell Harry to pay him off."

Twins read. Dale opens *Life* on his reading stand, follows a sentence with his finger. Nods but raises up again. Lowers his shaking finger into a page. "They can't write worth a damn anymore," he says. He squints down the living room. "Who are you? Oh. *Them,*" he tells himself.

"Want to lie on the couch, sir?" Teddy asks hopefully.

"Stay where you are, I'm very fine." And Dale wets his thumb and lifts a page of *Life* into *Look* and a page of *Look* into *Life* among shuffled mail ads on his reading stand. His finger tries to follow a story from *Life* into *Look*. "Can't write worth a damn," he says. Nods, again lifts out of a daze, says, "Take a right here, boy!"

"Bathroom?" Teddy suggests.

"That's what I said, didn't I?"

Wheel him to bathroom, walk him in, undress and sit him down. "Where are you taking me?" Dale asks.

"Nowhere," Teddy says. "You're home in your bathroom, sir."

"I know where I am. You can't get away with this. Punks."

"Let me tie your shoelace," Teddy says.

"Fatheads!" A fist nicks Teddy. "I gotcha, you basards!"

Twins fall back, the half-open door cutting between them painfully. Band pulsing, their faces wave with distress, eyes popping. Dale twists in awe and presses his head to the wall. "I'm sorry," he says, "pardon me."

"That's all right, sir," Teddy says. Walk him out to his wheelchair, twist him into it. Teddy off to one side, avoiding any kick, fits Dale's shoes to the footrests.

Martha stands in the kitchen doorway. "Did you let Mr. Summerfield *fall?* Well, of all the liars. Are you all right, Mr. Summerfield? Did these boys let you hurt yourself?"

"I'm very fine. Lay me down, boys." They wheel to the couch. Teddy lifts Dale to his feet, but Dale pulls back. "Pretty weak, aren't you, son?"

"You're pulling back," Teddy says.

"Hell I am. I'm trying to stand up." Teddy takes Dale's hands again, tries to lift. "Pull, pull," Dale says, half out. Teddy twists him to the couch, Dale tips over the wheelchair, lands kneeling on rug, chest on couch. *"God damn you!"*

Get Dale's arms on the couch, try to roll him up—he slips, bruises his head. *"Ohh-h-h you—goddamned—horses' asses!"* His lips puff open, teeth awry. "Get me up!"

Pull him up from rug, prop against couch, lift. "Let me alone!"

"You don't want anyone to see you on the rug," Teddy says. Lift Dale heavily, get his back on the couch.

"Get—me—on—this—couch!"

"Yes, sir, we're trying," Teddy says. Brace four knees under Dale, throw him onto the couch. Rolling off, push back on. The couch sags like a swamped lifeboat. Dale groans, barking in a whimper, "God Himself couldn't lift me!"

"What's going on in here?" Martha asks. "Is everything all right, Mr. Summerfield?"

"I want to go to the office," Dale says. *"Ohhhhh!"*—groaning anger.

"It's nearly suppertime!" Martha says. "Is everything all right, Mr. Summerfield? No? Why, what's wrong? What have you been doing?" she asks the twins. "Why is Mr. Summerfield's wheelchair tipped over? No reason! *Hmph.* Mr. Summerfield, your supper'll be ready in just a minute."

"Thank you, Martha. And call the police."

"Why ha ha!" she says. "Be ready in a jiffy."

"Hello, Daddo!" Dale's daughter, Kitty, says. "How're you feeling, old top!"

"Not very fine. This—these boys have been beating me with a club."

"Daddo, I'm sure the twins don't have a club."

"Hell they don't. I'm b-b-black and blue all over."

"Did Daddo have a fall?"

"P-punks don't talk much, do they?"

"Daddo, that isn't nice. Leo and Teddy do as well as anyone possibly could."

"P-punks."

Kenny the night nurse walks in. *"Good evening!* How's everything?"

"Who's that?" Dale asks.

"It's me, Mr. Summerfield." Kenny smiles—a refrigeration salesman who has nursed and chauffeured Dale for over twelve years.

"Hello, lad. How are you this evening? I'm d-d-dying."

"Why, fine! Ready for supper?" Kenny grins.

"I couldn't eat if I wanted to. You feed me too much."

"Daddo, just a little bit? Sweetbreads!"

Growls so deeply his teeth clack. *"Get me up!"*

"Okay, sir!" Kenny says. Swings Dale's knees around, pops him into his chair, wheels him off to the dining room.

"Oh, Fredric's at the door!" Kitty cries and lets in a spotted, mindlessly beautiful bird dog, which scampers into the dining room and circles the table, barking. Twins wave goodnight. Dale swoons into his sweetbreads, but Kitty sits him back up. His eyes saucer at the golden meal before him. "Good night lads," Dale says in candlelight.

"Paper, Daddo?" Kitty asks.

"No, no thanks, I've seen it twice before the last two times today." He holds up a card. "Thank you for the birthday card. But the year is wrong."

"My pen and I had a mutual misunderstanding, Daddo!"

"I'm going out to the flood," Dale says.

. . . Leo pulls in before a police barricade at flooded Cherry Creek. Dale sits up beside Teddy, smiling at cops as they wave the car on.

Pass an old wayside gas station with its sign hanging. "Turn off the water," Dale says. Sit quietly at the abandoned station in morning mist.

"Aren't you going to help me?" Dale tries to jam an elbow down, spring the locked door. *"Get me out of here!"*

Break out the wheelchair.

"What are you doing?" Dale asks quietly, his face fallen against the steering wheel.

The wet day settles into haze on pastures.

"You're doing very well, boys, very well," Dale says, now fallen to the seat. "We might just get somewhere. Pull me up." Lift and turn Dale. "I can't stand much more," he whispers to himself. Lift him toward the wheelchair, but he pulls back, knees buckling. "Get me into that chair!"

"We can't make you fit," Teddy says as the chair lurches away.

Dale slips down, hugs a warped gas pump.

"I know you, you're the boys who are always reading books instead of taking care of me. . . . Cross my legs."

"You'll fall flat on your face, boss," Teddy says.

"You're supposed to be my guar*deen,"* Dale says.

"I am," Teddy says. "So you shouldn't pound me in the balls, Mr. Summerfield."

"Tit for tat, boy. . . . Get me a candy."

"Up we go?" Teddy asks. "Hey! Am I getting through?"

Dale looks up wonderingly. "What faces to use on a poor old man," he says.

Showers flood Hotel King James alley. Rush the wheelchair from trunk, cart Dale indoors to the Prendergast Club.

"Hello, Dale!" says the elevator woman. "Eatin' with us today?"

"Yes, thank you. How are you, my dear?"

"I'm always better when I see you."

"Thank you."

Into the private club room. "Hang up my hat, please."

Businessmen playing rummy. "Hi there, Dale!"

"Hello! Hello! Get me a menu, boys." Dale watches card players.

"How's the furniture racket, Lean Wolf?" Barry Durham asks Dale. A dark, husky lawyer, Barry's married to Millie. "What's this about you selling?"

"I'll be sold down the river first," Dale says.

"I may have a buyer for you," Barry says, dark eyes devilish.

"N-n-n-not for all the t-t-tea in China."

"So your plant's not up for sale?" Barry asks, grinning broadcheeked.

"B-b-beans and frankfurters."

Rain picks the windows. Barry wins. "You gents ready to give up?"

"D-d-d-don't stop, Durham, they still got their pants left."

"What's that, Dale?" Barry asks.

"They . . . they . . ." Forgets. Everyone looks at him. "W-w-we went out to the flood at Cherry Creek."

"Oh, how was it out there?" Barry asks.

"Very bad. They've closed the gas station. T-t-take me to the table, boys."

Wheel Dale to long diningtable, lift into head chair. Leo fills a spoon with rainglow blue and gold pills. "Have you seen my glasses?" Dale asks. "I've lost my glasses."

Luncheon talk clanks down into mourning for lost members.

"What was that, Dale?" Barry asks.

"Keep to the dirt roads."

"Where?" Barry asks.

"Why, anywhere! There's nothing to see on highways."

Dale smiles at Barry slyly. "I'll play you a hand of showdown for the check."

Barry grins no, winking at Leo and Teddy.

"I'll throw in a bird dog if I lose," Dale says. "Name's Fredric."

"Ha, what kind of bird dog?" Barry asks.

"He barks at the table," Dale says, "bites babies, and reads *The Saturday Evening Post*."

"Dale," Barry says, "we were just talking about Sweets Gogarty."

"What happened to the boy?" Dale asks.

"Didn't you hear he died?"

"No. . . . That's very sad. I thought well of him."

"We're thinking of sending him a card," Barry says. "Shall we pop your name on?"

"Please. Thank you." Dale turns to Teddy. "Wh-why are they sending him a card?"

"Must be his wife," Teddy says, lifting a spoonful of beans for Dale.

Wind shivers the windows like flannel.

"I'm not hungry," Dale says.

Twins sit quiet. They buried Durwood in Ripley not a week before. He'd died in sugar shock on a windy corner in Erie while drinking.

Sawdust sunlight.

"We're experimenting with a new glue, Dad," Kitty's husband, Harry, says.

"The strongest glue in the world isn't fast," Dale says.

"What's that, Dad?"

Dale forgets. "Push on, push on, boys." Wheel Dale past saws, conveyors, kilns. "Stop here!"

Watch a gang feed sheets of plywood into an ancient press, a superflattening steam monster. Dale insults the machine for half the afternoon, singles out a man, tells the foreman to fire him. Goes up the freight lift to his office.

Sitting behind his desk, blind mail on reading stand, setting his finger into orders from firms and companies whose names he cannot say. . . . "Wheel me out there."

Wheel past clerks, secretaries. A secretary reads New Orders to Dale in his wheelchair. Afternoon dries away. "Wheel me back."

His office. "Lay me down." His couch a brown leather

barge. Swing the old man over, stretch him out, wrap his fingers on a buzzer.

Buzz buzz.

"Here, sir," Leo says.

"How long've I been laying down?"

"About two or three seconds, Mr. Summerfield."

"Is it time to get up?"

"No, sir, I'll be right outside the door," Leo says reasonably.

Buzz buzz.

"Think you're pretty smart, come in here spying."

"I'm your friend," Leo says. "I don't spy, sir."

Dale grinds his teeth. "Leave me alone, p-p-punks."

Buzz buzz.

"Back again, huh?" Dale asks wide-eyed. "Think I was sleeping? P-p-punks."

Get Dale up. He rabbit punches Leo's crotch. Wheel Dale to his desk, put his glasses on. Dale eyes Leo. "Iron balls, my boy? Get me the chief of police on the phone."

Harry and two vice-presidents are called in.

"Sell you down the river, what are you talking about, Dad?" Harry asks.

"And t-t-take those boys with you, that one's a convicted killer."

Twins hide in warehouse with the fired man and play cards till quitting time.

"Where you been?" Dale asks at his desk.

"Getting prescriptions filled," Leo lies.

"I w-w-want a haircut. Funeral tomorrow."

"It's late," Leo says. "Martha's waiting."

"I've g-g-got the money."

Leo pulls into the nightglow of Al's News. "Hey, Dale's here!" Sam the barber calls.

Get behind Mr. Summerfield, walk him in. At the barber chair, Teddy takes him alone, swings him up and in. Leo lifts the shoes onto footrest.

"Give these lads a haircut," Dale says in the chair.

"How about you, Dale?" Sam asks, lifting iron-gray curls.

"Might not be a bad idea."

Dale sits docile and wide-eyed, his great hands trembling under the pinstripe apron.

Twins sit reading a life of Mahler. "I'll be sorry to finish this, Anton," Leo says. "I really identify."

"Ya, Gustav," Teddy says. "But let's hope we turn up an Alma soon."

Empty stands during a night game. Dale has a season box but likes to sit on the grass by third base, wheelchair away. He never cheers and watches every play in wonder. He admires good plays in silence, grunts over larcenies. A batter hits a ground foul at them. Twins hop over Dale, field the ball.

"Good work, boys," Dale says. "You win the popcorn."

Leo and Teddy sit with their beers and hidden pints.

Wash Dale as he trembles, lay him across his bed, fill a needle, jab his wither, watch the old-man face flush gleamy pink wax. But a buzzer in his fingers. Cover him. "Turn out the light," Dale says.

Buzz buzz.

"Yes, sir?" Teddy says.

"I want to go to the operating room."

"The operating room?" Teddy asks.

"That's what I said, you horse's ass."

Wheel Dale to bathroom. "You're really out for blood, aren't you, boys?" He sits staring into the aquarium bathroom glow. "I didn't do anything to you." Waxen skin pink. "Gonna sell me down the river. Stand me up, this passage isn't easy to get through."

Sit him in his chair. "Wheel me down that way."

A tall mahogany bureau. "Get out those pictures," Dale says. Look at old photographs for an hour, Dale's eyes bronzed with Thorazine. Kitty at six in fern-banked sunroom, faded fleshcolor. His wife in golf knickers. Dale with the office staff, before his disease, standing in salt-and-pepper plus fours, dashing mustache, eyes cutting squarely into Teddy Roosevelt doom, no hint in the nerves, a man of grit trembling with force, no bogey in the spring grass. A colored photo of the dogwoods blooming by the front door, blood leaves a tubercular cough against sunwhite doorway, and here the gladioli's choked flesh. Lovely daughter. Matchless brick house. Sunday at the lake. Lovely days.

"Wheel me back. I'm a king."

"There you are, all tucked in," Teddy says.

"I'm very fortunate." Dale on his side, smiling. Wipe him here and there with a moist cloth. "Come here," Dale says. His eyes fix on the cloth. "Promise you'll never tell anyone about me. . . ."

. . . She stands in Dale's bedroom doorway, dim in the slashed smoky moonlight. Her shy face, boy lips pour over him with joy. Her fingers comb his rough hair. Dale sees bare artless feet on the varnished hardwood. "Where've you been?" he asks her. "You're so young!"

"I've come home, Dale. Didn't you expect me?"

"I'm an old man now. And you've grown young again."

"How I've missed you," her face says.

"How can we explain your being young again?" Dale asks. "There'll be a blazing commotion upstate when you're missed."

Her lips press down into his blood. His heart swells. In his dizziness, he opens his eyes. Empty night, heart pounding.

The twins eat chocolate mousse straight from a giant green bowl in the kitchen. Play Mahler in the living room. Burgundy.

Dale fights drugs and buzzes his buzzer until the venetian blinds burn. *Buzz buzz.* "What time's it?"

Tired twins, burgundy-rotting eyes. "Ready to get up?"

Groom and dress Dale, walk him downstairs between a set of railings. Serve grapefruit, oatmeal, eggs, Canadian bacon, sweetrolls and coffee liquid of sugar and heavy cream.

"N-n-not so damned much after this," Dale says, waking up in his redleather easy chair. Set up his cardtable. "We're late," Dale says.

"Where to today, sir?" Leo asks.

"To heaven. Are you ready?"

"You haven't started your grapefruit," Leo says.

"I'm done. G-g-get the car out."

Twins take his breakfast to the kitchen and bolt it down themselves, groaning. Out to garage. Rain on snow, pearl daylight hurting their hearts.

Drive in slush to Saint Luke's Episcopal Church. Put the wheelchair at the top of a great stone flight, pull Dale up step after step by his arms toward the chair.

"We're late," Dale says. "I can't go any farther."

Jump behind him reeling.

"I'm going down, lads!"

"We'll make it," Leo says.

"I'm falling!"

"I got you," Teddy calls.

"Please don't let me fall—" Dale buckles to his knees against Teddy and grasps him. Stares down the flight to the bottom, moaning, clacking false teeth with rage. *"You —damned—"*

"We won't let you fall!" Teddy cries. "You know we love you."

Dale's eyes roll. "I don't have to take this slop!" He pushes himself free, falls in his heavy coat, bruising his cheek on a stone step.

A ten-year-old girl stands at the bottom of the steps. "Bring that wheelchair down, will you?" Teddy asks her. She runs up the steps and tilts the chair. The chair gets away from her and bangs down the steps. Twins let go Dale to catch the chair, Dale slides headforward.

"—horses' asses!—"

The little girl turns backwards, hands on her eyes. The chair spills by. Leo grabs a wheel—but the chair pulls them over itself in a sickening dive with Leo's fingers locked in the spokes. His head whales a step.

"Don't *move!*" Dale cries, pulllng himself to the bottom. The little girl runs down to him. "Hello, darling, how are you?" Dale asks. She walks each step with him. Leo opens his eyes under a turning wheel, stares at rainweary March sky.

Brush off slush, wheel through the side door. Cross under pulpit as Reverend Lewis E. Ward starts his sermon.

"We partake of each other's spirit and each other's folly."

"Amen," Dale says from his chair.

Reverend Ward ends.

"Wh-wh-when's the funeral start?" Dale asks.

"There isn't any funeral," Leo says.

King James's new mayor, now an usher in striped pants and wet carnation, walks up whispering, "How wonderful you're here, Mr. Summerfield!"

"W-w-watch these big punks behind me, Stanley, they've got a gun."

A beauty starts the organ growling.

"How m-m-much are you gonna ask for me?" Dale asks. "I'm a poor man."

The organ trembles with a hymn. Dale tries to whisper to the nearby pews. "Help! Help!"

"You're all right, you're safe," Leo says. Dale swings at him, kicks feebly.

"Help!" he cries against the hymnsinging.

Teddy breaks open a roll of butterscotch, puts one on Dale's tongue.

"Thank you, very much. . . . I know you're there—can't fool me." Sucking butterscotch. Clouds dim the windows blindingly. Leo and Teddy, calm gunmen. Dale waves guardedly at the minister, whispering, *"Hey! Hey!"* Suddenly the organ spills and the hymn pours upward. Twins wheel the old man out through doves on the slush. "This is a federal crime!" he warns them.

Drive to a Randolph crossing Dale loves for its trains. Spring rain playing. "Trains . . ." Dale says. They park. "G-go ask," Dale says. Teddy holds up a train schedule. "Here we are." Sit for the afternoon watching trains pile by in the rain. "Wh-wh-when's the next express?" Dale asks. "Five-twenty," Leo says, "we're late for supper now." "That's all right," Dale says, "it's well worth the wait, my boy." The five-twenty piles by five minutes late with its light glimmering in the rainy nightfall. Drive home, Dale awake, happy, full.

Dale nods in his easy chair and wakes.

"Do you want the television on?" Teddy asks.

"Let's try it."

"Goodnight, Mr. Summerfield!" Martha cries.

"Goodnight," he whispers.

The chimes ring. Rollo Oscarson. "Hello, Dale, how *are* you?"

Dale tongue-tied, staring helplessly at his magazine covers. Little Rollo hangs over him, pats his shoulder. Dale looks up. "Hello . . ."

"I saw your sister, Ethel, yesterday," Rollo says, his eyes blue enamel.

"She told me."

"Now, now, Dale, you don't mind if I do a little courting in your family."

"Yes . . ."

"Fine!"

"Yes, I *mind* . . . dinky simp."

"I'd love a drink, thank you."

Dale tongue-tied again, sitting in agony. Rollo smacks

down his drink. "Well, I gotta go, Dale!" He waits. Dale turns to his magazines, ignoring him, benignly assured of wetting his wavering thumb as it flies about his shaking lip. Turns, looking over his glasses. "Did he go?"

"Yes, sir," Leo says coming back from the liquor closet.

"I guess it's time for the office."

"Bedtime, sir," Leo says.

"I want to go to the office."

"You mean the bathroom?"

"I mean the office!"

Drive down to factory, unlock a rear door. Wheel him all through the factory, every room, down corridors of lumber in the dim lights, Dale pointing *This way, that way* quietly, thumbing grains and finishings, the sanded maple, pine, poplar, mahogany, the cogs, belts, vats, presses, saws, lathes, forklifts, elevators, engines, scales, kilns, and steamrooms, and at last into his office. Blurting wet light and a day's mail at midnight. Sitting, reading, turning pages of trade mags, eyeglasses aghast in stale blue light. Twins rest their tired band on the couch's leather spaces, following carved leaves on the walnut desk, eying his lacquered Chinese cigar box, his *Leaders of the World Award* above the buck strength of his curls. An old man at a desk.

"Am I keeping you up?" he asks.

"Take all the time you want, sir," Leo says, blueeyed patience. Teddy nods agreeably. Beyond the window the lamps of Hospital Hill rise in eyenumbing stupor, grass green, shaven, spreading.

"Thank you. W-w-would you brush my teeth, please?"

The twins drink in the bathroom.

"Lay me down," Dale says.

"Your family's here and dinner's ready," Teddy says—his day.

"I want to rest. I believe I am going to expire."

"Dinner, Daddo!" Kitty says.

"Thank you, sweetheart. Wheel me in, boys."

During the meal Dale smiles at his family, listens from afar, chews tender meat endlessly, swallows on nothing, nods into his plate.

"Daddo! We're eating *supper!*—you don't want to sleep here. Push him up, Teddy, please."

"That's all I can eat, thank you," Dale says.

"Moon Brook Country Club has sent you a birthday cake, Daddo."

The family sings, the grandsons blow out the candles, Dale smiles, but his head droops into dying smoke. Twins lift him back into his wheelchair. They lay him on the living-room couch and try to feel his pulse. Spasming muscles in the wrist darken his heartbeat. Dale looks up. "What're you doing?" he asks.

"Taking your pulse," Teddy says.

Dale lifts his palsied hands and fiercely measures their tremble. "Get me up. My God, get me up."

They lift him, but he jerks peevishly and falls over his wheelchair. Kitty and Dale's sister, Ethel, rush in. He gasps, his arm twisted under him painfully. The women stand stock still.

"Are you choirgirls?" Dale asks. "Are you going to sing with your mouths like that?"

Wheel him to reading stand, seat him in his red easy chair.

"Would you like the *Post?*" Kitty asks fearfully.

"I've lost my taste for the *Post.*"

Twins build a fire. Blue evening burns on the street. The ladies read Dale's magazines by the french windows.

"Daddo, don't you want to look at the pictures in *Life?*" Kitty asks.

"Not especially," he says, watching the logs crackle. After a while he says, "G-g-get the car out."

They drive to Moon Brook's ninth hole on the service road.

"It's sprinkling," Leo says.

"So I see," Dale says. "Get my chair."

Break open wheelchair, sit him in it on the green, a blanket on his legs. The course stretches away between lanes of poplars. The sprinkle passes. The grass steams.

Whack! A ball lifts down the fairway, rattles into the poplars.

"Timber!" Dale cries. *"TIMMBERR-R!"*

Going home, they drive through Lakeview Cemetery. Moon Brook golf course lies beyond. They park by a large plot.

"That's my father," Dale says in the front seat.

"Yes, sir," Teddy says beside him.

"Th-th-those are my b-b-brothers. *That's* mine. I—"

"Yes, sir?" Teddy asks.

Tears fill Dale's eyes, he loses his breath.
"I-I-I-I w-won't be able to see the golf course!"

Drive to the lake and Sister Ethel's for lunch. She's older than Dale, a birdy crippled woman who drives, cooks, keeps her own home. After Dale's lunch they lay him out on her couch and eat with Ethel. She looks in at Dale sleeping and sits again at table, blind eye half-lidded.

"It's all part of a grand consciousness," she says.

"Quiet out there!" Dale whispers.

"Did you call, Dale!" Ethel rises nervously, goes in again, sits with him on couch. He lies slowly falling asleep, lip tremors fading, still.

Ethel sits at table. "Isn't it remarkable that Nature should think to pick my brother for this disease?" she asks them. "He was the strongest man I ever knew—he could drive across the country in three days."

"But it did pick him," Teddy says.

"Or he chose it," Leo says.

"How could he do that?" Ethel asks.

"I don't know," Leo says. "But it could be true."

"I don't see how," Ethel says.

"He tore himself apart," Leo says.

"He snapped every muscle in his body," Teddy says.

"You think he picked his own destruction?" Ethel asks. "Of course, he lived for his work—can you *imagine* owning five companies? Spread all over the country, keeping them together? He was possessed!" she whispers.

The twins balance on silence.

Light pours through windows coolly, red thread dripping from a needlework basket. Dale sleeps like a forge. Ethel cleans up. Twins go out and polish the steel-gray Cadillac.

Dale sits in his red easy chair. "How many candies have I had?"

"Whole top of the box!" Teddy says, fingering his gums.

"My mouth feels like mush," Dale says. "I'll try some whiskey tonight."

Dale drinks three bourbons before going to bed. "Take me upstairs!"

Wheel Dale to the stairs, give him a nightcap of pills, start walking him up quickly before he tires. Stops, giggling.

"We can't stall here, Mr. Summerfield," Leo says.

Dale faints to his knees, laughing and blue, grabs railing, a hand on his shaking side. Leo groans. "Ready to try again?" he asks. Dale's uppers, a pink crab on the step. His face turns hopelessly gaunt, eyes swollen and yellow, lids like tubs. "Oh, take me to the bathroom."

Downstairs bathroom is nearer, a narrow box. They start pulling Dale in step by step on his feet. A fist hits Teddy. "Where are you taking me?" Dale cries, pulling away, falling back.

"Hang on, for God's sake, Teddy!"

"He got away from me!"

Pull Dale into the toilet on his back, heave him up. The front door opens as Sister Ethel comes in. "Boys, *always* close the bathroom door!" They close the door. Dale falls asleep as his pills hit bourbon.

"What are we doing here!" Teddy asks the ceiling.

"Supporting ourselves," Leo says. "Wake up, Mr. Summerfield."

"Where am I?"

"You're falling asleep in the bathroom," Teddy says. The cramped room overheats.

"Th-th-the hell I am. . . . This train's on fire!" Dale sits trapped in a burning Pullman, pounding the wall *boom! boom!* screaming faintly, *"Fire! Fire! Fire!"*

"Are you all right, Dale?" Ethel calls.

"Save yourself!"

"What's that?" she asks. "Oh, I see, Dale, you lost your teeth. I'll wash them off and put them on the mail tray, brother dear."

"Get me out!" he tells the twins.

They stand him, but he pulls back in fear and sits again. "I gotta get off this train," he whispers, "there are people who love me."

"Let's go, then," Teddy says.

"Hurry!" Dale cries.

They walk, shuffle, and run in little hops upstairs into the bedroom. Dale sits abed shaking, or quaking, as they slip off his shoes.

"Ph-ph-ph-phone my sister that I'm safe," he whispers.

Dale's nightramble, fighting drugs. He calls his dead brothers from his bed, visits factories, cries, buzzes the buzzer, worries, laughs, swears. Drinking Dale's bourbon, the twins take two pills and their bed turns wheaten gold.

Something slouches down the hallway with shadow fingers and feet, stands in their doorway, black, heavy.

"Hey! Hey! Hey!" Dale cries from bed. *Buzz buzz.*

Go to his doorway, trembling. Dale's eyes gleam in moonlight.

"Go back to bed, boys. I'm fine."

"You *buzzed,*" Teddy insists.

"I know."

"What?" Teddy asks, his ear at the old man's lips.

"I—was—in—error."

"Take me to the high school, lads."

Park before King James High School. Doors open, boys pour out in ape-dance push, girls in knit sox, their calves tugboats. After a while, the brass doors suck back, stay closed. Kids gone.

"Go in and see," Dale says.

"See what?" Leo asks.

"See . . ." Forgets. A last girl sways past, hugging books. Dale nods his stetson. Her mouth tightens. "Ask *her,*" Dale says.

Twins sit still, watching her skirt in mirrors.

"You didn't ask her," Dale says. "Here comes a lad."

A last boy stands on the school steps. Wet black hair, red ears lifting a smile.

"Afternoon!" Dale calls.

"What?" the boy asks.

"Where is . . .? Where . . .?"

The boy shrugs, lights a fag, feigns dizziness to the twins, leaves.

"You won't go in for me?" Dale asks Teddy.

Twins go into the building, stand around, go back.

"What'd they say?" Dale asks.

"They didn't know," Teddy says meaninglessly.

"Hm. Well then, take me home," Dale says.

At the house. "I want a shower before supper, I'm wet," Dale says.

"You shoulda said something," Teddy says.

"Ooooh!"—clacking his teeth. "Get me upstairs!"

Undress, swing him into the shower—he clings to the taps. Sits on a stool in the stream while Teddy soapscrubs his curls.

"You're a big one, aren'tcha?" Dale says. "But I think I can take you on." Dale grunts, socks the metal shower-wall. It *booms*—he looks up in wonder. "Tearing the house down, boy?" he asks.

Kenny the night nurse comes into bathroom. *"Good evening!"*

"Hello, my boy," Dale says.

"Did you get out today, boss?" Kenny asks.

"Oh, yes. W-w-we parked in front of the high school all afternoon. They haven't found my wallet yet."

"He lost that five years ago at a football game," Kenny whispers to Leo. "Ready for supper, boss?"

"I can't eat till after supper," Dale says. "This big simp and I are going out back on the lawn."

"Oh! Looks like a pretty even match to me," Kenny says.

"The hell it is!" Dale cries.

Kitty stops by with her bird dog. "The company picnic's called off and everything's closed down, Daddo. The men are on strike. So why not stay home and let the car rest up?"

Open Dale's mail for him, sit reading a life of Bruckner.

"I want to go to the balloon race," Dale says.

"The picnic's called off, Daddo," Kitty says, leaving with Fredric.

"Take your big homely dog faces out of my living room," Dale says. Twins start to go into the sunroom to read. *Bing bing bing!* "I've been waiting two hours. What do I pay you boys for? I'd like to have the car out."

"Where to, sir?" Leo asks.

"B-B-Boston."

"That's two hundred miles!" Teddy says.

"You're out of your mind, boy. Let's go." Spills his reading stand over.

"We'd better pack, sir," Teddy says.

"Y-y-you're way beyond me," Dale says. "You're off in a f-f-fog!" Turns and bings and looks back. "Oh, there you are. Have you got the car out?"

Dale sits up front beside Teddy for the drive. At the corner Dale says, "Turn left."

"It's right to Boston," Teddy says.

"Turn right," Dale says. Leo makes a right turn, but Dale grabs across Teddy for the wheel, crying, *"Right! Right! Right!"*

They go left.

"That's better," Dale says. "C-c-come out of that fog, boy."

Park on Hospital Hill overlooking the factory and men with placards. Dale sits in his wheelchair in the sun while the twins hunker down.

"Go down there and tell them to g-g-g-go fly a kite," Dale says. "I'm not a rich man. I carried them through the winter. Deliver that message. To *him,* that's the man, the one who looks like he's not doing anything on the freight platform. I've seen that man before."

Go downhill into their old lumber yard, crossing the picket line to Harry Lillie, the timekeeper on the platform.

"Hello boys," Harry says shyly, gray, smiling.

"Hi," Leo says. "Nice day, Harry."

Harry looks up, checking.

Twins eagle the sky. Go back uphill.

"What'd he say?" Dale asks.

"He sent this coffee," Leo says.

"Oh. Did you pay them a dime?"

"No."

Harry waves from below.

Mr. Summerfield waves back, grinning. "It's always p-p-painful to fight a civilized man," he tells the twins.

Dale plans to visit his wife in Boston. Strep throat lays him in bed for a week. Clogged, he eats as much as ever, bloating. Purging fails. Kenny the night nurse walks into the bedroom on his shift. The boiled face on the pillow turns to him, saying, "Hello, Art," and turns away. Kenny goes out. "He's in the wrong ball park," Kenny tells the twins. "Did you call the family?"

"Yes, they think this is it," Teddy says.

"Shit, he's not sick," Kenny says. "All he needs is a good movement like the President just survived. When he gets double pneumonia up to here, *then* he starts to rattle like he had serious intentions."

And after a week Dale gets up for his trip. Pack fresh suits and pills, go to Boston in leandreaming benny glide and grease of trees. Twins flush, Dale's wallet loaded. Boston appears.

Coast down a brown river of elms. A nurse carries Mrs. Summerfield's elbow down to the car like a cupful of gold leaf. "We want her back in two hours!"

Drive off, Summerfields bouncing back.

"How nice to see you again, Dale."
"It's nice to see you, sweetheart."
"Thrilled with each other," Teddy whispers. Leo nods.
"Spin over the lake," Dale calls.
Lake waves, heat waves.
"Where shall we eat, Dale?" she asks.
"Wherever you wish, my dear."
"Let's park for a while!" she says.
Leo pulls under a shade tree by the lake.
Mrs. Summerfield says, *"We'll* just sit inside for a while."
Twins sit on a rock. Mystic Lake. Their tongues are shredded wheat. The Summerfields decide to eat at a hotel.

Green pewter. Hardwood dining-room floor, echoing. Sit at table, order, talk from caves. Dale, given a spoon of pills, speaks no more. He sits back stunned, blazing to stay awake. . . .

Home, Dale sits in his red easy chair. "Are you there?"

"Yes, sir," Leo says, drinking a tumbler of straight scotch.

"Take a letter. My dearest . . . It's raining out. The room is dim. The clock reminds me . . ." Forgets. "Business is urgent. I will come to bring you home at the earliest opportunity. Perhaps weekend from next. I am fine, hope you are same. Kitty sends love. Your loving husband, Dale."

Stares at glaring magazine pages, turning them blindly.

"T-t-take me to the phone," he says after a while. Wheel him to phone. He falls asleep, looks up, reaches for the receiver. Holds it in his lap, falls asleep. "Hello," he says, waking, and lifts the receiver. "Is she there?" he asks. "H-h-hello?"

"I'm sure she is," Leo says, smiling swimming.

"I'll n-n-never sell you down the river!" Dale says into the receiver and hangs up.

Dale abed, the twins lift a twenty-dollar bill from his wallet, bat to the liquor store, refresh the closet. Teddy sips a tumbler of sour mash, wears a lampshade, speaks Chinese to Leo.

Winter. The doctor gives Dale three days to live. Weeks pass. His heart pounds, he eats at the cardtable in his bedroom. Slatted sunlight burning his silverware, Dale says, "Let's g-g-go visit the triplets. I want to see the triplets."

Drive. Dale knows the exact house. "Back up the drive," he says. Twins knock at back door, see a petite redhead in shorts. "Mr. Summerfield!" she cries and goes out to the car in her shorts in melting snow. She leans in and they talk, Dale smiling like Texas at her. Her husband is a pressman at the factory. The twins walk Dale in, seat him in the kitchen. Three little redheaded girls walk into the kitchen in pink sweaters. Dale laughs happily, hand shaking on the table. Sticks a huge brute finger into a red curl.

Home. Dale goes to bed early. Kitty opens the front door in pouring rain and Fredric runs barking into living room, hall, dining room, upstairs to bedroom. The speckled dog slips on varnish, then whimpers and pleads by the bed. Dale drops a weak, meaty punch onto the dog's nose. *"Gotcha!"* he cries.

They hear Dale before he buzzes. His awakened hands rustle in the sheets. "I'm not h-h-hungry this evening."

Kitty walks in, kisses him, sits on bed. "How are you, Daddo?" Dale's mouth trembles—he thinks he has answered. She looks around the room wretchedly. "We've got to change this wallpaper, it's so gloomy! Boys, do you think we could put Daddo in Mother's room tomorrow? Let's look."

Mrs. Summerfield's Chinese bed burns with an embossed sunflower on the headboard, pagodas on black gloss, and on the footboard a burst of orange tiger lilies strangled in weeds. Twins slip Dale into this bed next day.

Paperhangers move buckets and rolls into Dale's room. Father and son, they stare at the large man dying in the Chinese bed.

"Did the paperhangers get here yet?" Kitty asks when she comes for Dale's Cadillac. "Oh, wonderful! Do you think they'll be finished before five? Oh dear, I should think they'd work faster than that. Daddo still in coma?" She looks stricken. "Isn't it a terrible world he's living in? —if he's even aware of it. Well, when he wakes up, he'll see new wallpaper!"

Henry Lamb, a housebroker, arrives at five. Dale in deepest sleep. Henry eyes every room in the house, the cellar, commends the strengthened living-room floor, the flowered sunroom, third floor bedrooms, Dale's new wallpaper.

The doctor cuts out Dale's pills—Dale can't swallow—

and says the end is near. Thirty-six hours at most. Next day the Met begins the *Ring* cycle on its Saturday afternoon broadcast and the twins tune in in the nurses' bedroom, sitting by winter windows. In the next room, Dale wakes up. *"I'm hungry!"* he croaks above the Wagner.

Twins hurry downstairs, mix a heavy-cream milkshake with ice cream and eggs. Dale sucks at his tube but has forgotten how to drink. "M-m-music," he says, the tube in his lips. *"V-V-Voice of Firestone!"*

"Would you like to get up?" Teddy asks.

Dale closes his eyes in a dream.

"We better try, sir," Teddy says.

Sit him in his wheelchair, his eyes opening. Wash him in the bathroom, shoulder muscles weak, bare toes tapping palsiedly on tile, body uprooted, tilting against the wall. Again sit him up. He tilts the other way, wide awake, shaking. He lifts his large brown eyes boyishly and looks at the frosted bathroom window. "Lovely day," he says as the window glares. He stares at Leo's hands gripping his own. "Let's go," he says, closing his eyes, falling asleep. He awakens. "Take me home, please."

Lift him into his wheelchair. *"Have mercy on an old man!"* he cries, eyes closed. Opens his haggard eyes. "I want to go home. . . ."

Sunday evening, Dale asleep twenty-four hours, the family departs. Twins hear his hands rustling. "What time's it? Why'd you let me oversleep? G-g-get me up. I want to shave."

Put in teeth, shave, comb the iron back. Sit him at his cardtable, lay out new magazines, mail, bell, and slip on his glasses.

In the kitchen Martha has set a tray with bright bell warmers: gravied sweetbreads on ham steak, yams, peas, asparagus, fruit salad, Roquefort salad, dinner rolls, sticky pecan rolls, relish, strawberry jam, butter, glasses for water and milk, a thermos of coffee, banana cream graham cracker pie, cheese, and napkin—her way of killing devils. They heat and carry the food upstairs. Dale looks over his glasses with interest, shredding his last piece of mail into a pile on the varnish. The great horn of plenty spills onto his cardtable. On with bib, in with pills. The twins sit beside him. "God bless America," Dale says, opening his mouth for the fruit salad.

Days, visits, opinions. Dale's heart pumps. The Met

sends out *Die Walküre.* The doctor raps Dale's lungs and says, "He won't pull through tomorrow, they're both full. The most merciful thing . . ."

Pulse fades wholly, returns stronger than ever.

Siegfried.

Dale wakes up on Tuesday but is mute. His lips blister and blisters break on his back. His back is too soft to salve—the salve lifts away good skin. Twins give him a fast, light shave for refreshment, wet his lips with water he can no longer swallow, and comb great rolls from his scalp. They bathe scales from his chest, a white wax from creases, rime from privates, white flakes from his feet—he mummifies in lard from his pores. Dull frost sweats his forehead and the crystals cannot be wiped without leaving skin cross-hatched with scrapings. Mushy soap in a bath tray: if touched, his skin catches fingerprints.

The family now eats dinner at the house daily—grandsons home on winter vacation. The doctor skips visits. Twins hoard Benedryl, Demerol, Dexydrine, vitamins, Thorazine, and needles. They plan travel to New York and really breaking into the music business—not for money, of course. Dale rattles through four-day sleep. Frederic avoids the upstairs. The twins wait for *Götterdämmerung* with a gallon in the closet. Martha runs up bills, baking and raving, restocking the pantry, the deep freeze, the fruit cellar, the bins, the tins, and the china.

Leo-Teddy sits in the kitchen with turkey, chestnut stuffing, gravied potatoes, baked pineapple, cream-cheese balls with chopped walnut, hearts of lettuce with whipped avocado dressing, cranberries, asparagus, rolls, butter, deep-dish apple pie and bourbon. Teddy drips a spoonful of straight bourbon onto his pie. *Ahh!* The buzzer buzzes after four days.

Go to the stairs, but Sister Ethel calls from the living room, "You sit still and eat." Follow her upstairs however. "Yes, Dale?" She sits on his bed, his flaking hornbacked hand in hers. Eyelids closed, trembling. "Do you want something, brother dear? I'm here to help you get anything you want. You can trust me, Dale." She grips his hand, the full force of her being directed from blue blind eye and good eye.

His lips bobble, too blistered to open. She looks up at the twins in agony. They wet Dale's lips with a sopping cloth. Finally the bulldog chops break open, his brows lift, and his eyeballs roll under his lids in dreams. "Please don't l-l-laugh so loud down there—I'm trying to sleep," Dale says.

Ethel's eyes brim. "Brother, we're not trying to keep you awake. It's just that the boys are home to see you."

"That's very nice, thank you."

"Could you drink some hot bouillon?" she asks.

His hands stop trembling and his breath rattles. She gets up, hobbles out weeping in her hankie. "How can he be so *mean!*" she whispers. Downstairs, mad and tearful. The family can't persuade her to stay. "He doesn't want to see me if he *does* wake up!" Ethel cries.

"Oh, Aunty darling," Kitty says, "he doesn't mean anything like that."

"I simply can't take it when he's mean. I can't!" Ethel limps out to her coupe.

The house falls silent. Grandsons look at each other. Suddenly Dale croaks upstairs. *"QUI-I-ET!"*

Ethel returns the next morning that the doctor forecasts the end. He is mistaken. Dale outlasts his disease twenty years past the ten once hoped. He now has double pneumonia, both lungs full, breathes in sniffs, his heart strains weakened walls, his nerves go unsoothed by deadeners he's taken for thirty years, his arteries are rock salt, his back a flame of blisters, he's not eaten in twelve days, had water in ten, penicillin in eight, his pores are clogged with wax, mouth sealed with rime, his skin pulls apart if washed, he is blighted with rashes, sores and lesions, he's lost fifty pounds, fungus cracks his feet, skin turns to horn, nails loosen, scalp infected, ringworm, chill, blindness, deafness—he is pulsing silt, a human Mississippi of infirmities in flood to the Gulf.

Reverend Ward arrives.

"Does Dale have a napkin?" Sister Ethel asks.

"Yes, he's wearing one," Teddy says.

She goes in, looks. "Really!" she says in tears. "Get a *clean* one! Always have a clean napkin for my *brother!*"

"Hello, Dale," the minister says. "Are you awake?"

Dale's lidded eyes roll.

Twins and Ethel go downstairs to the dim living room. Dale receives last blessings in his closed bedroom. She dries her tears and sits with hands folded on couch's edge. Frosty light halos her hands. Her injured eyelid droops, weary with evil. Drained strength in each bone and wrinkle.

The back door chimes. Twins answer. An old blueeyed tramp with emery wheel.

"Have you any scissors you'd like ground? *Hm*. Are you sure?"

The scissors-grinder goes out through garden snow. Twins go up to their room, look out the window. Dale sniffs in the next room. Listen. Dale snatching breath swiftly. Reverend Ward drives off in a new Buick, pomping his horn at the scissors-grinder.

Twins keep Mrs. Summerfield's weighty dictionary in their room, a bulky Shakespeare and her occult tomes. Dale rattles and groans through Friday midnight. Twins in the sickroom, their blood waiting for the true rattle. Shudder, turn away. Dale groans through his nose. They look back. Pinch that nose. Take away his pillows, let him drown. They try to read. Dale moans. "Look! Why doesn't he die?" Leo whispers. Sit in the dark, listen to breathing. "You're ready, Mr. Summerfield, let go," Teddy whispers. Dale breathes. Twins clap each other's knee for courage, rise, pull blankets past shaking rabbity feet, white body clenching for breath, falling, clenching, Pull out pillows, let head fall, open winter windows, sit down. Dale chokes and sniffs, nostrils bellowing. Get the great dictionary, the Shakespeare, pile books on Dale's chest. He drifts into overflowing resistance. The bed shakes. His sealed mouth rips open, brows clench, closed eyes hang in their sockets. A blood-red bush fills the bedroom and the twins' vision. They leap to the bed. Books off, windows down, pillows back, covers up. Dale breathes regularly.

Saturday the twins eat grape ice cream with grape jelly in their room, hit their burgundy closet with steady stealth, hear *Götterdämmerung*.

That night they fall asleep on the living-room couch, drunk. Kenny comes downstairs about 6 A.M. and says, "He just died." Twins sit up, still feeling the hand that wakened them. Go upstairs, nerves dry, eyes flushed, fatherless.

Dale's bedroom. Dust floats in sunlight. Dale is gray slate. His mouth gapes without teeth, his nose stone, closed eyes sunken ridges. Stillness dusts him, torn limbs at one with eternity.

WALLEYED scarecrow Flip Newquist staggers in hot sun up the high stony road to the reservoir and gasps over King James below. Blond brow wrinkled, sprung blue eye too-early wise. Scratched greasy glasses twined on his neck. His step clumsy, halfblind, agitated. "By God, it's hot up here!" he cries. "Too bad we can't go swimming in the reservoir."

Whitejacketed twins squint in noon sun by white Cadillac ambulance.

"This the famed Angelo's Ambulance Service?" Flip asks, spray jetting his lips. "Good Christ almighty, is this the wrong place to have an ambulance service! Why aren't you down in Brooklyn Square where you belong?"

"More people die up on the hill than down there," Teddy says.

"Hey, can I have one of those," Flip says, taking a fag from Leo. "I ran out Monday."

"Angelo knows what he's doing," Leo tells Flip. "He's nobody's Stupinsky."

"I'm not too sure about that," Flip says. "Hey, you're Leo and Teddy, I'm Flip Newquist from out West Ellicott way. We've never met."

"You wave to us on the library steps," Teddy says.

"Well, hi again! Hey, I thought you guys were musicians, not ambulance cowboys."

Flip starts to light his and Leo's cigarettes, searches for matches in his striped seersucker, finds a chewed pack, rips loose a softening match, loses it through bonethin fingers. "Just a second," he says, tearing another. Misses the scratch twice, a crumble blazes into his palm. "Drat," he says. Lifts hanging eyeglasses from his chest, jams them wildwavering over his ears. Third match spits perfectly. *"Ah,"* he sighs, flame jiggling under Leo's fag.

"We're not drivers yet," Leo says. "Just attendants—or

training to be attendants. We haven't had First Aid yet. And I'm not licensed to drive ambulance."

"We just started two days ago," Teddy says.

"Well, where's the fabulous Angelo?" Flip asks.

"Hollywood, Florida," Leo says.

"Opening a new ambulance service," Teddy says. "He wants to catch the fall season in stiffs."

"Fall season in stiffs!" Flip cries.

"September harvest." Teddy grins, eyes flaring.

"Jesus!" Flip says. "Remind me never to go to Florida in September. You got any water?"

"Like a glass of wine?"

"Sure would," Flip says.

Glaring whitewashed walls. Little room with cots, kitchen-stove, radio table. Churning low static, harsh police voices between cars and station. Flip jams on his glasses, glares at the police radio. "That's what I come to learn to operate."

"Operates itself," Teddy says.

"Well, you have to read the signals, don'tcha?" Flip asks. "And log things in?"

"We don't log anything but bills," Leo says, "and we send those *out*."

"Aw, heck," Flip says. "I was hoping Angelo'd hire me as a dispatcher. I'd have apprenticed for nothing. How many guys work here?"

"Well, for the summer just the three of us," Teddy says. "Since Angelo and Tony Victoria went to Florida."

"For harvesttime!" Flip shakes his head.

"You see pretty well?" Teddy asks.

"Heck, yes. I had twenty-twenty vision before my illness. I still read too much. I . . . I . . . my eyes are —well, I could see a hell of a lot better than I do!"

"What happened to you?" Teddy asks.

"Brain tumor at sixteen. They can't get it all out because it presses on the optic nerve, so it's in a rubber sleeve. I'm okay now though, no complaints. Well, hell, that's not true—I have so many complaints against everybody and everything that I have to draw the line or I'll go cracked as Ol' Ez. I can't be the only anarchist in town. You know Deacon Quince? I'm his protégé, he's educating me. I'm the lone anarchist in King James, it's too great a weight. And Deacon won't join me. Just when I need help, troops and assistants! There's a hell of a lot to be cleaned up in this country, starting here. We gotta have an intellectual revolution. I say burn City Hall, the *Post-Journal*, and can the capitalist toads on the Board of Ed."

Leo pours a plastic cup of wine for Flip, then he and Teddy chugalug. Hide gallon behind stove.

"Should I be drinking in here or not?" Flip asks.

Teddy checks the angle of vision on the stove's treasure, saying, "The driver's a lush. That's not for broadcast, though. *He's* in charge here."

"Christ, his secret's safe with me," Flip says. "Trust me. Do you mind if I hang around a bit? I'd like to learn more about this business."

"We don't mind," Leo says.

"We can practice our First Aid on him, can't we, Ygor?" Teddy croaks, eye gleaming as he straightens Flip's collar.

"Yes, Boris," Leo says sibilantly, "and our new Transylvanian suture technique."

"You can practice all afternoon," Flip says, "if I can have another butt. This wine's good stuff."

White Packard ambulance roars uphill, skids onto gravel drive. Buster jumps out, a skinny muscular man, humpish with blond brushcut, wild dead blue fisheyes. Sets a boxed pizza on the radio table, breaks open a beer six-pack for himself and the icebox.

"Buster, this is Flip," Teddy says. "He wants a dispatcher's job."

"Shit," Buster says, popping beer. "Dig in."

"Have a piece," Leo tells Flip.

"Say, thanks! How many ambulances you got in this service?" Flip asks.

"Four," Buster says, eyes numb. "Two that run. Packard has brakes."

"That's interesting," Flip says. "What's that big baby? Does it run?"

"The Cadillac?" Leo says. "Sure it runs. But it needs repairs Angelo can't afford just now."

"So you have one ambulance?" Flip says. "What happens when you have two customers?"

Buster smiles.

"You don't mean you use the Cadillac?" Flip asks.

Buster says nothing, chewing beer and pizza.

"Remind me never to get sick," Flip says. "How cathis one-car service support three people plus Angelo and Tony?"

"How d'ya think it manages?" Buster asks.

"By padding its bills and making no payments," Flip says.

Buster smiles. "You just might make a dispatcher."

"But," Teddy tells Flip, "*we* aren't getting paid until September."

"We're living with our mother until the jack rolls in," Leo says. "She has that big green house on Rose Alley by the library."

"She still married to George Fox?" Flip asks.

"No," Teddy says. "He sold the club to its members and took his dough to Florida. Started a tout sheet. He just got over stomach cancer."

"I met him a couple of times," Flip says. "Boy, he needed help!"

"Not George," Teddy says. "He stopped by himself."

"After they cut his stomach out," Leo says.

"What's your mother doing now?" Flip asks.

"Runs a rooming house," Leo says. "Very fancy, TV in the evening."

"I can't stand drugs," Flip says.

"Is that coffee?" Buster asks Flip.

"That's some wine Angelo left behind the stove," Teddy says, blushing.

"What!" Buster cries, getting the gallon. "That guinea greaser could have told us! Shyster leaves $300 for summer expenses that won't last three weeks. And a new guy coming in tomorrow. You done with this cup?"

Buster pours wine into Flip's cup, drinks it. "This homemade? Naw. Well, move your asses, let's pick up that transfer at W.C.A."

"I'll hold the fort," Flip says.

"You get any calls, flip this button and you'll get us on the radio," Buster says.

"I'll take all messages," Flip says.

"Just listen for accidents and write down the street address," Buster says.

Teddy onto back jump seat, a spare short stool for Leo —Buster hates three upfront. Pull out, bounce down a stony dirt road to English Street. They make Women's Christian Association Hospital in four minutes.

"Beat your record, Mr. Cody?" Teddy asks.

Buster reads his Bugs Bunny watch. "Naw."

"Better eat more carrots," Leo says.

"Let's work this broad for a tip," Buster says. "I need beer money."

Elderly lady with one eye, a heart patient released. Buster and twins walk her to their cot, strap her in, roll her outdoors, smoothly into the ambulance.

"Do you know where you're taking me?" she asks.

"You betcha," Buster says, pulling out. "Straight home."

"I won't jiggle off this, will I?"

"You're fastened in, ma'am, you can't fall." Leo smiles with Teddy.

Buster swerves. Her straps bulge, bad eye sunken, soft face quivering.

"Ain't nothin' to worry about, ma'am!" Buster calls, his cold blue shark's eye winking to Teddy.

"This car smells of peppermint schnapps," she says. She fastens her good eye on Teddy, its glitter holding him. *"Alcohol!"* she cries.

"How's it going out there?" Flip asks on the radio.

"Any calls?" Buster asks.

"Nothing. No speeding ambulance calls either, if you're worried about that."

"You must mean the city ambulance, I'm *sure,"* Buster says. "We have a bill-of-lading, ten-four."

"Roger," Flip says. "What's this ten-four shit?"

Buster turns off the radio. "Here we are, Arlington Avenue."

"This is the wrong place," the woman gasps, her eye rolling. "You're at the wrong place!"

"No, no," Buster says backing fast up the drive, braking hard. "Here's the right house—I remember it, ma'am." Winks to Teddy he smells a tip.

"Where are we?" she cries.

"Right at your house," Teddy says.

"Oh, God. Are you sure? Where's my husband?"

"He's showing Buster the way to the bedroom, ma'am," Leo says.

Roll her into living room, down a hallway. "Door's too narrow," Buster says, "we'll have to walk you in, ma'am."

"Look at those unmade beds. Oh, God," she gasps.

"Mama, that's all right, don't think about those things," her husband says. A little bald German, he rings a tiny gold dinner bell. "Look what we've got for you—just ring for service!"

Teddy and Buster get her up, walk her into her bedroom. Her husband tinkles the bell again, puts it on her bedstand.

Twins take the cot out to the ambulance, change sheets. Buster stays in the living room. Comes out after a while, says nothing, snaps on the radio. Beer money? *Tip?*

"Oh, you're back!" Flip says. "You're to make a pickup at King James General at one-thirty. Mr. J. B. Welles, the millionaire."

"Why don't he get good care somewhere?" Buster asks.

"Take him to W.C.A.," Flip says.

"Are you kidding?" Buster asks. "Why go from one bone factory to another? Is he good for a tip?"

"Don't ask me, ask him," Flip says. "Ten-four."

Silent ride to General, no mention of money. Tongues dry.

Stroke victim. Bald, white, wearing a green writer's visor, watching cowboys on TV in his room.

"Be careful. I'm paralyzed on the left side, boys," he says hoarsely.

"Don't you worry," Buster says, "we'll take good care of you!" Buster smiles like an iceman, kissing his fingers at the twins. *Tip?*

The old man trembles. "Will there be room for my TV set?"

"Yes, sir!" Buster smiles. "We'll fit it in."

"D-d-d-don't forget my *TV Guide*—it's got my whole week marked out for me."

Twins wheel Mr. Welles into the ambulance heavily. Buster goes back for the TV set. Twins sit beside the stretcher, brim down on the old millionaire. "Well, you'll be glad to get home!"

"Been in there eight months," the old man croaks. He eyes some stains on the ceiling skin above him.

"Grease," Teddy lies.

"I don't think so," Mr. Welles says. "It's something else."

He fingernails the scabby stain, raps the metal window frame, raps the glass. Can't stop rapping.

Buster slides in the TV. "Whew!" he says. "Heavy."

"Forty pounds," Mr. Welles croaks.

"Well, that's the heaviest forty pounds I ever lifted. *Whew.*"

"Me too," the old man says.

Pull into the W.C.A. Twins wheel Mr. Welles to Admissions. "We're not expecting any Mr. Welles," the nurse says.

"Don't abandon me here!" Mr. Welles cries to Buster from the floor.

The nurse calls King James General. "Mr. Welles was released to go home," she tells Buster, who is bluewhite with disbelief. "What's the address?" he asks.

Wheel the TV out with Mr. Welles's paralyzed leg resting on top by the aerial.

The Packard pulls onto Frederick Boulevard, backs up the drive. Twins roll the millionaire out as Buster carries the TV to the door. Mr. Welles looks blankly at his house. "I used to have a bigger house," he tells Leo.

A spotted bulldog on a rope in the yard barks, leaping, standing.

"Hal-loo, Tuffy!" the old man cries, sitting up.

The dog barks beside itself on grinning legs, leaping against the rope head over tail backwards.

"Didn't you tell me to take that millionaire to W.C.A.?" Buster asks Flip over the radio.

"Hey, you didn't *do* it, did you?" Flip cries. "Oh, *hell,* I was kidding!"

"You were kidding on the intercom?" Buster asks.

"You asked me where he could get better service!"

"Oh, man! Next time find out where we take the patient, Flip."

Back at the office, twins leave to buy cigarettes, have a beer. When they return, the office is empty. The intercom comes on and, over siren and roaring static, Buster asks, "Where the hell were you two?"

"At the drugstore," Teddy lies. "Emergency?"

"Now what the hell do you think?" the static cries.

"Who's with you?" Leo asks.

"Flip! Somebody's gotta help me, you know?"

"All right," Teddy says. "Where are you?"

"Now we need you guys in this wagon so we can pad the bill. Meet us at the corner of Maltby and Reservoir right now! Ten-four."

"Buster, got a fag?" they hear Flip ask.

Twins race downhill carefully, prickling in hot sun,

wait at Maltby. Buster hurtles up, grinds into the curb shrieking.

"Welcome aboard," Flip says up front, "and fasten your seat belts."

Twins clamber onto jump seats by the cot, their lungs pumping wine-brackishly. Flip turns, stares at them wide-eyed. The victim, a sixty-five-year-old bald man with snake-fold eyes and skin, lies moaning in the wind from open windows, stark see-through veinous white with his sheet blown down to his feet. Teddy takes out the man's false teeth, his jaw quivers, gasps in sips.

"Paralytic stroke," Buster says.

"How is he?" Flip asks Teddy.

Soft jaw drops with surprise, eyes open and clear in breeze and sunlight. Lungs empty, hissing. Eyes frost.

Leo drops the oxygen tank, but Teddy grabs it, taking the mask. Leo reads the meter, turns the gauge up. Teddy digs out the corpse's tongue, clamps it. Straps mask to heavy head. Oxygen jolts still lungs.

Leo and Teddy sit shamed past speech.

"What's happening?" Flip asks.

Leo empties liters of oxygen into the body, its blue chest arteries branching, hands Teddy the tank, scrambles for the sheet below. Error hatches like flies in their blood.

"We shoulda dug his tongue out first thing!" Leo cries, shaking Teddy's shoulder. Teddy agrees, popeyed.

"Shut up about that in the hospital," Buster says.

Hurtle up Hospital Hill's asphalt lane. They suffer in silence.

"God," Flip says, "you should have seen me with the stretcher. No, you shouldn't have. It's not as easy as it looks coming down a back way from the second floor. Buster, pad the bill for three attendants."

Wheel the corpse into Emergency. Buster gets a nurse to sign for delivery. Twins and Buster pick up Flip in the waiting room and leave.

As they roll downhill Buster holds up the receipt, clucking. "I told her he had a low pulse! She didn't sign him in D.O.A."

"Terrific," Teddy says. "Maybe he died of stroke anyway. Let's phone tomorrow and make sure about him."

"Check his condition," Leo says. "He wasn't a bad old fellow."

"Oh, he may even be alive!" Flip says.

"We haven't changed the sheets, Buster," Teddy says in a red haze.

Leo glares about the wagon.

"I wanted to get out of there," Buster says.

"You always keep a clean stretcher?" Flip asks. "That's smart."

"Man," Buster tells Flip, "you *want* to change those sheets."

Leo and Teddy look at the used sheets.

Back at the shack the new man arrives a day early—a half-blind squinteyed driver from North Warren mental hospital. He splits beers with Buster while the twins change sheets, sweep out the wagon—find *someone's* false teeth.

Supperbreak. Stella drives up in her green Olds. Twins take Flip home with them. "Aren't you Russ Newquist's boy?" she asks. "I know your parents from down at the King James Club. Your father is *revered* by some people."

"By me, too!" Flip says. "He does a lot of good works, especially for crazies."

Flip phones home while the twins crack Stella's fresh fifth in the kitchen.

"Stanley," Teddy says, "I was dying *all* afternoon. Pity me."

"We didn't dare ask him for a drink of our own wine!" Leo cries, sniffing on Teddy's shoulder.

"Yeah, I'm fine," Flip tells his father. "I'm down at Leo and Teddy's for supper, we met on Reservoir hill. I'm learning a trade. Stretcher-bearing!

"Hey," Flip says in the fluorescent kitchen, "should we call General to see how that old geezer's doing?"

"Later," Teddy says. "Let's prime our spirits first."

"We'll phone after supper," Leo says, pulling ice from the pink refrigerator.

Sit at table, savoring drinks. Stella serves clear stew. Twins crunch hot banana peppers pickled in brine.

"What're those?" Flip asks.

"Hot peppers," Teddy says.

"You eat 'em like celery," Flip says. "Should I try one?"

"They're hotter than blazes," Stella warns.

"Did you have a drink?" Leo asks.

"No, no liquor for me," Flip says, "I have to work tonight. You *know* what Shakespeare told Marlowe rather perspicaciously down at the Mermaid bar and grill, don't you? 'The wages of gin is death, buddy.' "

"Pour me a finger while you're at it," Stella says. "Well, how'd it go today, my sons?"

"The night's still young," Leo says, squirting Tabasco into both bowls while Teddy salts.

"Saved one, killed one," Flips says. "And we got J. B. Welles home by hook and crook."

"We don't *know* if he's dead," Leo says.

"We don't diagnose, Flip," Teddy says.

"That's not our job," Leo says. "We just walk or carry the body to the doctor or home or to the Henderson-Lincoln toga factory. Diagnose, no."

"But what if they're *dying!*" Flip asks.

"That's sometimes the case," Teddy says.

"Isn't that the truth?" Flip says. "And it's something to diagnose."

Stella shoves her dish away. "Do you mean to sit here and say you killed someone today?"

"Maybe," Leo says. "We got this paralytic stroke who was strangling on his tongue and we didn't know it."

"We're not doctors," Teddy says. "He *may* be alive."

"Boy, that'll be a miracle," Flip says. Twins stare coolly. "Though we can certainly hope for a miracle, Mrs. Fox! You gotta have hope in this business or you'll turn to a zombie the first day."

"You need hope by the rainbarrel in this business," Teddy says, drinking.

"To keep you breathing," Leo says, drinking. "You gotta keep your wind up or your spirit could get maimed for life."

"I don't see much elbow room for cheering," Stella says.

"Well, it was this or going out digging on the thruway," Teddy says.

"I think you'd make more money digging," Flip says.

"Come on, Flip," Teddy says, "moving dirt or moving bodies, what's all the talk about?"

Leo phones General. He returns. "They don't know who I'm talking about. The night shift's on."

"We'll read the obituaries tomorrow," Teddy says.

"Maybe he won't be there," Leo says.

"That's *one* thing the old *P-J*'s good for!" Flip says.

"Yeah, they cover death pretty well," Leo says.

"Are you kidding?" Teddy says. "Their obits are pure marshmallow. At least the *Sun* doesn't shed crocodile tears over death."

Flip holds up spidery fingers. "Ah, still here! Just checking, after all this funeral talk."

"I want to know more about this, my young men," Stella says. "Just exactly what happened? *Ahem!*"

"I shoulda taken his tongue out first thing," Teddy says. "I was nearest."

"You did your best," Leo says. "Hell, we'd just come running three blocks or more!"

"He might have already swallowed his tongue when Buster picked him up," Teddy says. "Flip, did Buster look at his tongue?"

"I don't remember but I don't think so," Flip says.

"There was no clamp," Leo says. "How'd he look when you carried him down?" he asks Flip.

"Oh, he was white," Flip says. "But I don't know if he was breathing."

"You know, he didn't turn blue," Teddy says, drinking.

"Christ, I thought he was transparent," Leo says, drinking. "Do you think Buster's detour to pick us up may have cut the old man's chances, Flip?"

"Well, you have to take the business aspect into consideration or there won't be any Angelo's," Flip says. "Unfortunately! And then there's the fact that I refused to ride in back with him when *I* might have got his tongue out—though I didn't know that much then. Next time I'll do better, I swear it," Flip says, clenching his bones on the table. "And no jokes on the transmitter!"

The office is empty when Stella drops them off.

"Hightail it out here!" Buster cries over the static. "This is an extreme emergency."

"I'm not licensed!" Leo says. No answer.

Twins run out to Cadillac, kick the wedges from the back wheels. Flip opens the rear, falls in clutching a white jacket.

"Get that door closed before you fall out," Leo says.

"Hell, I expect to go out through the roof," Flip says.

"Do you think I should turn the motor on?" Leo asks Teddy.

"Hell, yes, you'll have more control," Teddy says.

Motor catches. Roll down dark dirt road.

"Lights help, too," Teddy says.

"I can't find 'em," Leo says.

"Aren't you checked out on this meatwagon?" Flip asks.

"First time we been in it," Teddy says. "Where's the fucking turret light switch?"

He pulls a switch and Flip appears on the floor struggling into a white jacket in the strong inside cabin light.

"Leave that light on," Leo says. "It helps, I think!"

Roll slowly down Reservoir hill, red turret whirling over scattered houses in the tree-thick dark. Low-gear grinding.

"This is too slow! We'll never get there at five miles an hour," Teddy says. "Go into second."

Leo shifts into second in the dark. Wagon rasps faster, hood redly dimming and brightening.

"For Christ's sake, at least pound the siren," Teddy cries.

"Hold the wheel while I look for the lights," Leo says and ducks under the dashboard.

"We just passed Maltby, Captain Larsen," Teddy says.

Flip climbs up the jump seat like an untamed hawk. "Who's sailing this tub?"

"Wolf Larsen," Teddy says.

"I hope his sea legs are better than mine," Flip says.

"Can't find 'em," Leo says under the dash. Throws up his hands, takes the wheel. "Carry on, Hump."

Staring into darkness, sail Kinney Street intersection. *"Where are the fucking lights!"* Leo cries, stomping furiously. The siren screams.

"You're doing something right!" Teddy says. "Keep stomping."

The brights flood racing streetbricks. *"Ahh!"* twins sigh.

"Let's try the brakes as we come to Allen Street," Teddy says. "You may have to shift back to second."

"I don't want to strip the gears," Leo says. "If we don't have the right of way, we may be in trouble."

"Try the brakes," Teddy says.

Leo's foot sinks hopefully flat to the floorboard, pumps uselessly as the wagon picks up speed. "What's coming?" he cries.

"I don't see anything coming over Allen," Flip says. "Though I could be mistaken. Wait'll I get my glasses on."

"We go up Winsor to Sixth," Leo says. "I can't stop for this redlight. Let's hope they hear the siren."

Leo crosses to left lane, passes a car at the light, howls through the intersection into Winsor.

"Christ, how fast are we going?" Flip asks, jamming his glasses at his face.

"Sixty-five," Teddy says. "We gotta slow down for Second Street, Leo, we may not be so lucky there. Try the shift."

"We'll strip the gears at sixty-five!" Leo says.

"How the hell could Buster send us out in this deathtrap!" Teddy shouts.

"Buster has faith in Leo," Flip cries. "And I have faith in Buster. *Buster's no Stupinsky!*"

"That green light ain't gonna hold," Teddy says. "Try the shift."

Slow slightly going uphill to light. A car freezes in the meeting streets. The wagon screams through at fifty, runs a curb up Sixth Street hill.

"Slow down at the top," Teddy says. "We can practically coast the rest of the way. See any cops, Flip?"

"No. But I wasn't looking either," Flip says. "I believe I was praying sincerely for the first time in my life."

"Pray some more," Leo says, "we're not there yet."

"I will," Flip says. "I'd like a chance to use this white jacket, but there are a hell of a lot of fuzzy thinkers out there—behind steering wheels!"

Coast at forty through waiting traffic at North Main, pass Saints Peter and Paul Church in the dark. Black library fortress. Leo shifts into second, turns down Washington. "Let's stop at the Colored Elks for a bowtie," he says.

"Is that something you drink or wear?" Flip asks.

"It's for your spirit," Teddy says. "It makes you numb from the neck up."

"You guys dissipate and debauch a lot," Flip says. "If we live through this, maybe I can come along sometime."

"We'll stop on the way back if we don't have a customer," Leo says. *"Hey!"*

Buster bats toward them. They pass, screaming in bowered green lamplight.

A wreck by a Fluvanna fruitstand. A sports car plunged through a coupe. Leo coasts to a stop on the shoulder, slowly backs up. Get out cot, follow a sheriff's flashlight, Flip stumbling behind the cot. Down a dark shoulder. A blanket muffles the victim. Twins kneel, study her face for shock. Flip puts on his glasses. A woman, but a dead woman. Strong, high-boned cheeks, heavy dark hair, heavy lips parted—and a clean tiny wound under the point of her chin.

Twins spread a white sheet over her and snake the blanket from under the sheet so that her body is never exposed. The trooper takes his blanket.

"This is stuck," Leo says. "The cot won't drop its side-bar."

"We'll lift her over it," the trooper says.

"Watch out for broken bones," Teddy says. "There might be splinters."

Twins pull the sheet down, cross her wrists on her breast, but her hands slide off, and two troopers, now helping, lift her lifeless sack as the twins grab her calves and she flops onto the cot.

"We're worried about her bones," Leo says ablaze with error.

"I know her, a full-blooded Kinzua Indian," a trooper says. "I've seen her out in Red House many times."

"Is she breathing?" Flip asks. "Or am I diagnosing?"

Leo pulls out with the woman lying in strong inside light. "Goddamn switch!" he cries. The ambulance rolls down the darks of Washington Street like a gambling boat on fire within, Flip on the jump seat.

Leo hurtles up Washington hill, making the first light, breaking the second.

"I can't believe she's dead!" Flip says.

Twins embarrassed.

"Then cover her face!" Leo shouts.

Knock! Knock! Knock! Knock! Knock!

Twins stare at her faraway toes in rear-view mirror, their scalps prickling. "What's that knocking?" Teddy cries.

"I don't know," Flip says, "I thought you were doing it. Maybe I should be giving her oxygen, what do you think? There's that knocking again."

"Find where it's coming from," Leo croaks.

Flip looks under the cot. Leo turns onto First Street in second gear. A dead hand thuds onto Flip's back. "It's a big wooden board," he says.

"That's for fracture patients," Teddy says.

"Hey," Flip cries, throwing the hand off, "we didn't strap her in! Take those corners slow!"

Leo overshoots the hospital avenue, coasts up Barrett hill. "Shit," he says, "we can't stop in reverse. We'll have to go around the block."

"Go up Baker and over William to the back way," Teddy says. "If we don't get there pretty soon, we'll be fired."

Flip ties straps on the Indian. "How's that? I couldn't manage the buckles in this bouncing."

Buster runs to them in the emergency court, holding back the ambulance in whirling red light. It pushes him against the hospital wall. He leaps on the hood as the bumper grinds into stone. "Turn off those goddamn lights!" Buster whispers on the red hood. "You'll have every nurse in the place down on us for frightening patients."

"Where's the fucking switch?" Leo moans.

Buster turns off the lights. "What was your hurry? Didn't they give you a signal seven?"

"No," Leo says. "We looked at her but thought we might be wrong."

"We don't diagnose!" Teddy says.

Flip gets out unsteadily behind the cot, tucking straps.

"Where's the oxygen tank?" Buster asks.

"Up inside," Flip says.

"For Christ's sake, put it on her," Buster says. "We charge for that service."

"By all means," Flip says, getting the tank.

"Hurry up," Buster says, putting his half-pint into the new driver's safekeeping. "Keep a tight cork on that," he warns.

Spots, the squinteyed new driver, nods and heads back to the Packard, waving June bugs or mosquitoes away from his face.

Leo and Teddy mask her heavy head, lay the tank between her legs. Roll her into Emergency. Buster talks with the nurse while twins and Flip push the cot to a quiet dim room. Room 13. An intern closes the door. "Take off the mask," he says. He watches her a long moment, waiting for gleam or movement. Leaves.

"Communicative chap," Flip says, hands shivering.

"What's there to say?" Teddy asks.

"I swear she looks like she's breathing," Flip says.

"Stay here and don't let anyone in," Buster says, wheeling in a hospital stretcher. "Especially her boyfriend, he's wailing his butt off. Put her on this stretcher. Hey, you guys, always cover the face when you bring in a signal seven." Buster takes her sheet with him.

Guard the closed door. The body ready for breath. "You take the knees, Flip," Leo says. Lift her onto the tall stretcher. Flip swings the legs clumsily, knocks the stretcher rolling. They follow the stretcher rolling against the wall, work the Indian on heavily. Stand looking at her dark full strong face.

"She just can't be that hurt by a chin wound," Flip says.

Teddy croaks a breaking neckbone.

"Bring the tank," Buster whispers. "Walk straight past this bastard with the cane or he'll grill us."

Push the cot, following Buster. Good-bye, Kinzua. A man in a straw skimmer looks up wildly gaunt in the waiting room. Rises, leaning on his cane. "Where is she? What are they doing with her?" he asks, pleading to join them.

"The doctors are with her now," Buster says, "and they're very hopeful. They'll be right out."

Twins change sheets in the court. Flip hangs up the tank and mask in the cabin, shaking in his white jacket.

"You wanna drive the Packard back?" Buster asks and calls Spots from the Packard where he's sleeping. Spots and Buster get into the Cadillac, turn on the radio low.

"Wait a minute," Flip says in the cabin. "I think I'll ride in the Packard."

"What's wrong?" Buster asks. "The way back's all uphill. Don't need brakes."

"But I still think I'll ride in the Packard," Flip says.

"Hang on," Buster says. "There's a signal seven at the Boatlanding. You guys run down and take a look. Say you were in the area and heard the call."

"Right," Flip says. He gets into the Packard cabin. "There's a signal seven at the Boatlanding," he says. "We're to go down for a looksee."

"Signal seven!" Teddy says. "I can't believe it."

"Two in a row," Leo groans.

Flip looks at the clean cot. "It's a good thing we changed the sheets already," he says.

"Look," Teddy says, we can get a drink at Fish's when

we get there." He repeats the thought in his head. "Definitely, Stanley," he says.

"Then let's get there," Leo says. Veers out of General, hits forty in second gear, turret glaring in quiet back streets. They pass Lincoln Junior High School in the night. "The scene of our greatest failure," Teddy tells Leo.

"We're learning," Leo says.

"But *what* are we learning!" Teddy cries. "Will we ever use this in our music? Music's for skipping and dancing, Leo."

"Mahler did," Leo says.

"Where?" Teddy says.

"In his Seventh. He felt all this."

"But I hate his Seventh," Teddy says. "It's too grotesque."

"Maybe so, but he put it in, didn't he?" Leo says.

"I still don't like it. He sounds like he's cast out of the Garden."

Drive down green nightleaves of Fairview, cross Sixth Street bridge to the Boatlanding. Leo pulls in among police cars. Leave cot inside, cross through police headlamps beaming over black water into marsh steam. Twins sense glossy horror.

"Look casual," Teddy tells Flip.

"Oh, cool as a cucumber," Flip says. "I'd love a fag but I'm afraid I'd chew it up."

The night is seized and buzzing in an electric grip of crickets and marsh chirrings. The twins see the body and turn their backs, wheeling.

"What's wrong?" Flip asks.

"Just don't look," Teddy whispers.

"Wait back at the wagon," Leo tells Flip.

"Is that an order?" Flip asks. "I'd rather wait here. What's wrong with you guys?"

Twins nod to Coroner Samuel T. Showers.

"Whew!" Leo says. "Who is it?"

"Some colored guy," Showers says.

"He's been holding his breath a long time down there," Teddy says. "How long's he been under?"

"Maybe a week," Showers says.

"He's a Negro?" Flip asks, shaking.

"He's white now," Leo says.

"As the day he was born," Showers says. "Probably taking a leak and fell in. Ninety percent of these people can't swim. See, got his best shirt on, best pants, best shoes, and no socks. For God's sake."

Showers grips a big white hand firmly, severs it at the wrist, severs the other, drops the frogrubbery hands into a canvas bag and passes the bag to a cop. The cop jerks.

Flip turns away. "What's he want those for?" he croaks to a cop.

"I.D.," says the cop, a boy named Ray the twins went to Love School with. "He'll empty them out, blow 'em up and make prints. How're you guys?"

"Not complaining," Leo says hoarsely.

"Though we should be," Teddy says.

"I can't stand this smell any longer," Flip says. "Shall I get the stretcher?"

"You don't have to haul this mess," Showers says.

"We were in the area and heard the signal," Teddy says.

"The city wagon can take this," Showers says. "They got a rubber sheet."

Twins go back, radio Buster.

"You're goddamn right we're not hauling him," Buster says. "He'd smell up our best wagon for a month. Hustle back here. Ten-four!"

"That was too much for me," Flip says. "I almost had a seizure."

"Are you subject to fits?" Leo asks.

"Well, not *fits,*" Flip says. "Though I have blackouts and periods of blindness, deafness—and muteness! But not fits, I've been saved those."

Strip off their deathsweet jackets in the office, throw them out back to air until morning. Wash and wash their hands at the sink, smelling them. Flip lies trembling on a cot.

"Boy, I'm glad I didn't have to ride in back with that," he says.

Sunday Buster gives the twins six hours off after working them round the clock since the day they were hired.

Leo phones Thelma. "Don't come around me," she says. "I have some adoption papers for Stuart I'd like you to sign. Will you do that? I'd like to raise Stuart with his new father as his father."

"That might be best for him," Leo says. "Though I

don't think a telephone is any way to settle a matter like this."

"I'll be home for the morning," she says.

Twins drive down to Thelma's new flat on Chandler near her mother's worsted mill. Sit in kitchen, looking out over factories, while Thelma irons her wash. The morning sun a huge red ball on the roofs. As she kneels to her perfectly piled laundry basket, Leo sees valleys of her ear bruised with scrubbing. Stuart sleeps on a strange big bed-couch she's picked up somewhere.

"I greatly enjoy making love with you, to say the least," Leo says.

"You both do!" Thelma says.

"What can I deny?" Teddy asks. "I'm just a prisoner of love."

She fixes him. "One more like that and it's the firing squad, my boy."

Teddy looks in the cupboard for a familiar ship's decanter usually filled with sherry. "The sherry's gone?" he says. "I'll take vanilla." Sniffs a vanilla extract bottle, smiles, puts it back.

"I'm willing to remarry and start again," Leo says.

Thelma weeps. "I know you are. And I thank you for it. But you two boys will never be economically responsible. You call sex fucking. I hate that word. And that's all you think of me."

"That's not the whole truth, for Christ's sake!" Leo cries.

"Oh, I could never live with you again."

"I'll always love you," Leo says.

"And I," Teddy says, eying redgold sunlight on the kitchen table, peeking at shelves, corners. "Don't have a beer around, do you?"

"No."

"I'm really willing to try again," Leo says.

"No, I'm getting married. I want you to sign adoption papers."

"What's adoption?" Leo asks.

"You give up all legal rights to Stuart. And I don't want you to visit him either. Is that agreed?"

"Couldn't we be his Siamese uncles?" Teddy asks. "Lev and Fedya?"

"That'd never work," she says. "That's too many uncles by half."

"Divided loyalties," Teddy tells Leo.

"He should be told about the twin factor in his genes," Leo says.

"Let's let God worry about that," Thelma says. "By the way, I'm going to Moscow for three weeks."

"Russia?" Teddy asks. "You'll have to tell us what kvass is like."

"I probably won't be drinking any beer," Thelma says.

"Maybe you could ship us back a case of real vodka," Teddy says.

"It would take months to get here," Leo says. "Though I'll bet it's cheap."

"I don't think I'll be buying any vodka either," Thelma says.

Leo kisses Thelma, feeling her full breasts. "I will, *forever,*" he says.

"Thirst calls," Teddy says.

Leave, going carefully down narrow hallway to second floor back porch above glittering factory roofs.

Sit in Stella's green Olds for a belt of gin. "Tastes like starchy water," Leo says. Drive to Fredonia, where their poet friend George Gordon digs the state thruway. Gordon's not in on Canadaway Street. Walk to the Eagle Bar, stopping to think on a park bench. White shirts, nightblack pants, white suede hospital shoes Stella bought them. Breezy summer noon in the park, crossing their knees in rhyme, one beautiful feeling welded by gin.

"When are we ever gonna get laid again?" Teddy asks.

"Well, keep your eye peeled."

"That never helps," Teddy says. "I just see more I can't get my hands on."

"What does it matter?" Leo asks.

"Look, you can see Stuart when he grows up. *We* can."

"Do you think we're oversexed?" Leo asks.

"I don't know. I'll tell you if we ever get laid again."

"When you want it most it's not there. Boy, I'm hungry."

"And thirsty," Teddy says. "I could down a case of beer."

"That's about $3.60 with $1.20 deposit," Leo says. "We can afford it. Turn the case back in in King James."

"Hey, we'll have a ball with Gordon."

"Terrific," Leo says.

"My God, I wish we could get laid. D'ya think we're too strange?"

"Too strange for what?" Leo asks.

"Let's hit the Eagle. Remember that old dish—the drunken granny? Maybe she'll be there."

"I didn't like her all that much except to talk to," Leo says.

"If she'll spread I don't care if she's eighty-five. It's all good."

"I'd give a week of my life for a piece right now!"

"Me too. Any fish in the sea, Teddy says. "My God, that's the most beautiful girl I've ever seen."

The short dark girl walks up to them, hugging a book to her breasts.

"Are you Leo and Teddy, the musicians?" she asks.

They swallow and nod. Dark hair, open and hungry brown eyes, warmth, shyness, breasts.

"My name's Cynara Rosewein. Would you please look at a poem I've written and tell me if you think it should be set to music? I'd love to have it set to music. Like Sappho or Homer! But I'm not sure I'm worth it. I love Rodgers and Hammerstein, do you? Do you think they're worth anything? I'm trying to find out what I'm worth. I want to kill myself. Would you please read my poem?"

"Let's see it," Leo says.

"Have a seat," Teddy says, moving Leo.

She sits by Teddy, filling his nostrils with flesh, opens Skira's *Chinese Painting,* finding the poem. The twins read.

RUBAIYAH

The embers of my adolescence
Crumble to ashes; the incandescence
Fades. Reality bleak and stark
Stares coldly at me in the dark.

"Not bad," Teddy says. "Change *ashes* to *ash.*"

"It's beautiful but not musical," Leo says.

"Do you really think so?" she asks Leo. "I so want to write lyrics."

"Oh, you're lyrical," Teddy says. "How old are you?"

"Fifteen," Cynara says, looking down to be judged. "I

couldn't live if I'm worthless. I'm really desperate to know, I can hardly breathe! You both would do me a great favor if you'd tell me what to read and which composers to listen to. What music do you like? Who are your favorite authors? I'm reading Theodore Dreiser, do you think I should read Sinclair Lewis?"

"Theodore Dreiser!" Teddy says.

"My God," Leo says.

"What do you think of him? Is Theodore Dreiser greater than Thomas Wolfe?"

"They're both humorless," Teddy says.

"And demand patience," Leo says.

"Are they worth it?" Cynara asks.

"You gotta surrender to like them," Leo says.

"Yes!" Cynara cries.

"Surrender is everything," Teddy says. "If you're not gonna surrender, why read? Only to carp?"

"No, sometimes you read past your interest," Leo says. "You have to make sure there's nothing there."

"Oh, what insight," Cynara says. "Oh, I'm so overjoyed to have found you!" Her hair pulled back, cheeks mooning up, dark eyes white, boyish, open. "Comrades!" she cries. "Oh you are so full of right feelings, both of you. You've got to educate me. Please? You've got to come swimming with me this afternoon and I'll show you my reading list."

"We don't have suits," Teddy says.

"There's a store right across the street," she says. "I'll lend you the money if you need it. I have it home in my pig. Oh, you've got to come!" she pleads. "We've so much to say to each other. Can you come swimming with me?"

"With whom are you going?" Teddy asks.

"Daddy's leaving me at Point Gratiot. Will you come?"

"We have a car," Leo says. "We'll meet you there."

"Oh, this is late summer madness at its best!" Cynara says.

"When are you going?" Teddy asks.

"As soon as you buy your suits," she says. "I'll be sitting on the beach painting. You'll see me. You're not pretending? *Au revoir, mes chéris!*"

"We'll be there but suitless," Teddy says. Watch her walk past the firehouse, wave good-bye.

"This in *un*believable," Leo says in the Olds.

"Let's see what happens," Teddy says. "Let's skip that case of beer. I don't dare say what I think about this girl. You can't speak about anybody that alive. We're very nearly twice her age if she isn't lying. Christ, she reads Dreiser. We don't even read Dreiser."

"God never made a more beautiful bosom than hers," Leo says. "I swear it!"

"Let's use our heads and not get drunk," Teddy says.

"How right you are. Let's get some Lavoris and wash our mouths."

"Stop," Teddy says. "There's a drugstore."

Go in, buy a pint of Lavoris, drive to Point Gratiot, park.

"Let's find some place where we can rinse our mouths," Leo says.

"We'll find a cove."

Walk along cliffs of the point. A girl painting in a cove.

"Is that her already?" Teddy asks.

"I can't tell. Let's go down."

"She's waving," Teddy says.

Down the cliff, the pint in Leo's coat pocket.

She wears a great straw hat and sunglasses. Sink into sand while she paints and smiles. No Daddy in sight.

"I'm so glad you came," she says. "I'll try to be bright for you."

"Paint," Leo says.

"You are the most beautiful girl I have ever seen," Teddy says.

She smiles and paints, sitting in a one-piece turquoise bathing suit on a striped blanket. They watch her work. Teddy quietly feels his heart with his hand, and Leo his. Speechless. She does three watercolors in ten minutes, body hair dark and fine on her bosom.

"I'm wearing sunglasses because the paper glares," she says. "Will you play for me someday?"

"We didn't bring our instruments," Leo says.

"But we will," Teddy says.

Waves melt on sand, lazy as oil.

"Did you see the comet last night?" she asks, painting.

"No," Leo says. "I stayed in like Saint Anthony."

"I was in the backyard and looked over my shoulder," she says. "It was very frightening. Something like a train hitting an animal. It hurt me. It was a very powerful light, then it was gone. Then I dreamed that I saw my cat Laura hit by a truck."

"Did that frighten you?" Teddy asks. She nods.

"Didn't you feel anything hopeful about the comet?" Leo asks.

"Only that it would bring something I didn't know," she says. "Why don't you get some sun?"

Strip their wet shirts. Run with beersweat. "You're getting fat!" she says. "But it's not bad. Maybe you're what the comet meant."

"You have a rich fantasy life," Leo says. "It's all right at the surface."

"Yes," Teddy says. "Your subjectivity's boiling over."

"I'm very frightened," she says. "What if I'm not worth anything? How can I tell?"

"I'd say you're worth everything," Leo says. "What grade are you in?"

"Twelfth."

"Really?" Teddy asks. "You started school at *two?* Or three?"

"Eleventh," she amends. "I skipped seventh grade. That's really true."

"You had good marks?" Teddy says.

"Class valedictorian," she says. "My speech was printed in the Dunkirk *Observer*. But I look too drippy and Jewish in the photograph."

"Are you Jewish?" Teddy says happily. "I used to have a Jewish girlfriend!"

"Where is she now?" Cynara asks.

"God only knows," Teddy says. "I sure don't."

"She may have gone to Seattle," Leo says.

"That's a long way!" Cynara laughs. "Aren't you married?"

"Divorced," Leo says.

"Are you sad about it?" she asks.

"I cry about it a bit, yes," Leo says. "In the movies mostly."

"And I," Teddy says. Pang of sweet snake in his crotch. Salome!

"I'll send you the clipping but don't look at the photograph," she says. "Do you want to give me your address? We can correspond. Write me some *mad* letters. Will you?"

"We certainly will," Leo says.

"The madder the better," Cynara says. "Do you like monster movies?"

"Love 'em," Teddy says. "You too?"

"And I like a big black thing coming at me out of the dark," Cynara says. "There's a couple of Japanese monster movies playing in Fredonia tonight."

"Tonight?" Leo says. "Aw, too bad we gotta work this evening!"

"Oh, do you have to?" she asks. "Oh that's so bad. That ruins everything. We could rendezvous in the balcony! Couldn't you stay for even one movie?"

"We had to threaten to quit just to get the afternoon off," Teddy says. "We're ambulance drivers in King James."

"Oh, how thrilling. Tell me about it," Cynara says. Pad aside, takes off her sunglasses, smiles at them warmly.

"Ha!" Leo says. "I don't think you'd wanna hear about it."

"No, it's grisly," Teddy says. "We only do it for our music."

"You're writing an opera about ambulance driving!" Cynara cries. "Oh, *may* I read it? Have you written the libretto yet?"

"We're not writing an opera," Leo says.

"But eventually we have to write something, Leo," Teddy says.

"Oh, of course," Leo says. "I think we should start very soon."

"Would you write an opera for me?" Cynara asks.

"What about?" Teddy asks. Can hardly talk.

"Our late summer madness!" she says, sitting up, leaning earnestly, cleft. "Oh, *please!* My life depends on it."

"Well, what the hell," Leo says. "We could write a one-act opera, don't you think? If we put our minds to it? Look, we're nearly thirty, buddy. If we're ever gonna start, it's now. After thirty the sensibilities start to go, you know that. We won't have the sharpness. We should start now, I really feel it, Ollie."

"I do too," Teddy says. Beersweat twins squinting in sunlight, thinking.

"Oh yes!" Cynara says.

"So what'll we write about?" Teddy croaks.

"Please make it *commedia dell'arte,*" Cynara pleads. "That's my favorite kind of theater."

Leo eyes her turquoise suit. "Harlequin and Columbine?" he says.

"I don't think we could write the right kind of music for that," Teddy says. "That'd have to be *Parisian* and classical."

"Why not Italian!" she cries.

"We weren't born to write Italian opera," Leo says.

"We gotta write the libretto first," Teddy says, "then we'll dope out the music."

"We can decide on a subject on the way home," Leo says.

"You must write me every day how you're coming along," she says biting her lips under her huge straw. "Promise? But you can't write to my house, Daddy'll be furious."

"About us?" Teddy asks.

"Oh, he can't know about you! You're my great secret."

"What's your father do?" Leo asks.

"He's a bookie. He beats me terribly. I've got to get away from him."

"I can't believe that," Leo says.

"I've tried to kill myself twice already," Cynara says.

"Because your father beats you!" Teddy asks.

She nods. "He's terrible. He wanted me to be a boy. He calls me Si for Simon—that's *his* name. He won't be back for two hours, but if he sees me talking to you—well, I shudder. Let's go back into the shadow, I'm through painting."

They look at her paintings.

"May we keep these?" Leo asks. "Will you sign them for us?"

She signs them Laura. "That's who I want to be," she says sadly.

The paintings grow like pole-stars in the twins' eyes. Pick up her blanket, books, and paints, move out of sight under the cliff.

"How'd you try to kill yourself?" Leo asks.

Cynara touches her toes in a sitting-up exercise. "When I was eleven I cut my wrists." Her wrists—many tiny white scars. "I didn't cut deep enough and it dried while I thought I was dying on the bathroom floor. Chalk up one more 'almost' in my *catalogue des washouts terribles.*

You are the first human beings I've told about this. Nobody ever knew. When I was thirteen I swallowed a bottle of aspirins, but my father discovered me unconscious on my bed and had my stomach pumped, unfortunately."

"You must never feel like that again," Leo says.

"If we can be of any help," Teddy says.

"We'll give you our phone number. If you ever feel those feelings again, you damn well phone us," Leo says.

"Not that we mean to talk you out of it," Teddy says. "That's a private affair with your conscience. But there are two of us and we keep pretty well aired out—we're not suicidal, are we?"

"I get up with a bad taste in my mouth some mornings," Leo says. "In fact, sometimes I'm forced to keep good cheer through blinding headaches. Perhaps I drink too much."

"Come on, Nikolaevich," Teddy says. "Your intake's nothing to worry about. Don't make me mad."

"You're a *musician,*" Cynara says. "Both of you."

"But when you feel those feelings, phone us," Teddy says. "You shouldn't have recurring depressions. You might hurt yourself and live, you know? I'm saying you should say good-bye to us."

"I will," Cynara says. "I'll say good-bye especially to you. Perhaps you won't know it until I say it in your memories, but I won't forget you, I promise."

"That won't be enough," Leo says. "We want that phone call. What's your mother think about this?"

"She looks on the bright side," Cynara says. "She had an accident and now she only looks at the sunny side of things. My younger sister, Pearl, is a math genius. She doesn't go out of the house—I mean to school or anywhere—but she can do any math problem I ask her to do. I love her very dearly. Really, I live for her. She can multiply huge numbers in her *hair* in seconds, and she doesn't make errors. She's essentially a better human being than I am. And she's learning jazz piano!"

Twins move their heads out of bright sun into grotto shadow, Cynara seeming suddenly to appear out of a mist, taking shape in speckled minds as if from the past or from death, her shoulders white and whole, eyes boiling like root beer, smiling lips worried, eager, shaking with hope for her sister.

"Jazz piano!" Teddy says.

"Boy, we'll have to meet her," Leo says.

"You can't. You're my secret."

"Maybe we can walk by your house some night when she's playing," Teddy says.

"Yes, that'll be perfect," Cynara says. "Tell me when you're coming and I'll be at my bedroom window with a candle. When I'm in my room, I only read by candlelight."

"Upstairs or down?" Leo asks.

"Upstairs. I have some trees by my window and it's very dark."

Leo clears his throat, as does Teddy. "A tree?"

After a moment Cynara says, "I sort of take care of her—she can't stand to be by herself."

"Your mother or your sister?" Teddy asks.

"Both!" she laughs. "No, my sister, Pearl."

"I really can't believe that about your father," Leo says.

"It's true. I bruise very easily. I'll show you some bruises. Though with my birthday coming up next Sunday, he probably won't beat me this week. You'll have to take my word for it now. Why don't you come to my birthday dinner! My daddy's buying me dinner at the White Inn. Why don't you just walk in like old friends and you can have dinner with us. Then you can show me what you've *written* too. Oh, please come, I won't have a happy birthday without you! Say you will."

"Well, if we can get away," Teddy says.

"Oh, please don't let me down."

"All right, we'll be there! Okay?" Teddy asks Leo.

"You don't have to bring me a birthday present, the libretto will be enough."

"It may not be finished, Cynara," Teddy says. "We do work too."

"Oh, you've got to bring me something, even if only the scraps of an outline," Cynara says. "You really must, you know, if our great triangle is going to be real."

"We'll bring something," Teddy says. "Your family doesn't leave you much time for your personal life, does it?"

"Oh, you mean dates? I don't have dates, or very rarely. I'm hated. I'm despised at school. I don't have a single girl friend."

"I can believe that," Teddy says, "You're too beautiful."

"Please stop saying that! I'm very easily embarrassed."

"You're passionate!" Teddy says. "Of course you get embarrassed. Where shall we write to you?"

"How about care of George Gordon at 2 Canadaway Street?" Leo says. "Could you pick up mail there?"

"Oh, that's right on my way to school," Cynara says. "Perfect. Write to me as *soon* as you get back so that I'll know we're confirmed."

Her face drains. She stares at them searchingly. "Come back here," she says in shadow. "Can I trust you, Leo and Teddy? Shall we swear our faiths from the bottoms of our hearts?" Holds up her hands.

All cross hands. The twins burn with hope.

"Comrades?" she asks. "And perhaps more."

"Oh much more," Leo says.

"Much more," Teddy says.

"You'll be my personal musicians?" Cynara asks.

"We'll be anything you want," Leo says.

"And you will really, truly, without pretending write a one-act opera for me?"

"Oh, we swear it," Teddy says.

"We'll begin the libretto tonight," Leo says.

"Will you answer a question for me with absolute honesty?" Cynara asks, waiting for an answer. "Am I too full-figured?"

"No!"

"Don't you think I'm too freckled? and flirtatious? and too physical? I know I'm inarticulate and decorative. And too incapable of depth—it's really true, I'm not capable of any depth at all!—and too shy?—and just *too afraid?*'

They declare her virtues.

She bites her lip, her eyes searching them steeply to their heights. "I trust you!" she cries. "But I am determined not to be a kept woman before I'm eighteen, I warn you now," she says and pulls down her turquoise bathing suit to her waist. Leo and Teddy stare at nipples sunk within. "Kiss me," she says, both of you." Her dark eyes close on the puzzle-space between them.

They glide as one to hold her.

"We been drinking," Leo confesses.

"We need Lavoris," Teddy husks.

They pledge their hopes in the shadow, then quickly

get under Cynara's blanket. She resists their advances, surrenders, resists.

Suddenly she sits up with the blanket and cries, *"My own opera!"*

Flip sweeps out the sun-hot Cadillac. "Brakes at last!" he says. Watches twins walk down from the turf-covered reservoir of artesian well water where they keep their wine gallon behind a rock. "Boy," Flip says, "I wish I had your sense of balance."

"Whose?" Teddy asks.

"Either of you," Flip says. "In my condition I'm not choosy."

"You may have meant Leo's," Teddy says. "He's the quarterback in the family. I'm more of a spectator."

Hide their fresh gallon up front in the Cadillac until finding a better place. Noon sun burns.

"I'll put it differently," Flip says. "I like the way you both keep your feet on the ground. Oops, there's Buster!" Flip runs in, flicks on the radio. "I'm right here, Buster," he says steadily.

Buster says, "We're going to Allen Nursing Home and should be back in twenty minutes. If anything comes in, you go with the twins. Ten-four."

"Ten-four," Flip signs off. "Buster baby."

"I wish I had that license," Leo says.

"We ain't had a morning free to get it!" Teddy says. "Only *Sun*day."

He pricks two ales into foaming as the phone rings. An emergency. Twins drain, flatten, hide empty ale cans under the building while Flip scrawls a note to Buster: *Gone to Buffalo!*

"He'll think we went to the Palace Burlesk." Teddy belches and writes: *Heartbrook Hospital—Sick Child—Pulmonary—*

"Don't diagnose," Flip says.

"Hey," Teddy says, "let's take the last act of the opera. We can stop at Fredonia on the way back. Buster'll never know."

"If we hurry," Leo says.

"Let's not dawdle," Flip cries, "this kid is dying."

"Kick that beer can under the building farther," Flip, Teddy says.

Flip kicks the can sailing under with a clatter. "Don't want the boss to know you drink on the job, huh?"

"That, too," Teddy says. "But let's all keep our stashes separate, know what I mean? That fucking Spots is an alcoholic, when he's awake."

A black lady flags the ambulance at Gustavus Adolphus Children's Home. Cot out, follow her. Children stand in neat corridors. A girl eating a wiener at a beat-up card-table waves hello. A boy coughs blood in bed.

"How old is he?" Leo asks.

"Four," the lady says.

"What's wrong with him?" Teddy asks.

"He get sieges."

"You mean seizures?" Flip asks.

"He getting pneumonia now, though. Can't breathe in his little lungs. They fillin' with mucus."

"Is anybody coming with us?" Leo asks.

"No. They waitin' in Buffalo, the doctor and the grand-mother."

"Where are his toys?" Flip asks, looking about the room.

"He don't know how to play," she says.

The boy rolls great brown eyes, stares over his forehead at Flip, who is shocked by the stare.

Lock the cot into the cabin, scramble behind the wheel while Flip settles into the jump seat. Flip smiles down at the strapped boy whose head doesn't reach the pillow. "Should I give him oxygen?" Flip asks.

"How's he breathing?" Leo asks, goosing the siren.

"Kind of rasping, but regular," Flip says. "He likes the scenery. What about the pillow?"

"Let him lay flat until he looks like he might wanna be raised up," Leo says.

"But hang onto him, for God's sake," Teddy says, "this kid's really sick. By God, I can take coronaries, suicides and auto wrecks, but sick kids, man, they shake me."

"This one's too goddamn sad to look at," Leo says, pulling on the turret light.

The boy rattles blood but does not turn from the window. Flip wipes the bloody mute mouth. "He's got pale spots but no fever," he says, feeling the boy's brow. Big dull eyes stare at Flip, who fixes on the boy's sunshot ear.

Leo pulls around two cars at the Buffalo Street light and

lifts forward to a hundred passing Moon Brook golf course, siren burning the countryside.

They climb sunny hills. "Thank God we know where we're going," Leo shouts.

"Sure," Teddy shouts. "Heartbrook's out past Buffalo General. What's the name of that street?"

"I don't know—but I remember what it looks like," Leo says.

"Flip," Teddy shouts, "do you know the name of that street?"

"I wrote it down someplace," Flip says. "It was on that pad."

"Didn't you bring it?" Teddy asks.

"Of course I did," Flip says. Flip searches himself, bones trembling. "Are you sure I didn't give it to you?"

Teddy searches himself. "Did I give it to you?" he asks Leo.

"Look in my pockets," Leo says.

"I know everything in your pockets!" Teddy shouts.

"Look anyway," Leo shouts.

"Slow down for Sinclairville, we got a ticket there once," Teddy says. "Lift up. You don't have it. Look in your pockets again, Flip!"

Leo glances at rolling farmland. The speedometer cable grinds, snaps—the arrow sinks.

"Slow down through Sinclairville," Teddy warns again.

Leo slows through Sinclairville.

"What're we doing?" Teddy shouts.

"Five," Leo says, pointing at the speedometer.

"We're doing seventy!" Teddy says.

Leo pulls back to forty for the turn, hits the shoulder. "How's he doing, Flip?" Leo shouts.

"Are you sure I shouldn't be giving him oxygen?" Flip asks in the wind.

"How's he look!" Leo asks. "What's he doing now?"

"No change," Flip shouts. "He's watching the trees."

"How're your bowels?" Teddy asks Leo.

"Why the hell'd you ask?" Leo cries.

"I been tryin' to forget too!" Teddy says. "Whatta you think about that little filling station in Gerry?"

"I think we'll skip it!" Leo says.

"We shouldn't have had those banana peppers for breakfast," Teddy shouts over the siren. "When the hell will we learn?"

"Well, get your mind off it," Leo says.

"We haven't finished Gottlieb's last speech," Teddy says. "Maybe we can get it done before we see Cynara."

"We won't see her," Leo says, "unless we get back to Fredonia before she comes by Gordon's for the mail. Where are we?"

"Coming into Gerry," Teddy says.

"I mean Gottlieb!"

"This is where he shakes the pear tree," Teddy shouts, opening their springbinder. " 'You have driven a knife into my lungs in the middle of my work!' he cries. 'You're shaking me,' Melissa says."

"Perfect," Leo says. "Now he's really gotta shake the tree."

"Are you guys writing at a time like this?" Flip shouts.

"What other time is there!" Leo shouts.

They pass the little filling station, bowels yearning.

"I'm out of ink," Teddy says and takes a bottle of ink from the maps in the glove compartment. He leans toward Leo with bottle between knees, pen wavering. Bouncing ink spills through black pants. "Christ, my knees are soaked." Scribbles midnight circles with signature stub, puts bottle back with the maps. "How's the boy?" he cries over wind and siren.

"He's awake," Flip says.

"Is he suffering?" Leo asks.

"I don't know," Flip says, "but how would you feel? Boy, I wish I knew if he needs oxygen, this is terrible."

"Didn't you bring the First Aid book?" Teddy asks.

"I didn't think we'd need it," Flip says.

"You shoulda read that book ten times over by now!" Teddy cries. "If I could turn around, Flip, I'd strangle you."

"I promise I'll memorize it as soon as we get back," Flip sighs.

"Is he in shock?" Leo asks.

"I can't tell," Flip says, "but I don't diagnose!"

"Maybe we should give him a jolt to be on the safe side," Teddy says. "How's his breathing?"

"He has some kind of hemorrhage," Flip says. "But he's awake."

Teddy puts the springbinder aside, takes up his writing-board. "Should we describe the pear tree for a last time?" he asks. "I mean really let loose?"

"If we're graphic it won't be mad enough," Leo says. "Put it in the stage directions."

"We don't want stage directions in the fifth act, Leo," Teddy says. "She's just standing there like a pear tree, that's enough."

"But she's Persephone now and we should suggest her rising out of dead leaves," Leo says. "There has to be remorse at the roots."

"Does Persephone really ever bear fruit?" Teddy asks. "When do pear trees ripen? If we knew more details, we could give the tree validity."

"Good idea," Leo says. "Let's skip that passage until we can get to the Prendergast. Flip, when do pear trees ripen?"

"Spring, I think," Flip says. "At least they did when I was a boy."

"That's right," Leo says. "Remember Grandfather's orchard?"

"We only picked cherries," Teddy says. "The pears were on the ground."

"Hey, d'ya think the intercom works at this distance?" Flip asks. "Maybe we can get Buster to read the address back."

Teddy tries the radio.

"Come in, Angelo's!" Flip cries.

"Buster?" Teddy says.

"Calling Reservoir hill!" Flip cries. "Be there, Buster baby!"

"Wake up, Spots!" Teddy cries. *"EARTHQUAKE!"*

"A police escort will pick you up in Angola," Buster says.

"We'll try to slow down for 'em," Teddy yells.

"Where are we going?" Leo cries.

"Read from the pad," Flip says. The intercom fades in hill shadow. "Come in, Reservoir hill!" Flip cries from the cabin.

"Where are you now?" Buster asks.

"We're burning up Fredonia," Teddy says.

"How's the patient?" Buster asks.

"Where are we going!" Leo cries, letting up on the siren. "We're losing your signal!"

The radio fades in a cave of wind. Leo beats the siren.

"That's it," Teddy says. "Absolutely amazing. We picked up Buster twenty miles from Reservoir hill."

"It's the height," Leo says.

"Keep your eye peeled for Cynara," Teddy tells Leo.

"What's she look like?" Flip asks. "No, don't tell me—she looks like a pear tree."

"My God, that's her waving!" Leo says, waving.

"She heard the siren," Teddy says, waving.

Cynara in kerchief and raincoat on Canadaway Creek bridge, surprised, eager, glowing. Twins flood with unforeseen strength.

"She knows we'll be back," Leo says.

"Can't say what I thought of Miss Pear Tree," Flip says. "I didn't get my glasses on in time."

"How's the boy look?" Leo asks Flip.

"He's alive," Flip calls. "But he's still bleeding—if I may diagnose!"

"What about the light?" Teddy asks. "That cop parks right by the liquor store, Leo."

"I think it's high time we got to Buffalo," Leo says, harrying traffic with horn and siren, and swerves through the light in a straightaway, passing the White Inn, beloved for Cynara's birthday dinner.

"Let's swing into this," Teddy says. "If we finish today it'll be just three months since her birthday."

"When was her birthday?" Leo asks.

"I don't remember," Teddy says. "Hey, we better get rid of this wine before Angola. If we get stopped, our goose is cooked."

"Good idea," Leo says. "Get the cup."

"We shoulda decanted it into quarts," Teddy says, filling a stained paper cup, wetting his fingers with the heavy gallon.

"Hold it to my mouth," Leo says.

Teddy lifts the cup. "Clouds over Lake Erie," he says. Leo drains the cup, staining his white shirt. "Button up my jacket!" Teddy buttons Leo.

"I needed that," Leo says holding his wine down, belching. "I can feel the lift already."

"I can hear it," Flip says. "Did I tell you my Uncle Herbert died of cirrhosis? His liver got vulcanized out in Akron."

Teddy drains a cup and a refill.

"How much is left?" Leo asks.

Teddy holds up the gallon. "Better than half," he says.

"We can't throw that much wine away!" Leo shouts. "That's nearly full."

"Well, we can't drink it all," Teddy says.

"We can damn well try like hell," Leo shouts, eyes gleaming. "I don't want that boy to die!"

"How about us?" Teddy asks.

"I have all the hope in the world about us," Leo says. "How're you doing, Flip?"

"I'm praying again! You guys are making me awfully religious. Never thought I'd feel this way."

Teddy looks over Lake Erie. "I think we should put a storm in."

"What for?" Leo asks.

"To rock the tree!" Teddy says. "Maybe some lightning too, so we'll know the gods are around. Come on, Leo, wake up!"

"I'm awake!" Leo cries. "We gotta work up to that Strindberg line. Put it down for now."

"But we gotta rewrite it," Teddy says, writing, 'Hell does not flourish without Beatrice.' "There's the cops!"

A highway patrol falls in behind the wagon, closing up.

"Maybe that's our escort," Leo says. "God, I wish I had that license!"

"Christ! We should *never* have hidden this wine in the Cadillac," Teddy cries.

"We didn't think we'd be driving this boat already," Leo says.

The police boil past, wind shudders, air blisters with sirens.

"He's goin' pretty slow," Leo says.

"We gotta pass him and get rid of this fucking jug," Teddy says.

"Pour another," Leo says.

"The cops will see us!" Teddy says.

A hatless sheriff leans out his right window, warning and scolding cars ahead.

"Why are they going so slow?" Leo asks.

"They're doing the best they can, Leo," Teddy says.

"When Angelo gets back tomorrow, I'm asking for hazardous-duty pay," Flip calls.

"Does he even know you work for him?" Teddy asks.

"I hope so," Flip says. "Buster says he mentions me over the phone."

"How's the kid?" Teddy asks.

"He's making red bubbles." Flip says. "Small ones in the corners of his mouth."

"I think we should give him oxygen," Teddy tells Leo.

"Do you think he looks worse, Flip?" Leo asks.

"Well, he's still pinkmouthed," Flip says.

"At least he's not blue." Teddy shudders.

Traffic splits and Leo passes the police car on the outskirts of Angola. Ambulance shivers down to fifty at intersection.

"Slow up by that white steeple and I'll toss the jug out," Teddy says.

"Right on the sidewalk?" Leo says. "We could get reported."

"Let's hide it under a sheet in the cabin," Teddy says. "Then we'll still have it."

"Pour me a last one," Leo says. Teddy holds up the cup. Leo drinks through the running blot of Angola. "Hide it!" he cries as they pick up another police escort at the town line.

Teddy hands the jug back to Flip. "Put this under a sheet."

"A toga," Flip says.

"Throw the cup out," Leo says.

Teddy drains the purple cup, sends it dancing.

Another sheriff leans out his window, scorching drivers. A motorcycle cop falls in behind the ambulance but fades away.

Great steel towers of power cable run like windmills into Lackawanna. Steel mills spread in dirty daylight. Sun glistens on acids in blue air. Fumes shrink their nostrils.

"That sulfur and rubber stink makes my back creep," Teddy says.

"I think it's time for oxygen," Leo says. "Give the kid some oxygen, Flip!"

"Right you are," Flip says, reaching for the tank but suddenly bouncing from jump seat to floor. "Christ almighty, watch out for those potholes!"

"They're all over," Teddy says. *"Watch out! UNHH!"*

"Good-bye, Limbo, hello, Inferno," Leo says. "We still got an axle?"

"Damn it!" Flip says, falling still again.

"How's the kid?" Leo asks. *"Hold on!"*

"He's fine but the wine's rolling around like a bowling ball," Flip says.

"Put it on the cot so it doesn't smash," Teddy says, stuck to the road with Leo.

"We could always lie and say it's blood," Flip says crawling after the rolling bottle. Finds a paper under his hand. "My God, we're saved," he cries, "here's the address!" Raises gallon to cot, bounces, then raises it again, and lays it at the boy's feet.

"Are you getting oxygen into him?" Teddy asks, taking the note.

"Pronto," Flip says. "I can't even get onto my seat."

Leo slows to seventy for a four-lane bridge. Jounce onto it, Flip sailing, Leo gooses the motor, and they bob off the bridge downhill, Flip starkwhite against the back door.

"You're kissing their tail pretty close," Teddy says.

"Maybe they'll get the idea," Leo says. "Boy, I'm dry."

Flip scrambles up the cabin, pushing the wine back up cot, pulls himself onto the jump seat. "I'm sure glad that back door's secure," he says, bright and gasping. "My power of imagination's too strong!"

"Take a jolt," Teddy says.

"It'll make him dizzy," Leo says.

"Stay off the oxygen," Teddy calls.

"I haven't even got the mask unpacked yet," Flip says.

Leo peels into the wrong lane. "Hell, there ain't *anybody* over here!"

"Hallelujah, I got it on him," Flip says.

"That cop won't be happy if we pass him," Teddy says.

Leo flickers the-brights-the-brights with his foot, passes the cops like Pegasus. "Here we come, Heartbrook!"

Teddy claps in prayer, burning. He sees behind him the blown wet cheek of a sheriff hanging out a window. Hope floods the floorboards. *"Hit's the eleckprisspity a' Gawd!"* Teddy cries.

"How much should I give him?" Flip cries over the roar.

"Six liters!" Teddy says.

"I hope that's enough," Flip says.

"Give him twelve then!" Leo says.

"That's quite a blast," Teddy says.

A new patrol car pulls out in front of them. They follow him the last few blocks. Cops turn into emergency at

Buffalo General, not Heartbrook. The ambulance shrieks on by.

"They're all screwed up," Teddy says. "Here they come again."

"Now we run interference for them," Leo says. "Hah! Hang on, Flip, we're turning in."

"Thank God," Flip says, bracing himself over the child. "Damn it, I have a bloody nose."

"Hide the jug," Teddy says.

"Man, when I hit that door I thought my heart would burst, not my nose."

The siren dies as they burn through the gates of Heartbrook.

Phone Cynara from Gangi's bar in Fredonia, blow a brace of double martinis, wait in the wagon in the rain. Drink burgundy and rest on the cot in the strong inside light, Flip up front. The windows steam. Cynara raps, closes her umbrella, hides on the cabin floor in kerchief and wet raincoat—her eyes panicked.

"Turn off the lights, please!" she says. "And please ask Flip to wait outside for a moment. He can take my umbrella."

"No, I don't need your umbrella, Yum Yum," Flip says. Gets out, stands in a doorway, shivering.

"Daddy discovered our maildrop at Gordon's! He went raging into his apartment and accused him of seducing me. Just an hour ago!"

"What'd George say?" Leo asks.

"He made him sit down and listen to some Mahler," Cynara says. "And showed him his library. He told him I take books to read and Daddy finally believed him but said I couldn't go there anymore. Then he came home and beat me. I'm a mass of bruises, look at my leg"—a small mark above her knee—"I've got to get away from him! We've got to run away together. *Anywhere!*"

"You know what'll happen if we get caught?" Leo asks. "Twenty years."

"We can keep moving and hiding until I'm eighteen," Cynara says. "And I can dress a lot older."

"We're too conspicuous," Teddy says. "We can't hide."

"Don't you *love* me?" she beseeches palely, gripping her umbrella to leave.

"We can't get away with it," Leo says.

"I don't know," Teddy says. "I'm willing to try. Good God, life with Cynara's worth risk of jail!"

"I don't want you in jail, I want you with me!" she cries. "Don't talk as if we'll fail."

"Look, when Angelo pays us tomorrow, if he gets back, Leo and I can take off around the country and be conspicuously *absent* say for at least three months. Then we can drive back undercover, pick you up and nobody'll connect your disappearance with our going away."

"We can't do it any other way," Leo says.

"I could fly to you," Cynara says. "In disguise!"

"Cynara, what *you* are can't be disguised," Teddy says. "Running off together's insane. We three have been seen together in Gangi's and other places too often for the cops not to check us out in King James. We'd be caught in three days. We gotta separate first."

"I'm not so sure about all this," Leo says.

"Leo, we're pushing thirty," Teddy says, "this is our last chance! We'll never have this moment again. Are we gonna rot in King James forever? I'll bet my life we can get *The Green Wig* put on in Frisco or New York or Seattle or wherever we go. It's time we take the fucking bull by the horns!"

"Yes!" Cynara says. "If you don't give me this hope, I never want to see you again."

"This means we gotta separate for three months," Leo says heavily.

"Oh please, my sweethearts, both of you!"

They kiss her hands.

"Let's go down to Old Main and say good-bye," she says.

Drive to Old Main with Flip in back, go up alone with Cynara to third floor music practice rooms. A bust of Beethoven watches their farewell on an overstuffed couch. Flesh in a deserted, silver-dim room. The twins steal the bust, leaving.

They throw out the empty gallon by Moon Brook and in King James get a pint of gin for heart. Passing King James High School in the rain, Leo fades, drives through a metal lamppost on the school sidewalk. The pole falls, buckling the cabin. Shocked, they await the pole's crash onto the walk. At last they get out in the rain. The pole lies balanced down the dented roof.

White and shaking, Flip is sent to phone Angelo's, his

glasses solid steam in the downpour. The perishing scarecrow staggers into the night. Police haul the dizzy twins to the station two blocks away to record the wreck, then choose to book them as well. Humbled, Leo and Teddy cry abuse. Wander down a dark hall, piss in a showerroom drain. Found, they are herded into a cell with steel walls. They pound the walls for hours and cry filth down the cellblock. Stella bails them out at midnight for $210.

Angelo does not pay them. The city sues for $75 for its lamp. Stella pays.

Leo jumps bail, his operator's license yanked. Absent Teddy's fine is ten bucks, drunk and disorderly.

During the week Cynara comes to King James on "shopping trips," bringing many books, keepsakes, clothes and her paints, and meets Stella. In the kitchen Stella whispers to her sons, "That's the most beautiful girl I've ever seen!" She helps the twins pack and seal cases in the cellar. When Stella goes upstairs to make the boarders' beds, the twins show Cynara their double bed in the cellar.

The twins spend the day they plan to leave getting Cynara's boxes shipped West on the Erie Lackawanna. They post the boxes for San Antonio, planning to reship them to San Francisco, muddying their trail.

Stand sweating in the Erie freight office. "We should hold off leaving until morning," Leo says. "If we're out on the road by seven, maybe we'll catch a salesman going to Cleveland—or an early truck."

"To hell with that," Teddy says. "If we leave now, by seven in the morning we'll be four hundred miles away from King James. I can't wait!"

"Carpe diem!" Cynara urges on a farewell phone call from Fredonia. "Write to me every day, wherever you are. And *be sure* to take our bust of Ludwig with you. I love him and want him with us wherever we go."

"All over La Mancha," Teddy says.

Shower, change into fresh white shirts, black chinos, white suedes. A last bowl of Stella's chili and banana peppers. She drives them thirty miles to Westfield, not far from North East where she was born. The twins watch the lake hills fall away. They pass Chautauqua, a pang for their longago summers at the Ashland with Omar and the one with Beverly. Stella drives them across the long metal bridge out of Westfield and parks on the shoulder.

"Now you write me," she says reproachfully. "I can't say I like this beeswax, but your happiness always comes first with me. Would you mind answering one question before you go? Which of you is this little girl after?"

"Ahem!" twins say. "Honestly, she hasn't decided yet," Teddy adds.

"We're not thinking of getting married right away," Leo says. "Though that's our greatest hope."

"Well, it's my turn, Leo," Teddy says sternly.

"She loves us both," Leo tells Stella. "Anyway, she's worth everything we're doing, Mama."

"She surely is," Stella says. "Or I wouldn't be behind you in this scheme. Now *write me,* my sons, when you find work."

Kiss Stella good-bye. The green Olds turns, goes back over the bridge as they wave after her. She's given them $200 out of her savings for taxes. Twins stand by the road with their horn cases, suitcase and great laundry bag with their tall bust of Beethoven packed safely in the middle. Seven P.M. A ringed foggy moon in the dim blue sky, breeze lifting.

"Y'know," Teddy says, "if we're let off out in the wilds somewhere, we'll get mighty thirsty."

"We can't afford it but we deserve it," Leo agrees. "We'll just sip the cream off our traveling money—a last jug for the road."

"Right! For celebration, and to keep our spirits turning over," Teddy says. "Vodka, so the drivers won't smell us."

Walk back into town for two pints and a six-pack of ale.

The bridge darkens as they return, look both ways, snap open a pint. After an hour they walk farther out of town. The moon clouds over. Around midnight a cloudburst beats down. The laundry bag soaks through so heavily that Teddy can't carry it more than ten yards at a time. Beg rides fruitlessly from slowmoving cars in the downpour, struggle toward a bus stop they hope to find in Ripley. Run ahead with horns and suitcase, go back for laundry bag, hoist its waterlogged mass between them. Passing Ripley Cemetery, they hide their gear inside the gate, search for Durwood's grave. Their father's stone is lost on drizzling hummocks. Rain drives them back to their bag. Last pint, ale gone too. Remembering bodies hauled in their wagon. *"I wanna play!"* Leo cries. Break out their horns. Teddy screws his slide on, his breast pierced, head pulsing. "No Southern Comfort!" he moans. Furry, rich striving tones of "What a Friend" flood the small cemetery, rill and wind the soaking nightgrass. "Best we ever played it!" Teddy clasps Leo. Stand in cemetery in hard cold falling water in white shirts, drinking. Both start crying, heads raised. Lightning beards the earth.

"This is a hell of a start, Ollie!" Leo weeps on Teddy's shoulder. "And what the hell are we gonna find? No skills, no professions, just a pair of lost ninth graders!"

"Don't diagnose!" Teddy cries. "—God, are we *dumbheads!* We shoulda checked on the weather, at least."

"We swim too good to drown," Leo whispers.

They stand with palms out in the downpour.

"Stanley? Remember that magic trick Dad showed us in the bar?"

"The match burning in a shot of whiskey?"

"Yes," Teddy says.

"Sure do!" Leo says.

They see the flame on their father's glass, the alcohol a naked virgin, dancing, burning in a shameless blue frenzy.

Pick up their stoneheavy clothesbag, go out to the road. Two headlights burn toward them. Their hearts lift.

Thumbs up!

JANUARY 6, 1972
Jerome-Shakespeare avenues
Bronx, New York

THE DRUNKS

To Jack McManis

but hug the lifemask till it shrivel up

Will you smile at the enthusiasm I express concerning this divine wanderer?

—MARY SHELLEY
Frankenstein

TWIN snores of Leo-Teddy in shadowblack cellar. *Bing!* Steer-heavy, waking cell by cell, burning eyes cracking through sulfur-crusts. Hip band stretching over ridge of dead bedsprings. BRINNGGGGG*!* Three A.M. death-thirst.

"Ohhhh!" Teddy groans.

Leo groans. "My brain wants to pop out some new lobes."

"I feel like a boxcar of dead dogs."

"What's that stink?"

"Must be comin' in the window."

"This whole basement stinks of armpits."

"Did we kill that second gallon? I feel a wineball sloshing."

"When will we learn? *Muscatel Kills.*"

"Are you awake?"

"I don't think so. Are you?"

"Let's not be late three days in a row. Today's payday."

Leo-Teddy bolts upright. "*Three-thirty!* WE'RE LATE."

Their pink bedlamp brightens. Stone walls, basement clotheslines amazed with roomers' bedsheets. Crawl to bed's edge, limbs droop throbbing, limp as an octopus. Sand-flames in shrivelled eyes. They tote up their week's wages, today's cash refreshment. Cooling beers midmorning at the Colored Elks. Ahh!

"We'll make up for lost time," Teddy mutters. "So we're not docked."

Teddy eyes Leo's nose, fingers his own carefully, still eying Leo's. Leo's nose seems to have swollen overnight.

Piss hardons, dig scum from glanses, lint from bellies, hairs from rear clefts. Teddy cleans stinkum from squishy toes while Leo rubs dinge from ankles. Pull on fresh jockeyshorts. Teddy measures the hardcentered strawberry boil on his haunch. "Glad that's not on Boris," he says, grabbing his bulge. "Bride of Boris, where are you?"

Crack open yesterday's socks. "Let's shower after work," Leo says, "and put on clean socks then."

Fingering flakes from their ears.

Take up icecreamwhite starched pants, split the flat legs, stand white-trousered. Starched white shirts, clip-on black bow ties now greasecurled. White hip band sleeve, sewn by Stella. Uncrack starched white jackets, push fists down starched sleeves. Work stiffly caked starch apart with coarse ripping. Loop softworn belts on swelling waists. Stand wholly encased in starch, jacketbacks red-threaded—

HOKUM BREAD
King James Baking Co. Inc.

Payday surges through Leo-Teddy. "Let's give Mother fifty bucks today," Leo says.

"That'll only leave seventy-eight," Teddy lectures.

Gliding through Stella's sheets, ducking.

"She deserves it," Leo says. "My God, we make one-fifty a week. We've never earned so much!"

"Not after taxes, Leo. We only take home one-twenty-eight. You know how long seventy-eight bucks'll last us. I mean that's only thirty-nine apiece for drinkin' money. Thirty-nine! I mean one-fifty *sounds* like a shitpot—but let's be realistic. We'll give her forty bucks."

"Hey, we took that ten-buck advance. We'll only get one-eighteen."

"Okay, Stella gets thirty," Teddy says. "Don't forget, today we get a fifth of sour mash. We *promised* ourselves. Let's not go back on that, right? Let's not forget anything that important for our spirits."

"If this fuckin' town only had a cat house," Leo cries softly, "I bet we'd have a lot smaller liquor bill."

"We spend too much time chasin' tail in bars where there ain't any! That's our problem. We haven't picked up a cunt once. Bars are a sheer waste of spirit. We gotta get in focus. We gotta use our drinkin' money for composing, not for chasin' tail. We should find our *optimum drinking level* and be sure to be *writing* at that hour. Religiously."

Brush teeth at laundry cellar's large zinc tub. Leo spits bloody foam from running gums. Teddy rams his toothbrush too far back, suddenly heaves midnight muscatel.

Hangs drooling over the tub, sloshing curds down the drain. "Good God," he says happily, "I feel a hell of lot better! Try it, stick your toothbrush down your throat." Leo heaves too as Teddy smiles benignly. "You're right!" Leo cries. "Hey, we really discovered somethin'!" "Damn right," Teddy says. Rinse swollen eyes, quietly piss in dry sink. "Goodbye," Teddy says, Boris fading.

Leo glares into the tiny sinkmirror. "My nose is gettin' bigger!"

"So's mine." Teddy glowers. "Think it's booze? Maybe we need more ice in our drinks."

Leo-Teddy growls at his image, eyes racing from nose to nose.

Tiptoe upstairs in clodhoppers. "We gotta get some god-damn normal shoes!" Leo whispers.

"Well, we haven't had a cent to spare."

Stella sleeps in a very tiny room just off the kitchen. Twins go into kitchen closet, get two empty pop bottles and a vodka fifth, brightening. At the sink they fill each pop bottle with Stella's vodka, promising to replace it, then run some water into her bottle. Teddy sips from her watered bottle, grimaces foully. "We *gotta* replace it!"

Leo sips from Stella's bottle. *"Piss!"*

They add a few drops of red food coloring into one popbottle vodka, a few drops of blue into the other.

Teddy winks, smiling blissfully. "Mine's cherry."

"Mine's grape!"

Corked bottles into lunchbuckets. Softly open Stella's bountiful, soundless pink refrigerator. Take out four hard-boiledeggs for diets, two redhot banana peppers to munch on their walk to work. Slip out the backdoor, go up Rose Alley to Sixth Street and downhill to the bakery at Five Point. Muggy unclear night, lamps yellow as starchwhite Leo-Teddy glides downhill.

"Let's remember to dump the gin empties when we get outta town," Leo says. "Me with no license—if we ever have an accident with all those pints in the walls, our names will be written in dogshit."

Heat-lightning crackles in the lake's dark clouds.

"How the hell are we ever gonna save twenty-five hundred for Las Vegas?" Teddy asks.

"Hope for the best. Keerist I'm hungry!"

"I need about six hours of penetration without with-drawal."

Five Point lies deserted and damp as the four-legged white flood of starch marches under fogged streetlamps, hard heels grinding a beat on redbrick. Fresh bread fumes spread from the bakery, dizzyingly delicious. Leo-Teddy aches for food, ale, heavenly sex, fame, glory, travel, and work well done. Sucks down bread fumes like a horse. ***Hungerpains!***

Flip Newquist hails them from a dark bakery doorway. "Hey, I been waitin' a half hour for you guys! Late again, huh?" Staggers toward them blindly, as if on stilts, scratched glasses bouncing around his neck. Wild blue eye glittering, awry. "Can you guys lend me a buck? I'm flat busted and need a taxi home. Been up all night out at Tiny Johnson's Wineybrook Farm. You two gotta get out there to meet Oscar Harpur the genius. He's expected today. He's the real thing. Deacon Quince—I'm his protégé—says Harpur's a polymathic genius like Leonardo or Isaac Newton and that crew. How about that buck? and a butt! I'm all whacked out after a night of halcyon joy and dissipation and debauchery at Wineybrook. Can ya get me some cupcakes? I'm starving!"

"They count every goddamn cupcake," Teddy says.

"Then forget it."

Punch clock seventeen minutes late, go back to heat-boiling ovens. Hurried hellos to bakers, look about carefully, snatch a hot whole wheat loaf unsliced, glide to the men's room. Crushed bread burns under Leo's jacket. In the john, rip the loaf, wolf it down moaning, the soft puffy dough molding into plugs in their cheeks. Suck, suck, spitlessly.

Teddy sniffs the toilet air. "There's that stink again!"

"Well, we know it's not us. It's still there the minute after we step outta the shower. Smells like stale innertubes to me."

"It hangs over the whole town," Teddy says. "It's amazing nobody mentions it. Hey, our new toothbrush vomiting technique's a life-saver—I feel terrific, Stanley."

"A real medical discovery, Ollie. Let's try it every morning. Whether we need it or not."

"We may be able t' drink more," Teddy says.

Weariness lingers—up with Stella past midnight studying their toy roulette wheel over stiff lime rickeys, muscatel, stolen swigs of gin in the kitchen. They get their delivery book, stack their truck with breads, cupcakes, donuts, rolls, and sponge cakes. All the deliverymen are gone already. Fat black Mouser watching them, floured fur filthy-gray.

"Wish this damn bakery baked some real food," Teddy says. "Danish! or almond cakes or oatmeal cookies. Nothin' but bubble-bread."

"Nice wheat flavor," Leo says, sucking.

They sigh at their loaded truck and stand behind the steering wheel, the sliding door racked wide for breezes. Leo pulls out Hokum Alley. Teddy's into his lunchbucket as the boxlike orange truck grips into North Main hill, and pops his bottle in the breeze.

Leo sips. *"Ahh!* that loosens my elbows. There's Flip!"

Singing Chinese jazz Leo-Teddy drives Flip to West Ellicott.

"I feel this fourwheel-drive's a helluva lot safer than your mother's Olds," Flip says in back.

"Stay off the cupcakes," Teddy tells Flip. "Hang on."

Leo turns onto Sixth, Flip flops to the wall. *"Warn* me!"

"I did!" Teddy says.

"I just love orange cupcakes," Flip says licking his fingers.

Unleaning twins steadfast, four feet planted into floorboards, Leo gripping the fat wheel, Flip flopping.

"Maybe this truck isn't safer!" Flip says. "What's that rattle?"

"Bottles," Leo says. "In the walls."

"Didja have to tell 'im?" Teddy asks. "Now you've told Tiny Johnson and Deacon Quince that we drive around with bottles in our walls. Not very smart."

"Hey, mum's the word with me!" Flip says.

"And next week it'll be broadcast at Community College," Teddy adds.

"I'm not that bad," Flip says. "I keep secrets worth keepin'. Hey, you guys gotta tell me more about the joys of coast-to-coast thumbing."

"We walked the aisle down in Dallas," Teddy says. "At a rescue mission—for three days of meal tickets and bed checks."

"The preacher got to you?" Flip asks.

"We were carried away," Teddy says.

"Felt that higher power!" Leo says.

"My head's solid cement when it comes to all that Bible guff. I've heard too many nuts spoutin' off. Don't wanna join 'em. Boiling oil wouldn't make me believe! But if you fellas ever need help with a drinkin' problem, I know a guy who can help you."

"Who?" Leo-Teddy asks.

"That's a goldarn secret!" Flip says. "When ya wanna know, just ask me about Bill W."

"We don't have any drinkin' problem, Flip," Leo says.

"We don't drink much whiskey," Teddy says. "We like a good burgundy."

"*If,* I said."

"It's religious with us," Teddy says.

"A musician's gotta have some kind of religion," Leo says. "Or else he sounds depressed."

"I can't stand depression," Flip says. "Whacks me out."

"That's what we're sayin'!" Teddy says. "Musicians shouldn't be depressed. We face it constantly. Even Louis really believes—that's why he has more windpower than any man on earth."

Flip's house. Early dawn glistens in heatbringing midsummer haze. "Boy, I can't wait until you guys meet Harpur," Flip says. "Maybe we can all go out to Wineybrook together. Well, hasty bananas."

Wave goodbye, drive back to town. Empty lots. Clouds drink up earthglow. King James, fast asleep.

Teddy drinks. "You noticed this vodka's beginnin' t' taste like water?"

"We didn't water this vodka."

"Sure we did," Teddy says. "Last night. Took a glass of vodka to bed with us."

"I don't remember finishin' the wine."

"We gotta switch to gin," Teddy says. "Juniper berries got more flavor than this damn vodka potato booze. I can taste the starch!"

"We gotta cut out that loaf of bread every morning. We gotta stick to hardboiled eggs and grapefruit for a month."

Teddy drinks. "By God, I *can* taste the starch." Drinks from Leo's bottle, testing. "Sure do!"

Leo drinks eighty-proof red vodka, once-watered. "Well, it's not hundred-proof," Leo apologizes for the vodka. "Gin sounds good though." Drinks, racks the bottle in the bracket beside their delivery book. *"Need it,"* he says, patting his bottle "—flavor or no flavor."

Glide bread into Elias's and the Victory, then restock

the all-night diners on Second Street down to City Line Diner in Falconer. Head out of town toward Kennedy.

"Well, there's my Kennedy hardon," Teddy says. "This road does it every time."

"It's boredom," Leo says. "And *loneliness*. We need New York."

"And Cynara. What's that smell?"

"Cows," Leo says.

"No. It's more like athlete's foot. Christ, it's—it's even out here in the country. . . . that *fungus!*"

A cloud bursts over Kennedy road. "My God!" Leo cries, "Somebody stole my wiper!"

Teddy's wiper scrapes perfectly. "Is this our truck?" he asks, listening for the wall clinkings.

"Can't see a fuckin' thing!"

"Stick your head out," Teddy says.

Leo leans out his open door, steering into the downpour. "I can't see around the curve ahead!"

"Lemme handle the wheel," Teddy says, "you hang out there." Teddy grabs Leo's waist as Leo leans straight into wet wind. "God, you're gettin' fat."

Leo grips the roof. "Start turnin'!"

Teddy watches rain pour through his open door. "Our french bread's gettin' soaked. I told you that wiper was loose."

Leo pelted heavily, jacket billowing. "*You're* perfect?" he shouts.

"*I* can't see a damn thing!" Teddy cries at the wheel.

"Pull right, you're on the wrong side of the road."

On the curve a gasoline truck passes from the front, the driver in a yellow mackintosh running down his window. He sees the breadtruckblur, no lights on, a man leaning past a window's solid water, the wrong wiper pounding away—his white eyes think hard at Leo-Teddy. Leo-Teddy smiles to him in the rain, waving. The driver shakes his fist.

Lightning. A reddish rogue cow gallops lowing toward a near barn, its hide a radium glow. A herd crowds mooing at the barn door. "*Lucky bitch!*" Leo cries.

Glide soaked into the Ellington Hotel at eight. Borrow on Hokum, bag three quarts of ale. "In case one apiece isn't enough," Teddy winks.

Windows ashine and dry, doors open, twins upright,

whipping down two-lane highway. Teddy holds an ale quart to Leo's mouth.

They toss hidden vodka pints from the walls out Teddy's door. Wet, sunshot hill, littered in rear-view mirror. High June morning, blue-boiling. More bottles sailing.

"God, it's a beautiful day," Leo says, Gordon's orange boar skimming the gravel. "Vodka, farewell!" he says.

"Nice t' get the truck even half cleaned out!"

"I'll drink to that."

Leo-Teddy holds the bottle up to Leo. Teddy's eyes close in the breezes. Fourwheeled drive gripping highway underfoot. Leo-Teddy yawns. Teddy stretches, raps ceiling. "We gotta rest after we get paid this afternoon. And shower—my socks are oozy. We can't go in and play tonight all whacked out—we'll fluff every other note. Sigy'll can us."

"He likes us."

Teddy laughs. "He knows how bad we play."

"Doesn't he pay us?"

"We gotta take lessons," Teddy says. "Then we can get union cards. Man, we should be rollin' in dough! When the hell we gonna make some real bread?"

"This time next year, we'll be over the hump. I feel it."

Teddy silent, then his eyes kindle. "What if I could take two dollar bills and suddenly fan them into two hundred bills?"

"I'd praise your cleverness."

"I mean I'd be fannin' and fannin' bills out like Jesus! Someday, Stanley. Someday."

Teddy sends a no-deposit plastic alebottle bouncing. Uncaps a fresh beauty. "If we play the Baghdad Lounge for ten years, he still won't let us play with our mutes off. I'm sick of waltzes."

"Look, ya keep this up and we'll be crackin' and flubbin' all night. Let's buck up. And we gotta rest before class today."

"Sure do," Teddy says. "Dya realize you passed out at the cafeteria table Wednesday night?"

"Fuckin' sherry sandbagged me."

"We'll never pick up any tail down there when we're in that condition."

"Let's keep our spirits up," Leo says. "Remember Leadbelly? He couldn't even read as much as we do now. I feel that really learnin' to play scales will be like a five-year-old kid learnin' Chinese. I mean if a five-year-old can read Chinese, *we* can learn t'read music."

"But why'd Sigy take us on in the first place? T' marry Wilma and Wanda? Those twins are twenty-two already, maybe still virgins. He wants 'em off his back."

"You're crazy!" Leo shouts.

"Why? Hey, *on* the road or *off* it—okay?"

"I'm a divorced father," Leo says scornfully. "Those twins won't even look at us. It's just like down at Community College, we're ten years older than all the available tail. We're gonna be lonely all our lives, Teddy. Adjust to it."

Teddy, silent pity. Pulling up to Pat's Superette at Winsor Hill. Glance uphill at Thelma's parents' house. Load loaves into delivery boxes, hurry up superette steps. Thelma's coupe stops on the hill.

"Hello, strangers!" she calls. Wry smile through car-window.

"Daddy!" Stuart calls standing on the front seat.

"I see you're getting up in the world," Thelma says.

"Hi there!" Leo-Teddy says. *Pang*. Son's bright blue eyes, weird Swedish smile. "Hey," Leo says, "we got weekend gigs at the Baghdad."

"Why don'tcha stop by tonight?" Teddy says. "Be our guest."

Thelma thinks twice. "Well, there's a little matter I want to talk about anyway. Okay."

Twin smiles. "Howdya like our truck, Stuart?" Teddy says.

"It's four-wheel drive!" Leo says. "And brakes."

"I'll betcha need that," Thelma says. *"Ahem!"*

Leo-Teddy waves as Thelma drives uphill to Grandma Karen's.

"Hmm," Leo says. "She thinks we're workin' beneath our abilities. I felt it. Multilingual Teacher's Ex-husband Drives Truck."

*"Gin*mobile," Teddy corrects.

Bald Pat calls behind his counter, "Hey, you guys're late today."

"Had a flat," Teddy lies. "Near Ellington."

Leo-Teddy racks fresh loaves. Hunger! Garlicky salami and pepperone spices. Buy a pepperone on Hokum money, cold six-pack. Pluck a bunch of watercress from Pat's sidewalk vegetable bins.

They drive up Swede Hill, find an inclination and drink ale from redplastic cups held low. Hit two stores. Chew watercress before hitting Fairmount Avenue Red and White.

"Fairmount, we are here!" Leo-Teddy sings.

Teddy chewing watercress, sucks hard for chlorophyll. "Chew some deodorant before we go in, Ygor."

"Your teeth are still purple from Wednesday," Leo says.

"You're terribly considerate," Teddy's Karloff lisp. "And so are yours. Very gr-rapey indeed, my friend."

Lips buttoned, Leo-Teddy services the rack, breath filtering out by molecules. Ale fumes spreading. "We stink like fresh horse manure!" Leo whispers. Both suck hard on watercress.

They wait outdoors for three customers to finish, then go in for payment. Teddy nudges cow-eyed Leo that payment's been made. *Hunh?* Glide out to truck.

Cross town. Gliding in and out of Spano's Super Market.

"Didn't we originally used t' hit Spano's before Fairmount?"

"I forget," Leo says. "We've rearranged our route so much, I can't remember the original. But we hit our *waterholes* just right."

Leo turns down Winsor Hill. "Now where dya think you're goin'?"

"I wanna see Stuart," Leo says.

"Not again this morning!" Teddy sighs. "Must you always be carried away by your impulses? Stay off the gutter."

"Thought ya knew what it felt like t' be a father."

"And a brother!"

Leo pulls up at Grandma Karen's. Empty yard, breaking sunshine.

"Let's go in," Leo says.

"Leo-Teddy!" Stuart cries through the screendoor.

"Let's not," Leo says suddenly. "We owe Karen for that fifth."

"It's my day," Teddy says. "We go in! We'll borrow from Hokum t' pay 'er back."

"We shoulda done that yesterday. Instead of borrowin' from her."

"You get scrupulous beyond my fathoming. Okay, we

don't turn in our route money until after we cash our paychecks. And let's not forget the Hotel Ellington ales or Pat's goodies. We gotta make those up too."

Climb walksteps, glide up blue porch. They carry Stuart into the kitchen as Suzie Beagle lies down growling and barking by the gas stove. Thelma's mother Karen is washing dishes in the blue and yellow kitchen.

"Dya know," she asks seriously, "I think you guys are really *sunburned!* Have a can of beer. I think there's one can in de box."

"Nothin' for us," Leo says. "Thanks."

"We just stopped by t' see Stuart."

"Ve have some blended vhiskey if you don't mind dat."

"We're workin'!" Leo says.

Leo-Teddy looks at himself strangely Swedenized in Stuart's face. Their round forehead, now square. Sensuous lips, tempered. Blue eyes framed in Swedish lids. *Innocent.*

Watch Stuart at the upright. "I think he's grown," Teddy says. "Sure has. Seems a lot quieter than we were."

"Introspective," Teddy says. "Poor kid!"

"He don't play the piano any better than you fellers," Karen says. "Of course, he's only t'ree."

Leo-Teddy sits at the piano, Stuart on Leo's neck. "Fu Manchu!" Stuart cries.

"That's the wrong chord," Teddy says. "Give it that pentatonic mystery or somethin'."

"Where the hell's that chord?" Leo searches the keyboard.

"This," Teddy says, repeats F-sharp liltingly. "Make it swing." Raps out Chinese bells in upper tones. Leo enters, stumbles. "It rocks," Teddy says. "Now vamp it."

Leo-Teddy sings—

> "Chinaman wash 'em laundry,
> Chinaman smoke 'em pipe,
> Loves his little twist of smoke,
> Oh he's feelin' ripe!"

"Fu Man-chu!" Stuart sings. *"Fu Man-chu!"*

"I got those Dr. Fu Manchu blues!" Teddy sings.

"Limehouse gal I'm cryin' to you!" Leo sings.

Leo-Teddy swings, "WON'T YA LOAD MY PIPE AND KICK MY GONG?"

"Limehouse gal, won't ya kick my gong?
Limehouse gal, won't ya kick my gong?
Limehouse gal, feel my habit comin' on!"

"D sharp," Teddy tells Leo.
"Don't confuse me!"

"Hello Cholly, she cries,
Whassa matter for you?

"I GOT THOSE DING-DONG HONG KONG
DR. FU MANCHU OPIUM BLUES!"

"Aren't you fellers workin'?" Karen asks.
"Yes!" Leo-Teddy rises glowing.
"One shot wouldn't hurt us," Leo says, Stuart on his shoulders.
Teddy agrees thoughtfully. "No, it wouldn't."
Leo, red-faced, asks Karen, "How 'bout one for the road?" He leans forward so Stuart can reach the bottle in the cupboard.
"You want one?" Teddy asks, shotglass out to Karen.
"Today I don't feel like it."
Leo pours. Teddy belts a shot, shudders. *"Green,"* he tells Leo. Leo downs blend. Stuart stares below at shots vanishing.
"Now that does it!" Leo tells Karen, tasting green whiskies. "But I need somethin' t' wash it down."
"We don't have time for the beer," Teddy says.
"Look, we'll cut our lunchhour short."
"We should go."
"Maybe Teddy's right," Karen says.
" 'Chopsticks!' " Leo insists.
Karen goes upstairs to rouse Julia. Twins glide silently to the cupboard, steal a round. Stuart puts the bottle back. *"Green agh! Too fast!"* Stuart repeats after Leo, shaking his head with foul face.
Tall Julia clomps down in sweater and skirt. "Hi guys," she says. "Thanks for the breakfast music! Who's been drinkin', Ma!?"
Twins nonchalant, casually superintense.

"Ya mean us?" Teddy asks. Sudden understanding floods him. *"Oh,"* he tells her, "we had a beer before we came!"

"Ya know," Karen says seriously, "I couldn't tell it, I t'ought you smelled like grass."

"Watercress," Teddy says. "Cleans your blood."

" *'Chopsticks,'* " Leo says. "Then we'll see about goin'. This is a great day, Teddy. We wanna remember it *for the rest of our life*—right?"

Leo-Teddy beats into "Chopsticks" without stumble.

"That don't sound like 'Chopsticks,' " Julia calls.

"These are our own variations!" Leo says.

"When we can't remember how to play it," Teddy says.

"Let's play it straight," Leo says.

"That's as straight as I remember," Teddy says. "I get lost in the upper registers. How's it go?"

Leo beats treble, corrects himself.

"I get it, I get it!" Teddy shouts.

"Somethin' like that," Leo says.

Twins beat "Chopsticks" too slow, start again. Leo-Teddy nods knowingly to himself. "Chopsticks" fast and chastened chimes whiskeybright. Teddy's Chinese variations in the high tones, hope ripening. Magnetic, weird Chinese gaiety fading. Sadness.

"Perfect!" Leo-Teddy cries.

"Best ever!" Teddy cries. "We *never* played it better!"

"Hey, wasn't dat somethin'," Karen says to her ex-son-in-law and Stuart's uncle. "You boys on your lunchhour?"

"Guess we better cut our lunchhour short, Teddy. Why don't we eat here?"

Leo-Teddy brings in his buckets, opens tomato-sardine-bleu-cheese-ryebread sandwiches at the table. Julia, Stuart, and Karen watch them crack and shell hard-boiledeggs. Stuart gobbles a cold hamburger patty, both hands stuffing.

"Chew your food, you lilla shaver," Karen says.

Stuart smiles, both cheeks lumpen. Stuffs in more.

"Are you *chewin'* dat?" Karen asks.

Shakes his head. Stuffing.

"He likes cold hamburger," Teddy says.

"Chew your meat," Leo says.

Stuart gulps. "Done!" he cries. *"Jello!"*

Julia opens the icebox, hands Stuart his lime jello.

"Chew your jello, Stuart," Leo lectures.

Stuart foulfaced over his jello. *"Green agh! Too fast!"*

"Who chews jello?" Teddy asks, uncorking purple vodka.

"Where'dja get the grape pop?" Julia asks.

"Don't give her any, boys!" Karen says. "You drink it all for yourselfs."

"Mo*ther,* I didn't *ask* for any!"

Teddy suddenly sweeps with good feelings. "I'd give ya some, doll, but it's gone flat."

"Say, that's not sodapop!" Karen says.

"I put in too much food coloring," Teddy says.

"Is that grape juice and milk?" Julia asks.

"You put food coloring in grape juice and milk?" Karen asks.

"Looks like paint," Julia says.

Leo-Teddy giggles, red-faced.

"What's so funny?" Julia asks.

"Hey, lemme smell dat!" Karen says. Sniffs dyed vodka. "Boy, are you guys somethin'!"

Leo-Teddy rocks and weeps, the hound growling at their bared teeth.

"What's so funny?" Julia asks.

Affection for Karen and Julia rises through Leo-Teddy as he laughs himself sickwhite. Wipes his eyes. "We *needed* that," Leo sighs.

"We should hit Fairmount Red and White," Teddy sighs.

"Didn't we hit Fairmount Red and White before we came here?"

"That was Wednesday."

"Goddamnit, we were just there two hours ago."

"Christ, you're right," Teddy says. "What was I thinkin'? Ah, well. *Listen to those hopsmokin' blues, da da!"*

"Limehouse gal, I'm cryin' t' you!" Leo sings.

"I GOT THOSE DING-DONG HONG KONG DR. FU MANCHU OPIUM BLUES!"

"No more!" Teddy cries. "We gotta hit the road."

Leo lifts Stuart's bubblepipe. "Can you blow bubbles? Where's cup?"

Leo-Teddy works soap in warm water, carries Stuart onto the sunstruck front porch. Billowing skins, runny green-violet bubbles streaming, lift in a flood from the porch. Float over the hot orange truck roof and grandly up Chadakoin valley. A huge oily rainbow udder dangles from Leo's pipe.

"Boy, these are real bubbles!" Teddy cries. "Not those damn plastic bubbles from Woolworth's."

Watch wobbling bubbleshadow, a white watery light in a dark ring on the porchsteps. Leo softly fills the soap-running bubble, larger and larger, Stuart wideeyed at silver quivering sunsparkle. A breeze catches the bubble. It slops loose and the great globe rises dripping sunlight.

"My God! it's still holding." Leo-Teddy glows at Stuart.

The bubble rises above low leafy branches, glitters bigger than a clear bowling ball against June clouds, lifts over the Swansons' roof.

"Where's it goin'?" Teddy shouts, saddling Stuart on his shoulders.

"Over the roof!" Stuart cries.

Leo-Teddy chases off the porch and through backyards after the bubble rising over Winsor Hill. Soft breeze lifting. Follow the bubble, sprinting uphill in the street. Water burning, the bubble skims over the hill houses and highest leaves. Twins gallop red bricks, surefooted, unafraid of slippery cinders. Bubble in the blue.

"It can't last!" Teddy cries. "I can't either."

"Let's keep after it."

Redwindowed bubble rising, higher, higher, Leo-Teddy cresting Winsor Hill Stuart points.

"It went down Falconer!" Leo pants.

"Can't go on," Teddy groans.

"Daddy, Daddy!"

Chase down Falconer, Stuart a ton on Teddy's shoulders. "Our runnin' days are over," Teddy gasps.

"Bubble!"

Pant to a stop on the playground.

"There, Daddy!" Stuart points. His searching blue eyes, Thelma's cat smile.

Bubble falls toward warm gravel. Superbelly swimming, stretching to split. Swelling upward-downward, blue membrane straining to stay soapbound. Eyes fix on the silver gut, its falling clear glass shimmer, thinning upward yawn for higher breezes. Nearly halving, quivering, bursts, violetgreen fading from air.

"Ahh!"

"Gone!" Stuart cries.

"Soapman got it," Leo says. "Boy, I'll never forget this day!"

"Boy!" Teddy says. "Really bountiful!"

"We're pretty damn late."

"You're not goin' a mile over 35 miles per hour!" Teddy warns, sharing Stuart with Leo's shoulder.

"I'm in good shape," Leo says. "Now aren'tcha glad we stopped?"

"Aw, this is what life's all about," Teddy agrees, trotting downhill.

Leo-Teddy breaks to a walk, heaving, beersweat pouring.

"How 'bout that cold one in the icebox?" Teddy asks. "Hell, let's leave it and pay Karen next week for that fifth."

They lift Stuart onto the blue-blue porch. Into hot sunblazed truck. Goodbye to Stuart behind the gate, his bubbles streaming. *Pang.*

"We better drink these warm ales before they explode," Teddy says.

Leo drives uphill, stops dead, swings back, drives downhill.

"We *been* to Spano's!" he rasps slapping the wheel.

"We're gettin' stoned."

"Believe me," Leo says, "the one or two people in town who don't drink won't notice us."

"If we don't dodge all over the sidewalks, *ahem!*"

"Just keep your *friggin'* hands off the wheel."

". . . . Yes, God, I *could* stand a cold one."

"You're reachin' me!" Leo says.

"If we zap down t' the Grapevine, we can have pizza with it," Teddy says. "With that baconfat crust."

"We *can't* go down t' Falconer!" Leo cries.

"I bet we could make it."

"Today's *payday,* Teddy! We gotta get back or the office'll be closed."

"You're right. Make it Kliney's for kummelwick."

"We're just runnin' in for a draught," Leo warns.

"All right, skip the fuckin' sandwich! *And* the pizza." Teddy sighs heavily, deprived. "But I can *taste* that baconfat crust!"

"I'm glad somebody here can make an adult decision," Leo says.

Drive brightorange breadtruck furtively through downtown noon traffic, far from any Hokum breadracks. Third and Main dims with cloudshadow, suddenly glows lemon. Doddering below their windshield, purplish Uncle John Pealow crosses slowly with the walkers, his walleye rolling blindly at the truck. Twins wave, honk hello to Stella's roomer. Uncle John snorts at the truck, raises his closed umbrella.

"Whatcha think you're doin'!" he hoots, hoarsely, and toils shaking to the curb. Pitted nose, blue veins, red picklebulb. Curious Leo-Teddy eyes his own noses in rear-view mirror. Brightening engorgement, clear daylit veins, oily pores.

At Kliney's Leo bolts into a golden parking space, his rear bumper hooking the front bumper of an orange Volkswagen. A harsh squeal spears him. Motor dies.

"That's *it!*" Leo says. "There goes my license—which I don't have anyway."

"We're just hooked, grandma, calm down."

"I'll back out."

"Hmm, we're not movin'."

"There's a police car comin'!" Leo cries.

Cops pass the oddly angled breadtruck, wait at the redlight, turn. Leo tries to back out silently. Bugfender crumples, shrieking.

They get out to read tombstones: the longish dent in the truckwall, the Volks bumper twisted like taffy. Twins hop onto the Volks bumper, pushing down hard, up down, up down. The Volks bumper screams from its bolts, snaps loose, strikes ringingly onto bricks. Fear rings Leo-Teddy.

"I feel that my adolescence has come to an end," Leo says.

"You may be right."

Leo-Teddy hangs the Volks bumper loosely in place. Drives truck into tarnished golden parking space.

"We gonna scoot outta here?" Leo asks.

"Skip the ales?" Teddy, thoughtful. "We been recognized."

"But we can't take a chance on the cops."

"You sure can't. But they'll throw the book at us if we drive off."

"We better wait," Leo says, "and offer to pay for repairs."

Teddy darkens. "What if he wants t' do it through our 'insurance company'?"

"Don't remind me! It's cash if we don't want Hokum t' know."

Leo-Teddy revamps the truck dent into a soft crush. Waits over ales on the first two stools in Kliney's fan-cooled cafe, watching for the Volks driver.

"I'm dizzy," Leo says. "Seein' spots!"

"Me too. We never been this late before! How long we gonna wait? Maybe we should just leave a phony note under his wiper."

Leo eyes the Volks windshield wiper long and hard, seeing a phony note. "We gotta pay."

"Why the hell'd ya drive in *forwards* anyway?"

"Why else I got fourwheel drive?" Leo says. "A perfect fuckin' parking place! I couldn't believe my eyes."

"Ya got excited thinkin' about these ales."

Twin smiles at Mr. Kliney at the taps—blue lips, bald head hanging and trembling.

"Shall we have a few beef on kummelwick?" Teddy asks.

"I'm too nervous." Taps for another draught.

"I thought you were dizzy," Teddy says.

"This one'll straighten me out."

Kliney skims foam with an ivory flatstick, fills glasses brimming. Leo in pain. "At least we have *Stuart's bubble* t' remember this day for!"

"And these ales," Teddy breathes thankfully. "Where'd we be without ale? Staff of life, a few cool ones daily. Christ, we mighta gone t' work for First National Bank and been stuck into a drive-in window. Let's chew some watercress before this bastard shows up—it may be a woman."

Tap for another ale. The Redcap Ale clock, rainbow electrons capering on its face, races, time draining as nerves shrink tight. Soft sleepy fireworks of pink and blue sperm. Glaze.

"What about the dent in our wagon?" Leo asks the barmirror.

"Sit tight until somebody asks."

"They may ask *today,*" Leo says. "Maybe we should quit this job."

"Well—we were sideswiped by a hit-and-run. In Ellington. They'll never check. Though if Colonel John wants to collect on the truck, he'll wanna see your license."

"My God, it's just a *dent,* Teddy! We could hammer it out and he'd never know!" Leo throws sweat with a finger. "Shit, why aren't we in New York with Cynara? Outta this fuckin' town!"

"Start fresh! Cut down on our intake."

"Drink on weekends," Leo says. "Stick t' simple beverages—in our own Village pad. *Only* on weekends—a fifth and a few six-packs."

"Maybe stop altogether," Teddy says. "Y'know—for half a year? Once we're outta this burg. Put everything inta savings! An' compose in peace for awhile! *GOD!"*

"Grand idea. I'm for it. Cut out booze for *a year.* Okay?"

"Ter*RI*fic." Teddy slaps the bar.

"Wish that goddamn bastard'd get back. I think we're gettin' smart at last. This was a lucky accident! We need a nest egg. Let's lower our sights. Set a $300 goal. Agreed? Las Vegas on $300. And no booze when we play the wheel. I'll bet we could get union cards in Vegas. Nevada must have terrifically low standards for musicians. Then maybe we could parlay that for a card from 802 in Manhattan. We gotta start somewhere! And I don't mean the Salvation Army. We play with Sigy at the Baghdad and that's band work, ain't it? We gotta gear up and produce, Teddy. Where's our fake-book of tunes for Chinese jazz?"

"We haven't perfected 'em yet," Teddy says. *"But they're comin'!"*

"Right. We gotta come up with an absolutely new style. Remember, there's not a single Chinese trumpet artist in the States. Nobody's ever thought of pentatonic jazz!"

"Only us."

"We start writin' the first day in Vegas. A *raft* of Chinese blues. First day—after our stint at the wheel."

"Terrific," Teddy agrees. Capering rainbow sperm melt and waste on the Redcap clock.

Leo-Teddy sees himself in a motel, composing, horns on bed and bureau, ink pot, music paper. Bottles, ice-buckets.

"Can't do it on *beer,"* Teddy says. "Why don't we treat ourselves? We'll lay in seven fifths of Hennessy the first day, a case of soda."

"Limit ourselves to one a day," Leo affirms.

"Cognac goes pretty fast—even with soda."

"We'll see. Maybe we better wait out front. That Volks bastard might think we been drinkin'."

"One last one?" Teddy asks.

"I don't feel good."

"Me neither. Maybe we need a sandwich. An alibi for bein' in here."

"Smart thinkin'," Leo says. "We'll *say* we had one."

Old Mr. Kliney, squirrelbacked, eggskulled and shuffling, punches up their last ale, slides change over the bar, his sleeves gartered, long fingers shaking. "Goodbye," he says.

"Got any watercress?" Leo asks Kliney.

"Watercress? You want wild parsley," Kliney rasps, beckoning.

Follow Kliney's slow shuffle. Big old wooden icebox. Kliney presses a trembling bunch of pale wild parsley on Leo-Teddy. "Been eatin' onions?" he asks as they chomp.

Parsley's cool, piercing camphor fills their lungs.

"Sardines," Leo says.

"Nothin wrong with sardines," Kliney says.

"We like t' be careful for our customers," Teddy says. "Maybe we'll bring our mother down for supper tonight. Have a dozen beef on kummelwick—get our fill of 'em at last! Let's go."

Leo-Teddy passes the ale and beer taps, lingers, walks on, stops hard. "Perfect ale weather," Leo says.

Teddy looks out at the breezy blue June day.

"It'll wash down this parsley," Leo adds.

"And leave us stinkin' again. *Hey, look!*"

Hurry outdoors. Orange Volks gone.

"Let's get lost!" Teddy says.

"Maybe we'll get away with it!" Leo cries.

Lock hands for luck. Leo shoots out nervously, turns up Washington Street hill. Waiting for the redlight at Fifth, Leo-Teddy is shocked white. Three police cars are parked out front of *their house,* a fourth squad car in Rose Alley. Guilty sunlight.

"My God!" Teddy cries. "We were *recognized.*"

"It's only a minor traffic accident!" Leo shrieks.

"Maybe we should just drive to Hokum. Pick up our pay and come home. Say we're sick."

"We *tried* t' go on deliverin'—but we're sick!"

Leo-Teddy grips his spirit, drives into Hokum's silent garage. Parks. All the other trucks are unloaded, at rest for the weekend. Shaking twins unload their stacks of undelivered breads. Floury Mouser sits up yawning on the cold oven, fixes his bitter green stare on fourfooted Leo-Teddy. Twins hide a warm quart of ale in the truck wall, go up to the office.

"Maybe the office heard about us already," Teddy says. "My God, we might be walkin' into real trouble. Maybe a clean breast is best."

"Didn't get his license number. Slipped our minds, right? We have *our side* of the story."

"What's our side?" Teddy asks. "Oh shit, just don't lisp!"

Bertha, Colonel John Hokum's heartstopping secretary, seats Leo-Teddy on a bench. Bosom locked up in see-through blue blouse and bra, diamond wedding ring, baby picture on desk. Porcelainblue eyes.

Teddy whispers dismally, "How can one man alone deserve all that?"

"Remember that knockout wedding ring I got Thelma?" Leo rasps.

"Oh, she was thrilled. Until we mentioned they were rhinestones."

"Look—we were waitin' for this guy and it *just dragged on.*"

Feast on blond Bertha of chinadoll eyes, bowels longing. Her father in terrific trouble. Manslaughter. Driving while. . . . Leo-Teddy breathes lightly through half-closed lips, hardly exhaling ever. "Smile," Leo whispers, "let's not stain her picture of us." Smiles, their eyes a feasting windshield of loveglances. Bertha smiles back. Gentlemen nip up crumpled pantlegs, cross knees, uncross, can't sit, up, wait by window, impatient as a horse. Sweating, keeping down the waitingroom's alcohol content. Misery rising, horseheads sinking. Bertha's cups of honey, heavy-hanging yellow hair. Oh hunger!

Colonel Hokum, a retired young fighter-interceptor turned baker, greets Leo-Teddy with his dark chiselsmile. His desk, his flags, his jet-fighter unit pennant. Commanding cloudy eyes, granite heart.

"You're not here for a raise?" he warns.

"No," Teddy croaks. "We didn't finish our route today."

"We had an accident," Leo whispers. "I—*urp,* pardon me—drove into a lady's fender!"

"Bumper," Teddy says.

"Where?" Colonel Hokum rises—stumpy, erect ape, agleam within.

"On Wes' Second," Leo slurs.

"East," Teddy says, hitting the *t.*

"East," Leo says. Head swimming, stare at Colonel's family photo.

"Why didn't you finish your route?"

"Her fender came off," Leo says. *"Bumper!"*

"How hard ya hit 'er?"

"Oh I was parking!" Eyes white innocence.

"But our bumpers got hooked," Teddy hears himself say. "So we stood on her bumper to get it loose and it came off. We didn't *knock* it off—it fell. It was just a little Volks!"

"So we were waitin' for the owner t' show up," Leo says without breathing. "Well, what can we say?—time just *dragged on."* Inhaling. "And finally when we went outdoo—*uh,* when we came *in*—t' phone the office!—this damn orange Volks drives off with the bumper balanced on front."

"Don't even know who we hit," Teddy says.

"Damaged," Leo corrects.

"Didn't get her license," Teddy says.

"How'dya know it was a woman?" Colonel Hokum asks. Crosses round his desk toward them—a human ice floe.

Leo-Teddy shrugs, binding breath, lips buttoned. Red flashes prickle skin. Blue eyes withering them. Their old friend Jack Hokum of Lakeview Avenue days!—who first *sought* their friendship.

"The truck's all right?" Colonel Hokum asks.

"Just a little hammering out," Leo says. "Do it ourselves."

"And the windshield wiper fell off. It's nothin'," Teddy judges.

"But why didn't you finish your route?"

Smile, please, Jack, please smile...

"We didn't think they'd want bread this late in the day!" Leo says.

"Maybe we were wrong?" Teddy asks Leo.

"Teddy, we thought we were doin' the right thing—comin' right back t' report the accident."

"Well, did you get West Ellicott?"

"No," Leo says.

"Lakewood?"

"No," Teddy says.

"Celeron?" the Colonel asks.

Leo-Teddy feigns a sigh, not breathing, heads hanging.

"But that was this morning." Colonel Hokum gleams. "You're through with the Falconer Red and White by nine-thirty or ten at the latest."

"Oh more like ten-thirty," Teddy fixes.

"Sometimes quarter to eleven," Leo drawls. "We have a very long route from Ellington t' Lakewood—longest in the fleet!"

"Not that we're complainin', Jack," Teddy says.

Colonel Hokum smiles straight through Teddy. *Engaged to their sister Millie. Jilted her. Millie three days weeping. Smile, Jack,* Leo-Teddy pleads massively, eyes sweat-reddened, lips pursed innocence.

"What you two get me into! Well, don't worry about it. We're covered, whatever happens."

Teddy grins. "I'd love t' see her face when that bumper drops off! Oh, sorry."

"Lemme think about this," John says. "Didya report it to the police?"

Leo-Teddy cannot move, fake, or bluster.

"No!" Leo croaks. Blushing.

"Didn't know what t' say." Teddy blushes, back running wet, hands clenching. Smile, Teddy.

"Well, the world isn't gonna end over this," Leo sighs. "But I feel pretty damn stupid, John."

"Don't John me. What were you doing on East Second?"

"Oh, that's a shortcut." Teddy coughs, diverted by a faraway chimney with a sparrow on it. Divine, that sparrow?

"Between which stores?" John-Jack asks mildly.

"Uh, between where we had lunch and where we were goin'," Leo says.

"Lunch? When do you eat lunch?"

"Quite *early* today," Leo admits.

"But—what time did this accident happen?"

"Gee," Leo guesses, "—today. Early this afternoon."

"I can't understand why ya didn't get farther than the Falconer Red and White," John says. "Didya stop off in Ellington to shoot rabbits?"

"Took a long lunch hour," Teddy says. His breast clean at last. "We were tryin' a new dogleg in the route. Didn't pan out."

"Piss poor," Leo agrees. "Let's not try to improve on the route after this."

John looks out his window at his garaged trucks. Remembers his father's horsedrawn delivery wagons—these very yards. Same sunlight. Coarse oats puffing from nosebags, stables fuming in morning chill. Horseshit pyramids sweetening Third and Main.

"Whatever made you boys want to drive a breadtruck? Didn't ya know how early ya'd have to get up? And that it might cut into your drinking time? *Lay off* the Colored Elks on my time. Or you'll lose my friendship. Bakery first—it's family, see?" Leo-Teddy, decent boys, nodding. "You boys amaze even me. Not that you're hopeless. Don't you like driving for me? Would ya rather work in the bakery? It's clean work. But hot, I'm afraid."

"Somebody complain about us?" Leo asks.

"Nonsense," Teddy says. "Our service is excellent."

"We don't take long lunchhours usually," Leo says. Eyepains, breathpains.

"Jack, the truth is, our life's an open book. It's true!" *Pains.*

"We just stopped off on Orchard Street after the Falconer Red and White—t' see Stuart." Cleanbreasted Leo-Teddy searches John's fatherhood. "We were playin' the piano and blowin' soapbubbles, frankly . . . and the time flew!"

"We're sorry about it." Teddy groans at their stupidity.

"But don't think we're givin' poor service," Leo says.

"With us, it's Hokum first," Teddy says, glinting. *Chokepains.* "When we're workin' we give a little extra. A smile to all. Really! We're all smiles on our route—and conscientious to a fault."

Leo scratches his head. "I'll feel a lot better when this accident's settled."

"I'll go halves on the damages," Teddy says. "You can dock us both, John—Jack."

"For what?" Jack asks warmly. "What damages?"

"Whatever it costs," Leo says. "We're perfectly willin' t' be docked."

"It's only fair to Hokum," Teddy says. "Your insurance premium—"

"I can't report this accident to the insurance company!" John laughs. "We don't have a suit, so let's not project one. But I think you should call the police and tell 'em about it. Let's keep covered."

Leo dials the desk sergeant downtown, on John's phone, reports his accident. Teddy burns with Leo's pains. Hot-iron daylight, spirits parched. *Long long long rest! Not rested for years!* Jack puts on his golf hat. Leo-Teddy longs for John-Jack's warmgoing friendship.

"No, I did *not* leave the scene of the accident," Leo tells the desk sergeant. "I waited over an hour!"

"Over an *hour!*" Teddy croaks into the phone. "We got a witness!"

Leo-Teddy hangs up, promises himself deep sleep. Balm.

"We gotta go down in person," Leo says, hoarsening. Teddy claps his forehead, groans at the news. "Well, okay," he adds, "if we gotta."

"Who's your witness?" Jack asks.

". . . A Mr. Kliney," Teddy says, bloodfaced.

"Kliney!—All right, I'm not dockin' you for anything." Jack says. "I'll bail you out once more but that's it. Gimme a call at the golf course if anything happens."

Leo frowns seriously. "Phone you at Moon Brook?"

"Or at my home. Keep me posted." Jack bores into Teddy. *"You* phone the customers you missed. See if any of 'em want a special delivery."

Their hearts sink. Colored Elks fade, cool amber ales removed afar.

"Gee, they'll be closin' in a couple hours," Leo says.

"Wake up, this is their weekend delivery!" John says. "We can't leave 'em high and dry. Anybody you can't service today, service tomorrow morning. *Early*."

Leo-Teddy nods. Sure oversleep—must stay up all night, or fail John. Bertha stands in the doorway, sweepy Italian hat in hand. Cataracted left eye. Her father's day in court, long past, staining her. "Will that be all, Colonel Jack?"

"See you Monday, Bertha. And don't colonel me. You can use my phone," he tells Teddy.

"We gotta go down for our delivery book." Teddy hesitates.

"All right," Jack says, "go down for it!"

Leo-Teddy quickly glides out after Bertha, follows her downstairs. Her beauteous jouncings—heartbreak! Gasp, quietly reviving, sucking in great bags of air. Lock inner arms for steadiness, brains popping, bursting. Hope spearing them—to hold her bones, that evenly folded meat and fat, that honeyhair. Narrow wooden stairs, pass a window. The whole sunny day canted, sliding into a chasm. Silently get delivery book—*strong men ready to weep.* Bertha!—run through a brick wall to hug you for five seconds. How long must we go womanless, O Lord? Sniff for beer odors, watch Colonel Jack walk toward them eying the truck's dent. Leo-Teddy grips his nerves as John looks inside the truck.

"Sure ya wouldn't like to work in the bakery?" he asks. Smiles, at last.

Relief fills Leo-Teddy. "Jack, we've quit drinkin'—right, Teddy? So don't worry about that anymore."

"We've *finally* settled down to work on our opera," Teddy sighs.

"That's good to hear," he says. "Don't forget to phone me."

Colonel Jack rolls back his Chevy roof, snaps it down. Drives out, golf clubs on back seat, a warning fist to his ear—*phone!*

"Now there's a right guy," Teddy says.

"Real gentleman," Leo says. "We fibbed a bit, maybe, but we were *essentially* honest with him. It pays, it really pays."

"Oh sure," Teddy agrees. Looks in delivery book. "Shit! This is eighteen phone calls. We could drive it faster!"

Leo-Teddy clumps upstairs to Jack's office. Offices empty, Bertha's picturebaby beaming. Innocent. Twins glance over their shoulders, close the Colonel's door tight.

"Now," Teddy asks, "where's he keep the body hidden?"

Look about the Colonel's files, drawers, desk. Bottle, bottle?

Leo gnashes his teeth. "I can't go down to the police station! We *meant* to go but we just didn't get there physically, how's that?"

"How's what?"

"Didn't we phone in to show honorable intentions?"

"Sure did," Teddy says. Looks behind, then inside watercooler. Leo tries closet. Locked. Guilt steals over Leo-Teddy, staring at Colonel John's family photo. *Thirst!*

"So, let's hit the phone," Leo says.

"We need a fast trip to The Brass Rail."

"My God, we'll never get outta here!" Leo cries.

"Look. We're not gonna deliver anything this afternoon, not after eighteen calls. We're too thirsty for this horseshit. Let's do our phonin' at home over some *icy* lime rickeys."

"But he really wants his fuckin' bubblebread delivered," Leo says. "He mighta fired us today, Teddy."

"So?—we got today's *paychecks*. Anyway, he'll stand still for this. Keep cool. What happened, Stanley, is that we took so long phonin', we didn't have time to deliver before goin' to class. It's admirable that we put education before employment."

"We know what's important," Leo says, amazed with craving.

"We really do," Teddy states, checking under the desk. "This bullshit is not for free spirits. Truthfully, I'm gettin' very strong waves from Vegas."

Paychecks steaming, soggy white suits head straight for The Brass Rail for early evening starters. Route money dwindles on doubleshots. Must cash checks! Banks closed. Pant back to the garage, drive breadtruck to Colored Elks for fast cash. Race in for bow-tie tumblers of bourbon. Lifesavers. Lavender club, damp blacks smiling in sleazy pinstripes. Janitors, yardhands, twins welcome and merry, fat men on Sugar Hill. Teddy's check is cashed, Leo's saved in rigorous new savings policy—hot flashes for Vegas. Back to the bakery. Park. Saved.

"Sonofabitchin' John don't dring at the office, I guess," Teddy says. "An' a jet pilot at that!"

"Well, his father's a minister."

"That's no excuse for a dry desk."

"He's not a bad guy," Leo says. "We should take him to the Colored Elks sometime, as a treat. Show him our appreciation."

"Help break his zombie routine," Teddy says. "Work and golf! Frankly, he's not the kinda guy I like t' *drink* with. My God, my socks are mush. Let's get home, face the music, shove off fast. Baghdad beckons."

Blue twilight falls on Stella's huge white rooming house as Leo-Teddy glides up Rose Alley. Comfort ahead, cash in Teddy's pocket.

"Gotta rehearse," Leo says. "We can't go on cold tonight."

"Whole high register's shot," Teddy agrees. "One solid week's practice'd do it." A shout burns from Teddy's blood. "MY GOD! We left our delivery book at the Colored Elks!"

"SHIT!" Leo rages.

"Left it right on the stool beside me. Our memories are collapsing like shit." Taps his temple. "Sometimes it's touch and go with us!"

Sky turns brown, clouded with stool. Strengthless, breathless.

"D'we dare borrow the car?" Teddy sighs. Slaps his pocket for extra reassurance their cash is there, wadded flat.

"We *walk,*" Leo says. "She's just had the taillight repaired after our last fiasco. We'll get a fifth of Dixie Bell eighty-proof vodka for her and a pint of hundred-proof Smirnoff for us. Finish off her watered bottle and pour the Smirnoff pint into her empty fifth—it *looks* like more. But we can't touch the Smirnoff until we kill that watered piss."

"But I love that Smirnoff label! It means somethin' to me. You can't pour Smirnoff into a Dixie Bell bottle—*Christ!*"

"We steam off the labels and dress up the Dixie Bell bottle."

Leo-Teddy turns still again, walks sweating back up stony Rose Alley. "Where's the delivery money?" Leo asks.

"This is it. Everything."

"But where'd it go!"

"I dunno. We didn't collect all that much today."

"Whew," Leo says. "Frankly, money's just too trivial to agonize over. Though we're not gonna have much left!"

"We better replace Stella's fifth outta your check. *Monday.*"

"We're savin' *my* check."

"Let's be realistic," Teddy says. "My God, Leo sometimes you just—*whew!"*

Green showermist hushes through milkleaves. Soothing wind, steaming forehead prickle, sweet life on his tongues.

"Thank God our morning hangover problem's ironed out," Teddy praises himself. "That toothbrush technique's a godsend."

"Shoulda thought of it earlier. I dunno where our brains are."

Twilight glide onto back porch. White springmetal chairs where Leo-Teddy typed his *Tales from the Precipice* libretto, afloat on cold ale, burgundy gallons. Pang. Into bottlepink kitchen. Stella's Fridaynight drinks with Ragnar, star roomer, hopeful suitor still married.

"Eyah, here are de boys, *Stel*la." Ragnar waves stumped knuckles—fingers lost over long years in King James furniture factory saws and presses. "Help yourselfs to a drink, fellas. I yust stopped down to start de evening vid Stella."

"Before he closes up Main Street," Stella says.

"Vy, how you talk, Stella!" Ragnar says. Stickumed hair stiff, tight, straight back off his skull like woodshavings. "I yust go out for a schnapps or two."

Stella's spine straight, hairwaves graying. She gulps wonder. "Do you gentlemen know that this house was surrounded by the police this afternoon? In broad daylight! Why, I was *white."* Shoves shotglass. *"If* you please, mister," she tells Ragnar.

"Your names vill be in all de papers from King Yames to Buffalo!" Ragnar says. Lips clench over his great club jaw.

"So what happened?" Leo says.

"Uncle Yohn Pealow is in yail!"

"Oh, you're getting it all mixed up," Stella sighs. "He's in Gowanda, not jail, my good man."

"Eyah, eyahh!"

Leo-Teddy cracks cubes flying, washes two from the floor, floods two glasses with Ragnar's greenblended horsepiss. Strength rising.

"What's Uncle John done?" Teddy asks.

"Why, he's been writing threatening letters to the mayor," Stella says. "What's more, he had a doublebarreled shotgun! And cartridges! Why, doesn't that daze you?"

Leo-Teddy says, *"Korsakov's Syndrome!* Picklebrain!"

Ragnar, horrified. "Vy, ve all t'ought he vas in A.A.!"

"He was *not,*" Stella says. "Look in my trash barrel. You won't trust your senses!"

"May I have a glass of icewater?" asks Dr. Ahmad Basra, young Iraqi brain chemist-roomer. Tailored; crisp brown eyes. "And a knife," he adds, "I want to kill myself."

"Haff a drink," Ragnar says.

"No, just icewater, thank you very much. Actually, I am quite lonely. I have fantasies!" Smiles, coolly studying himself as an acid. "I am very *eentent* tonight! Perhaps eet was all the police cars while I was reading *Crime and Punishment* in my room. I am normally highly repressed, nothing moves me. But when I see those cops' eyes over their guns, my knees turn to noodle soup. I was extremely emotionated. But the interns deed not even use their strait jacket. They just walked Uncle John down to their ambulance and drove off. And now—hees room is empty, *phtt!*"

"Tell these boys what the police found in the garret!" Stella says.

"Thees ees like Dostoievsky!" Ahmad says. "He has one-hundred cartridges and two bags of spanish peanuts—hundreds of eendividual peanuts wrapped in teenfoil. Complete proteins for energy. Very interesting. What does he want these proteins for?"

Leo-Teddy sees Uncle John Pealow, his bloodshot walleye rolling, oiling his bores with rod and patch. Lipless upper lip coldly ridged, cracked at the corners. Warts raging on red face as he sits pulling hairs from his blue nosebulb. Clips stock to barrel. Delicately unwraps nut, nibbles protein for headlong energy high. *BLAM! BLAM!*

"Believe me," Stella says, "there's something wrong with that man."

"But Uncle John doesn't drink," Teddy says.

"He was looped to the gills today," Stella reports.

"Vy, he vas Yekyll and Hyde!"

Leo sighs. "Uncle John Pealow has too much will power to drink."

"Told us he couldn't even stand hard cider," Teddy says.

"Don't think he wasn't nipping," Stella says. "I could smell his breath through a closed door. They found twenty-four empty pints as part of his stash."

"He vas not goot in de head." Ragnar taps his head for utter clarity.

"Crazy people shouldn't drink," Stella says. "Even I know that. It's like giving whiskey to an Indian."

"We're part Indian," Teddy says.

"Keep that to yourself, my son. That's like being colored."

"Ah, eet ees in the evening paper!" Ahmad says. "And a quite beautiful photograph too." He returns brimming from the front porch with a *Post-Journal.* "All our names are spelled correctly!"

"My stars!" Stella cries—a three-column Staffoto of Scene of the Arrest, 210 West Fifth St. *Home!* Poised and firred, sculpted in sunshadow by a nameless P-J salon artist. Stone porch, white chairs. White arrow at garret window. Crime.

"Vy, you could knock me over vid a fedder. Dat is vort' framing, Stella." Ragnar sighs reverently. "Yust shade out de arrow vid a pencil."

"I think not," she says.

Leo-Teddy puts on reading glasses. By TONY TRIPI. Reads first paragraph three times. Words floating away. Takes off glasses, unable to read.

"He's been in and out of trouble like a fiddler's elbow," Stella says.

"Hm!" Teddy says. "He told us, 'I've used up all my tickets, boys. A.A.'s all that's left!' "

"Classical niacin deficiency," Ahmad says. "You notice his skin is like sunburn? Hands dry and scaly? Tongue coated, breath foul? He complained to me, 'I get dizzy for no reason! Can't sleep! I got mouth sores, constipation, I'm all nerves and nightmares, Dr. Basra! I hear pistol shots, telephone bells, soft door chimes, and a weird radio whine from outer space—you know that ringing in the ears? Sometimes I feel awful weird, doctor!' Classical symptoms of lack of B-vitamins. Thees causes more schizophrenia than all the neuroses put together."

Leo-Teddy swimming. "Hey, we're late!"

Flip Newquist says, "Can I come into this beautified annex to Gowanda?"

"We're all sane here," Stella claims. "Or we think we are."

"You guys drivin' down to Community College?" Flip asks.

"Too late," Leo says. "We gotta warm up at the hotel."

"I am very eentent," Ahmad says, "especially to find a girl to study the classical effects of beer with."

Leo-Teddy downstairs to cellar. "Don't spill your drink," Teddy warns. "We shoulda turned on the light."

"I have eagle vision."

"I melt steel bars."

Pink bedlamp, caterpillared bedspread, two hairy wave-rippling worms. Twins peel off sticking socks.

"You boys like your socks ripe," Flip says. "I change mine every day like a dratted slave."

"I belted too much of Ragnar's bottle," Leo says. "Ready t' heave."

"Am I drinkin' your drink?" Teddy holds a glass to the light. "Mine was darker."

"Drunker," Flip says.

"Le's get up t' the bathroom fast," Leo says. Slips off his pants. "I don' wanna use the laundry drain." Looks about madly. "How can I lose a drink! Let's nab the watered vodka."

". . . . Why don't you guys wise up?" Flip asks.

" 'Bout what?" Teddy says.

"If ya don't know, I can't tell ya. Goldarn it, I'm goin' upstairs and get dissipated! I only wish I could say what I know."

"Who's this guy Bill W.?" Leo asks.

"His name's Bill Wilson," Flip says. "He's quite a guy."

"Never heard of him," Teddy says.

"He's from New England," Flip says. "He used to drink more than you two guys put together."

"Hurry!" Leo whispers, "I don't need a toothbrush this time."

Beerfat twins jiggling in jockeyshorts, carrying suits, shirts, clodhoppers, burst barefoot through kitchen into pantry, nail vodka, rush up back stairs to the big white fir-shaded bathroom. Door closed, Leo lifts seat, spews into bowl. "Really fat," Teddy sighs holding him.

Leo bittermouthed over greenwhiskied water, nose drooling. Reads the toiletseat's printed legend—

CRANE

Teddy wreathes Leo's back, his other arm curving between bowl and wall. Leo stiffens, retching again. Salt red eyes. "Dry heaves," he whispers.

"Is that more blood?"

"It's not pizza. Water!"

Teddy runs a glass, unscrews the vodka for himself. "Wash your face," he says, "I don't dare get into the shower with you this dizzy."

Leo sips water, then painfully from the bottle. Heaves vodka and water out mouth and nose. Teddy sips stoically, toasts his enlarging nose in the mirror while Leo swats water on his face. "Fuckin' optical illusion!" Teddy mutters.

"What is?" Leo whispers.

"These jowls! I'm too young for jowls."

Leo wads his own puffed pink face, crinkles red swollen eyes. "Nah. It's just a doublechin."

"We gotta get strict about the diet."

"Right." Leo drinks. "That helps!"

"We better lay off the Dixie Bell until we pick up some hamburgers. *Let's concentrate on gettin' outdoors with our horns in our cases.* And hope we'll, *ahem,* get a grip on ourselves."

Leo's hanging head stares about the bathroom—a skulled cow. "Sure can't phone in sick," he says. "Le's take shower. We go work with our hair soaked, we'll stay sober."

"An' look like gangsters."

Step into deep graysteel white tub, close white curtains. Peace. "Jus' medium hot," Leo says. *"Please."*

"Scalp massage cuts fuzzy thinkin', right? We walk outta this house pretty near sober. Right?"

"An' no booze while we practice down at the hotel—le's get that straight," Leo says. "Boy, I got red eyes, huh?"

"You have. Often."

"Las' one before we shower?" Leo asks.

"Ya just said we wouldn't!"

"How can anything I said anytime in the past apply t'

now? Will ya tell me that? When I feel a true thirst? Don't be insane, wouldya mind?"

"Now we're not gettin' inta trouble tonight, Stanley. We'll drink *after* the shower."

"Then le's just rinse."

"Turn it to as hot as *you* can stand," Teddy says. "'S that all?"

"I wanna drink before this torture! Then I won' feel th' heat." Stretches for vodka on toilet tank, misses. Bottle bounces from lid into toilet bowl, loudly. "My God!" Teddy cries.

"It *didn't* break," Leo insists. "Fuckin' lilyliver."

Scramble from tub, loosen upsidedown vodka from bowl.

CRANE

"Saved some," Leo says.

"Now it's really watered. Can we drink it?"

"Why, tha's pure wellwater."

"You first." Teddy eyes the level carefully. "How is it?"

"Watery." Leo drinks on.

"You're cuttin' inta my half!"

"Needed that! Lot better now. Cool as branchwater! —*mmm . . .*"

"Don't wanna get sick t' my stomach," Teddy says in the tub, eying the bottle closely. "Sediment," he says. "Some kinda fishfood."

"Le's not have broken glass in the tub again," Leo warns.

"Shut up!—ya want me t' pour my half down the drain?"

Leo shields himself with a towel. "Take your fuckin' steambath."

Teddy measures him finely. "You think I'm selfrighteous?"

"Please shower, shithead."

Hot streaming steam, Teddy red awake.

"'S comin' through the towel!"

"Five more seconds!—*aaAAgh! Agghh! Aggg*HHHH!"

"I'm boiled!"

"That did it!" Teddy turns tap. "Here, cool off."

"NOT SO COLD!"

* * *

Leo ties a rosetted blacksilk necktie on his redsatin shirt. Crimps his fat knot, stares through mirrorsteam at Teddy—deep wonder.

"What're ya lookin' at, Hyde?" Teddy asks.

"Am I Hyde?"

"I never know."

Leo grunts. Charcoal pinstripe, stale hot-iron crotch-stink. Brush bankers' suitcoats, eye rosettes on black silk, valentine shirts. Filthy allweather clodhoppers, steel-tipped. Homburgs. Leo gives himself a hardeyed sheriff's squint in the mirror, deepens it to Promethean intelligence. Teddy watches, longsuffering.

Hurriedly sop floor, tissue a gleam into the sink and mirror, police the toiletseat for vomit curds.

CRANE

"What're we doin'!" Teddy cries. "We should be at Fourth and Washington by now!"

Push shoppingcart, tall black trombone case stickered genius, rich brown chesterfield trumpet case, fake-books, mysterious paper bags. Utterly clear greenevening, yellow-starred.

Leo coughs waking wonder, carrying front-end of shopping cart down steep cracked stone steps to Hotel King James alley. Steps flooding upward, Teddy with the weight. "Steady," Teddy says, "let's not rest until we hit bottom." Greasy rainfilminess.

Profound wonder flooding from clear evening of a moment past, now misted. "What's in that bag?" Leo asks, oddly clearvoiced.

"Ragnar's Four Roses. He won't miss it, they're carting Martha home. She passed out over her sherry."

"Martha!" Leo says. "She's not comin' until Saturday."

"Today is Saturday, Hyde."

". . . . I feel absolutely *sober.*" Breathes deeply, dry-mouthed, lightheaded. Sober!

"Ya should—you just had your first drink of the day." Teddy belts from the Four Roses bag. "My God, that's foul. Let's dash over to Fisher's for a fifth of that one-fifty-one West Indian. We can't drink this piss, it's degrading."

"How much money do we have?"

"After the rum we'll still have thirteen bucks and the fresh gallon under the cellar steps."

"We have an uncracked gallon?"

"Tomorrow's Sunday, Hyde! Frankly, I could drink a keg. But if I had any moral courage at all, I'd throw this piss away."

"Well, let's go careful on that West Indian voodoo juice." Leo foresees rum delirium with fear and desire.

"Oh, that proof stuns the metabolism," Teddy agrees. "But we can handle it. We're cold sober. My tongue tasted good all afternoon."

Stormgreen sky boiling. Run over side alley.

"I sure hope you got 'Star Dust' outta your system," Teddy says.

"Did I play 'Star Dust'?"

"Sigy gave us his first and last warnin' about unauthorized debuts!"

Into Fisher's, breathing heavy. Teddy snags the long longed-for rum fifth, pays fast, holds dynamic love—one-hundred-fifty-one proof. "We left our instruments in the alley," he explains to Fisher's new clerk.

"Alley?"

"Across the street. We're hornplayers! Catch us at the Baghdad. What's your name?"

"Ray."

"Great t' meetcha. We're Leo and Teddy. Dig ya later, *R-r-roy!*"

Uncorking by the horn cart.

"Well," Teddy says, "we laid in a solid foundation with Roy. First impressions count. Don't give up the ship," he toasts Leo. Sips one-hundred-fifty-one proof lovefire. Gasps bitterly, lobster-eyed.

"UGGGH!*—Delicious!*" Leo whispers, lanced. "That sting has no bottom to it!"

"Fortitude! Look, we're takin' in too many bottles. Let's finish the Four Roses."

". . . How'd my 'Star Dust' sound last night?"

"Exuberant. But there were a few cracked notes."

Leo's shoe splits on the arch. *"Shit!"* Grits his teeth at tragically snapped shoelace. "Goddamn cheap shoelace!" Leo-Teddy sips first, dips to shoelace. "Well, I'm glad we slept today."

"Two hours ain't much," Teddy says.

"Two hours! But I feel so good."

"Well, that was our first pussyhop in five months."

"Christ," Leo says, replacing thricebroken fuzzy lace of knots. He freezes, drained, agape. *"Our* first—that sure wasn't Thelma!"

"She never showed. We were down on Metallic Avenue."

Cork up. Shoppingcart into hotel's alley entrance, carry cart by hand up to mezzanine ballroom.

"Don't remember a fuckin' thing. I can hardly follow what we're talkin' about now. Did I really lose a whole day? We were in the shower—" Leo recalls reading the toilet seat—CRANE. A day ago!

"A vicious habit, Holmes."

Snap on ballroom bar lights. Set up musicstand, chairs, music. Hide bottles in trombone case. Teddy tips back his homburg, sets up "The Memphis Blues" as Leo warms up. Tones bounce powerfully from ballroom walls. "My God, hear that!" Leo cries.

"Sounds good."

"Restin' up pays off. What happened t' Stella's vodka?"

"We killed it in the shower."

"Were we drinkin' in the shower again? We better watch that, buster. This has been a sobering experience, Teddy. I dunno why I feel so good. I should be exhausted."

"Ha!—we got the adrenals of a seventeen-year-old boy. This—GA-A-ASP!—Foul Roses *twists* me! How c'd we stoop so low? Let's save it for horn polish."

Blow "The Memphis Blues"—as written, note for note.

"Ah!" Teddy says. "We swung for about twenty seconds."

"Felt it," Leo agrees. "Say, I didn't get a drink."

"Don't waste your sobriety on this crap." Leo sips rum instead. *"Oh,"* he sighs. *"Ohh. Ohh.* Can feel every turn it takes! Ya think this high-proof could give us ulcers?"

"Nah. Ya can't swallow more'n a teaspoon at once."

"Took an ounce," Leo whispers, tears risen.

"Then ya deserve t' burn." Teddy shifts to a Louis transcription, "Two Deuces." "We gotta keep tempo on this."

"This is slow blues. It doesn't swing."

"Louis swings everything."

Leo blows high A, quavering, muffs the first bars. "I haven't rested enough."

"Take your time. I can wait."

"This is difficult fingering!"

"Rest a minute!"

Leo blows scales feebly. "I-yi-yi, I'm a sparrow with lung cancer."

"I'm sweatin' already. This fuckin' bucket takes twice as much wind as your trumpet. Buck up!"

"I feel a knife goin' through my chest." Studies the music. "Sixteenth notes! This passage is so obscure Louis himself couldn't play it."

"He plays sixty-fourth notes."

Leo silent. "How'd we wind up on Metallic?"

Teddy smells his greensludge tubes. "Real sewage in these pipes—too much onions and Albanian hot dog sauce. You remember Frank Roosevelt? No! Well, we bought 'im a bow-tie at the Colored Elks, afterhours. So he looks us over, he's just a goodhearted submarginal, and says he's pimpin' for his beautiful sister. It takes a while to get to like Roosevelt—he has slanted beetle eyes and a faraway stunned look. We heard Tiny Johnson turn 'im down."

"Tiny Johnson! I was fried, huh?"

"We were. You and I walked Roosevelt over to his sister's on Metallic—the house is about ten feet back from the Erie tracks. Hey, they got a Coke machine filled with beer for fifty cents a bottle! It's hot."

"The beer?"

"No, the machine. Stolen. We were the only customers."

"What was she like?"

"Oh, that body! *Ideal, just ideal.* Unfortunately, Roosevelt's submarginal, but Helen's mentally incompetent. Pure foambrain. She's twenty-six and her thirteen-year-old daughter took a knife to one of mama's beaux last week and the Bureau of Child Welfare has put li'l Butterfly in Gowanda for the second time. Second time, right. Helen's asleep on the couch when we walk in. Well, she might actually be awake, but it's hard to tell, *ahem.* Bigmamma knockers, but pale and slim—and almond eyes like Roosevelt's, almost *Persian.* We sit around the kitchen for a half hour, but she won't sell us a piece until

Roosevelt promises t' go downtown t' get her some asthma pills. He won't go. 'You wanna be my butter an' egg man, you gets me those pills! I can't fuck these nice boys without any *AIR* in my chest, Franklin. I wants my pills!' "

"Did he find a store open?"

"He wouldn't go! *We* did. We *ran* all the way to General Hospital."

"Two miles uphill?"

"We were eager. And the sonofabitchin' intern only gave us two pills. So we were the first customers at Davis's drug store durin' the cloudburst this mornin'. And we got her some breakfast steaks at Anderson's. We liked her!"

"This don't seem too bad."

"Oh, we banged her three times apiece. We needed it."

"How much we pay Franklin?"

"We paid *her* forty bucks—she wouldn't give a nickel t' Frank. So he went next door to see how his girlfriend's business was and didn't come back until breakfast."

"She gave us six rolls for forty bucks!"

"She *loved* us! And we paid more 'n that. Emptied the Coke machine."

"Now I really wish I been there."

"Ya don't remember that bed? Well, maybe that's best."

"Why?"

"Noble knockers, weak kidneys. Well, beautiful boobs don't last forever, either. We can't make it on the couch, where she earns her livin', so she takes us on the bed. Baby Ruth wrappers and orange peel ground into the floor, clothes in the corners, crayons scrawls and lipstick pictures. A big yellowstained bedsheet—so unwholesome. Even the mattress has piss rings like a sequoia. She digs into a corner and uncracks a used coffee filter and, *gosh,* it's a bedsheet, not a coffee filter."

Leo nods solemnly at the bedsheet, shocked.

"She uses these two sheets alternately—and keeps a lard can by the bed for *fast* relief . . . when she can't make the john in time."

"How'd she like us?"

"Oh, man, she was stoned! We were part of her double-vision. Sighin' and cryin'—she loves t' screw! 'Makin' it with twins is so groovy! oh you studs, you stone studs!

oh mama! papa! You charlies is sex artists!' Screamin', man, and *gurglin'*."

Leo beams.

Teddy sighs. "No feelin' at all when I came. Not once."

"None?"

"Let's play."

"Did *I?*"

Teddy shrugs. "Ya jacked off into the sheet once. Maybe ya felt that."

Leo longs for Helen's unremembered breasts. *"Doggone it!"*

"Then we all went nighty-night. Next thing I knew the bed's soaked. I nudge Helen. She jumps on the can and gives such a long load I know it has t' be somebody else."

"I wet the bed!"

"AHH!" Teddy nods.

Leo silent. Burning.

"Like a baby," Teddy sighs.

"Why didn't ya wake me up?"

"I did. You changed the filter."

A cold frog branches in Leo's throat. "She didn't toss us out?"

"Not at forty bucks a visit."

Leo hits Louis's flowery blues three times, cracking. "I'm wearin' my lip out on that fuckin' high A!"

Stare down empty ballroom darkness, the service bar at their backs. Years ago, at Ham Knudsen's fraternity's New Years Eve ball, when the lights went out for midnight kisses, Leo-Teddy lifted two sealed fifths of scotch from this very bar and vamoosed. Most massive blizzard in seventy years outdoors. Woke up next morning with a heavensent full fifth waiting on their bureau. Drove singing up the lake for maplesyrup Sunday morning pancakes. Ran through two pumps at a gas station, knocking 'em flat, Teddy yawning as the pumps fell, quietly sliding fifth under the seat, whistling "Rose Marie" as the slack-jawed boy attendant ran out of the garage. "Terrible ice ya got here," Leo tells the boy.

Leo-Teddy feels someone hovering behind him.

Catsmile manager Mortimer A. Johnson takes shape in the dark. Smiling, not smiling, hair thinning, ears appearing. "How are you getting on?" he asks. "I'm afraid we have sleeping guests who can hear you boys. Use your mutes, would you mind?"

"We just finished," Leo croaks. Suddenly shaking wet.

Teddy smiles, closes trombone case on voodoo juice. "We're just goin' down to the lounge to work." Smiles.

Mort smiles. "Fire, flood, theft, sickness, death, I've had all the natural and unnatural phenomena," he says. "Whatever happens in a home, happens in a hotel. And now—musical twins. I plan to take a rest. After thirty years of this, it's time, don't you think, gentlemen?"

"You retirin', Mr. Johnson?" Leo asks. Hold back dark molasses rumfumes.

"I have plans. Not immediate, but plans."

Teddy beachcombing in Hawaii, palmy nightbreezes, sweet rum tang. *Forever!* "Gee, how'd ya ever get into *this* business?"

Mort smiles mildly, almost moaning. "Through accounting. Went to King James Business College!"

"Gosh," Leo-Teddy says.

"Had a lot of famous people here! When the big band business was in full swing, we had overflow crowds. The Dorsey Brothers, and Gene Krupa—swing musicians. Of course we still have Stew Snyder's band. He's a really fine person, and I like his playing—a touch of Harry James. His music hasn't ruined him."

Leo-Teddy beams silently, stomachs trembling.

"Louis Armstrong," Leo says "—we sat with him in his dressing room for half an hour between sets."

"*He* didn't stay here," Mort says. "Coloreds stayed at the Samuels."

"*We* offered him a drink!" Teddy says, largeheartedly. "He wouldn't take it—not on a gig. Like us."

Mort, thin lips pursed, catsmile.

" 'S all a myth about alcohol helpin' a musician's playing," Leo explains, drawing a myth in the air. "Louis's still the greatest trumpeter in the universe."

"On a level with Beethoven," Teddy says.

"He's just havin' a hard time now." Leo sighs. "He's accused of playin' for money!"

"People think Dixieland's dead, Mr. Johnson," Teddy says. Sneers, "That damn bop."

Mort smiles. "I always wanted to be friends with musicians. Well, I'll leave you to your work. *Hideho,* boys."

Leo-Teddy licks his hot lips as Mr. Johnson dries into mezzanine darkness. *Air!* deep, lungflooding. Frozen grins of safety as Teddy hazards 151-proof ounce, hands rum to Leo. Teddy's eyes boil, cheeks blotch, lips flap like a horse, he rolls like a ballbearing on his chair. Ahhh ahhh ahhhh ahhhh ahhhh!

"Snot on your brush," Leo says. Teddy coughs long and purple into hardened handkerchief. Pounds chest for breath—firetight windpipe. Leo eyes the level, slips down *two* ounces, corks up—fire branching downward. Leo-Teddy's fists clench. Eyes answer eyes, tear for tear. Sunset throb in breast, one-hundred-fifty-one proof, as their fearful dragon's tongue flickers within.

Fan faces with homburgs. "This won't go out without water!"

"Overdid it!"

Carry loaded cart down marble stairs. Push through lobby, chests burning. Fourfooted fast swerve around seated guest's crossed legs. Brownsuit with old brown vest —whitehaired, slim, whiteeyed.

"George!" Leo-Teddy says and shakes hands with his seated ex-stepfather. Groom mustaches through dizzying rum pain. "Haven't seen you in years," Teddy says. Rum-numbed bitter burn.

"How are you boys?" George Fox, caved in, vacant, defused. Irish dragon out to pasture. Last days. Soon lie down, cool to asbestos. "Still with John Hokum?" he asks, taking in their gangster pinstripes, homburgs.

"Sure," Teddy says. Rum dottles his sight.

"You look overqualified for truckdriving."

"We're musicians tonight, George," Leo says.

"Been nice t' see ya," Teddy says. "We're late. You got a room here?"

George grunts. No more cashmere coat, pearl Stetson, shined yellow gloves. Or Cadillac. Room, bed, dresser, a little chat with pensioners and old age wards rooming here. Stomach cancer survivor, bottle corked forever. Drained, bland, luckless grasp—but more alive than dead, still a bit distinguished. Leo smiles warmly, released from his vow to hate Fox forever.

"I have that," George says about his room. "Your mother has great expectations for you boys."

"We're writin' a new opera," Leo says.

"What happened to the last one?"

"We gotta get it put on," Teddy says. "Opera's the hardest thing in the world t' finance, George."

"Impossible," Leo says, the world's weight upon him. "That's why we gotta go to *New York*."

George eyes their scuffed clubtoe boots. "New York? Say hello to Stella for me," he says hoarsely.

"Bye."

"Now that the sonofabitch's sober, he's useless," Teddy whispers.

Leo, wideeyed smile. "I didn't know the Irish drank!"

Push into Baghdad's watercool air. "I always feel excited when we come through this door," Teddy says. "Even t' play waltzes." Empty the shoppingcart in the band's little corner. "Christ—at least we're not out there in Sheepland with the Rotarians and CPAs. *We got a real life t' live!* Let's limit ourselves to two beers."

"Apiece," Leo says.

"Of course. And *after* work," Teddy winks. *"VOO*-doo!"

"Ahh!"

Teddy thumps his chest. "That's *real-l* juice! I was seein' spots in front of George."

Wheel their cart back into the lobby to hide it under the mezzanine staircase. Their step cadenced, swimming.

"Boys!" George calls, rising. Intense secret smile, Irish prisoner's pained eyes. "I want you to tell Stella something for me. Tell her," he says looking both ways and dropping his voice, "I'm teaming up with some friends of Bill W. Got that? Bill *W*."

"Sure," Teddy says. "Is that Bill Wilson from New England?"

George's mouth drops, cheeks flushing. "What do you know about him?" he asks hoarsely.

"Nothin'," Leo says. "Flip Newquist knows him."

"Russ Newquist's boy?" George asks.

"Yeah," Leo says. "Ya know Russ?"

"I surely do," George says. Pale blue eyes fierce. *"Russ Newquist is a saint."*

"Oh, we like him a lot," Teddy says.

Leo smiles. "Always good for some zinfandel when we visit Flip."

George puzzled. "Russ doesn't drink. I know he doesn't."

Teddy laughs. "Maybe that's why he keeps such lousy wine for guests!"

George grunts disdain. "You boys've got a lot t' learn." Nods, looks at his watch. "I got a meeting to get to. *Bill W. . . .*"

Leo-Teddy tucks shoppingcart into stairshadow, Foul Roses in bag.

"Same old hidebound bastard!" Teddy says.

Homburgs off at last, hair clipped high, parted, combed back harshly like reeking woodblocks.

"We take it easy," Teddy says, "so this jug lasts the night. Let's be clearheaded for Thelma. Boy, last night's catchin' up with me!"

Leo squints at rum in Teddy's case. "God, 's half-empty!"

Blue orchestra stand goldlettered and sparkling

LEO-TEDDY

as Leo-Teddy strives through "Play, Gypsies!" on muted horns. Grayhaired fiddler Sigy Redfield bears down on buttery tones while his Sidy pumps the piano. They don't look much like Wanda and Wilma, their twins.

Tiny Johnson and Rob Grapevine scrounge into the Baghdad. Twins rest their horns. "W-w-w-we left your car out front," Tiny says hangdog in overalls. Nineteen, craggy, callow, strawblond boyhair falling. "It's all in one p-p-p-piece! How *are* you?" he asks Leo. "Some b-b-blast at the Colored Elks! One guy tried t' sell me his sister!"

"Great," Leo says, "I don't remember last night. How was your trip to Kentucky?"

"W-w-w-we m-m-made it in thirty-six hours," Tiny says. "On b-b-b-benzedrine. This is Rob Grapevine, he's a p-p-p-poet from Allendale Avenue. W-w-w-would ya like t' come out to the farm after work and m-m-meet Harpur? He w-w-w-wants t' meet you fellas and thank you for the loan of your car." Tiny glowers slyly. "Then you'd be givin' us a ride home too!"

"Sure," Leo says. "My wife's droppin' by. May I bring her?"

"Hell, yes," Rob says. Plump Kaiser mustache. "Man isn't whole without woman, sez the Lord! And Plato."

"I was astounded when ya let me have the car," Tiny says. "Ya didn't know me at all and when I asked to b-b-b-borrow it, Teddy just said, 'Here are the keys!' "

"That's pretty impressive," Rob Grapevine judges.

"Our pleasure," Teddy says.

"D'you fellas play anything besides this cocktail schmaltz?" Rob asks, stroking his dark bush into loops.

"Jazz," Leo says.

"Jesus, I could stand some hot jazz!" Rob says.

"Bring your instruments," Tiny says. "We'll have a two-man jam session tonight. If ya feel up to it after this corn oil."

"We never tire," Teddy says.

"But sometimes pass out," Leo says.

"That's my kinda drinkin', pardners!" Rob says.

Sigy announces, "And now Leo-Teddy vill play 'Den You'll Remember Me' from *De Bohemian Girl*. Okay, boys!"

"Yo ho ho and a bottle of terp!" Rob says. "Let's grab a beer at Kliney's, Tiny."

"See you at one," Tiny says, and fakes a *bwahh* on the bardrinkers.

Leo-Teddy clips open his Arban exercise book. Starts slowly on the same notes and stays there but for rare harmony by Teddy. Sidy hammers rhythm, smiling about, but biting her lips at the twins. Their mutes pillow split tones and fluffs.

"And ven you learn to transspoze, you'll be even better!" Sigy says.

Singing in the moonlight. Turn off by the golf course, up stony Horton Road to Wineybrook farm. Thelma whistling in white linen suit beside Teddy. He whispers, "I've prayed for this—for both of you."

"Drink for today, write for tomorrow!" Grapevine cries, and sings in angel tenor—

On top of Mount Codeine
All covered with snow
I lost my connection
For paying too slow

Oh that monkey will get you
He'll jump on your back
A hard-hearted connection
Is worse than the rack!

"JESUS!" Rob cries. "That's by Jack McFin, he should be up by now and you can meet him. Wineybrook, we are here!"

Windows burning, the moonlit farm leans on a hill, its barn bleached and shadowed. Beethoven's *Grosse Fugue* assaults the screens. Slide out under the wheel. Tiny hands out their horn cases groggily. Foureyed Leo-Teddy, sweeping hilly moonfields. They go down to the kitchen in starlight.

Beethoven swells the looseboarded house. Tiny's wife Becky and Harpur's wife Janet, two countrygirls—frank, worn smiles—wash metal harps from the stove and the icebox. Barelightbulbed kitchen shimmers in the twins' wide vision, pinpoint eyes squinting pain.

Shy, darkhaired Janet grips their hands. "I can't thank you enough for rescuing us! We were *stranded* in Pippa Pass—that must be the most depressed village in Kentucky."

"Well, all the children know about you boys!" Becky says.

"We're the village idiots," Teddy says.

Beethoven ends. Choptalk splits from the livingroom. A black Mexican racing dog sniffs the twins' seats nervously, whimpering on rotted linoleum.

Purple bathrobe bulging, a mammoth strides in from the livingroom. *"What are you doing out here!"* Oscar Harpur cries, head ducking under lintel, ham hand outstretched. At first sight of Oscar, an opera composer, Teddy thrills with fear: whale forebrain, long silken hair, wicked iceblue polar eyes. X-ray, creamlicking smile at Thelma in her creamwhite suit.

The "Venusberg Music" begins.

Rob plucks a stove harp from the dish tray. *"Tannhaeuser!* Lush nights in steamy old Venusberg! Play for us, Oscar!"

Oscar strums the stove harp, holds it to his ear pinging wires and asks the ceilingbulb, *"Kenst du wohl den Weg?* —Janet, that bulb is only *forty watts,* you girls can't work in this gloom! How *are* you, I'm Oscar Harpur. You must be Leo, how do you do, and you're Teddy. How pleased I am to meet you both. I've heard nothing but good reports about you." The "Venusberg" swells. "You're Thelma, if I'm not mistaken—and white as a lily!"

"I'm no lily, believe me!" Thelma laughs, trembling.

"A truly Nordic figure," Oscar says. Licking. Thelma colors to her roots. "Oh, I've embarrassed you. You mustn't let my enthusiasm bother you, my dear." Oscar folds her hand into his. "I mean no harm. I'm the gentlest man on earth. You'll find that out when we really know each other."

"Are you going to be teaching here?" Thelma asks. Her hands hide under her arms, her body trembles at his superbright anxieties.

"Oh my God!" Oscar cries. "I've *served* my time in King James. They don't want me here. But that's a long story we'll go into another time. I can't tell you two gentlemen how pleased I am that you came out tonight so that I can thank you for your great kindness in getting us out of that pest hole. Come in, meet our guests—you drink wine, don't you? We have a case, thank heaven. Janet! three glasses. This must be a trombone and that's a trumpet or cornet case. Marvelous! Are you going to play for us? I play the flute myself, though it's long gone to the hock shop—a magnificent three-hundred-fifty-dollar flute—but it couldn't be helped. We were so strapped in Manhattan, I mean utter poverty, my dears—I was stealing *milk* from the thugs next door for my children! So there went my flute, *phoof,* forever! But you're not interested in my sorrows. Come in, come in!"

Oscar, brushing his locks, leads them to Deacon Quince, a gray Greek scholar and linotypist for the King James *Morning Sun*. Buddha smile, cigar, plump Mongol eyes. "By Gemini, I'm happy to meet you all finally! Wineybrook spirits are now assembling and we'd like you to join us. There may be a little deviltry tonight, or let's hope so, ha ha ha. How's business at the Baghdad Lounge?"

"Business is great but we're not," Teddy says.

"I suspected as much," Deacon says. He feigns worry that does not seem feigned.

"We only get paid as one musician," Leo says.

"That's all they can afford down there," Thelma says.

Jack McFin walks into the bare livingroom. Redhaired,

freckled, athletic, Jack has the stunned look of a man befuddled to his backbone. He looks about in wonder with blank blue eyes as if finding a rapids or the Bayreuth Festival at full tilt.

"He has arisen!" Deacon cries. "It's a great day, isn't it, Jack?"

"Gee, I don't know. Is it?" Jack looks about. "Where's the sacristy, I need a drink. I've got wine fleas dying in my stomach, Oscar. They need help, pronto."

"Janet!" Oscar cries. "Bring Jack a glass."

"Don't bother," Jack calls. "I'll get it myself and pack in a breath of fresh air out back."

"How about some b-b-b-breakfast, Jack?" Tiny asks. "I'll have B-B-Becky m-m-m-make you some *huevos rancheros con salsa cruda.*"

"Christ, no," Jack says. "That Mexican fartfodder is a soporific. Thanks anyway."

Oscar pours, first handing Thelma a carefully brimming glass pinched in his terrific fingers.

"Jack, this is Leo-Teddy," Tiny says. "And this is Leo's wife Thelma."

"Hi! I've heard a lot about you lads," Jack says. *"All good.* But this is the first I've heard of you," he tells Thelma. "I'll bet you have a lot of courage or you wouldn't have married this lucky guy."

"Oh, love conquers all," Teddy says.

Thelma's smile tightens—Leo's happy she doesn't say "ex-wife."

"I really mean it," Jack tells her. "Boy, I wish I had your problems, Leo. Yours too!" he tells Teddy. "Ah, mana, I feel the heavenly city rising—a mellow breakfast. This all we have, Oscar?"

"Deacon bought a case!" Oscar glows at Deacon. Deacon bows.

"Sweet Christ," Jack says. "You're not a deacon, you're a saint."

Deacon bows again. "It's not every day that King James is visited by such a congregation of vapors—I mean *spirits!*" he says. "Drink while ye may, my boy."

"I need more wine," Oscar says. "May I freshen your glass, Deacon? Oh wait, you've got a wine fly, let me get it out."

"Kamikaze paradise," Grapevine says, asleep under the Bayreuth Chorus. "Battle aces of the grape!"

"How much did *he* drink today?" Jack asks, eyes smokeblue funerals.

"Who can measure the Euphrates in spring?" Deacon asks.

"Check his eyes for vital signs."

"You should talk!" Deacon tells Jack. "Your eyes used to come down like shutters."

"Shit, yes," Jack laughs. "In the old days—not any more, I hope. I'm through with that dreary L.A. muscatel. Sherry's more aristocratic. But I like this red eyewash just fine, don't get me wrong, Deacon."

Tiny rouses from his rocker, crying, "Rebecca! *Comida, comida!* God, I'm just comin' down from the b-b-b-benzedrine, Oscar."

"I'm just going up," Jack says. "Christ, what a fagged crew. Come on, Oscar, let's climb over the roof. We need exercise."

"That roofbeam won't hold Oscar," Deacon says.

"I'll go up as a trial balloon," Grapevine says sitting up. He struggles up glowering. "Better piss first. Wha's so funny? You don't think I can make it over the roof?" he asks, shucking his shirt.

"You better have another drink first," Jack says. "I want you in shape if we need each other up there."

"Ah, you're back with the Manicheans, Harpur," Deacon says. "We've missed you. It's been dull without you."

Oscar smiles sacredly, leans on Tiny's livingroom wall. The wall buckles, shuddering. Wine-red, he glares at Tiny. "This place is held together by Scotch tape!"

Tiny shrivels, worm-eaten smile, lashed.

"What are *you* doin' here?" Leo asks Jack.

"Wish I knew. Leeching, I guess. As Kafka says, 'Just look on me as a dream.' "

Rob lists against Teddy. "Leo and I were thinkin' of marketing an oxygen-mask hangover killer," Teddy says. "That pure oxygen drives the brain-fatigue poisons right out in five seconds."

"I've tried it," Jack says. "After five minutes the hangover rolls right back in again. Along with the whole bag of whims, manias, compulsions, obsessions, and megrims. Paraldehyde's the true elixir—concentrated alcohol—but you can only get it at the clinics. A beer breakfast's best —great, in fact, with burnt bacon for protein. You need protein early in the day, don't you think? Don't get me wrong, I'm no food faddist! Of course, pure oxygen is a great high by itself—it's not nitrous oxide, but it's nice."

"Shit," Grapevine says, "fuckin' dentists got no right keepin' that laughing gas to themselves."

"You an old friend of Oscar's?" Teddy asks, eying Oscar.

"You could say that," Jack says. "He saved me from the happy farm. Pulled me off the Bowery, got me headed for my degree at Columbia. I was on the Embarcadero in Frisco—and Main Street, L.A. Lived in a rusted out stationwagon in an empty lot in Hell's Kitchen for six months. Talk about maelstroms! Had a few deetees there, mainly auditory, nothing to worry about—it's the visual hallucinations that mean real brain damage. A few old friends I knew were dead were standing around talking with me. Boy, when Oscar found me I was pretty as a shithouse rat. Not boring you, am I? Drinking that fucking 'squeeze' every morning, then going up to some Central Park stables to curry horses. I could never panhandle—didn't have the guts."

"Wow," Leo says. "That's like Edgar Allan Poe or Hart Crane."

"Not without getting the work done," Jack says "—aside from questions of genius."

"What's 'squeeze'?" Teddy asks.

"Oh, jellied alcohol—canned heat for cooking fuel. Cheaper than rubbing alcohol—rubbing alcohol's the harshest drink on earth, but it's still better'n Sterno, believe me. You squeeze Sterno through a handkerchief for the juice. Don't spoon it straight!—it's bad for your lining. In fact, stay away from that pink-elephant jelly altogether—you get the gremlins from that shit. Terrific fears. And it burns out the brain cells. That crap would give a dead horse the deetees. I remember squeezing a can of it, then stealing some raw lamb chops out of a gin-mill's kitchen on lower Broadway and asking myself as I was running, What the hell am I gonna do with these fucking things? I like lamb, but not raw."

"What'd ya do?" Leo asks.

"Ate 'em in an alley. Just the meat though—I gave the fat to a mutt. If it wasn't a gremlin. It just sat there watching me gnaw the bones—it had red-orange mange and human eyes and was pleading with me."

"Pleadin'?" Teddy asks.

"Crying. Not to let it die, I guess. Looked a helluva lot like me! Don't get me wrong, I don't drink like that anymore. I'm more on the beerwagon. Are you gonna play those things I saw in the kitchen?"

" 'S pretty late," Teddy says.

"Kids're sleepin'!" Leo says. "Dya like jazz?"

"Hate it," Jack says.

"Ya mean you just never listen to it?" Leo asks.

"I've listened and I hate it," Jack says. "I used to like ensemble jazz before those ego-soloists started shitting all over the music."

"Oh, Louis plays good ensemble," Leo says.

"Louis!" Jack laughs. "He's the one who let all those shitheads loose, for God's sake. I won't say I haven't heard him hit some good strong notes himself, but what came after is catastrophe."

"Ya play an axe?" Teddy asks.

"Hell, no," Jack says. "Well, I've wasted many hours on the fiddle, roasting chestnuts—you know 'The Old Refrain' by Kreisler? But I don't play. Music's such a timewaster, don't you think? What do you play?"

"Trumpet. But I haven't mastered it yet."

"That's honest," Jack says, voice mild and flat.

"What kinda dance music dya like?" Teddy asks.

"Oh, 'Goodnight Irene' or anything by Leadbelly. I sat around with him one night down in his kitchen on the Lower East Side and he played for me. 'Ole Riley Walked the Water' and 'I'm Dancin' with Tears in My Eyes'—you know he wrote that for an insane girl? Christ, I'll never forget that evening. I'll write a poem about that man if my spirit ever feels equal to it. I feel kin with him—though *I* never killed anyone. Up, Rob?"

Rob Grapevine drains a full glass and turns. "Did I hear Rob Logic mentioned in vain?" Fills his glass, glares at it on the table and, plump waist running sweat, says to his drink, *"Wake up, winebuggers!"* Staggers out to the porch. Gripping his bladder, Tiny follows, saying, "Gotta empty m-m-m-my b-b-b-basketb-b-b-ball!"

"Don't souse the fairies, Tiny," Oscar calls from the kitchen.

"Christ, they're swimmin' t' Mexico on Grapevine's p-p-p-piss!"

A shadow gets up from the porch and walks in.

"Locke!" Jack cries. "When did you get here?"

"The fireflies are raving over the lawn," Bob Locke says. Thin, longhaired, wispy mustaches, darkglittering far-off Chinese eyes. "Hi, Jack!" he says softly. "Have you seen the fireflies?"

"Out back," Jack says. "God, that night air's delicious. When'd you get here?"

" 'Bout two hours ago. You were sleeping."

"How's the poetry going?" Jack asks.

"Just finished five hundred stanzas of terza rima about my first wife," Locke says. Now his eyes seem pink, rimmed with wine-worries. "I'm between marriages."

"Gee, that's too bad," Jack says. "I know how you feel. But that damned terza rima will sure help get your birds singing. Boys, meet Bob Locke, King of the Purple Bohemians."

"I'm more hermetic than bohemian," Locke tells Jack. "I like that pressure in classic forms."

Leo whispers to Thelma, "What's *hermetic?"*

"I haven't the slightest idea," Thelma says. "This place is a madhouse, I will not stay here another moment. That music has given me a driving headache. I can see that this is *not* a place to have a talk about our mutual economic responsibilities."

Oscar walks Thelma and Leo-Teddy out to their car. He slides an arm around her as they walk, the twins strolling ahead, and clamps a palm on her bosom.

"Truly Nordic," the twins hear Oscar say behind. "You *must* come back, Thelma. Very soon!"

Thelma drives off, white, wordless.

In the fireflies. Oscar crimps a cigarette into his long Zeus holder. The sharp shock of the stars fills Leo-Teddy.

"Oscar," Leo asks. ". . . do you believe in God?"

Oscar's face flames with a match. "My dear boy, of course I do! Look at the beauty of flowers, the gorgeous uselessness of sunrise and sunset, the miracles that come in through the eye. These have no use in a purely mechanistic universe. A spirit is needed to receive them, a divine spirit. That's us, His image, our minds reflect His glory. I believe with Beethoven, Mozart, and Bach!"

"Thank you!" Leo breathes. *"Yes!"* Teddy breathes.

"I'm sorry you'll have to walk back to town," Oscar says. "You must have terrible problems. But let's not talk about them tonight. You're enjoying yourselves and that's what counts."

"What problems?" Leo asks.

"Do you have any children?" Oscar asks.

"A son," Leo says.

"Why, how wonderful. And are you happy?"

"We live for our music!" Teddy says.

Tidal pity fills Oscar as he widely grips Leo-Teddy's outer shoulders, Oscar's polarblue eyes moonlit, ablaze. Leo-Teddy cannot breathe. "Well, not tonight," Oscar whispers. Twins silent. "I mean," Oscar says, "if you should ever need advice and I can be of help, please feel free to call on me and I'll give you what poor power of insight I may have. Understood? Now let's go in."

Janet and Becky serve the twins Mexican tidbits while Grapevine's piss again gurgles into grass by their window. Leo-Teddy blushes, swallowing dryly. From the porch Grapevine declaims to the moon, stars, and fireflies—

> You, glowworm, sleuth of the rainy night,
> Go look if her couch is rocking like the sea.
> Rain, drown this dynamite of fright—
>   Come comfort me!

"Now he's talking about his cock," Jack tells Teddy. "Though it's my four-liner."

Teddy feels Leo listing and nudges him. They watch Oscar's purple bulk sink into his easy chair, shoes on hassock. The Mexican racing dog shrieks under Oscar, squeals sliding over the chair arm. *"Sofia!"* Oscar cries as the dog trembles cowering on the floor. "Come here, little one, I'm sorry I sat on you." Pulls the dog onto his great lap, petting and rubbing it. "But you've got to watch out," Oscar tells Sofia, pulling the dog's long black ears tight and giving its dark nervous eyes his X-ray stare. "Do you understand? Have some meat." Oscar pinches a large chunk of beef from his taco, gives it to Sofia. Oscar's brow suddenly crimps. *"What am I doing!"* he cries and digs the meat out of Sofia's mouth, bolts it into his own mouth. "We can't afford to be giving you meat! You'll have to bear up with the rest of us this summer. My God, I'm giving this bitch meat out of my own children's mouths—and this near the poorhouse!"

"Yes, O Leviathan!" Deacon says, "yet even the dogs eat the crumbs that fall from their master's table."

"Jesus, that four-liner creams me, Jack!" Grapevine

says coming back in. "That's on a level with Waller or Herbert or I'm a lead centavo."

"Not any Waller I know," Jack says. "Unless you mean Fats."

"You're too modest," Oscar says.

"Am I? Explain my modesty to me, Oscar, maybe I'll get over it."

"I'm not joking, I'm very serious," Oscar says. "Look at that marvelous velvet texture—and *'sleuth'!*—it's like the whole verse is set up to make that word work. You've exhausted *sleuth* forever, nobody'll ever be able to use it again."

"Oh, I'm just sucking a rain-tit for comfort," Jack says.

"But *sleuth* condenses the poem into a perfect drop of spiritual light," Bob Locke says, a black chinese cat sitting midlivingroom floor, eyes dark sparks under heavy lids. "You've got a whole reach of words you've made your own, Jack. By the way, I've dedicated my 'Sixth Station' to Oscar."

"You have!" Oscar cries. His eyes brim. "Oh, I'm very moved. You'll have to sign my copy, let me get it out." Oscar dips into a crate of loose poems by his chair

"Ya gotta hear this," Grapevine tells the twins. "It's one of the great poems. Oh,

> Pass me through, Beloved, as light through glass,
> but stain me, too, with tinctures earth delivers
> to plead the prism-love Thy Way uncovers—

Prism-love! *God!* It's like the Rose Window at Chartres. Dya see it? Dya *see* it! *Pass me through, Beloved, as light through glass!"*

Leo-Teddy thrills. Rob weaving with hard stunned blue eyes beside Leo. Rob swallows, sucks nostrils wide and, overcome, says, "I gotta go out again—an' look at the moon. . . . Gotta study the roof logistics too." Lurches, wine in hand, to the porch, bouncing against the doorway. *"Oh my God, what a night!"* Rob cries.

Oscar shuffles poems by the hundreds in huge batches and sighs and sighs. *"Janet!"*

"I think they've gone to b-b-b-bed, Oscar."

"Bed already?" Oscar says. "But we'll need coffee later! Why, the night's just blooming. I've found it!"

"I've found it!" Oscar cries.

"The Snowman surely is no human thing," Grapevine speaks from the porch. Comes in bare and steaming. "God, that's Locke's poem," he tells Deacon, "where Faust leads Don Quixote and Don Juan and Helen of Troy up the icefalls to the Snowman's. *I dread the Abominable Snowman's skulking might!* My God, Bob, did you bring it?"

"I'm afraid not," Locke says taking his poem from Oscar. "Pen? Let me think about this for a while, Oscar. I like to germinate my dedications."

"Ah," Oscar sighs at Locke, wine-red, forebrain gleaming.

"Ah!" Tiny cries slyly, eating Grapevine's taco while Rob talks with Deacon. "Hey, Oscar, let's hear some jazz!"

Oscar rolls his eyes, about to suffer.

"That'll wake us up," Grapevine seconds. "Christ, I'm almost sober. Oscar, did I ever describe my ideal library for you? WHOO! Every other book's a dummy with a pint of sneaky-pete or brandy in it. The best books have the best drinks. What a library!—ya spend half the night reading Rochester and sippin' muscat."

"How about *writing?"* Jack asks.

"Ya know what the Persians say, Jack," Rob says, "Write in drunkenness, revise in sobriety. Remind me to show you the new stanza for my 'Public Drunk Number 1' poem. It really creams me now. Forget the version I sent you, it had too much ground glass and rusty razorblades in its rhythms. *Now* Ol' Bayzo's out walkin' the foggy dawns of Atlantic City and packing muscat in both raincoat pockets. Ha ha, and He said unto them 'Let the rain be wine!' Hell, why doesn't the Lord even do that for us once in a while?"

"You're goddamn right," Tiny says grimly, looking about his old farm walls. "B-b-b-break loose up there!"

"Don't tempt Him, Tiny," Deacon says. "He has a way of sending things in excess. Well, this'll be some summer! You have these twins thinking all you wordgiants talk about is wineflies and beverages."

"Gosh, no," Teddy says.

Leo's painfully stiff winegrin begs for faith.

Leo-Teddy lifts his burgundy. "This is life," Teddy says tenderly. Twins drink to burning, blushing, wineglowing

Now. All eyes meet, highly pleased, their wine spiked with the clove of Teddy's toast.

"Oh, we do a lotta work," Rob tells Teddy. "Tiny's in the middle of a novel about Southern Mexico, Oscar's writin' an opera about the Collective Unconscious—"

"—Now, Rob," Oscar says, "that's not it at all—"

"Christ, Oscar, Jung'll flip in his grave—" Rob says.

"—That old man doesn't interest me one iota," Oscar says.

"Say Yeats will flip in his grave," Jack suggests to Rob.

"Thank you, Jack," Oscar says. "Let's call it the mythical unconscious, if we have to label it—*unh!*"

"Right!" Rob says. "And Jack's finishing his 'Darkness of the Mountains' sonnet sequence, Deacon's translating Homer's mermaid music into English, and I'm turnin' out a poem a day myself. Even if most of 'em are exercises, I'm puttin' my queer shoulder to the wheel too."

"Don't steal that," Tiny says, *"you're* not queer. So don't you fellas think we're just b-b-b-bayzo hounds. We don't really drink that m-m-m-much, do we, Oscar?"

"Alas, no!" Oscar says opening their third gallon. "Let's let that air for awhile." Blows a tarry cigarette from his long Zeus holder, screws it together with a fresh cigarette-as-filter inside, and plugs in a Chesterfield. Leo-Teddy watches, the devil building a mill. "I try to stay as far away from tobacco as I can," Oscar says, lighting his faraway cigarette tip, then sucking blue smoke, refreshed in every cell.

Leo weaves, seated. "Le's have another. Dya think *all* these guys're geniuses?"

"They sure talk good," Teddy says. "I'm gettin' tight. Could we ever train Thelma t' act like Janet?"

Leo stares deeply into Teddy. "That's a noble suggestion."

"Work on it," Teddy says. "Bring 'er out regularly. Oscar can give us a pointer or two about female psychology! I'm willin' t' learn. And get 'er a Mexican cookbook."

"Janet's without exception the greatest woman I ever met," Leo says. "Oscar's really liberated every beautiful quality she has."

"We can't really hope for so much," Teddy says. "Though Becky's great too."

"Yeah, but Tiny's too Napoleonic, don'tcha think? He has her draggin'. But she'll be another Janet someday!"

"Give ten years of my life for either of 'em," Teddy says. "Maybe twenty."

Rob Grapevine, eyepoints piercing, leans over, pats both their hands, unable to speak, then kisses his fingers to heaven, crying, *"Caramba!* Man izzn whole without woman and those two are queens from heaven! I like you two guys very much. Ya gotta come out here often this summer."

Tiny pulls off an island of loose wallplaster, eyes sullen. "Need'n axe," he mutters.

Tiny goes out. Through their window they see him kick the house, then try to kick his foot through their window. Falls on his back, gets up and staggers up to the hard-leaning barn in search of an axe, looks around and staggers back in big moonlight.

"Where do you work?" Jack asks. "I'm a teacher, in better moments."

"Drive a breadtruck," Leo sighs. "We're sort of nurses and ambulance drivers too." Winebelches and a fellow belch rises from Teddy.

"How about cadging me a few happyjacks?" Jack asks. "I like Miltown, Equanil, Serpasil, Thorazine, Dexamyl, Sparine, Frequel, Suavatil, or any of those tranquility pills. I like pep pills too—whatever you can cop, I'll be glad to reimburse you. I don't drink much, but I love my happy-jacks! Where I am, I can't even get dexies. But no Phenolbarbs—*please*. They bore me."

"We got some leftover Thorazine," Leo says. "We'll bring it out."

"Demerol too," Teddy says. "But that's pretty boring."

"Oh no!" Jack corrects. "I'd be much obliged."

"But we only give it in ampules," Teddy says.

"Christ, no needles!" Jack cries. "Thanks just the same. They scare the hell out of me. I've been bled by so many blood banks, I'm needleshy. Forget ampules."

"Well, there are some other things in the chest," Leo says.

"Oscar," Jack says, "when the hell are we going to take our long portage across the Northwest?"

Oscar deathrattles in his big easy chair. "Don't ask me now, Jack. This has been the worst year of my life, bar none. I couldn't carry a paddle to a duck pond, much less cross the country in a canoe."

"In a canoe!" Grapevine cries.

"W-w-w-we haven't heard a-b-b-bout this, Oscar."

"Oh, the whole Northwest's connected by water," Jack says "—I just found out over my last drink. Maybe it's all connected by drink, I'm not sure. Christ, I mean the whole country's connected, not just the Northwest. We're going to start on the St. Lawrence. We'll carry the canoe a few miles here and there, but mostly it's paddling or gliding. Lay off the fucking lighterfluid and Chesterfields. Jesus, Oscar, we've got to get going if we're ever going. Look at our ages. You know, when you turn forty, the nerves start to go. We won't get the full benefit if we wait much longer. Christ, I looked at myself in the mirror tonight and nearly fainted. Get that man out of his grave! I cried. I wish somebody'd put the fear of God into me, I need it. We can't go on pissing our lives away in these cuntwater college towns. That's what it takes, the fear of God to get us moving. Might improve our writing too. I really believe that. Until you can put the fear of God into another man, you aren't alive yourself. I've been reading David the Psalmist, that sonofabitch has the message, *Fear God like a chancre sore*. I'm misquoting, of course."

"You don't have enough fear of God?" Oscar asks.

"Hell, no! Do you?"

Oscar pats his pockets. "Can't find any—but it may be the wine. Deacon, how's your fear of God?"

"I am already prostrate before you, O Prince!" Deacon spouts, Buddha bending.

Rob falls into a coughing fit while Oscar feigns a broken puppet. *"Dry!"* Rob coughs, reaching for Tiny's glass.

"That'll only give you a *wet* cough," Rob, Jack says. "Shit, I can't tell if you look more like a bank robber or a Mexican bandit."

"A Mex general!" Rob says, coughing purple. "In my next incarnation, I'll be a general and shoot up Chiapas. I'm gettin' strong vibrations about reincarnation for my Egyptian poem."

"Reincarnation?" Deacon says. "You need *de*incarnation—if you only knew it, my boy."

"Let's hear that jazz!" Tiny cries.

"Uh, Jack really don't like it," Teddy says.

"Oh shit, don't worry about me," Jack says. "Go ahead and play, I'll bet you're great!"

" 'S late," Leo says.

"Later than you think," Deacon says. "But play!"

"Play!" Tiny says. "That's why we have this fuckin' farm in the country, for Christ's sake. Aside from it only costin' thirty b-b-b-bucks a m-m-m-month."

"We're supposed to be repairing this despondent fart-box," Oscar sighs. "Though don't get me wrong, Tiny, I'm thankful for everything you've done."

"Gee, I rather like it here," Jack says. "I wouldn't piss on this place myself. Plenty of fresh air if nothing else."

Oscar shudders, drawing up his purple. "We'll make do, Jack, *barely*. It may turn into a very *dry* summer. We might all be out planting potatoes, if Tiny loses his job at the tool-stamping factory. Rob hopes to get a job as a shoe salesman—"

"—Peeping Tom," Rob says, smile swerving.

"—though he'll barely make enough for himself," Oscar adds.

"—I'll help out on the food and wine, Oscar," Rob says. *"Faithfully."*

"—but," Oscar says, "if that nincompoop thinks we're putting any work into this place, he doesn't know his new tenants."

"W-w-w-well, I'll have t' do *something* around here, Oscar. Christ, w-w-w-we're just b-b-b-back from havin' our own place in San Cristobal with two p-p-p-patios and three SERVANTS."

"Lo! how the mighty have fallen," Deacon says.

"Anyway, this is where I'm regrouping what's left of me after Pippa Pass," Oscar tells Leo-Teddy. "You've heard about me at King James Community College, haven't you? Kicked out! Kicked out! Failed four-fifths of my students and wouldn't upgrade their marks."

"And they deserved to fail!" Tiny says grimly. "Grapevine and I were in those classes and it's true."

"God!" Grapevine cries. "The first course in humanities Oscar announces his class'll read *The Iliad, The Odyssey, The Aeneid, Paradise Lost, Don Juan, Prometheus Unbound,* and just about everybody including Dante and Chaucer by Christmas—and they all nearly *fainted!* 'Cept Tiny 'n me."

"And B-B-Becky," Tiny says. "These were kids just out of King James High School who could just about spell their names with p-p-p-prompting. They were *slaughtered!* I m-m-m-mean these kids could just about m-m-m-make it from the high school to the army recruiting station and w-w-w-w-wandered into Oscar's classes by m-m-m-mistake."

"Boy," Rob says, eying the floor passionately. "I'll forever be indebted to your course in Mahler's *Eighth,* Oscar."

"Why, that's very kind of you. Thank you, Rob. Your glass is empty. Tapering off?"

"What!" Rob cries. "With this hundred-proof halo? Moderation's for the fuckin' birds!"

"Say," Jack says, "let's hear that jazz."

Leo-Teddy's hearts sink as he rises against his better judgment. Brings in his horns, shakes out spit, sighing heavily, stands in the diningroom facing the bombed-plaster livingroom. Teddy whispers to Leo and lifts his trombone. Taps the downbeat.

"Don't gimme the beat or I'll get lost," Leo says, shaking his trumpet.

"Now there's an honest man," Jack laughs shaking his head, "he can't find the tempo. I know this will be glorious already. Let me leech another drink, Deacon, before we get underway. Christ, I came here without a cent, can you lend me busfare to New York?"

"Salivatin' too much," Leo whispers.

Teddy's blood rises—he starts solidly on "Goodnight Irene" and, eyes closed, blows two soft and lifting choruses before Leo joins on the bridge. Blow two more choruses, playing the same notes.

Bob Locke claps and Grapevine dances. Tiny sings.

Twins split and ramble through the last bridge and chorus and say goodnight with held harmony.

"Christ, that was great," Jack says, "although I got lost for awhile. You guys can play all night. Shit, Oscar, if Irene turn her back on me, I'm gonna take morphine and die. *Boy, that's writing!"*

"That's mighty impressive," Rob agrees.

"If Irene turn her b-b-b-back on m-m-m-me, I'd write that w-w-w-well too."

"Hey, play some more!" Jack says.

Two small boys, a little girl with blazing blue eyes and a six-year-old girl in pigtails stand smiling in the doorway.

"We came down to hear that funny music," Curt says, rubbing four-year-blue eyes.

"That's Leo-Teddy," Chris whispers up to Curt.

Julia, the smallest, crawls onto Oscar's lap, her eyes burning at Leo-Teddy.

Leo says, "We'll play one more piece."

"And that's it," Teddy says, placing music in Rob's hands. "There won't be anything left to us after this piece."

Oscar sits like Hitler ready to bite cyanide.

Leo-Teddy starts *Cornet Chop Suey* with full-wind, chiming tones. Rob sways with the musicbook. Sock out the stop chorus. Grinning children jump. Halfway through, twins split perilously, striving to find each other in racing phrases. Thankfully hit the Solo flourish together and burn their high A. *"I'm creaming, I'm creaming, Jesus!"* Rob cries.

"Somebody prop Grapevine up," Deacon calls, "or there won't be any music."

Mid-Solo Leo-Teddy blows apart, horns snarling at each other. Teddy lowers his, waiting for a light from Leo. At a pause, Teddy blows the last chorus with Leo overblowing thinly. End in a washout on high A, trembling wanly.

"That piece's too long to play all at once," Teddy says hoarsely, blushing.

"There are supposed t' be piano interludes to rest in," Leo gasps, pink cheeks streamingwet.

"Piano interludes!" Oscar cries.

Leo-Teddy's hearts turn.

"Do you mean like Rachmaninoff?" Oscar asks.

Leo-Teddy laughs, red, wet, pierced.

"We never learn!" Teddy whispers.

"Gotta memorize this bitch note for note!" Leo says. "And we better do it before we make bigger assholes of ourselves than we have tonight."

"Stole the words outta my mouth."

Leo-Teddy packs his horns in the kitchen, takes a breather at the back entry, wiping his eyes. Turns to watch Wineybrook spirits in the far livingroom.

Grapevine afar pours wine for Jack, who sits forward as if waiting to catch a ball that never appears. Through their sidewindow, Deacon rocks his rocker, merrily sucking a cigar butt, ordained, ale-fatherly.

"For sweet shit," Grapevine cries, "let's hear Mahler's *Eighth!"*

"Good God, *no,*" Jack says. "I can go along with Oscar's man Bruckner partway at least, but not Mahler. Cuntheaded incurable jackoff artist sucking his own lollipop. His handjobs drain me, I can't stop laughing. *No* Mahler, please."

"Oh now, Jack," Oscar says, "Mahler's *Eighth* is the greatest piece of religious kitsch a Jew has produced since the *Song of Songs*. You've got to admit that and admire it for what it is. And Scherchen's performance is out of this world. He has Emmy Loose sighing and fainting right out of the choruses—I mean fainting in ecstasy!" Oscar kisses his fingers. "I'm sure that old man was getting into her pants, she couldn't sing that way otherwise."

"Goddamn right," Grapevine says. "Christ, she's creamin'!"

Leo-Teddy breathes cool stars to still himself. Goes indoors.

"Well, let's read some poetry," Jack McFin says. "Hell, let's read *Song of Myself!* Turn off that goddamn jukebox, Oscar. Music's too simple to write, don't you think? Any shithead can put those symbols together. Let's read Whitman."

"Song of Myself!" Oscar cries. "Do you realize how long that is? We'll be up until daybreak."

"Let's read it," Teddy says.

"Sure!" Leo says, swimming.

"I'm game b-b-b-but I'm goin' t' b-b-b-bed after an hour."

"Now Tiny," Oscar says. "You get entirely too much sleep. At your age you should be getting by on two or three hours a night."

"Four at the most, Oscar," Jack laughs. "Two screwing and two resting."

"You're p-p-p-probably right," Tiny glooms.

"I only need six hours at my age and I rise like a lark," Oscar says.

"Of course, you don't go down to Crescent Tool every day either," Deacon says. "With that infernal tool-stamping, which is louder than Mahler's *Eighth* on top of Beethoven's *Ninth,* I might add."

"That would mean nothing," Oscar says. "The working hours, I mean."

"You gotta read more Blake, Harpur," Locke says. "How can you send this boy into those satanic mills?"

"I don't send him into the mills!" Oscar cries.

"And your other poor slavey hired out to measure feet off the street," Deacon says. "I refer to our blooming shoe salesman, Tom Peep."

"I resent that!" Grapevine cries. "You don't understand the situation at all, Deacon, if that's what you think. *Shit!"*

"Have another drink, Rob," Deacon says.

Rob stares at the gallon dumbly. ". . . Don't understand the—*hiccough*—fraternity prevails among mastersingers. . . ." Falls forward between knees, hiccoughing, sits up, spasming regularly.

"Ah, I see what's coming," Deacon says.

"Let's get off this sleep kick," Rob hiccoughs. "What I wanna know, Oscar, is what has art got to do with *real* problems, such as the cattlemen versus the homesteaders?"

"Answer that vile question, Harpur," Deacon says.

"Dear Rob, art is useless," Oscar says. "Pour me one too, Tiny, if you will."

"Hear, hear!" Deacon cries. "Of art it may be said, Its uses are as lobsters on the moon—very rare!"

"I'll never b-b-b-believe it," Tiny says.

"Well, I do," Rob says. "Art is fuckin' useless. Jack?"

"You may be right, Rob," Jack says, "but I can't say for sure. I guess I'm just grateful I'm a poet—or think I am. The greatest sin against that little bit of spirit I have is ingratitude, and I don't want to intellectualize that spirit away. But Christ, Oscar, what's poetry *in* eternity for? Some wisdom strikes me as so profound that I know it's God-given. Look at Kafka. He didn't write for us, he wrote for himself out of religious purpose—spiritual purpose. Just because his stuff's in print doesn't mean he wrote it for print, or much of it. I really believe him when he says he wants it all burnt—it's not artistic shortcomings he's worried about exposing, it's that all his best stories are prayers and personal and not compromised by hopes of publication. I mean he's striving toward those heavenly gates, for God's sake, not the critics' blessings. Kafka, Blake, John Clare in the madhouse, Christopher Smart in the madhouse—Christ, they're the only ones who had freedom in eternity, and the God-given wisdom to hang onto it like a barefoot African running off with a chicken in each fist. I don't call prayer useless, why should I call poetry useless?"

"Hear, hear!" Deacon cries.

"Poetry's the most useful thing I can think of," Jack adds. "I hope you don't mind my being a little religious. Usually I'm not religious enough."

"Christ," Grapevine hiccoughs at Leo, "somebody should tape Jack and Oscar together. All's glorious conversation's bein' *lost!"* Shakes his head. " 'S terrible! I'd give my right ball to have all this taped! Then we c'd hear it all over 'gain t'morrow when we feel better."

"Wake up," Teddy nudges Leo. "What 're ya doin'?"

"I'm awake." Leo squinches at Rob, who squinches back. "We're awake," Leo says.

"Sure we are," Rob says.

A car pulls up the drive. George Gordon and Tony Tripi come in the back entry. Oscar rises, widewarmingly, and grips George in full embrace. "Let me look at you!" Oscar says, wet-eyed.

George Gordon holds a straight pipe, a white sailor's hat pulled down around his ears and turned up in back like a racing scull. His wolfhead burns with Faustian goatee. *"My God, you look great, Oscar!"* he says lifting Oscar off his feet. "And you haven't lost a pound either, I can tell!" He marches and dances about with Oscar's head brushing the ceiling, the floor sinking like a springboard.

"My God, I didn't think that was possible," Jack tells Teddy. "Oscar needs two scales to weigh himself."

"How'd you ever plan to get into a canoe together?" Deacon asks.

"Oh, we're going in separate kayaks," Jack says.

"I wondered about that when the subject came up," Deacon says.

"Well," Jack says, "Oscar's not a bad kayak amateur. He's coordinated like a one-man string quintet."

Locke leans over to nodding Leo. "Jack's the ninth ranking kayak racer in the States."

"Not any longer," Jack says. "George, you'll burst a blood vessel!"

"He can row backward faster than I can run forward," Locke says. "We raced on the Erie canal once. I lost."

Jack laughs. "You should have seen Oscar in his first kayak. Flipped over—he couldn't get out!"

"My God, Oscar, what happened?" Rob cries.

"Now, Jack," Oscar says from the ceiling, "I didn't *want* to get out. It was completely waterproof upsidedown—not a drop got in, you know. I was simply unwarned about the lightness of canvas. There's an entirely different stability from any other craft."

"Sure is," Jack says. "That's why it throws us."

"B-b-b-but Oscar. How w-w-w-were you saved!"

"Saved?" Oscar asks. "I floated up the other side."

"A full turn," Jack says. *"Boy!* I'll forego any analogies—for Melville's sake."

Oscar descends from his ceiling tour in George's grip. "I missed you," he says simply with feeling. Holds Gordon's face in pale meat-palms, kisses him flush on the lips, then steps back clapping his shoulders while Gordon grips Oscar. "Let me look at you!"

"Lest you get any wrong ideas," Deacon tells Teddy, "that's a show of purely Platonic affection."

"You're just jealous," Tiny says.

"Ah, my boy, what you'll never know about Zen." Deacon bows.

"Wake up!" Teddy nudges Leo.

"I'm awake! Gimme a cigarette."

"You're *Tony Tripi,* aren't you?" Oscar says. "I hear wonderful things about you."

"Well, I had to meet *you,*" Tony says—a dark rakethin bird from the Italian section down on Victoria Street. "Yep—had to!"

Oscar mocks surprise. "I'm glad you think so! But why?"

"Oscar Harpur, human gadfly—*had* to meet you!" Tony laughs nervously. "Go on talkin', I just came to listen, forget about me."

"Rosencrantz and Guildenstern!" George Gordon cries.

"Laertes!" Teddy cries.

George grips Teddy. "How's Leo?"

"Restin'," Teddy says. He senses a strange fear under George's hale glow.

"His hair's on fire," Jack says calmly across the room.

Teddy claps Leo's smoking forehead. "What's burnin'?" Leo asks.

"You!" Teddy shouts.

"Hey," Tony says, "you guys were in *Hamlet* together, weren't you? Missed that production, drat it."

"I hear a trumpet," Leo says softly. "Hi George, when'd ya get here?"

"Tony's a fine and mellowing writer," George says.

"I heard that and seriously question it," Deacon says. "How are things down at the dear benighted *Post-Journal?"*

Tripi cringes. "I wish I were at the *Sun!* Dya need a lousy sportswriter? I can spell—better'n Fitzgerald!"

"You'll start at the bottom," Deacon warns.

"I'll do it," Tony says. "I'll write deep purple football prose. Get anybody anything? St. Francis, the galloping doormat, at your service."

"George! George! Talk to me!" Oscar cries from his deep chair, feet hassocked, arms wide.

"Who's blowin' that trumpet?" Leo ask Teddy.

"What trumpet?"

"I thought we were going to read Whitman?" Jack says. "Christ, I'm awake. I could drink till noon—and may do it if the grapeshit holds out."

"George, you don't love me anymore," Oscar says wearily.

George tamps his pipe coals. "Say, how was your visit to Tate, Oscar?"

"Very charming! I brought some Jack Daniel's and showed him the first part of my *Poorhouse Poems."*

"Athing!" Rob tells Teddy solemnly "A *thing*—dya see? He's Oscar's hero in the poorhouse."

"And what did Tate think?" George asks.

"Oh, he loved them."

"What were his reservations, Oscar?" Jack asks.

"For the life of me, I couldn't figure 'em out," Oscar says. "I think he meant they needed more resonance."

"Christ, you're resonant," Jack says. "What'd he mean?"

"Oscar, read the poems or I'll *give* 'em," Rob says.

"Hell, yes, read them!" George says.

Oscar takes up his springbinder, turns to his poorhouse hero.

" 'S that a published book?" Leo asks.

"No," Oscar says, "this is just a binder, poor thing."

Deacon stops rocking—room quiet, porch crickets grating shrilly. Oscar reads with full surrender. Yellow words detach and fall in utter glory around Oscar's poorhouse. He ends deeply moved. *"No more,"* he whispers and leans his book against his chair. Rob falls back, glazed.

"That's sublime, Oscar," George whispers. "That defined a lot for me."

Oscar sighs. "Maybe I should give up verses and become a millionaire."

"I can't imagine what Tate meant by resonance," Jack says.

Drained, Oscar sits looking out at crates and empty boxes filling the kitchen. "Tiny, dear boy, do we have to wake up in the morning and see all that shit in the kitchen? Why don't you take it out back and burn it? Rob, go help him. Looks like a boneyard out there."

"Let's all pitch in for Janet and Becky," Jack says.

All pile boxes onto the ash drum out back. Tiny goes up to the barn, rips off a sixteen-foot tall board. Gordon cracks it to pieces.

"Tiny," Deacon says, "I thought you were supposed to be repairing this place, not demolishing it."

"What does it really matter?" Oscar asks, face sagging.

Baking-hot fire grows in a yellow blossom of suet and bones, marrow hissing and spitting blue flames in gas jets.

"Boy!" Jack sighs at the blaze. " 'Our God is not out of breath, because he hath blown one tempest, and swallowed a Navy.' I've been reading Donne's sermons. I need 'em!"

"Wish I was blowing your trumpet," Locke tells Leo.

"Not out here," Jack says.

"Or Oscar will throw himself on the pyre," Deacon says.

"Now I'm not that bad!" Oscar says. "My God, what are you kiddies doing up again?"

The four children hop starknaked into the yard, Sarah in panties. Shoulders pumpkinorange, Chris streaks to Tiny. "We couldn't sleep, Daddy!" Curt cries.

"You mean you didn't want to," Oscar says. "Is that right, Julia?"

Julia's wordless joy blazes at orange gods. Sarah bends to the flames, heavenhearted. Curt dances and hops.

"Goddamnit, if we're not going to read," Jack says, "I'm for a walk."

"Great," Tripi says. "We passed Moon Brook comin' up. The fairies are holdin' their midsummer open nationals tonight."

"Christ, we can't miss that!" Jack says. "I despise golf—though it's not as bad as tennis—but I love shaved greens."

"That ninth hole's like the river Jordan," Tripi says. "I only say that because it's St. John's Day at midnight."

"John the Baptist or St. John the Apostle?" Jack asks.

"Jack the Baptist!" Tripi says. "Down on Victoria Street tomorrow we'll have more baptisms than you can shake a forked stick at."

"Are you practicing?" Jack asks.

"Wish I could tell!" Tripi says. "Don't want to commit myself until the last moment."

"I know what you mean," Jack sighs. "I'm a chronic backslider myself."

"Compadre!"

"Let's have coffee before we go on this walk," Oscar says. *"Janet!"*

"We don't want that shit espresso, Oscar," Jack says, "we want wine. Somebody get a gallon, a full one."

"I keep hearin' a trumpet somewhere," Leo tells Teddy.

"Why don't I take your trumpet?" Locke asks Leo.

Leo-Teddy goes into the vacant kitchen, hits the voodoo juice in Teddy's case, brings out the trumpet and mute. Sarah totes a gallon wonderingly as Tripi wafts about her. "I'm batty as a bat, don't mind me!"

Rob Grapevine throws his arms up the fire, dancing. "I wanna be translated into the Egyptian! I gotta have my reincarnation poem in Egyptian, gotta see it in hieroglyphs! And then I'll die satisfied forever! WHOO!"

"You'll have to go out to Nashville," Oscar says, "and visit Sidney Hirsch for that."

Leo-Teddy carries Sarah and Julia on his shoulders as Tiny spins Chris aloft.

"Heavens!" Janet says in the back doorway. "Where are you all going, Oscar?"

"Moon Brook," Tripi says. "Come along!"

Becky follows, nightgown a wing of moonlight.

Leo-Teddy lurches into a fox-trot with himself, girls screaming on his necks. "Be myie*EE LAAWV!"* George tenors. *"Mario!"* Rob cries.

"Madness!" Janet says.

"Don't discount madness," Deacon calls. "We'll all grow new heads in the morning."

"We'll need 'em," Jack says.

Fire dies as singers cross field to road. *"Damp raiders of the dew!"* Rob Grapevine cries, barewaisted. Fireflygreen moonlight.

"Let's keep this down a bit," Jack says. "We may hear something worth hearing."

"The stars on their pivots!" Rob whispers.

Walk down the still road in roaring silence. Cows in a barn awake and chafe at passing voices. Pale fences where the pens stand empty. Drowned fields. A dog barks afar.

"Oh what this air does to my rheumatic bones," Deacon says, cigar fluming ghostblue.

"I'm arthritic," Tiny says. "The night's hard on me too."

"This isn't night, it's eternity," Jack says.

"I list where the winefly lists," Rob Grapevine tenors, stumbling.

Cross to the golf course, circle the slope below the white clubhouse high in the moonlight.

"It's the world's largest graveyard," Jack says.

"Heavenly," Tony says. "There go Peaseblossom and Cobweb!"

Slopes of liquid pearl fall before them.

"Oh, with eighteen perilous holes for golfers!" Rob cries on the green.

Leo-Teddy gallops, girls riding then rolling on the wadded green.

"Leo-Teddy's a centaur," George Gordon says.

"Drinks like a horse too," Jack says.

"Hey, Deacon!" Tony calls. *"Purple golf balls sped over Moon Brook to holes in the perilous green!* Can I show that to the *Sun*? Will they hire me?"

"Say Shakespearian golf balls," Jack says.

"O O O O that Shakespeherian Rag!" Rob cries. *"It's so elegant! So intelligent!"*

Grapevine runs after the children, hallooing. Leo-Teddy rolls forward on the damp, stomachs sloshing. George Gordon walks on his hands, stiltedly. Rob falls down. "I lost her, I lost her!" he sobs on the grass.

"What's wrong with him?" Locke asks Oscar.

"Leave him alone for awhile," Becky says. She hikes off in her cotton nightgown, sits marbled with Tiny and Chris in a white shadow-trio.

"Rob used to go with Becky before Tiny did," Tony whispers to Leo-Teddy.

Rob falls over on his back, passed out.

"Tony, put some wine on his eyes," Deacon says.

"Leave him alone!" Becky says. "My fanny's *soaked."*

"So'm I," Tiny says. Chris's white ribs heave, tow hair shocked white.

"Ollie," Leo whispers, "Jack thinks we drink like a horse."

"Well, we got two stomachs," Teddy says.

"AHHH!" Leo-Teddy cries.

Tony and Deacon go up to Grapevine's white bread-body in the moonlight.

"Go ahead," Deacon says, "see what happens."

Tony dips a finger into the winegallon, wets each eyelid. Grapevine snores. "Two drops won't do it, Deacon," Tony says.

"Two tankcars, you mean," Deacon says. "We can't let this poor useless wine poet just lie here all night, he'll catch pneumonia."

"That's not possible the way he's fortified," Jack says.

"*We* could carry him back," Teddy says.

"That's hopeless," Tiny says.

"Stop tormenting him!" Becky says.

"We're not tormenting him!" Tiny cries. "He's not even *awake*."

"Don't be too sure of that," Deacon says. "I see signs of life."

Rob Grapevine snorts, sits up on his elbows, looks blanky, unbelievingly about at figures flitting above him, others moonsculpted—children running whitely on the slope. His eyes shutter.

"Christ, he's not even here," Jack says. "I know that look. I wasn't there when I saw it on myself a couple of times."

Rob's eyes open on a greenglowing sleuth in the grass.

"Roar, Grapevine," Deacon says.

"Where'm I?" Rob looks at Jack. "I see a light comin' outta your eyes," he says.

"Out of my ass," Jack laughs. "I'm farting fireflies."

Rob lifts his fingers, a burden-bearing stargazer—

> "And why do I often meet your visage here,
> Your eyes like agate lanterns?"

"I'm not Poe," Jack says. "Man makes the world with his cock, not with his pen, Rob. Wake up, for Christ's sake."

Leo-Teddy shakes, marveling at Jack's rockdeep obscenity.

"All right, Grapevine," Deacon says, "if you can't roar,

repent! And be new-baptized! I see I'm not getting through."

Rob staggers to his feet, slumps on Jack. *"John?"* he asks.

"Don't call me John, I'm Happyjack McFin."

"Happy Jack? *Hiccough!* Oscar? *Hiccough!* HICCOUGH! HICCOUGH!"

"Stand back," Deacon warns.

"Where am I?"

"You're eclipsed," Jack says. "How do you feel?"

"HICCOUGH! HICCOUGH!"

"Rob, go off in the trees," Oscar says. "Let's be sporting and not heave on the green." Oscar turns Rob, gives him a gentle push toward the woods below.

Rob turns, violently hiccoughing. "Where you all goin'?"

"Don't stand near him," Deacon warns. "Go down to the woods, Rob, and do your duty."

Rob staggers downhill toward the dark woods.

"We'll meet you round the bend at Ninny's tomb," Deacon calls.

Rob fades into trees and thickets.

"By God, I think he'll make it," Deacon says.

"Help! Help!" Rob cries from the woods. "I'm murdered by thorns!"

"Christ, he's lost," Jack says. "Serves him right."

"Chris," Tiny says, "run down and help Rob get back."

Chris runs naked downslope to the woods.

"Ah, the plains of Athens—reborn in King James," Deacon says. "I was there, you know, and saw all those naked fellers out running."

"Hey, you fatties used to be great runners," George tells Leo-Teddy. "Why don't we have a race? Out past that sand trap and back."

"You darin' us?" Teddy asks.

"In a friendly way," George says rapping Teddy's shoulder.

"Can you run," Teddy asks Leo, "or should I show him up alone?"

"Don't wanta but I will," Leo says. "Of course, it's not fair."

"Yeah," Teddy tells George, "there are two of us."

"For God's sake, I know that! Oscar, you judge."

"Not so fast, my fine feathered friends," Deacon says.

"This must be done by the book. True Athenians will run stark naked or not at all. Now if this is to be a true decathlon event, I advise you to strip down or it won't be registered among the immortal races."

"Christ, yes," Jack says. "Bareass or don't run."

"You wanta run too?" Leo asks.

"I prefer fishing," Jack says.

"Somebody go down there to hold a light so we can see where the hole is," Teddy says. "How'll we know where to turn?"

George hands his butane lighter to Tiny. "Go down and stand on the hole like a goodfellow."

Tiny sighs, trying the flame. "All right. But don't trample me!"

As George Gordon and Leo-Teddy strip, Tiny runs past the sand trap to the far hole and sends up a brief blue flame. *"Ready?"* he calls.

"I'll call out!" Oscar cries. "Okay, you're to circle Tiny and come back here and pass the gallon."

"Boy," Teddy whispers, "are we not in shape for this, Ygor."

"Who's worried?" Leo unbelts his stomach roll.

George drops to wet grass, swiftly pumps twenty push-ups, jumps up, swats his palms clean. "Ready?"

"Line up," Oscar says. "Kiddies get back."

Locke blows call to colors on the muted trumpet, badly. Naked runners bend in moonlight, knuckles on the green. *"Put yourself into it!"* Teddy whispers.

"Now I've seen everything!" Jack says.

Girls laugh, roll back, sit up wideeyed.

"On your mark," Oscar says. "Get set. *Go!*—and bless you all."

Foameyed, Gordon slips on his face on wet grass as Leo-Teddy hurtles off.

"Drat it!" Tony says, "I wanta get in this too. Can I have special dispensation to run with my clothes on?"

"Your moment's past, my son," Deacon says.

"I'll run anyway," Tony says, chasing Gordon and the children. Gordon flies toward the galloping twins.

"This feels great!" Leo says.

"Too much bellyvash," Teddy gasps.

"I don't dare let out on this grass!"

"He'll be lettin' out downhill," Teddy puffs. "Let's save

ourselves for the turn. We goin' around or over the sand trap?"

"Straight through," Leo says. "I hear 'im! *Let's go.*"

Chris comes out of the woods leading Rob Grapevine. Looks up startled, *"Wha-at!"* Rob sees three naked shadows running at him. *"Aghhh!"* he screams and rushes back into the woods and briers. Chris takes off after the twins.

A butane starflame wavers blue and yellow on the far green as Leo-Teddy hits the sand trap with Gordon beside him. Gordon goes down on his knees as the twins leap up and out. Pound through the rough surefootedly, head toward the weird blue flame, hearts thudding.

"Sweat in my eyes!" Leo whispers.

"Keep hopin'!"

Thump down the straitaway, not looking back, full out. Suddenly Gordon strains beside them as they hit the green. Tiny screams at the white mass charging at him, drops to his knees covering his head, the burning lighter above. Gordon grabs the lighter, crying, "This is mine, old man!" as Leo-Teddy piles into him and all go down on Tiny.

"Tripi wins, Tripi wins!" Tiny screams in the tangle.

Gordon up and gone, Leo-Teddy on his heels, band throbbing.

Tripi sees them coming, turns and starts back ahead, cheating. Gordon sprints past him. "AGGHH!"—a terror-stricken scream again rises from the woods where Grapevine plunges, *"I'm cut, I'm cut!"* Leo-Teddy pours his might into wineburning arms and legs, gaining Gordon's side. Gordon lights the lighter as he runs, returning like Pheidippides from Marathon to Athens. A steel-mill flame shoots into his goatee. *"Sheist!"* he cries beating himself on the chin with both hands, lighter falling to grass. *"God damn it!"* Turns for the lighter as the twins beat past, breaking their necks for the sand trap. *"Tripi! Get that lighter!"* Gordon calls back, running again.

"This hurts!" Leo cries, strangling.

"Forget it!" Teddy urges.

Cross the rough and leap like lead into the sand trap, then push off. Faraway girls and children shout with Oscar, Jack and Deacon. Locke drops his mute and more or less blows "Bugle Call Rag." Small childbodies jump in the moonlight, circling moths. Leo-Teddy hears Gordon hit the trap behind with breath bursting as if punched in his chest. Wet grass slips underfoot as toes dig into the turf. Chris runs toward them, they wave him aside. Behind, Gordon cries, *"Goddamnit, Chris!"*

Leo's horn blares under blueburning clouds over the ninth hole. Leo-Teddy fixes his being on the urgent trumpet. Legs burn and mouths foam wineslather, straining for the gallon where Oscar rises like Karloff, arms gigantically aloft in the moon, slowly waving. Gordon flies by Leo's side, leg muscles pumping. They race uphill to the moon.

Now Leo is the light, Teddy the fire. Breathburning strength. Dew floods the floor as milkbright mares boil into Oscar's circle, throats howling, nostrils snorting, eyes rolling in frenzy, thudding on muscles of luck and motherspirit.

"Gordon!" Oscar cries.

"Gosh, I'd say it was the twins from where I stood," Jack says. "Or at least a tie."

"A palpable tie!" Deacon says.

Locke and the ladies agree.

"Let's let it go at that," Jack says stripping his shirt. "Oscar, give George your robe while I sweat these boys out. Christ, that was the craziest race I ever saw, I'm sorry now I didn't run." Jack rubs down Leo-Teddy with his shirt. "I wouldn't have minded losing, in fact—not too greatly. *Boy,* that was worth being here for! How do you feel?"

Leo-Teddy gasping and naked, legs rippling.

"Anybody seen Grapevine?" Tiny asks coming up. "I looked in the w-w-w-woods b-b-b-but he's vamoosed."

"How many times you take a dive, George?" Jack asks. "About thirty-eight?"

"Grass was slippery an' beard caught fire!" George gasps.

"Breakneck as a dream," Jack says.

"We mighta had unfair advantage," Leo gasps.

"Do it again sometime!" George warns.

"Why, you're hardly winded," Oscar pats George. *"Hercules!"*

"Maybe Grapevine went back to the house," Deacon says. "There's still another gallon back there."

A car passes as a deer's green eyes glare from the wood.

Wineybrook spirits wind over dreaming Moon Brook,

float on mist to the farm. Spreadeagle at last in the cracked livingroom.

"Perhaps Grapevine's finally on the roof," Deacon says.

"Only by a miracle," Oscar says.

"Why on the roof?" Gordon asks.

"He's been threatening to climb it all night," Oscar says. "But he couldn't have, do you think?"

Oscar and Gordon step onto the lawn, scan the roof. "Well, what the hell," Gordon says. Leaps onto porchrail, swings up to the lower roof. Tests the drain, heists himself to the upper roof, scrambles on ridged soles to the high gable and straddles the house. "George, watch yourself!" Oscar cries at the high roofshadow. George seated, spurs the roof. "Xerxes' elephant!" he cries. Stares down the tapeworm road. *"Lo! the Egyptian comes*—if I'm not mistaken."

"Egyptian, hell, it's a zombie," Oscar says.

Rob Grapevine staggers up to the farmdoor, red skin scraped, drenched with winesweat. They help him into the livingroom. Redeyed, torn with whipstings, he falls on the gallon, wet back filthy, flying curls shot with leafmeal.

"Where w-w-w-were you!"

"Lost on the Jurassic highway!" Rob cries, biting back tears. "Came to in the fuckin' woods durin' the rainstorm, fell on the gravel—!"

"What rainstorm, Rob?" Oscar asks.

"Didn't it rain up here?" Rob asks. "Jesus, the toilet overflowed where I was, look at me, I'm soppin'. *God!*—what a walk! Slipped on the grass—kept seein' *wild mares,* I swear Bucephalus galloped by on the golf course, all four hooves off the ground. There mus' be wild horses from here to Sinclairville! Next thing there'll be cattle rustlers. I'm sore all over, ankles, shins, knees, elbows, ribs, shoulders—I musta been *trampled* on, or hit by a car maybe, I'm not sure which! Woke up in a gravel ditch. Limped up to a farmhouse—Christ, it was a trooper's house and he threatened t' run me in for *prowling*—sonofabitch wouldn't even tell me which side of Horton Road I was on!"

"You poor boy," Becky says.

"Well, I'll be all right, maybe. Christ, if I don't get a poem outta this nightmare—alls I remember is this inhuman bluewhite teevee moonlight!"

"Wonderful!" Jack says.

Rob looks at Jack queerly. "What're ya all grinnin' about? It wasn't funny, I tell you! Christ, *look at me!*—it'll take me a week to knit back t'gether."

"Read some Whitman," Jack says.

Rob out back, pissing in eternity with Leo-Teddy. "We *piss* like a horse," Teddy sighs.

"Listen," Rob says, "you guys're gonna learn more here this summer than in four years of college. I hope you'll be comin' out some more with your horns—it isn't always this *fuckin' upsetting* out here—we'll have some quiet nights with Wagner and Mahler and Bruckner. Just sippin' to keep the gremlins at bay, y' know?"

Tripi dances out behind Locke. "I see we missed the micturation contest," Tony says. "Grapevine piss over the moon?"

"Ah, a metapiss!" Locke says. "Who doused all the fireflies?"

"Listen, you guys," Rob tells Tony and Leo-Teddy. "We can't fail the spirit Oscar and Jack have *given* us—know what I mean? Put your hands on mine. Oscar tol' me confidentially he thinks you twins have the sensibilities of angels, Teddy especially, but the minds of morons." Leo-Teddy blazes through moonlit masks. "Whatever he means by that—but don't *worry,* he gives me the whip too! 'S all out of love, believe me."

"What'd he say about me?" Tony asks, hopefully.

Rob looks away, unable to lie.

"I see," Tony says. "And here—I felt like an angel all night!"

They clasp hands, a vote by starlight, go in and read Whitman. After awhile George and Tony go. Behind his wheel, George crimps a cigarette into his long Zeus holder like Oscar's. "Wonderful workout!" he wolfsmiles. Tony leans out his window, taking Leo-Teddy's hands. "To smile is to bless," he says. "That's my lifework—make everyone happy!"

Oscar swales off to bed with Yeats and a candle. Deacon sleeps in the easy chair and hassock. Locke nods over his imperfect dedication for "Pass me through, Beloved" for Harpur. Leo-Teddy awakens at orange first-light, sitting against cracked plasterboard. Rob's at peace in his sunbolted greasygreen snoring bag in the back entry. Tiny's feet hit the ceiling like a die-stamp as Becky comes down to make coffee. Jack sits in the rocker, glasses on, reading, sipping. He looks up, blankblue.

"Let's go out for a stretch," he says, "I've still got five pages to go. God, *Song of Myself* is glorious! The Spirit is moving in every word."

Stretch in the front yard. First sun-needles in the tree-line.

"Thank God, we finally got that foul phonograph off and into some serious poetry," Jack says. "Christ, it's great out here. Smell that air. Maybe we can get up to the lake for some fishing today? I have to leave tomorrow. I hear this lake's full of muskies, four and five footers. Ever catch one?"

"Caught a sturgeon in Lake Erie once," Teddy says. "But nothin' up here."

"Just some sunnies," Leo says.

"Oh, I like sunnies," Jack says thoughtfully. "How'd you boat the sturgeon?"

"Dad gaffed it," Leo says.

"It was a whale!" Teddy says.

"That must have been thrilling. Love to 've been there. How old were you?"

"Four or five," Leo says.

"We were in a rowboat out at the nightline," Teddy says. "And suddenly there it was beside us in the water. Huge. *A whale, a whale!* we cried."

"I'll bet that put the fear of God into you," Jack says.

"We were with our father," Teddy says.

"It was almost as big as the boat!" Leo says.

Jack laughs hard at Leo. "There speaks a true fisherman!"

Twins' Grandfather Kerris rises. His hands dip into cool water, he sprinkles his face and shoulders. Rocks on his porch, full cheeks splitting with sap. Orchard fog lifting, a far groundhog catches his eye. He stirs with thoughts of fish in the red morning.

Leo comes to behind the wheel of the breadtruck, harsh headlights passing him in the night. Teddy stares ahead at the road. Glance into inner rearview mirror: Jack McFin and Rob Grapevine on the truckfloor amid littered orange loaves of Hokum, passing a winegallon. Half-empty.

"Boy, I wish we had more of that voodoo rum," Jack calls out. "You guys drink good stuff—and powerful! *Lautermilch.*"

"If we all sell blood," Rob says, "we c'n get another happiness jug in New York."

"Good idea," Jack suggests. Stan-Laurel brokendoll blanklook.

"Or maybe *two* gals of vino veritas," Rob says. "And we could leave one with Jack when we come back tomorrow. Manhattan junglejuice!"

"I'm needleshy, I'm afraid," Jack says.

"Christ, me too!" Rob says. "But I'm willin'. How about it, you guys?"

"Oh sure," Teddy says. "How much they pay?"

"St. Luke's gives four bucks a pint for beginners," Jack says. "But I'd hate to have you sell it just for me. Gosh, no!"

"Think nothin' of it," Teddy says. "Leo and I should be good for eight bucks. Though we may need gas and doughnut money t' get home again."

"Hell," Rob says, "we just siphon gas outta some parked crumple-car—we c'n get a hose for a quarter. Let's put all live cash to good use."

". . . . This flat floor's like a raft," Jack says.

"Rides smooth as a cobweb," Rob says. "Wow—martini moonlight! *And the hills danced with champagne sardines!* Jesus, lend me your notepad, Jack, I feel a pome comin' on!"

"Too bad we can't get in some catfishing off the backend," Jack says. "Well, this is enough. I want to thank you guys, and Hokum too! I wouldn't want to be anywhere else but right here. Now."

"Aristotle," Rob says.

"No, not Aristotle," Jack fleers. "He's dead, I'm alive. Here, now."

Rob kisses his fingers at the ceiling. "YAHOO*! Crane, thou shouldst be with us at this hour.* Calls for a drink, yesirree," he sighs.

Raft rounding rockchiselled Allegheny mountainside, a deep channel of wooded moonlight falling below the windblowing open sliding door. Leo stares at doped hills, peagreen skyshine. "Where are we?" he whispers to Teddy.

"*Huh?* We're on 17 comin' outta Horseheads."

"*Horseheads!*" Leo cries softly.

"Coming into Elmira," Jack says. "I used to teach up at Watkins Glen. Couldn't stand the drunks, though. Christ, never trust a drunk, their word isn't worth shit. I drink a lot myself—but I always keep my word, I'll say that about myself. It was a girls school. *Ugh*—a spring day, all those little cuntsicles batting their asses at you—I hated it! Drove me to drink."

"Whoo!" Rob cries. "Yowzah, why don't we make a detour up to Watkins Glen? Dip in, chilluns!" Rob splits open a loaf of Hokum.

"God, no," Jack says. "Though I love Seneca Lake and the cascades, don't get me wrong." He laughs flatly. "Talk about cuntsicles. Out in L.A.—that fruitstand—I had a banker's daughter who lent me her Cadillac. I hated driving it, kept losing the damn thing. It was as big as a tin dinosaur but I kept losing it like a cuff link. Had a job waiting tables at a ritzy inn at Rancho Santa Fe, but I woke up stoned in L.A. and that Caddy was nowhere in view. Hopped a freight out to Rancho Santa Fe—was dead asleep on top of a boxcar, kept nodding out, which *is* dangerous. I had a jockstrap with me, so I tied my wrist to the coupling wheel. Had a good two-hour snooze up in the breeze. When I got there, this cottage was having a champagne breakfast and I was just on time to serve it. Outdoor table surrounded by icebuckets—tubs of champagne and fifths of Jack Daniel in the kitchen. I pour down a tumbler of bourbon and sail out with scrambled eggs for these movie execs yipping on the lawn—bunch of egofucking cocksuckers, they're the worst shitheads in the world. I pour icewater into a woman's waterglass—but it's upsidedown and I stand watching icecubes bounce off it unbelievably and dance all over her scrambled eggs. Boy, was I surprised—and blotto! Yeahh—you twins drink like a horse—fuck like one too, I'll bet! I'm more of a steady drinker. Not a whole lot at once, just steady. And eventually everything in sight and ready for more. At that pace I can outdrink even Oscar, and *he* buckles walls when he's juiced. He'll finally hit the sack but I'll still be up at eight or nine, still sipping, if there's a drop left. Not too blotto either. I love to watch that muscat sunrise, smell the world waking up, say a few prayers to Walt. Or maybe God. Coasting on wine wings like Whitman's man-of-war-bird—'thou art *all* wings,' Walt says. Or wine! ha ha."

"God," Rob says, tears standing in his eyes. "GOD! Do you really pray, Jack?"

"Oh, sometimes."

"How dya go about it?" Leo asks.

"Spare no details!" Jack cries. "I'm getting a book of my poems together—at last—and there'll be a little religious touch in it. That's fashionable. Nothing holyroller, of course. I just want to be honest with God—not distraught, for Christ's sake, just honest. I detest these poetasters who cornhole God whenever His back's turned."

Leo's nerves grip the wheel, an urgent melodious trumpet purling somewhere on the mountain. Coldprickling forehead and arms, shortness of breath, wet nose, sudden eagle clearness of eye. Some wordless thought warping him, an unfocused urge fighting back. Shallow breath near tears. Pull the truck onto the roadside, headlights burning the valley shadow. Switchoff. Listen. A far horn, echoing, urging, his heart hooked into his throat.

"What're ya doin'?" Teddy asks.

"Tyin' my shoelace, I felt it snap. Goddamn motherfucking sonofabitch shoelace. PISSES ME OFF!"

"What kind of knot do you use?" Jack asks. "Oh, those bowknots aren't worth shit. Let me show you my kayak knot." Jack lifts Leo's shoelace, ties the burst strands, draws the laces snug, ties a bowknot and knots the loops also. "That'll last all day," he says. "And night!"

Leo sighs. "Feels good! Piss call, Teddy."

Step down into the night, piss into sloped darkness.

"That Leo's a powerhouse," they hear Jack tell Rob. "He's going to make it. What did he say back there at Horseheads? I want to jot that down."

"Christ," Rob says, "don't let me mangle it. 'A universe of solid time is all around us, melting like a drop of hot wax wherever we move.' "

"Talk about an expanding universe," Jack says, "—wow. That boy's a mystic. He's the drop of hot wax."

"Caramba!" Rob cries. "That's worthy of Donne or Herbert!"

"Oh, I don't know," Jack says. "Maybe it's just head shit. I'll wait until I read it tomorrow."

Leo stands quaking. "I said that? I need a drink."

Teddy snags the gallon, hands it to Leo. "Feelin' okay?"

"How the hell'd we get this fuckin' truck?"

"*Your* idea!" Teddy says. "We were just drivin' Jack to the bus station, then we decided to take him on to Randolph, *then* Salamanca. Then we just kept on goin'."

"Oh my God. What's Colonel John gonna say?"

"We didn't plan t' go this far!"

"We're almost in New York, moron!" Leo whispers. "They must be missin' the truck just about now."

"We'll phone in and explain," Teddy says. "We're bringin' it back t'morrow, it's not like theft, ya know. We were bombed when we sneaked it out—I didn't even want to!"

"Jesus. How much dough we got?"

"We're flat."

Leo's heart sinks. "Shit. What'd I do t' my finger? Feels numb."

"You don't remember, Hyde?"

"Don't be so fuckin' superior! Would I ask if I knew?"

"Ya belted Mama, asshole. That's what."

Leo's eyes close on dark night. *"Ohh!"* he moans. Stands silent. "Did I hurt her?"

"A shiner. And her face is swollen."

"Ohh, ohh!" Leo moans. "What was I thinkin'?"

"Salvation!" Teddy whispers. "Ya wanted to wake 'er up, save her from Demon Gin. She egged ya into it but you were a real tornado, buster. Smashed her bedlamp—ya even pulled out the telephone, so we *can't* phone home for money, either. You burned our bridges."

Leo shakes his head. "Why didn't ya stop me?"

"I did," Teddy says. "I broke your finger."

"—I don't feel good."

"I'll bet ya don't. We'll get it set back in King James."

"—Will she let us back in the house? Do I dare ask!"

"Shit. She's had worse from George and Hermann and Durwood."

Leo chokes, shaken. "Gimme another drink!" Brackish red shower into stomach. "Dya hear a trumpet? What's that tune?"

"I don't hear *anything*."

"I'd like t' shoot myself and explode my brain like a cauliflower."

"You must like loud noises."

"Don'tcha understand how I feel? You got no heart at all? You're insane! You're just a monster, Teddy, that's all you are. Don'tcha realize how I'm sufferin'?"

Teddy plays a tearful ghostviolin.

"Hopeless," Leo says. "That's all, brother. Let's go so we can get back, shithead."

"Leo?" Jack says softly within. "Oh, he's a hopeless alcoholic. I think Teddy may make it, though."

"You just said Leo," Rob says.

"Did I? I could be wrong about both of them. I could be wrong about everything."

"Why'd you say Teddy'd make it?" Rob asks.

"I don't know," Jack says. "The way he talks about his grandfather. The ancestral tree's the most important source of spirit. It's genetic, it's a gift from heaven. That's from Hirsch."

"It was Leo who was talkin' about his grandfather," Rob says.

"Oh, was it?" Jack says.

Leo-Teddy pulses with embarrassment, gets in the truck. Leo switches on, pulls out, eyes full of water. Long silent drive past Elmira.

"Whattaya think about language as gesture, Jack?" Rob asks.

"My God, I don't! Maybe language as God. I don't shortchange language—or God."

"The man without God in his bed is dead," Rob says. "And doesn't know it!"

"Or maybe he *does,*" Jack says. "I sure did."

"Hey, handy-dandy!—hadn't thought about that," Rob says. "You know that poem by Whitman with God as his bedfellow? Damn litcrits are always thinkin' he's talkin' about a faggot."

"Whitman's no faggot," Jack says. "I knew a Village faggot, among others. Used to hear music under his hair-dryer. Muzak came pouring right out of the dryer. Needed help, that lad, tons of it. The auditories are terrible—though not as bad as the visuals. When I lived in an empty lot by the Salvation Army in Hell's kitchen, I could hear their band all night—was always 'Nearer My God to Thee'! ha ha. They weren't playing, of course. Did I tell you about my fainting at the blood bank?" Jack calls to Leo-Teddy. "Soon as they jabbed the needle in, I fainted. Wham, right out. So they quit and gave me a doubleshot when I woke up. Boy, I thought, this is the Promised Land! Next week I'm back and faint again—on purpose, of course. But this time they snap an ammonia ampule under my nose. They'd cut out the whiskey ration. I decided to change my bank!"

"When was that, Jack?" Leo asks huskily, just keeping his voice from breaking.

"Oh that was years ago. Years and years ago. I was a terrific lush then."

RAINDARKENING bankwindow, hellshine within. Villagers rushing corpsebright. Black noon falls on West Fourteenth.

Mrs. Alice Anchor, Chemical Church Bank vice-president, weighs Leo-Teddy's loan papers—his damnable finances. "Are you as foggy as ya look?" Teddy asks Leo quietly. Stan-Leo scratches his head, tries to focus, leans forward as if to catch a ball that never arrives. "Oh, thtop imitatin' Jack!" Teddy says. "That big drunk."

"Frankly," Alice says, "I'm curious. You have an income of twenty thousand dollars!"

Ghostmoney! Shined, rotting shoes, musty shoppingbags stuffed with stolen music, stolen books, stolen records. Burgundy.

"But only Leo wants this loan?" she asks.

"He has credit," Teddy says. Smiling gap, his two front uppers missing.

"What's wrong with *your* credit?" she asks.

"The National Credit Athothiation," Teddy lisps. "They thent me a red letter thayin' my credit ratin's gone. I owe Columbia, RTHEA Victor, and Time-Life for bookth and records."

"National Credit?—never heard of 'em," Alice says. "We'll set them aside for the moment. Now, a joint application will be much stronger. Not that I minimize your obligations. You do intend to pay these mail-order clubs?"

"We wanna contholidate our debts!" Teddy says. "Sure we'll pay."

"How much do you owe?" she asks. Brown eyes, beauty-shop waves.

"Maybe forty buckth. I shouldn't have ordered the junk."

"What are your other debts?"

"Bond Clothes for these trenchcoats." Teddy shrugs, punches his chin for his idiocy.

She eyes his missing teeth. "Are you a boxer?"

"I was hit by a flyin' manhole cover," Teddy says.

"My heavens! Lucky you weren't killed. *You too,*" she tells Leo, who nods blankly. "How'd it happen?"

"Uhh," Teddy stumbles. "It muthta been thteam built up in the thewer thythtem. We were walkin' down Maiden Lane when thith cover flew fifty feet into the air. Wow. Damn thing came down on a truck—no one was hurt, thank God." Teddy smiles, ending his tale with an eyeroll.

"Except *you,*" Alice says.

"Oh, it didn't *hit* me," Teddy says. "I was jutht so fluthtered, I banged into a lamppotht."

"Truck was ruined," Leo reminds Teddy.

"Dya read the *Daily News?*" Teddy asks.

"Never," Alice says.

"They reported it. Latht week, Leo?"

"M? Yeah, last month."

Teddy sighs forbearingly. "Well, two weekth ago, Mrs. Anchor."

"You don't own a car?" she asks.

"Not anymore," Leo says, wishing he were clear-headed. "Streets are so unsafe to drive on. But we got a big hifi and library."

"And musical inthrumentth," Teddy says.

"A piano?" she asks.

"No," Leo says. "Just horns." His head cocks, he hears radio signals afar. Teddy nudges him: *pay attention.*

"Expensive horns?" she asks. Leo-Teddy smiles forlornly. "Then let's forget about musical instruments," she says. Looks over her shoulder, drops her voice. "I *like* your beards—they're very distingué."

"Vandykes," Teddy says through chlorophyll breath-mask. Leo blushes bitterly at Teddy's idiot gaptooth grin, averts his head.

"You look like musicians!" she says, eying their shined split shoes, striped ties, steel specs. "Sort of European," she adds. "But don't try to softsoap me. In fact, I'd prefer to talk either with one or the other of you. This seven thousand combined yearly income from the Virginia Chirpists Service—what do you do for this, Leo?"

"Chirpiththth reviews music," Teddy lisps quickly.

"We're quoted in the *Times*."

"Virginia Chirpiththth is quoted," Teddy corrects him.

"But it's us."

"Yeth, but that means nothin' for a bank loan, Leo."

"Of course it does," Alice says. "That's excellent! Do you like *Time* magazine?"

Leo frowns. "Oh, they don't sign their work."

Teddy shrugs. "We don't either."

"Well, we're staff."

"No we're not, we're freelanthe."

"I see," Leo says. "We put in so much time for 'em, it feels like we're staff. We're paid by the review, Mrs. Anchor."

"How much?" she asks.

"We—we started out at four dollars," Leo says. "Now we're up to six dollars a review."

"And you make seven thousand a year at this!" she cries.

"It's exhausting," Leo says.

"There's an awful lot recorded and published each year," Teddy says.

"So you're established critics?"

"Reviewers," Teddy says.

"Well, I don't know anything more about music than I read in *Time*."

"It's our inner life," Leo says.

Teddy groans. "That *doesn't* go into a bank loan, Leo."

"Do you publish your music?" she asks.

Teddy laughs. "We never even met a published composer!"

"But we're doin' a soundtrack for our movie *Trumpet*. That's why we need the loan."

"And for dental work. I need some choppers for blowin' my ax. Like to thee the thcript?" Teddy digs into his bag.

"Let's hold off on that. So you've been with the Department of Welfare for six months as social workers. That's your big income?"

"Aside from benefits," Leo says. Teddy bumps him.

"What benefits?" Alice asks.

Leo-Teddy, quiet. Close, damp bank, hearts pounding. Leo eyes dried ooze on Teddy's redscraped jowl. Teddy clears his throat. Leo hears floodwarnings. "Benefitth from Virginia Chirpithtth Thervithe," Teddy says at last. "Bookth and records. We thell a lot of review bookth and records over at the Thtrand and Dayton's."

"Are these benefits reportable income?"

"Ha!" Teddy says, wiping his grin. "We couldn't begin t' report 'em."

Leo eyes books in their bags. "We have quite a turnover," he says.

"Jutht about everything that patheth through our hands. Terrible. We can't hold onto anything."

"We *hate* to sell these books and records," Leo says, breathing shallowly. "We're forced to. T' keep ourselves in music supplies."

"But now that we're workin' for the thity, maybe we c'n give up thith other busineth."

"How much do these extra benefits add up to a year?"

"Never figured it out," Teddy says. "We'd have t' keep inventory."

"We wouldn't have time t' write, Mrs. Anchor."

"Are these books and records valuable?"

"Honethtly, it'th amusing. We get a quarter on the dollar at thecondhand shopth."

"How much *are* your music supplies?"

"All depends on what ya include," Leo says.

"Include food and liquids," Teddy tells Leo. "We can't divide what is from what isn't music thupplies. We can't thtop eatin' and expect t' write. We drink at leatht a cathe of Coke a week—that'th fifty-two catheth a year. Without our Coketh, Leo, we'd run dry inthtanter! Coke is urgently needed."

"I appreciate that," she says. "But can't you suggest a figure for me to consider?"

"Boy, ya know," Leo says, "I think everything we make goes into music supplies and Coke! If we ever really analyzed it."

"Are these supplies tax-exempt?"

Teddy flushes. "Maybe we should report 'em for exemption. We don't. They're too trivial t' report—just fringe benefitth."

"Music supplies are a legal exemption," she says.

Leo-Teddy balances his unpaid taxes and music supplies, quietly sinking under churning Federal machinery. "What should we do?" Leo asks Teddy. Teddy snakes out

Leo's hardened handkerchief, wipes his palms, cold forehead, eyes his burgundy gallon thirstily.

"Let's see one of those books," she says. Leo pulls out *Antique Guns,* big leatherbound silver pictures. "Oh how handsome," she says. "My God, *this* is worth thirty-six dollars! Are you experts on guns?"

Leo reddens deeply. "No!"

"We don't know anything about guns," Teddy says hoarsely. "It was jutht lyin' around Chirpitht'th offithe. We're writin' an *opera.* A gun book could be handy."

"Well, I think I've heard enough about your benefits."

"We're NOT gonna sell this book!" Leo insists. "This is for our music."

Teddy nods. "That'th why we have it in the bag."

She eyes their stuffed benefits bags uneasily. "Now, *uh,* you make six thousand *apiece* from Welfare?"

"It keepth uth in thafflower oil. That'th our thtaple."

"We diet."

"On safflower oil?" Alice asks.

"Oh, it'th the betht. Ya gotta get with Dr. Taller."

"But isn't he the crackpot being sued by the government?"

"Maketh no differenthe. *He's right!* We dropped thirty pounds apiethe. That means thomething. Mrs. Anchor, when you weigh four-hundred-eighty pounds."

"Safflower oil cuts fat to urine," Leo declares. "Uremic acid!"

"It's my lunchhour," Alice says.

"We're down t'four-twenty," Teddy says. "We were nearly a quarter of a ton."

"I'd like to lose eight or ten pounds," she says.

"Drink an ounthe of thafflower oil fifteen minuteth before eatin'. It depretheth th' appetite."

Leo pushes up his oily glasses. "We always carry a quart with us. Is there a good place around here for lunch?"

"I like Cervantes on West Fourth," she says.

"That thounds nithe. Are you eatin' there?"

"Well," she says.

"Mrs. Anchor," Teddy says, "we're reviewers. We don't go around influenthin' bank presidentth."

"You can't influence me. But I'd like to hear more about your movie. Off the record."

"We promise not t' talk business," Leo says. Head

cocked, a weather report flooding in. Teddy humps their band: *Close your mouth.*

"All right, I accept. But let's just meet there. And this will be Dutch treat—understood?"

"Wear boots," Leo says. "There's a flood comin'. I heard the warning."

"It *is* dark out. Thanks."

Leo-Teddy carries shoppingbags into glaring blackness on the way to West Fourth. Dirty gusts whipping.

"Need'n alley. I'm burthtin'."

"Let's hold off until we get to the restaurant."

"Dyin' of thirtht!"

No alley, they gasp into a doctor's basement doorway, pretend to read mailboxes. Teddy hooks out the gallon.

"God, I gotta pith," he sighs, drinking. Glass grinds his teeth.

Leo watches deathpale walkers in the wind. "Oh, man," he says, "we gotta get there before it rains. Our bags'll melt!"

SShssshh pelt the first hard wild drops outdoors.

"Better carry the bags in our arms," Leo says. "These are splittin'."

"Gotta get new ones. *New bags!*" Teddy tells heaven.

Streets aghast in the first whippings, thunder shuffling above.

"Wet already!" Teddy cries. "I thought trenchcoatth were waterproof! Thomebody *took* uth, thtanley . . ."

"Let's try that organic foods store."

Leo-Teddy steams prickling into noon diners and waits for service at the checkout counter. A redhead with large nipples works the register. Leo-Teddy grits his jaws. She leans over the counter to look at the white uppour, goatbubs wallowing. "Oh, this is terrible," she says, chilled. Twins choke. She rubs her nose, her register-bell rings. An elderly black in white straw hat and white Vandyke turns with his small purchase of ginger root and smiles at them with tingling eyes, nodding, and passes outdoors. Leo-Teddy stands stuck with quills, watches him shoot his umbrella and walk blissfully into the rain. Thunder whitens the stones, Leo-Teddy speechless.

"Yes?" she asks through orange lashes. Freckled bubbycleft.

Leo-Teddy dumb, purple teeth grinning.

"Who was that man?" Leo whispers.

"He shops here. He's a missionary."

"To Manhattan?" Teddy asks.

"Why not?" she says.

"He has the Spirit," Leo says.

Leo-Teddy pays for two shoppingbags. Slip old bags into new bags, go out with bags abreast. Soaked, wind-driven, run to West Fourth.

"I get confused over here!" Leo cries.

"Use your fuckin' noodle," Teddy shouts.

"But it says Twelfth Street!"

"Then let'th athk for help, Thtanley." Teddy, longsuffering. "AHEM!"

Shoes leaking, Leo-Teddy leaps a burst main like a shot off a shovel, rises hopefully with bags held tight, lands short, ankles deep. Crosses between hornblowing cornyellow cabs to a plugged sewer, sunken curb. Wades to the corner. A short dark girl, glowing flesh white and red, stands lost in thought under a checkered umbrella. Black and white harlequin rainbonnet and slicker. "LEO-TEDDY! *What're you doing here?*" she cries. Rainlight fills her skin. Leo-Teddy's hearts flow up in the downpour. Her face falls at Teddy's toothless howl.

Teddy kisses her. "We're makin' a bank loan!"

Wetness beating them, she grips Leo in a kiss, gets a four-armed hug.

"What're *you* doin' here?" Leo asks.

"I live here!" Cynara says. "We moved down from Riverside Drive to be in the Village and *find ourselves!* I married my cousin Byrdie."

"What happen' t' Thterling?"

"We're divorced!"

"But you were childhood sweethearts!" Leo cries in the hard rain.

"I read his philosophy thesis," Cynara says. "Sheer babble! The *first page* disillusioned me! I tried to kill myself in Texas, yipes. I rented a motel room for three days, told the manager I was writing a paper and didn't want to be disturbed. Then I swallowed a whole glass of pills and slept for three days. When I woke up I'd lost fifteen pounds. Then I went to the airport and flew to Byrdie."

"Next time ya wanna diet, try thafflower oil."

"You were supposed t' phone *us* when ya got that feelin'!"

"Oh I know. I tried twice but you weren't listed. Oh, I

gotta tell you everything—all my symptoms! When can we meet? Can I come to visit? I want to see you both desperately and have such a heart-to-hearts. Oh, Christ, I had my first orgasm."

"Terrific," Teddy says, heart sinking. "How?"

"I forgot to work and it just bloomed. What's your number?"

Teddy hands her a card: *Leo-Teddy Prometheus Productions*. "We're makin' a bank loan for a movie."

"A movie! *Get under.*"

"Underground," Teddy says under her checkered parachute. "Like t' be in it?"

"Oh God yes! OH I'M PRICKLING!"

"We'll write ya in," Leo says. "Expect our call. What's your name?"

"Laura Goldstein now. I changed it legally from Cynara. Oh this is glorious—first an opera, now the movies!"

"Hey, where the hell's Wetht Fourth?"

She groans. "I can never remember! My memory's hideous. I'm terribly sorry—I know it's—it should be—"

Water beating through rotted shoes, no clock in the blackening air. No shadow on foxfire skin, eager brown eyes binding their love.

"Dya know what time it is?" Leo asks.

"Twelve," she says. "Don't you think?"

"Twelve a long time ago," Leo says.

"Feels more like twelve-twenty," Teddy says. "Let'th grab a cab."

"Oh, West Fourth isn't far," she says. "You can walk there in three minutes. It's *in there!*" Pointing. *Jumblestreets.*

"My bag's got a hole already," Teddy blubbers. "Let'th carry 'em under our coatth."

Beards pearled, bags stinking. Unbelt and wrap coats over crumbling bags. Nerves stretched dietbright, teeth grinding. Teddy holds the umbrella while Cynara cinches the winebag under his trenchcoat. Steaming on him, a nearness strong as jasmine. His pipe grows hard in the gale.

She belts Leo, bulging with books, records, music, thirty-six-dollar block of *Antique Guns*.

"We're late, we're late! *Goodbye, thweetheart!*"

"Call me soon!"

Rush with hands in coat slits, wine jouncing, books shaking. "Married Byrdie!" Leo cries. "SHIT! We'll never sleep with 'er again!"

"Don't bet on it. She jutht made my organ growl—on purpothe!"

Leo glares at Teddy's toothless determination. ". . . I'm gettin' old."

Sprint down a long block of basement steps and windowplants.

"Thith ain't right! Let'th go left."

"I don't know *where* we are."

"We're lotht, idiot! Hey, that corner's familiar."

"Right. West Fourth's down there."

Rush carefully with burdens, turn the corner.

"Very familiar!" Teddy cries. Rain hacks his squint. "Haven't we seen this corner before, Ollie?"

"Sure, latht year. Thay, those harlequin coatth are gettin' popular."

"Ah CRAP! We've run around th' block!"

Their sidewalk harlequin, checkered in the wind.

"Hello, again," Cynara says. "You didn't find it?"

Teddy howls, *"We couldn't find shit in a shoeshine tin!"*

"If we had a flat tire, we'd change the wrong fuckin' tire!"

Deer eyes offer fellow feeling, then lift with fear. Teddy's gasping mouth pumping steam on her. She stares at his winepurple tongue, rolling eyes—Leo's piercing dietstrain, heart-seethe. She bites her lips, steeped in their pain, their sunken, wrinkled, brown-circled eyes.

"Gotta take a cab!" Teddy cries.

"Ya haven't moved from this spot," Leo tells her.

"I live here. Just stepped out to feel the lightning."

"Oh Alithe Anchor, we're thorry. Ya don't know her but she's our angel!"

"Okay, let's give up and get a cab."

"We c'n have a nip in the backtheat. Well-deserved!"

"Teddy!" Cynara whispers. "What happened to your—?"

"I fell athleep on the Thyclone at Coney Island. It'th a roller-coathter." He damps heroic agony. "A real neckbreaker ride!"

"Phone me," she begs. *"Remember!"*

Bus her goodbye. Hooves sink into ankledeep sewage,

wade over cobbles. Rooted with arm out in flailing rain, begging cabs, hands under swollen coats.

Leo boils. "Put your heart into it."

"Cabs don't care about my heart. Only Alithe Anchor cares—maybe! Dya think she wantth thex with uth?"

A yellow glory urges itself toward Leo-Teddy, and passes, waves spraying his calves. *"That fat rat didn't even thee uth!"*

"Here comes another. Beg, Teddy, beg!"

His four-hundred-twenty-pound being yearns for the bright yellowbulb cab to take him into itself. Hard clockwork wipers pass, Leo-Teddy weary, tongues gluey.

"Thome moron getth all the cabs! There's gotta be one for uth!"

"I need drink."

Look back at Cynara, his whole brace of bones parched for her. She bends her head, extends a hand in hope, ardently.

"Goddamnit, I don't want thympathy, I wanna fuck 'er! Right here an' now!"

"Work 'er up, wouldn't we?"

"If nethethary, right on thith goddamn thewer. Here comes another. *Jesuthfuckingchritht,* I'm cold!" Thumbs out.

"Put your heart into it."

"That isn't enough. That thimply isn't enough."

Cab turns on a far light, glides toward bulging Leo-Teddy.

"Gonna stop!" Leo cries.

Teddy quakes for joy, fist up in idiot triumph.

Wet yellow glow slowly grazes their feet, rippling, glides by.

"By God I wish I had a gun!" Leo rages, hoisting his books.

Teddy's fist bolts. "Pith on em! Pith on all Yellow cabs!"

"FUCK YOU!" Leo-Teddy howls after the cab.

Wave hardeyed, hardluck goodbyes to Cynara, slog over Twelfth's rivering cobbles, fingers clenched under belly bags. Lightning branches above Con Ed—Leo-Teddy looks back. Cynara ages in meatgreen darkness. Shivering twins, jaws gritting, brackish winegasses belching. Eyes burn with cold, four lungs laboring. Looking up at streetsigns, West Fourth, and catercorner West Twelfth.

Leo-Teddy stands where Fourth crosses Twelfth, awash at his own funeral.

"We were here and ran away," Teddy says. *"Fools!"*

"Ah!" Leo says, eying the senseless streetsign. "Professor Moriarty again, Watson."

Go into a small linened restaurant below the walk.

"She's not here yet!" Teddy cries happily.

"Good afternoon," the gaunt gray manager says, his left hand in his suitcoat pocket. "Mrs. Anchor will be here shortly.

Gasp, unbelt each other. The manager's chestnut eyes glisten as Leo-Teddy cradles his bags into a footrack, lifts out a quart bag. "Thafflower oil," Teddy says. "For our diet," Leo says. The manager's warm surprise heats their marrow. Shaking their coats, he agedly one-hands each coat back on a hanger, his left still pocketed with menus underarm. Guides the twins to a bay window. Leo-Teddy sits back in greensilver streetglow. "Bad weather for busineth!" Teddy says, gaping blissfully in the room's mercies.

"The worst." His marked, scarred hand offers a wine list.

"Dya therve martinis?"

"Yes."

"That'th too bad. We'll have two."

"Doubles," Leo says.

The manager speaks erectly to a short irongray waiter who brings them water, examines their red eyes witheringly, departs for their drinks.

"That thteward's a nithe old gent. Why's he keep his hand in his pocket?"

"Because he does more with one hand than we do with four."

Teddy grips himself in prayer. "God, may we come through today!"

"Success," Leo says, crooking Teddy's little finger for luck. "But it's still easier t' stage a mass murder!—here we're makin' a fuckin' movie so we can produce an opera! Gotta be a shortcut."

"We jutht don't know where t' go t' thell out. I'm nervous. Let'th have our oil—get our thtomachth coated tho we'll be coherent with Alithe."

Drain waterglass, fill it brimming with safflower oil, splurt Tabasco and Worcestershire sauce. Stir brown bubbles, each. . . . swallows. . . . half, gives a hot, oily burp, napkins his lips. "Chritht, we forgot th' vinegar. Vinegar's half the reason we drink thith thtuff."

Cool gin spills on their laps as John the waiter stands up their drinks, mops the spillage.

"Shut up about that flood when Alithe gets here. She'll think we're both cuckoo."

Leo smiles largeheartedly over his gin, watches the waiter's head float away.

"Thometimes you got a beautiful thmile. *Thometimes!*"

Moses and Aaron Katz hurry in dripping. The horn-rimmed Katz twins, slim, husky, bald and studious, halloo Leo-Teddy, join him at table.

"Goot, goot, Ygor!" Teddy gurgles over his glass. Signals the waiter for two more, asks the Katzes, "Want thome gin an' garbage?"

"We're wine drinkers," Aaron says. "This is our favorite restaurant."

"We don't p-p-p-plan to change it after the Rev-v-v-volution," Moses says. Hooks his cane on his chair. Though bald, Moses's hair hangs over his collar, his eye a mad-financier glitter. "We turned down your ghetto libretto," he tells Leo-Teddy.

"We feel it's premature," Aaron says.

"And too serious," Moses says. "You really don't understand the spirit of radical 'P-p-p-pataph-ph-ph-physics. You're b-b-b-both too serious," he adds solemnly.

"Shall we mail it back?" Aaron asks.

"Or just b-b-b-burn it?"

Leo-Teddy tingles pain. "We'll pick it up," Leo says.

Twins drain gin. Teddy puts his arm around Leo, grinning spongily. "Me an' my brother, we can take rejection! Thweet are the utheth of adverthity, right? *Right.*"

Alice blows in on a gust, still beauty-waved. The manager one-hands her coat, folds in scarf, gloves, dry umbrella and hangs them. Leo-Teddy fixes admiringly on the manager's deft, grave one-handed jugglery.

"Look," Alice says seated, "call me Alice. I may be middleaging rapidimento, but I feel a lot younger than 'Mrs. Anchor.' "

"A martini, Mrs. Anchor?" the manager asks.

"Yes! My God, it's Judgment Day out there, Miguel—I didn't expect it so soon. Well, are you twins musicians too?"

"Poetth," Teddy says.

"Radicals," Aaron says. "We edit *The East Village Mother.*"

"Is that for housewives?" Alice asks.

"It's not even for marriage," Aaron says.

"Oh!" Alice laughs. "What is it for?"

"Poets," Aaron says. "We're legislating."

"Legislating what?" Alice asks.

"The Rev-v-v-volution," Moses says. "W-w-w-we're the v-v-v-vanguard."

"Well, I'm curious!" Alice says. "What're you revolting against?"

"The total culture," Aaron says. "After us come the anarchists."

"W-w-w-we're just p-p-p-pointing the w-w-w-way."

"For whom?" Alice asks. "For what? What revolution?"

"*We* are the Revolution," Aaron says.

"You two guys sitting here?" Alice asks.

"Yes," Aaron says. "It's all gonna spring from us."

"W-w-w-we can give a comp-p-p-plete r-r-r-rundown on it."

"I wish you would," Alice says.

"When we were exiled from the old Les Deux Megots on Seventh Street," Aaron says, "we led the underground poets to Le Mètro on Second Avenue for readings, then to St. Mark's on-the-Bowery and finally we dispersed through the West Village. There weren't any poetry readings in the West Village either before we began our readings there. By then we must have had fifty poets."

"F-f-f-five hundred!"

"Ya can't call all of 'em poets," Leo says.

"Yes, they are," Moses says severely.

"Of course," Aaron says austerely, his face cold and weighty. "What else would you call 'em?"

"Well, thome of 'em can't *write.*"

"You're too serious," Aaron says.

"You've gotta dig 'P-p-p-pataph-ph-ph-physics!"

"What's 'Pataphysics?" Alice asks.

"It's the Revolution," Aaron says. "It's from Patagonia."

"This is maddening," Alice tells the Katzes.

"It's supp-p-p-posed to be."

"We're crushing Pharaoh's army," Aaron says.

"Yes," Moses says. "The exodus is over and we're going

b-b-b-back to the East V-v-v-village to b-b-b-build the Holy Land."

"And that's this *East Village Mother?"* Alice asks.

"That's right, Alice," Aaron says.

"What's 'Pataphysics?" she asks again.

"W-w-w-we're 'P-p-p-pataph--ph-ph-physics."

"But what are you! Or what is it!"

"It's the same thing," Aaron says. "Either one of us. Take your choice. You've heard of the Crucifixion?"

"I believe so," Alice says.

"Too serious," Aaron says. "Sheer anti-'Pataphysics. Nothing gets accomplished that way—look around you at the results."

"What's 'Pataphysics?" she asks Leo.

"Oh, you're in it," Leo says. "Ya work for it!"

"I work for it?"

"Don'tcha think the credit system's pure fiction?" Leo asks her.

"The entire financial structure," Aaron agrees.

"Well, yes," Alice hedges.

"The Revolution ith pure fiction."

"P-p-p-poetry!" Moses affirms.

"You mean," Alice says, "since it doesn't mean anything, you're having a revolution?"

"That's right," Aaron says. "But it means a lot to us. *A nation is remembered for its poets!*—it's time they got PAID."

"Never happen," Alice says.

"W-w-w-we're w-w-w-winning! They can't f-f-f-fight 'P-p-p-pata-ph-ph-ph-physics. W-w-w-we're psychic guerr-r-r-rillas. W-w-w-we're b-b-b-bombing everything!"

"Who can't fight 'Pataphysics?" Alice asks.

"Anybody," Aaron says. "Your bank will be dust in ten years."

"W-w-w-we're legislating."

"Who SAYS you're legislating!" Alice cries.

"Oh, we're unacknowledged," Aaron says. "That's how we win."

"You two guys are gonna turn my bank to dust in ten years?"

The Katz twins grin at each other, nodding.

"Are these guys serious?" Alice asks Teddy.

Teddy claps Leo. *"We're* the theriouth ones."

"Too serious," Aaron says.

"I'm not getting too much of this," Alice says. "Let's get off the revolution and order. Myself, I take a serious interest in eating and drinking."

"Oh, eating and drinking are v-v-v-very imp-p-p-portant. You can't take them seriously enough. They're so serious you have to turn your b-b-b-back on 'em or they'll b-b-b-blind you."

"And just eat *anything,*" Aaron says. "Abandon reason, like the Christians."

"It doesn't matter?" Alice asks.

"Does it?" Aaron asks. "Order for us. Order anything."

"Me?" Alice asks.

All twins nod.

"All right," Alice says. "Let's all have paella."

"*That* has shellf-f-f-fish."

"You can't eat shellfish?" Alice asks Moses.

"Oh, w-w-w-we eat it b-b-b-but w-w-w-we're Jewish."

"So am I Jewish!" Alice cries. "What're you?"

"Oh, we're Christians," Leo says.

Teddy nods. "Can't ethcape it!"

"You can eat shellfish?" she asks.

"We love shellfish," Leo says. "They're God's creatures."

"We got thinging oythters in our opera."

"Wagnerian oysters," Leo says.

"W-w-w-we don't like Germ-m-m-man m-m-m-music," Moses mumbles heavily.

"It's too serious," Aaron says.

"You don't even like *Tristan?*" Alice asks.

"Oh, that's horrid! P-p-p-pigs and snakes caterw-w-w-wauling."

"Never heard such dismal singing," Aaron agrees.

"W-w-w-when w-w-w-we get the deathr-r-r-ray, w-w-w-we're gonna w-w-w-wipe out all of Germ-m-m-many."

"All seventy-million," Aaron says. "We'll turn 'em to bacon."

"The R-r-r-red Sea w-w-w-will have been child's p-p-p-play!"

"What deathray?" Alice asks.

"What good's a deathray that isn't a secret?" Aaron asks Alice.

"I'm sinking, boys," Alice says. "Let's start ordering—paella?"

"I thought we were perfectly agreed," Aaron says.

"What about the clams?" Alice asks.

"Oysters are our favorite," Leo says.

"John!" Alice calls.

The harsh waiter returns, a short potbellied Irishman with bluebrilliant eyes, stoneserious nose, withering lips. He reviews Leo-Teddy's gnawed shoes, beards, nails, frayed cuffs and ties.

"John," Alice asks, "can you make paella with oysters instead of clams?"

"I think clams would be better," John says. "They're meatier, Mrs. Anchor."

"Oythters on th' thide! That won't offend you fellas?"

"Well?" Aaron asks Moses.

"W-w-w-we'll m-m-m-make an exception."

"Otherwise we'd have to leave," Aaron says.

"Isn't that taking the dietary laws rather seriously?" Alice asks.

"What else do we have?" Aaron asks.

"Well, I begin to wonder," Alice says. "How about poetry?"

"The *Laws* are sheer poetry," Aaron says.

"No f-f-f-finer by anyb-b-b-body," Moses says modestly.

"Moses slaved over those Laws," Aaron says.

"It took a long time—they b-b-b-built the b-b-b-bank while I w-w-w-was w-w-w-writing 'em! Now I have to tear the b-b-b-bank down."

"Only the force of poetry can melt the Golden Calf," Aaron says. "You gotta fight fiction with poetry. It's in Moses' *Coffee House Cantos."*

"Tompkins Square P-p-p-press."

Thunder burns the window white.

"Was that a bomb!" Alice cries.

"Not yet," Aaron says.

John returns. "Two more with olives. Alithe?"

"Well, I shouldn't," Alice says.

The restaurant glares in outer darkness.

"But I will."

"We'll have a bottle of Rainwater," Aaron says.

"Madeira with paella?" John shakes his head.

"W-w-w-we like R-r-r-rainw-w-w-water. It's so sunny!"

"That's 'Pataphysics, John," Alice says. "Give it to 'em. But I'd still like a simple explanation of It—and singing oysters."

"W-w-w-we p-p-p-prefer obscurity."

"How about the oysters?" she asks Teddy.

"On the Theventh Day, God rethted because He'd made the oythter and brought all His workth to perfection."

"Perfection?" Alice asks. *"Oysters?"*

Moses and Aaron avert their heads, Moses's fingers in his ears.

"Ya don't wanna hear thith? It'th all in the Bible!"

"W-w-w-we'd p-p-p-prefer not to," Aaron says.

"P-p-p-pretend w-w-w-we're not listening," Moses says.

"He'd produced the hermaphrodite," Leo says.

Alice's brows wedge with curiosity. All sit quietly. Leo eyes his rotting shoe, its kayak knot. John brings the paella, clams steaming.

"Is everything perfect?" Miguel asks.

Leo-Teddy smiles, but Leo turns from Teddy's mongoloid grin.

"If I ever meet God, Miguel," Teddy says, "He'll remind me of you!"

"May you survive your fantasies by many years," Miguel says.

"VENI! VENI, CREATOR THPIRITUTH!" Leo-Teddy bellows. Soaked boars, climbing six flights to their apartment, arms loaded with brown bags flagged with celery, crushed full with delicacies, large and small bottles, rotten shoes stomping joyfully, foreheads dripping fatness.

"Pay the rent!" Teddy cries.

"I WILL PAY THE RENT!" Leo cries.

"GLORY GLORY HALLELUIAH! GLORY GLORY—"

Out of silver darkness, a man appears coming downstairs, and above him Nancy Mars suddenly leans over the top railing.

"Jack, I'll do my best," she calls. "Oh, here they come!"

The man comes nearer to Leo-Teddy, a shiver leaping through them at his strangely intense face. His hair, orange-silver, finely clipped, his face pale red, he wears dark coat and suit, checked vest, Highlander tartan tie. His shoes shine, his right eye glitters through them, reading their spines.

"Hello," McFin says, hardly smiling.

"Jack!" Leo-Teddy cries, shouldering brown bags.

"Bringing home the fatted calf?" he asks, eying their haunch of groceries. "Boy, you guys sound happy."

"Golden Calf!" Leo cries.

"We jutht hit the bank at Monte Carlo for a thousand buckth!"

Jack follows them back up and into harsh kitchen-shine where Nancy waits. Rain whips the window. "I see you were successful," she says.

"We *nailed* those bathtards."

"Wonderful," Nancy says. "I'm so happy for you. Jack's been waitin' over an hour. We've had a super talk—or at least I have!"

"Look! Look!" Teddy cries, handing her a dozen wrapped chrysanthemums. Grinning Chinese. "Tho hoppy t' therve mithy."

"For me?" she asks.

"Put 'em all over the houthe!" Teddy pecks her cheek. "And thith is thomethin' thpecial." Unwraps a wreath of ox-eye daisies, places it on her head. Teddy shines at Jack, at Nancy—Leo's eyes drip sugar. Rip off coats, ties, refreshed for the feast.

"What're these for!" she asks, eying her wreath in the sink mirror.

Teddy winks. "I have a quethtion to athk ya later. Ah, beautiful!—*you—are—beautiful!"* Nancy grips her forehead, blushing.

Four arms outstretched. Jack backs off.

"No gush, please. I'm not really one of that Harpur crowd."

Leo-Teddy's zest flags, returns. "God, Jack," Teddy says, "we hardly recognized ya. Ya look *great!"*

"What's happened to ya?" Leo asks.

"Oh, I got some answers to what was bothering me," Jack says.

"What was that?" Leo asks.

"Mainly delusions of ego," Jack says.

"Well, ya look like a professor," Leo says.

"Gosh, no," Jack laughs. "Though the dean of my department's making overtures. Testimonials, in fact. How're you doing on your horns? Writing anything?"

"Hell, yeth!" Serenely excited, rips brown bag spilling. "Thmoked oythterth. But wait'll ya thee thith!"

Leo-Teddy sets out fifths of sour mash, cognac, scotch, chocolate gin, and one-hundred-fifty-one proof rum.

"Have you come at the right time!" Leo grins. "It's just

incredible, heavenly luck. Wait'll we tell ya what we did t' that bank!"

"Gee, I can't stay," Jack says. "I have some friends to see. I was down for a refresher walk through the Bowery, my old home, and thought I'd stop over to see how you two are doing. But I've already spent my hour here. I'm only in town for the day, I'm afraid."

Groans. "Hell, but ya can have a thnort for the road. Hey, it'th not tho often we have a thpread like thith. Thtay a minute at leatht." Teddy smacks the sour mash lovingly on the label, kisses it all over.

"No thanks," Jack says. "I've had enough."

"Well, have *one*," Leo says. "Name yer pizen, pardner, as Rob sez."

"Haven't had a drink for a year and three months," Jack says.

Teddy still gasps from stairclimbing. "It'th bad for your health?"

"It gives me cancer of the ego. Say, may I use your phone? Where's the phonebook?"

Nancy clears the grocery-strewn table as Leo-Teddy snaps on livingroom lamps against the dark rainlight.

"We're on a health kick too," Leo says. "We took off thirty pounds apiece with safflower oil!"

"Gives uth oily shortth. But it delays abthorption of alcohol too."

"Why delay that?"

"We don't like t' get drunk!" Teddy says.

"We just like that creative glow." Leo nods meaningfully at vast binders of manuscript over their desk. "Need it for our work."

Jack looks untouched by the statement.

"Hey, the *flowers*?—I'm athkin' Nanthy t' marry me today!" Grins, gaptoothed serenity silking his eyes—Leo's too.

Jack looks out at tall Nancy in the kitchen, her long brown hair, brown eyes, cupid lips, and heartshaped face. "She's a powerhouse," he says.

"Big as one too," Teddy says. "But we love'er."

"Don't sleep with her. She has our bed, we sleep here on the couch."

"It doesn't look wide enough," Jack says.

"We sleep sittin' up. We're used to it—don't need much shuteye. Just a few hours, like Oscar says. We wake up like fire-engines! We stay up late workin' and she goes to bed early."

"Early? She thleepth eleven-twelve hours a day! She's only nineteen, ran away from college back in Cleveland. She doesn't know *anything!* We're teachin' her how t' peel oranges. Well, really, how t' cook like Janet Harpur. She can't even underthtand the thtreetth, she goes by the *thun!* Comes up outta the thubway, lookth at the thun. She was livin' here with a guy who took off but left 'er all thith furniture, that big hifi, thith dethk. She felt unthafe in thith area an' wrote uth a letter care of Thtanley's Bar invitin' uth to room with 'er. Tho we moved in latht month. She's jutht home from the hothpital yethterday."

"So she told me. She makes great coffee—but I guess you take credit for that. Does she know you want to marry her?"

"Well—she doesn't like thentimentality. Talkth about only goin' out with fags from now on. She's down on emotional relationshipth."

"Not that *we're* fags."

"What happened to your front teeth?" Jack asks.

"Bit of panic. You tell 'im, it'th too painful for me."

"Friday afternoon," Leo tells Jack, "we three were in Times Square—"

"—in a thtate of dubiouth ebullienthe." Teddy sighs forgivingly.

"—and we wanted t' sell some records at a secondhand store in Union Square," Leo says, "before the store closed. So, not usin' our horsesense, we took the fuckin' subway on the rush hour. When we got off in Union Square, it was mobbed. Couldn't move, we just swayed here and there. It was inhuman, we couldn't get off the platform!"

"Suffocating!" Nancy says. Chrysanthemums deck the livingroom in empty Jack Daniel's bottles, her head still crowned with ox-eyes.

"Both of us got hit by a panic attack," Leo says—

"—me worthe. Don't think we're always thkulled though."

"This colossal, ironjawed German—wide as us together and four times tighter—starts plowin' his way t' the stairs. He'd gone crazy. We thought we'd get torn apart in the crush—"

"Really thcary, Jack—from the mental athpect. Our band was throbbin'. I flew outta my *tree!*"

"Teddy bolted right into a steel stanchion," Leo says. "*I-yi-yi,* blood everywhere. I thought he'd pass out. Then we'd really get trampled. But Nancy and I got 'im out safe."

"Made the recordthtore too. Bloody but unbowed! We needed a fresh gallon."

"Yeah," Jack says, "those subways are pretty defeating. I stick to buses."

"Thay, what happened to your eye? It lookth different."

"Oh, it burst," Jack says. "About a year and half ago. My blood pressure got too high. I was under no particular strain—just drinking—and the lens burst. Believe me, I'm not suffering. I'm in good company."

"Fuck, yes," Leo says half-enviously. "Homer!"

"Milton!—*When I conthider how my light is thpent—*"

"No," Jack says, "*A. A.* I could get sober, but I couldn't *stay* sober—not alone. So I joined."

'But you're not an alcoholic, Jack," Teddy says.

"*I* think I am."

"—You mean," Leo asks, "ya can't take one single drink for the rest of your life?"

"I'm not worried about the rest of my life. I'm just not drinking today."

"Well, when ya get back in shape—" Teddy grins, pours thick brown chocolate gin.

"Oh, I don't miss it."

Leo-Teddy, stunned.

"Ya don't mind if *we* drink?" Leo asks.

"Gosh, no, go right ahead. I'll make that call now. Don't let me dampen your spirits. You guys need it."

"Oh, we use booze like Mobilgath. Hey, we wanna show ya our movie thcript!"

"Why don't you mail me a copy? I have to leave in a minute."

"*Hm,* okay." Leo sighs. Looks at Nancy in her wreath. "Hey, doll, we'll hippityhop down t' Avenue C for some scallions for the welsh rarebit. It won't be *perfect* without scallions."

"We brought thtout inthtead of ale. It'll be brown rabbit! *UMM?* Were ya gonna thay thomethin'?"

"Nothin'," Nancy says. "I have something to talk about after Jack leaves."

"We need more lampth. More light, for God's thake. Thith cave maketh my eyes thore. We'll pick up a floor lamp when we go out for the thcallions. Okay?"

"Wonderful. I think you'll need it," she says.

"Ya ever have chocolate gin?" Teddy asks Jack at the phone. "It'th my only weakneth."

"Oh?"

Dry heads on kitchen towel, light up twin chairleg cigars. *"Ah!"* Teddy lifts a fat desk jar of glowing green leaves vivid as steel shavings. "How 'bout thome pot, Jack? Thith is really fresh and potent! *mmMMMH!"*

"No," Jack says flatly, bluntly.

"Well!" Teddy toasts Leo's half-waterglass of brown gin liqueur. *"Cheers!* To a new world, Jekyll, of operas an' movies."

"Success!" Nancy cries.

"Nancy!" Leo says, horrified, "where's your *drink?"*

"Nothin' for me, thanks. I don't think I'm well enough."

"Nonthenthe, old girl. Ya gotta try thith chocolate gin. It'th what ya been dreamin' New York'th all about!"

"I'd rather not."

"Oh, come on, for Chritht'th thake. Join th' party. Thith shit is nine buckth a fifth—*cherryflavored!* THWITH CHOCOLATE! It'th *real* chocolate, no kiddin'. Ya love chocolate, ya know ya do." Pours her a dollop, undoes her fingers, shoves the glass in.

Housemates toast the future, Nancy sipping lightly, twins gulping.

"Refills," Teddy says.

"Chinatown, my Chinatown!" Leo sings. "Let's break out our horns for Jack."

Teddy tonguetests his lip through a Mongolian grin. "When ya gotta blow, ya gotta blow!"

"I'm leaving," Jack says.

"But ya gotta hear our new Casals record!" Leo cries.

"Bach'th Fifth Thuite for Unaccompanied Cello. It'th tho great!"

"Heavenly!" Leo says.

"Whatta lutht for life. With a thpirit like that, I'd have twenty kids too."

"Hello, Doctor Deer? John McFin. I'm in town for this afternoon and hope I can see you. Oh, I'm sorry—I should remember your Friday schedule."

"Look what we ripped off from a mail-order cookbook club!" Teddy whispers to Jack, holding up a bright red fondue pot and burner. "We'll have a rarebit *hors d'oeuvre."*

Leo-Teddy spreads the kitchen table with cheeses, stout, kirsch, sauces and spices, then flexes his brains for fondue.

"I'm at the apartment of those hornplaying Siamese twins I told you about—those city heathen. Yes, they are —they want to stuff me with viands and music and smoked oysters."

"We don't need *all* this kirsch in the rarebit." Leo half-fills two sideglasses. Teddy grates natural cheddar into melted butter. Nancy opens a greenplastic shutter on the bedroom doorway and disappears. "What's she doin'?" Leo asks. Teddy shrugs, toasting the stormrattle window, drinks with a deep sigh "I LOVE LIFE!" Waltz about the kitchen for Jack's benefit, singing, "WHEN YOU ARE IN LAWV!"

"Yes, that's *them,"* Jack says. "The state hospital?—it was about as up to date as Bedlam. I was in the deetees, Doctor."

Quiet twins eavesdrop in the kitchen, working noiselessly. Surprise and wonder at the change in their old wine mate seeps through their drink-heavy being.

"It was a debacle, Doctor. No snakes or tiny animals, but men with knives and guns, and threatening voices and Negroes and Mexicans I tried to defend myself against! Ha ha. Oh, it all seemed terribly real—Mexican bandits after me with guns and machetes! I ran seven miles crosscountry, Doctor, and into a police station crying for protection. When they put me in a cell, that didn't help a bit. Those Mexes were everywhere."

Nancy closes the bedroom shutter again. "You make the toatht!

"The nerve doctor asked me why I drank—"

"THHCALLIONS! Let'th not forget fresh thcallions."

"—I told him I didn't need any reason! I'm an alcoholic!"

Leo-Teddy uncaps three bottles of brown stout, pours one slowly into creaming cheese on the burner, his eyes spiring wildly at Nancy. She leans her flowerwreathed forehead against the wall, despairingly. Teddy eyes her large shoulders and long hair, his heart pouring, winks at

Leo with their secret. "Think I'm doin' the right thing?" he asks Leo, who nods with hope.

"I decided to go into A.A. to save my life."

The hifi suddenly crackles, its hum fades, tubes dying out. The apartment lights flicker, rooms sinking into silver dimness.

"Whole houthe is out!"

"It's the flood," Leo says.

"I'll get out the candles," Nancy says. Rises large and shapely on the metal bathtub lid. "Hey," Leo says, "lemme do that." "I'm fine," she says, gets down a bag of white candles, works candles into fat wine jugs.

"Well, we've had a power failure down here, Doctor Deer. How's your metabiology book coming? Remember, sir, I think of you as Whitman said of Thoreau—a 'real force.' Stability isn't so bad, you know? I see powerhouses everywhere—inspiration galore!"

Candleflames flicker in livingroom and kitchen. Jack rises, face glowing red, pale blue eyes flat.

"Well, I hope to stay longer my next trip. Nancy, do right by these boys."

"Nothin' can staunch *their* ebullience!"

"Jack," Leo cries, "ya didn't even hear us play our horns!"

"I've got to get up to Thirty-third Street and First Avenue—that's the A.A. workcenter." Jack shakes hands. "Write when you can."

Leo-Teddy runs for his horns as Jack goes out the door.

"Open th' door!" Teddy cries to Nancy.

Nancy opens the halldoor as the twins burst into CHINATOWN MY CHINATOWN! Nancy looks out the door. Jack shakes his head, goes downstairs as Nancy waves farewell. "Godspeed," he says, "and remember—hit 'em right between the eyes." A wounded look crosses her as she closes the door.

Leo-Teddy lowers his horns, gasping. "My lip'th mush." Teddy pours cognac. "Boy, he left fatht!"

"I must say," Nancy says, "Jack bears *no* relation to Edgar Allan Poe that I can see."

"That was years ago," Leo says. Sips, *sighs*. "Oh Lord, I'd forgotten what this tastes like."

"I *know* you thneak out here for a little brandy every night, Thcarlet." Teddy thumbs his mustache. *"Thcal-*

lions! Can't eat rarebit without thcallions. We put the kirsch in yet? Well, let'th put more."

"You're not goin' out on a rainy day like this for scallions?"

"Brainy day." Teddy taps his skull slyly. Sniffs pot as kirsch, cheese, stout, and mustard fumes rise bitingly. "Ah, frankinthenthe an' myrrhhh!"

"So near perfection," Leo simpers. "I swoon for scallions."

"I'd like t' sit down and talk for a moment," Nancy says. Smiling, not smiling, big brown eyes fearful.

"You are *tho* BEAUTIFUL! That wreath is—is—"

"—sublime," Leo says. "That's our highest accolade."

"*Thublime.*" Teddy swells, lifting her fingers to kiss them.

"Please," she says, drawing twins onto livingroom couch.

"*Oops!*" Leo-Teddy hops up. Kitchentable for scotch. Returns, inhaling the ecstasy of a stormtossed powerfailure Friday with candles and thousand-dollar bankbook—now down to eight-hundred-thirty dollars.

"We *paid* the grothery bill. Have no fear."

"Our tab is pure as the virgin snow. Ya can show your face again, kid."

"We're clear at the liquorthtore too. We were in for one-hundred-and-twenty donutth!"

"But that's not gonna happen again," Leo says, pouring. "We learned our lesson there, believe me."

"Never again." Teddy raps his knee. "We're goin' *thtraight,* Nanthy."

Nancy places her wreath on Teddy's head. "I'm leavin'," she says.

"Goin' home to see mama?" Leo asks.

"I'm movin' in with Jenny," she says firmly.

Teddy chokes—"She's no fag!"

Leo sighs. "We'll miss ya, Woody. And your guitar."

"When ya get thith idea?"

"In the hospital."

"Ya didn't mention it," Teddy says.

"We didn't visit her. She's mad."

"We were gettin' the thcript ready! Tho we c'd make thith fuckin' bank loan an' pay the rent, *for Chritht'th thake!"*

"Yeah," Leo says, "but they didn't even look at the script."

"We didn't know that! And Nanthy was only in for three days."

"Well, that doesn't matter," Nancy trembles. "What I wanna figure out is what t' do with the furniture and hifi. I know it's worth somethin' but I won't need it at Jenny's. I'd like ya t' buy it from me. The hifi too. Altogether it's worth about five-hundred dollars. I'll let ya have it for one-fifty. Is that fair? Can ya afford it?"

"Sure," Leo says. Teddy nods.

"May I have the check today? I gotta help out on Jenny's rent."

"Thith is tho thudden!" Teddy near tears.

"I'm tryin' t' be diplomatic."

"Well, tho'm I. Why dya think I—*ohhhh!*—bought these f-f-flowers?"

"I'm afraid to say."

"I w-w-wanted to athk ya t' marry me. And I thtill do."

"Thanks, Teddy. I sure hate t' turn down my first proposal! And maybe my last. But it just wouldn't be possible."

Teddy's face hangs dripping in his hand, covered. . . . "Why not?"

Nancy, silent.

"Because of me?"

"*Oh, no, Leo!* If either of ya'd asked me just last week, I'd've jumped! Don't think it's because I don't love you boys—both of you—*deeply*. Boy, I made up my mind not t' cry about this. But—thank you both, I'll remember this moment the rest of my life."

"Then why can't ya thay yeth!"

Silence.

"Teddy's serious, Nancy."

"Well, I'll tell ya. I went t' the hospital for a miscarriage."

Leo-Teddy, stunned. *"Ya did?"*

"I'm afraid that I had it in the hallway toilet. It was just a foetus—but it already had features. I think it was a boy."

"What'd ya do with it?" Leo whispers.

"Wrapped it up and put it in the garbage."

Stare at the racing downpour, lifting weights that will

not rise through mindfog. Heavy breath. A whaler's sip at their straight scotches, arms rhyming.

"Thomethin's utterly wrong. *I* jutht thought ya'd lotht a lotta weight!"

"Ya didn't mention a miscarriage in your note. Ya just said ya'd gone t' the hospital."

"Jenny thaid it was for female troubles. That didn't thound like anything important."

"She was protectin' me. I didn't say a lot of things in that note. When I came back from the bathroom, I tried for twenty minutes to wake you both t' take me t' the hospital. I was still bleeding. But you were zonked out on the floor—I couldn't even shake ya awake! Not that I'm blaming you—if I blamed *anybody* it'd be that big German who pushed us so hard in the subway. Ya'd just had too much ebullience for one day. I mean sherry."

"Muthcatel."

"So I phoned Bellevue myself and they sent an ambulance. The house was filled with interns and doctors and oxygen tanks. They took me out on a stretcher. All those people were in here Monday night and you boys never woke up for a minute. Not that I blame ya for *anything*. It's only that—well, I invited you to board here for my protection. And the first time I really needed ya—I'll feel safer with Jenny."

"We want ya t' stay," Leo says.

"Can't we thtart fresh? We're willin' t' turn over a new leaf."

"Sure are. Anything ya say. Teddy's goin' to a dentist Monday."

"It may shock you boys, but I don't think change is possible."

"Oh, that'th not true." Studies the wire wreath on his knees. "Ya been talkin' with Jack?"

"We talked for an hour. But this is my own decision."

Teddy smells the daisy wreath. "What'd Jack thay? Didn't he thay we were composers and needed t' drink?"

"He thinks you have a modest musical talent. Very modest."

Leo-Teddy flushes hard red. Teddy's head hangs side to side. Suddenly he crushes the wreath onto his head. "*Awrrh,*" he growls, "the bells are ringin' for me an' my gal. Jack muthta thaid thomethin' worthe!"

"He say somethin' about our drinkin'?"

"He suggested—he merely *suggested* that I keep my friendship for you boys, but detach myself from your drinking or any idea of reforming you."

"Reformin' us?" Leo says.

"He says you're two different people."

"Of courthe we are!"

"When you're drinkin' and when you're not drinkin'," Nancy says.

"He's never theen uth when we weren't drinkin'! Sure, we're *happier* when we're drinkin'! Everybody is! That'th what alcohol does, maketh ya happy! For cryin' out loud."

"Well, I can't argue with you," Nancy says. "And I can't argue with liquor."

"With *liquor?"* Teddy asks.

"It's stronger than all of us."

"Oh balls. Don't give uth those girl-thcout turds."

"Really," Leo says, "that's just plain silly. Frankly, Nancy, there's no reply t' such a misinformed attitude."

"Complete mithinformation. What you need is about a thixth-month *thoak* in Baudelaire an' Poe an' Rimbaud an' Hart Crane, the real *geniutheth* of poetry! But Jack thaid thomethin' *more*."

"No, that's all. Well, that's not true—he said a lot—I can see why you boys love 'im. He also said that he thought his favorite drunken poets would've written a lot better and had a lot more work t' show for themselves if they hadn't died early deaths as alcoholics. But I can't argue for Jack. He *suggested* that I was doin' the right thing—that the best thing I could do for ya both was t' slam the door in your faces."

"*WELL!* I'm jutht thtunned. How can he think that way?—it'th amazing. He's tho fucked up, it'th mythtifying. For one thing, he's mithed the whole ethenthe of those poetth—they *died* for alcohol!"

"I guess they did if you say so."

"Jack's thinkin' must really've deteriorated," Leo says. "I bet he thinks *we're* far gone."

"That's for you to decide," Nancy says, eying his bacchic wreath.

"I can't follow thith. When I'm as far gone as Jack was, I'll quit. Won't we?"

"Well, we're not alcoholics." Leo grips Teddy's knee.

"Of courthe not." Sighs deeply, bargaining with the

ceiling. "Thtill, if it'd make a differenthe with your acctheptin' my proposal—well, *thonofagun, we'll thtop!"*

"Not this minute!" Leo blurts. Looks at the ravishments on the kitchentable. "Tomorrow morning."

Nancy smiles. "Ya think ya could drink all that t'night?"

Teddy ponders heavily. "I think we could. An' if we can't, what'th it matter? We'll have thomethin' on hand for guethtth."

"I think the bottles are stacked against you," Nancy says. "Anyway, I promised Jenny I'd move in with her. May I have the check?"

Get new checkbook off the desk. Leo's fat-stub pen blots an orange Hawaiian sunset. "Need my glasses," he sighs.

"Lemme," Teddy says. Slowly forms letters running up and off the checkbook.

"They won't take that," Nancy says.

Teddy helpless. *"You* write it." Hands her the pen.

Teddy inhales cigarette smoke, plants his lips on Leo's ear. Smoke plumes from Leo's mouth. Twin grins at Nancy.

"Oi!" Nancy says. "That's a new one."

"Thlam the door in our fathes? What'th that mean?"

"He thinks we're hopeless drunks!" Leo snorts, drinking. "Fills ya with wonder, don't it."

Nancy bites her lips, revealing, "The worst he's ever seen, he says."

"Oh that. What the hell's thith door busineth?"

"Nancy's the door. Here, sign this. He wants us t' join A.A.?"

"I detetht groupth!"

"I didn't say we were gonna join!"

"I WON'T THIGN! *Thith converthation's got outta hand!"* Teddy shudders disgust, turns away, mouth twisted with scorn. His thighs tremble. Stares into kitchen, silent upon a peak crowned with daisies. Loneliness slowly throttles his breath. He eyes his nails royally. "Would ya marry me if I did join?"

"Jack thinks you're beyond A.A.," she says.

"Beyond A.A.?" Teddy reels.

"He's never seen anybody recover from your condition."

Teddy thinks through raging fog. "What condition?"

"I don't know," she says.

"Our drinkin' condition!" Leo says.

"—He mutht think we're *alcoholicth*. Why—I c'n thtop drinkin'! I'll prove it. I won't have another drink today."

"Would ya marry *me* if I join A.A.?" Leo asks.

"Oh, I gotta hold myself together. Please, Leo, I'm goin' to Jenny's."

"Then I won't do it."

"Ya won't do it? You'll do it if I thay tho, thir."

Leo presents his middle finger.

Vast, scorning resolve fills Teddy. Signs the check, rips it free. "Ya sure thith is enough?"

"Oh thank you! I'll never forget this. You're sure ya can spare this from your movie?"

"There's always more where that came from." Teddy pats her hand. Looks about at the apartment, the new owner. "Well, let'th eat."

"I'm afraid Jenny expects me for supper." Nancy rises with a full breath. "I'll leave now. I'm packed already."

"You're not stayin' for supper! This is so quick!"

Nancy puts on her coat as twins gape forlornly. Goes into shuttered bedroom, hauls her suitcase into candlelit kitchen. Whipping rain, her cherished face warmburning.

"Oh, that'th too heavy for you in your condition."

"I'll be all right. I'm just goin' to the bus stop."

"No, no, we'll carry it downthtairs for ya."

Nancy's last look, tying her headscarf. Twins moon at her big browneyed child's face. "Don't worry, I'll be back t' visit. And I really can't thank you enough for everything. Jenny and I'll have ya over for supper. Macaroni!"

Cover the rarebit, follow her with suitcase.

"She hates men," Leo says.

"No, she's just had some bad times. Anyway, she's what I need right now."

Goodbye at the front entrance.

"I'll be joinin' A.A.," Teddy says.

"One of these days." A laugh spasms over Leo's dogteeth.

"If ya don't shut up, I'll do it right now. Nanthy, b'lieve me, I'll join thith minute—*I'll run right up!*—if you'll jutht thay yeth to my proposal. I need you! I'm dyin' for you! I cry in my thleep about ya, Nanthy!"

"Well," she sighs "—if ya join, I'll think it over. But I don't wanna give ya any false hopes. Really, it's too soon after my accident to think about—"

Teddy's bowels thrill. Her queenly eyes! Her breasts! *"I'll do anything for you!"* Tears stand in his eyes. Looks to heaven, grabs her hand. "Thay you're not a rock!"

"I'll always love both of you." Kisses Leo-Teddy's cheeks, goes out into hardfalling afternoon rain.

"To the buth thtop, idiot!" Teddy races out after her. Rips suitcase from her, smiling joyously, tromping at Nancy's side, chin-high to the bus stop.

"BOY!" Waterdrops bang his crown of daisies. "FRESH AIR!"

"You're soaked!" she says. Their wineblotched white shirts stick like decals.

"We don't mind a little mitht!"

"Gotta get some scallions anyway."

Nancy's bus heaves up through curbflood. Suddenly Teddy pulls Leo on behind her. "We'll pay for you." He hands the driver a five-spot.

"Can't change this." The driver eyes Teddy's wreath.

"We want three fares," Teddy insists.

"I have it," Nancy says.

"Thith is ludicrouth. We'll pay ya back," he assures her.

"Oh, the sonofabitch was lyin'," Leo agrees, staggering.

Follow Nancy down the bus, sit in empty seat behind her. Teddy wreathed in smiles and flowers. Nancy asks, "What're ya doin'?"

"Good crazyass question." Leo watches Tompkins Square Park wash by his steamed window.

"Don't worry," Teddy tells him. "We'll take a cab on Firtht Avenue. We c'n afford it."

"A cab where?"

"To Thirty-third Thtreet!"

"You're joinin' A.A.?" Nancy's face lights, candled with joy.

Teddy's gelded heart lifts. "I'll do anything. Therioutly. An' I hope I'm provin' it."

"It may be too late," Leo suggests. "Probably is. Look, *I* wanna go back for my trenchcoat! This fuckin' weather calls for a cask of cognac."

"Come on, buthter, it'th been rainin' *long enough.* Let'th let a little thunshine in. Ya can't carry a bottle inta the A.A. offithe, for Chritht'th thake. Where's your horthethenthe? My God, Leo, let'th be honetht—we *gotta* be thinthere."

Stare at each other's bloat, silently. Suddenly Nancy's crying, holding their hands, gripping them to her cheeks.

"Oh—*this is wonderful!* Leo, you'll join too?"

"I'm not promisin' anything, Nancy. I'll look into the matter. *WELL-L!* I'll admit I wouldn't mind learnin' t' drink like a gentleman! But—"

"He's thinkin' of the bottles back on the kitchen table." Teddy sneers. "I c'n read his billboard like it was a brain. It thays *Jack Daniel's 8 Years Old*. Eight years old, ho ho. Whattaya thay we grow up, kiwi. What's Whitman thay?—I believe in those winged purpothes—thomethin' like that."

"You're starry-eyed."

"Yeth! Thtarry-eyed—an' happy about it!"

"You'll be drinkin' tonight." Stares into Teddy's glow. "Okay, I'm sorry—I take that back. Rant on, Walt."

"It'th really pothible t' change, ya know. How many times've we quit and failed? Maybe A.A. can do for uth what we can't do for ourthelves. How about *that?* Thtop and thtay thtopped!"

"Cool it." Leo shakes pearls from his Vandyke. "Let's keep this anonymous."

"Yeah? Well, thomeday you may bleth me for thith little talk." Teddy looks down from a great height. "How dya like the idea that Jack thinkth we're incurable thtew-bums?"

Leo reads the floor. Flattened.

"He says *he's* a miracle," Nancy says.

"He's not kiddin'," Teddy says. *"We know.* Boy, I feel like shoutin'. What an *example* that man is! What a pow-erhouthe, Nanthy."

"Oh, Teddy. Somethin's got into you!" Teddy looks away modestly. "Here's your stop. Good luck to ya both. Hope ya get a taxi right away! Oh, I can't stop cryin', I'm so happy."

"Phone ya t'night," Teddy says.

Flag cabs in downpour at First Avenue and Fourteenth Street.

Leo cocks his ear. "Dya hear a guinea pig squealin'?"

"No—an' I don't hear any radio! Let'th thtart hikin'."

"Sonofabitch. We'll never get a cab."

Lope up First Avenue, rainwinds whaling and pushing.

Lightning leaps out of the east, shines to the west. Heaven shakes their hidden hearts. At Twenty-third burst mains gush fountaining over corners. Wade through flood-tide crossstreets. A bus passes, shaves by, water beating their calves, Teddy holding his five-dollar bill. He stands yet is hurried.

Leo holds him back. "I need a drink."

Teddy silent, passing Bellevue. A bar appears.

"Tho do I!"

"Wait a minute. There's a liquor store. Let's not waste money in a bar. Let's get a farewell fifth of Rainwater, somethin' really tastey."

"Terrific idea. Finish it before we get there. Wait a minute! What am I thinkin'?"

"Mira!" Leo cries. "Ya think I wanna give up drinkin'? My God, anybody who lives in this fuckedup city deserves t' drink. *I mean on this planet!* We're livin' in the worst horror in history. Don'tcha know how many people are bein' burned to death every single day in Vietnam?" Teddy listens intently. "Ya got any idea how many people in India and Africa die like flies every day from famine, pestilence, *earthquakes,* beri-beri, and starvation? Look at the junky deathrate right in this city, the muggings, the greatest crime-wave ever known! For Christ's sake, Teddy, we deserve a drink!"

Teddy's arms fall. "I can't fight that logic."

Solemnly into liquor store. Marches out with bagged fifth of Rainwater. Uncorks on the street, drinks long lilt of sunlit Madeira.

"Oh God, that'th heavenly. Now let'th get there."

Passing a market Leo cries, *"Scallions!"*

"Forget 'em."

"No, I want scallions for our rarebit."

"Boy, have you got no control over your appetiteth!"

Twins go up to the vegetable bins, find a tall pile of long green scallions. The purplelipped, deadcigarsucking shopowner waits beside them.

"Top ones're never any good," Leo says. Digs under for buried bunches, holding each up and eying it carefully.

"I'm chilly!" Teddy grips his bladder.

"Just a minute." Leo digs deeper.

"What's he lookin' foeh?" the shopowner asks.

"I'm lookin' for a perfect bunch," Leo says.

The shopowner eyes Teddy's wreath. *"He's* a scallion-freak?"

Leo reddens. "I want a bunch that isn't wilted or bent. That askin' too much?"

"A bunch of onions is a bunch of onions, buddy." Fishygreen eyes, blood vessels brightening his cheeks.

"Not to me," Leo says severely.

"You'll cut th' tops off anyway. Look, yoeh ovehhandlin' my produce."

"You wanna sell me some scallions or not?"

"Let'th blow."

"Yeah, leave." The shopowner measures Leo-Teddy finely.

"Okay, keep your fuckin' onions," Leo says.

"Get outta heah!" The shopowner growls, abruptly pushing them outdoors.

"This is UNJUST!" Leo's eyes roll, heels skidding. "This is unbelievable! Just what the hell dya think you're doin', ya moron! Ya stupid imbecile! *Ya fuckin' insect!"*

Teddy thoughtlessly back-elbows the man's chest, driving wind and cigar out of him. The owner staggers, turning, gasping, then pushes past them and runs into the street, crying, *"Police! Police!"* Stands waving a long butcherknife in the rain. *"Police! Police!"*

"Let'th beat it. Maybe I shouldn't 've butted him."

"He *deserves* every bit of punishment he's got comin' to him. *He's evil!* I'm not budgin'. I'm makin' sure he gets his just fuckin' deserts. We're in the right, Teddy."

"We're thtandin' here with a bottle. Copth won't take kindly t' that."

"Justice is justice. Your opinion is not needed. You don't see what a *foul worm* that guy is?"

"Look, let'th come back later, after we join A.A. We'll be in a thtronger position."

"No!"

Teddy holds Rainwater aloft. "Still half-full!"

"All right, all right. I recognize some abstract value in bein' A.A. members before we put this utter imbecile in his place."

Race up First, fade into an alley doorway.

"Let'th not get arrethted on our way to A.A." Drinks.

"It would only be the hand of heaven."

"Yeah, well, it'th my future marriage you're toyin' with."

"No fuckin' *vegetableman's* gonna call me a freak and get away with it. I'll be back tomorrow picketin' that bastard."

"Thith Shop Unfair to Thcallionfreakth?"

"I'm cold. We been runnin' too hard." Bends, vomiting. Teddy holds back like a Greek, then bends, vomiting unstoppably with fellow-feeling. Points at Leo's winewhiskey vomit. " 'S that blood?"

"Who cares?"

"Well, I feel a helluva lot better."

"Let's finish this an' get on." Leo drinks.

"Can't wathte it." Drinks.

Abruptly, wine pumps out of Leo's nose and mouth. Teddy holds back, hand on doorknob, breast stiffened, stomach lifting and falling.

"I'm through," Leo whispers. Takes bottle, drinks again, long, slow, numbing a small pulsing in his stomach. Grins brightly, "Stayin' down! I think I need food. As long as we're uptown, let's hit a skinflick after we join A.A. Eat, rest up, dry off. Get a bottle for the flick."

"Sure. We thtill got two twenties. Though maybe we should go home and write?"

"Bottles'll be there temptin' us."

"Gotta fathe 'em thooner or later."

"We'll just put 'em in the cupboard an' forget about 'em."

"They won't go t' wathte. I've heard that alcoholicth often have liquor in the houthe, jutht t' show how thtrong they are. Fightin' booze's all will power and we got *that* to thpare."

"Obviously we're not alcoholics. Not in any manner, shape, or direction."

"No, but we wanna cut down. Be thocial drinkers."

"Not so com*pul*sive."

Sneak back up the avenue, hiding in doorways. No patrol car. At Thirty-third, lightning again bursts in the east, eyes filling with falling brown specks, a gathering of eagles above East River. A sign appears—on a narrow doorway: A.A.

"After you," Leo says.

"Wait a minute." Teddy shakes their Rainwater. Hides the bottle by an empty pint beside the short steps. "Let'th not mention those bottles we have home." Leo winks. "Nanthy, it'th all for you!" Teddy sweeps in.

Short hallway, into an office with three desks, a few wallchairs with pale, shot men holding foamplastic coffeecups, a man behind each desk, cleareyed, healthy. Jack sits talking with a short, hardy redheaded adviser behind a desk. "Yeah," Jack says, "I've had it with the Irish virus." He follows the adviser's surprised gaze.

"Am I still drinkin'?" the adviser asks Jack.

Twins sopping, Teddy's daisywreath dragging about his ears.

"Lo!" Jack says, "the bridegroom cometh."

"Jack! We came t' join up! Whatta we thign?"

Jack rises, gets another chair. "Sit here, I'm just taking up valuable space. John-Bob, these are my Village friends, Leo and Teddy. Boys, meet John-Bob Burns—or should I say John-Bob B?"

"Any relation to the poet?" Leo asks hoarsely, sitting, trembling.

"Same booze," John-Bob says, smallvoiced. Neat, cleanjawed Scot with bright hazel faintly cocked eye. "One of you thinks he's got a drinkin' problem?" John-Bob asks in whispery tobaccocroak.

"I'm open for thome thuggethtionth."

"How about you?" John-Bob asks Leo.

"I'm seriously thinkin' of cuttin' down."

"How do I know if I'm an alcoholic?" Teddy asks.

"Or if I even have a problem?"

"You're sittin' here, right? You got a problem or you wouldn't be askin' for help. How much dya drink?"

"Well, thometimes a gallon of red a day."

"Apiece?" John-Bob asks.

"Yes," Leo croaks, "if we *must* be honest." Looks for Jack who's faded into a back hallway.

"We try t' make a gallon apiethe thtretch through the day and night. Thometimes we gotta break into a third gallon."

"We buy it by the case. 'S an engineering feat t' get rid of the empties."

"Onthe a week we throw 'em off the roof into the vacant lot nextht door."

John-Bob grins, whispering, "I c'd never afford cases. Dya feel your lives 've become unmanageable in any way?"

"Well-l," Teddy hedges. Lights a fag superintently. "How dya mean?"

"You tell me," John-Bob says.

Stare at each other profoundly. Jack returns with steaming cups. "Here, plenty of milk and sugar. You'll need it."

"Jack," Leo says. "Honestly. Dya think our lives're *unmanageable?*"

"Do you?" Jack asks. "Talk with John-Bob. I'll be out back when you're finished. This is great!"

"Ya thee," Teddy blows a great blue smokecloud over John-Bob, "Jack'th prejudithed! He's known uth quite a few years now. I mean, thomebody who *knows* ya can't be as objective as you are. I wouldn't thay our lives were unmanageable. In fact, the reason I'm here is to put my life into greater manageability! I'm thomethin' of a perfectionitht."

"We're composers. We may drink excessively, true, but we get an awful lotta work done. Jack only knows half the facts."

"We're exthtremely conscientiouth. Overly thcrupulouth about our work. We thpend *hours* erathin' and cleanin' up pages tho they have a beautiful appearanthe."

"Faultless," Leo says.

"Of courthe, *Leo,* now, he's throwin' up blood—an' keepth hearin' radio thignals."

"That may just be an ear infection!" Leo says. "Or vitamin deficiency. But we've composed *seven* operas. That doesn't sound unmanageable, does it?"

"Seven operas!" John-Bob says.

"Unperformed. They're too ecthentric. But they will be performed!"

"They surely will," Leo says.

"What are these radio signals?" John-Bob asks. "You hear music?"

"Sure he does."

"What dya expect? I'm a composer!" Leo knocks Teddy's knee. "I feel that that subject's personal and entirely beyond the realm of alcohol or our present discussion. Let's get back t' booze, huh?"

"Whatta we thign? We're goin' to a movie."

"There's nothin' to sign," John-Bob says. "You never been to an A.A. meeting? Here's a meetingbook. Perry Street Workshop has a meetin' at six o'clock. Why don't-cha make that?—it's right near you in the Village."

"Well, we're in the *Eatht* Village, not the Wetht Village. That'th awfully far to go for uth."

"Won't even be outta the *movie* by six, will we, Ollie?"

"Why go if we don't even know if we're alcoholicth?"

"That's where ya find out," John-Bob says. "Nobody can tell ya you're an alcoholic but yourself."

Leo looks about unhappily. "Well, this is certainly painless. There must be more to joinin' A.A. than this!"

"Oh, there is," John-Bob says. "When'd you gentlemen have your last drink?"

"Wasn't it jutht before noon?"

Leo peeks around for Jack. "Oh, I think it was *early* this mornin'. —Are *you* an alcoholic? Or's that too personal?"

"If I'm not, I'll *do* until the real thing comes along. Where I was born, I'd have to be."

"There's an awful lotta Burnses," Leo says.

"Sure are!" John-Bob whispers. "I had seven older brothers and they were all drunks. All middlenamed Robert too. I'm the only one still livin'. I'm an orphan!—the disease wiped out my whole family."

Leo giggles. "They needed A.A.!"

"You're from Thcotland?"

"I got out as fast as I could. But I nearly died anyway."

"We had a little drinkin' in our family," Teddy says. "Nothin' that bad, of courthe. Maybe *I'm* jutht a heavy drinker."

"Mama's always said we come from drinkin' people."

"Let'th not dramatize heavy drinkers as alcoholicth. I'll thtand up for mythelf even if you won't. Not that I'm pigheaded. Gimme the factth—*jutht where's* the line drawn, huh?"

"Between heavy drinkin' and alcoholism?" John-Bob asks. "It's the effect it has on you—not the quantity. Maybe ya feel you've hit some kinda bottom?"

"Frankly, I don't. I'm here more for my brother's thake, if the truth mutht be known."

"It was *your idea* t' come here!"

"Only because Nanthy thaid she wouldn't marry me unleth I joined. Let'th not make my cathe thound worthe than it is."

"You're not here for yourself?" John-Bob asks Teddy.

"Not really! I got a different conthtitution from Leo. Couldn't that make a differenthe?"

"I dunno. You're throwin' up blood, Leo?"

Leo sighs. *"Yes."* Glares at Teddy, who looks away. "It comes and goes."

"Does it worry ya?" John-Bob asks.

"Not particularly. I suppose it should. What dya think it is?"

"Bleeding ulcer?" John-Bob suggests. "I dunno. Why don'tcha stop drinkin' for ninety days and see if it stops?"

"Ninety days!"

"We recommend ninety days as a trial sobriety. Your head'll clear up even if your stomach doesn't!"

"But ninety days!" Leo reels. "That's *three months."*

"If ya don't feel better, we'll refund your misery. It's only one day at a time—don't drink anything one day at a time. This is a twenty-four-hour program."

Teddy snorts gently. Leo lifts weights through mind-bloat. "One day at a time?" he asks. "That's ridiculous. Why don't I just stay sober ninety days and prove I can do it? One day at a time, that's for boy scouts. I stayed sober for thirty days just two years ago."

"Tho'd I. No alcoholic could do that."

"How long ya been drinkin'?" John-Bob asks Leo.

"Well-l!" Leo says hugely, measuring downriver and upriver. "Ya mean heavy drinkin' or just drinkin'?"

"I don't know," John-Bob says. "You tell me."

"Well, we been drinkin' about twenty years. But heavy only this past six."

"Frankly, Thtan, I *don't* think we qualify."

"After twenty years," John-Bob says, "ninety days isn't such a long time to wait for your head to clear up. We build up an awful lot of alcoholic thinkin' in twenty years, until it saturates everything we think."

Double stonewall stare, massive blankness.

"What if ya don't even *have* alcoholic thinkin'?" Teddy asks. "Then you're not an alcoholic?"

"What year's this?" John-Bob asks Teddy.

Teddy sighs, studies Leo. "What'th thith? June?"

"I mean what year?" John-Bob asks.

"What is—thith is—the date on our loan we jutht thigned. No, that'th nextht year. Now I *know* what year it is, let'th not be childish. I didn't come here t' play games. In fact, John-Bob, you thit here talkin' t' me like you were an *intern,* not a *doctor.* Ya don't have anthers for any quethtion I athk ya. Not one thtraight anther! Are you completely devoid of an honetht reply? Or of thinthere thympathy for thomeone who might be thufferin'? I could be quite a thick man!—but I'd never know it from you. Maybe I should be talkin' with thomebody elthe—or is thith whole plathe filled with *interns?* I think I'm wathtin' my time here, Leo."

"How about you?" John-Bob asks Leo. "You wanna buy ninety days?"

"Well, I don't know. Sometimes I let Teddy do the thinkin' for us. . . ."

"I think ya should," Teddy says. "Look, Bob-John, he's the one who's the alcoholic—we've both thought that for years. He's the one who has the two-day blackoutth. *He's* the fuckin' Jekyll-Hyde in thith fuckin' freak show! He's the one who hears trumpetth! He's the one who wetth the bed and needs the rubber mat, *hah!* It'th not me, for Chritht'th thake. I'd *like* to thee you thober up, buthter, then maybe we c'd get thome *manageability* into our lives. Right? Wouldn't ya like a little manageability in your pithy, utheleth exthithtenthe? Ya got any idea how many times I've had t' *carry* you into the kitchen so I could pith in the think?—inthtead of on the floor like *you* do? You got no toleranthe for alcohol, buthter. *None!"*

"You threw up same as I did just ten minutes ago!"

"I got an iron conthtitution!"

"Famous last words." John-Bob smiles.

Trembling hard, Teddy bores into John-Bob with steely eyes. "Ya thee who's thittin' on which thide of thith dethk, don'tcha? When I want advithe from a fuckin' drunk, I'll athk for it."

"How's it going?" Jack asks John-Bob mildly.

"I'm thurrounded by failures!" Teddy eyes the office. "That'th my whole problem. Look, you *go* to these fuckin' meetings, they'll be good for ya. I don't want anything to do with 'em—but *you* go on *your* days. *Okay?"*

Leo looks left and right, shaking, deserted.

"AHA!" Teddy cries. "You're thinkin' of those fuckin' bottles home on the table! Ten minutes away from booze an' you're shakin' already! Like a baby! Well, I'm through with your drinkin', dummkopf, I've had it! That'th *my booze!* If I thee you take one drink in the nextht ninety days, I'm perthonally gonna thmash your imbethilic fathe into pure shit. Got my warnin'? *Hnh?*

GOT IT? *My God—thith is the motht deprethin' afternoon of my life, Jack.* I want you t' know that."

"Gee, I'm sorry you feel that way, Teddy," Jack says. "I feel *up,* myself. But then I always do. *You're* going to a meeting, Leo?"

Leo nods, whispering, "Happily! Ya sure know how t' grind a fella down, Teddy." Tears springing. "You've told things about me I wouldn't tell God Himself."

"So ya pith on the floor, tho what? Thomebody hath t' be honetht around here."

Leo's head slides down his arm on the desk. "Well, I gotta get outta here. Because I'm really gonna be cryin' in a minute."

"Ya'll get no pity from me," Teddy warns.

"Drink your coffee," Jack tells Leo.

Waves of selfpity drive through Leo, spurt from his eyes. "I'm sorry, I can't stop," he wails at John-Bob, who sits checking off meetings in Leo's meetingbook.

"I know how you feel," Jack tells Leo. "Felt the same way when those chains dropped off. Boy, what a relief. No more blood banks, no more slavery to the next drink and the next bottle—that one we have is never enough, is it? We're always worried about the next one. You're not giving up alcohol, Leo, you're giving up insanity, hangovers, the wine shits, bloody gums, nightmares, insomnia and about five dozen other symptoms you thought were infections and bad nerves. You won't miss those horrors."

Teddy, hands clenched between his knees, ears stuffed. Leo drenched in fog, kneading his forehead. "Talk slower, Jack," he says.

"I gotta get outta here!" Teddy cries. "Get up! *I'll* take care of Leo. Come on, Thtanley."

"Here's your meetingbook," Jack says, slipping the book into Leo's sidepocket.

Teddy rips the book out, pulling Leo to his feet, bounces the crumpled book off John-Bob's desk. "Not one word from you thonsofbitcheth."

"I want that." Leo reaches for the book.

"Come on," Teddy says, "I know what you need."

"I'll write you, Leo," Jack says. "And congratulations on being born. You may find that this is the greatest day of your life. Just don't take that first drink and you'll make it—one day at a time."

Teddy's rage bursts at Jack. *"You've come as a thief in the night and thtolen my brother from me!"*

"I'm sorry you feel that way, Teddy," Jack repeats.

Teddy stares at him powerlessly. Leo shakes Jack's hand, stuffs the meetingbook back into his pocket.

Leo-Teddy goes out into the drenching light.

JAW set, eyes shut, Teddy whales giant chords from the hifi speakers, bloodying the last movement of Bruckner's *Seventh,* his grunts, his triumphant harpoons serenely darted. *AHH!* his arms fall, last note faded. Leo nods, half-asleep on his feet. *"That'th thublime."* Teddy takes a glass of white wine from the desk. Leo glances at his three-hundred-dollar check from Whippoorwill Records: *Advance against royalties for Song, "The Minnow."* "Jazz is a dead end," Teddy adds *"—tho* repet*it*iouth. Though I admire your little minnow ditty, don't get me wrong."

"Thanks. We'll have a peaceful evening, won't we?"

"Sure will. Ain't everyday ya get married. Lend me two-fifty for a pint of vodka."

"A *pint?"* Leo's back prickles.

"Medithinal purpotheth!" Feels his jaw tenderly. "My fillin' fell out. I don't want the cavity t' thtart *rottin'* before I get to a dentitht."

"How about half a pint? Just for tonight."

"Aw," Teddy says lowly, "Wanda's wise."

"Yeah, but she has *hopes.* For my sake, just half a pint tonight. I'll get ya the other half tomorrow."

"Ya'll get *uth* the other half."

"I'm *not* drinkin'!"

"Joker." Teddy lifts the sauterne gallon, rolls its dreggy leavings about. "Thith won't latht. We don't want me havin' nightmares—not t'night, ya know?" Stares at their deskphoto of the Redfield twins, Wilma and Wanda. "Too bad Wilma's in Parith. She'd be a nithe thedative. You've thought about that?"

"She's also *married.*"

"Well, maybe thomeday we'll make a beautiful four-thome."

"Let's go!" Wanda calls, hangs up dishtowel.

Teddy assembles vast notes for his *Prometheus* libretto, fixes them into his clipboard. "Ready! You're not takin' your clipboard?"

"I'm on vacation tonight," Leo says.

"I never tire." Teddy empties the gallon, swirls his glass. "Remember—Bruckner didn't even thtart writin' thymphonies until he was forty. I got a few years to prepare, huh?"

"I'll excuse your modesty."

Teddy drinks off his wine with a smack. "Oh, laugh all ya want. I know ya do."

"Where? Behind your back?"

Teddy eyes the empty gallon, hooks it for the garbage. "I'm willin' t' have a peatheful evenin'. No reason for argument. I want ya to have a beautiful evening filled with beautiful feelings, and I'll do everything I can t' help. Ya deserve it, every conthideration."

Leo nods thanks, holds Teddy's trenchcoat for him. Teddy holds his, lifts Leo's hair over his collar. Leo-Teddy sits at kitchentable while Wanda brushes their hair quickly.

"Boy, was that somethin'!" she says. "Come home broke from City Hall afteh gettin' married and find a check fa' *three hundred dollars* in th' mailbox! Guess that's the Higheh Poweh watchin' oveh us."

"I call it thynchronithity. Jung has all about it."

"I call it Higher Power," Leo says.

"I'm still an atheist," Wanda says nervously.

"Oh no!" Teddy cries, taking her under his wing. "Not that! Even I'm not that. Jutht be willin', Wanda, and it'll come. Look at th' miracles of the earth, the thunrise, the flowers, all th' beautiful things that've no uthe in a mechanithtic univerthe. Thtands t' reason, a divine thpirit'th needed t' receive 'em. There's a utheleth gorgeouthneth in nature that'th only meant to inthpire. Ya'll thee for yourthelf thomeday. You'll make it."

"That's beautiful, Uncle Teddy." Wanda brushes her own hair. "Ya just make that up?"

"Yeah."

"Oscar said that years ago," Leo says.

"Oh, did he? Well—I think I improve on it. Ya believe it, don'tcha?"

"Oh, it's beautiful."

Foxcollared Wanda in her blue winter coat, snaps out the livingroom lights, turns on the radio loud. Kitchen-light on, doublelock the door, go down six musty flights, Wanda's French perfume rising through sour Ukrainian cabbage acids. Curved fox, lyreshape hips.

"What kills me," Teddy laughs, "is your mother showin' up thith morning to help ya dreth while you're in the tub!"

"Was she shocked?" Leo asks. "We weren't dressed ourselves."

"What if she was? I'm a big girl." Wanda's a small Jewish girl with auburn hair, foxy face and steelrim glasses. "I wish this meeting were open to women. I'd love to heah Holy tell his horror story."

"I don't think you'd like Riker's Island," Leo says. "A prison's no place t' visit on your wedding day, honey. I musta been really mocus, tellin' Holy I'd go with 'im on my wedding day! I tell ya Holy's an architect?"

"No," Wanda says.

"His uncle designed the Empire Thtate Building. No kiddin'! That mutht be thomethin' t' live with, bein' an architect himthelf. Be like being Wagner's nephew an' tryin' to write operas. Always outclathed!"

Teddy talks tirelessly. Leo thinks of ear plugs he bought at a drugstore to help him think—useless! he still hears every word Teddy or Wanda says. *Supersensitive? Try Our .38 Calibre Ear Plug. POW!*

Thanksgiving weekend snow laps neon streets to black carbon, falls into blue darkness of Tompkins Square Park. Evening cops patrol the parkfence, slickers glistening black under bluewhite lampglare. Tall steel tulips blind the park paths, light lighter than light under snow-birthing darkness. Deep homefeelings for upstate hills, far snowfalls.

"Are you all right?" Wanda asks Leo nervously.

"Sure! Why shouldn't I be?"

"I thought you were suddenly sad about somethin'."

"I'm high-energy! I been high-energy for weeks. Don't

worry about my goddamn nerves so much—I'm not a victim of my moods—*or* my whims, ahem. I spent two months tryin't' get a handle on this program and I don't wanta blow it now."

"Leo's terrific," Teddy tells her. Smiles at Leo. "She thtudies your nerves like a chromatic fantathy. Why, here's Frank'th Tank Shop!"

"Teddy lost a filling—" Leo begins.

"You don't have t' explain," Wanda says. "It's Teddy's choice."

"Thank you," Leo says.

"Por nada," she says.

"Play, gipthies, danthe, gipthies," Teddy sings, opening the liquorstore door, *"play while you may!"* Stares about tenderly at the bottles. "I almotht married a Jewish gipthy," he tells Wanda.

"Salome?" Wanda asks.

Teddy nods. "Used t'wear Egyptian eyeshadow—tho blue! *But when a beautiful woman breakth your heart*—two half-pintth of vodka, Frank."

"Singin' tonight?" gray Frank asks.

"Gilbey's hundred proof, please," Teddy sings, *"if that'th all right with Leo!* My brother got altared today."

"Did it hurt?" Frank asks Leo.

"He means *married!"* Wanda cries.

"Oh, congratulations," Frank says flatly. "You the lucky girl?"

"I'm the lucky man." Leo pays. "In every possible way."

"That's interestin'," Frank says.

"I sold a song today," Leo says.

"About a minnow!" Teddy pockets his pints.

"What's so interestin' about a minnow?" Frank asks Leo.

"This minnow finally finds a completely undisturbed place," Leo says. "And can look down into the pool he's in and see the pebbles on the bottom."

"Maybe it *shoulda* been about a whale," Frank suggests wisely over his cigar.

"Very good, Francis!" Teddy says, flushed as Leo. "And working itth way up a brook to thpawn, ha ha."

"A whale couldn't make the first step," Leo says. "It'd struggle and struggle just to get up a tiny falls."

"But that'd be more interestin'," Frank says, not budging.

"It's a *lovely* song!" Wanda squeezes Leo's hand.

"Ya finish yoeh opera yet?" Frank asks Teddy.

"Oh, I'm thtill perfecting my libretto. Got over thix-hundred pages of noteth t' pull together. Then I'll compose the music, no thweat. I got it all up here." Taps his skull. "And here." Riffs his thick sheaf on the counter.

Frank looks at a large rosepink wine-ring on Teddy's top page. "Good luck," he says.

Climb six flights to Holy's topfloor pad. Leo reaches up, pushing on Wanda's bottom.

"Thanks! I needed that."

"You Wanda, me Tarzan."

Teddy uncaps, swigs. "You Tarzan, me Gilbey's."

Holy's buzzer muted, a slip of paper taped over it. Leo knocks, Holy stands before them—the tallest recovering drinker in Manhattan.

"My God!" Wanda says. He's all in black with black knit tie, white carnation, his tonsure slicked forward over bald crown. Bright veins fleck his nose, his long narrow face slouches with dignity. *"Good evening!"* he sounds forth with loving harmony. "Come into my parlor, such as it is. How *are* you this evening? I've been thinking over my fifty years of drinking—I had my first spoonful of wine at two hours, did I tell you, because I wasn't expected to live—and I was recalling three universities I'd chewed up like separate tins of Dutch biscuits in my youth." His mouth sets with victory. *"Three of them! Ha!* Those bastards couldn't teach *me!* I don't know if I believe in God yet but—me, a year sober!—I surely believe in miracles. After what I went through. . . ."

"Oh, now I'll miss your story twice as badly!" Wanda says. "But I'll be at your birthday party up at Yorkville."

"You will!" Holy cries. "You're coming? Marvelous! I was so mocus last year, I don't know the exact day I came into the fellowship." His each utterance highsounding. "But I know that everyone was eating turkey and I *wasn't,* so it must've been around Thanksgiving." Shakes his head with wonder. "Oh, it has really been hell!—this last three weeks. They talk about the first-birthday blues, and now I know. But I want all of it, everything the fellowship offers, and I've got it. It is *hell.* I mean I am destroyed in pieces."

"Want some advice from my fifty-nine days?" Leo asks.

"I certainly do not."

"I haven't any."

"I doubt that anything *anyone* could say would help," Holy declares. "My God, I went to the dentist today—I'm determined to have my teeth rebuilt, each one separately—and that *thief* wants four thousand dollars for the job! But—I've decided it's worth it. I even took a job today at that secondhand shop on Eleventh and B, restoring furniture. I'll pay that bastardly dentist every penny, the *first* honest act of my life. And when are you going?" he asks Teddy.

"I'm afraid of gettin' a dual problem with Novocaine," Teddy says.

"You're fearful of becoming a Novocaine addict? That's new."

"Well, really, my lip getth numb and I can't blow my trombone."

"Can you blow it with your teeth *missing?"* Holy asks. "Besides, you don't need drilling to get a denture, dear fellow."

"Oh, I'll probably be givin' up the horn. There's no plathe in a thymphony orchethtra for trombones. I'll jutht retain an amateur's interetht."

"I didn't know you wrote *symphonies!"* Holy says.

"I'm workin' in a new form—thymphonic opera. I may have t' go to Juilliard t' get a few bathicth under my belt. But maybe not. Geniuth is nine-tenth' enthusiasm."

Holy sniffs spirits in the air. "I didn't know you admitted to a single problem, much less a dual problem."

"I don't." Teddy gleams. *"Obviouthly!"*

"Obviously. But that's your problem, not mine. Let's be on our way. Hop, hop!"

Down and out into huge snowflakes. Walks bare, flakes melting as they hit. Across the street the park stretches roomily in falling whiteness.

"Lousy weather for polo." Teddy, glittereyed.

"Heavenly!" Holy turns to Leo. "How're you fixed?"

"All right," Leo hedges. "About twenty bucks on me."

"Good," Holy says. "It's *my* birthday and I've *got* to take a cab. I'm too shook up to take a bus to the Queensboro Bridge."

Leo kisses Wanda goodbye.

"Where are you off to?" Holy asks.

"Shopping," she says. "Ya didn't congratulate me."

"Oh my heavens, that's right. Let me kiss the bride. Were you childhood sweethearts?"

"They used to play with my parents in a cocktail lounge back home. I'm more New York—I only lived in King James a coupla yeahs."

"You make a lovely bride," Holy says.

"Thanks," she squeaks.

"I feel well blessed," Leo says. "And goddamn happy!"

Catch a cab and soon wedge into solid holiday traffic on Second Avenue. After a full hour, they rush about the ramp to Queensboro Bridge, lost. Holy strides straight into traffic to ask a cop where the bus stop is. Soon they cross the right bridge in the wrong bus, sweating, nervous, late. Holy gets three transfers to the right bus. Steam blows up from Queens factories under the bridge, neon like red cellophane turning floating factory wraiths infrared: allsnowing Queens a red shore below the bus. Beyond the bridge, change buses in front of a Spanish fortune-teller's storefront where young blacks spit like sharpshooters between front teeth. "Thtill thlaves." Teddy belches. "Too much shrieking music. Well, even the thubway kills the top of your hearing. I should thue the thity for what it'th done to me professionally."

Bus through Queens, narrow, smalltown boulevards, shop-jammed, neonwaved. At last only Holy and Leo-Teddy left on the bus. Silence. Teddy sips behind Holy's back.

"You spoken at a prison before?" Leo asks Holy.

"Not this one. And I shouldn't be. I'm too depressed."

The bus lurches up a gloomy turnoff and drives into blackness. An airliner lifts overhead, vast thrumming buzz above blinding flakes. Snow lathers the nothingness, bus climbing a bridge over snowfeathered nightslide of East River. Blue and pink bulbs dottle La Guardia runways. Pull into prison terminal.

A black guard takes them into a housetrailer.

"Bus'll be back in forty minutes," Holy says. "Damn! We gotta catch it to make my birthday party. *A.A.*," he tells the indoor guard. "We're twenty minutes late, I'm afraid."

Sit on bench, wait for prison bus.

"It'th the Big Houthe, athe!" sidewinder whisper to Holy.

"No, actually these are all low-termers here, three years tops," Holy says. "It's not really the Big House, ace." He beckons. "Sign the register." Clip plastic numbers to trenchcoat lapels. Holy beams nervously above the plastic clip on his black alpaca collar, the brighthearted funeral director.

A dismal brown bus arrives within the gate. Drive into darkness and dark one-story buildings. Round a traffic circle, stop by a low building with sealed slab doors. The driver leads them into an anteroom. *"Boy—"* Teddy eyes the room's wallfacings showing Industry's future—*"Work Thaves!*—like Jesuth."

"I'm *not* gonna give away my cigarettes," Holy says suddenly. "Not when I only have two bucks and they'll cost me sixty cents in a machine."

Leo-Teddy clutches his own packs possessively.

"We went with Marty O'Dublin t' the psycho ward at Bellevue," Leo tells Holy, "and *he* gave away two packs in half an hour."

"Those guys'd really bounthed their marbles. I'll never go there again! Damned jumblies gimme bad dreams. Really, I dreamt about 'em! *Ghathtly dreams.*"

Holy stares about their tomb, depressed. "You know what this décor is, don't you?"

"Flash Gordon Conquers the Univerthe?"

A barred door slides open on silence. A black guard appears in a cagelike chamber.

"A.A.," Holy says and inner bars slide magically open.

"Go down there and turn lef'," the guard says.

"Wow." Teddy stares ahead.

"Incredible," Leo agrees.

"It's like the Empire State Building laid out on its side," Holy says.

Start hiking down the one-story cellblock series toward a barred door specklike in the distance. On each side, deep cellblocks, fellow monsters milling in undershirts and prison pants. Pass a mess hall, a recreation room, on and on, a dozen cellblocks, all barred. Guilt presses Leo-Teddy so hard he can't bear to look into a cell for fear of catching a black prisoner's eye.

"We're the only guys in here with beards!" Teddy whispers. His half-pints swell to quarts in his pockets.

"Christ," Leo says, "talk about the last mile." Clutches

the fresh hard cigarette pack in his trenchcoat, trembling with oceanic embarrassment.

Holy, taller than Lincoln, paces Leo-Teddy's glide. "A.A.," he says again and barred doors flow electrically open—pass through without breaking cadence. Follow a black guard's finger. Turn, come into a mammoth blasting room howling hard-rock from a jukebox. Casual men everywhere sleepwalk like taffy figures in sedating sound. Walk through a door lettered *Hebrew* in childlike letters.

"It's a temple," Holy whispers.

A glowing white prisoner in hornrims cries, "Hello! I'm the chairman. We'd about given up on ya! You wanna wait and speak last?" He grimaces fellow feeling for Holy.

"I'll speak now," Holy says.

Goes behind a lectern, still in his black alpaca overcoat. Frowzy room filled, every seat taken, A.A. slogans hung about. Leo-Teddy finds only an empty bench beside Holy, sits barefacing the prisoners, cigarette packs gripped, half-pints like pistols.

Holy stretches his watch on the lectern, slowly thumbs its glass face. Several white prisoners among the blacks glue their bugged eyes on Holy. Silence. Jaded basketball star? blacksuited carnationed banker?—this bald. . . .

"My name is Holy and I am an alcoholic." His voice bites into the back row. "It's really Holbrook, but I'm called Holy.

"By profession I'm an architect but I've never practiced my art in this country. I have in Europe and the Far East but not in the States. Since I still draw, I'm not embarrassed to say I'm an artist.

"I was born to a very great deal of money, and was raised as a rich boy with every bit of the trimmings. But money has very little to do with our disease, so I won't waste our precious time talking about my glamorous youth. Alcohol is not a class problem, nor an intellectual problem. It's a physical, mental, and spiritual problem.

"I had my first drink the day I was born."

Licks his lips. His rocklike thumb clamps over the watchface, his outdoor blue eyes beam through puffy lids, himself the sheriff of his thirst.

"I was born at home and not expected to live. My parents gave me up for dead and so did the doctor. But my French nanny, who cared for me, believed in wine, and she spooned wine and water into me. She saved my life with wine, and I drank every day of my life until I started stealing my father's brandy at four, and by five I was addicted to every form of alcohol in my father's house. He was a world-respected connoisseur, with precise tastes, and in our cellar we had at least one bottle of every wine and every liquor on earth worth drinking. He was not an alcoholic. But at eight I was a confirmed drunkard and had tasted everything I cared to taste and from then on, taste meant nothing, I went straight for the alcohol.

"But I have to skip this so that I can get to the only part of my story which means anything to me—the present and what I do with it. I had my last drink one year ago today. Today is my birthday in sobriety. I am fifty years old in body but only one year old in any way I care to remember. Today I celebrate my real birthday. It hasn't been easy. The last three weeks've been as hellish as any time when I was drinking. I'm thirsty tonight. And that's the truth! I mean ungodly thirsty. I won't go into the reasons, they're there and they're mine. It's my thirst.

"I won't dwell on this. I stopped attending one group's meetings in the Village because I can see they're only haggling over ways to have a slip. Under the fog, that's all they talk about. But *I* need health, not discussion, and faith, not analysis. I can't toy with the faintest idea of a slip. Just one slip and it's the padded walls and police guards twenty-four-gray-hours-a-day, every day, forever. I can't afford that, not for a drunk. So if I thirst, I thirst for what you can give me tonight.

"My God, I've seen you all before, each one of you. In my nightmares—and I was sitting out there."

The room roars as a prisoner comes in from the jackhammering recreation room and closes the door. Holy smiles faintly.

"When I finished my first ninety days sobriety and gave my first A.A. talk, I was afraid that all my fine insights would be lost unless I gave my first talk in a room tailored for pindrop silence. I didn't know then that a really grand idea is louder than a gang war." He grips the lectern, eyes glittering, lips wet. "I know you, I've served time—but never again. And I'm not here to compare prison experiences. So. . . .

"My uncle built a very famous skyscraper and my mother thought I should conform to the family's style of accomplishment. She thought I should conform in every detail to what she had in mind for me. I mention her only because I've just recently come into my own as a free human being—despite some abortive marriages. Now I am released from all institutions, utterly released, from mother, school, war, marriage, and work. Freedom is hell.

"I redecorate muddled up apartments. My whole life has been odd but expensive, like my redecorating. During the war I had influential friends and was assigned to bar duty in Washington. My job was to sit around bars and inform on officers who unwittingly leaked out secrets. But I took to the work too assiduously and was never sober enough to inform on anyone. I requested transfer and was sent to India where I built air strips and rationed opium to the laborers. I did that for a year, doling out raw opium—"

Teddy grins, head lolling, arms prickling, amused by opium, his gaptooth face sweeping the prisoners' eyes shining at Holy. Leo sees dull demons.

"—and drinking vodka at fifteen cents a fifth—"

"Hah!" Teddy laughs. Prisoners ripple, shifting to see him.

"I ran through four or five fifths of vodka daily on top of my opium habit. I was hooked, but it never interfered with my work. After a year, to kick the habit, I had myself transferred to China, away from my source. In China I built a few things which are still there. I did my cold turkey on a lake of vodka."

Teddy recalls a hole in his left coat pocket, thanks himself for quick thinking, grips his bottle more tightly and makes a note to hold onto it when he rises.

"To show you how far gone I was and could still function—I did a news program. A friend of mine had collected enormous quantities of radio equipment, very powerful, and I monitored the news in a huge tent hung with walls of equipment. I speak three languages, including Spanish and French, but over this transmitter I suddenly found myself listening fluently to programs in Urdu, a south Indian dialect called Tamil, a Cantonese dialect, German, Japanese, and a Setzuan dialect. I was writing and delivering magnificent news stories nightly, derived from languages I couldn't speak.

"At the time I took in a Eurasian girl, whom I got with child. When she was about to deliver—even then she walked three paces behind me—a friend I admired, a priest, suggested that the correct thing to do was marry her. So I did. She died two weeks later when she was blown up—by the Americans—"

Teddy sniffs loud indignation, chin high.

"—I tried to find my son—for over a year and by every means I could—but he was lost. I never found him. I know I tried!—but I don't remember so well. I was mocus, just about wet-brained.

"Back in the States, I was invited by my brother to stay a week in Mexico. I stayed five years. I did production design and some murals. Then I went to Buenos Aires and fished for shark livers on a three-masted schooner, which was heaven with vitamin A. We'd take out the liver, then throw the shark back, then follow the rising price for shark livers on the wireless. That was my only lucky year.

"Later, I opened an art gallery in the Village and ran it with a friend for four years. I sold nothing of my own—I simply don't know how to evaluate my own work, don't ask me why.

"Then last year I had my crucial experience with alcohol. I had a cold for three months which laid me up. I just stayed home and drank gin until at last I couldn't get out of bed. I couldn't turn two pages. I was *flojera*—utterly flat. A vegetable! I told myself I was finally going to stop, I couldn't go on. Caving in under sheriffs chasing me, debts, dunning letters—and the *bells*. The only thing that could get me out of bed was the phone. If the doorbell rang, I might peek under the door to see if there were feet on the other side—and there often weren't! I complained to my landlord that my doorbell rang by itself. I finally stuffed it with paper. But it was the phone I feared most. My creditors, everyone I hated most, people out to injure me had my number. The phone company interrupted my service for nonpayment, but the bell kept on ringing independently. It frightened me so that I tiptoed by it even when it wasn't ringing. Then a repairman came and took it away, and when it kept on ringing I hid in the bathroom until it stopped. Oh! I'd lie on the bathroom floor. I cried so hard that I didn't know I was praying.

"Praying? I was starved. My existence was totally unpeopled. My liquor was delivered to the door which I'd open just enough to take the bottle. Finally, I made a last effort. I went out and phoned a girl I knew in A.A. That was a year ago Thanksgiving—everyone was eating turkey and I wasn't. The next day she took me to A.A. and there were all these *delicious* people. I liked them. I liked them and couldn't understand a word they said for months—"

Teddy studies his ragged nails, fishes out a matchbook, starts filing his nails with the striking surface. Beet-red, Leo nudges him. Teddy draws back, wounded. Goes on filing his nails.

"—I couldn't speak to them but I liked them. I who had thought myself all these years a brilliantly impressive bar conversationalist found myself unable to say one word, because now I knew: I was really a pressing bore, and always had been. My whole glamorous life was a bore. *Empty! No growth!*

"I hung around the Intergroup office for four months, just sitting there. Very gradually I've begun to awaken, but I'm not awake yet. When they finally allowed me to start answering phones, the calls from all over the city—*that*—was heaven. That was the greatest blessing of my life. . . . because here were the voices of people worse off than myself, whom I could help. I arrived at Intergroup each morning panting to answer the phones. Those voices, they were all my pigeons! I couldn't hear enough of them! On the Easter holidays the office was almost empty and from Good Friday through Easter Sunday, I was in ecstasy. At night I'd lie awake in a passion. I got up at dawn and couldn't eat I was trembling so, and I chased to the office for more of this miracle I'd been blessed with. And I drank all day at the phones."

Holy stands quietly at a loss.

"There's nothing easy yet. I can't live normally. I'm not very old yet—one year. I can't do a great many things that other people take for granted—including crying. I have no companions, not one outside the fellowship. But that's enough, I get by, and the things I miss most are those I've never really had anyway. I'm beginning to hope that I may take up my true art here in the States. I have food, I'm my own boss, I can hear my phone ring today and welcome the conversation. That's miraculous. I pay all my bills, have paid many old ones. Most of all, I'm happy to be standing right where I'm standing. They told me when I came into this fellowship, Stick with the winners. Save your best for those you can help, don't bother with the hopeless. I can't do that, I'm sorry. *I* was hopeless once.

"I said I was depressed when I came here tonight. I've been terribly, relentlessly depressed for three weeks. But action is magic, speaking with you, and you have given me something, your interest, which I see and feel. Something is trying to stay alive in this room—all these eyes and minds focused on simple, powerful ideas—something in here is fighting death and disease and insanity to stay alive, call it species survival, call it group conscience, call it higher power, call it God. It's here and it's getting itself in focus. Thank you. I feel released. All of you, you have lifted my sickness from me. Again, thank you."

The prisoners' applause shocks Leo-Teddy, a stack of plates falling without stop. Holy, his eyes piercing and contrite, pleads with Leo. "Did I reach them?" Then prisoners stand, applauding. Holy can't look at them. Teddy rises, eyes rimmed and glistening, grabs Holy's hand. *"I loved that drinkin' on the phones at Eathter!* BEAUTIFUL!"

Clink!

"I wasn't *drinking!"* Holy edges toward the door.

The glowing chairman, his glasses buttery and gleaming, shouts, "Can'tcha stay?"

"No," Holy shakes his head.

A tall, thin, older black prisoner shakes Holy's hand, then thanks Leo-Teddy, shaking. "Here's your package, man." He slips Teddy his bagged half-pint. "Lucky it didn't break!"

"Thankth!" Teddy, shaking red. "It'th jutht rubbing alcohol."

"I dig shaving lotion," the black says. "That rubbing alcohol's too spaced out for me. My name's Luckie. R. U. Luckie."

"Mine's Teddy. Dya thmoke?"

"Just cigars. You need a butt?"

"Nah, I was gonna give ya mine."

"Keep 'em," Luckie says. "Hey, you're the kinda A.A. cat I dig." Luckie nudges Teddy, his voice soft and happy.

Teddy hangs his head happily, comes up smiling.

"Maybe I could mail you thome shaving lotion? What kind dya dig?"

"Hey, man, Polynesian Jade! But it's four-eighty-five a bottle. Aw, they wouldn't let me receive it."

"We can try! Write your name on my clipboard."

Luckie writes his name and number. "You are some cat!" he says admiringly. "Comin' in here with a package! An' half a load on!"

Teddy winks, shakes Luckie's hand hard. "It may come in a loaf of bread—but ya'll get it, believe me."

"We can't wait for the Lord's Prayer," Holy says, hustling Leo-Teddy toward the door. Trenchcoated twins and Holy roll out of the meeting, thieves on a bank heist.

Walk back the Last Mile, steps cadenced, barred doors gliding open, closing noiselessly.

"Boy, thith has been one of the great nightth of my life. Tho much more friendly than Bellevue! And that cat I was talkin' with, R. U. Luckie, is about the greateteht gentleman I ever met. Shining!"

"You really think I got through?" Holy implores Leo.

"Wow," Leo says.

"Sure." Teddy says. "But thith was the fathtetht A.A. huthtle in hithtory. Twenty minuteth topth!"

"I never can remember what I said!"

"That lake of vodka really creamed 'em. Whatta conthept—I could thuddenly thmell it with pine needles."

Into the anteroom. Leo takes out his unopened cigarettes, unbends the crushed package. Holy pushes on a sealed brass exit slab. "It gives," he says.

"Don't go out there," a black guard calls from a cubicle. "Wait for the bus here."

"Ha!" Holy says, "they frown on visitors larking about the grounds in the dark." Looks about the room. "I hate this period! Industrial futurism—real lobby art. Anyone who could draw lightning with his ruler or arcs with his compass was an architect—a little god. Not an engineer, mind you, who built things. Go to Radio City if you want this mentality at its most ghastly—murals of Labor, turning gears, and stone bas-reliefs of Zeus with a beard of lightning. Really depressing."

"Don't mith Prometheuth bringin' fire down to the little bobtails in th' thkating rink." Rubs his knuckles, the sexbrained gnomic mad scientist.

They slake themselves on cigarettes.

"I didn't look one man in the face," Leo says. "Maybe a guard or two."

"What!" Holy asks.

"I felt strange. I couldn't look at the prisoners."

"My God," Holy says, stricken. "All I could think was, All this youth and beauty locked up!"

The driver calls. Go out into the dark. Snow falls in a sweet clean chill on jelling slush. The dark lies condemned about them, snowwhite grass glowing as if moonlit. Leo gnaws at himself about the prisoners. "I guess I'm not Tolstoy!" he tells Holy.

"Listen!" Holy says. "Thirty thousand men under bars in a storm and you can't hear a sound. . . . It's eerie."

Bus to the terminal. Turn in lapel clips, sign out. A twelve-minute wait for the city bus. Time. . . .

Teddy nudges Holy, shifts into his rattlesnake whisper. "What were ya buthted for, athe?"

"Loitering," Holy says. "In bars."

Leo, wellmannered, hopes Holy won't hit him for a loan. Reckons his cash against another cab to Yorkville.

The city bus pulls up, parks for five minutes while the driver lies down on a bus seat and smokes. Walk to the outdoor bus stop in the prison parking lot. A sign over a sandfilled can says Discharge Your Gun Here. Teddy looks both ways "—Gotta pith." "Well, not in here!" Leo says. Leo-Teddy goes behind the concrete cubicle, relieves himself, Teddy writing a big T in the slush. Sips deeply. Rejoin Holy. Snow falls, the island windchilled from the river. Leo squints through limp air and fat flakes toward the prison buildings, the sky turns ruddy as a forge and he sees men working great furnaces and steel pouring moltenbright where tiny men-devils tend carts on rails, nightstacks milling smoke, and sees hearted within the prison a vast white bed of coals caked with pure heat, light lighter than light as bus headlights drive toward him through snowfall, the busdoor racks open and a smoking corpse asks, *Ready?*

"I feel half-tight," Leo says, boarding.

"I meant to ask you about that," Holy says. Turns in his seat to face Leo-Teddy. "Do you two have the same bloodstreams? Do you mind my asking?"

"I don't mind," Teddy says. "Sure we do."

Holy nods, turns forward again.

Leo swallows. Wanda's wise. Or is she? Intent! Doesn't

intent count? His tongue, dry. His *wife* waiting for him in Yorkville. His wife and his vows—no more wine, no beer, no gin. But, oh, something bounding in him warmer than wine, hotter than gin, more quenching than ale. In the mornings, the shades high, light falling on table salt, on her blouses and sweaters and dresses, her eyes milk-white at breakfast, her face slept and new, the spirit in her blue birdpupils eying him, Leo-Teddy wet-combed, Leo fresh for work, pleasure, buoyance, on his energy-high. Being born.

The bus jounces through outer darkness, a raft slapping upstream. Queens reddens ahead. Cold trenchcoats wet, flakes dying on the panes. Leo's prison-nerves drink at her face.

"Well, over half those guys on Rikers are alkies," Holy tells Leo-Teddy. "Not just heavy drinkers, but alkies."

"How dya know?" Teddy asks. "I really don't go along with that bullshit about heavy drinkers and alkies."

"I *know* you don't." Holy smiles. "That's *your* problem."

Teddy tightens. "Do you know what fear is?"

"I know a lot of it went away when I stopped drinking," Holy says. "I've had my full quota, dear man. The push in the middle of my back while waiting for the subway, and always keeping to a stanchion—"

"I don't mean guilt fears. I mean fear of thmoke. Fear of fire. I don't mean fear of gettin' shot in the head through your houthewindow—I'm used t' that fear. I mean of thirens, fear of *bells*—"

"Now that I know about!"

"Real fear! Don't tell me about *fear,* pal! I have fears you never thought of. You ever have fear of flies fillin' your mouth and ya can't cough 'em out because you'll jutht thwallow 'em? That'th *fear!"*

"Have you thought of Antabuse?" Holy asks.

Teddy snorts hugely. "Sure I have. Ya wanta kill me? You jutht don't understand a fundamental differenthe between you an' me. *You* are an alcoholic—I don't wanna take your inventory, of courthe—but you are an *admitted* alcoholic. Admit it. Are you or are you not an alcoholic?"

"I damned well am."

"Thee?" Teddy shrugs. "That'th it. You may need Antabuthe—but not me." Smiles. "I'm not an alcoholic.

Now, Leo, *he* may need Antabuthe, but I think he knows better."

"You'd *both* go into convulsions?" Holy asks.

"I would first," Leo says. "And if I lived for awhile, they'd hit him too."

"I think I'll shut up for awhile," Holy says. "As Bill W. says, Avoid argument like the plague. I hope I haven't offended either of you."

"Have no fear. I'm thtill lookin' for a genuine alcoholic in thith program. Haven't found one yet."

"What about Fat Tom in the stockingcap?" Leo asks.

"Oh, he's a mental cathe. What I object to, firtht they tell you it'th a physical disease, then they thuggetht you take a moral inventory. What brainwash!"

Queensboro Bridge. Red steam writhing from the tiers and grottoes of the river. Leo sits pleading for release from complicated horrors.

"Ha, lookth like devils live on those wharfth."

The bus rounds a ramp and stops. They hit the snow traffic. Squint in fresh heavy flakes. "We better grab a cab!" Leo says.

"We'll never get one in this weather," Holy says. "Bus will be faster."

Stand at the bus stop under last-century stones of Queensboro Bridge. A blond kid with a pint of sweet on his hip bums a fag, his pupils tight blue, weaves his thanks to Holy.

"Are you all right?" Holy asks.

"Sure, why not?"

"You look out of it," Holy says.

"Man, I am out of it!"

"Do you need some money?"

"Money? How much money?"

"Oh, a thou' or so," Holy laughs.

"What's a thou', man? I been away."

"A thousand dollars! Naturally, I haven't got a thou', just some change."

"I could use fifty cents for somethin' t' eat, I guess."

"Be my guest." Holy gives him two quarters. The blond raises a fistful of change and folds in Holy's offering. "Thanks."

"Where've you been?" Holy asks.

"You know, man, just out of it—not in town! Hey, have a drink."

"Not for me," Holy says.

"Come on. It's port."

"No."

"How 'bout you guys?"

"Oh, a thip of port never hurt anyone." Lifts the package. "Mucho grathiath." Teddy, silent about his own bottles.

"You won't drink?" the kid asks Holy.

"I never learned how."

All four get on the uptown bus, bundle to the rear. Leo-Teddy sits behind Andy, a sot friend of theirs, whom Teddy thinks is a quicktongued phony, and his girlfriend Lynn. Leo eyes Andy's blond Gainsborough ringlets. "Well, you look sober and freshly washed."

"On my way to A.A.!" Andy laughs. "Let's hope it takes this time."

"Another miracle for Bill W.!" Leo says. "When'd this happen?"

"He finally got the message you been pounding through his skull," Lynn says. Pulls back long black hair.

"This is my second week," Andy says. "I had a slip two days ago, came up to see you guys. Sat around your hallway talking with your Polish neighbor—and I don't speak Polish! Lucky ya missed me, I was six sheets into my paranoia. Whoo! Blotto."

"The paraldehyde kid rides again?" Teddy says.

"Well, I went up to Bellevue to get off the juice but the bastards wouldn't give me even five c.c.'s. Paraldehyde's a great high but I need A.A. What happened to that song you wrote about the minnow?"

"Got recorded by the Dobell Gang," Leo says. Leo's amazed how much he likes Andy when he's sober and not boasting about languages he knows or making vicious, spitty comments about Lower East Side poverty poets. Lynn is always turning him outdoors and he comes begging Teddy for any booze in the house. "When you're sober, Andy, you look like an angel," Leo says.

"Well!" Lynn says, giving Andy her Mona Mystery smile.

"The Dobell Gang!" Andy cries. "Hey, that's great." Shakes his head violently, throwing his hands up. "Christ, I gotta get with it. This A.A.'s gotta *take*. I'm ready for it, I couldn't slap two spondees together for fifty fuckin' dollars apiece. When your spirit's a short piss in a tin can, you're washed up—you're ready! If I hit bottom once more I'll turn mineral and you can put a stone on me. What've *you* got now?"

"Fifty-nine days," Leo says. "I been in a lot longer—nearly five months—but I had some slips too."

"Thlipth! Ha! Glad I don't have t' worry about thlipth."

"Oh, you might slip and get sober," Leo suggests, adding, "Give this man a double of Old Grandiosity."

"How's your French?" Teddy asks Andy, ignoring Leo. "I might like t' take lethons—read Beckett and Prouth in the original."

"I don't read 'em in the original, why should you?" Andy says.

"How'd your slips happen?" Lynn asks Leo.

"I was high on energy but couldn't get a note on the page."

"Aha! you see?" Andy says, the British scientist. "This disease is baffling, cunning, and insidious, sir! Without help it is too much for us. But there is One who has all power—that One is God. May you find Him now! Well, I'm ready—like a blind virgin in a nunnery."

Across the aisle Holy takes down the name of the blond kid with the port.

"I'm a photographer," the kid says. Teddy hears *fartographer*.

"I'd like to see your work," Holy says.

Leo sits embarrassed by the talk. The kid seems a shrewd, road-wise drunk and maybe ex-con, his eyes helplessly snarled inward, blueglittering, spent, obscene.

"What kind of work do you do?" Holy asks. "Portraits?"

"Well," the kid says, "I have *some* salon work in my portfolio, but I prefer available light. I just shot over three-hundred smalltown churches back in the Bible Belt. I'd like to interest a publisher in a softcover edition."

Leo suddenly envies the kid, seeing pages of aspiring, heart-deep photos he's never seen. Weatherbeaten grace, praise for old boards.

Yorkville. Leo-Teddy and Holy shake hands with the kid, get off with Andy and Lynn.

"Gee, I didn't even like him at first!" Leo tells Holy as they cross York in the soft snowfall.

"That little punk on the buth?"

"He was no little punk," Holy says, "he was an artist."

"He's got a problem. You can thee it, it'th a mile wide."

Andy glows at Leo-Teddy. "You hear what this bastard Ray Angel did to me? Sold all my books for a fix! Three thousand paperbacks, seventeen years of collecting! My life's work—gone!"

Lynn's dark smile riddles Andy's drama. She's A.A. too, and slips.

"Of course," Andy says, "I knew he was boosting a few hardcovers, yes. But to clean me out, sell everything in one swoop! That bastard's a failed poet and he's gonna stay a failed poet."

"Don't get obsessed," Leo says. "He burned me for a twenty."

"I know he did and I'm gonna pay you back," Andy says. "I'm responsible for introducing him to you."

"Who's this?" Holy asks.

"Oh, thith guy's hopeleth. A real burn artitht, hophead exth-con with eleven years in the jug."

"He's the worst," Andy tells Holy. "This guy lives just to burn you, steal you blind, play you for a patsy—he'll steal the boxtops off your cereal, he'll steal *anything*. The moss on your grave isn't safe with him around. Never grew up, been in the pokey eleven years. He's insane, of course."

'He's the motht worthleth bathtard I ever met."

"What's his name?" Holy asks.

"Ray Angel," Andy says. "Though that's just his poet-alias. Nobody knows his real name."

"He's a poet?" Holy asks. "Do you have his address?"

"Hell, yes, he lives in my apartment!" Andy cries. "Moved his wife and kids in and moved me out. Over the liquorstore on Tenth and B."

Holy writes in his address book. "I know a farm upstate that might help him out."

Leo laughs. "Holy, this guy's really hopeless."

"Are you God?"

Leo's jaw falls, high-energy fading. "No, just warning you."

"Is he a good poet?" Holy asks Andy.

"Oh, he has his coterie. But he's not an alky. He's out burning so many people for a fix he can't slow down for mere alcoholism."

"Has he hit bottom?" Holy asks Andy.

"He's plastered to it like a squashed beetle! He'll take one look at you and his eye'll light up like a kid with his first Christmas tree."

"He's merthileth. He'll chew you up."

"I'll go by tomorrow. When's he usually home?"

"He doesn't have *hours,"* Andy says. "He's either manic or scoring or zonked out."

"Holy, don't ya have enough pigeons?" Teddy asks.

"He's not a pigeon, he's a sitting duck."

Fat fallingflakes cling to eyelashes.

"My flesh shrivels," Holy says, "when I deny anybody anything."

"I deny seven times daily," Leo says. "Not meaning to, of course."

"Bullshit," Holy says.

"I've got the cork in the bottle, Holy," Leo says. "That's the best I can do."

A fountainshowering breeze flakes their faces as they walk up the steps to St. Monica's. Holy laughs, stopping Leo-Teddy. Solemnly, he brushes the snow from their beards.

"I baptize thee Leo in the name of Bill W.," Holy says.

"What about me?" Teddy asks.

"You're not born yet," Holy says, going in.

"Fuck him. He's Bill W.?"

Leo-Teddy sees Wanda seated up front in black corduroy pants and blue velour blouse, nibbling her cuticles. He sits waiting for the speaker to end. Wanda looks bird-bright and intent, her skin flushed and ivory from the snow. From afar, Leo sees her eager spirit in her cropped damp hair and face, and vows lifelong love.

Red-rinsed hair burnished upward in copper swoops, the speaker's in her late thirties. *"This program has ruint all my defects of characteh!"*

Pretty dull, Leo's look tells Teddy, who begins writing on his clipboard. Wanda laughs aloud, a friendly grunt from listeners as the woman's story catches them up. Leo grunts, despite weariness.

"My last act as an earthperson," she says, "was t' snatch off my landlawd's glasses and punch and punch 'im in the nose. Forty minutes lateh I was sittin' with 'im at my first A.A. meeting and plannin' my first slip! I haven't slipped yet but I married my landlawd."

Teddy holds up his clipboard for Leo to read. *Do you*

realize we can never play polo? Teddy reaches over and adds *!!* after ?, eyes Leo tragically. Leo takes the pen and writes through a winestain: *Maybe water polo.* Teddy sits back thoughtfully, then writes: *That's* not *like horses!*

Fat Tom, the meeting's huge stockingcapped filthy-bearded lone young vagrant, his heavy hairy belly showing in the front row as he sits in a bent over boxing stance, drops his jacket on his chair, crosses jerkily with loud toothsucking to the coffee urn, refills his foamcup with sugar and a little milk and coffee, fills a hand with sugar biscuits, returns to his seat still sucking his teeth, takes a hairy short comb from his winter shirt, stirs his coffeesugar hairily, ticks the comb dry on his heel, pockets it, sips his syrup, tunes in on the speaker intensely for five seconds, turns his head in wonder at the speaker's insanity, his eyes rolling, hunches up defensively, unable to follow a single phrase.

As the woman ends, she thanks her listeners for saving her life.

"Bullshit," Teddy whispers. "Phony gratitude grabs my ath."

Applause. Leo-Teddy sits by Wanda. She shakes her head in a daze. *"My God!*—was she *brilliant!"* Wanda says.

"Her?" Leo asks.

"Honey, the first thing she said was, My name is Edna Sherry and I came into A.A. t' save my ass. My kids make so much noise durin' Thanksgiving dinner that I invited my two ex-husbands oveh to share-the-horror yestehday. I didn't drink!"

"Wish I'd heard her," Leo says.

"I detetht people who thay things they don't feel. All that bullshit gratitude. Who needs it? She wantth t' drink —why hide it?"

Wanda kisses Leo. Hugh Winecellar stands over Leo-Teddy, sucking a vanillarich thin cigar. His groomed black beard graying, he waits, smiling benignly as if ordering yard goods. Leo-Teddy's wedding suits are gifts off Hugh's back. His own suit burns in a blue flame.

"Where *were* you?" Hugh asks. "I'm concerned about you dear boys. Why are you staring? Oh, these threads?" Hugh thumbs his blue lapel, brushes the pile. The suit pours powderblue velvet light, then turns evening purple, a corduroy pile fingerprinted like face-powder—a man tailored into a nimbus. "This is their first outing, the dears," Hugh says, brown eyes amused. "I'm quite happy with them. Told my tailor, Nothing dismal now, have to cheer myself up. Saw a bolt of this and thought I'd sunk into the Mediterranean. Where *were* you?—we missed you. Oh, *this* was scout night! How were the lads on Riker's rock—bearing up?"

"We left them well-refreshed with Holy," Leo says.

Teddy yawns. *"Jesuth!* Dullsville. Nothin' really to chew on."

"I'm sure they'd have enjoyed your more secular font," Hugh says sniffing at Teddy. "But we must each work our own side of the street, mustn't we, Teddy? And he who quotes scripture drinketh at the fountains of heaven. How about that? I speak in gems. But I bandy myself. What else, when I'm so depressed! Remember, the first aim of sobriety is self-esteem. Visit your tailor faithfully for the advance threads, for the spirit oft proclaims the man, don't you think? Wear heavenly threads, I say. Now, *Leo* and I can work together, see an eye for an eye and a suit for a houndstooth. Oh, did I lose you? Ah well, I lose my wife, my analyst, my rabbi, though I speak with a silver tongue worthy of a crown prince. You're lost again? It matters not, only the heart counts. Cleave through a wall of human flesh to shake your hands! But seriously, what do you think of me? Can you judge from my suit? Don't you think that I'm *past* all this heavy guzzlers' chitchat? Graduated?" He pulls his mustache curls. *"Cured?"*

"Ha, cured!" Wanda cries. "Ya can't get cured."

"My dear, of course you can. I met a Doctor Feelgood in Iceland, cured me like that! Made a social drinker of me in three sessions. Now I'm fit as a label—like to see that doctor again. Row all the way there with two swizzlesticks just to grip his hand for what he did for me. Unfortunately, he passed on, a victim of bad advice. Choked to death on a piece of lemon peel in his martini."

"Have you ever played polo?" Teddy asks, ready to weigh Hugh's reply.

"Wha-a-at!" Hugh asks. "No, I haven't. Why?"

"I was thinkin' of takin' up thkydiving. To compenthate for polo."

"Wait until I screw my head around so I can hear

with the other ear," Hugh says. *"What* are you asking me?"

"Well, have ya ever done thkydiving?"

"No, nor do I play the trombone. Why?"

"I'm lookin' for thome kinda real recreation or ethcape. I should do *thomethin'* bethides compose. I'm thinkin' of bein' a merchant theaman three month' of the year."

"And," Hugh asks Leo, "what kind of geographical escape would *you* like?"

"I'd like to take A.A. to Moscow."

"There's a slight problem there," Hugh says. "They don't believe in the same Higher Power."

"The Life Force will do," Leo says. "Shaw was a socialist."

Beside Hugh a lady novelist who pitches A.A. at prisons and hospitals says, *"Crap!* Intellectually knowing I can't drink doesn't mean a dogturd to me. I need the emotional identification with others who are giving me an education in hope."

Tim the chairman says, "That bloody identification can go too far, darling. Now wasn't Edna brilliant on that? Lay it on the line, I say. When my pigeons phone me all lushed up at holy-christ-two-A.M., I don't futz around: *Drop dead!"*

"Right!" she croaks, lighting a tiny Dutch cigar. "When he's down, shove a foot into him. Give the shithead the message."

"You weren't at work today," Leo tells Hugh.

"No, thank God. Hewing at canvas like all World War II. Beat myself down to my socks at the studio. Rough work sometimes, easel painting. Then I went to my seance this evening. I'm afraid of the old doctor. You know, I thought I had my inordinate grandiosity well in hand, but Dr. Deer was quite shocking to me about those paintings of mine I took in for him to see. I wouldn't dare tell you what he said. I think I should ask him to lower his fee."

"What's he charge you a session?" Leo asks.

"Sixty-three krillion dollars—but money isn't everything. Cigar? You know, if we stand close together, we might be mistaken for the Dancing Bear Triplets. Except you're not as depressed as I—or hypoglycemic—A.A. can't cure that. Still, I'm hopeful. It's better to be aware and depressed than drunk and depressed. Still waiting for that flash of lightning! You know what they say about

Bill W., don't you? Every year his flash of lightning grows brighter when he tells his horror story. I like that, shows there's hope even for a modest sinner like myself. Shall we sit?"

The last speaker, a Washington reporter, keeps setting his heartbeat with a pacemaker under his shirt. Eyes his listeners, rolls his limegreen eyes back in a huff. "My name is Jack Barleycorn and, God be praised, I'm an alcoholic. Look at you. Face after sober face. I was wonderin', sittin' here lookin' at yer orphan faces. What would ye look like if ye each looked like ye looked after yer last drink?—I mean the minute after yer very last drink, each and everyone of you. *Ha!* My God, it's hideous to conceive." His eyestraining draws a great laugh. "Back when I fairst jined this deterioratin' organi*za*tion, a call for help meant a fast trip with a pint of whiskey for the aid and comfort of a dyin' man somewhere. And a second call for help after the fairst man arrived meant they'd killed the pint between 'em and someone had better come instantaneously with a quart. That was when the old clubhouse was still on Twenty-fourth Street. . . ."

Teddy sighs disgust, doodles, plans a drink in the men's room. Leo too is maddened by the Irishman—his cocksure humor while resetting his threatened heartbeat. Pity for limegreen eyes presses on Leo—he closes his own, blinking, banks of selfpity giving way in his chest.

"I need air," he tells Wanda. "Be right back."

Heads for the men's room, but groans suddenly and pushes straight outdoors into the snow. Gnashes his teeth, wringing his hands on the top steps, tries to hold back his tear-fit. Teddy looks about, uncaps a half-pint. "What'th bugging you?"

"I dunno!"

"Me?"

Leo eyes the package. "My brother, drunk or sober."

"Aw. I'm peatheful, don't worry. Your dandruff is incredible—ya oughta do thomethin' about it."

Hugh steps out. "You boys all right?"

"I sure don't feel good," Leo says.

"May I ask what's wrong?"

"I'm goin' crazy!" Leo says. Teddy shrugs.

"Have you talked with Wanda about this?" Hugh asks.

"She gets scared and pulls the blankets over her head," Leo says.

"Do you want to tell me about it?" Hugh asks, suit burning purple, long mustaches curled barbwire. *I am him,* Leo thinks. "Let's go down to my rent-a-buggy," Hugh says. "I rent it by the year to save on taxes."

Hugh lets Leo-Teddy into the rear, sits up front. The car is an upholstered crypt, the windows marble facings of ice.

"I'm in a trance all the time," Leo says.

"Oh that," Hugh says, "that's *real life,* my boy! you're seeing it at last."

"I can't understand what people are sayin'!"

"Perfectly normal," Hugh says. "You couldn't understand them before either, only now you think you're supposed to. Right? Don't worry about it. They'll clear up."

"Queer dreams—sometimes I go t' sleep thinkin' I've slipped back into the nervous system of an eight-year-old. Last night I went back to my mother's breast and suckled, with this powerful magnetism flowing between us—just a blushing little hot-flashing ball of a baby. Then I dream I'm pursued by juiceheads—Bowery degenerates—and no way t' stop 'em."

"*I* know those goons. Bronze Agers in thecondhand thuitth."

"Eight-thirty this morning, I wake up, Teddy and Wanda asleep, my eyes wide open in broad daylight. Then I notice—and I'm fifty-nine days sober!—I'm in this wet-dream bliss, without emission. An amazing buzz, pulsing and rippling. Felt very natural—what was amazing was that I'd never known I had this power in me before. But I'm into this scary moaning. Don't dare close my eyes. I'm a boneless idiot baby at my mother's breast. Drooling. Then I see I'm floating six inches off the bed on a sheet of blue fire, with combers of blue light comin' at me from the livingroom. I think perhaps I can summon up this blue shining energy at will. It strikes me this is some kinda spiritual experience like Bill W.'s. My sickness has been lifted!"

"And where was I through all thith? Havin' a long thnore, ha!"

The door opens. "It's over," Wanda says. Banked snow blueglittering behind her. "Come in for the pahty."

"Thank you for taking me into your confidence," Hugh says.

Leo eyes Wanda waiting above. "Dya think I should tell her?"

Hugh cocks his head, peaceable as a dancing bear, eyes slashed with a swagger, tamed with agony. "You've got to, if you're going to live with her. But not when she's too tired to cope. She's just a bride, my boy."

"May I have a thigar?"

Hugh drives cigars into Leo-Teddy's breast pockets, leads him up the fluffy steps. Wanda waits nervously. Holy opens first-birthday presents at a serving table, encircled by sober, cleareyed, cake-eating alcoholics sipping coffee. Holy tearily holds aloft a winecolored handkerchief necktie. "Oh, my God, I'm getting the whole bit," he gasps, "it's too much, I'm just not ready for all this. All these corny emotions! Look," he tells Wanda, "these gifts, the A.A. daybook, all these *cards,* and this dear cloth cat to hang as a lightpull. It's not fair yet—I haven't been among people long enough for this kind of attention." Tim hands him a paper plate of cake with *Holy* in a blue stripe on yellowdye frosting. "Oh, for *Christ's* sake," Holy cries. Shoves the cake back at Tim, rushes to the kitchen. Mobbed! *"Oh,"* he cries vexed and runs upstairs to a schoolroom.

"Why don'tcha ask Holy if he wants a cab ride home with us?" Wanda asks.

Into the schoolroom. Cloud-towering Lincoln, Holy weeps in a tiny kindergarten chair at a tiny table, a murdered accordion, head hung upsidedown, arms spilling to the floor. Damps his eyes on a shoulder.

"Ya'll be glad when *thith* meeting's over!"

"I'm at a permanent meeting." Holy sits straight. "I have to be."

"Wanta ride?" Leo asks. "We're takin' a cab."

"No, thanks. Well, the party's over. It's not fun anymore."

"What isn't?" Teddy slips behind a blackboard. Leo eyes him hard. Teddy rinses vodka through his cavity, smiles swallowing.

"Anything," Holy says, wiping his table with a blackboard eraser. "I'm even getting picky about meetings. I *have* to get picky. I'm not coming back here for two months. What do you think has been so hellish for me these past three weeks? They know here just how to get me to do this or that. And I don't like it. It's not fair,

they're taking advantage of me and I'm not gonna do one more thing for this group. Not *one* thing! This group's *eating me up!*" His fist raps the child's table. "I'm sorry but I've had it!"

Going back, Holy stops. "Oh God, John-Bob's back!"

Seated alone, redhaired John-Bob nods asleep into a fuming cigarette. Shoes rimed and waterlogged, his tie askew in a filthy loop.

"We invited him to our wedding!" Leo tells Holy. "He gave me my first A.A. pitch down at Intergroup."

"Thee! Feet of clay! Everybody's jutht one drink away from a drunk!"

Wanda says, "I thought he was away carin' for his invalid motheh!"

Holy snorts. "His mother's dead and buried in Scotland along with his seven brothers and all his uncles. Well, *I'm* not taking him home. He can get back to Staten Island by himself."

"Are you gonna help him?" Wanda asks Leo.

"Hurry! Let's blow before he sees us."

"He'll be all right," Teddy says.

Into coats. "Please hurry," Leo says. Wanda hops into a boot. "I *don't* want 'im to see me."

Snow. Streetlights iceblue, dumb bliss and energy, the snow blue. Intense silence sparkles on trackless walks. Scuff into fleece. A current suddenly runs up Leo's spine.

"Are you terribly unhappy?" Wanda asks him.

Leo, silent. "He's losin' his energy high." Teddy says.

"Honey, what are you thinkin'?" Wanda's eyes brim. "Don't be unhappy," she squeaks.

"I'm all right." Leo stops, knotting his face into his hand. He holds her cold cheeks, kisses her helpless open mouth. *"His whole family!*—At least we can take the bastard down to the ferry."

Sit on the ferry's middledeck, spirits drained, coming back from Staten Island.

"I'm sorry," Leo says. "Our wedding night!"

She grips his hand. "You didn't know it would take so long."

"Or that he was so godawful drunk."

"Not very kind of ya to pour his thcotch down the think. He may have nightmares or convulsions and need that juithe."

"Let'im shake. You got yours, didn'tcha?"

Teddy still tastes a huge nip of scotch. "I gueth we did!"

Leo kisses Wanda. *"Smell me."*

"It's hard to say," she says. "I can't tell if it's you or Teddy."

"Well, I don't *taste* anything," Leo says.

Her head on his shoulder, staring out at Liberty Island. Spot-lighted Liberty rises, pale green toga swept with nightflakes. Teddy toasts her lamp with his last half-pint —Stella, the trademark for Columbia Pictures. Cheers, Mama!

Out of nowhere, mountain birds warble wildly.

Teddy knocks his skull. "You hear what I hear?" Leo nods, popeyed. Wanda sits up, looking about. "I can't believe my eahs!"

Beautiful as park birds at dawn, but more rilling and hopeful, lirruping, whistling singing, silvery and wailing, an inhuman, lamenting birdy happiness.

"What kinda bird's that?" Wanda asks.

"It'th one voithe with a lot of birds in it."

Chwangg! a guitar chord comes down. *Plunka-plunka-plunka* banjo. A voice sings out like Leadbelly, *"Hey Black Betty, Black Betty, Black Betty!"* Birds warble in a hail of string rhythms.

"Boy! lithen to those pea-pickin' shitkickerth!"

Leo shrivels, embarrassed by public show, eyes his lap. But Teddy soaks in the music, beaming. "Let'th go look!" Teddy boosts Leo. "All right, all right," Leo says, "I can't resist either."

Round the coffeebar. A suitcase lies open on deck with pennants sticking out and huge lapel buttons shouting GOOD CHEER! and THINK HAPPY!—and uplifting mottoes, giveaway items, handkerchiefs, stickers saying LEAD A CLEAN LIFE! A sign propped by the suitcase says, All Items FREE. Swiss Warbler 25¢.

Two blacks sit on a bench, at their feet a tambourine with a mess of change in it. A little heavy fellow with old clothes and popped gut thrashes a bango and at the same time blows a mouthorgan braced around his neck. He leans forward, puffyeyed, picking strings, singing coal-black and thickvoiced. His partner flashes a tambourine, beating his knee while looking both ways for the law. Leo brightens, spirit waking with a prickle as he feeds three quarters into the floor tambourine. He grins, hoping to break onlookers' embarrassment, telling Teddy loudly, "*He's* great!"

"The dark Raphael of the harmonica," Teddy rasps grandly.

"LEAD A CLE-EAN LIFE!" the banjoist sings and suddenly wild birdsong erupts from nowhere. He sits with mouth wide as an astonished kid's, jamming chords. "LEAD A CLEAN LIFE!" His partner sits dopeymouthed also, thumping his tambourine with a jingle.

"Oh man, hit'th a shitkickerth' holiday down at Cabin Holler!"

Birdsong swoops in and out from nowhere.

"Wheah's the birds?" Wanda asks. Leo-Teddy shrugs, beaming.

Abruptly the partner jumps up, dancing in a tailored shiny black suit, a green plaid tie and red tam. His shoes, glossy Italian points, chatter like Eleanor Powell's as he picks up a silver salver. The banjoist sits back half-lidded, head lolling as he thrashes, beating hard, ecstatic.

"He's Doctor Halleleujah!" Leo says.

Callow teenagers and hidebound city folk stand and watch, smiling through prison bars at the free black spirits released on deck and surrounded by warbling. The dancer spins the salver on a finger overhead, points tapping, twists and dips under the spinning silver, his eye nerved for cops. Coins hit the tambourine on the floor.

After a while the banjoist says, "Here's a song I calls, Happiness Is a Cloud Called Jesus. He'p yoselfs t' this stuff, folks, it's all free today." Starts singing from his chest and jangling strings.

"He's got a heart like a bird thanctuary."

"A great healer," Leo says. "I feel renewed."

The two blacks fall into a duet, though the dancer just hisses and sputters to himself as birds swell out. The nervous dancer falls to the deck in his red tam, doing handclaps under pushups in rhythm, then spins around with one palm on deck, feet tapping, his other hand finger-snapping. More coins in kitty, birds swirling. At last he sits again, never having unbuttoned his one-button roll, now more nervous than ever, and keeps up velvet finger-snapping. Mouths open, sputtering, birds, birds, birds.

The banjoist falls into a pitch for happiness, staring straight into Leo. "Hey theah, God is a man an' woman, brothuh! You wanta feel good? Well then, you looks inside and just make sure you see somethin' good in theah! Thass all the heaven you needs, brothuh. Don't take too many of yoah own doctor's medicine 'cause thass drugs too."

"Whoo, yes!" Leo says.

"You're easily moved," Teddy says quietly.

"Hey-y!" the black tells Leo happily and suddenly twangling birdsong erupts all over Leo, shot right through him as he sits ringing with a thousand warblers in his chest, stomach and wealthy fork. *Rrnh!* Teddy growls, fighting back invisible birds. Leo can't bear to look at the birdman nor turn from his half-lidded rapture. Unable to swallow, he's pinned naked by the black's sleepy gaze. The singer stops strumming, leans into his partner and now the ferry vibrates with freed birds, Leo's head floating, blood turned to running silver. Mercifully, the banjoist thrashes once, twice, eases into a rhythm and attacks the mouthorgan while passengers applaud. His partner sputters accompaniment among the birds.

The song ends. "Everybody's invited t' take somethin' from this suitcase, the singer says. 'S all free." The dancer goes around with the tambourine for gifts. A broad-brimmed whitebearded older man gives a whole handful of change, thanking the musicians, his ruddy face as serene as if he'd waited a century of crossings and floodtides to hand them this money.

As the ferry docks, the passengers move to the front exit. Leo rises to look in the suitcase while the banjo struts. The dancer brings back a heavy haul of change and lays his tambourine on the floor beside Leo-Teddy's feet. Coins still pour in.

"How dya make that GREAT bird sound!" Leo asks. The dancer reaches into his suitcase, hands Leo two ricepaper gift packets, meanwhile packing the salver and pennants into the suitcase and staring about nervously.

"Afraid ya'll have to pay off a cop?" Teddy asks.

The dancer grunts to himself desperately, not answering Teddy, while the singer closes up his banjo case. Leo reads the ricepaper packets. The Wonderful Double Throat Swiss Warbler Bird Call, studies the directions for hissing through a pinked-leather reed-whistle—

"Ya just put this on your tongue and *hiss?"* Leo asks the dancer.

A blue reed appears on the dancer's tongue and a loud birdcall stuns Leo. Then, as if raised by a magic call, the tambourine lifts from the floor, flies down the deck toward a black porter with a pushbroom, change spraying everywhere in a money shower. The elderly porter looks up amazed by twirling coins.

"Why you do that?" the dancer asks Leo.

Leo, shocked by the dancer's red eyes.

"He did it!" the small popbellied singer says.

Teddy, unsmiling, selfcomposed, crosses his arms, says nothing.

The dancer looks about, harried, starts picking up change as if fearful of cops with drawn guns. His coal-black partner jams his hands onto his hips, purses thick-banded lips. "Now why you *do* that?"

Teddy, veiled, the servant from on high.

"You think you Jesus comin' through the temple kickin' out the moneylenders?" the singer asks.

Teddy's soul rises, solemnly looks down on cowshit, says nothing.

"I'm sorry," Leo says.

"You thtay outta this." Quietly. "Your help is not needed in thith affair. Really. Jutht keep quiet—I'm only thinkin' of you."

The black porter stops sweeping, stands in the spilt money. Leo walks forward with Teddy, bends from the waist to pick up change.

"You are going againtht my wishes." Teddy not bending. "And you're makin' me dizzy. Please get up."

Leo, strangling, picks up coins with the dancer and Wanda while Teddy stands blankfaced.

"I'm gonna fall," Teddy announces.

Leo stands, purple. *"I'm too fat!"* he cries. Teddy sways, falling backward pulling Leo with him, strikes his forehead on a thick bench. Leo falls back on his elbows, hands still clutching coins, the wind knocked out of him. "Now I *know* I'm too fat," he groans.

"I tol' ya not t' bend." Teddy sits up as the black singer helps Leo. Teddy tenderly measures a knot already swelling on his forehead. "Well, there's nothin' to be done about that now," he says. "Yeth, there is," he adds to himself, pulling Leo back down, and sinks several coins from the floor into his sidepocket.

"What're ya doin'!" Leo asks whitely.

"I'm makin' damned sure these public nuithanthes make rethtitution for the injuries I've thuffered as a direct result of their totally uncalled for and ridiculouth public performanthe. Am I clear?"

"How much've ya got in your pocket?" Leo asks, still seated on deck. Teddy silent, Leo digs into Teddy's pocket.

Teddy, white, yanks Leo's hand out. "Jutht whattaya think you're doin', thir!"

"I wanta know how much you're stealin' so I can pay this poor sonofabitch back! *So tell me!*"

"You're not rethponthible for me." Teddy sneers and pulls at the hand but Leo gets it in and pulls out a fistful of coins. *"Gimme my money!"* Teddy cries, tugging Leo's fingers open. Suddenly, Leo's arm springs loose but the coins go flying again. Teddy, anchored, watches them roll away from himself, wild despair rising. *"Why'd ya do that!"* he screams, then throws himself sideways to pick up fresh coins. "You damned, *damned* idiot!" he cries at Leo, again stuffing coins into his pocket. Again Leo digs at the pocketed money. Teddy grabs Leo's neck and starts strangling. "LET GO OF MY MONEY!"

"Uncle Teddy," Wanda squeals, yanking his head by the hair, *"you're not nice!"*

"I'm thurrounded by morons and little children!" Teddy rages through tears. Leo pulls Teddy from his throat. Teddy's eyes sweep the two blacks, then pop at Leo. "You've put me through the motht humiliating night of my life. Please don't conthider me your brother any longer. I'm a thtranger to you."

"THANK GOD!" Leo cries, rubbing his neck. "I could have you put in jail, ya know? For *assault!*"

"Jutht you try it!" Teddy's beard snarls in Leo's face.

"Oh get up," Wanda pleads, "please get up. I'm sorry I pulled your hair, Uncle Teddy."

"You gonna gimme my money?" the short singer asks Teddy.

"I don't have to anther you." Teddy's granite glint fails to stare down the black.

"Leave him alone," says the dancer, still picking up money with Leo, Wanda, and the porter. Curious passengers watch afar, leaving. The whitebearded rosy old man has the porter's broom and calmly pushes coins into the main aisle. The dancer warily picks up coins around Teddy's shoes.

"Please get up!" Wanda cries. "Don't worry about them," she explains to the old man, the porter, and the blacks. "I've known 'em for twenty years—they're high-strung, ya know?"

"Give them five dollars," Leo tells Wanda.

"Don't be abthurd!" Teddy rises.

"What's buggin' you, man?" the singer asks.

"I don't have t'tell you anything."

"Well, you come through heah kickin' my tambourine and my money!"

"You wanna make thomethin' of it?"

"No, man. I jus' wanna heah some sense."

"Let's blow," the dancer says, tambourine full of coins.

"Wait a minute." Leo bends again for more coins by Teddy's feet. Teddy stoops a bit for Leo. "You wanna play with me?" Teddy asks the short singer.

The singer sighs, "No, man, you got the devil in you."

Leo eyes Teddy oddly, seeing a glitter that pops his heart into his mouth. Leo trembles, hands the singer his coins.

"I don't have five dollars," Wanda says.

Leo digs out his bills.

"Jutht a moment. Let'th be fair to the latht jot and tittle about thith." Digs out the change in his pocket, appears to weigh seriously some vast money matters, touches his tender head lump for its value.

Leo tells Wanda. "He's figurin' out where his next drink's comin' from."

"Ya thimply don't underthtand anything, do ya? I'm trying t' go by what'th fair and equitable for *my injury*."

Wanda shuts up, sits down, waits for Leo to think. Leo squeezes her hand, seeing himself and Teddy through her eyes as Wanda looks back at herself from his eyes, their love flowing to and fro.

The musician waits for Teddy to hand him his money. At last he slams down his suitcase. "You wanna go outside and mix it up? You want some roughhouse?"

The dancer tugs him. "Le's go, le's go!"

"You wanna fight, I fights!" the singer tells Teddy.

Teddy smiles, keeping the cash, letting out line.

"I'm leavin'," says the dancer. The singer picks up his suitcase.

"What'th wrong? You don't wanta fight?"

"No man, not now. I'll meet you when you haven't got the devil in you."

Teddy smiles, letting out line.

"You can't be yourself," the black says. "You musta been drinkin'. I'll fight you when you're sober."

The dancer hooks the singer and plows ahead. Teddy follows, money in hand.

"I don't like your music," Teddy says at their backs. Stops, looking about, motions for the porter. "These public entertainers mutht be a great nuithanthe for you," he tells the tall thin black. "I want *you* t'know that I act out of unimpeachable motives, tho you take thith change —for all your trouble. Don't believe any athpersions you hear againtht me. I'm thuch a jutht man that I'm often tempted t' join the minithtry or take holy orders at a monathtery. Remember that—I was conthumed by juthtithe."

"Try Gray Moor," the porter says. "That's a Franciscan retreat about twenty miles up the Hudson."

"Franthithcans? I'll keep that theriouthly in mind. There's thomething tremendouthly appealing about the vow of poverty."

"It's more of a halfway house, you don't take no vows. Tell 'em Luckie sent ya. They know me up there. They're waitin' for a spiritual gentleman like you. You're always welcome at Gray Moor, anytime of the day or night. Don't even bother callin' ahead, just *go* there."

"I've theen you thomewhere before tonight."

"I got a twin brother but you couldn't have seen him —he's put away."

"Really? *I* have a twin."

"I can see that!" Luckie says.

"Thank you again. You are about the greatetht gentleman I have ever met."

"Just tell 'em B. Luckie sent you."

"Bee Lucky?"

"That's right." The porter smiles. "Take my word for it, they have a beautiful bed waitin' just for you!"

"I shall look into it, thir."

Walk onto the upstairs ramp around the terminal. The dancer is far ahead, the singer slower with his suitcase, sunken, sullen. As the twins pass him, Leo's back trembles, alert to any craze.

"Will ya tell me why you kicked that money?" Leo asks.

"I hate his music and I don't like him."

"Don'tcha think it's unfair of you to deny him his rightful gains?"

"That'th my busineth."

"Well, it doesn't seem fair to me."

"And I don't like you either," Teddy says. Leo shakes. "You thaid thomethin' about fighting?" Teddy calls to the singer.

The dancer returns. "Why don't you leave us alone?"

"I'm not talking to you."

"Tomorrow when you're sober," the singer says.

Leo trembles like a bridegroom.

"I'm thtanding here right now."

"Well, you come back tomorrow."

Teddy smiles, letting out line. The singer slams down his banjo case. "All right, I'm ready!"

The dancer drags the singer off to soothe him. Teddy reaches out with his toe, topples the banjo case.

"Take it over to him, honey," Leo asks Wanda.

Wanda bends shaking in front of Teddy, takes the banjo case to the singer. Follow her. All ride down the escalator silently, Teddy glittering above Wanda and the blacks. Leo descends into hellshine.

Teddy freezes near the pizza bar. Leo whispers to Wanda so that Teddy can't hear, "Get a cop, if you have to." Wanda, pierced, looks pleadingly for confirmation, then starts moving. "I'm goin' out and look for a cab!" she lies hoarsely. Watch her step through deep wet snow, turn, disappear. Leo's eyes close in prayer. "Don't wanna go to the hospital, I'm a brand-new bridegroom!"

Teddy's saintly granite measures Leo. Leo looks away. The whitebearded old man loafs in the pizza bar, droopy-lidded eyes averted. When Teddy looks back, the two blacks are gone. "They got away!" he cries, making no effort to chase them. "Jutht incredible!—when you really *need* a cop, there isn't one within twenty blockth! Though I was ready t' handle those two devils alone." Again, Teddy measures Leo. "Weird," he says. "You don't have the thlightetht idea what I'm talking about and yet you were my brother. Thtill, it'th only to be exthpected, when thuccthetn thtriketh. The inward eye is dulled, the finer inthighttth lotht."

Leo catches the maroon old man watching them—the

old man nods his broadbrim, gives him a friendly wink. "Let's go home," Leo says.

"Don't you underthtand anything?" Teddy, rivetted. His face swells like a human bag.

"You want to fight with me?" Leo asks at last. "Is that it?"

Teddy, silence, letting out line.

"Why don't we see a cop," Leo asks, "and let him decide what's right or wrong about what's bugging you?"

"I don't thee a cop."

"We'll *find* one."

"I don't need a cop. You're what'th wrong with me."

"I think we need some authority to decide."

"I don't need an authority, ethpecially not a Tranthit Authority cop." Teddy's wick brightens. "Do you think Bruckner needs an authority? Beethoven needs an authority? That any *real* artitht needs an authority? *My authority is from heaven!"*

"I'll be a bearded Chinese miracle. Who told you that?"

"God is telling me that."

"Whattaya think you are—an angel?"

Teddy hesitates. "Don't athk. We each have our roles in this farthe, and thome are inferior. I'm not content to remain a moron with angelic thenthibilities, as Othcar put it." Leo-Teddy goes outdoors. "You aren't even aware of the erosion of character, the thimple thpiritual damage that worldly thuccthetn has on you. For example, these two coons, these incredible devils can earn four or five hundred a week—I mean apiethe—for a little minthtrel routine while an artitht devoted to the higheth thpiritual urges of the rathe mutht thtarve for recognition and go without the bare nethethities. But you don't even thee how thith fact inthultth your exithtenthe. If it were up to me, these musical beggars would be banned from the thtreetth, thubways, and ferries. Are you lithening?"

"And airport lounges," Leo suggests huskily, looking for Wanda.

"Yeth! Do you have the thlighteth idea what an inthult it is that these thinging roaches should take our rewards while we—?" Takes out his package, strips the bag, measures the corner of vodka. "No, I thee it'th quite beyond you."

Heavenly six-inch snowflakes fall into brilliant drifts.

Wanda shrugs, cabless. "I'm too weak, you'll have to carry me," she says.

"Why don't you give Wanda the rosenkavalier attentions she needs? Here it'th her wedding night and you're hanging around Thouth Ferry. For Chritht'th thake, Leo! Thith should have been a night of thoft music, danthing and candlelight, an intimate little evening in our apartment with half a dozen thteamed lobthters. Not thith trudging around with drunkth. Well, idiot brother, perhapth it'th brain damage."

"Are you friends again?" Wanda asks Leo-Teddy.

"Chums!" Teddy winks.

"Tells me what a beautiful night we coulda had."

"Didn't we?" Wanda asks.

"You didn't mind the twelfth-step work?"

She grips his arm. "Don't you knock A.A., Teddy!"

"Me? I got 'im into thith program! Thpiritually thpeaking, it was all my idea. Why I practically put the words into his mouth at Intergroup. Not that I think Leo's a full-blown alcoholic, mind you! I'm thtill lookin' for a genuine alcoholic in thith program. Haven't found one yet." Teddy digs out change, winking at Leo. "Didn't think I was broke, did you, ol' buddy? Lend me a latht nickel for a thixpack."

Trudge across South Ferry to the late, late beanpot bars. Wait for the late, late subway. Home at twenty of five. Teddy pops a cold ale, sits on the dark couch while Wanda undresses in the bedroom. Leo spoons rum raisin ice cream straight from the tub.

"I think you're making *me* fat with all thith late-hours ithe cream. Thome of it getth inta my blood thtream! I can't even bend over for our shoes."

"Sedative," Leo says, spooning. Teddy drinks with disgust at ice cream.

"Look, if I thaid anything to offend you, forget it. 'Th your wedding night. I like you."

"You hate me. I'm a miracle."

"Oh? I rethpect your illneth, that goes without thaying. I don't forget we been through a lot together. Remember the purple bathtard we found thtuck with his ath in the air in the bathroom? Thome of those things we thaw and did drivin' ambulanthe—nothin' can ever grow there again."

"Grow where?"

"I don't know where. Can't you follow a thimple conversation? I'm thaying we lotht our latht illusions pryin' that thtiff out from between the toilet and the tub. He was cold as thith ale. Remember?"

"Not very often. Why should I?"

"Well, if you wanna forget the motht profound exthperienthe of our life—"

"Not of my life."

"Oh shit, you're high as a kite right thith minute. Don't jazz me. Admit it, aren't you high?"

Wanda brushes her teeth in a queenly aqua robe at the kitchen sink. "I'd say so," Leo says.

"Then what'th the point? I rethpect your disease and all, but your thobriety's a joke."

Leo shrugs, sees his own eyes in Teddy's bloated lids. "I'm hopeful, Teddy. At least I try not to be cynical."

"Thynical? *Boy!*—what underthtatement, after what I've lotht." Teddy stares at the street's deep darkness, touches the throbbing lump on his brow, buckles his empty ale can. Shaking tears flood him. *"Thalome!"* he sobs. "She got away from me, Leo! My *beautiful* danther! Oh my God, how do I deserve thith? She was all mine, I uthed t' hold her like a teddy bear! *All right!"* Looks about wildly, plucks the penknife from their desk. Opens its snapped, ragged blade, eyes it blurrily. "Thynara. . . . *Thelma!* I loved her too, Leo. Don't think I was the itheberg I pretended t' be. Oh God, can't anyone underthtand how lonely I am? Can't even my own brother underthtand? THTUART!—he's *my* thon too, ya know? He's my thon, Leo!"

Leo claps Teddy's knee. "Let's call it a night."

"I don't wanna drink! I wanta big knife! I'm gonna kill mythelf!"

"Well. I'm going to bed."

BLISSFUL Baby Teddy watches blue sleet run down the window like bits of fat in a pan, blue windowlight bursting through Dr. David Deer's pearlgrey forcefield of hair. Soft cigarette smoke dries Teddy's balsawood tongue . . . Leo sips black coffee from a cup on the servingstand before them. Dr. Deer's pen stops scratching, his serpenthooded green eyes X-ray Teddy with dreaded insight, making an instant photo of Teddy's soul-state. He spreads Teddy's libretto *The Ass* under the desklamp's cupped shine. As Teddy watches, the Doctor's fair face turns scarlet, terrible, fiercely mirroring Teddy's innermost offenses, lies, baseness, the groaning ass his work urges the reader to see—though what he's left out brings a cell-deep shame and trembling.

"I'm workin' on a bestiary, Doctor," he explains loudly. "First *The Whale*, then *The Ass*. These animals help me DEFINE THEMES in my life that otherwise are very VAGUE! I got an awful memory! Whole periods of my life I can't remember! I seem to be swallowed up in the present."

Leo crawls with distaste as the doctor reads Teddy's work.

" 'Women are fuckle!'—Am I reading correctly? *My, my!* you seem to have known a lot of women." Dr. Deer firm, serious, crisply Southern. Half deaf. "And *this*—'The apartment hangs with lead windowweights like huge sausages in a delicatessan—everywhere he moves, lead weights knead his shoulders.' *Very* interesting. What are these sausages—or windowweights?"

"They mean I'm DEPRESSED!" Teddy croaks, pouring sherry into his tiny goblet. Raises his glass. "First today, Doctor. I like to come here with a clear mind."

Leo smiles too, his own tongue toasty from Teddy's opium pipe.

"Oh, that's empty, dear fellow." Dr. Deer slips the quart

into his wastecan. "Please let me get you another from the kitchen."

"Don't bother!" Leo bursts, then shuts up. "Sorry."

"Steady, steady," Teddy warns Leo, his nose prickling with a leaden cold. "I'm in good shape. I came SUPPLIED, Doctor!"—raising a shoppingbag beside his chair. "Though I'm CUTTING DOWN."

"I see." Dr. Deer sits again, keen green eyes curious. "I have to watch myself with you gentlemen. Especially Leo—I never know when he's not drinking."

"I'M NOT. I sit home stuffing on ice cream while Teddy belts the wine."

Quiet. Echoes swim in Teddy of his morning practice, a ghost trombone clamoring "None But the Loney Heart," black and dripping rain. A patient's portrait of Dr. Deer's elder brother Sidney the Fugitive, who lived alone for forty years in an ecstasy of languages, hangs on a wall of this small room. Dr. Deer sits very erect, tall and fair, his eyes snakegreen, lids hooded—blind on the right, deaf on the left, but memory fit and strong. His body swells in Teddy's drugged eye.

"You remind me of that big Greek statue of Zeus on his throne!" Teddy says.

Dr. Deer smiles. "You'll soon be calling me sonofabitch and Hebrew bastard. *That sheeny Deer!* What is this amazing word 'fuckle'?"

Teddy grins. "Just somethin' I made up!" Leo looks away, forlorn. "It came to me while listening to *Cosí fan Tutte,* ha ha. It means FICKLE. I hear lots of words like that—all day long! TINTINNABULATION, Doctor."

"Oh! Like Edgar Allan Poe?"

"Yep!" Teddy admits. "But he never uses 'em."

"Then how do you know he heard them?"

"Juiceheads do. He was a terrific juicehead."

Dr. Deer cups his good ear. "You mean drunkard?"

Teddy nods into his shrivelled wet tissue wad, sniffing. "It's a kind of ECHOLALIA."

"I meant no criticism," Dr. Deer says—and smiles. "Of you *or* Poe."

"Oh, Poe is my heart laid bare," Teddy swears.

Dr. Deer pens this, adding many X's and dashes. "You're a great admirer of Poe—or an adept?" Dr. Deer's eyes fill queerly. "You feel some *spiritual kinship?* I mean, he was devoid of ideas, wasn't he, old chap? He died in the gutter."

"HE DIED IN BED!" Teddy cries. "He just had no tolerance for alcohol—one shot wiped him out. That dying in a gutter's just FIGURATIVE, Doctor. A friend picked him up and got 'im into a BED." Teddy nods hard assurance.

Dr. Deer smiles. "You think that makes the difference?"

"Oh, Doctor," Teddy says, "Poe's our greatest COSMOLOGIST, nobody equals him. You read *Eureka?*—that's his greatest work. I'm into it now—a fantastic description of the universe as the heart of God—tremendous! He makes it THROB. God's heart is a big, throbbing, superexpanding and contracting erectile machine of live atoms. *Terrific.*"

"I'm not up to Poe."

"He foresaw the expanding universe, Doctor! *And* relativity—'space is time.' "

"No!" Dr. Deer smiles. "You seem uplifted by him. Your eyes show it."

"I AM. Ya know, in *Eureka* he proves that we can't have intellectual belief in God—only FAITH. Same thing Lecomte du Nouy says in *Human Destiny*. Intellect is USELESS!"

"Oh, really! Why is that?"

Teddy leans foreward, smokeblue eyepoints burning. "Well, did ya ever try to *see* the universe in your imagination? We're so ridiculously bound by our eyes we can't even imagine SPHERICAL VISION—up, down, and AROUND! When I was a child I'd try to see the universe inside a huge ball of dirt—but then I figured this dirt must be just so deep and then there'd be space again. All we can imagine is a PIECE OF SPACE and make that stand for the whole. We can't see behind our heads! Same with God—nobody can IMAGINE GOD, only some piece of Him, some flower or man or sunrise. We take the rest on faith."

"Isn't that intellectual?" Dr. Deer asks.

"No, it's INTUITION."

"*Ah!*—What about pain?"

". . . What about it?" Teddy blank.

"Pain and suffering—where are they in Poe's cosmology?"

Teddy sips, then shouts, "That's the TENSION: expanding particles want to fall back into their original unity. Every action has an equal and opposite force—that's *Newton,* Doctor. The universe is powerfully attracted to falling back into its original ball of pure beginningness—it explodes and pulls back together over and over. GRAVITY IS SUFFERING."

Suddenly Teddy's eyes pop, he clicks his ballpoint and notes on his clipboard, "giant pots of shit"—"Shitty Dishes"—"Shitsong" . . . "My first tragedy: *Turdus Giganticus*" . . .

"God is gravity?" Dr. Deer asks. "How does gravity suffer, dear fellow?"

Teddy sighs. "Why's it have to suffer?"

"Didn't Poe?"

"IN EVERY ATOM!"

"Well, I'll borrow it when you're through—maybe I can give it thirty minutes. Though my time is precious!" Dr. Deer stares with pain at his shelves. "So much to read! But I *must* keep abreast. When I retire I'll write my book straight off, without reading. I'll do all three volumes in a year. I wrote my Genius book in three months. And the *Times!*—I lose forty-five minutes a day on that."

Teddy snorts, throwing up his hands. "That's SILLY, Dr. Deer. NOBODY has to read the *Times*. All those big front-page events are sheer fiction—just reporters souping up a skirmish into a byline. It's a fact-fiction MISHMASH! The reporters gotta make bylines to keep their paychecks comin'. What's worse, they all DRINK! I don't believe *anything* I read in the *Times!* Liars, Doctor, every one of 'em. Can't you just FEEL the fiction oozing outta the front page? BOOZE INFLATION—it's their occupational disease. Doctor, I despair when I think of you sitting in here wasting YOUR VALUABLE TIME on the *Times*. But then I don't believe anything I read. Words don't mean much anymore. They're all phony. Empty. PURE FAKE."

Teddy stares at his clipboard, draws an arrow from *Turdus Giganticus* and notes "the *Times*." Hooks a gallon of muscatel from his shoppingbag, fills and drains his goblet, refills with a gasp of improvement.

"I see." Dr. Deer's pen scratches, dips to the inkstand, adds X's and dashes with a hidden, or blank, meaning. "You're remarkably well read, aren't you? Have you read Bruno or Leibnitz on the Monad? Or Hirsch on Metabiology?"

Cold lightning fills the twins' spines, their breath goes shallow, eyes brighten. Is Dr. Deer about to reveal himself? Is their lifelong search about to be answered? Teddy barks, clearing phlegm. *"No!"*

"Try them someday. When you finish Poe."

"What's the Monad?" Leo asks, Teddy silent.

"One who is many, many who are One," Dr. Deer says. "The vertebrae and the spine at once, the stones *and* the arch—the Monarch and the Anarch." Dr. Deer's voice falls to a whispering rasp; beside himself, he wipes his lips. "But don't tell the pope's wife!"

Teddy's intuition spirals. "Oh sure!—the many sparks of the Divine Fire. And the Great White Brotherhood—it's in *The Secret Doctrine,* the physical, astral and mental bodies on the seven-runged ladder to Nirvana. I know all about Madame Blavatsky and theosophy. She's impossible! Nobody can read her. But, uh, vague as she is, she may be right anyway."

"Right about what?"

"Revealed knowledge! The Great White Brotherhood!" Teddy erect, kneading his scalp for sparks. "A chain of supergeniuses around the earth who never contact each other but know each other's work. Oscar Harpur told us all about 'em. They scared him so much he gave up the whole study as TOO DISHEARTENING—they rule the world! Greek shipping magnates, oil monopolists, even Moscow and Washington are only front men for the Brotherhood's secular power. Their wealth's so vast that money has no meaning! I mean HEAVING WEALTH, Doctor—like oilbeds! It's hard to believe, but it sounds true. Whatta you think?"

Dr. Deer laughs. "You *are* full of surprises. Does *Eureka* show revealed knowledge?"

"He's sure a better cosmologist than Madame Blavatsky," Teddy said, pouring. "She's seven layers of Buddhistic BULLSHIT, but even Edgar reads like OPIUM writing. He's high on *something,* Doctor, his prose has PINPOINTED EYEBALLS."

"Hm." Dr. Deer looks down to see if the twins' ankles are crossed. "You've tried opium?"

Teddy nods casually. "We both have." Leo nods, prickling sinfully. "Very mild drug—but fantastic. You see ALL THE EVIL in everything, people, buildings, taxicabs—the whole world's evil is revealed. There's a halo over everything."

"That's what *Eureka*'s about?"

"That's *cosmology,* Doctor," Teddy says. "It's NOT about good and evil."

Dr. Deer's mock perplexity. "But you said it's about the Divine Heart throbbing."

"RIGHT!" Teddy squirms on his itchy pile and ancient shorts, soothing himself against the chair, sips muscatel, his opiumtoasted tongue still dry as ash. "But it's a *poem,* Doctor."

"Oh? Then in writing it he wasn't 'touched by God'?"

" 'Touched by God'? Like who?"

"Why, like Moses on Sinai, or Isaiah, or Buddha under the fig tree, or whoever wrote *The Tempest."*

"That's by Shakespeare."

Dr. Deer smiles. "Have you studied the cosmology of *The Tempest?"*

Teddy thinks. "But *that's* about freedom and bondage."

"And *justice,* Doctor," Dr. Deer says. "Divine justice. But let's get back to and then *down to earth.* Doctor, for your last five minutes—*the time!* I must say you twins are the most interesting patients I've ever had." Dr. Deer looks above at the source of his blessings. "You were sent to me by heaven, rest assured of that. *Look here,* old chap, you're saying a poem doesn't have to be sensible—that intuitional genius doesn't have to account for pain and suffering—that you're happy with a half-baked opium dream. Is *this* what you're saying?"

"Doctor. I don't KNOW if Poe was touched by God! I don't read the Bible!—that goddamn book is nothing but suffering and pain from Moses to Revelation. There isn't ONE MOMENT of *laughter* or *humor* in it, just doom, doom, doom, not one word of GOOD CHEER! I can't live by doom alone."

Dr. Deer amazed. "You of all people—what've you got to laugh about? I should think you'd find great comfort in the Bible. But I'm only trying to understand you. Don't you know that there's a great battle going on and that suffering is our highest education in fighting that battle?"

". . . What battle?" Teddy asks.

Dr. Deer points upward fiercely.

"Doctor!" Teddy asks wideeyed "—do you mean you believe in *heaven?*—and *angels?"*

"Hierarchies," Dr. Deer says fiercely, then quickly covers his mouth. "Ah, I mustn't let the cat out of the bag."

Leo-Teddy mute, tingling.

"How can you believe in that?" Teddy asks.

"Because I've been wounded, sir. And I am suffering. Every day is the sabbath but I am condemned to sit here and work. Listening to the problems of wealthy women when I should be writing my work on the Great Memory. And I've been waiting over thirty-five years to write it! Instead, I must sit here and be educated—not by my patients—but by *my* patience and suffering."

"Doctor, you should GET OUT MORE," Teddy says.

"Oh, I do," Dr. Deer says "—once a week. Just to walk around the block is exquisite delight—though I shouldn't be doing it."

"Now *there!*" Teddy says. "You take this suffering business altogether too seriously."

"I'm in torment daily. Aren't you?"

"Yes—but I LAUGH A LOT. In fact, I laugh more than anyone I know!"

"I believe you."

"I'm always laughing *somewhere* inside."

Dr. Deer nods.

"It's painful," Teddy says. "I'm always gritting my teeth and laughing."

"It takes great courage."

Teddy nods. "What does?"

"To admit God white-hot into your spine. It takes more courage than you have yet, doesn't it? I admire you, don't mistake me. You're having a tremendous trial, it's no wonder you drink. Now, *Leo,* do you have a dream for me?"

"Doctor," Teddy says, "we didn't get to *my letter.*"

Dr. Deer studies his desk clock. "Dear, dear! Ten minutes—I can give you an extra ten minutes, and make it up with Leo next visit. Where's this extraordinary letter?"

Teddy points into his libretto *The Ass.* "Read it aloud so I can hear how it sounds." Pouring. "It's part of my sex-opera but I *am* sending it to some girls I know."

Dr. Deer reads Teddy's

WINESTAINED RESCUE LETTER

Outta bread. Outta butts. Outta wine. Out. Inert.

I'm in bed, girls. Groaning. Gushing out my guillotined heart. SIGH! SIGHHHHH! Ravenous for a little white body to sink into. I haven't had a piece in eighteen months. That's too long! While *you* enjoy yourself and possess everything I desire, I, penniless of your beauty and sexual vigor, have to scrape up some action. *Inertia!* Sheer yoga—make the mountains come to Mohammed. I admire you deeply, even love you. Won't you give me a picket off your fence?

Yes, inertia. I've been inert on my bed for three days (and so's Leo, but he goes home to Wanda on *his* days), flogging my flagpole in, like Custer, a last stand against death. Visit me in my distress and adversity. Please help me get standing again. Things, particularly sex, aren't going well for me. I am poor, obscure, and need special attention. I am a sexual desperado. But I'm gonna keep going and write the great opera of the Siamese monster Boris & Ygor.

Ah, I can just hear Judy cry, He can lie there till hell freezes over! SHIT!—Judy just loves to beat up on Uncle Punch, who bears up as best he can. But he remembers at his heart's core the night he saw Judy bare, plain, slim and burning, brown eyes sugared, bush burning—but not for me! (Still, dear old Frank'll be big-spirited about it.)

Nancy could be moved, she's approachable, pliable, kindhearted. But really there are Marty's feelings to consider. After all, they're married—how generous can a friend be? But she's haunted me for years—I once proposed to her! I'm only human, I can't resist her memory when it steals over me, prickling!

I'm considering every corner of the action! Adie wouldn't really understand—though she might, she might! And show up at my door, a glowing angel of mercy, my apartment flooded with candles, music, wine, the two of us in the altogether, leaping from room to room!

"And what will *you* be doing?" Dr. Deer asks Leo.
"I'll be dressed."
"*Ahem,* you're nearly finished, Doctor," Teddy says.

Though I suppose it's Rebecca who might understand most deeply what a kindness she could do. Paul—be kind. But I fear I hear Judy rasping, "Look, if you want a piece of ass, get out and beg like every other man!"

Judy shows a grievous lack of heart! I don't want a Times Square pavement flower! No bought red mouth! I want the deep sweet peace and heartbreaking simplicity of a twenty-minute YES from one I admire, someone largehearted, a friend to make me dizzy with life again. Your heart will be as happy as mine! It doesn't take much to brighten a fat man up.

A touch.

Yours in blanket admiration,
Teddy

"You can't send this boorish horseshit," Leo says.

"Why not? It's beautifully written! It's some of the finest prose I've ever read! For Christ's sake, this piece of writing has INTEGRITY—though I guess I shouldn't expect you to see that."

"Everytime one of these girls shows up at your pad you're walkin' around naked with a half hardon and pissin' in the sink. And you're *bombed!* How in hell can you expect 'em to wanna screw you?"

Teddy's head rises to heights. "That Bengali girl doesn't mind me."

"She doesn't even speak English! She's in love with our bust of Beethoven."

"Well, what's that got to do with it? How about Delores? Should I put Deedee into the letter?"

"Never! Teddy, she's seen you at your *most* disgusting."

"Boy," Teddy sighs, "you're sure out to castrate me—and undermine Dr. Deer's confidence in me!"

"Ya gotta be less VULGAR!"

"I don't need your carping."

"You haven't sent this letter yet?" Dr. Deer asks.

Teddy, pouring. "It's not perfect yet, Doctor."

"This is quite curious," Dr. Deer says. "These are all *wives* of your close friends? And you think their husbands should share them with you? Who's this Bengali girl?"

"She's very unimportant," Teddy says. "Well, she's been flown over from Calcutta for bone disease treatments and stays with a houseful of girls on the Lower East Side. Her father's a rice exporter—"

"—Jute," Leo says.

"Well, she sure eats a lot of rice—she likes bowls of rice mixed with melted American cheese."

"My word!" Dr. Deer laughs. "Oh, I shouldn't laugh. Tell me more, old chap."

"Well, first time she stripped for me I couldn't believe my eyes. She's *built,* Doctor, I mean grapefruit bosoms."

"But a small waist," Leo says. "Relatively."

"She's taken a fancy to me."

Dr. Deer's pen scratches. "What's her name?"

"Shit, I can't pronounce it, Doctor."

"Well, what do you call her?"

"Jumbo."

"I see! She's white?"

"She's white enough for me!" Teddy says. "And she likes to dance. On the bed, standing."

"My, my! Didn't you have another ladyfriend who liked to dance? A Salome?"

"Doctor, nearly *all* the ladies I know dance. All girls live in a world of fantasy—then they're hysterical when the world doesn't conform. It's pathetic. She wears American clothes but she has a stone in her nose—you know, a diamond on her nostril. She wants to marry me! It's impossible!"

"Why? Isn't she wealthy?"

"God, no, she's a checkout girl at my A&P and always undercharges me. But she talks so damn fast, it POURS outta her, Doctor, this gibberish! I keep fallin' asleep. You can only listen to gibberish about fifteen minutes, Doctor, then everything fades. You go numb. And then, her bones creak. When we make love, I hear her bones creaking. It's eerie, like she's becoming disjointed. Well, it's all over now."

Leo nods. "I liked her."

"She don't ask *you* to marry her. *Ha!* Doesn't she put you to sleep? And she's not only insatiable, Doctor, she's frigid. Well, that's not unusual, the last ten girls I bedded were frigid. Boy, she kept my prostate throbbing like the heart of a Galapagos turtle. I mean I *hurt.* She nearly killed me. Then during our last argument she had the nerve to tell me she'd never had an orgasm—a parting cut to the balls, Doctor. Well, how could she come through all those NOISES?"

"She talks during intercourse, old chap?"

"Her bones, Doctor! She's a bundle of rusty hinges. She always sighs as if she's had a climax. But she says she faked every one of 'em—for my sake, ha! And besides, she loves Leo."

"But you're not seeing her any longer?"

"I hope not! *Yi!*—like to see her picture?" Digs split wallet from inner pocket, shows snapshot. Seated on a floormattress in a dingey room, Leo smiles patiently while Teddy buckles sideways, his gallon hovering over a glass held by a grinning little girl, his face blurring, jiggled, jowled, joyous.

"Well, *Teddy* looks happy," Dr. Deer says.

Leo snorts. "Damn DEATHPHOTO. He's got corpse-eyes."

"I'm not sure I see what you mean."

"He looks dead! *Glassyeyed!* Like a cocaine addict."

Teddy sniffs. "You're really out for character assassination today, aren'tcha? *Whew!*"

"This little girl's *Jumbo?*"

"Ha!" Teddy cries. "You should see her stripped. A phenomenon, Doctor."

"Very beautiful," Leo says.

"Oh, Christ, he doesn't have to put up with her EMOTIONS. Ugh!"

"Is that a mole?" Dr. Deer asks.

"A hole," Leo says.

"That's where her diamond was," Teddy says. "She hocked it—to get my horn outta hock. But in her twisted mind, Doctor, it was really more like GETTING ENGAGED. I plan to get it back for her—when I have the cash. Believe me."

"Oh, I do. But see here, doesn't that diamond have some religious significance for her?"

" 'Religious significance!' My God, she's an adamant atheist, a rationalist. Her total intellectual equipment comes from crossword puzzles and detective novels, though her English is childish. That's what puts me to sleep all the time, Doctor, the sheer torrent of trash she spouts! She's a Niagara! She hoses me down with trivia. I get DOPED, my only defense is to get her stripped for action on the bed, shove a novel into her hands and hide out at my desk. But she's a fiendish reader, three or four mysteries in two hours! I obviously can't work with her around. She's always dancing in a circle to the icebox after each book and rehearsing plots over cold cheese-rice. Thank God for Leo, he *listens.*"

"I don't understand. Why have you written this letter if you're so exhausted by this girl's sexual demands?"

"Oh, Doctor, she doesn't count. I don't include her in my sex life. It's been eighteen months since I had a girl I liked. I gotta get that diamond back so she'll lemme alone—she's always showing up, that detective brain of hers follows my every movement. I mean, twelve-thirty at night, knock, knock, there she is and it's two and half hours of babble before I can persuade her to shut up and get into bed. I'd trade my horn in for her diamond but it's already in hock, sonofabitch."

"But why string her along? Can't you just not admit her?"

"Well, she slumps, Doctor! I'm so desperate it's killin' me. I feel PAIN. When am I gonna find a girl I can love? Doctor, my heart can't stand this much longer—lying on my bed my heart feels like a dying pigeon fluttering on its wings—it's tachycardia!—I get PALPITATIONS like heart failure. I feel FANGS in my chest. All my life all I wanted's a girl—I can hardly remember not wanting a girl. How can this go on year after year? Life is INHUMAN! I'm so hungry the whole world's EROTICIZED—even the *air* makes me sex-sick. Oh God Almighty, how long must I wait? All He sends me is—JUMBO! with a hole in her nose!"

"You're too idealistic," Leo says.

"IDEALISTIC! I'm sufferin' and you talk like a nitwit!"

"Now, now, there are plenty of places to meet attractive women," Dr. Deer says.

"They don't drink," Teddy says. "Doctor, if you could hear my *sighs*. It's incredible—for hours I can't BREATHE and these long sighs—UNNNHHH! UNNNH! UNH! UNNNNNHHHH!!—I can't stop 'em! I just lie there like an elephant in rut with the *must* comin' outta my eyes. It's desire beyond belief, it collects in my crotch, in my chest—drink can't touch it! Nothin' helps, I can't sleep, I masturbate seven times running, my whole body feels like soft taffy on an anvil. And it's just over girls! Is it any wonder I wrote that letter? That letter's a complete understatement of my despair, Doctor. My high hopes! my ridiculousness, my embarrassment—it's all a hundred times worse than I can tell you. I get eroticized just by a girl's EYELASHES on the subway, Doctor! Just a fringe! By IRISES, by eyes ALIVE in a girl's head! But all that's the easy part of suffering. Because then there's the FULL MOON."

Dr. Deer cocks his ear. "What happens then?"

"I'm completely defenseless. I'll sit in my apartment not knowing why I feel so upset. Then I see the full moon at the window. CHAOS comes over me, I break down into some original, vegetative ROT. I'm pregnant in my chest and can't give birth, I get a big watery BALL in here and can't prick it. I could cry for a year and not get cried out. And I CAN'T GET AN ERECTION, not if I try for an hour! I'm impotent, I lose all sex interest for weeks. Suddenly I feel FUNGOID, my flesh rubs off in balls in the tub, I get bloody cracks between my toes, my CROTCH ROTS, I keep smellin' this hideous STALE ODOR all over the city, I've smelled it for nearly three years now!"

"Do *you* smell it?"

"Sure do," Leo says. "It's Teddy."

Teddy sighs. "This is a little argument we have, Doctor."

"You sweat wine," Leo says.

"Doctor, this is simply not true. That's the Phantom A.A. talkin'."

"The Phantom A.A.?" Dr. Deer asks.

"He makes a meeting once every two weeks," Teddy says, *"if that.* If he doesn't watch out, he'll be drinking."

"Well, these symptoms are most interesting," Dr. Deer tells Teddy, "but—"

"It's NOT ME! I'm healthy as a horse! But I feel like Hitler sucking on a cyanide coughdrop!"

"We only have twenty minutes left for Leo. So A.A.'s losing its attraction for you? You feel you're getting a grip on yourself?"

"I feel I'm terrifically embarrassed by a certain person to my right talkin' during the meetings!" Leo says. "Anyway, I'm giving my first talk tomorrow night. Telling my 'horror story,' Doctor. I think I've mastered the field of information in A.A. A meeting every two weeks is about what I need. After all, I have to do my work, besides working at the hospital, and I don't get much writing done on Teddy's days."

"Aren't you gentlemen due for a raise?"

"I hope so!" Leo says. "But we gotta pass our six-month inspection first and bring in our college degrees for a record check—that's a terrific stumbling block."

"But you've shown you can do the work even though

you don't have degrees," Dr. Deer says. "Won't they take that into consideration?"

"We could get canned for a phony telegram we sent 'em. We went down to the Western Union nearest the New School and sent the Welfare Department a telegram verifying our 'degrees' in World Lit—and signed it 'The Registrar'! They could take this amiss. We either gotta forge some degrees or 'fess up."

"My, my! And which do you think you'll do!"

"Come clean," Leo says.

"Ridiculous," Teddy snorts.

"Look, it was six months ago we did this," Leo says. "I was a different person then. Maybe you haven't changed but I have."

"I get an *awful lot* of this HOLIER-THAN-THOU, Doctor."

"Soberer," Leo says.

"Everybody's SWAMPED," Teddy says. "But we try to keep a little more caught up in our reports than the other workers. These reports are a tidal wave, we're all DROWNING. But *we* put in a little extra effort—a helluva lot extra. WE WORK"

"I'm sure you do," Dr. Deer says.

"We need the dough," Teddy says. "I mean look how far we are behind with you."

"Thank you for thinking of me. But I'm willing to go along for awhile. You *are* my most astonishing patients—don't forget, I published a book on twins."

"And they *like* us." Teddy smiles.

"Ha!" Leo says. "They don't like your humming at your desk."

"I can't help it. It helps me concentrate. Anyway, it's not loud."

"It's schmaltz."

Teddy pours. "It keeps me awake."

"Let's get back to Leo," Dr. Deer says. "Have you heard from John McFin?"

"He's standing right behind me."

Teddy jumps, gulping.

"Everytime I think of a drink," Leo says. "Frankly, I'm haunted by him."

"I see. You admire him very much, don't you?"

"Saved my life! His power of example got me sober. I only wish I knew Russian."

"Why Russian?"

"I'd like to take A.A. to Moscow. They need it, Doctor! Their alcohol problem's staggering."

Dr. Deer glances at Leo's ankles. Leo quickly uncrosses them, sits up.

"I wanna form Drinkers Anonymous," Teddy says. "Show people they can drink, given proper guidance."

"You gonna be president?" Leo asks.

"At least I'm not goin' to Moscow! I'm workin' my own program, buddy. You're not workin' any *I* can see."

"Just put the cork in the bottle," Leo says. Digs a cigarette from a pack with two joints in it. Teddy quivers, unfocused, resourceless, forcing a smile.

"Now let's be serious," Dr. Deer says. "Tell me, if you would be so kind, sir, how *you* feel about this Bengali girl?"

"I try reasonably hard to stay faithful to Wanda."

"That's quite noble of you. How does Wanda feel about, uh, Jumbo?"

"Well, she's Jewish, Doctor," Leo says.

Dr. Deer laughs despite himself. "I must say, you astonish me at times. What does being Jewish have to do with her feelings about Jumbo?"

"She's just not jealous."

"Oh? That's hard to believe. How does being Jewish make her immune to jealousy?"

"Well, you know Jewish girls, Doctor. Wearing miniskirts—without tights!—goin' up subway steps utterly blasé, men bending to tie their shoelaces for a fast peek—it's appalling."

"I know how you must feel, old fellow."

"New York! All my bedmates are Jewish. I'm terrifically impressed by their sense of family. What first impressed me about Cynara was her warmth about goin' to temple."

"Oh," Dr. Deer sighs, "you mustn't put any stock in that. Does Wanda observe holy days?"

"Well, no. But she's trying! She's bought a prayer book and tried to get her family to go through the Passover text when we went up for dinner. She was a lot more serious about it than they were. I guess I set her some kind of example," Leo says hoarsely, clearing his toasted throat. "Whenever I talk about religion with her she falls asleep—but she's *trying*. Right now it's all gesture. Her relatives joke about Christ—that *meshugana* who thought he was

"I mean in bed. I'm a gentleman."

Leo squirms at this incredible description, says nothing. Silence.

"See here," Dr. Deer says, "you've got a life to live, music to write, you need recognition, money, security."

Leo, startled. "I don't think I want all that. My spirit's my security."

"One for the road," Teddy says, pouring. Bags his gallon in shoppingbag.

"You take that to work with you?" Dr. Deer asks.

"Not every day—good heavens!" Teddy says. "It's just that our paychecks don't come through until this afternoon and I'm broke." (And have an exhaustion hard-on.)

"I see. And when can I expect another token payment from either of you?"

"Don't lump me in with Teddy, Doctor. I pay as well as I can."

"I plan to do better," Teddy sighs. "But I only make so much! I gotta get my horn outta hock, got back rent to catch up on, I've worn my sox and shorts to rags, I'm dyin' under my grocery tab—it's stupendous—I need music supplies, our carfare's fantastic—you have no idea what we spend on subways and busses. Expenses are TERRIBLE! But I plan to catch up on my debts *today* and perhaps I'll be able to make you a DOUBLE PAYMENT next payday."

"Please try. It's been two months since you've given me anything, Ted. And *my* rent's gone up."

"Doctor," Teddy says, "you mentioned there are plenty of places to find attractive women. Where'd you mean?"

"Why—churches! they have a lot of mixing. Or Ethical Culture groups. They have very attractive young women. Or music societies, the ones in the Sunday *Times*, choral groups—"

"—I can't sing," Teddy says.

"—dances at the girls' Y's—innumerable places to meet nice girls."

Teddy sighs, holding Leo's coat. "Like I say, Doctor, they don't drink."

"They couldn't sing with Teddy breathin' on 'em," Leo says.

"My, my," Dr. Deer says. "We'll have to work on your drinking problem, won't we?"

"No problem, Doctor. I takes it or I leaves it. Mostly I takes it."

"I see. You don't wear hats on a day like this? You really shouldn't take such chances with your health! Leo, good luck on your talk tomorrow night—I'll be with you in spirit. I imagine you'll get a standing ovation? Be sure to phone me afterward. And bring me a dream next visit!" He shakes their hands with a binding grip and fierce eye. "Bless you both! I think of you nightly in my prayers."

"It's hard to believe that anyone still prays," Teddy says.

"Oh, I'll be flying with the angels when my time comes." His grip deepens, then he closes the door after them, his smile a fiery gray force.

Trenchcoated tent, Leo-Teddy lurks below in the building's foyer. "Shall we?"

Leo says, "We'll be too foggy to work this afternoon."

Teddy belches. "Oh, I'm terrific."

Leo lights an opiumloaded reefer. Twins go out holding their breath and, trading the cupped joint, head up Park for the Eighty-sixty Street subway. Blue sleet pits their faces, shoes chilling in slush. Park blowing hard and empty—the twins smoke brazenly. Cross over Eighty-sixth where traffic lamps and deep red neons of Yorkville clutch their eyes under hard sleet. Leo-Teddy stares at Yorkville's eternity, a village on the Great Divide, the raw boil over the ridge. Twins floating.

"I wish you'd clam up about my breath," Teddy says.

"You got no idea what that sewage flow all night smells like."

"Okay, I'll do something about it—*Uh, shit!*" Teddy stops, a stitch under his rib. "Damned liver's flopping like a dying fish." Hand under trenchcoat. "My God, it's shaking. Feel."

"I know, believe me."

"This must be 'chill on the liver,' don'tcha think?"

"It's the kinda stomach ulcer ya could put your finger through."

"Bullshit. I don't toss blood." Icewater floods his shoecracks. "D'ya think I could rainproof these with candlewax? It'd freeze and snap off, huh? Shit. I'm not ready to shell out ten bucks for shoes."

"They're *your* feet.

Teddy sweating, belches painfully, bounces against Marboro's bookwindow. "Lemme breathe! We gotta get back to oatmeal—that spaghetti omelette's rubberized in muscatel. *Unhh!* Last night I dreamed I was walkin' starknaked out front of Dr. Deer's, too ashamed to go in."

"Don't heave here, Teddy. Let's find an alley."

"Not gonna heave." Drags on smoldering roach, grips his breath. Cold bluehaloed slush, blowing sleet. Eyes frogging back, rubber belchfumes croaking. *"Whoo,* close! Oh man, I wish we were at your pad digging Beethoven's Thirtieth piano sonata—pure Happy Cloud Land."

"Today's *payday*. We'll be on our way in four hours."

"Thanks for the tip—you have my sincere gratitude and respect." Teddy looks about, brightening. "Hey, ya know those fiddling students out fronta the Eighth Street Book Shop? How about right here?—this is virgin turf. Throw a hat down and start blowin'." Teddy wipes sleet from his forehead. "Not today of course . . . Let's drag ass."

"We're goin' to work."

"Correct." Teddy moves toward the downtown stairs slyly.

"We gotta cross the street," Leo says. Leo-Teddy waits for the light, Teddy glaring at splashing cars. "Want me to hold the bag?" Leo asks.

"If I wanna drink, I'll drink."

"Don't think I'd stop you, Edgar."

On the uptown local platform, Teddy races for a half-empty bench. "Made it!" he crows, grinning with his denture on his tongue, the bucktooth British colonel cheering his troops. *"Good boy, Din!"* he says, settling his chill gallon between his shoes. Looks at the platform's deserted end. "I don't wanna sit here." Leo-Teddy drifts down the empty platform, stops with his back hiding Teddy's chugalug. "Cheers. *Cold!*—that'll see me through," Teddy sighs, face rubied, palm on twitching ulcer. Stare down-tunnel for the local's rolling glimmer from Seventy-seventh, the long darkness attractive, inviting their gaze to dwell upon the far platform's webbed outpour.

"Fuck my rent," Teddy burps. "Think we can make

the Second Avenue Pawnshop by five-thirty? I gotta get my ax no matter what."

"With your lip! What for, fat man?"

"Cocksucker." Wipes winespittle, blue pupils pinpointed. "If it wasn't payday, I'd throw you on those fuckin' tracks. I suppose you're gonna take my inventory tomorrow night—when you tell *your* horror story. Go ahead! I don't give a fuck. Say anything you want about me."

"Whatever I say you'll think it's about you . . . I'm gonna give 'em a story like they never heard before. And lay it on the line about A.A. too."

"You do *that* and I'll buy you an ounce of Panamanian afterward. *Be sure* to tell 'em how boring their fuckin' meetings are. All that drivel night after night—a sane man can't hold his eyes open! *Tell 'em!* And we'll hit Dr. Sunshine's—I'm not kiddin' about that ounce. It'll be worth it to hear some sanity in those damn church basements. Like a draft of cold air in a smoky room. They'll be takin' *notes!*"

Cold tunnel rankness of bloody butcher's paper. Teddy gags. "Hate that smell!"

"At least it's not you, for a change."

Arriving train's chill breeze washes their eyes. Rushing cars, rainbow blobbed with airpaint. Teddy takes out his filtertips, checks his joints carefully, stuffs pack away. Doors open, Leo-Teddy sits back in an empty doubleseat, bushed, buzzing. Eyes a redwigged black schoolgirl's plump white skeletonglowing kneebones.

"Oh God," Teddy moans, "that spaghetti omelette's really jitter-buggin'."

"Suffer, nightowl! Try givin' yourself some rest."

"Can I help it if I don't come alive before midnight? That's when I get my best work done."

"Yeah? And then we wake up at your desk and say, Good God, it's morning!"

"That's when that ol' incandescent winecloud starts its semaphore. Don't wanna drain my daily ecstasy off into sleep. I live full intensity—fuck the consequences. That black girl's gonna drive me into Selfabuse Anonymous. Christ!" he groans, pressing his anxiety-hopping stomach, "we're ten minutes late!" Pains cut his breath. Loud belch. GROAN. "How can I have this killer hard-on?"

A dapper, curlygray, hawkhatted black ambles on with

a tenor case, sits thinking and, knee crossed by a polished Italian point in soft lowcut rubber, his half-lidded eyes wander coolly to two vandykes in trenchcoats regarding him, then he retires amazed into his godhood, clipped mustache primed against further tumult or ruffling of his calm, hawklike—

GROAN!

Teddy bent forward, clutching himself.

"The Hawk!" Leo whispers . . . the world's greatest tenor sax, Louis's buddy!

The car jerks hard, starting.

Labor pains. Blood drains from Teddy's head. Slugged by stomach spasm. "Oh God, I'm gonna be sick."

Leo glares, eying The Hawk. "You can't be sick here! *That's the Hawk!"*

"No place else!" Teddy groans, pulling gallon from shoppingbag. Letters, bills, blank music paper, cigars, cigarettes, a *Times,* A&P cashregister slips, peanut shucks, all spill from the upturned bag Teddy beats on its bottom. Passengers watch Con Ed bills breeze down the carfloor as he makes sure his bag's empty, his half-spent Paradise muscatel gallon awash at his foot. Leo, redfaced, sees the copperwigged schoolgirl's jaw drop, The Hawk speared, round-eyed, a blank sheet of music paper creeping by his shaped-leather tenor case. Whimpering, Teddy smiles wildly at The Hawk, begging the car's forgiveness, jams bag to face. Abruptly, Leo raises him, drags blind Teddy and bag through the door to the between-cars platform. The roaring train picks up speed toward Ninety-fifth, rocking and windy as Teddy belts the passing darkness with muscatel and fried spaghetti. The platforms roll and fall as Leo holds him, wine drooling onto their shoes. Teddy looks up stricken.

"Where's your bridge?" Leo asks.

Teddy's tongue searches his gaping upper row for his front teeth. *"Shit!"* Bends below to comb his vomit for the bridge. "It'th gone! *Thonofabitch,* I puked out thixty buckth! *I'm a cretin again!* I can't fathe Thophrosyne without my teeth, she'll can uth! Let'th phone in."

"We'll just say they're bein' repaired."

"You idiot!" Teddy shakes his bag like a tambourine. "If I'd jutht thrown up in *thith* I'd thtill have my choppers. Why'd I follow you!"

"Hey, this is our stop."

Eyes blended with self-hate, Leo-Teddy crowds back to his seat, jams bottle, letters, paper back into bag, Teddy wiping red eyes, wet cheeks.

"Hey!" Hawk says, picking up a red Con Ed bill by his sax. "Better pay this or you be a pair of frozen ducks."

"We're payin', we're payin'!" Teddy lurches down the car as passengers hand them bills, letters, music paper. Doors open. *"Thay hello to Louis for uth!"* Teddy wails.

"Louis who?"

"Popth!" Teddy races for the door. "He's our thpiritual advisor!"

Teddy's damp bag splits, gallon falling sharply, rolling back inside. He turns in the doorway, lunges back for the bottle just beyond his fingertips as the door closes. Leo outside, leg inside, tries to force the door open, Teddy within bending for the bottle now rolling up the aisle. Suddenly the black schoolgirl leaps up, hands Teddy his oily gallon, her rosered lips drawn with disgust.

Teddy's thanks pour. "THANK YOU, I'M THORRY, I'M THORRY! How'dya like t' be in a movie I'm gonna make?" She shakes her head. Teddy attacks the door, feeling his shoes ooze. "THUBWA-A-AYS!"

"Just be patient," Leo says outside.

"Tell 'im to thtop the train!"

"You're losing all your letters," the girl says, picking up envelopes.

"Be an angel and thtop the train."

"Train ain't movin'."

Teddy, hands stuffed with letters and gallon, searches for the red cord to stop the train.

Leo calls, "Help me push!"

Arms full, Teddy shoulders the door just as it opens, and falls flat onto Leo on the station platform. The door closes on his foot and as he yanks it out he finds the base of the gallon snapped off cleanly on the platform and sees his big toe sticking filthily out of his sock—his shoe still inside the car. The train moves slowly down the tracks.

"SHIT! SHIT! SHI-I-IT! MY SHOE, MY SHOE!"

Leo-Teddy limps shouting down the platform, the car pulling away. A window drops, the sopping shoe thuds off a stanchion. The Hawk, amazed by Teddy's blown kiss of toothless gratitude, waves back stoned.

Teddy fights his foot into soaked leather, ties his lace.

"These fuckin' trains are a *menathe!*" Leo picks spaghetti off their trenchcoat skirts, silently. "We gotta thtart takin' buthes, buddyboy."

"Look at these coats. We can't stink up the office with these."

"What'th that look mean? I'm thupposed to feel guilty? Over an accthident? *Boy!* I jutht hope Hawk don't tell Popth he thaw uth pukin'."

"Maybe he'll say something minor, like convulsions."

Picking up letters, Teddy measures Leo's thickheadedness. *"I* have problems you apparently don't know about."

"Yeah, mental problems!"

"I'VE got a lot of difficulties t' overcome, SHITHEAD!"

"HA!" Leo kicks the winegallon bottom onto the tracks.

"Hey, man, how about two minutes of THERENITY, huh? Or wouldya prefer a butht on the jaw?"

LATE, LATE! Judgment overhead.

Freezing on the windy corner of Ninety-fifth and Lex, stinking trenchcoats stiffening as Teddy fights going to the dry cleaner, *"I'm a bad ax, man, don't* FUCK WITH ME! I'm the greateth librettitht thinthe Lorenzo da Ponte. Wagner? Don't make me laugh. Tell me, these fatthos thtand there thingin' for hours on end and what'th it all about, man? What'th it all about? Maybe *Trithtan and Isolde,* okay. It'th only 'Body and Thoul' carried to vatht exthtremes. But there's an idea there, not bad! It coulda been shorter but I'll grant him *one* opera. And there's a great one-hour operetta hidden in *Die Meithterthinger.* But the *Ring Thycle?* You tell me what it'th all about—go ahead, Einthtein, tell me! Look, I'm down to thixthteen thentth, you wanna lend me a buck-twenny-five until we get our checkth cashed? No wine! I jutht need a doubleshot of tequila. I'm wathted, Leo. Then we go t' the cleaner, or before, I'm with you one hundred perthent."

Leo-Teddy argues the cleaner into a rush job on the trenchcoats, evening pickup. Race and skid carefully downhill to Metropolitan Hospital, detour to Tiger's Bar. Quick double, lemon wedge, salt. At the bar Teddy Sierra turns stickup artist, knocks off Tiger's till, is struck down on the sidewalk by comforting gunfire. "Lucky the hospital's right across the street," Teddy whispers to Leo, blackness bubbling his blood. *"Now you're free!"* His lights sneeze off in an orgasm. *"Ahhh! . . ."* Crippled Leo blowing "Body and Soul" at Teddy's memorial, followed by Bruckner's *Seventh* over the parlor's sound system, loud enough to wake the—TEQUILA CLOUD masked by chlorophyll, glide smoothly through raggedy hallflow of nerveshattering Spanish squawk and ambling blacks, pass Admissions, gliss on oil past Sophrosyne's office and the older caseworkers' office, into Welfare's superclutter of fresh college grads at their paralyzing hills of unfiled financial investigations, sweep up clipboards and S.R.675's, hit the front elevator, Teddy clamping his breath for thirteen floors in the visitor-crowded lift, both twins soaked in an agreeable, life-fulfilling, somewhat opiated trip, speak to the guard who unlocks 13B and lets them into the psycho ward. Sedated nerveshamblers mill in pajamas, cadge cigarettes, forbidden matches.

Leo-Teddy reads the previous admissions record on Jack Daniels, twenty-eight, a black now readmitted for alcoholic hallucinations. Jack Daniels lies staring out his window, unshaven, slumped, sapped.

Leo whispers. "He's not even *here*."

"Sure he is. We'll get through. Hi, Jack! My name's Teddy, thith is my brother Leo."

Jack's head, still. Move into his line of sight. Jack looks from Teddy to Leo, Leo to Teddy, lips gravely drawn, his eyes seemingly wet with death.

"Feelin' better?" Teddy asks. No answer. "We're from Welfare. We're here t' thee you don't pay a fuckin' thent for thith hothpitalization. You're gettin' a free ride! After all, thith is a thity hothpital, your taxes built thith trap. Right? Jack?"

"You prowlin' round here for?" Jack whispers rapidly.

"What'th that, Jack? We're here t' thee you don't worry about your hothpital bill."

"Ain't ready t' go yet! Ahm in *pa-a-ain* . . ."

Dreambound horrorgaze, queer narrow skull, stiff tufts flying in a nappy frightwig.

Teddy nods agreeably, scribbles on his clipboard: *Not much reality development!*—a real baby. "We're not here to throw you out, we're here t' pamper you. We wantcha t' feel abtholutely free t' thtay here—in every financial rethpect." Teddy glances at his S.R. 675. "Are you a U. ETH. thitizen, Jack?"

"Can't frighten me. I'm all frightened out."

"Nah, we're not tryin' t' frighten ya. Are we, Leo?"

"Tol' the doctors all about you." Jack's voice jerks. "You take that damn icepick outta here. An' take them dead peoples with you. I tol' the doctor!—mah heart can't take much more of this."

Leo says softly, "We're welfare workers."

"Wanna kill me one way or th' other, huh? Well, I can't stan' no more."

"Nobody could get your addreth outta you latht night, Jack. You thtill live on Ninety-fifth with your mother?"

"Jus' take my body if you wants it." Red eyes wide. "But please don' torture me!"

"What! Look, thith is *your* hothpital. Feel free to use it. Look, man," he whispers, *"we're* out to fuck the thythtem. *Sure we are!"*

Jack's eyes stand with tears. His hand shakes over his mouth, then lies quivering on his white sheet.

"If you're too tired to talk now," Leo says, "we'll come back later, Mr. Daniels. I think we better go."

"Wait a minute! You boys got a cigarette?"

"You're not allowed to thmoke in bed. Here, I'll leave one on your thtand."

Jack gasps, shaking, mouth flexing to speak. "I ain't never gonna see my mama no more!"

"I'm sorry," Leo says. "She pass away?"

"I ain' gettin' outta here! They gonna get me tonight." Stares at something beyond the whistling window. "You tell them nurses not to turn out mah light tonight—or they gets me for sure. They come inside."

Leo-Teddy eyes the window. "Who'll come inside?"

"Dead peoples. Out there."

Teddy says. "We're on the thirteenth floor, Jack."

Jack stares at Leo-Teddy hard. "Which one of you gonna sign my death certificate?"

"Well," Teddy says, "we're not doctors, we're with Welfare."

"You be sure to tell my mama, so she can claim mah body." Jack starts crying again. "I don' wanna lay down in the basement like a sack of coal!" Stares past Leo's shoulder at the window. "They tryin' to keep me nervous an' discouraged an' frightened. When the lights out they come inside. Want me t' join 'em. Sometimes they don't even wait for the lights! Already stole mah face."

"How'd that happen?" Teddy asks.

"Don' know! Woke up at my mama's two days ago

an' it was gone. Ain' had a drink for four days. How you think mah kids feel, they daddy ain' got a face? Mah brothers won' talk t' me. Then I sits around makin' this cracklin' sound in mah chest—no wonder nobody can't stan' me."

"How can your fathe be gone when I can thee it?"

"'S all numb! Can't feel a thing. Jus' ain' there no more. Ahm heartsick and discouraged! Fail mah children so bad —*uh, uh, uh!*— can't bear the sight of 'em, *uh, uh, uh!* —so miserable mah chest is cracklin'!"

"Well," Teddy says, "we'll come back on Monday."

"Jack," Leo says, "maybe that crackling's just your pneumonia."

"Nossir. It's *everything.*"

"Didya ever think you might be an alcoholic?" Leo asks.

"Sure I am! Ahm always seein' an' hearin' things. But I ain' had a drink in four days. Seein' an' hearin' things right now, tha's why Ahm here. I don't *want* t' be here, Ahm a steady worker—stockboy fo' Pioneer supermarket on Amsterdam. But I can't drink no more'n a third of a pint of wine. Won't nothin' go down anymore."

"Ever try A.A.?" Leo asks.

"Ain' nothin' t' be done. He comin' with that icepick."

Teddy slips out a W.S. 11. "Jack, would ya thign thith for me? It means ya don't have to pay for your thtay here."

Jack's hands rise shaking. "I can't write." Eyes the window in terror. "Don't let 'em turn off the light tonight, doctor! Ahm gonna die!"

Sleet boosts the panes, rattling, a high flowing scream that doesn't die. Jack Daniels twists, agitated hands hiding his turned face, brown eyes burning at the frosted window. Howling garble, he scrambles off the bed's far side, sweatdrops flying, falls to the floor and crawls out of the room, whining with terror, looks both ways fast down the hall, then creeps mumbling toward the locked entrance.

"Hey, Jack, what'th the matter?" Teddy beside him. "Nobody's chathin' you!"

"I gotta go now or I never get outta here!"

"Come on, get up."

"Let 'im alone," a young Spanish woman says in quick clear English. "He's got a political right to crawl if he wants to. You bastards tear my ass. Why don'tcha go back to the C.I.A. where ya came from?"

A skinny black with muscled arms and Afro raked straight up says, "Watch yo' ass with her, mothers. She got a Black Belt an' throw you both all the way down this hall. She already cream me once."

Leo-Teddy squats by Jack. Leo says, "There's nothin' to fear, Mr. Daniels."

"Ahm gon' die in here." Jack slips against the wall, tears falling through sweat. "Ahm gon' die! Ahm gon' die!"

A flame prickles Leo's spine, Dr. Deer passes through him, and his voice wells, "Jack, you have eternal life. Hear me? You'll never die."

The Spanish woman knocks the guard's window. "These goons are attacking a patient!"

A small black guard in hornrim bifocals and green jumper comes in with Miss Hanson, the ward's elderly head nurse about whom Leo-Teddy's warned.

"What's goin' on in here?" Her auburn wig, gimlet eyes bending toward Jack. *"You?* You get back into bed and stay there, buster—or it's *phfft* back onto the street."

Jack stares in terror at Nurse Hanson's ugly blue corpse. "Ah wants t' go!"

"Ha! You're too sick to ride an elevator," she says.

"These C.I.A. finks are hounding him," the Spanish woman says crisply.

"Tuck him in," Nurse Hanson tells the guard. "Who are you guys?"

"We're financial invethtigators with Welfare." Teddy holds back his tequila cloud. Lips prim over lost bridge, fighting his lisp.

"Christ," she says. "Where's Jack McCarthy?"

"Takin' a week off in San Juan," Leo says, churning out charm.

"Well, I'm givin' that Sophrosyne a piece of my mind. I can't have *financial investigators* upsetting my ward."

"We don't invethtigate anything!"

"Gosh, no," Leo says.

"We're abtholutely *againtht* financial rethponthibility."

"Ya don't say!" Nurse Hanson says.

Leo says, "We just try to get the nearest relative to come in and sign a form sayin' the patient can't pay. We don't bug *anybody*."

"We give it away!" Teddy smiles a primrose.

"Give what away?"

Teddy swallows. "The hothpital's thervithes. The thity pays part and the thtate pays part."

"That means *I'm payin'*," Nurse Hanson says. "I wish you'd never explained it to me. If you two *investigators* are finished in here, please be so kind as to disappear. *Phht!*"

Teddy measures his stack of S.R.675's, peeved.

"*Vamoose!* But don't go away mad—you guys may be in the right place!"

Going down Leo-Teddy meets Anne Quist with her clipboard full of completed 675's. Smiling Swede, her blonde bun over their heads, the first girl ever to discuss with them frankly the power of marijuana orgasm.

"How ya doin'?" she asks down her bosom at their eye level.

"We were just chewed out for invading the flight deck," Leo says.

"Jutht doin' our job!" Teddy not breathing. "Watch out for that old biddy Hanthon."

"I never get psychos. I'm not sure I'd like it, I identify too much. Do they suffer a lot up there?"

"People thuffer everywhere. They jutht don't know it."

Leo touches her softly rounded hand, whispering, "I didn't know *I* was a suffering alcoholic until I got sober!"

"Oh you poor man." Her hand lights on his arm.

"I'm all right," Leo says. "Ya only suffer when you can't put your energies to good use."

"How wise of you! That's wonderful." Brown eyes admire him to his depths. "And *you'll* be all right someday too," she tells Teddy.

Teddy swallows, says nothing. The elevator ride is pleasurable, fulfilling, sensuous, dry-mouthed, the calm before the paycheck. He nudges Leo as the door opens and Anne heads toward Admissions record room. "Hey," he draws her aside, "I'm gettin' an ounthe of Panamanian tonight."

"Panamanian's overrated, don't you think? I like Persian but it's so fucking hard to get."

Teddy asks hoarsely, "But you do get it?"

"My boyfriend's a Muslim."

"How 'bout thome coffee? You can pay."

"I'm sorry, I can't. Some interns have invited me downstairs for a dissection—a woman. Like to come? It's in five minutes. Wear your white coats though."

"*Agh!*" Leo says. "I'm married. I think we'll skip it."

"I dig, man," Anne says, brown eyes concerned, her hand stroking Leo's. She binds Teddy's eyes in X-ray study. "And I'm sure *you* respect Leo's sensitivity."

"Like my own," Teddy says. "You plannin' on marriage?"

"Not unless I get pregnant. I take an awful lot of chances that way—I'm too susceptible. But birth control pills dry up my period and I miss it. I like to feel a healthy, productive rhythm in my body and not have my ovaries pinched off by chemicals. Maybe I'm too emotional—but you wouldn't want a vasectomy, would you? Wouldn't you feel half dead? Seriously?"

"I've never conthidered the thportth model."

"You'd be a zombie." She hurries off, pitched forward, bent to her 675's.

Teddy arms the wall to keep from fainting. "That'd be a thteam fitting!—right? Cunt all over, no matter where you touch. Look at my hand shake. I need a boothter shot. Think our checkth are ready?"

Glide into Welfare, stand in a short line at Sophrosyne's desk as younger caseworkers come out studying their deductions. *"Screwed again!"* littlegirl Cynthia mutters, smooth childface fiery, "When're those dogfuckers downtown gonna learn how to make out a check?" Leo-Teddy smiling coolly, hearts racing in dry heat as her yellowblue eyes flash at them. Cynthia, let me take you away from all this, Teddy thinks. Feels a draft in his rear—sly fingers uncover a six-inch tear in his seam. *"Thonofabitch!* I been walkin' around with a hole in my pantth."

"Y'mean in your crotch?"

"Not those wear-holes, I mean on the theat! Muthta thplit fallin' off the train."

Shuffle forward. Anne scoots in behind them, planting herself with a pounding sigh. Teddy casually clasps his clipboard against his backside, twists toward her and asks chokingly, "Don't happen t' have a thafety pin, do you?"

"Not on me, Teddy. May be one in my drawer. Want me to look?"

"MMM!"

"Hold my place."

Sophrosyne smiles at her twin subjects, her dark Haitian mouth drawn up duchesslike under powerful cheekbones. She thumbs her checks slowly, lovingly, savoring the identity of each staffmember, his salary, his time in service, his work-aura. Setting Leo's check aside, she traces her pencil down a yellow pad to his name, looks up with her full being pursed on her sandy lips.

"How far you behin' in your caseload? Just a estimate, if you please."

"About forty-five interviews."

"Forty-five! *Mm-mm.* How you expec' your clients to know what benefits they available if you don't get to see 'em while they still in the hospital? Don't you think it be wiser to get to 'em before they leave?"

"Well, some only stay a day. And I inherited half this caseload, ma'am, when Mr. Troutt resigned."

"But is you really *trying* to get out to them wards?"

"I sure am! But the more time I spend in the wards, the fewer 675's I can get done at my desk."

"Maybe you isn't dividing your time prudently. Maybe you should work the wards mornings and do your write-ups in th' afternoon. I realize you under a handicap but you really *mus'* keep your caseload current."

"I work very hard. Some of these darn patients left three months ago and can't be reached except by field visit."

"Well, your review comin' up, you know. And your caseload is got to be up-to-date."

"—I *suppose* I could take 'em home! . . ."

She smiles at his thoughtfulness, hands him his check, enters 45 on her list, snaps Teddy's check beside her pad. "How far *you* behin'?"

Teddy swallows held breath, considers his stagnant caseload. "About thixty," he lies, face bloating.

"Sixty? *Sixty!*"

"Well." Teddy coughs. "Motht everybody's behind eighty or ninety."

"Sixty. *Mm-mm!*"

"Thometimes ya don't get the full interview, ma'am. The patient'th groggy, or thleepin' and when ya get back, he's gone!" She says nothing, painfully weighing his uselessness. "And the Thpanish are impothible—a lot of 'em jutht off the plane from Puerto Rico, don't thpeak a word of English, don't *intend* to, and don't even read or write Thpanish!"

"But you always can get a X on their WS-11, can't you? That's our state aid! State will accep' just a X with your name as witness. Can't you get just a X?"

Teddy nods, faking faith in his power to collect X's. Sophrosyne sees no one behind Leo-Teddy, then eyes Teddy as a field not worth the planting—though he is her tenant. "Step closer," she says. "I have a complaint from Nurse Hanson of Psychiatrics that you been drinking on her ward and upsetting patients."

Fear glows in their band, charges their stomachs. Teddy longs to escape into her turkey breasts.

"I have spoke to you about your drinking—whenever you gentlemen walk by my door I know it without looking up. Look at this S.R.675," lifting Teddy's form from her in-box, "I can't even read it." Teddy glances at yesterday's smeared scrawls—a sign of genius, Dr. Deer says, though Teddy's nerves also recall Colonel John Hokum chewing him out at the bakery. "How can I send this downtown for review? Don't you think you could practice a little moderation in your penmanship? Am I *clear?*"

Teddy crimson. "We were *not* drinking in 13B or anywhere elthe in thith hothpital—that'th jutht crazy! As for —I had a beer for lunch because I'd brought an exthtremely dry cheese thandwich—*one* beer, that'th the truth. *But*—if it offends her I'll cut out even a beer for lunch. Nurthe Hanthon's an elderly lady who thinkth one molecule of beer—"

"—smell like a wet turkey," Sophrosyne says. "Half her patients alcoholics! And you go up there all filled with beer fumes? You gentlemen are my responsibility, I have to speak up for you whenever a hospital staffmember complains. How can I defen' a cloud of beer fumes? You get yourselves together, this my las' warning. Now would you go down to clinic and relieve Mr. Coeur so he can get paid? And mind *your* penmanship!"

Leo-Teddy steps backward into Anne, Teddy's clipboard spills to the floor. Anne kneels to help the twins, handing Teddy a blue diaper pin as his seam splits with a fartburble of leaking wine. Teddy, beating purple, jaw tight on waves of suffering, snatches up his clipboard to mask his threadbare crotch, split seam. "Thankth," he whispers, measuring the pin's big prong, "think thith'll reach the heart?"

She pats his hand.

"Body'll be in the men's room."

Into the numbing mess and decay of the men's toilet and shooting gallery. Teddy pulls down his pants in a wide open stall, wipes and wipes himself, pins his seam together while a Spanish teenager with a filthy cast on his arm leans nodding against a wall, cigarette smoke spiralling up his cast, face stiffened in half-death.

"That gives me an idea." Teddy lights a joint. "Lucky ya can't be fired for farting."

"Worried about your image?"

"With Thophrosyne? That old cunt. Ya remember the time she rubbed her boobies up my arm?" Teddy swallows smoke; Leo drags deep.

"I thought she fell tryin' to get around us."

"Ha! I'll get her alone in her offithe thometime. She'll melt. Jutht grab her on the boobs and look hungry! I been thinkin' about givin' her a phonecall at home. Latht drag."

Leo drags, wets his thumb, pinches the ember. Leo-Teddy savors his held breath, watches the junkie nod. "Feel anything?" Leo gasps.

"King Kong!" Teddy gasps, whetting his moist nose on his shoulder. Studies his nose pores in the cankered sink-mirror, wets a towel with steaming water, scrubs his nose bulb. "Oily pores!" he complains.

"Mmmmm!" Leo sighs. "Toasty!"

Flow down to clinic's tiny Welfare cubicle. Gerard-Philippe Coeur, thin, darkcurled, eloquent-eyed, looks up from the Puerto Rican mother and babe he's interviewing in Spanish.

"Thtill on the firtht page?" Teddy glances at the 675. "Thophie's waiting to lay you. But hold fire, we're gonna zap acroth the thtreet and cash our checkth."

"Have one for me," Coeur says.

"Thith is the good life, ma'am!" Teddy winks at the PR mother. *"La vita bueno!"*

Leo-Teddy gallops down the side-entrance, wades into freezing wind off the East river, passes a forsaken playground to Nipsy's basement check-cashing service. Nipsy, the smoothfaced young Sicilian manager, looks up, chewing gum behind bulletproof glass. "Hey, howsa moosic comin'!" Rubbing his belly as they sign their checks. "I'm waitin' for you guys t' hit a big one. How ya doin'?—gettin' any? Must be *somethin'*, both you guys goin' down together." Nipsy sits back on his stool, withholding their money. "Someday I spring for a fifth and we get together back here and you tell me all about your 'adventures.' *Whoo,*" he shakes his hand, "I wanna hear that! Someday you guys'll both shit jackpots. *Hey, honey,*" he tells his wife, "here's those Siamese twins, say hello. Look at those beards. *Va-va-va-voom!* I bet you two muffdivers are somethin' ta see in action! Sloppy, huh?"

"We're pretty crude," Leo says.

"Real anteaters," Teddy agrees, counting bills. Teddy reads the Pay Your Con Ed Bill Here sign, touches the red Con-Ed turn-off warning in his breast pocket, grunts "Fuck it—*Monday*. I may need the cash thith weekend."

Passing Tiger's, Teddy pauses for a double. Lemon, salt. *Thaffron rithe! thaffron rithe! luvs dat yaller thaffron rithe!* Sings senselessly, then sobers up at once, playing to their mirror-image with a papal cloud of sainthood over his head.

Gerald-Philippe's nose twitches in his cramped cubicle. "Something's in the air!"

"Sure is!" Teddy says merrily. Slips a half-smoked joint into Coeur's shirtpocket. "Hit the shooting gallery on your way back. There's thtill a double order of chop thuey in that roach."

Coeur sniffs his toasty pocket, smiles deeply enriched, claps a faint hand onto Teddy's shoulder. "This truly *is* payday—bless you, Boris-Bela. The new *Dr. Strange* is in the middle drawer!"

"Take your time," Leo says. "Drink life to the full."

"Give 'er a jab for uth."

Boris-Bela forces a second folding chair behind the desk, beckons to a waiting black with a dishtowel around her head.

"Ah cain't make it in there," she moans.

Twins squeeze behind their desk, Teddy on his diaper pin. "*Try,*" he suggests. The thin black seems stuck to her chair, arms open between her knees, long horseface dead, eyes wandering with token life. Leo-Teddy lifts her forlorn body to the camp chair by his desk. Her eyes raise, slimegreen and speckled, haunted by some forgotten memory of spawning or breeding.

Leo eyes her pale-banded lips. "Hi! I'm Leo, he's Teddy. What's your name?"

". . . Wummin . . ."

"Wummin? How dya spell it?"

Shakes her head, her dark coat shoulder gray with flakes.

"Can you thpell your name?"

Long, dead stare.

"What's your first name?" Leo asks.

"The habla inglés? What'th your addreth?"

Stupor.

"What seems to be wrong?" Leo asks.

". . . Wuhms . . ."

"Thquiffo?" Teddy sniffs. "Maybe she came in for dandruff—that'th the wortht cathe I've ever theen."

"Fell down," she says.

"When'd that happen?" Leo asks.

Shakes her head. "Three weeks ago . . . in my 'partment. Hit mah head . . ."

"Hurt yourself bad?" Leo asks.

Nods, holds up her middle finger and thumb for wide measure. "Hit mah head open . . ."

"And ya haven't had any treatment?" Leo asks. "Why didn't you come down earlier, honey?"

". . . Couldn't move . . ."

Teddy's bound by her dandruff wriggling in the draft. Takes *Dr. Strange Master of the Mystic Arts Comics* out of Coeur's drawer. "How'd ya hit your head, thweetie?"

". . . Drinkin' . . . Made up mah mind, get dewuhmified or kill yo'self off. Wuhms in mah stomach, in mah mouth . . . *all* mah organs . . ."

"Poor thirculation! Her nerve-ends are goin' numb."

"Don't worry, ma'am!" Leo says. "We've got great drugs these days, all sorts of special treatments. With penicillin, even syphilis isn't much worse 'n a head cold."

"Ain' got no dose," she sighs and unwraps her head towel. White flakes shower from her wound. Leo-Teddy jumps back, shuddering, Teddy gasping, holding his breath and his stomach.

"Maybe we better get you down to the emergency ward," Leo says.

"Cain't move."

Shaking, Leo phones Emergency for an intern and

wheelchair. Teddy groans, stomach lifting in slow waves of lemon acidity. "Tell 'em right away!"

Leo groans, his bones shipwrecked. "Dr. Bowerman'll be right here, ma'am!"

Teddy grips his palms at heaven. "Hit the braketh, please!"

"You ever been a patient here before?" Leo asks.

". . . Don't know . . . Maybe deetoxication . . ."

"Give 'er the rateth. Get that *Xth!*" Teddy croaks.

Leo breathless, choking. "Uh, the rates at this hospital are fifty-three-fifty a day—everybody pays the same. If you have radium treatment or gold put into your veins or heart surgery or anything at all, the rate is fifty-three-fifty a day. Can you pay that?"

She looks silently at the ice-howl at the window. Leo-Teddy pulsing.

"Fine!" Leo says. "I don't want you to pay a damned cent—you be my guest! Just sign your name on this line. This means the state'll pay. *This* line."

She grips his ballpoint, staring at WS-11.

"Just make an X."

"—That ain' mah name—"

"Then write your name."

Teddy trembles. "She don't know her name. Hell, write anything, ma'm."

Surprise rounds her eyes as she turns from Leo to Teddy, her heart seeming to give a bound of interest in the twins. Licks her lips, leans forward breathing heavily. She pulls out a fresh bar of Ivory soap and lays it on Dr. Strange's occult mistress. "Ah wants to take a bath! Inside an' outside. Write that down."

"Sure thing," Teddy says, eying her gray shoulders.

"D'ya know your birth date?" Leo asks. She shakes her head. "Well, d'ya have any friends or relatives?"

She nods. *"Sixty."*

"I see," Leo says, hearing the intern approach whistling.

"Ahm sixty years old! Put that down."

"Well, what have we here!" the intern says, all tall sparkling impish innocence and curly dark hair. "I've brought you a taxi, ma'am. Ready for a ride?"

"You the doctor gonna gimme a bath?"

"Heck, yes. I'm your man. Shall we get into this wheelchair?"

"Cain't move. Take mah soap."

"Hm! What's the trouble besides B.O.?"

"Look under the towel," Teddy says, his eyes drilling into the deskblotter.

"You mah doctor?" she asks as he lifts her head towel.

"You can call me Noble," he says. "Ah ha, head wound. Beautiful!"

Under matted dark gray hair, her skull is split and dented, a teacup-size hole seething with tiny, diving, capering maggots. Her green eyes question Leo-Teddy as if her spine is exposed.

"Lucky for you you have some flies in your house," Noble says. "Fly larvae are benign, you know," he tells Leo-Teddy.

"I can't look," Teddy's drained white.

"Well, that takes some gettin' used to. They only eat dead flesh. We're happy to see 'em—they leave the most perfectly granulated wound you can hope for, just swab and bandage. Time was when surgeons kept 'em on hand to put *into* a wound. Practice has been discontinued, you know, ha ha. Not very efficient."

"Less expensive, though," Leo says.

"Hey, you're right about that! What could be cheaper than a fly?" He claps his hands eagerly. "Well, shall we get these frisky fellers outta there, ma'm?"

"Thee if anything's left," Teddy mutters.

"Nothin' fancy!" she says, handing him her soap. "Ivory's all I can afford." Noble wheels her out, humming. "Thank you, gentlemens, I will pay later."

"Thank you," Leo tells Noble.

"Anytime! Happy to oblige."

Leo-Teddy sighing at each other.

"Thith is my life! I felt those fuckin' worms right under my thkin!"

Leo looks out at a line of clients.

"Let the pithheads wait. Okay? *Right,* man. I need tequila. Let'th go."

A young Spanish girl with baby waits in their doorway for her interview.

"Let's wait for Gerard," Leo says.

"I can't thit here. I'm afraid there'll be worms wherever I lay my hand. I jutht wanna bang my head againtht the gong and thlowly thcream t'death! Ya know, *you* are jutht too weird for words. How can you thit here tho

calmly, tho *coldly,* not feelin' anything? Huh? Let'th go." Teddy looks up at the girl. *"The hable inglés?"*

"Un poco, senor." She smiles graciously.

"No importante." Teddy rises in bliss toward Tiger's. "Have thith chair, mother, the man'll be right back."

She backs off from Teddy's eager eyes.

"Have a theat!" Teddy gives her *Dr. Strange.* "Here's a visual aid."

Stonebleak snow whips the playground, harsh wind molding kneebones. "Whoo, do I need tequila! Gotta get me thome new threads before I freeze my balls. I thpeak literally. Why not hit a Harlem pawnshop for thuits tonight?"

"You're gettin' your horn!"

"Maybe I'll thave a bundle and con Jumbo inta gettin' it."

"Phone 'er up for macaroni and potatoes, huh?"

Leo-Teddy draws stools together, Teddy crying, "Hit me with a triple, Tiger!" Beams at the bountiful tequila bottle on the pretty bar.

"All out," Tiger says, tossing the empty below the bar. "Somethin' else?"

"Ginger ale," Leo says.

Teddy droops, slack, lost, razored. "No more *tequila?"* Tragic eyes rove the whole pretty shelf, then Teddy stands, bitterly scanning the lower shelves of backup bottles. "UNH!" he grunts, lifeblood running down his stool. "Thith is a blow."

"What'll it be?" Tiger asks.

"Gee, don't you *thtock* tequila? That'th my favorite, Tiger."

Tiger waits under ring pics of himself as middleweight contender, handsome, redblond, nose, eyes, ears faintly swollen, forever. He shrugs. "We don't get that trade."

"I drink it. God, ya thtock Fockink gin and that'th a thpecialty item."

"I got that case at a discount." Tiger glances at three hatted men muttering in a dim corner. "Let's not argue," he rasps.

"Triple vodka and lemon. Uh, hundred proof."

Tiger sets up Teddy with a salt shaker and whole lemon in wedges, watching Teddy sniff at his shredded wet kleenex. "Murderouth potht-nasal drip," Teddy sighs.

He pays for Leo, snorting at Leo's glass. "How d'ya drink that garbage day after day?"

Leo squints at the Fockink label. "Ain't easy."

"Boy!" Teddy laps salt from his fist, sucks wedge, belts half his vodka. *"Ahh!*—that really does hit the thpot." His eyes water. "But it'th not tequila." Eyes the Fockink label. "Remember Thtella's collection of miniatures in the diningroom? Raspberry liqueur, banana, crème de cacao, crème de menthe—"

"—peach and apricot," Leo says.

"—yeah, an' Thouthern Comfort, Lemon Hart Jamaica rum—what a shelf she had!—"

"—before we got into it—"

"—talk about thrawberry fields forever, it was like a thoda fountain with a fantathtic kick in every flavor."

Leo's nerves lift in a powerful wave of homefeelings for alcohol, a cell-deep blush for the past.

"I only wish—"

"What?"

"I wasn't givin' my first talk tomorrow night! Whattaya think I wish?"

"Idiot. Dya think *I'd* thqueal? It'th nithe t' have you as a compath for gettin' home thtraight, but I could give that up. Go ahead, have one."

"I don't want a drink, I want a drunk. I just wish—I'll stick to pot."

"Your choithe."

"The fuckin' pot don't reach me like it used to, though! I like that disorienting, synergistic high with the lush boosting the tea. That's a bitch t' give up! Let's get some LSD at Dr. Sunshine's tomorrow night."

"Tonight! Why wait?"

"No, tomorrow night I gotta have a clear head. Maybe I'll have one joint on the way to the meeting—just for the lift, so I can belt out my story. But—I think I could handle one beer right now. Maybe have another in three months, so I don't get a habit." Leo eyes the clock for months. "Maybe early Spring . . . Smell should be gone by the time I get home."

"Wanda can't tell *who* she's thmellin', you know that."

"Oh God, one beer. Just one bottle."

"Have a Canadian ale. More kick. Pep up the pot."

"Damn good idea." Leo's will cuts loose, a horse bolting downhill, he orders an ale, watches Tiger pour. Lifts the glass, focused utterly on the brisk bubbles. Memoryless, guiltless, remorseless, sips off half the glass, sighs "AHHH!" right down to his soles, refills to the breaking brim.

Teddy, gaptooth grin. "How's that?"

"Instant hope," Leo whispers. "I feel *good!*" Lifting cells prick open, the soft punch of happiness, a brightening heavy soak of beautiful feelings. "Boy, one sip! 'S already goosing the tea. Floating! *Goot, goot!*—But one's enough."

"Ya know what A.A. thays. *No guilt* about drinkin'—it'th a wathte of energy. Drinking's the natural thtate of the alcoholic."

"Oh, it's a disease, it's not a matter of moral choice." Leo grins. "My God, that's good. If I were an alcoholic, I'd be in trouble."

"Don't feel guilty." Teddy gnaws his filtertip.

"I don't! Feel good. *Sprach Zarathustra!* Well—back to work!"

"I mean don't let thith little indithcretion interfere with your talk tomorrow night."

"Far from it! I feel a lot less tense already. Probably speak all the better—think of all those A.A.'s who can't drink even one beer and are committed to blind acceptance. But I'm an artist and I have to know both sides of the question. Right?"

Step into street stript of its masks. "Eureka," Teddy whispers. Wonderbearing winter day, snow lathering heartbreak playground, high lifebush of tree limbs mirrored in Leo-Teddy's longing nerves, the high hospital haloed with humanity, Himalayan snows winding twilightyellow windows.

"This really is eternal life," Leo says.

"Welcome home."

"Oh I'm not drinkin' again. But I just learned that I don't have to sit in any goddamned eternal fear about one drink now and then when I *need* it."

"Right. I could fathe anything today. *Is that Jack McFin!*"

"Where!"

Race to the corner. Jack's image gone like Marley's ghost.

"Couldn't've been him, he's in Pennthylvania."

"I didn't see the guy."

Back at Coeur's cubicle. "How was Thophie?"

"Like cold mutton. Your left-wing Lucky was better."

Leo rifles his clipboard. "Let's clear up this damn Delgado 675. Bastard ain't signed out and ain't in his ward. Maybe he's down in the icebox."

A three-year-old wails beside his Spanish mother, his lips pulled down in tragedy, a rubber nipple strung around his neck. "Shit, that little cockthucker's thtill at the easy part. Thuck up, kid!"

Leo eyes the squawking hall through beautiful blue veils. "Hey! how about a pill that moves you t' the country instantly?"

"A gassuh!" Teddy grins, slapping five on Leo's upturned palm.

"DREAMY, DREAMY CHINATOWN!"

Tippytoe downstairs to morgue, shuffle fingersnapping after an intern with a small, shiny roundbladed power saw. Their eyes follow him into a passing basement lab, catch a fat starknaked white body on a distant table off the dissection room, breadmountain belly so mounded her breasts can't be seen past the yellow soles facing Leo-Teddy. Pleasurehigh falling fast, glide past a long room with a huge smooth wall like a refrigerated filing cabinet, into the morgue's record room.

Leo pulls out the D tray as Teddy tightens his belt, harassed. "God, all that fat. She couldn't've died of fat poisoning?"

"Hm," Leo says. "Three Luis Delgadoes died here! But none admitted this year."

"Why don't we go back on thafflower oil?"

"Go ahead. But that's doin' it the hard way."

"Look, I got a bigger build, that'th why I'm heavier than you."

Leo eyes Teddy's gut. "You could use a few shirtbuttons, Ollie."

Noble comes humming into the record room with a male nurse and tells the attendant, "Delivery needs a toe tag."

Leo-Teddy at the doorway, sheeted feet lie on the end of a roller table. Fear charges his spines. Leo coughs hard. "Noble! that's not Delgado, is it, from TB?"

"Sorry," Noble says. "It's a psycho."

"Thanks. We can't find this sonofabitch Delgado. Musta sneaked out in pajamas."

"Lousy day for it," Noble says.

"Maybe his thirtht overcame him. Pthyco? That'th our ward for two weekth—maybe we got thith guy's 675. Who's thith?"

"Jackson Daniels," Noble says. "He ain't signin' anything, fellas."

"We were just talkin' with him!" Leo cries.

"Can't be the thame guy. What'd he die of?"

"Don't know," Noble says. "Nurse came in to give him Demerol and he was cold. Looks like he died of fright." Noble smiles at the cool, vein-ravaged morgue attendant benignly. "I *closed* his eyes, sweetie."

"That's your problem," the attendant says.

Teddy looks up at the clock, shoves D tray closed. "I'm through. I've had it for today. Let'th fold our tent and thteal off like the A-rabs."

"It's payday—Sophie's on the lookout!"

"Goddamnit, I don't care if we do get fired! We're too good for thith job."

"Yeah? This is the first *professional* job we ever had."

Leo-Teddy in the hall. The fat woman's table gone.

"Chritht. They're in there thawing her up right now. Maybe thith isn't the thame Jack Daniels."

Leo lifts the sheet, lowers it, his eyes closing. Sighs loudly, shaking his head hard. "Okay," he whispers, "let's blow."

"Eternal life," Teddy sneers, a rubbery gargoyle smile on his heavy lips, fleshy cheeks. "Ya had more thenthe when you were fourteen, Leo! *You're really thlippin'!*"

Anne Quist skids around the corner, thuds flying into the dissection room, slow breasts lifting in a ghostly aquarium.

Derek, the exseminarian chairman of Village Open Discussion, reads the A.A. Preamble, then introduces Leo to the smokebound roomful of coffeedrinking alcoholics. Wanda knits an eight-foot purple scarf for Leo.

"My name is Leo and I am an alcoholic. Mostly. Sometimes it slips my mind."

Teddy grins, his front pearlywhites absent, his ego ready to beg marriage from the Queen of Sheba, breaks open *The Brothers Karamazov* on the small table and begins reading, ignoring Leo, floridly. Words wash senselessly on the page, phrases twisting like metal filings drawn in circles by a magnet. Clicks his felttip over a fogbound nickel tablet, inspirations fastfading.

"Before I came into A.A. I was a two-fisted, souped up, barhopping, girlhopping, trumpet-playing, obsessive-compulsive insane maniac with my both eyes fastened squarely on the next drink and the next bosom—and my two feet planted squarely in midair. Or four feet. I was a compulsive eater, a guy who'd run anywhere to satisfy a craving—*zap!* The outside of my icebox was a solid mass of female breasts I'd clipped from magazines—and other organs! If I saw a picture of a martini in a subway, I had to have one. If I thought of roasting a sixteen-pound suckling pig, I'd go up to Spanish Harlem and buy one, have it roasted for me in a Puerto Rican restaurant, then take it home and *eat it*—or take it to a girl-friend's house for her birthday, a huge, stuffed burnt pig, total garlic. My whole life's been a series of compulsions and gratifications. I'm a sort of tube of endless desires, gulping down something I call life. I see a bare hip in a movie and I fill with anxieties because I can't have it. My will power melts before a pizza parlor, a delly, a bar or a liquor store—despite an obsessive desire to better myself! my extraordinary Puritanism. It takes a Puritan to be so locked into the longings of this baby mammoth I have inside me. Life is short, my stomach's bottomless—I mean I gotta have whatever I want! I'm a pleasurholic.

"I been suckin' my thumb, suckin' bottles, suckin', suckin', suckin' since I was born! This somehow carried me into trumpet-playing with a dream of becoming independently wealthy. I like music that's UP, that's gratifying, that makes me feel tremendous. I play the hifi so loud the floor trembles. How *go-o-ood* Baby Leo feels goofing along with Bruckner or Louis at a hundred-thousand decibels all through the purple midnight and into those wonderfully elastic late hours where all the city quiets down and I can stay awake with all my cells alive with good feelings like lyin' in a fragrant tubfull of warm maple syrup—doped to the gills!

"The message is that I'm an addict of my beautiful feelings. I just can't seem to grow up outta the crib! Show me a kid with a heroin problem and I identify—though I never liked downers. I like opium and pot. I don't know what you people think but I think that anything that keeps me from drinkin' is terrific. For me, marijuana's perfect, my grass crutch, it satisfies me, it takes my addiction, it derails my desire to drink. So I'm all for it. Other folks take Valium and Librium and vitamins—I take vitamins too—they take Demerol and all sorts of sedations and ups and down, and *I* take pot—which keeps my ass outta the bars.

"So I started drinkin' when I was thirteen. My mother used to keep a livingroom display cabinet of miniature bottles of the world's greatest booze and Teddy and I—uh, my brother *drinks,* but I don't take his inventory, if he ever decides he's an alcoholic that'll be up to him since alcoholism's a self-diagnosed disease where only the victim can say whether or not he believes he has it— . . . Well, my mother's miniatures, we used to get into 'em and pretty soon we'd drunk a couple hundred bottles of fruit liqueurs and gin, bourbon, vodka, rye, it was a world survey of distilleries. People with hardhitting horror stories cringe when I tell 'em that for years my big drink, aside from burgundy, was vodka and root beer, half an' half. I was ashamed of it. At restaurants or at parties, they never had *root beer* but I'd ask for it, humiliating myself. Sheer abasement—but for five or six years rooty-tooty was my passion. Passion? It was lust! I'd walk miles for a gallon of oldfashioned root beer to mix by the pitcherful with vodka. At any party just lemme make my pitcher of rooty-tooty and the hostess could forget about me—I'd bring my own root beer and vodka and a big windmill drinkin' mug that held a full pint. I finally got over that when I discovered Bloody Marys and got hooked on Tabasco and Worcestershire sauces.

"My God, my time's flyin'! This is my virgin talk, so bear with me! I'm happy to be speakin', I remember my first meeting down at the Workshop. A sixty-two-year old nurse was tellin' her story, I couldn't identify a bit, but somethin' about her had me running out on the street three times to bawl. I felt the chains fallin' off—such a tremendous relief that I no longer had to know where my next drink was comin' from! No more blood banks, no more rip offs and unpaid debts to my mother and my wife and my friends. I don't worry about the drink I'm drinkin' but about the next one—should it be a double-vodka for the road? a six-pack for the nighthours? What about tomorrow's gallon of red, Mussolini's revenge? *I'm freed!* But I'll be frank. When I sit at these meetings I don't understand half what's said—The Steps are still gibberish to me, it's hard to believe that all that banality has somethin' to do with *me.* Or The Big Book, some of the worst writing I've ever read. Anyway, people here rattle on and on in a fog—of course, maybe I'm in the fog, ha ha. Then when it's my turn to speak, I been polishin' up my comment like the Hope diamond but a red passion fills my head and I don't know what I'm sayin' until after I finally shut up. I tellya, I stare hard and I *listen hard,* but it's like tryin' to lift hundred-pound weights with my mind to discover what half of the people here are talkin' about, that's the brassnuts truth.

"Oh, hell. I'm an American boy! I was raised to drink. Independence, I learned it in the first grade, swore allegiance. The idea that I should *stop drinkin'* goes against every damn thing I ever been taught. Don't give up the drink! Fight to the last drop! Baby Leo will not be stopped! Selfishness is my most important possession. Anybody suggesting I don't drink is puttin' a knife deep into my individuality. Somehow, I guess, I gotta reeducate myself. My first couple of months in A.A. I could *not* get the message. When I drink—when I break the seal and heft that full bottle to my nose and sniff that silky bourbon, the anticipation's incredible, and what the sadist gets outta layin' on the lash, or the masochist gets outta the whip biting in, *I* get outta the first drink. My whole nervous system lights up, instant chemistry, I feel pleasure bone-deep. So when I came into A.A. I was quite relieved when a new product hit the market—low calorie diet beer, just a trace of alcohol, but essentially I'd be on the wagon. Well, I was in A.A. two months before it got through to me that diet beer lowered my resistance to regular beer—when diet beer wasn't available quite often—and to hard booze. I have not had a drink of hard booze in ninety days—"

Teddy nods, vouching for Leo.

"—or diet beer! *Or* Bulmer's Woodpecker Cider—that's five-and-one-half percent alcohol, eleven-proof, no different from wine, but I was on that for three weeks after I came in because, frankly, it seemed innocuous. Then I heard it was gonna be DISCONTINUED!—it's imported from Britain—and I found myself runnin' through every borough in New York buyin' up the last bottles on the shelves. I was drinkin' so much cider my pores oozed a stale apple odor—I couldn't get off my bed, I stank of apples like an empty vinegar vat—or a full one. I was paralyzed to my couch, my whole apartment was deliquescing around me, I had fruit flies everywhere! When I admitted that I was obsessed I quit that shit. It was just like burgundy! I can't put my new A.A. spirit into my old alcoholic mind. Woodpecker cider and diet beer will not hold back the sea of alcoholic thinking I'm *tryin'* to build some dikes against. Sometimes I don't know if I'm having a dynamic recovery or a disaster but—

"I'm not gettin' my story out! Why'd I drink? I told you why—it's my *right* to drink. Social drinkers say alcoholics lack will power, but I find I'll go to any lengths to drink—if the whole Eighth Army was standin' on my arm I'd still get that drink up to my mouth. That's will power! I'm oversupplied. I'm a goddamned American boy and nothin's gonna stop me from exercisin' my rights—and justifying my daily suicide. I don't mind suicide but not every day!

"I drank because I come from drinkin' people and was surrounded by drunks all my childhood. My father drank and never worked—one day when we were six-months old, my mother was suckling us when Dad dropkicked her right on the chin and left a scar. My first stepfather was a German bastard who managed a three-story German beerbarn in Erie and whose favorite Sunday morning pastime was shootin' bear and woodchuck from his carwindow—and punchin' my mother in the eye. My second stepfather was an Irish sonofabitch who managed a fancy restaurant and whose hair had turned white in his twenties from the sheer enormity of his guilt. He was a mispracticing Catholic and always in mortal sin and if you mix mortal sin with alcohol you get an insane, wifebeating Irishman."

"A menathe!"

"I drank because I deserved to drink. I've been an ambulance driver and a private nurse and, uh, I'm on suspension from a hospital right now—I faked some academic credentials to get a job as social worker and it was discovered yesterday afternoon. Now we're waiting for a ruling. But I'm not gonna drink about that! Anyway, I handled some damned grisly victims, you can use your imagination, heart attacks in bathrooms, automobile fatalities with teeth stickin' outta the forehead—I mean *horror*—it tore my faith in life. I was an utter cynic year after black year, and I deserved to drink if it kept me from suicide, right?"

Teddy nods.

"Frankly, life was a pisscolored windowshade! For years I couldn't get outta this amber swamplight I was sloggin' through daily. I was a walking corpse. I needed BOOZE IN LARGE QUANTITIES just to work up a faint smile or croak of laughter. Unbearable! *just unbearable!* I deserved my booze! Meanwhile, everybody thought I was a happy, smiling musician."

Teddy nods ruefully.

"I got fears you never heard of. Bein' torn apart by a subway crowd—how do I manage that one? Just by not drinkin', I guess. My loneliness and sex misery've been indescribably tearful and slimy. I was not only decadent, I was actively decaying like a buggy manure pile. It's unrepeatable in mixed company! But most of all I deserve to drink because I'm a musician and composer. A hornplayer needs wind, lots of wind, and when you're depressed there ain't no wind—all ya get is a pinched squeak. When you walk around with every day like a death in the family, you aren't gonna be blowin' a trumpet! It just won't come. So you drink. And there's about a half hour of good spirits before the fog moves in. Then you have twenty-three-and-a-half hours to get through before you're clear enough for another great half-hour. *That's* the con job on myself I fight daily. My art demands that I lift my spirits. Alcohol is *so* productive. *Hah!* But the pure shit I've written while drinkin' would overflow a garbage scow. Whole scores, MUCK from start to finish! This dope is so beautiful when you're writing it, and such crud when you're sober. There's a song by Mahler from a Chinese poem, 'Always Be Drunken.' I can't. I just can't do it. I'll be dead. I gotta be intoxicated by sobriety.

"I'd like to say that since I've been sober I've been fantastically productive. I haven't. I've written and sold one song in the past three months—but I did the first sketch for that song on diet beer. Sure, I want an emotional bender to get me writin' again. I'm still fogged up! I'm on a pink cloud, feels great, but the music is *not comin'*. When Teddy snaps open a fresh gallon of red and his mug fills to the brim, and he *sips* and AHH'*s*, and shoots up on beautiful feelings, sure—that friggin' odor near knocks me over. Baby Leo cries, *I want! I want! I want!* And things get a lot goddamn worse than that too. One reason I stopped drinkin' was I was throwin' up blood regularly. For the first time in my life I'd come into some real money—my wife had a job, I'd got a job and *he'd* got a job, and we all got paid on the same Friday, I mean we were loaded, and we were walkin' over to O. Henry's bar for a beautiful evening of the best booze in the house —*at last* I had the freedom to drink as I wished, no more compulsive goddamn gallon wine, I was a gentleman drinker at last, gracious living had arrived, I'd survived the damn Mussolini red and blood banks and now I could drink in the manner I'd always deserved and, by God, just as we're goin' into O. Henry's I burst into tears, a hysterical cloudburst, couldn't stop it, and I collapsed over the roof of a parked car, sobbing. Howling self-pity. A tidal wave! At last I'd been granted my heart's desire —and my stomach perforated! Just as I found perfect freedom and largesse to kill myself on the finest booze in the city! And that was my breakthrough to A.A.—an ulcer. Just as my life became the most manageable it'd ever been, I had to quit booze.

"Stopping just when I was ready to start has been very hard on me. A.A.'s First Step, 'Admitted that we were powerless over alcohol—and that our lives had become unmanageable . . .' Well, it's just the reverse with me. My life's never been more manageable. So to a great degree, I have to admit I'm an alcoholic on a purely abstract level. I mean, it's nothing I believe deep down. And that's the truth. I may be sittin' here sober but I'm not at all convinced I'm an alcoholic.

"What's more, I feel that my sickness has been lifted. A while back, I awoke at eight one morning, my wife asleep beside me, Teddy snoring. And I was *floating* six inches off the bed on a sheet of blue fire and I could see these combers of blue light washin' toward me from the livingroom. I felt a bliss more powerful than sex. It lasted about ten minutes. And I saw a face of burning embers above me, lifting and falling over me. I was so blissful I nearly died of fright. I thought my heart would stop, it was fluttering like a pigeon dyin' in the gutter. My whole being filled with happiness and a voice told me, 'Your sickness has been lifted.' I've not had a desire to drink since then."

"Bullshit," Teddy says.

"Thank you all for sharing your experience, strength and—"

"Tell 'em about the demons."

Leo coughs. "All right, Teddy. I gotta be honest. For the past three weeks I've been havin' a terrible spiritual insight, which I can't shake. And this is simply that we're all demons. I'm a demon, Teddy's a demon, and so's every single person on earth, from the Pope down to the White Rose janitor. We're all strugglin' with our flesh. When I look at a person I see him depersonalized—I see his animal gums and his teeth and eyeballs in their sockets, every organ distinct and beastly. When I look at you out there, I see a room full of Frankenstein monsters. It's the same on the street, or lookin' at actors in movies—they're just erect monsters with herd responses mobilized on their faces. I see people mainly having stock responses to each other, a set of stock positions they defend or expose, stock laughter, stock comments, stock looks. We're all in agony, we're all strugglin' to become angels out of this mass of herd instincts, while every act is in the grip of a demonic force that refuses to allow us any real freedom. We aren't free, we're demons. We're magnetized by an electric current of herd instincts that moves us about like so many filings. Into bars, out of bars, into movies, out of movies, into the A&P, outta the A&P, into the A.A. meeting, out onto the street again. I'm sorry but that's what I see. What I *hope* though is that this is a necessary passage to eternal life. Thank you for listening."

Polite applause, somewhat thin. Abstracted. Teddy glances about—the idiots, no one taking notes!

Leo swallows. "Well, shall we have our discussion?"

A pretty black raises her hand. "What I wanter know, how do this A.A.A. help you keep 'way from your drinkin' frien's who don't wanter let you go? An' it's Christmas! What I do on *New Years Eve?* They come 'round with their eyes beet-red offerin' me gin and whiskey—what I do? What about my image?"

Leo sinks in darkness, groping. "Uh, I don't know. I haven't been able to solve this problem myself."

Teddy turns blurred page, blurs turned page, glances

over his rims at the woman. Can't get a sentence to read properly.

Harshgreen eyes and hatchet nose, Derek the exJesuit lowers his cigar and raises his hand. "My name's Derek and I'm an alcoholic. You tell your friends you're sick with a killer disease and if they keep offering you booze, they're *not* your friends. Or they're sick themselves. It's that plain, anybody who tries to force you to drink is sick himself. Most of our friends are not social drinkers and will be happy to have one less mouth at the bottle. Anyway, none of 'em is gonna bend you down onto the floor and jam the bottle down your throat—none of your *friends*. You are the only one who has to decide about drinking or not drinking, you're the one who lifts the glass. Why should you keep an image for drunken schmucks who are some of the most boring people on earth? I mean your old drinking buddies. You ever sit back and listen to your friends talk while they're smashed? Makes you wonder how you could've sat there talking so stupidly yourself. If you wanna live to see *next* Christmas and next New Years, you better remember that your system can no longer handle alcohol the way it used to. And it never will again, no matter how long you stay sober." Derek eyes Leo. "This is the weirdest A.A. meeting I've ever been to. You two guys look so much alike I get double vision—like I'm drunk! I wonder if you *think* as much alike? All my life I thought I was the perfect intellectual. What other people had to say was bullshit—and what I had to say was too profound for them to understand—too philosophical, epistemological, phenomenological, theological, esthetic, or existential. So I was perfect in my loneliness. But this disease and A.A. have freed me from my Napoleonic selfinterest and perfection, my total mental and spiritual isolation. But you two guys —identical twins—"

"—Thiamese."

"Siamese! Leo talks about everything *but* that. I should think you'd be able to laugh at each other's foibles and nonsensical alcoholic thinking. But you sit there as solemn as two tombstone salesmen and tell us you're not convinced you're alcoholics, both of you ready to defend to the death your intellectual and artistic need to drink, and other pretensions. Your *need!*"

"He didn't thay that."

"Maybe I heard with the wrong ear," Derek says "—forgive me! Leo tells us about a spiritual experience like Bill W.'s as if he were relieved forever from following The Program. You're some kind of special case, huh? What kind of weirdness is this? I mean, what's this demonology and blue-light bullshit in the practical world of day-to-day sobriety?"

"I feel I've been touched," Leo says.

"I'll say so," Derek agrees.

"As for me—" Teddy says.

"I don't wanna hear from you," Derek says. "You're not even sober."

"Well, fuck you, you're gonna hear from me!" Teddy rises, pulling Leo up. Glistening eyes sweep the room like Christ's. *"As for me,* I intend to devote my life to humanity, not thit around with my thumb up my ath wonderin' whether I'm a drunk or not. I'm gonna become a conthultant." Leo nods in hard agreement. "Open a thtorefront on Avenue B. Become a conthultant on *emotional problems. Real work!* Now let'th get outta here, I've had enough crap for one night. I feel let down enough by thith group, don't you?"

Leo sighs. "Bill W. says, Avoid controversy like the plague."

"I am! These thelfimportant bathtards couldn't get the methage if it was printed in big yellow lightbulbs! LET'TH GO!"

Leo-Teddy takes his coats, glides through crowded smoke to the stairs. Wanda follows, face to the floor.

"Hey there!" Chris Sunshine cries gleefully, letting Leo-Teddy and Wanda through the heavy redmetal door to his "Firm" in the factory district. Dr. Sunshine's a slim, short balding dealer with laughing blue eyes, bad teeth and a welling, pot-soaked bursting gargle *"ha! ha! ha! ha! ha!* Brought your trumpet, huh? *Terrific!* Where's your trombone—still at the Second Avenue pawnshop? Guess what I got for *you*—a real Japanese plastic junior trombone! *Miniaturized!* I got it just for you HA HA HA HA HA HA HA HA!"

Teddy grins, rubs his hands, bows with palms joined. "Doctor Clean and Mithter Toad, a musical corporation, at your thervithe, thir. Break out those wild Arabian bombers, we're ready t' blow, man. We jutht came from an A.A. meeting where we worked up a powerful thirtht thtompin' those deadath Puritans."

"What's the liquid refreshment?" Chris asks cheerily.

"Ouzo!" Leo says. "I showed 'em I could go ninety days without a drop. I'm no alcoholic."

"Eight-nine days,"' Teddy says.

"Don't be petty." Leo pops a mouthpiece into his trumpet, rips loose.

"How 'bout that!" Chris asks Wanda. "Gave up juice myself—for my health! I dig those meetings though—been to a lot of 'em on the Bowery. Not for myself, of course! Well, maybe just a little bit for myself."

"They make their own decisions,"' Wanda says.

"Aw," Leo says, "I wanna write."

"Live, ya mean." Teddy's arm around Leo. "He's mailin' back his Purple Heart."

"Hey man, dig this!" Chris cries. "Betcha haven't seen one of these since you were *kids!"* Chris holds up a small metal red-white-and-blue wheel with a plunger that spins the wheel on flints and shoots off pink-and-blue sparks in a gush of nostalgia. "I got one for both of you—guaranteed Japanese imitation 1939 Japanese toys! HA HA HA HA HA HA! THE JAPS ARE IMITATING THEMSELVES!"

"HA HA HA HA HA HA!!" Leo-Teddy cries.

"HA HA HA HA HA HA HA HA HA!!!" Chris cries.

Leo-Teddy's thumbs plunge the toy wheels spinning hard, pink and blue sparks flying lushly, happy hearts borne back to the Woolworth counters of their Erie childhood.

HUGE pink breast, mashed and blubberish, blind monstrous nipple lifting through soapbubbles, blooms on the Metropolitan grindhouse screen—Leo shot, yawning, Teddy nodding, bloated liverlips ballooning. Halfway again through this numbing skinflick with its bouncy sax-trumpet track estranged from the action, sourly punning narrator, heavy rapture of studio-dubbed sighs. Teddy's week-end, Wanda at New Hope in a crosspour of self-analysis with Wilma. Cocksoft Leo sips from the gallon, gagging on sherry brassflavor, unmoved by the giant push-ball tit. Glances at the spare male audience, porkfloggers anonymous, apart as assassins. Gasps tragically, poached eyes rolling, *"Goddamn A.A.'s ruined my drinking!"*

Boring hours staring at magnified skin pores—incredible the boredom! All for a nipple, bare tits in a pool, a stray crotch wisp that's always snipped out so the house won't be raided. Twins have great hopes for sex films—perhaps filmmakers will even show screwing someday. Superhallucinogenic screwing, *Wagnerian screwing!* Oh, Cynara!

Knocking on Leo's door last month, there she stood. Dark-glasses wanting to show us her pregnancy. Pretending she'd just dropped in—Show me your new song. It's for me! *Yipes!* Wanting to lie on the bed to rest her back while we read aloud. Wanda at work. Couldn't resist. Eternal vow years ago, whatever marriages arose. Let's make love. Quiet day, undersea bedroom. Nipples wide, brown, bulging, all of her cool and bulging under four ravishing hands until Teddy zonked out. Her eyes pleading, pretty little boy-mouth open, softly panting, sucking her lower lip as her eyes close. Her arms around both our necks, pineapple breasts spilling sideways, oh so willing, her warmth kissed all over. Blue breastveins, blueskeined velvetsheen bellymound, can all these baked goods perish? We'll still be lovers thirty years from now! Never lose this heartfelt lust, handheld ripeness. Teddy out after first shot—still hasn't forgiven me for not pouring coffee into him—he'd still've been drunk but wide-awake drunk. Studying coverlet for wet spots, hiding towel in bottom of hamper. Shaking! Teddy hysterical at not getting a second lay. Screaming on the bed, calling her a twisted fucking Chinese commissar. Took her home by cab, terrible depression, all my A.A. mysticism sounding phony even to me as I pumped it at her. A separate peace with myself about adultery. How could I resist? Lost when I opened the kitchen door. My heart! Justified. Ever come again? *Goddamned Teddy!* I hope you're getting The Program, *wherever you are!* Me too. Gotta sober up before Wanda gets back tomorrow. Smell like a used tank car. Tomorrow the cure!

"My God," Teddy rasps, waking. "This the last show?"

"You only been out half an hour."

"Don't hand me that, I been asleep four or five hours. You just wait, sometime you'll be out and I'll lie to you. Just like you deserve. I got a headache." Raises trembling hand to his eyes, twitches in his seat. "Boy, I'm numb! You tingle all over?"

"Let's get outta this deathtrap."

"Can't move," Teddy whispers. Stares ahead, stunned by the screen's right side: all redjellied with cometing microbes. Suddenly his breath fails, a flush shoots through his limbs, his jaw clamps tight. He falls away from Leo, then lifts out of his seat, electrified, board-stiff, arms and legs jerking.

"Jesus Christ!" Leo cries. Teddy foams, drooling through clenched teeth. Fear rattles Leo, an undertow of despair sweeping body from mind. *"Help!"* he cries, trying to force Teddy's jaw open and get at his tongue. Digging at tight teeth. *"Agh!"* he moans. *"Help!"*

No one moves. The theater fills with an actress's climax.

"Help! Call an ambulance!"

Teddy convulses without stop.

"Is there a doctor in here?" Leo cries. Looking back he sees three men get up hurriedly and leave.

"Mawmawmawmawmaw!" Teddy cries, eyes rolled back, pelvis beating upward. As he bellows a fart, a man in the next row shakes his head at Teddy's humping and leaves cursing. Leo digs out his filthy ball of handkerchief and, fear springing tears, tries to stuff it through Teddy's teeth. "You'll be all right, Ted!"

A skinny young Spanish usher flashes a beam. "Hey, man, you scarin' everybody outta here!"

"My brother may be a diabetic," Leo says. "Can you call an ambulance?"

"Wait here."

Teddy relaxes. Sighs on the soundtrack fake gratitude.

A woman, the Cuban ticketseller, pokes a beam at them. "I call ambulance, you wait."

"What the hell ya doin'?" Teddy pushes down the handkerchief.

"Ya had a diabetic sugar shock attack! How are you?"

"You crazy? Nothin's wrong with me. What's *she* want?"

"You feel better?" she asks. Hen-staring curiosity. *"Hey, hey?"*

"Yeah! Gracias, senora, I'm muy bueno."

"You were screaming," Leo says.

"Balls. We sleep through the last show? This place is empty."

"You wait," she says. "I call ambulance."

"You *called* an ambulance? Oh bullshit, let's get outta here before this female fog gets violent."

Leo hooks the shoppingbag. Follow the ticketseller, arms shouldered. "How dya feel?" Leo asks.

"Like the worst case of coffeenerves ever. But pretty good! Hey—my pants are sopping. Christ, that's *shit!*"

"We'll hit your pad so you can rest."

"I'm soaked!"

Breathless nightheat pops Leo-Teddy's pores on the sidewalk. "Boy, your eyes are red."

"Smog," Teddy says. Wet backs to the poster for PANTY PASSIONS. "Fuckin' combustion. My God, this stink's unbearable. Let's trot."

"You want a heart attack? You just come outta sugar shock!"

"Then why'm I up and walkin'? *Hm?"*

"Because you got the constitution of a horse's asshole. When *you* crack, you're gonna die. Iron constitutions are killers—everything goes at once!"

A far siren, burning higher. Twins leap, cutting from the curb through midblock traffic. Trembling zigzag toward Teddy's pad. Hit a dark doorway for sherry breathers.

"Seven-thirty," Teddy says. "We still got time to make the rushes at Andy's. No bath, though."

"But a good scrub," Leo suggests. "You don't remember shaking, and shitting your pants?"

"Man, I was asleep. Stop exaggerating, it's just the wine trots—could happen to *anyone* on Paradise sherry."

"Yeah? Well, what about last night? Ya woke up hangin' off the bed."

"So?"

"Ya flipped right outta bed!"

"So? That's perfectly normal. It's happened several times. I musta had a nightmare."

"Dad died of this."

"Will ya cut the bullshit! If I gotta pay a coupla shakes

and nightmares to drink, I'll pay. I DON'T SCARE! GET IT?"

Avenue B's fagged blue nightmare, a Spanish shout of loping beerdrinkers with laughably small cans in tiny bags —surging eyes, drained razor smiles, stickball kids dodging cabs and curbgarbage, a smashed phonebooth's yammering tragedy, glass-sugared split concrete, dead cat in ashcan. Leo-Teddy pale blue, headsludge bottomless.

"Damn!" Teddy cries. "This is real life! To think we mighta missed all this back in King James. Ha, and Stravinsky sits out there in Hollywood peddling abstractions. Let's have a beer."

"Look, we gotta change pants, get over to Andy's for our screen test."

"Hey, right! Good thinking. Why don' we go down to Bowery afterward? I'd love a taste of Five Star."

Teddy stops at a newstand, fixed on a Spanish paper with a picture of Marlon Brando. "Let's get that."

"We can't read Spanish."

"Sure I can."

Stand for several minutes reading headlines, scanning bosoms on covers. A black blind man with gluey slits buys cherry lifesavers, stands sniffing—"There's a bakery of shit around here somewhere!" Teddy snorts loftily and eyes a girl in a yellow bikini walking out of the Caribbean, crotch folds dividing. "Tha's one of the most beautiful girls I've ever seen," Teddy judges weightedly. "I'm serious! She could give a guy a lotta home comfort. A Venus—I gotta phone Jumbo."

Walk home singing, papers underarm. Hailed at Seventh and B by Martin Longmoon and Nancy Mars. Martin, a pocky, penniless Canadian student always in a dark suit and tie, walks tall with his broken back in a brace and bites his lip like a frightened bank teller. Nancy's holed up again on the Lower East Side, waiting out another unwanted baby, father departed.

"Martin's on my shitlist," Nancy says. "He just proposed again."

"Why not accept?" Leo asks.

"He's just *horny,* goddamnit—look at him!"

"I only asked out of a sense of humanity," Martin says. "You're upset tonight."

"How's A.A.?" Leo asks Martin.

"Oh, he's on a three-day slip," Nancy says. "He still has two days to go."

"Approximately," Martin says. "Just beer, of course. I'm too weak for gin and tonic."

"Come up to our pad," Teddy says. "We're celebrating Dionysian Festival Month."

"It only comes twelve times a year," Leo says.

Nancy eyes their shoppingbag. "Some of that crappy-assed wine?"

"Paradise!" Leo-Teddy says.

"You two are too young to be alcoholics," Teddy says.

"Why thank you!" Nancy says. "That's one of the nicest pieces of bullshit you've ever laid on me."

"Gosh, Nancy," Leo says. "How you've changed."

"I don't think twenty-six is too young," Martin says. "Kafka'd say you're *never* too young for a crime against yourself. Not that I read Kafka. Not that I read anybody!"

"What *do* you do, Martin?" Nancy asks.

"Why—I drink."

In the streetlamp's blue aura, Teddy bows at his steps. "Welcome to Rat Crumb Manor." Watermarks of a flood leave a white acid kiss on the building's facings. A long soft rat scrambles under the staircase within.

"Utopia Now!" Leo cries.

Teddy draws back, studying Leo. "Oh, *you* here?"

"Better warn you," Leo tells Nancy. "No Con Ed, so try not to step on the roach paste in your bare feet. It stings."

"You know," she says, "I like you twins better when one of you's sober. But don't worry about it—I'm thirsty!"

"The price of drink is eternal vigilance," Martin says. "Sure smells of catshit here."

Teddy unlocks, the twins go into the dark. Winebottle candle suddenly burning on kitchen table. Nancy watches roaches bolt from the sink. Three kittens cool on the metal bathtub lid.

"Boy, Teddy," she says, "why don't you make a geographical escape to Bellevue?"

"Not my cup of tea," Teddy says. "Never been hospitalized since I was five. No auto wrecks, no divorces, no operations, no dryingout farms. That's why I never joined A.A. I'm too healthy."

She opens the dark warm icebox. "No beer, huh?"

"Sissy drink," Teddy says. "Beer's somethin' ya have with ham sandwiches. But we got a wonderful sherry."

He lights livingroom candles as Martin and Nancy sink to the baseboard pillows, apart.

"You'll never get up again," he tells her. "Like to borrow my brace?"

"With Paradise I may need it." She looks at the desk's bust of Wagner wearing Teddy's shiny black Nazi motorcycle helmet with a sidewilted candlestub on top.

"That's for sitting in the john with the lights out," Martin tells her.

Leo-Teddy searches the dark cupboard for jelly glasses, brings the gallon to Nancy.

"All for me?" she asks. "You wanna put *me* in Bellevue?"

"Ha!" Teddy cries, pouring. "You kids drink for three days and need a hospital—I go on a ten-day binge and bounce back healthy as a horse."

"Christ," she says. "This afternoon I was stark staring sober! Sitting home, having a little pity party all by myself, when this crappyassed fink shows up with a bag full of bananas and Danish beer. You have no consideration, Martin!"

"I couldn't let you go on worrying about the rent. It's too trivial."

"You're right!" she says. "And my clothes are too trivial, and my baby's too trivial! I've come to a decision. Life is shit."

"Oh, 's not that bad," Leo says, drinking, belching. "Hey, you gotta wash, Teddy."

"Gotta hit the toilet first." Teddy lights his Nazi helmet from a candle, snatches up his half-empty Manhattan phonebook. "We're outta paper."

Down the outside hall, unpadlock Teddy's john. Teddy unzips, sits sideways on the splintered seat while Leo waits on a stool in the Nazi flicker. Teddy feels his stiffened, paperthin trousers. "That last one went right through me. Now I know how Boris felt all night in those muddy pants. 'We belong dead!' "

Leo holds his breath, gagging. "Let's dump you inta the tub fast!"

"Will ya SHUT UP! Just a scrub. Don' wanna be late to Andy's. *God, I'm bushed.*"

Ceilingwater trickles down the toilet's greenslime walls into the cellar below.

"Sonsofbitches," Leo says. "Still haven't unplugged their toilet up there."

"We oughtta complain," Teddy says. "Christ, ya'd think I live on the Bowery!" He swells heavily, sighing sobs, wiping his wet eyes. "Tha' Fucker Up There's sure puttin' me through the meatgrinder! But I'm standin' up okay—better'n those two-faced A.A. bastards with their secret drinkin'. I ain't no fuckin' secret drinker, you can sure say that for me."

"You aren't in A.A.," Leo says.

"Hell, I'm not! What the fuck ya mean, I'm not in A.A.? I got as much right t' be in A.A. as you do! *You're not in A.A.!*"

"Shit—you hate A.A. You never spent ninety minutes sober since I been in."

"I'm gonna prove somethin' to you once and for all," Teddy says. "I'm gonna stay *sober* tomorrow."

"Some miracle. In fact, it could be dangerous. Don't do it, Teddy, you could get sicker."

"Never been sick a day in my life. Why, I feel better already, just thinkin' about it. Fuck, yes. Cold turkey! *Me, sick?*"

"Sobriety poisoning—ya might get to like it."

Teddy thinks, drooping over his knees. Tears spring, dripping. "I wanna go to Gray Moor," he sobs. *"Tomorrow!* Will ya go with me?"

"I don't need Gray Moor!" Leo stares hard at the mosswet floor.

"I DO!"

"That bunch of homeless drunks. I don't wanna go to a halfway house. I got a home. And a wife!"

"I don't have anything!" Teddy sobs. "Oh my God, I'll get down on my knees and beg you! Go with me to Gray Moor."

"I-yi-yi. Okay, sure. Tomorrow."

"I'll thank you for the rest of my life, ol' buddy. *Write it down.*" Teddy rips out a telephone page, hands Leo the book. Leo prints GRAYMOOR in big red letters. "Paste it to the kitchen door so we don't forget," Teddy says, gripping Leo's knee. "But don' say anything about it to Nancy and Martin—*shh!*—we don' wanna spoil their evening."

Back into kitchen, the flaming Nazi crosses almost steadily to his writing table, kicking a black mama cat aside, glues the page to the wall over his desk.

"Gray Moor," Nancy reads aloud.

"I'm throwin' in the sponge," Teddy says. "Goin' to Gray Moor!"

"Isn't this rather sudden?" she asks.

"Well, I didn't wanna tell ya," Teddy says. "Goin' early tomorrow. Like to come along? They got a ladies dorm out there."

"Why don't you, Nancy?" Martin says. "We'll go together."

"They *won't* let you sleep with me, Martin. I'll wait until my crappyassed landlord throws me out. You go."

"You need someone to light your cigarettes."

"You phony intellectual," she says, sniffing. "Are you sure that's *cat*shit?"

Leo-Teddy skims the metal lid off the kitchen bathtub, kittens scrambling, blasts steam into milling roaches. Teddy kicks off his shoes, drops his pants and shirt, sets taps, plugs the tub with a wad of telephone paper. As the tub fills, they search Teddy's closet for a pair of pants with a crotch left.

"I don't have one *whole* pair of pants!" He finds some bermudas but no shirt with buttons on the belly, settles for a tee-shirt with holes only in one armpit. Lays his clothes on the kitchen table, lies down in the tub as Leo balances on the rim. Teddy lies thoughtful, staring down at his black sox and Harvard garters, filthy toes through the holes.

"I'm worth saving," he says.

"Sure," Leo says. "It's twenty-one days out there, though."

"Teddy needs twenty-one months," Nancy calls.

"Twenty-one years might be more like it," Leo hears Jack McFin's sarcastic, haunting voice in memory. "For both of 'em!"

Teddy studies a big bruise that seems to have wandered from his shoulder down his arm. "Hey, little mother," he calls, "scrub my back!"

"Goddamnit," Nancy says, "everytime I come here he jumps into the tub."

"Well, I'll cover my animal, if you're modest," he says. "In fact, I can't even see myself. This water's *black!*"

"Take off your socks," Leo says.

WHAM BANG BANG BANG BANG on the knobless red firedoor to Andy's Factory. No answer. Creamsherry sky moving in nightclouds. Twins in bermuda shorts, rubber Jap sandals, flapping red-checked shirts, heads strapped into greencelluloid editorial visors. WHAM BANG BANG! Leo-Teddy sucks at the gallon's last drops, plants the empty by Grand Central YMCA with papal blessings.

"Need another half-gallon to last the night." Teddy burps rubber. "We can just stretch it and still buy tokens. But we won't have anything for tomorrow."

"That figures," Leo says. "If we spend everything tonight, we won't drink tomorrow. Good thinkin'."

"Why not drink tomorrow?"

"Gray Moor, lunkhead!"

"Christ, my memory. Ghastly."

Stare up at a Gallo wine billboard of a girl coming out of surf.

> *"A pretty tit—is like a melody—*
> THAT HAUNTS YOU NIGHT AND DAY!"

Blunder down to fancy plague shop, blow ten sweating minutes in passionate study of shelves and prices, tempting import wines in straw bibs.

"Hate to buy our California piss in here," Teddy says, tucking his teeshirt down tight and stretching the rotted armpit over bare ribs. "Really feels cheap!"

"Drink positive," Leo says. "Power of alcoholic thinking."

Wham bang bang bang bang on Andy's door. Stricken, Teddy hugs their farewell half-gallon, eying Leo. "D'ya realize this may be my last drink!"

"Shit," Leo says, banging. "I've quit everyday for the past ten years."

"Maybe they'll have us up every morning singin' Gregorian chants." Teddy snaps the plastic seal, holds the bottle out thoughtfully, his palm shaping the bottle's shoulder. "Too bad it's not Benedictine," he sighs. "I'd like a little brandy to say goodbye on." His zeal rises quickly. "Well, I'm gonna enjoy it!"

The firedoor opens. Twenty-four-year-old Greta Garbo stares at them, harsh music pouring past her. "Oh hi," she says, shaking her head. *"I'm* leaving! Fucking place has given me a headache."

"Andy upstairs?" Leo asks.

"Yes!—that tightfisted freak! Could you lend me sixteen bucks?"

"Haven't got it," Teddy says. "You're the girl with the lovely Band-Aids."

"What Band-Aids?" she asks.

"In *Ondine*."

"Oh. Well, I was still new, and shy of being seen stark-naked. I didn't wear 'em in *Fuck*."

"Haven't caught that yet," Leo says. "But we will!"

"That's my best," she says. "I really give in that. *Ciao*."

"We should write something for her," Teddy says, going in.

"Maybe she can't act."

"Boy, they could use light in here. Three flights, *unh!*"

"The first step's the hardest," Leo says.

"Stop ruinin' my drinking! And keep the fuckin' booze in the bag. We only got enough for ourselves. When we need a booster, we'll hit the toilet."

Climb dismal flights through growing growling pounding static guitars singing whining screeching galactic explosions twisting girders rivets squealing free human bone mashed by python sound flesh crushed eyebulbs popping, pass through a silversprayed firedoor with a pair of shadowblack darkglasses stenciled on it, into vast space slumping with faggy freaks and hear hurled from a far rock group's jumble of electrical equipment and speakers an amplified horror forest of cheetahs, tigers and orangutans at the top paranoid power of soundwaves, the floor thundering like naked stone under the howl of Niagara.

"They kill ten times louder than necessary!" Leo shouts.

"And are PROUD OF IT!"

A slender handsome lad in an eloquent shaped bouffant stands listening, turns to Leo-Teddy tenderly and says, "Do you dig it? There aren't any musicians! The band's playing all by itself without 'em!"

Twins eye the musicianless rock group instruments with their amplifiers.

"Very mysterious!" Leo hedges. "How do 'they' do it?"

"It's all on tape loops so the musicians can rest while the band plays on!" the lad shouts benignly. "This is a replay!"

Leo points at the guitars lying untended on stools and amplifiers. *"They play very well!"*

"YOU SEE," the lad says, "there's nothing mysterious at all! In fact, it's so beautiful! It's like the painting that's left after the painter dies. What could be more tender than for a band to survive its musicians? It's a very human longing—so very projective and satisfying—this band could play for a thousand years without resting! It's fabulous, your music floating through eternity, past all buildings, all civilizations—past life itself! If we can just get a solar battery! Andy wants HIS OWN HALL so the band can run PERMANENTLY!"

"Like Con Ed," Teddy says. "But it's too loud!"

The lad pulls himself up. *"Any* human being should have a tolerance for anybody's music! This band is working very, very hard!"

"But you can't even hear the songs!" Leo shouts.

'It's extremely TRADITIONAL MUSIC! And they play it because NOBODY ELSE WILL! Just *listen*— how straightforward can you get about the incredible suffering we go through daily? Don't you realize we're talking about a VERY, VERY GOOD BAND, a very, very CONSTRUCTIVE, GOOD, HONEST BAND that's ENORMOUSLY TALENTED? Very *close,* and *real,* and *working together?"*

"They're nice people," Teddy says.

The lad smiles sweetly, blows them a kiss and goes up to a microphone to sing. His face agonized, voice soundless as dust. A Swede with straight nylonblonde hair joins him, her bland face hard as a wax apple, singing soundlessly, words crushed. They stand in the raging music, jaws opening and closing, mouthroofs pink as voicethrower's dummies. Shivers yank Leo-Teddy, crawl into his hair.

Leo cries, "Let's not do business with Andy if *that's* what happens to you!"

A shadow catches the corner of sight, leaps away, hiding.

"What was that!" Leo asks.

"I don't know, I'm pretendin' I didn't see it! Let's find Andy."

A boy with a centurion's helmet of nitty hair stalks about blowing a harmonica into surprised ears and blows it into the knees of a teenager on a couch with her ratty dress hiked above her silkstockings.

"Have you see Andy?" Teddy asks Harmonica.

"Andy's dead."

"You must be jokin'!"

"I am."

Ambles off blatting his mouthorgan at Leo-Teddy, sneering.

Larry and Mario, Leo-Teddy's friends, sit in Mario's small dressing room while a girl helps Mario attach his false lashes and Mario stuffs his bra coyly behind a sweater held modestly over his bosom. Larry, Mario's costar, is a weightlifter and bleachblond bull moose.

"Darn that Andy! He wants me to sing for de whole movie today!" Mario complains, batting his calfskin eyes at the twins imploringly. "How do you like my new red wig? Do I look like Lana Turner?"

Larry purses a kiss at Mario. "Gorgeous."

Mario's Spanish pout flames. "I'm so MAD at Andy! He just pushes me out dere and makes me do everything. For two reels! Are you pulling your cock out today?"

"Gee," Larry says, "the whole situation, it's so embarrassing! I can hardly get a hardon even thinkin' about it. Reality's *too much!*"

"Just KISS ME!" Mario cries. "You'll get it up."

"I *hope* so."

"You'll be lipstick from chin to forehead before I get t'rough with you," Mario insists, his deer eyes gaga with starpower at Larry. "I want this to be our greatest love scene, *Larry*."

"Boy! I'll try," Larry says hopefully and falls to the floor for push-ups. "Gotta get in shape. BROADS! Should I put my hand in your twat, Mario?"

"Would you put it in Lana Turner's?" Mario asks.

"I'll think about that," Larry says, counting pushups. "Maybe you should put some kind of bush down there. Red!"

Mario eyes her costar mournfully through blue eyemakeup. "Larry, *just pretend!*"

Leo-Teddy walks past three color teevees playing different programs, nobody watching. A silversprayed old desk—everything on or by it is sprayed, the taped and bandaged nineteen-fifteen telephone, the glass of a standup photo, inkwell and pen, a silver cast of Larry's cock signed Larry Supercock, swivelchair, wastebasket, file cabinets, worktables, barbells, a bicycle exerciser, a theatrical traveling trunk, all silver, even the tall windowpanes. A stripped brick wall as long as The Factory is silversprayed, the vast ceiling's coated with silverfoil, all overhead pipes wrapped in foil where several gasfilled aluminumfoil pillows float—the open toilet's walls are silverfoil, its washbowl silversprayed, the toilet silverlidded and porcelain throne silver right down to the waterline.

A silverhaired boyman in blackleather biker's jacket and shadowblack shades appears from a dark room carrying an aproned Aunt Jemima cookie jar, like a dream in a dream. His silverhair falls forward in strawstiff, widerumpled bangs. He walks delicately on highheeled silverboots, his slim body gentle, lazy, a giant one-pound fruitnut chocolate bar wedged into his jacket pocket. He sidles up to Leo-Teddy, his shades like popped black rubber unyielding to light, his lips wide and utterly emotionless, his nose pink with split blood vessels.

"Wonderful," he says softly. "I'm glad to see you. We've got the rushes on your screen test."

"Hey, *we're* gonna make a movie!" Teddy says.

"Great," Andy says softly. "What about?"

"Well it's modest," Teddy says. "Color. Uh, eight millimetre."

"That's the best size," Andy says. "Use the cheapest Kodak you can find. What's it about?"

"An epic! We're buyin' about fifteen reels for this. This masterpiece is *simple*. We receive a fifty-buck windfall in the mail and the camera just follows us from bar to bar all over the Lower East Side while we blow the cash. We start out with five shots apiece lined up on Stanley's bar and wind up flat broke on the pier under Brooklyn Bridge blowin' our horns. It's after a story by Dickens called 'Making a Night of It' in *Sketches by Boz.*"

"It's about *fellowship,*" Leo says. "Real friendship. By the end of reel fifteen, you should love these two guys. That's our company, Friendly Films."

"Are they Siamese twins?" Andy asks.

"We're gonna shoot *around* that," Teddy says.

"Right," Leo says. "That's not a necessary element to your liking these guys."

Andy's sidekick with the harmonica listens intently.

"Do they go to bed with each other? You don't have a winner unless there's a big fuck scene."

"It's not a sex flick," Teddy says.

"It's about fellowship," Leo insists, asking Andy, "Don't you ever feel a *thrill* of friendship?"

"Sometimes things just go through me like waves," Andy says. "They get scary. But it's not friendship. I think friendship can get too involved anyway, and it's not really worth it. It's easier without it. You've gotta *learn* how to really not care, like the kids nowadays—they do it with boys *and* girls. It's frigid people who really make out. Really. If you like somebody, wonderful—just don't think about it. Not when you're making love. It's not worth it."

"But what if your friend really upsets you?" Leo asks.

"Just pretend he's on television. I try not to feel anything. Do you boys dance together?"

"No," Leo says.

"That's too bad," Andy says. "I'd like to shoot something cute like that. In costume."

"Well—" Teddy says. "I wrote a kind of Brechtian song, 'The White Slavery Waltz'—*maybe*—"

"One of you in drag!" Mouthorgan suggests.

"We used to wear our hair like Andy's," Teddy whispers.

"Rogers and Astaire," Andy says. "Don't you even tap dance?"

"Not well," Teddy says. "We have a Jekyll and Hyde act we do."

"Oh, that's precious," Andy says. "We could do that with a lot of blood in it. Just *buckets* of ketchup—something scary, with real feelings in it."

"In this act we strangle each other," Teddy says.

"And somebody's eyes pop out?" Andy asks. "We could get some glass eyes. Dr. Jekyll stands there screaming with his *eyes* in his hands! Which of you plays Hyde?"

"I do," Teddy says.

"Teddy can sound real degenerate," Leo says.

"Our first horror film!" Andy says. "Oh, I wanna see your screen test and think about it."

Leo-Teddy sits in camp chairs before the makeshift sheet of a screen. Silver dustbeam. Andy plops by Leo, Mouthorgan by Teddy.

"Gee," Andy says, "I think I'm getting excited."

"There's real money in blood these days," Mouthorgan says.

"Buckets," Andy says.

Leo-Teddy bottlesafe and thoughtful, planning a blood-dabbled script, Blind Man's Bloodyfingers and Clues All over the Walls—Friendly Films shelved.

We used to wear our hair like Andy's," Teddy whispers.

"But not with hairspray!"

"Sure we did—that greenglop hairset Mama got from Woolworth's. Where's your memory?"

"Boy, we were five once?—I think it's a silver wig."

Numbers puzzle the screen, then Teddy-Leo looks out stilly, life larger than life. Headshot, no motion, four eyes staring, lids shaped stone. Stillness. Diseased innocence rings their eyes. Suddenly—did the four eyes blink? Or is this freezeframe? Teddy-Leo stares into Leo-Teddy, unmovingly. At last, Teddy-Leo swallows. Mouthorgan applauds with a harmonica zip, others clap after this long wait for action. "Marvelous," Andy sighs, lifting his shades and revealing the wide brown eyes of a querulous lemur.

"Looked like we swallowed some goldfish," Leo whispers.

"We look tight," Teddy says; Leo nods, *"—as fish."*

Teddy-Leo stares, tightpupilled public enemies in a bathroom mirror. Teddy's eyes more deeply ringed, swollen, piercingly farsighted, fulfilled, looking through the camera lens at the mountains of Bruckner, stone heights of Valhalla. Leo quieter, hidden in some recess of Teddy's, weakened with secret spite. Teddy-Leo blinks, guiltily.

"Christ," Leo whispers, "I thought I was comin' on noble and it looks like I got the clap."

"We needed sleep, obviously. Or maybe we shoulda had our horns."

"Awful! I can't look."

Teddy-Leo flickers a smile, winestained separated teeth appear in their Vandykes. Teddy's red shaving rash dries in blood on his throat. Their lank hair droops. Foreheads gleam winedrops. Veined eyeballs fishslimed, halflidded, force open with naked ego-power.

Teddy tells Andy, "We shoulda danced!"

"Oh no," Andy says. "This is the best screen test I've ever shot."

Teddy watches, remembers jacking off the morning of the screen test, reads anxiety in Leo also. Remembers jacking off twice this morning—will it be read when the lights go on?

"You don't look too good," he tells Leo. Looks away from the screen, sighs loudly. "This is shit, we can do better than this, Andy. Take it off."

"Shhh."

"Let's hit the toilet for a booster," he asks Leo.

"Wanna watch."

"What's there to watch? *Nothin'!*"

"I'm not movin'."

Teddy's bored fingers beat his knee. "Butt me, I'm out." Slakes his thirst on smoke, unconsoled. "This flick gets four stars for lousiness," he sighs. Closes his eyes, snores loudly with boredom. Looks again, a rubbery gargoyle smile passes over his screened face, he's noticeably *walleyed* while Leo isn't. Shock. Watches himself loosen his denture with his tongue, run his front teeth in and out grinning idiotically while screened Leo ignores.

"Christ," Teddy jeers, "you're a resentful bastard. Can't you even smile? You weren't in the spirit at all."

"What spirit?"

"Of the fuckin' *screen test!*"

"Andy told us to just look into the camera."

"But not like asshole idiots! You make me embarrassed for you. Christ. Now I see you for what you really are. Fuckin' prude! Goddamn Puritan, look at ya up there! It's *pitiful.* My God, I gotta look at your sorrowful puss for another *fifteen minutes?*"

"What about yours?" Leo rasps.

Teddy shrugs at the screen. "I got absolutely nothin' to hide."

"Lost your brains a long time ago, huh?"

A grieving, hungering ache comes over screened Leo.

"Glorious," Teddy mutters. "What's that shiteating look all about? *Acting?*"

Silence.

Teddy-Leo's ironman stare grows whitehot, but melts, ba-baaah sheepfaced, wet winefarts withheld, the spotted leprous underbelly of selfpity.

Silence. Criminal. Craven.

"There's gotta be a warrant out for those two guys,"

Leo says. His voice catches. "Fuckin' pair of moral sieves, if ya ask me!"

Screen-Teddy abruptly twitches, a rubber smirk big enough to deliver a grapefruit stretches for a vast belch that leaves him blissfully weteyed. "I'm so funny," his eyes say. Teddy applauds himself alone. Leo joins screen-Leo in spineshaking, lavaburn resentment, breathing hard, deep, quivering, lips drawn murderously tight.

"Look at you!" Teddy sneers. "While I'm up there belching out charm by the barrel.

"Cocksucker. You were blacked out the whole test."

"Didn't hurt my acting," Teddy says.

"Acting! Ya call *this* acting?"

"Hey," Mouthorgan asks, "can you guys suck each other off?"

"No!" Leo-Teddy croaks, shriveling, lying.

"Shit."

Silence. Andy's oversized eyes, aghast with secret satisfaction.

"My God," Leo mutters, "I hope Jack never sees this. Remember, we're goin' to Gray Moor tomorrow."

"Maybe. My life isn't so unmanageable."

"Why'd ya shit your pants tonight?"

"They had to throw chairs away after Beethoven farted."

"You got a stupid, fuckin' precedent for every fart you've ever blown!"

Teddy babbles to himself as Larry leans forward to Leo and whispers, "Teddy's just an extravert, go easy on 'im."

Mario whispers to Leo, "Teddy has tons of personal magnetism—it's really amazing how he comes across. Andy could do a lot for his career, get him a portfolio of glamor shots. He *wants* to be an actor, doesn't he?"

"He wants to be Hitler."

"I *made* him!" Teddy raves at screen-Leo. "He'd be shit without me. I even got him SOBER once—an' he's a genuine alcoholic! I been lookin' for you for years, never saw you right beside me. Know what he did yesterday?" Teddy asks Andy. "Dropped a full pint of gin on the shit-eatin' kitchen floor, sponged it up into a saucepan, then strained it through cheesecloth—not a drop lost! Boy, if that ain't fuckin' alcoholic! Falls outta bed constantly, it's pitiful. Thinks he's in the Red Cross—wants to carry alcoholism to Moscow. Should see 'im in the morning—

jumping muscles, sits on his hands for a half hour before he dares piss."

"I might miss your sink, huh?" Leo asks.

"I'm married to a monster." Teddy shakes his head hopelessly at screen-Leo. A long sigh lets go and rises in anger. *"Gonna get rid of you an' get a dog!"*

"Heil."

Teddy huffs, opens the bagged sherry, slugs watching the screen. Leo reaches for the bottle. Teddy yanks it away.

"*No.* I'm watchin' out for you. Takin' you to Gray Moor tomorrow."

Leo grips his seat in red frenzy. *"Gimme that bottle."*

"Nope. Don' you realize you're a sick cookie?"

Leo throbs. Sees screen-Teddy as a strange being blurted out of screen-Leo's body, an awesome alien body much like his but strangled of all acquaintance, loathsome features queerly bloated, sinister, split off from screen-Leo's hope and warmth, chilling, similar, abandoned. Something in screen-Leo hits him with hard pity, drives the wind out as Leo fills with love for his image, hatred for Teddy. His fists clench to keep from exploding. Abruptly, screen-Teddy swallows, fear brightening him and without warning a rat of vomit bolts straight from his mouth into the lens.

Applause, whistles, cheers. Andy sighs gratefully as Mouthorgan blows wildly at blurred ghosts beyond the runny lens. Teddy-Leo's racing shadow darkens, a tissued finger wipes the lens, then Teddy rises back into view clutching his mouth with Leo's hands clamped over his. His nose drools over the four hands on his mouth. Suddenly Teddy gasps in his chair. Leo claps his palms over Teddy's mouth. Teddy roars, biting Leo's thumb bloody.

"AGGHH!"

"Take your goddamn hands off my mouth!"

"I was only tryin to help!"

Teddy flames at the screen as Leo rocks with pain, sucking his bleeding thumb.

"THAT'S IT!" Leo cries. "WE'RE THROUGH!"

Teddy impaled. Horror. Shame.

"I don't remember that at all!"

"Did we clean it up?" Leo asks Andy.

"Fuck you did," Larry says. "I cleaned it up."

Teddy rises, yanking Leo up. "I gotta get outta here!"

Hooks the bottle, then burns into Leo. "This faggot factory's *insane*. They're all FREAKS!"

"Wait," Andy says. His big ghostly brown eyes blink. "It's a *very good* screen test—you should adore it. I think I'm quite proud of it."

"Stars!" Teddy shouts. "Stars for lousiness! *March.*" He heads Leo toward the silvergleaming exit. Leo tries to cry back to Andy. *"Don't apologize!"* Teddy shouts. "I'm gonna *sue* this bastard! Takin' advantage of a sick man—it's cruel and obscene!"

Wind down halfdark stairs, Leo sucking thumb in silence, Teddy raging aloud. On the street Leo inspects terrible teethmarks in his thumb.

"You'll be all right," Teddy says. "Have a drink. And *my stomach's* perfectly all right."

Both take long slugs. Teddy measures the wineline fatefully. "We may not make the night. Can't we get anymore?"

"We got grass, acid, ups, and downs in the icebox. Look at my thumb!"

"No acid. Absolutely no acid in my condition."

"My thumb!"

"Sorry." Teddy stares afar, exhales decisively. "It doesn't matter. In the long run it really doesn't matter. Buck up until we get home. Can you do that? I promise you, things will get better. *Tonight.*"

"How?"

Teddy, silent menace, prods Leo toward the Fifty-first Street subway. Stopping for a boost, he eyes Leo's wrapped red thumb, smiles from on high, tightpupilled. "You're lucky I didn't bite it off. I was angry enough. And still am."

"Teddy, I've had enough of your puke for one night."

"We needn't refer to that again. This is gonna be a great night—the greatest of our lives."

"I'm bored already."

Teddy tops his boost with a longer slug. "Have another! You'll need it."

Down into sweltering Cathedral Station, Jap sandals flapping. Fast to the token booth, train pulling in. Booth empty! A pencil-mustached, potbellied Puerto Rican with insane eyes races to the booth from the other stairs, trounces Teddy's bare toes while beating a coin on the wooden sill for a token. *"Aghh!"* Teddy cries, limping backward. The PR ignores him, beerfumes pouring, eyes rolling wildly at the train. A black woman in wireframe glasses enters the booth with a bucket of tokens. The PR hammers his coins while the subway woman frosts him from inside her cage.

"Geev me token!" Sweats like a beerglass.

"You wait your turn." She looks at Leo, waits for his money.

"I mees train!"

"You wait," she says. "Can't you see you stepped on this man's foot?"

Leo slides in their last dollar as Teddy bends up and down in pain.

"I no onderstand inglés! I no learn thees crazy language! I go home San Juan quick when I make money, no leev in thees crazy country like you! I no be slave like you!"

"Don't you think—" securing glasses on her nose "—you should apologize to this gentleman for stepping on his foot?"

"I NO ONDERSTAND INGLES!"

Traindoors close. She slides his token out at last, still lecturing. He steps back with his token, sees the closed doors, draws himself up, savage and grave. "I mees my train!"

"You deserve to," she says.

"Slave," he sneers fiercely, *"you* learn inglés!" Boils through the turnstile, glaring at all in his way as the train pulls out. Leo-Teddy limps behind him, arms ashoulder.

Teddy looks at his scraped toes. "I'd take him on right now but for these fuckin' sandals. We'd be sittin' ducks."

"Probably thinks we're sweethearts."

Twins limp upstation, lean over to stare up empty tracks. Nada. Down the bare platform the PR blazes, harassed, persecuted.

"The natives are restless tonight," Leo says.

Teddy sets down the shoppingbag, farting. "Gas bombs ready, sir."

"Carry on, Thundermug."

"Kill!" Teddy says. "KILL FOR THE LOVE OF KALI!" His eyes roll, he keels forward over the tracks. Leo screams, grabbing him. Unbelievable pain smashes Leo's leg, Teddy's body knocking him breathless. He lies under Teddy on a steel rail, leg throbbing. Far down the track

a train glimmers toward them. Leo gibbers, paralyzed, trying to pull back under the platform.

Suddenly a voice crackles over him senselessly, two strong arms pull him to his knees. The PR shouts at him to get up. Leo points at Teddy. They try to lift Teddy, Leo kneeling.

"He's out cold," Leo says. The PR stares at him. "He's *out!*" Leo cries. "You get on the other side."

Slowly they lift Teddy but Leo's outer leg won't lift himself. The PR shouts at him in Spanish to get up. Leo can't.

A high whistle screams down the tunnel as Leo falls to his knee. The PR lets Teddy hang in Leo's arms, lifts Leo's leg under him as Leo rises clutching Teddy. Rest Teddy against the high platform.

The PR waves back the oncoming train. *"Leeft!"* he cries, lifting Teddy.

"No!"

"LEEFT!"

"NO!" Leo cries, grabbing their band. *"Dos uno!"*

"Dos uno?"

The PR stares at bare flesh joining the twins' summer shorts, not grasping that Leo-Teddy is one.

"LEEFT!"

"NO!"

"LEEFT!"

"NOOO! Teddy, wake up!"

"You no leeft?"

Leo one-handedly unbuttons his shorts, works them off his bare ass and points to the band. *"Dos uno!"*

"Dos uno? DOS UNO! The PR stands frozen in his vain works. Suddenly he turns, stamping toward the train, shaking his arms as if grossly wronged. "DOS UNO! DOS UNO!"

"Si! Si! HELP! You lift *me!"*

Leo tries to hold Teddy's inner arm on the platform as Teddy slides under the platform, dangling, his arm above. The PR grabs Leo's legs, braces himself and lifts Leo slowly as Leo elbows onto the platform still holding Teddy's hand. But slowly the PR buckles under Leo-Teddy's four-hundred-and-forty pounds, Teddy dead-weight. Now the PR grabs their middle legs and slaves to lift them as Leo again elbows forward trying to raise his smashed outer leg to the platform. Bolting pain, his knee grips the edge. Slowly he rolls onto the platform as the train glides screeching into the station, whistle hooting.

"Somebody *help!*" Leo cries, looking up at a girl walking out of the surf in a Gallo wine poster, her crotch fold divided. He hangs braced on the edge and cries to the dripping face below, *"Si! Si!* Now lift *him!"*

The man disappears beneath Teddy as Leo lies on his side pulling Teddy's arm. Slowly Teddy rises, cheek scraping. Leo grabs the head's hair, yanking it onto concrete, and inches onto the platform. The train squeals to a halt midplatform.

The twins lie side by side, Leo white with fear. "WAKE UP, TEDDY!"

Teddy's eyes open. "What?"

"You're alive!"

"I'm fine. Why? Where are we?"

The PR stands over them, mute, gasping, then lifts Teddy again as the twins hobble to a bench, Teddy carrying the shoppingbag. Leo-Teddy slumps back, watching the train pull in. The PR studies them keenly, his face twisting. Teddy sets down the bag, *CLINK*.

"I pass out?" Teddy asks.

"Anything feel broken?"

Teddy snorts, wipes his nose on his shoulder. "Sillyass question—God watches over drunks."

"Borrachons!" the PR cries, whiteeyed and stalks away.

"Gracias," Teddy calls. "What's with him?"

Leo's eyes close as he fingers a huge bony lump on his thigh. Passengers pour past, staring.

"For Christ's sake, Leo," Teddy complains, buttoning Leo's hairy fly.

Spiritualblueneon shades the Seventh Street funeral home near Teddy's pad. Hobbling twins pause to read the lighted whitemetal letters of Ukrainians resting within . . . *V. Marmeladov* . . .

BEAUTY, DIGNITY, SERVICE
AIR CONDITIONED
Terms Arranged
24 Hour Service
Come in for a chat
about your Future

A haggard, largenosed woman weeps in the parlor, looks up at bluelighted twins at the window.

"We should look into a doublesized box," Teddy says. "Something special. We gotta watch out we don't wind up pickled under glass as curiosities. I'm *serious*—I don't feel long for this world."

Drinks, seeing himself in a see-through casket, an easy-going smile arranged on their faces, under hundred-proof vodka, pickled in death as in life. Opens door to a narrow hall, Leo too fagged to argue. Teddy whispers, "We tell 'im we have a very fat grandfather!" The old woman catches her breath, whimpering fearfully at limping twins, their torn shirts, wild hair and beards, dried blood on Teddy's split forehead. She grips her purse as they scrape up to her, Leo's leg dragging.

"Manager around?" Teddy asks, winehoarse, smiling.

"What're you doin' in here?" a man asks—lip lifting at bare sandled feet, addressing them in his neat suit, neat hair, false teeth, junkie Ukrainian stormtrooper blue eyes. "This is a place of business! You'll have to leave."

"We're here t' see about a casket," Teddy says.

"Have you ordered one?"

"We *wanna* order one," Teddy says. "But I won't lie, we got a problem. 'S gotta be for the two of us. See? We wanna be buried together. Right, Leo?" Leo nods.

"That's illegal. We can't help you. Please to leave."

"Screw the law!" Teddy says. "We can at least be cremated together, can't we?"

"No!" He tries to turn Teddy's shoulder. "Come back when you're feeling better."

"But we're here now!" Teddy says.

The man pushes. "Get out."

"This is an indignity!" Teddy cries, falling back against a chair. "I'm not leaving!"

"Holy Mother!" The woman cries as Leo moans loudly, pains shooting his cracked thigh. His head turns white and he growls, *"We'll be back, little man!"*

"Don't bother, heepies!" the manager warns.

"Oh yes we will," Teddy says, fresh anger rising. "We're famous musicians, buster. We'll be back with a brass band to wake the dead!"

"Ohh!" the old woman groans, crossing herself, falls-back onto the couch under her handkerchief.

"Don't worry, Mrs. Marmeladov!" the manager says

and draws himself up full. *"You gentlemen are barred from thees parlor."*

At last he gets the twins out front, stands guarding his door.

"Hah! We'll be back in ten minutes with our horns," Teddy says. "You asked for it, schmuck, you're gonna get it."

Arms ashoulder, Leo-Teddy's wide earthbound skeleton drags itself along the sidewalk to the big intersection at Seventh and A. Stand afire on the corner, eying maddened Saturday night traffic.

"We gotta run, if we can," Leo says, "or we'll never get across."

"What nerve." Teddy fumes at the light. *"Barred* from a stinkin' Ukrainian funeral parlor! Lowbrowed bastard —poor racial stock if I ever saw it. WE'LL CREMATE THE FUCKIN' BASTARD!"

"Run!" Leo cries hobbling, stiff with pain.

Teddy stops midintersection, shaking a fist at a one-eyed crumple car skimming by, horn blaring. "SCUMBAG! This is a public thoroughfare! You got any idea how many *madmen* are behind these wheels?"

"Let's not think about it, they're probably drunk too."

Passing Tompkins Square Park blacklands.

"Any spic kids come out with their shivs tonight," Teddy says, "we jump 'em. I've hit bottom with this neighborhood. I'm through takin' shit. I'm ready to kill for my rights. We're insane not to have pistols. Gonna sue that bastard for defamation of character. *Heepie!"*

Drinks. Through euphoric fuzz of swollen blood vessels, Teddy envisions V. Marmeladov, corpse, a Ukrainian smile on his face. Really happy. Deliciously serene. Dead.

Dead!

A magnificent blue-and-yellow dog-headed solar boat, ornamented with scarabs and rams-heads, painted with small birds, ibises, and Eyes of Horus, sails up South Ferry into the setting sun, bearing the massive double-coffin of Leo-Teddy, twins' gold images carved on the chalkblue lid, their four eyes large mild dots contemplating the Gates of Heaven as the shavenheaded pilot steers the barge and its oarsmen into the Beautiful West and House of Eternity. Osiris, I rise toward you! Gold stars glisten on bluegreen twilight. Evening tranquility . . .

"Someday we'll get justice," Teddy whispers. "Everything that's comin' to us!"

Stand gasping at Teddy's steps. Go up slowly, middle feet first, gingerly lifting outer legs one stone stair at a time. The street alive with Spanish—nobody speaks to them. Groan into Teddy's, light candles, get drug bags from dry-stink icebox, creak slowly to living-room where Teddy lifts his black Nazi helmet from Wagner's bust, lights the candlestub on top, slips on the helmet as they sink to the floor pillows, blitzed. Leo moans long, Teddy bends over his belly gently working his scraped toes, finds on his shoulder a yellow bruise boiling up from deep flesh.

"I thought this was lower down on my arm," he says. "Or maybe it's growin'! Leo, we never woulda fallen," he says carefully, "if we'd had supper. I fainted from sheer malnutrition. Gotta watch that. *An'* it was sweltering down there."

Leo pulls at the lowering wineline. *"I'm dead* . . . Don't feel any different from bein' alive."

The wallphone shakes them. Teddy tips the receiver until it falls to the linoleum. "I'm not here," Leo says.

"House of Frankenstein . . . Oh hi, Dr. Deer. No, he's not here."

"Yes, I am!" Leo clears and clears his hoarseness, shakes his humming beeswarming head until his brain wobbles painfully like custard. "Good evening, Dr Deer. How're you tonight?—I'm just tiptop, thank you for callin'. No, I'm not asleep. It's just a slight headache or a foggy connection.—No, really, I'm fine, Doctor, I'm an American—I wasn't raised t' feel pain even if I did feel it."

"Always a pill," Teddy mutters, rolling a joint.

"She's down in New Hope visiting her Siamese twin. Oh, yes, you're right, they're not Siamese. Yeah, it's a dangerous time, the restraints are off, ha ha—but I'm only intoxicated by A.A. this weekend, Doctor. Went to three meetings already. Didn't we go to three meetings?"

"I'm not here." Teddy watches candleshadows on his portraits of Mahler, Bruckner, and Wagner, red firelight playing on sculpted rococo frames. *Tasteful,* he thinks with a pang. Busts of Wagner and Beethoven. Sees someone seated at the dark kitchen table.

"Oh, we been workin', Doctor—very hard. I had a bit

of a fall in the bathtub. Well, my thigh's all sort of black and blue and yellow and red. Got a big lump on it too. Should be better by morning. Oh, sure it hurts, but I ignore it, Doctor! I can't be bothered."

Teddy's scalp ices as he stares at Shadowman seated in the kitchen. "That's not Martin. Who is it?"

"I'm thinkin' of goin' directly to bed, Doctor. Bite to eat and last smoke! I may read my Bible too, conditions permitting. Where d'ya think I should start? The New Testament? Oh, you don't read that! Well, maybe Exodus will be entertaining."

"Hey, you sonofabitch!" Teddy calls at the kitchen. "Come in here!"

A feathered white shadow leaps beside him. He turns to see a scrawny chicken on the streetwindow sill. The bird's head cocks, oneeying him intently, the eye sick with a milky membrane, neckfeathers torn off.

"Look at that!" Teddy giggles. "The sky's fallin', Chicken Little! You come all the way from San Juan?"

The thin white bantam stalks through the livingroom. Teddy's cells freeze. "Tell Dr. Deer there's a Puerto Rican housefly walkin' through our livingroom. A killer chicken! Slightly underfed. You peck my toes, you self-important bastard, I'll gas you in the oven."

Shadowman moves. Teddy watches the huge kitchen blob scrape slowly to the lightless icebox, take out a month-old loaf of sprouted rye. The chicken walks fearlessly into the kitchen, puck-puck, its head jerking forward, backward, a big cake of droppings stuck to its bottom. Master of all it surveys.

"Leo?" Teddy calls.

"What?"

"Oh. I thought you were in the kitchen. *Hey!* close the icebox, buster!"

Brk, brk, brrk, brrk-brrk-brrrrrk! the bantam squawks and flaps into the high milk shelf just as the shadow closes the icebox, growling *"Arrngh! Goot, goot!"*

Teddy's vision doubles and blurs. "I know that voice!" He breaks out his reading glasses, drops his head into wobbling frames, peers at Leo's eyes. "Ahh! Put on your glasses, you'll see better. 'S the heat. Who you talkin' to?"

"Dr. Deer."

"Idiot. I haven't paid the phone bill in six months."

"Well, you handed it to me!"

"Gimme." Teddy takes the phone. "Dr. Deer? *Dr. Deer?* Ha, Christ it's dead—no dial tone!"

"Must've hung up—I fell asleep. Ohh, damn. Wanted to ask him something. Forget."

". . . We got a fuckin' chicken nesting in the icebox," Teddy says.

"You squirrelly again? Show me."

A high, smug smile fills Teddy. "I can't!"

"Why not?"

"There's someone in the kitchen!" he whispers.

"Who?"

"I dunno. But I know his voice."

Leo eyes the flickering kitchen, sits back halfasleep. "Okay, you answer the phone, smartass."

"It's not ringing! Here, *listen!*" Teddy dangles the receiver against Leo's head.

"Boy," Leo says, "you must think I'm really far gone. Did I *say* it was ringing? I *meant* when it does ring. What's wrong, you afraid to answer the phone?"

"I hate fuckin' bells. Fuckin' thing's dead!"

"Ha!" Leo sneers at Teddy. "Can't teach a dumb dog old tricks. All right, I'll answer it. Might be Wanda. Where's that joint?"

Teddy wobbles sideways, trying to pinch up the joint. "Shit." Falls back fagged. "You pick it up, 's right there."

Leo leans past Teddy, weaving on his spine as Teddy grabs him from falling. Deep inspiration burns Leo's face, he sums up their situation. *"Maybe* we don't need any more! I don't want pot slurrin' my speech Wanda calls. She'll think *I* been drinkin' too."

"Right. You're shut off. I'll drink yours."

"Aw shit, I'll smoke too."

Teddy pinches up the joint at last, holds it shimmying before his lips, hands it to Leo. "Put this in my mouth."

Leo plugs the wavering joint into Teddy. Leo-Teddy beams at his awe-inspiring wickedness.

Teddy grins. *"Gustav!"*

"Anton!"

Military kisses, both cheeks. Glitter into each other's big blue eyes lovingly.

Leo-Teddy looks for confirmation from the Mahler-Bruckner-Wagner over the desk, reads GRAY MOOR.

Teddy groans, moves the sherry to his side. *"I* may get

sick if I don't have enough." Chills pierce him. "Got a match?"

Leo eyes Teddy's facewaver in his helmet's candleflame shadow. "Maybe we should split the bottle evenly, *ahem.*"

"I don't think tha's fair at all. You have smaller capacity. Stands to reason I need more." Listens to dragfooted shadow crinkling bread package open.

"Goot, goot!"

" 'S not enough for both of us as it is," Leo decides. "We may as well split it."

"Don't insist an' make me angry, Gustav. I'm not easily swayed." Teddy thinks of the shadowman they saw at Andy's Factory.

"I can't sit here dry while you drink! I already tried that for half a year, remember?"

Leo holds up their bag of red diet pills, green downers—red-green boyhood recall of Norwegian sweaters with reindeer-Christmas tree-diamond patterns jagged with homefeelings.

". . . Those were good days!" Teddy recalls strongly. "You in A.A., all the booze for me. Never come again! Now *I'll* be in A.A. Of course, you're stoppin' too, you'll help me. You wouldn' drink in fronta me, wouldya?"

"Sure! You're not easily swayed."

"TORTURING me?"

" 'S all in your mind. Don' project. Start workin' on your First Step."

"My name is Teddy an' I am POWERFUL over alcohol!"

"Powerless."

"Ridiculous. If I stop, I'm powerful. Besides, I don't have t' say I'm URRP! alcoholic. I only gotta desire stop drinkin'. Ya think I don't know my rights in A.A.? I know ALL my rights, buddy. I'll do the wine-splittin'. Where's . . . le's go kitchen. Glasses."

"Can we make it? I don't think I can . . ."

Teddy brings the bottle as they crawl toward the kitchen—stops. *"Shh.* Watch out for that selfpitying bastard at the table. He's a prize pig. Kept me awake for hours last night."

"Somebody's been comin' in here?"

"Oh, he's a terrible leech. An' what a temper! I think he's got worms in his brain. He's habitual meatbeater, really, chronic. I hear 'im at it for hours."

"Wha's he look like?" Leo asks, his bruised leg wobbling.

"Never seen 'im. Jus' hear him *moaning*. Sometimes he sounds dangerous. Keeps cryin'."

"About what?"

" 'Peace and quiet! Peace and quiet!' Scares me shitless. Stops by the bedroom doorway to listen to *you* snorin'. It gets on his nerves. You're lucky he hasn't whipped you. Ignore him," Teddy warns wisely. "If he *sighs*, pretend you don't hear it."

"He's got a whip?"

"Not yet. He wants to break off the TV aerial, whip the shit out of us. *Shh!*" Shadow at icebox snatches out bantam squawker by its neck, whirls bird overhead cracking its neck, runs it under boiling sinkwater, plucked feathers falling on tub and floor, soft, steady pressure of chicken thigh cracking off—

"Goot! Goot!"

"Maybe we better skip glasses," Teddy says, dripping headsweat.

"Are ya sure he's really out there?"

"Man, he comes in here every night! I'm lucky I get an hour's sleep."

Leo-Teddy backs kneeling into livingroom. Turns. Suddenly Teddy shakes I-I-I-I-IEE! rises quivering to his knees spine frozen.

"What's up!" Leo whispers.

Teddy roundeyed at giant Shadowman hunched over his desk. *"There, he's there!"*

"How'd he get in *here?*"

Shadowman leans over to read a long redcrayon poem lettered onto wallplaster by Teddy's desk—

BLOODWINE
I sit by my bulletproof window
over Seventh and Paranoia
singing
There is a gallows made of wine!
National Blood Bank
barred me for life today—
even the vampires reject me.
I'm missing
my little wine treats,
I'm missing the action today.

Shadowman SIGHS, an earthdeep quaver, thrumming bass drawn on bone. Hands thrump heavily to desk, head hanging hopeless. Shaking—is Shadowman sobbing? Something weirdly familiar about that square head, the slumped huge shoulders, neckplugs. SIGHHHH! Shadowman lifts a raw thigh sandwich on moldy rye, great molars crack chickenbone, ketchup leaking. Spots on the floor, too smooth for ketchup! Ripples convulse Teddy's jaw, chattering, jolting him upright as Leo listens to Teddy's kneebones jiggle on the floor.

"Serves him right," Leo hears Jack say, "give the sick sonofabitch a drink."

Leo nudges Teddy onto their floor pillows. "Ignore 'im! You need a drink."

Teddy falls on the bottle, heart fluttering, a sobbing moan fishboned in his throat. Drinks brassy sugarheavy cream sherry. Everything since the movie comes up instantly, shooting, drooling, his pillow curded.

"He's lucky," Jack tells Leo, "it didn't come out his ears."

Teddy drinks, heaves again. *"Can't keep it down!"* Falls convulsing on hands and knees, tears dripping. Nothing helps, stomach orgasms without stop. *"Can't breathe!"* Leo slaps him on the back, his own thigh pulsing.

"Try drinkin' slower," he says.

Teddy sips, convulsing, scratchy glass grinding on his denture. Sherry on chin and throat, again he vomits, nothing left, spasming emptily. "Terrible, terrible. Can't lay down." Crawls onto his sopped pillow, sits up spasming. "Can't go on! Cigarette. Whersh joint?"

"You're sittin' on it. Maybe pot'll only make it worse."

Teddy digs out the wet joint. "I'm bad shape!"

"Things could be worse," Leo repeats after Jack. "Think of Jack with the Mexican army after 'im."

"Not UHH! not UHH! not gonna UHH! *live!*"

"Buck up! You jus' need li'l booze."

"How'm I gon' DRINK MORE to keep *him* away? Can' take in any MORE! Not daily, man!"

"We gon' Gray Moor tomorrow."

"Won' UHH! be alive tomorrow UHH! if I'm lucky." Eyes his pillow. "Shit my pansh again."

"Nah, thash jus' puke." Arms ashoulder. "You past th' crisis. Hang on."

"HANG ON?" Teddy reels aside, spasming.

Leo takes off his redcheck shirt, wipes Teddy's beard. Teddy grabs the shirt. "Is tha' blood?"

"Hm! How's your ulcer?"

Teddy breaks down, sobbing without stop, loudly.

"Buck up, for Chrissake!"

"He needs A.A.," Jack says. "Hit 'im when he's lowest, really sock it to him!"

"You need A.A.!"

"I'M PAST A.A.!"

"Come on, jus' conshentrate," Leo says. "Tomorrow your firs' big day of sobriety at Gray Moor. Month from now you be sittin' in Stark's or Schrafft's affer the meetin's—with all *The Sobriety!"*

"I HATE THAT WORD!"

"I'll never use it again."

"How's A.A. gon' help me *now?"* Teddy weeps.

"We could call for police amb'lance."

"Idiot!" His face contorts gruesomely. "The *pho-one's* dead!"

"We try booth on corner."

"I can' CRAWL tha' far! Anyway, the Puerto Rican army polished it off."

"Try th' Serenity Prayer."

"Tha' won' help. D'ya remember it?"

". . . No!"

"You SEE! I'm HOPELESS!"

Leo's head hangs as churning spasms bend Teddy double barking seal barks.

"Tell your story!" Leo says. "Like I did."

"Lotta good tha' did you," Teddy gasps, "you lyin' potfreak."

"Maybe you can be more honest."

"Opiumhead!"

"Yeah, well . . . I wasn't at my besht. Tell *me* your story—but be honest. Go ahead. Start!"

"Start where?"

"For Chrissake," Leo says, "you heard a hundred, two hundred stories."

"I never listened," Teddy said. "How'd they start?"

Leo's mouth clamps.

"My name is Teddy an' I'ma alcoholic! HA! DON' DRINK!"

Shadowman shoves his sandwich violently aside, turns

slowly in his chair to face Teddy. Teddy belches, horror releasing him at last from spasms. Shadowman smiles, grimly familiar, listening, his peering, suffering, liquid black eyes yellowrimmed, half-dead, lizardlike, gravely intent, begging, insane. His great highdomed powerbox skull, smoothed over pale putty flesh with his maker's thumbprints still embedded—and yet his head seems healed of old scars, reborn awesomely fresh—his slaughterlidded eyes and quick lipless tic, even his neckplugs and damp black hair capping his steel-clamped brow, chop Teddy with cleaving recognition. An image, soulmirrored, flashes from the ghoul into Teddy's brightening spine. The monster gnaws his lips, waiting, skin bloodlessly green-gray, his two front uppers missing.

"AGGGHH!"

Teddy bursts into tears. "Pull 'em out," he pleads, "so I don' swallow 'em!"

Leo loosens Teddy's teeth, solemnly shimmies them onto a bookshelf. "Come on, *give!*"

"Mine is the thaddetht thtory ever told! NOBODY'S EVER THUFFERED AS I THUFFER!—AGHH! AGHH! AGHHHHH!—I AM THE THADDETHT MAN ON EARTH! AND NOOBODY CAN H-HELP ME!"

Leo sprouts tears. *"You tell it honest, Teddy! That's* REAL *honest!"*

"*Arrnngh!*" the monster warns.

Teddy glares wonderingly and at last sees a two-foot being growing from the monster's thigh, a shriveled, humpspined, brokennecked crazy shepherd in a laced jacket, his head a mat of short hairs, Baby Leo-faced, fawning at the monster, then questioning Teddy severely. "*Be honest,*" the shepherd warns, hanging angled from the monster's hip, his eyes accusing as Stella's. Little Ygor twists, wiping the monster's desk crumbs onto the sandwich plate, polishes drops of chickenblood into his jacketsleeve, unlaces his top and stuffs the dripping sandwich against his breast, licks his fingers clean. *"You tell the truth, little man,"* he tells Teddy, lacing himself up chickenbreasted.

Teddy tonguetied, reeling. "Don' tell anyone 'bout tha' chicken!" he warns Leo. "They'll think I'm *crazy.*"

Leo sucks his bloody thumb, cheeks shining wet. "Wha' chicken?"

"Forget about it! Oh, what'th it matter? I'm hopeleth! I wanna *kill* mythelf!"

"Arnh! Arnh!" the monster urges him, nodding. Ygor looks as if this might not be enough, spiritually—that much more is called for.

"Tell your story, Teddy. *I'll* understand you."

"I thtarted drinkin' at theven when we thtole two ales from a fire ethcape an' drank 'em in the Shea's. I'll tell you about loththes!" Teddy's helmet spills candlewax. "Give you a horror thtory like ya never heard!" Firefly red waxdrops drip and drift down his wrists. "Oh my God, how I've thuffered. Loneliness, misery, dethpair. My life'th been hard thailin', buthter. Loth' the two women I loved, Thalome and Thynara. I'm curthed!"

"Arrnh! Argnnh!" the monster agrees.

"No guilt! I'm not remortheful. I'm even col'hearted at times. Gotta admit it! Gotta be—t' achieve my greatetht. I admit I'm not perfect."

Ygor applauds quietly, head nodding on broken neck.

Teddy decays to his knees, rises again inspired. "I need a devoted woman who will thacrifithe herthelf to my art."

The monster squeezed Ygor. *"A bride, a bride!"* Ygor calls.

"I won' compromise. I need total devotion. I may be th' motht perfec' musical mind twentieth thentury! I'm capable of vatht achievementth. I can't be dependent on anyone—the plan for my latetht libretto already dwarfth th' *Ring Thycle*. I profoundly believe tha' mine ith the greatetht thtory ever tol'—who has ever thuffered a greater cruthifixion?

"I deserve limousines, a patron, the Russian Tea Room, caviar, Thtolichnaya vodka, champagne breakfaththth! But my needs are modetht. Day isn't long enough for me t' fulfill my great effortth exthpec' from mythelf. Am underwhelmed by thmall minds! Debt collectors, need to thurvive—conthtantly dragged down—*unexthprethed!*"

Hot anxiety fills the moaning monster. Ygor soothes his scarred wrist. The monster grips Ygor's hand, Ygor returns intense support, sympathy, kisses Boris's green-glowing hand.

"But all shit I take, I thtan' up PRETTY WELL! Pain woulda killed lether men. Never been happy day in my life. Either conthtipated or my athhole's blithtered from athids. My crotch rash's terrible! How many times lose my front teeth? Bleedin' gums, ulthers, hoppin' thtomach. I'm leprouth, my toenails crack, my toes bleed, my hair falls out like tumbleweed, my breath paralyzed, pores are ranthid, eyes itch conthtantly, I can't thee acroth the room without glatheth. Poor brain thirculation, no memory! My teeth are purple and wobbly, what're left. No thex life! All th' girls I fuck are frigid—but maybe I'm a thwine, I admit it. Can't help it! Fuck a telephone booth if it'd have me! Thteal from the library in th' name of American music. Thteal from thupermarketth an newsthtan's, caught onthe by Brentano's thtore detective, twithe by dickth in th' A&P! My houthe's a roach palathe, toilet'th rottin' from upthtairs overflow an' may fall into th' bathement, don' have a thtick of livingroom furniture an' my lightth are off! Hifi dyin' of rotten tubes, motherfuckin' TV won' work! I'm musician can't earn a living off his horn—I'll never have a great lip again, not like when I was thirty. Tholes flap, gotta wear thirty-nine thent rubber thandals tha' pick up glath. Even thtagger when I'm thober! Balanthe is shit on the thubway! Thith ain' life! I been shanghaied! Fear th' doorbell, can' open my mail, grothery tab's thtaggering. Wortht of all, I even got a Thiamese twin who's almotht thickeningly NORMAL! Who could pothibly live thith way? His complete dithregard for my health and thpirit is dithguthting—I been deprethed thinthe birth. Do better alone. Can' thtand his eternal dependenthy another minute! Takin' care of him my every wakin' moment! Don' have a friend on earth! No future! No one underthtan's me! When's life gonna thtart payin' off? *I wanna kill mythelf!*

"THERE!" Teddy cries terribly, glaring at Leo.

"So what else is new? Suicide! CAN'T YOU BE HONEST?"

"Thaid I wanna get rid of you!"

"Stick me in th' oven, Adolf."

"I HATE YOU! I HATE MYTHELF! WE SHOULD BE DEAD!"

Leo's eyes close, head drifting away in sleep. "Oh, you make me tired."

Ygor's arms cross, he bores with relentless sternness into Teddy. The monster twitches, his great black nails open and close, scarred naked arms stretch out of black suitcoat, hungering for rape.

"Don' leave me!" Teddy grabs Leo. "Wake up, wake up!"

"Oh shit, lemme alone." Leo fades. "Ya *couldn't* be honest. . . ."

"You're leavin' me alone with *them!*"

A winding, growling, whiplash winefart rasps from the monster as Ygor grabs him by the coat. *"Down, down!"* Ygor commands. The seated monster reaches for Teddy's long TV aerial, snaps it from the machine. Teddy lifts his arm to save his TV just as the monster stares at him harshly.

"Doesn't work!" Teddy cries, pointing at his set. "Dirty fuckin' machine!"

"ARRGNNGGHH!"

Raging monster whips TV, Ygor jiggling vainly.

Teddy's set bursts. *"Bomb General Motors!"* he cries in tears.

Unchained, the monster's fury rises, he roars to his feet, Ygor's legs flying as he clings for life to the monster's shrunken mudcaked sleeve. Scummed hifi tubes splinter under the whip, the turntable lifts like a flapjack, the speakers' filthy cloth facings hang shredded. Teddy cowers as the silver scourge whistles above him. *Slam* the aerial cracks onto Teddy's desk, handwriting curling as pain shoots through Teddy.

Ygor screams at Teddy. *"Now see what you've done!"* Deep guilt pierces Teddy at Ygor's whiteeyed fingerpointing. The dwarf pleads with the monster, cuffing his green ear. *"Stop! Stop it before you hurt yourself, you big fag!"*

Teddy barks under upraised arms, strangling on fear.

The whip backlashes the bust of Wagner, a wedge of plaster forehead flying in chips, then smarts into the framed glass likeness of Mahler's sideview, Bruckner's white hair and large gentle nose, Wagner's purple cap, flowing locks, hard blue eyes. Books leap from shelves, written sheets burst tinnily whipped in air. The howling monster whales into the unusable old trombone hanging on the hat tree, Teddy's stolen library records of the *Ring Cycle,* incomplete, lashes the huge, aged, rented broken-down electric monster typewriter, then lifts it overhead as Teddy gibbers below and heaves it out the open airshaft window. A grinding crunch on concrete dies into the marginbell's horrible echo.

"He doesn't *like* you!" Ygor cries at Teddy. *"Sing to him!"*

Leo's head lifts. "Wha'?"

"Thing, goddamnit! Thing, thing, thing!"

Leo stares at the face of alcohol made flesh blustering into his. His thumb throbs.

"THING!"

"Wahh!" Leo cries, and bites Teddy's nose. Pain blooms in his own crotch.

Teddy rips back bleeding, his nose half bitten through. Shaking fingers lift fearfully to touch his pouring nose, the tip's loose wobble. Barking, indignant groans cough from him, his face clouds with pain, dripping blood—he eyes Leo unbelievingly. "My brother?!" he says.

Leo's blue with hatred, suddenly bats Teddy's throat, his thigh on fire. Teddy twists Leo's ear so hard Leo screams.

"You!" Teddy glitters, helmet askew. "You're deranged! What the hell's got inta you?" Leans forward, his eye swelling, nose running red. "You've ruined me, you fool!"

"Die!"

"Thtop shouting!" Teddy groans, his shuddering hands filling with blood.

"I'll shout all I want to." Leo dangles sideways, sobbing.

A big thumb of shit mushrooms from Teddy as he sobs into his wet red fists. *"I'll kill you!"*

"I'll *sing* all right! If I had a knife I'd cut your feeble-minded head off! I can't stand your goddamn yakkin' another minute!"

"Juth' shut up," Teddy cries. "Moth' inthane bullshit I ever heard in my life. I did nothin' t' hurt you, thuddenly you try to bit my nothe off. And *thtrangle* me! You've lotht all loyalty for me. It'th juth' incredible. We're quitth! —don' think I'll ever accthept you back as my brother, y'blitherin' athhole." Teddy can barely touch his flaming nose.

Leo snorts at the nose. "It was gettin' too big anyway. You should be hanged!" Holds his swollen cut thumb up. "How dya think my thumb got this way?"

"Ya exthpect me t' remember every idiotic thing *you* do? It was an accthident! How'd it happen?"

"Up at Andy's, moron! Ya got any idea what's happened to us today?"

"—Perfec'ly normal day. Why? Wha'th that got t' do with *bitin' my nothe* an' *chokin'* me?"

"First ya had a diabetic convulsion at th' Metropolitan an' tossed your cookies!"

"Firtht we did *not* go t' the Met today, buthter, and thecond I don't have diabetes! HAH!"

"The Metropolitan grindhouse? for the meatbeaters matinee—remember the ambulance?"

"Oh that—that'th not why ya bit me."

"Shitting your pants there?"

"I never shit my pantth in my life! Twithted—you're really twithted! Why can't you be honetht?"

"Then why're we goin' t' Gray Moor?"

"You muth' be crazy t' think I'm goin' *anywhere* with you."

"How 'bout throwin' up inta the camera durin' the screen test?"

"Ridiculouth. Our thcreen thetht was a howling thucctheth. But I'll thue the bathtard anyway. He didn' pay me an' is gonna make a million off that li'l piethe of film. Can ya imagine what a film clip of Mahler'd be worth today?"

"Howlin' success, huh? That why you bit my thumb?"

"I exthplained that! I don't remember it. Ya thmall-minded creep, ya sure know how to put things in their wortht light."

"How 'bout fallin' off the subway platform?"

"Don't blame me if *you* path out, buddy."

"Gettin' thrown outta the funeral parlor?"

"Nobody could throw uth out—we *left.* Got that thtraight? I'm not thrown outta anyplathe. You are a math of thuthpicions—you're thick! And shut up on the convulsion bullshit."

"You just been havin' the dry heaves for half an hour—you're sittin' in the shit! Gonna deny this fuckin' vomit right on the floor?"

"Thith converthation's ended. Fuck off, willya?"

Leo reaches for the wine. Teddy slaps his arm down, moves the bottle back.

"Gimme that wine."

"Buthter, *you've* had too much."

"You'll regret this."

"Look at my blood! *My nothe, my nothe!*"

Leo clips Teddy's denture from the bookcase, pitches it clattering against the closet. "HAH!"

Teddy stares unmoved, snorts at the teeth. "I won't need those anymore," he whispers. Turns his head, swigs at the wine. Leo takes up the bag of red uppers. Teddy snatches the bag of green downers, lifts his chin in self-sacrifice, starts sobbing quietly. Unknots his bag, licks a deep handful of downers into his throat, washes them bellyward with creamsherry. Eyes Leo with a haughty snivel, bursts into deep sobs, sits back as if knighted, sobs wretchedly staring straight ahead, nose dripping red into his beard.

"Fuck you!" Leo whispers grandly. Empties bag of uppers into his mouth. Stretches for the wine, Teddy watching disdainfully, his lips swollen with sobs. Leo washes down his own pills, sits against the wall, leg pounding brightly.

Leo-Teddy sits glassyeyed. At last Teddy's sobs work on Leo, his breath catches and he too doubles over gripped with self-pity.

Teddy's beard and throat, bloody as if his throat's cut. He gasps tragically, *"We shoulda done thith before, Thtanley! We 're Goats!"*

Leo nods vigorously, sobbing. *"Feels good t' die!"*

Weird shadows leap as Teddy's helmet candle gutters out. A lone winebottle flames on the bookcase. Too dim for farewell notes. Teddy's pulse a slow long throb, their breath and sobs from one body in rhyme.

"Goot, goot!" the monster whispers.

Widegrinning metal-clamped boxskull, he's seated at the desk again, blissfully beaming Ygor riding his knee, the monster's lead-gleaming cranelike hand calling gently to Teddy. Something more real than movies lights his huge powerhead, give his skin green-bright life—it is his smile, teddybear splitting wide, hesitant, pleading, and the fellowship his rich black shining corpseeyes beg Teddy to give. Here is the monster Teddy has always loved! charming Teddy's very soul! and nervous with gifts for Teddy he shoves his chair back revealing a set of clear belljars lined up on the desk. *"Look!"* the monster's open heart implores, "look at my *friends!*" Gloating, licking his lip, he gently lifts the tall glass bell from a jar holding a white ballerina. At once the Lilliputian dancer smiles overpoweringly at Teddy with her tiny red mouth and starts dancing on the desk. Her leaps and turns, deep runnings and high flights bind him with their grace and small swanbeating bones. The scherzo from Tchaikovsky's Sixth corkscrews from the walls. Teddy hopes she'll never stop dancing. She leaps from the desk, landing on point on the linoleum, whirls ever more swiftly, dips away, hops floating over Teddy's denture and flutters to the kitchen. His heart suddenly beats hard as he sees something move in the darkness of the open icebox. Her tremendous familiarity floods Teddy as she smiles from afar and at last he sees that she is his old flame—a long soft rat jumps heavily from the icebox, short red penis gleaming, scuttles across the kitchen and bites into the ballerina's white hips as horror blooms in waves from Teddy's feet to his scalp. The fat rat runs under the sink with Salome limp in its muzzle and, tail beating excitedly, is gone. The monster, busy with his next jar, doesn't see Teddy frozen and openmouthed or miss his dancer. Teddy's skin feels splitting and about to shed itself of a fearful, loathesome speckling. The earnest monster again lifts a glass bell and reveals a glowingly eager white stallion ridden by a noble erect baby wholly encased in glittering armor, the horse's loose white hide flicking in quick folds over brimming muscles, rigid arteries. The Swan theme from *Lohengrin* wells from the bloodred walls. The armored baby holds a great red, white and black flag stuck into a pole rest below the saddle as the shining horse leaps onto the desk, liquid banner jiggling from a spear with a tall threadbound blade holding an old hammerhead nail. The white horse nervously, slowly parades about the desk. Baby rolls in the saddle, sprawling backward, then against the banner's spear, falls forward nearly off the saddle, never grasping pommel or reins, then slips off the saddle's flagless side, twirling on his armored butt, and marvelously recovers. The monster and Ygor hurrah in glee. Awe fills Teddy for the wonderful horse, its slow singing march in small high steps, but rolling baby sets him trembling again. At last horse and rider halt at the next belljar, baby rolling back as if awaiting some grail from the sky. A loud WAHHH! and hungersobs scream from the closed helmet. The monster lifts open the next belljar. A nippled quart of clear Russian vodka towers over horse and baby, label beautifully lettered, the bright vodka pure, spellbindingly clear, perhaps holy. Ygor's hairy finger flips back baby's visor. *Goot, goot!* Now Ygor loosens and lifts away baby's helmet and Teddy sees baby's black toothbrush mustache and black crow's wing across baby's forehead—painful familiarity! baby Adolf?—the eyes seem Teddy's, hauntingly his own, blue, piercing, the round skull, wide large beating temples. As horseman he does not cut a good figure! Yet now he sees the banner's white circle and black swastika on bloodred field, terrifyingly attractive, hateful—deep satisfaction floods from its liquid shock, energy, brilliance, its rapturous power like a roaring in his ears, *mein lieber Schwan!* its staff spearing his inmost being to grip work, work, work as his salvation, whatever the sacrifice in personal emotions, strangling all pity on himself. No pity for Teddy! he must Work. My God, *forever?* No choice, big sigh of duty, he's divinely handpicked. And for work he needs pick-me-up, gallons of it. *Juice!* WAHHDKAAA!! The grinning monster lifts the bottle, steals a long suck from its nipple, bubbles gurgling upward as little Ygor tugs his sleeve. The wetchinned monster, richly inspired now, tucks Ygor underarm and shoves the nipple into his foul yellow teeth. Eyes closed and cloudborne with joy, Ygor suckles eagerly. Baby rages on his saddle while Ygor moans, guzzling. The monster glances virginally at Teddy, asking forgiveness, then clucks comfort at the rolling little mustached knight. Still baby Ygor drinks in bliss. At last the monster licks a lingering drop from the nipple as Ygor rolls on the monster's knee, both of them shiningeyed. The monster's great bony arm cranes the bottle over baby Teddolf, who tearily watches a fresh clear drop waver on the giant nipple's amber slit. Green muddy fingers hold the colossal bottle in midair as baby Teddolf slurps the quivering drop, his lips just covering the slit. Swallowing, swallowing, his neck balloons and strains after more vodka, the bottlewash sparkling, his wet red eyes now opening and closing parrotlike pupils. *At last I'll get enough!* Teddy thinks. But baby Teddolf, his face and neck flushing red, swelling, veins and eyes popping, can't stop. The monster smiles, grim with joy—a creature more stupid than himself, what triumph! Ygor points out gladly that the bottle's still three-fifths full, there's a long way for baby to go. Teddolf's pink, splayed rigid hands swell past his wristguard armor. His round body seeks every split and chink until the armor swells, creaking. Brownflecked vodka leaks off the saddle under baby Teddolf's rump—the monster and Ygor giggle. *Stop, stop!* Teddy tries to cry, but now baby Teddolf convulses in the saddle, still drinking as the horse's white flank pipes with blood-streaked vodka. Fevered baby gulps and swells, raging to put out vodka fire with more vodka. Teddy loves Teddolf, loves his balance and black mustache, even the sucking swollen lips mashed against his face by the bottle. Ever bigger Teddolf arches and bends in the saddle, perhaps to snap his spine as his very soul flips fishlike. Some fact in baby's buttoneyed stupor of guzzling hooks Teddy's imagination. Baby's nose is growing! Not only that, horsey's trampled wahdka into muddy muck on the desk and already sinks up to his girdle in bog. Growing roses of rust speckle and pit baby Teddolf's armor until baby's hot pink fat swells through the holes. Baby's bare legs appear as leg mail bursts its rotted threads and armor plates fall into mud. At this coming appearance of the bare hero himself, violins soar radiantly from cracked walls. Breastplate and waistplate rust and fall. Shockwaves shaking him, naked Teddolf drinks on, his skin—belly, arms, legs, head—drumtight with vodka as horsey sinks. Teddolf's inflamed pisser pisses an acid hole into his saddle and straight into his wildeyed sinking horse's spine. The saddle falls in two, steaming. Teddolf squishes on the bare, rotted spine, vodka piss steaming into horsey's bloating belly. Baby's falling jowls wobble, wide pink gristle grows on baby's nose, his mouth splits like a horrible puppet's, his upper lip's notched under a wrinkling long hairy snout. As horsey sinks out of sight, his ears fly to baby Teddolf's head! And now Teddolf lies alone in the muck, a bristled pink pig big as a horse, licking the bottle's last drops, a superacidic, gagging mash smell bursting sourly from every pore as, *mein lieber Schwein!* the violins crest, sweetly crest, the squealing pig struggling to lick inside the amber nipple, penis-tongue shooting inside for more, the snout itself working inside until the pig's head goes licking up the glass neck, piggy's forelegs scrabbling at the nipple's slit to get in, back legs humping piggy's great head through the narrow bottleneck until the hooved forelegs are into the clear glass womb, the obscene pink tongue licking the wall's liquor, piggy's convulsing body urging itself at highest labor through the neck, curled tail inside, back hooves wiggling and at last *whoosh* stuffed air blows from the bottle as the great pig stands within, snout licking the bottom in circles. Teddy's breath blows at piggy's unbelievable WORK at getting into the bottle. Great pride slimes Ygor's and the monster's loving dead eyes. Selfsweetening sugary fiddles build loudly and turn into a drumthumping goose-step victory march, *Sieg heils* rocketing as marching legs swing high, straight and stiff, the monster holding the stuffed bottle up to his eye as he shakes happily his still pissing, clever pig-in-a-bottle, sets the bottle back and the belljar comes down on upside-down Teddolf on his nose within, doomed black mustache whisking in piss, snout snuffling, tongue rooting out the last vodka vapor on the glass, big blue eye pressed outward at the candlelit room and coldly intelligent to the roots of its being.

Pining grief sweeps Teddy for the piss-drowning pig. But nothing can turn the monster's hooting good will toward Teddy as It opens the third and largest belljar. Here's a two-story cottage of cutaway rooms—sills banked with potted snaps, porch blooming with glads, giant hocks nodding giraffelike against the raintrough. Teddy's longing leaps painfully—the lake cottage always desired! A framed sampler over the fireplace reads

FEAR THE LORD

The motto cleaves him with second thoughts. On the diningroom wall hangs

MILK AND HONEY
COMING LATER!

You won't be around for milk and honey, a shadow warns Teddy. His grief deepens. Wordless question, the space filled by his being—sheer questionless question! Boneshaking trembling strikes him speechless with forewarnings of nonbeing. Leo and Teddy sit in the livingroom, musicstand up, horns in hand. Look about five-years-old, barely able to read words, much less music. A tall lean silver-haired shadow heads the diningroom table, Jack sits at his right and around the table bright shadows sit wreathed like leafy vines and olive branches. Wholeness and grace hang over the shadows—they are at a continual feast, filled with terrific contentment. Teddy yearns for the pleasure of their company. Jack reads to the group from a big blue book on the table, abruptly laughs at himself and cries out, *"Then those two interns bundled me up in a canvas sportsjacket!"*

The twins begin playing "What a Friend We Have in Jesus"—Teddy's never heard them play so well. Overpowering melody wells from the small horns, their tones flowing gold. The monster silent, eyes streaming, little Ygor stricken with eager melody. Teddy rebukes himself for never having joined a Salvation Army band, vows he will next chance. Always loved that four-square gospel music on horns! Grayblue shadow darkens the cottage, snowflakes falling. The lake freezes. Twins in their Norwegian sweaters run out on the lake, with a heavy pick jab a hole through the hard gray hood. Crinkle nightcrawlers onto their hooks, drop lines deep into the lake, red bobbers floating on green water. Raked iceboats skate on edge from Chautauqua. Other lake fishermen unbudging at far holes this gray winter afternoon. Leo-Teddy fixes on the hole in the lessening light, a chill breeze washing his ribs, pricking his ankles. Suddenly both bobbers sink, lines yanked taut. Something below tugs unbelievably hard. Twins booted heels dig back, the fish like the lakebottom itself spinning about. *Rock of Gibraltar!* they cry—this isn't a fish they've hooked. They give no line but hold fast, slowly pulling back. Something THUMPS underfoot, a tremendous shadow floods darkly by under the heavy ice. At last the twins back onto the shore, line twined on their arms, Leo pulling Teddy. A pale, rubbery, almost see-through lip rises through the icehole. More lip appears, and more lip, and now a great glistening bulldog fishjaw pulls up. The hole swells with a long cavelike fishmouth, longer and longer, still rising until the head of an enormous largemouthed bass slides onto the ice, its head taller than the twins themselves. Still they pull, up the shore, back slowly up the cottage's snowfilled yard. The bass grows taller, taller, the more that rises from the hole the more immense the fish gets. Now they pull the fish, higher and plumper than a railroad car, off the lake and onto their front yard as they back onto the porch. The long fish lies in the yard, big mouth ready to swallow the cottage, tail switching heavy snowbanks. The huge mouth closes on ugly tractorshovel hinges, opens again, long and deep, a mammoth cave, daylight gleaming through thin blue gristle. The bass stills, waiting, its tremendous eyes lidless, unblinking, eyes tall as stagecoach wheels, silver-rimmed eternity saucers. The twins go down to rip their hooks from the rubber lip, find baits still wriggling, call it a day with one fish. Jack watches from the porch, ashine. *"Boy,"* he says, *"fishermen's luck!* The lake dropped four inches, I'll bet." Leo-Teddy stands by a high gill opening on spongey red plates slowly feathering with unmelting flakes. The great gill closes on snow, opens for more. Twins pass chest fins splayed on snow, the black, greenish body, pale white belly an armored bank of gloprunning scales, and round the tallbranching tailfin. As they crunch back to the porch, spiny backfins rise above the cottage roof, nervously settle. Nightfolk twins on the porchsteps, staring down the bass's huge throat halfway into the body. "Maybe you'll let me still-fish with you someday," Jack says going indoors, "you guys sure have what it takes." Twins sit considering their gifts, look above at clear stars, pieces of light going deeper and deeper into the heavens. For the first time, awesome depths draw a peculiar wonder as Leo-Teddy ponders the nightheavens. Deeps beyond deeps above the aura of lake ice, eyebinding deeps asking a wordless answer from their still wonder. The tremendous wonder demands a sound, some word from pieces and pieces of light within them, a private, pure reply as their being mirrors the Being above. The live fish shines in the dark. They come out with their giant redplastic flashlight, study the fish's eye in the night. Too high up! Off to bed, second floor. In the night they wake to find their bed walking to the window. The bass has writhed next to the house and, hardly a breath away, gleams a great fish eye, black, glimmering, a bottomless pool of intelligence staring at them—unblinking perpetual attention from the lakedepths. Their breath steams the eyefilm. "Is it dying?" Leo whispers. Teddy studies the black brilliance. "I don't think so, I see somebody inside." "That's us!" Leo says. "You're right." The harder they stare at the eye the more the white moon and blacklimbed trees, the very cottage itself flow from the eye, surround and cluster to it magnetically. The eye contains and gives off everything, a mother-darkness and secret birthplace of all germs awaiting life. Aim their giant flashlight at the eye—snap! redplastic lights up like optic nervematter.

Twins jump as if dashed with icewater, for the whole fish lens leaps alive, catching light like perfect water, the powerful shock of light distilled into intelligence so clear and deep that the flashbeam narrows sharply into black infinity within a lake of darkness. "Maybe it comes out the other eye!" Leo whispers, inspiring Teddy to rise and see. Downstairs, the house silent, creep off the porch with bare feet in galoshes. Walk narrow passage between fish and house, the light on the high sill still shining into the bass's eye. Curve around the high, open mouth to the far side, look up at the deep black eye catching the moon. "Nope," Teddy intently, "you're wrong." Leo insists, "But it's all lighted up *inside*." Stand before ridged teeth looking down the bass's throat, paperthin cartilage pinkly lighted, the bright beam sinking through flesh, shadowed by skull bones. "Curious t' know what's in there?" Leo asks, "How deep d'ya think it goes?"—"Well," Teddy says, "let's find out." Step over the lower jaw's sharpbladed teeth, walk fourfooted and sure down the slippery tongue, the roof arced and glowing above. "Long walk!" Teddy says after awhile. Beyond, a red railroad lantern burns on a cardtable where four men sit in the darkroom redglow, arguing. Silent twins creep near, pressed to a cold damp live wall, listening. The memorystabbing red railroad lamp, sleepy, whitehearted—it is Durwood's nightlamp which hung from his bow when rowing in from sturgeon fishing on Lake Erie. Jack sits with Jonah and Bill W., who rents the cottage, and Bill's old bottlebuddy Ebby T. Jack reads something aloud from a notepad, his breath spuming pink, but Ebby looks hot and sweaty, like he's just crawled out of the lake, and snorts from a hip flask. At last he thrashes in his chair, agonized at Jack's notes, the red railroad lamp wobbling on the table.

"Call this a Preamble!" Ebby cries, "why just look at it and see what it's like!"

Bill W. hugs a ratty patchwork quilt around his shoulder. "Shut up," he says.

But Ebby won't shut. "Don't show a damn thing about all the *anxiety* an' *work* that goes inta bein' a genuine alcoholic. Nobody'll believe it! *I* don't believe it! A man whose drunk six thousand bottles of bourbon won't listen t' this pap for ten seconds. Call *this* a Preamble!"

Bill sighs a damp red cloud. "Shut up!"

"I resent that!"

"Why?" Jack asks.

Ebby T., long Roosevelt cigarette holder, skinny black pencil-mustache. Castoff clothes, pocket kerchief elegantly draped, sole flapping. A sneer that involves every muscle in his body.

"Here you specimens of society sit," Ebby snorts, "ready to take a man's bottle away from him—with a piece of paper! A man's rights and property! His independence! An' all for a two-cent Preamble that jams him into a trap of sobriety he's gonna fry in for *weeks* until his head clears and he gets his senses back."

"Nobody has to *sign* this, Ebby," Jack says.

"Mealymouthed hogwash. I'll never vote for it."

Jonah's fingers crinkle through icy stiff white hair. "Ya don't have a vote," he croaks.

Ebby's mouth twists at Jonah, ghastly with hate and distaste. *"You* don't have a vote either, juicehead. Ya gotta be awake t' vote."

"I got more vote than you," Jonah says. "I'm sober one day—"

"I resent that!" Ebby cries. "I've had more sobriety than you'll ever have, noddy. You don't even know what year it is, hah!"

"He has showed me his mercy!" Jonah shouts into Ebby's face. Shreds of lake weed hang from Jonah's head and shoulders. Ebby turns with unbearable disgust, even fright, and spits on the wall—his spit stiffens where it lands. The pale pink wall is lettered with greasy purple crayon slogans

FIRST THINGS FIRST!
BUT FOR THE GRACE OF GOD!
LET GO, LET GOD!

"Showed it," Jonah adds, "ever since I fell inta this fish." His eyes roll white with high-intensity selfpity. "I got twenty-four hours *soberiety,* Lord!"

Ebby examines black fingernails and says from a great height, "He's *never* gonna make this Program."

Teddy feels strong kinship with Ebby's mighty self-assurance, disdain, filthy nails, even his gargley laugh.

Jonah rises with fists clenched, chair falling. "I may not make the Program! But it's not for you t' say, slacker!" He thumbs his squashed nose like a boxer, sniffing loud.

Ebby watches mildly. "Threw ya overboard, didn't they?"

"Whattaya mean!"

"You didn't *fall*, Whitey, you were pushed."

"I was asleep!" Jonah cries.

"Or didya jump?" Ebby asks languidly.

"I'll *tell* you!" Jonah whispers. "I went to sleep over the oars an' when I woke up agin, all the lake was covered with snakes, wild an' skippin', an' great serpents crawled all over the oars an' one bit my cheek—*pulled* me in! An' the snakes swum ever'where, up and down Chautauqua, waves of 'em passin' over me, closin' over me, wrapped like weeds around my head! An' I went down t' the bottom, snakes ever'where even underwater, wrigglin' an' glidin', and I was beggin' God t' finish me off, an' throwin' up every drink I ever had, chokin', until I got just so plumb tuckered, I fainted. An' woke up in here. That's the truth! An' if ever I see land agin, I'm gonna put the cork in the bottle an' preach abstinence the rest of my days. I'll pay every vow. His mercy is with me!"

"Was he rowin' on ice?" Teddy whispers.

"Beats me! I never saw any snakes out there."

"Good intentions bore me," Ebby sniffs. "Your trouble, kiddo, is you don't know when t' stop. You have no *control,* absolutely none. Weak character, it's written all over your puss. Ya oughta stop puttin' your head in the washing machine. It makes your eyes look stupid when they're in focus. Talk about ugly! Didn't your mother warn you your face might freeze that way?—Don't look at *me* that way, Wilson!" he cries suddenly at Bill. "I got *you* sober!"

"Thank you, Ebby," Bill says, "wherever you are."

"An' don't ya ever forget that! That sackcloth don't fool me! I know you want a drink as bad as any drunk who walks this earth. Sit in your ashes, you two-faced welsher. Turn your back on your ol' buddy, huh? You'll be back! I always say there's nothin' grimmer, more fiendishly puritanic, holier-than-thou and humorless than a reformed drinker—and one look at your sour mug proves it!"

"Uhh!" Bill groans. "Jack, I'm depressed—I am wildly discouraged. Six months and only one sober pigeon to show for it—just you!"

"Gee, I'm sorry you feel that way," Jack says. "I feel great."

"Yeah? I guess I get steamed up," Bill says. Sits tall and lean in his patchwork, his face long, bony-nosed, crisp eyes kind. "Hah! even my sponsor's an active drunk—listen to him!"

"Have some skim milk." Jack shoves a half-gallon carton at Bill.

"Make mine ginger ale," Bill sighs.

Jack lifts ginger ale from crushed ice on the bass's belly, uncaps the bottle, hands it to Bill with a chipped blue enamel mug. Bill ignores the cup, drains half the bottle, two fingers locked on its neck as on a cigar or tapered pilsner bottle. A soft lager belch dozes from him—sounding to the twins as if he sat right beside them—his blond hair parted in the middle, eyes wandering sharply. "When I get angry I'm one step away from a bourbon," he says. "Whattaya think, Jack? Should we set up a booth in Grand Army Plaza? Would one booth be enough for the turnover?"

"Gee, Bill," Jack asks, "how could we man them and stay anonymous?"

"I'll do it!" Jonah says. "I don't care who knows I'm an alkyholic!"

"I demand a booth," Ebby says.

"Give *him* Coney Island," Jack laughs.

"You're right," Bill says, "we can't blow our anonymity."

"Wear *crepe,"* Ebby says with a thicklipped grimace. "It goes with sackcloth."

Bill considers. "How about veils?"

"I'll sit *under* my booth in the shadow," Jonah says.

"I need a black mask," Ebby says. "I refuse to steal men's souls without it."

"How about a gag?" Bill says.

"And a straitjacket," Jack says. "That might be a powerful example."

"I'll do it," Ebby says. "For a pint every two hours. A gag *and* a straitjacket!"

"You can't drink through a gag, Ebby," Jack says. "And we sure wouldn't take the jacket off. But we could pour a few ounces into a saucer and let you get down and sniff it."

"I'm in deadly earnest, Jack—you men aren't takin' me

seriously." Ebby winces, his face twists horribly. "Sittin' with you guys is the greatest disgrace of my life. I'll *sit there* though in clothes that aren't fit for a hog! I'll wear the filthiest, most torn hat we can find on the Bowery, I'll—I'll pretend I got the snakes like Jonah!"

"Why pretend?" Jack asks. "Take the cure."

"*Aghh!* the snakes, the snakes!" Ebby cries. "Don't let 'em touch me! Get 'em off, they're *cold!*—How's that? By God, I'll do it—if it'll help deliver some poor bastard from his grief."

Ebby's efforts silence them.

"What's wrong?" Ebby asks. "It's not convincing?"

"Not very," Jack says. "What do you think?"

"I'm depressed." Bill shrinks into the depths of his blanket. "Let's take stock of our options. First we gotta wind up this Preamble. 'The only requirement for membership is an honest desire to stop drinking'—what's wrong with that?"

"*Nothing!*" Jack says. "My heart leaps up everytime you say it."

"You fellas don't think I can act."

"What do you think, Jonah?" Bill asks.

A sun beats upon the head of Jonah. "I'll take off *all* my clothes!" he cries fiercely.

"That's not wise," Jack says. "What do you think of the Preamble?"

"I have been exceeding glad of the gourd. But God has prepared a worm in the morning." Jonah holds his pounding head. "Better for me to die than to live, Lord!"

"We can't put that howling idiot in a booth," Ebby says. "He'll give us *all* a bad name. That voice alone makes my back prickle and my blood run cold. I think one booth's enough, an' Coney sounds good t' me. Jack, I'm with ya one hundred percent."

"We're *not* gonna pay for your next drink!" Bill cries at Ebby.

"You boys misunderstand me!" Ebby says, wavering fag snuffed into a wavering ale bottle. "I'm not askin' Bill t' hock his golf clubs or you guys t' pay anything! Why can't we just have a collection basket on the counter? That's the sensible thing."

"Oh Christ," Bill says, "let's leave the poor devil alone."

Ebby digests this. "Boy, Wilson, have you become baffling, cunning, and insidious! If you guys think ya can run this show without me, go right ahead and try. I'm gonna shut up. You can beg me t' talk an' I won't. *Shit!* Call this a Preamble!"

"Can a drunk have an 'honest' desire?" Bill asks Jack.

"An' I'm not sittin' in any goddamn booth in Coney for love nor money!"

"Hell, no," Jack says, "but he can *get* honest."

"You can all go hang."

"Frankly, I like honest desire," Bill says. "How about 'driving honesty'?"

"I'm shuttin' up!"

"That's asking too much of the poor bastards," Jack says.

"I DISAGREE!"

"Why?" Bill asks Jack.

"Christ," Jack says, "that's asking for terrific focus right away."

"I have a right to speak!"

"Stop hollerin'," Bill says.

"I was incurable!" Ebby shouts. "They were gonna lock me up an' throw away the key. But I'm here today! Threw off wet-brain completely and sit before you in this kitchen as a miracle, the livin' proof that alcoholism can be overcome! Complete remission of symptoms! *Raised from the dead! I bring great tidings!* You guys wanna know what this paltry organization needs? A skywriter! Gotta put the message right up where it can be read—in smoke!"

"That's the best thing you've said all night," Bill says. "A bit starryeyed, maybe."

Jonah looks cast down. "I don't like it. I can't fly."

"Whole Preamble!" Ebby says. *"In smoke!"*

"In gin," Jack laughs.

"Sounds desperately expensive," Bill says. "Maybe we could sober up some pilot and he'd do it free."

"That's not possible with any pilot I know," Jack says. "Besides, they can't spell."

"Or get 'im drunk," Ebby says thoughtfully. "Nope, I'm agin it. Brevity! Reduce it all t' one word." Thinks deeply, pounds the table. "Let 'im write: MODERATION!"

"Now that's genius," Jack says. "How about *abstinence,* Ebby?"

"In all honesty, Jack, I've tried that an' it don't work."

"Maybe you didn't try long enough," Bill says.

"Or vigorously." Jack sharpens his curvebladed Finnish fish knife on a small whetstone. "Moderation's for the fuckin' birds, Ebby. Half measures avail us nothing."

"Half measures!" Ebby glares at Jack. "I know what yer thinkin'. All right, so what! I had a li'l slip! I saw Bill sober up an' I got a *li'l cocky,* I admit it. If I could get tha' hopeless drunk sober, I sure could get myself sober again, if necessary. My success went t' my head! But I'll sober up again—alone if need be. But I don' wan' anymore a tha' spiritual guff! Put the cork in th' bottle an' stop—tha's all ya gotta know. I tried God an' He don' work either. Back with the Oxford Group—f' Chrissake, I'm practically member a th' Washingtonians! *I go back!* Too much God. If I ever need Him again, I'll phone Him. An' don' gimme any of tha' *fellowship* bullshit neither! I'm *all right!* There's nothin' th' matter with ol' Ebby T., absolutely nothin' get alarmed about."

Ebby stands, staggering backward then sidewards toward the twins, slips on his rear. On hands and knees, he searches crushed ice lining the belly. "Now where'd I hide tha' ale?" He looks up thoughtfully. "Those ancient Aztecs," he says, "used t' execute drunken priests who were pulque addicts."

"Good idea," Jack says.

"Let's start now," Jonah says.

Unbearably depressed, Bill watches Jack get up and, by the gill, drag a five-foot muskellunge out of ice, start dressing the long silvery fish. Bill broods on flying scales, Jack's knobby digging bloody knuckles. "Finns make the best fishknives in the world," Jack tells Jonah. "I stayed sober many a night scaling blue-gills until I saw 'em in my sleep. I dream about fish! ask Bill. The first few days out of the nerve farm I heard a choir of children singing to me in my backyard, but I'd keep scaling. Man, thank God for fish. Even bluegills, the little pests! When're we gonna get some women into this fellowship, Bill?"

Bill grunts lucklessly. "But I do have a prospect," he admits. "She's got three children. She always has a fifth of brandy waiting after she leaves the maternity ward—wants to make sure she gets a mother's glow . . . Maybe I preach too much! Maybe I should tell her she hasn't a blue-baby's chance in hell at beating this disease, *before* I come on with the spiritual approach. Maybe I get the cart before the horse."

"Scare the shit out of her," Jack says. "Tell her it's fatal. Then tell her there's nothing better than a natural glow."

Bill watches his first sponsor Ebby slip on his face, cheek shooting through soft crushed ice. Ebby draws an arm under his head, his coarsely thickened face and sneer relax in sleep; a throat cough reawakens the sneer, then Ebby's mouth opens in a trance like death. His two front teeth are missing.

"Could work," Bill says, his eye drifting back to Ebby. "I GET THESE WAVES OF SELF-PITY! I CAN'T CURE ANYONE PERMANENTLY!"

"You're not God!" Jonah cries loudly.

"I resent that!" Bill steams, and leaps up in his patchwork.

"Tell 'er that a natural lift is everything," Jack says, beheading the musky. "Then *glow*—but not too obviously, if you know what I mean. You don't want her to think you're a lapsed priest."

"Or Jesus Christ!" Bill cries. "I'm just a lapsed Wall Street broker."

"You're just Bill W.," Jonah says.

"I'm just Bill W. from Vermont. And I couldn't get one alky ward sober if I preached until Doomsday."

"Hell," Jack says, "try just one man at a time and see how it goes."

Bill stands over Ebby. "He may be full of antifreeze but he'll die if we leave him like this. Help me, Jonah."

Bill stretches his blanket by Ebby and he and Jonah roll the deadweight drunk onto it, tuck it around him. Teddy feels a strange warmth for the wrapped up man, as if even in near-death a passionate comfort might be drawn from the looselimbed snorer. Bill grips himself, rubbing for heat. "You and Ebby are both right, Jack. These prospects aren't gonna listen to any God guff. I gotta polish up the medical aspects until you can see your face in 'em."

"Our best pitch is power of example," Jack says, setting his bloody knife aside. He stretches the long pink quivering body on his palms, scaled of its long mask of armor. "*Boy,* let's have some steaks! Where'd my knife go?"

Teddy prickles—the darkstreaked knife slithers across the frosty floor as if magnetized toward the hidden twins. Suddenly Teddy sees a sitting savage hunched beside him. The wildlooking man wears only a skirt of soft pelts with a single shoulder strap, tangled pheasant feathers grow from his back and shoulders—feathers sprout from his very skull. His face and bare skin are spread with dreadful specks like carroway seeds. He smiles at Teddy, his eyes warm dark brown without whites, like Coca-Cola. "I should have *known* an angel would look this human," Teddy thinks, "—more human than human!" This upper being seems sunk into animal nature, into patchwork fur and hairy feathers, pitted flesh, and Teddy thinks that the man should be horrid with his ugly blackheaded pores but that his otherwise freezing ugliness adds a superhuman warmth to his backcountry smiles, dark Coke glimmer. The man's magnetism grips Teddy's limbs, holding him stiff as Jack's bloody knife drops through the air and severs Leo-Teddy's band in a single stroke. Teddy stands cloven from Leo. *"Come along, boy,"* the dark angel of death says softly, electrically, and Teddy feels himself walking out of the red room beside the warm fearful man-angel, and glances back once to find Leo standing wideeyed and watching Teddy's wordless leavetaking. It is a tearing of flesh from his bones to leave Leo but at last he surrenders, amazed at the angel's love for him, hopelessly hopeful in the grip of death.

Leo throbs in the candlelit livingroom, his eyes close, his head hangs on his chest a long while, then a blue light appears. Silent snow, blue night, a lonely steel park lamp burns soft whiteblue over blue snow, blue firs. Leo present, can't see himself, he is shadow. The soft, pulsing radiance of the blueglass lamp washes the still snow with unearthly peace and quiet, peace and quiet. Leo's heart enters the night, he breathes this scene in his breast. Never has he known such deeply sought after, flowing peace. He hopes it will never end, the King James of wealth and elms and vast blue lawns of snow glimpsed in childhood.

Somewhere above sits the great stone fortress of Prendergast Free Library, its tall, narrow stone windows buttery and attractive in the nightpeace. Someone's inside whom he cannot see but dimly loves, she's checking out *The Idiot* and goes to her car and drives off before he gets even a hint of her face. Parched for her company! Is it Thelma? Is Stuart, now fourteen, in the front seat? Why is he always sexstarved in the library, hungering for some meeting, or lovestarved, desiring plenty and fulfillment from women reading titles on shelves? Is it even a woman he wants? Or some longvanished meeting in the basement of the Great Books Friday night roundtable, or of The Saturday Night Shakespeare and Sharp Cheese Society? Some damned meeting! compelling, slaking, offering a deep ravishing comfort he's sought all his life and may never have. Loss, oceanic, terrible . . .

But the library's lights are out. Midnight in the still black branches of the cloudriding moon, the full moon lifting naked out of cloudfilm, washed white and dripping from its bath, hiding again in blue clouds, see-through blue, again rising steeply above racing steam. Leo's shadow enters the darkbright tall stone church of Saints Peter and Paul, waits in a pew while two or three parishioners pray in empty vastness. A gold blare shines from the altar. Why hasn't he been here for so many years? Is this the overflowing home toward which his whole life tends? Too late for holy orders? Some eternal shadow forever at his side is missing. His estranged shadowheart hammers and shakes, he shudders in his sleep. Where is the long-awaited, unreserved fulfillment?

A balalaika playing "Moscow Nights" haunts Brooklyn Square which has become Red Square. Leo's shadow sits in an empty hall in blizzarding Moscow. The Twelve Steps suggested for recovery hang lettered in Russian from a bleak wall, A.A. slogans tell alcoholic Muscovites TELEPHONE THERAPY—EASY DOES IT—SOBRIETY, SANITY, SERENITY, also in Russian. A lectern waits for Leo's first horror story to the Russians, a second lectern for his translator. A table stands spread with pamphlets, The Big Book is already translated, an Intergroup central exchange phone number has been printed daily in *Pravda* and *Izvestia,* all Russia awaits the American messiah and his Program for Recovery. But the hall cannot open until Leo's ninetieth day of sobriety arrives at midnight. A tall samovar steams on the tea table. He waits on a hard camp chair for the last five minutes to pass before midnight, sensing outdoors a vast river of vodka spreading through the streets and alleys of Moscow. Will he fail? Lotta drunks in Moscow—chairs stretch so far he can't see the back wall.

He goes down cellar to shovel coal into the furnace for the subzero hall but can't find the lightswitch. The furnace is frigid—even his central heating's a failure! In pitch darkness he finds the shovel, the furnace door, the coal pile and starts shoveling coal into the furnace, hoping grimly for a last ember to take flame somewhere inside. He shakes the grate, hears ashes fall, waits praying for one spark, a miracle to fire his message to Moscow. Dread crawls over his skin, doom hanging overhead in the darkness—a twangling fear that he will be drunk shortly, or is drunk, or has been secretly drinking for days. I thought it'd happen in Paris or Rome! Have I really taken up *social drinking* in *Moscow?* Oh my God, so unbelievable! so TYPICAL! He recalls a bottle of kerosene on a nearby sill, finds it in the black and spurts ounces blindly into the furnace. No lighter, no matches!—rapidly search every pocket again, anxiety mounting, molars grinding as if on oyster shells. Abruptly, a broiling orange and black mushroom explodes overhead and oilflames burst along the rafters. A door flies open above, the lights flash on brightly. Leo sees three policemen hurry down cellarstairs, feels steel fingers clamp his arms, carry him up the stairs. In the smoking hall a policeman takes the kerosene bottle from Leo's grasp, glares at him. *"Stolichnaya!"* the cop cries. *"Nozdrovya!"* Leo says, "thank God you've saved me." But the growling cop holds the bottle up to Leo's eyes. Stolichnaya Vodka! Leo's hope bursts like a waterdrop, a deep groaning sigh pours from him, two cops keep him from fainting. He stares guiltily at the vodka—he'd known all along he couldn't resist the clear power of Stolichnaya. It's a planned slip. A peasant in a muzhik blouse sits across from him in the police wagon, a long wide red scrape down his forehead, stoned eyes rolling, his nose queerly dented or smashed. He groans hoarsely as if billied in the gut and breathless. Leo watches dumbly as a seated officer books him at a desk, the arsonist's vodka bottle tagged for exhibit. He tries to get a tear-wet cigarette into his mouth but the cop points to a red and white stenciled warning on the wall. Leo fails to fit the wet fag back into its pack, squirrels it shredding into his shirt pocket. "It was an accident," Leo wipes his eyes, "I didn't mean to take those pills! I thought they were vitamins," he lies, his brave smile inviting belief. Terrific innocence shining through tears. "You can't put me in jail for a common error in judgment—*Nyet, nyet,* comrade!" But a barred door slams on a general cell and he stands beside a fat shirtless Asian with his bloodied shirt tied around his skull. About thirty moaning men sit, stand, or even sleep in piss in the seatless, bedless drunk tank, mashed men, shaking, talking to empty spaces. Leo's mouth's numb, feels cut up inside and bloody, fear thrills him that they will peg him for a Yankee imperialist pig who lynches niggers, firebombs Asian villages, and rapes gook children. He sits on damp concrete, trembling hand searching for a match, finds in his fingers a wet kingsize American cigarette. Slowly crushes it into his palm unseen, hides the shreds behind his back. Sits mumbling like the others as he slowly finds that he can speak Russian—Booze! the international language. "I am not an Americanski, I am a world citizen, comrade, come to Moscow to dry out in your famous drunk tanks, perhaps the finest drunk tanks in the Soviet Union. How about you, comrade? Is your life unmanageable? D'ya ever feel powerless over alcohol? This your first bust for public intoxication? *Your sixty-fourth!*" Night falls on the Moscow drunk tank, pure night, not a bulb burning in the darkness. *"Fedya Mikhailovich?"* a low hoarse whisper at his ear. *"Nyet, nyet!"* Leo cries, "I am not Fedya Mikhailovich the drunk, I am Lev Nikolaevich the puritan! Fedya Mikhailovich looks exactly like me, there is a mistake! The wrong man has been imprisoned! I am not a criminal alcoholic!" But a blinding light flares on and he finds himself waking from sleep on slimy duckboards in a tiny bathhouse with sixty naked shavenheaded alcoholics, some of them thickset women, all with skin sores and dead red eyes. Everyone stands with a pail of hot water, washing himself as fast and hard as possible. All are so closely cramped that everyone stands on each other's bare feet in the stinking slime. Steam pours constantly from cold water poured onto skinburning bricks along one wall, while each convict beats himself red with wrapped birchsticks. In the shouting, screaming horror, Leo finds a red A branded onto his chest. His ankles can barely move, steep pains from shackle sores paralyze his legs. The fat Asian with the bloody head stands popeyed beside him, whipping himself as best he can. "I have heard, Fedya Mikhailovich, that you've been sentenced to four years in Vodkagrad!" the Asian whispers. "Don't worry, about half of these people in here are the best citizens in all Russia! You'll be in excellent company!" *"Nyet, nyet!"* Leo sobs and in a landslide of misery every hope in his breast is buried, every gram of will—the last cells of freedom freeze in his blood as he glances at his four-year convict companions. *"He hit me in the face!"* the Asian cries suddenly.

"Guard, guard, this international criminal hit me in the face with his switches!" Leo is hauled to the front of the bathhouse. The convicts push aside into solid walls of flesh to make a gauntlet for Leo to run and be whipped. A guard kicks him forward. Leo runs back and forth as birch switches swat his back, the guard crying, *"Harder! Harder! Lay it on! Touch him up, touch him up!" "—I have a mother!"* Leo cries. But the switches don't hurt much and Leo feels release, the light pains welcome. At last he's held over hot bricks by companions as reviving steam boils over him opening every cavity in his body. But now he's cold —cold sober—colder than he's ever known. Midnight stars butter the sky over his Vodkagrad barracks where Leo wakes on his hard plankbed. He shares the bed by the passageway. Despite footshackles, he rises quietly in the great groaning room and stands by the single frigid window in the dark passageway. His heavy prison jacket and the four-year shag hanging from his face strangely comfort him—he has come through. Outside, minus-thirty-degree frost sparkles on sheds and hills, every boardcreak and frosty footstep carries to him clearly in the blue, blue night —for the last time! An alcoholwashed moon, so white his heart hurts to look at it. "I have paid," he thinks, and an overpowering fullness of expiation swells through him. "Today is Easter. They're sending me home, dried out. My fourth birthday in sobriety! Will they recognize it at Renewal East? at Yorkville? It *hasn't* all been in vain." He watches a friendly spider cross the sill in the white moonlight, a dreamy webweaver. Leo sees himself sitting in the front row at Yorkville, his ankles still shackled, the shacklechain held up by a cord from his waist. Wanda beside him, dimly, eyes damp, chin up. "I won't shave, or say a word for the first year—won't tell my story until my fifth birthday." His eyes tear. "Then they'll know I paid! If only the governor will let me keep my chains, I'll wear 'em to the grave. Only in my last moment, at the hospital or wherever it happens—perhaps at a meeting!—I'll give thanksgiving and permit myself . . . *a last smile!"* His tears flow hot. And now—his dehumanized brain shrunk to a pea staring out of a big shaggy pod at the ice plains—it's time to wake up.

Leo wakes weteyed beside Teddy, curiously alert, palate amazingly dry, senses rising, almost rocketing. The desk candle down an inch. He zooms UP, awake as a fly in heat, crotch buzzing with anxiety. Teddy hangs forward, mouth open. Leo pulls his head up by the hair: Teddy's breath shallow, lips blue.

"You damned IDIOT!" Leo cries, but falls back as flame shoots up his cracked thigh. An unspoken terror crosses his mind. He feels Teddy's cold forehead, pulls back in panic. shakes Teddy's head like a rattle. "You pea-brain, WAKE UP!"

Fear spirals upward, his mind races farsightedly, a deathdeep shuddering grips him. *"Gotta walk him!"* But Leo's numb leg turns whitehot. He snags the desk chair, gets it under his elbow, tries to lift himself on his good inner leg and raise Teddy too. Inches up the wall, Teddy's arm around his neck. Teddy's dead weight, heavy as ice, heavy as death. Never has Teddy been this heavy when Leo's dragged him stupified to bed. At last the wobbling twins balance on Leo's inner leg and the chair. Fears his injured leg, clamps Teddy's arm hard.

"Come on, Teddy, *walk!* Just walk, buddy. You need oxygen, RIGHT?"

Teddy hangs like a big greased engine. Crippled leg forward, Leo moans, hops fast to his good leg. Steps, hops, dragging Teddy to the kitchen doorframe. *"Walk, Teddy, walk!"* Leo pulls up his pantleg, finds his throbbing flesh bluerotten with a spreading yellow bruise around their band. Drags Teddy into flickering kitchen, grabs the staggering icebox but Teddy pulls him straight down, heavily scraping the stove. Bluebolt pain. Teddy's big bloody nose squashed flat against the floor, oozing. Leo crawls under the sink for ammonia, unscrews the dried-empty plastic, holds the faintsmelling bottle to Teddy's nose. Rises with Teddy's head hitting the sink, shoves it under the running tap. Teddy's nose bleeds onto crusted dishes. His breath, so slow and shallow. Leo jams a finger deep into Teddy's throat—nada. Wildturkey panic.

"Throw up right on the floor!" Leo implores.

They slip against the bathtub. Leo digs a filthy spoon from the sink, slicing his thumbcushion on a butcher knife, drags Teddy to the spice shelf, fills spoon with Tabasco. Slowly spoons hot red peppersauce into Teddy until sauce mixes with blood in Teddy's beard. He rubs Tabasco over Teddy's gums. No action. Spurts Tabasco carefully into Teddy's nose wound, draws back shuddering at the pain Teddy should feel. Trembling, fright, terrific loss ahead.

Gibbering, he grabs the shaving mirror, hobbles club-footed to the desk candle, holds the mirror to Teddy's mouth.

"Come on, Teddy! No ambulances, I ain't hailin' any more ambulances. We're pullin' through this on our own."

In the skimpy flame he can't tell if Teddy's alive or dead, but prickling certainty numbs his last hope. Sits down hard on the desk chair, sobbing, Teddy on his chest. Again he holds up the mirror, bitten thumb bleeding from its knifewound. No hint of mist. White fear tells him to finish the twinning abandoned by nature—cut Teddy away, save himself. Set loose this divine, fat, nosebitten idiot with his lisping daily decay—it's right in his eyes! A dying slug! wasting blue lunatic boor. No more of this loathesome mirrorman, Teddy's railing remorseless lies, misdeeds, pigheadedness. *This hopeless bastard!*

Self-pity thrills Leo, hatred showers from him. At last to be rid of this public fart who sits on the sidewalk when they pass a bar Leo won't enter, both twins stubborn, asses in cold slush,—rid of Teddy's moaning hangovers, world-*sighs,* half-dream horrors, twitchings, jabber of terror-ramblings beyond Leo's threats or bargains as Teddy flails on the bed,—rid of his insane, heedless rotting, and twi-light smile of triumph, blasted spirit, tormented nothing-ness, bloody jackingoff beyond orgasm, burnt bedsheets, blisters, sores, nicked head and fingers, bruises, mental strangeness and confusion, setting a glass down in empty space, then casting his own sins upon Leo, his endless be-littlement of every lifeline to sanity, his blackouts, likely brain damage, masking of utter weakness with an iron fist, his tidal self-pity, his ulcers, convulsions, vomitings and mania for more while the last still drools from his nose, more pain, more punishment—rid of his delusions and laughable posturings as the greatest living composer, his insults, his sweats and doom and self-absolving suicide for the spiritual betterment of mankind, for ART, his dustiest and most stupid alibi. To be rid of this helpless haze. *To be rid of Teddy!*

The butcher knife. Freedom beckons from the dark sink with the force of miracle. Escape, no return, out of bond-age to the suffering body on his chest. At last to let Teddy be Teddy's keeper entirely, alive *or* dead. Leo sits before his first drink of freedom, ready to bear Teddy to the sink. Shaking in every bone, he rises, Teddy's arm clamped about his neck. Deep, marvelous power floods his better leg, a healing hope, as he scrapes erectly to the sink, digs through dishes for the butcher knife handle, then with his ordinary strength returned hauls Teddy into the dark bedroom and pulls him painfully onto the winestained altar of Teddy's thirst.

Knife beside him, Leo grips his hands in prayer. His spine shakes from neck to sacrum. Horrific blue bliss burns from soles to scalp, a fear so harrowing that his flesh feels laid open, cloven to the bones.

"Dear Father, I'm not prayin' for myself, I'm prayin' for Teddy. He's a pig! And so'm I! But wouldn't he be better off without me as his damned crutch? I enable him t' keep guzzling until he's gonna drink us both t' death! He'll wake up the same old madman, if he's not dead already! Please grant me an answer!"

Walls faint with candlelight, Leo's eyes open. Calm power stems from clenched hands. Purposeful fingers open, creep over Teddy's breast for a heartbeat. Can't bear his hideous face. Pulse faint beyond feeling, deadly still. Leo grips the knife, slides his pants down, measures their band with the blade. Cut closer to Teddy I'll hurt less but leave a big lump—and Teddy may bleed to death. His hand explores their band and, centered underside, their common navel. Should *I* take the navel? He really may bleed to death! But then he may murder us both with his drinking—that's manslaughter at least! Or suicide. Goddamnit, I'm not murdering him. The worst crime's a bad job of cutting and goddamn infection! Boy, am I full of alcoholic thinking, he groans. You gotta boil the knife first, idiot!

Looks at Teddy, the bitten nose unusually long and snoutlike. A black bubble hangs from the snout. The bubble bursts. Slowly another bubble builds.

The swine! *Alive by miracle!*

Fearful hope lifts Leo, a spirit blowing upon him, catching him up. A vision fills him of himself and Teddy free, sitting on a still dawn lake in a rowboat, waiting and patient, their lives in the mountainmisted mirror.

Teddy turns slowly in the dream and smiles. Leo's heart reaches out, beats with his cleareyed brother's. Joy rises that this vision is worth every measure to achieve.

SATCHMO DEAD,
A JAZZ ERA ENDS

BLUE noon over battlements of Seventh Regiment Armory on Park Avenue where Louis lies in state. Leo-Teddy in line on sidewalk—a few yards away TV reporters nab mourners coming out. Big white steamboats cruising heaven, soft wind blowin' through the pine-wood trees *ba baz da ba dez ba ba da da ba doo da ba doo da dez buddya da be da da* DA ZOT! *Good mawnin', everybody-y-y!*

Hair breezing, Leo eyes their tufted shadow underfoot, a mustard sunspot breaking Teddy's phantom. Teddy braced on canes, stiffly overerect. Leo's eyes princeblue, crisp. Teddy stout, florid, pufflidded—longing for blue Hawaii, yellowbrown breasts, palms bound with orchids. Leo whiffs Teddy's lime lifesavers, his sigh as the line moves up steps. Teddy takes a throwaway from his denim-shirt, reads MRS. ROSARIO, Spiritual Reader and Advisor, People come from far countries to see her, You are just a few steps from a New Life. Gives true and sound advice on all affairs. Are you an unhappy, hopeless failure?—this message is for YOU! I promise to bring you a full and happy life. Come to me! Feel NO embarrassment. Go up the red stairs to the red light. Teddy prickles, gripping her melons, his passion spilling in Mrs. Rosario's palm as she geev him an extra Spanish twist and mama's wink of endearment. "Mrs. Rosario, sex isn't everything, I need a mate." "My spiritual power is a gift from God!" she cries. "Lick my breasts."

"Think she sells it?" Teddy asks.

"You don't wanna blow twenty bucks on a handjob, Teddy."

"Nah." Teddy balls the handbill away.

"KONG!" a passing black cries.

A gray wirehaired Irish Wolfhound towers over Teddy, paws on his shoulders as it whimpers eagerly, its great tail wagging the earth. Teddy stares into giant brown hound eyes, his retrieved handbill in the dog's hot wet mouth. The beautifully tailored black pulls on the hound's tiger-striped leash.

"Down, Kong! He's very people-oriented but just a puppy. Sorry."

"P-p-puppy!" Teddy cries. "Saint B-b-bernard!"

Kong wags and whimpers, waiting for Teddy to take the handbill. His vast brown pleading eyes swell with love. Teddy's heart lurches, wags in his breast before the god's naked affection. "This is the most b-b-beautiful dog on earth!" he blurts. "Where'd ya b-b-buy him?"

"Look, ya got eleven cats already," Leo says.

"This is the p-p-pet I've always w-w-wanted!" He takes the handbill, digs Kong's hardrough massive head as red dogtongue instantly wets his whole hand like a salt lick. "But he m-m-might take up a lot of room. What's he weigh?"

"Just one-hundred-fifty," the natty black says. "He's not fullgrown yet."

Leo decides by the black's clear eyes he's not a drunk, and asks, "Eats a helluva lot?"

"He eats beef, horsemeat, liver, kidney, tripe, fish, whole chickens, cottage cheese, bacon fat, honey, crunchy kibbles, vitamins, table scraps, and dog food. An' this cat's a heavy drinker too."

Kong's great brown eyes lap at Teddy. "I can't resist 'im!" Teddy cries. "He loves me, don'tcha see he loves me! He's w-w-waitin' for m-m-me t' throw a cane!"

"They very affectionate breed," the owner says.

"Sure are!" Teddy says. "Feels b-b-beautiful just lookin' at him lookin' at me. How m-m-much does one cost?"

"That's the easy part," the black says. "You might get one for three or four hundred. It's the *upkeep* that counts. An' runnin' him seven or eight miles a day. Keeps *me* in shape!"

"You run seven miles a day!" Teddy asks.

"No, man, *I* bicycle."

"W-w-w'ed have to get bicycles," Teddy says. "W-w-we'll look into it. Thanks a lot. *Bye, Kong!"*

The black waves, pulling his whimpering puppy. "An' keep your toilet lid down or you'll find *that* empty too."

Teddy glows. "That p-p-puppy got m-m-me right where I live. Those eyes! they're practically human. Once in a while your dreams are answered—it don't happen often b-b-but when it does it's b-b-beautiful. Of course, I can't face a b-b-bicycle."

Leo stares at a red splotch on Teddy's hand—for the past week Teddy's been painting a fresco on their bedroom wall. The full works, wet plaster and tempera, copying Goya's fresco of a dog's head staring at heaven, its eyes sad, fearful, head shivering in fluid light.

"But m-m-maybe someday," Teddy says, searching blue sky. "Or we w-w-weld some b-b-bikes together and *you* p-p-pump."

"Great," Leo says. "I'll look forward to it."

"Terrific."

Move inside with the line, Teddy sweating on his canes.

"Now hold onto yourself in here," Leo warns. "Okay?"

"Sure. I don't hear any m-m-music. I'm only w-w-worried about my talk tonight. I don't remember the Seventh Step."

"It's not a Step meeting, you're just tellin' your story."

"B-b-but I'm havin' trouble with my Seventh Step!"

"Look at me!—a perfect Seventh Step, but I *still* got character defects. I'm still rotten with perfectionism."

Teddy sighs. "M-m-my defects hang out like Christmas tree ornaments."

Leo-Teddy passes banks of fleshy gladiola, gazes hard on the dark face in the roses and twilight purple burgundy satin. IN SATCH' WE TRUST. *"I'm layin' this one on you, Rex!"* Whooping Big Daddy Winesprinkler, hornblowing hillhigh dancing black goat under the goofing moon, drooling Big Baby Bacchus borne on orgasm. Dionysus unleashed in divine trance, leaping notes whipped, naked, bent, flattened, trilled, riding high, meteoric C's, D's, E's, F's wheemed in silver tones of steaming Good Time Charlie ginmill pandemonium, a pang as his spirit wings away over the grapedancers' fading frenzy in their tubs, a string snapping in Leo-Teddy's hearts, Louis so small, pale and dainty, his lip scar a white button.

Gripping homefeelings for wine nights on the starry hifi with Doc Sunshine's waving midnight grasslands of beautiful feelings, Louis stretching out on "Wild Man Blues," "Two Deuces," "West End Blues"—purple bottleshine burgundy gallon, bombers laced with hash, the long night's slow throb, gin brilliance, heartbeats one with Louis's up-pouring and overflowing mad lifeloving flood of feelings —*aghhh!* Teddy's eyes leak for the past.

"W-w-we should hold a w-w-wake," he whispers. "Sit up all night with his records!"

"You're tellin' your story tonight."

"How about tomorrow?"

"Tomorrow night's fine," Leo says, smiling. "A little pity party all by ourselves."

Leo-Teddy turns from the casket.

"D-d-dig you later, D-d-dipper."

Mourners file out past Louis's widow Lucille.

"Gee," Teddy says, tall on the sunny steps, "I got such a rush of stinkin' thinkin' in there. I could smell the California red. And grass!"

"I didn't feel he was dead at all." Leo grips Teddy as his canes work down the steps.

"Remember L.A.? W-w-we sat w-w-with him for half an hour in his dressing room!"

"He's not dead."

"Healthy as a horse," Teddy says.

Leo-Teddy in Leo's Bronx livingroom blowing Louis's "Struttin' with Some Barbecue," tones strong and dancing. Teddy's canes hang from a bookshelf.

"Juicy!" Leo says.

"Phrasing," Teddy says.

Buzzer hums. Twins hurry slowly to the intercom, cry, *"Red Onion Jazz Babies!"*

"Your transportation's arrived!" a happy voice cries back.

Leo-Teddy waits as the hallway elevator opens on Nelson Winespear and whiteheaded Charlie Parnell.

"We heard you guys from the street," Charlie says hoarsely, grunting.

"Sounded like King Kong," Nelson says. *"Loud!"*

"But not bad," Charlie admits. He's a redfaced, goodbellied man with amused, sly seablue eyes, a building contractor with a whim of iron who not so long ago left wife, home, and fourteen years sobriety for a year-long drunk in Puerto Rico during which his girlfriend stabbed him in the back—he pulled out the knife, stuck on a Band-Aid, kept on cantina-hopping, allowed nothing to faze his drunk. At High Watch, a drying-out farm upstate, he met Nelson, who fastened to him like a son. Nelson's a blond ex-cattle king, with a thousand head of Angus steers back in Missouri, an ex-TV football star, ex-army officer and teacher of Russian, ex-Hollywood scriptwriter of outdoor adventures, ex-high ironworker who walked around blackout drunk on bare steel one-hundred stories above Wall Street, ex-father, ex-husband, ex-suicide, and ex-drunk who is now a recovering alcoholic. Nelson's trim and rocky, his eyes deepset, worried blue, he sucks an unlit Italian stogey, wears khaki with redblooded polkadot kerchief sprucing his back pocket like a badge of unbending manliness—though it's actually just his chewing tobacco chinwiper. He has a widesmiling Missouri voice, forceful, amused, no-shit. "Where's the phone?" he asks. "We found a three-year-old that can't lose."

Nelson dials his bookie. Charlie looks around at Teddy's paintings. "Your wife still in Europe?" he asks Leo.

"Whole year now."

"The restraints are off, huh?" Charlie says. "Take my advice, get a replacement fast. There's nothin' like a broad t' keep ya wise to yourself—you know the kind of thinkin' when you're alone all the time? Maybe I should visit my ol' drinkin' buddies, see how life's treatin' 'em. Next thing you're downin' scotches like a carpenter's elbow. Don't be alone too much."

"Alone?" Leo says.

"Alone! What am I, talkin' to myself? I gave that up when I met Nelson—he's got a terrific tin ear."

"That's what they told me in Hollywood!" Nelson says, then asks the receiver, "Hello, Tommy?—Well-l, I *do* have pneumonia. But I'm in divine right order, thanks very much. Put Charlie and me down for ten to win on Mustard Seed in the seventh. Yeah, man, he's a natural—sired by Bill W. out of Serenity. Some trainer must be runnin' a straight-arrow stable up at Saratoga." Nelson hangs up, sees twelve shoppingbags of books and records in the bedroom hallway. *"My God,* are those what we're takin'!"

"I told ya w-w-we'd need a stationw-w-wagon."

"Don't worry," Charlie tells Nelson, "these guys always tip with a fifth of bourbon—*don'tcha?* Just what you need to break up your grippe."

"It's not grippe," Nelson says, "the doctor says it's walkin' pneumonia. He's mad as *hell* I'm not home in bed."

"We could take these books and records back next week," Leo says.

"Nossir," Nelson says, hard and serious. "I've never missed a meeting of Renewal East since I joined A.A. and I sure ain't missin' *tonight's.* Teddy's first talk!—I been waitin' for this a whole year. I wouldn't miss it for a barrel of bourbon! I never heard of such a moving act by a recovering A.A.," he waves at the shoppingbags, "it has a kind of historic magnitude. Most marvelous Ninth Step I ever heard of. I may even ask Teddy to be my sponsor after his talk tonight—if it really hits me right."

"He's not kiddin'!" Leo tells Teddy.

"I surely am not," Nelson says, with an unnervingly tense blue stare at Teddy. "But I gotta see how he carries the ball first."

"How can you have Teddy for a sponsor and not Leo?" Charlie asks.

"Aw, Leo," Nelson says, "he's still off with his blue lights and damned mysticism—very flaky, even though it keeps *him* sober. But you can't pitch that highflown crap at a guy just off the street. Now Teddy's got the message like nobody I know! *Don't drink and go to meetings.*"

"Bill W. says—" Leo begins.

"I don't care what Bill W. says," Nelson says.

"—hit 'em right off with the Higher Power."

"The group's my Higher Power," Nelson says. "I'm not much for prayer and that guff yet. Maybe it'll get me—an' I hope it does!—but I only know the feelin' I get when I walk into a meeting. I'm hooked the first minute. That's the only Higher Power I know. So far."

Charlie totes four bags, shakes his head at Leo-Teddy. *"Heavy!"*

"This is Teddy's idea!" Leo cries.

"I mighta known *he'd* think up such a practical step," Nelson says. *"Ahem!"* Leo reaches for two bags but Nelson knocks his hands away. "Now you two guys just wait here—Charlie and I'll make this easily in two trips. Go back to your horns—we're treatin' Teddy like royalty today. So *you* just feel lucky about any side benefit you get from Teddy's sobriety." Nelson strains with four bags, follows Charlie to the elevator. "Remember, Leo, there are men in the ranks who will stay in the ranks because they *just—don't—get—things—done."*

"How can I b-b-be *his* sponsor?" Teddy asks Leo.

"He'll *tell* you in great detail!"

The phone rings. "Leo?" a soft voice asks, "This is Byrdie Goldstein out in California."

"Hey, Byrdie, how are ya!"

"Hi, B-b-byrdie!"

"Not so good. I have bad news, fellas. Laura's dead. She killed herself yesterday. I know you're her best friends back East."

"Cynara!" Leo says. "—I'm terribly sorry, Byrdie."

"Good God! She m-m-musta been really depressed, B-b-byrdie."

"She was. She'd been writing suicide notes for months and savin' 'em up. They're even dated, so I can remember what we did that day. She really planned it good for once."

"But what about her baby!" Leo asks.

"I know!" Byrdie says. "She really knew how to hurt a fella. But it's all the Flux—she's flowin' with universe now. I'd even given up my law practice for her, let my hair grow, took up the guitar. Began seriously observing the Jewish sabbath, all for her. But it wasn't enough. Something in her never changed. I don't know why she did it—she just says she felt unworthy of the baby."

"She had a powerful case of low self-esteem," Leo agrees.

"Was it p-p-pills?"

"Gosh, no. It was a .45 automatic. I didn't see it. The coroner calls it a cannon. She bought it at a hardware store over a month ago—'for protection!'—and kept it hidden."

"That's no ladies gun," Teddy says.

"She wasn't takin' any chances!" Byrdie gasps. "She knew about this for a whole month. Then we went to bed night before last—she'd been very pleasant and kind for weeks—then got up at one o'clock while I was asleep and pinned these notes all over the house. And she put on a sequinned cape I bought her in San Francisco, very beautiful with all sorts of starry scrollwork, which she said she hated when I gave it to her—she never wore it for me once!—and walked out into the woods and sat down by a tree by an old mill. I f-f-found her there in the morning when I missed her about five o'clock. There was a little blood on her head but I didn't look or see the gun—I'd read the notes. I just walked around her for a while howling and went home to hold my baby."

"How're you now?" Teddy asks.

"Well—she wanted to join the Flux. She was deeply depressed six months at least—acting strange, thought she was bein' followed. I just gotta flow with it. She's bein' cremated this morning at nine—noon your time. I thought you might wanna say a prayer for her. I'm callin' from the crematorium! Say a prayer, fellas!"

"We sure will," Leo says. "For both of you."

"Thanks for callin', B-b-byrdie."

"I wanted to kill myself too, but I made a vow to the baby instead. It doesn't hurt so much when I remember Laura's part of nature again. We're all in the Flux, fellas."

"She's not dead," Leo agrees. "But a life is a terrible thing to waste. Please write us when you feel up to it."

"Mill Valley's so pleasant!" Byrdie shouts. "It's the most pleasant place in the whole United States! But it has the highest suicide rate in California—it just doesn't make sense! She shoulda been happy here! Well, I gotta get in the chapel."

Leo hangs up. *"Dead!"* Teddy cries. "And just a little niacin coulda saved her! Plain niacin and she'd be alive! If she took as much vitamins as we do, she'd've been lifted right outta d-d-depression!"

"First Louis, now Cynara."

"Are you guys sure you don't have a fifth?" Charlie asks in the doorway. "Nelson's really sick."

"Whoo!" Nelson cries. "Don't think I haven't thought about it. Just three ounces of Nelson County's finest bourbon and I'd be reborn in half an hour! Hell, in *seconds!"*

Teddy says, "I heard it m-m-might have a d-d-different effect."

"Don't I know it."

"We sure oughtta thank these guys," Teddy says, shoving cigars into Nelson's and Charlie's shirtpockets. "Royal Crown Flats, nineteen-forty-two, real Havana—I get 'em in Chinatown! They're p-p-pure sunshine an' only get better the farther d-d-down you smoke 'em. *Perfection!"*

"Hey!" Charlie says, "how come you don't stammer as much when ya talk about cigars?"

"Maybe I don't feel ridiculous."

"He's a helluva lot better than a year ago," Nelson tells Charlie. "Five hundred percent!"

Teddy smiles. "I was gonna replace *B-b-b-b-b-b-b-b-Beethoven*—before I got well."

"He's recovering," Leo agrees. "I don't even notice his stammer."

Leo-Teddy turns on a squalling Spanish station loud, slides a five-foot steel bar into the door, locks double locks. They go down amid the elevator scratchings: SCOWL LOVE BLACKSPADE MARIA SANCHO PIZZA KING KOOL

"How's this buildin'?" Charlie asks.

"Goin' fast."

"Three years ago it was mostly Jewish," Leo says. "We'd like to move."

Nelson tenses. *"Where to?"*

"Iceland."

"You're still drunk," Nelson snorts.

"I'd like Connecticut," Teddy says.

"That's sane," Nelson says.

"Martini country!" Charlie warns Teddy.

"It's *all* martini country," Nelson says. "From the great Atlantic to the wide Pacific shores. One big cookin' liver, heh heh! Feel lucky? Shit, I'm so goddamned lucky, I'm overwhelmed! The luck of bein' the one drunk in twenty who doesn't die from this disease is too much t' think about."

"Ya haven't run the course *yet,"* Charlie says.

"I'm runnin' on my knees."

"I thought you weren't religious," Leo says.

"That's not religion, it's gratitude. It slows me down when I get stinkin' thinkin'. A big whiff of *that* can kill ya. And ya might not be as lucky as I was," Nelson says, tapping a plate in his skull.

When Nelson's first wife left him, taking their kids, he was so shaken that he tried to drive a truck over a cliff with a shotgun in his mouth. He hit a stump. When he came to, deaf and bloody, he was looking through a hole in the truckroof and in some high limbs saw a squirrel leaping between branches. *"Oh God, I want to live!"* he thought. He convulsed on the operating table and later, couldn't hear a sound for a month, then drank for ten more years while thinking himself insane.

Leo-Teddy (heads burbling "Struttin' with Some Barbecue") remembers Cynara on a visit with Byrdie, returned from Europe, their daughter six months old, Cynara giving Leo-Teddy a stolen (farewell) kiss in the study with a deep, pleading, hopeless, silent look whose despair the twins could not understand.

"I'll call you w-w-when I get stinkin' that w-w-way," Teddy says. "An' you call me."

"I haven't taken you as my sponsor yet," Nelson says. "You gonna come on strong tonight? I can't have a lily-livered, snivelling sponsor who can't stand up an' tell me I'm full of horseshit. I want the best. This is a big responsibility I may give you. Understand?"

"Sure do!" Teddy says.

"And try not to be too spiritual. I like a simple message and get easily upset by galloping horseshit and flyin' blue lights."

Charlie tells Leo, "He's not mentionin' any names."

"Right," Nelson says. "I keep all my criticisms anonymous."

Past Yankee Stadium onto East River Drive in the loaded stationwagon. Lightbulbs on the stadium flash the last seconds before noon.

Leo-Teddy silent in dripping July sunlight, praying in the backseat, Cynara in the furnace. Judgment Day in California.

Teddy grips Leo's knee, whispers, "We gotta be tough about this!"

Leo's filmy eyes sting. *"Not me!"*

"Both of us," Teddy says. "Remember our vow? No matter who dies, we don't drink. Not even if our asses drop off."

"Ya didn't remember that at Louis's this morning!"

"I'm *me,* I forget things. You gotta remember for the both of us," Teddy says. "I dunno why I thought that way. I wasn't thinkin'. Louis went *peaceful,* so we gotta be double strong about Cynara."

"No fuckin' promises," Leo says.

"You need a sponsor!"

"Bullshit! Don'tcha think that if she were sittin' here right now, she'd be tellin' us *to live?* That all our fuckin' restrictions and puritan crap are bullshit?"

"Some expert she was. Goddamnit, I need your support, I gotta give a talk tonight."

"Wouldn't she? And wouldn't Louis?"

"Your self-pity's revolting," Teddy says.

"Fuck you," Leo says clearly, insultproof.

A giant billboard looms by bearing twelve-foot green bottles of scotch in a row. Leo-Teddy sits thumbing his catalogue of threats against himself, either half: the crippling Swedish operation, withdrawal and powerful silence, income halved like flesh, hairsbreadth justice, old sins to sharpen casually, failures, slips, asshole embarrassments.

Nelson asks Charlie, "Get a whiff from the billboard?"

"That's what I drank on my last slip."

"I'm a bourbon man myself," Nelson says.

"I mean a hundred-fifty gallon bottle," Charlie says. "I mean it! Two fifths a day for a year comes out to about a hundred-fifty gallons. That's about what that bottle holds."

"What'd ya do with the empty?" Nelson asks.

"What'd I do with the *year!* I still don't know."

Doublepark at Donnell Library in midtown, start carrying books and records to the overdue counter. A heavy, ashwigged blonde reads *Don Quixote* on a stool by the cash register, looks up at the stoneserious hairy ambush of Leo-Teddy, four eyes glaring.

"W-w-w-we have several overdue b-b-books and records to return."

Leo empties dusty albums onto the counter, hauls up a second bag. The librarian looks over the counter at the gathering comber of overdue sins. Electricity clouds her wig, disbelief shakes her. Her eyes drill sharply into Leo-Teddy for the roots of evil. Nelson rushes up with the last bags, his jaw burning worriedly.

"All these are overdue?" she asks. "This is unforgivable! You'll have to pay the fines! *Why* have you kept out so many books and records?"

"W-w-we checked 'em out or stole 'em w-w-when w-w-we w-w-were active alcoholics."

Punchy unwillingness to believe.

"We don't drink anymore," Leo says. "We joined a band of recovering drinkers."

"W-w-we'll p-p-pay the fine."

She opens an album. *"This has been out eight years!"*

"Some 've b-b-been out for ten," Teddy says.

"I can't handle this," she says. "Wait here while I get the head librarian. Don't go away!"

"Tough cookie," Nelson says in cold sweat.

Twins silent at the bar. Judgment Day in Manhattan.

She returns with a tall, intense young Chinese-American woman who surveys the bags. *"Why* have you kep' these out?"

"W-w-we took 'em out or stole 'em w-w-when w-w-we w-w-were active alcoholics," Teddy says. "W-w-we'd like to m-m-make restitution."

The Chinese librarian, not smiling, smiles less, sick. "I-I—We have to see what the fine is. I.I—*Why* have you kep' them out!"

"W-w-we're recovering alcoholics. W-w-we took 'em over the p-p-past ten years w-w-when w-w-we w-w-were drinking."

She stares hopelessly at the bags. "This is *too much work!"* She takes in Nelson. "What have you got to do with this?"

"I'm makin' sure they recover."

"But I have not seen these two men in here before! I would *remember them!"* the Chinese says triumphantly.

"They been here," Nelson says.

She eyes Leo-Teddy keenly. "You *couldn't* have taken all these from Donnell."

"No," Leo says, "but we're returning 'em here."

"The b-b-books are from all over. But they're your records!"

The overdue librarian studies the first album. "Why this was a *one-week* record."

"It must have been new!" the young Chinese says. "Charge them for a new record."

"At ten cents a day?" Overdue asks.

"W-w-when w-w-we took it out it w-w-was *five* cents."

"Fines have gone up!" the Chinese, solemnly.

Leo-Teddy feels the first harsh stripe of blood oozing, girds himself. Nelson shakes his head at the ceiling, stuffs a pinch of tobacco under his tongue for support, mops his neck with polkadot kerchief.

As Overdue multiplies and adds, bloodlessly, the horn-rimmed head librarian adds up Leo-Teddy's purpledyed bluejeans, purple summer shirts, clearrimmed glasses, beards, pontytails, sober bright eyes. "Frankly, you gentlemen don't look like alcoholics."

"W-w-we don't drink anymore, ma'm."

Nelson says, "I'll vouch for 'em. They're drunks. I'll sign anything."

"That's not necessary." She watches the figures add.

"But ten years! You could have returned *some* of them before this!"

"W-w-we just stopped drinkin' a few years ago. W-w-with some slips."

"We're just gettin' definitely sober," Leo says.

"Approximately," Nelson says.

"But—*this is appalling.*"

"W-w-we'll m-m-make restitution!"

"I'll cosign anything necessary," Nelson says firmly.

"Oh no!" Teddy swats the counter. "W-w-we're responsible."

Overdue turns distastefully from a stack of dustballed albums. Leo-Teddy tightmouthed.

Nelson smiles ruefully. "They did it for American music. They're musical Michelangelos! And for American literature, didn't ya? Of course, that's no excuse."

"Then why make it?" the Chinese asks, pained.

"Better than suicide," Leo suggests.

"Huh?" Teddy asks. "W-w-we always stole w-w-when w-w-we w-w-were drunk and happy and *up*. Well, or else nervous and down."

"*How* did you steal these records?" she asks, hoping Leo will answer.

"Under our trenchcoats," Teddy says. "W-w-w-we belted 'em under our p-p-p-pants. W-w-w-we look p-p-pretty fat anyway."

"Pretty cool," Overdue says.

Teddy recalls their shakes, the wine oozing from their scalps and every pore under their hot trenchcoats as they trundled like pregnant swine past the doorguards, showing their innocent shoppingbags for inspection.

"W-w-we w-w-were insane."

Deep silence, the last figures totalled.

"$3,167!" the Chinese cries. "This can't be right."

"Oh yes it is."

Leo-Teddy chills, a Siberian dimness filling Donnell.

Nelson cries, "Why the books and records alone aren't worth that much!"

"That happens," Overdue says, fighting the glitter in her eyes.

"What are you going to do?" the Chinese asks.

"W-w-we'll have to pay in w-w-weekly instalments. That's the w-w-way w-w-we incurred it."

"That'll take ten years," the Chinese says. "How much of this can you afford to pay now?"

"I'm on w-w-welfare. But I can p-p-put five dollars a w-w-week into it."

"Are you working?" she asks Leo.

"I'm a songwriter! I make about seventy-five dollars a week. I can put in five."

"Faithfully," Nelson says. "And I'll match their ten! That way it'll only take five years."

"No you won't," Teddy says, *"we're* responsible."

"Well, why don't we reduce the fine to something reasonable?" the head librarian asks. "How about one thousand dollars? We can't carry this bookkeeping forever."

Leo-Teddy ponders in silence.

"Hm. How about five hundred dollars?" she asks.

Twins seriously consider their income in silence.

"Three hundred?" she says. She smiles. "How 'bout *seventy-five dollar?"*

"W-w-we still can only p-p-pay five dollars apiece w-w-weekly."

"Well," she pleads, "how 'bout fifteen dollar *right now?"*

"And that's *all?"* Nelson asks.

"Yes."

"Yes!" Teddy says, digging up a ten and five one-dollar rolls of pennies. "They're all there, I just counted 'em this morning."

Overdue rings up the cash coldly.

"Thank you very much," Teddy says, restitution made.

"D'ya need a receipt?" Nelson asks Leo.

"No receipt!" the Chinese says. "This is several weeks work already." She stares at them, strongly dismayed, still looking for scars of addiction.

Teddy lifts a cane in thanks, turns hobbling, erect. Soberfaced, Nelson and Leo-Teddy leave the library in silence, caning past the guard coolly, climb into the sunny stationwagon.

"How'd it go?" Charlie asks.

Nelson kisses heaven, releasing a great sigh with sparkling eyes. *"Everything is in divine right order!"*

"Oh, I expected no less," Charlie says, "with you masterminding the deal."

"They did it all by themselves. You'd've been so goddamn proud of 'em you'd've popped your buttons. *Boy,* this is already the greatest day of my life—an' there's so much ahead yet! How do you men feel?"

"I'm happy," Leo says.

"You don't sound it," Nelson says. "You sound constipated."

"Don't let it worry ya."

"I *do* worry!"

"I thought I'd feel terrific," Teddy says, "wanna dance in the street. I just feel confessed. Shoulda done it long ago."

"By God," Nelson says, "it always pains me to hear you guys arguing, but when you both come on like a pair of old queens I really get disgusted. You guys are supposed t' be towering examples of A.A. strength. People look up to you for support! *I do!* This is a miraculous step forward you've taken today—I wanted to cry in there, I was so happy for you. That was one of the most painful moments I ever saw two men stand up to. Those broads weren't givin' an inch! All I could think of was reachin' for the flute—*glug, glug, glug!*—when that Chink kept cuttin' you down, an' I kept sayin', *My name is Nelson Winespear and I am an alcoholic! Never despair! Never despair! Never despair!*"

Teddy grips Nelson's shoulder. "I'll give you my canes someday."

"That's better," Nelson says. "I hope you're gettin' your senses back. How're ya doin', Leo?"

"Oh. All I need is a little money t' ruin my happiness."

"What's that supposed to mean?" Nelson asks.

"It means I'm fuckin' glad I don't have any more money than I do. I'd be tempted to take up 'gracious living.' "

"You don't want gracious living and wine in a basket," Nelson says. "You just want that flute. Sonofabitch—you're drunk already!"

"No inventories," Charlie warns.

"Sorry," Nelson says. "I get carried away. I don't wanna take your inventory, Leo, you understand that?"

"You couldn't," Leo says evenly.

"Right," Charlie tells Nelson, "and Leo couldn't take yours."

Nelson agrees softly. "That's for damn sure."

Drive through hopping boredom of Times Square—a seventy-foot vodka bottle pouring into a mammoth shot-glass—"I knocked that one off too," Charlie says—down

Broadway's sunny hopelessness. Pull up at Intergroup on East Twenty-second. Charlie smiles sun-red, his white hair flying back in a great corona. "See you guys tonight."

"Thanks a helluva lot," Teddy says.

"Muy gracias," Leo says.

"I'll never go there *anymore!"* Charlie sings.

"San Juan or High Watch?" Nelson shakes Charlie's hand. "Ya know what I think everytime I look at you?"

"There, but for the grace of God—" Charlie asks.

"I'm serious! I see you the first time I saw you, walkin' down that path at High Watch with a big Buddha smile on your puss while I was dyin' on cold turkey. What's that bastard got t' smile about? I asked. Brand new on the grounds and there you stand with a big golden grin as if no hangover on earth can touch you."

"It couldn't!" Charlie laughs. "The doc who sent me up gimme a three-day shot of B_{-12} and morphine before I got in the car. I'd've smiled in a Mexican lockup."

Leo-Teddy and Nelson wait for the selfservice elevator, eye an empty Rainwater fifth under the stairs. Terrible-tempered Tyrone Hargis, a graying, calicobearded ex-story department head for a movie company, hurries in, glasses gleaming, a library underarms. "I'm late! My first time on the phones, and I'm late! Unforgivable, Hargis, *unforgivable, sir!* It's the lash for you."

"Take it easy," Nelson says.

"What do I do? What do I say? What if I get a DRUNKEN LUNATIC on the phone! What do I *say*, sir?"

"Whatever comes naturally," Nelson says. "You'll recognize each other."

"I see. *Hmm!* I get your point. I'll tell him, quietly and calmly, that he's a damn fool to drink. How's that?"

"Just—just take it easy," Nelson says.

"I'll try, sir. I'll do my best. But remember, I've hit the halfcentury mark. I'll tell 'em not to waste as much time as *I* did. *Drop that drink!* Make haste to a meeting!"

"Just listen to Teddy operate for awhile," Nelson says.

"I will. You show 'em no pity, I take it, Ted? They're impossibly full of self-pity, right? I'll use the rational approach. *Supercool!"*

"Don't project," Nelson says in the rising elevator. He asks Leo, "Ya really loved that spade, didn'tcha?"

"Who?"

"That trumpeter, Fatso Armstrong."

"*Satchmo,*" Leo says. "Sure did."

"I knew somethin' was gettin' ya down."

"Oh, he died peacefully," Teddy says. "Just the way he lived."

The elevator opens on the hospital desk where Leon Bones, a rakish, tall elderly black argues with a hazy, hawknosed goldmustached mulatto. A halloo goes up from workers down the desks. "Ya can all go home now!" Nelson cries back, "Renewal has landed and will secure all lines."

Leon throws up his hands. "Here's a guy who insists *real* alcoholics don't recover! Why don't you two boys talk with 'im—I can't get through. Go with 'em, Malcolm."

"Leon," Nelson says, "this is Tyrone H. from Renewal. He's come up to hold hands with some sufferin' alcoholics. It's his first crack at the phones."

"Ohh, really!" Leon says. "You intend t' read all them books while you're here? Or you gonna read to sufferin' drunks on the phone?"

"Ha ha!" Terrible-tempered Tyrone H. says. "We'll be pretty busy, eh?"

"I'm glad my subtlety isn't lost on you."

"Which subtlety?"

"You jus' follow them twins, they'll give you the modus operandi."

"That's my language!" Tyrone cries. "I see I'll be at home here."

Tyrone draws an extra chair to Leo-Teddy's big desk, sits beside it while Malcolm glitters goldenhaired from the far side.

"My name's Leo, this is Teddy—we're alcoholics. You havin' a problem with booze, Malcolm?"

Malcolm sighs loftily. "I don't know *really.*"

"People without booze problems don't come here," Teddy says.

"The very fact that you're here shows you have a problem, don't you think?" Leo asks.

"Yes. Well—I can't see it as a problem."

"Why not?" Teddy asks.

"I shan't discuss it, it's too personal."

"Do you have a desire to stop drinkin'?" Leo asks.

"No, I don't *want* to, I *have* to! I'm going to lose my job, I think, and it's a lovely job. I travel a lot and get all the bottles I want duty-free."

"What's your gig?" Leo asks.

"Well, my *job* is ticket agent for Air France. I'm actually a composer."

"Whaddaya write?" Teddy asks.

"Opera, to be precise. I'm now working on the libretto for a three-act opus I call *The Phantasmagoriacs.*"

"Where'd ya study?" Teddy asks.

"Oh God! I *went* to Harvard for two years but just could *not* hack it, you know? Actually, I'm self-educated. Musically, that is."

"You compose on the piano, Malcolm?" Teddy asks.

"I don't *write.* I *sing,* rather free-form, or serially, if you know what I mean. Are you familiar with *Pierrot Lunaire?*"

"Schoenberg!" Tyrone cries.

"Sure," Leo says. "All those dying twangs in the moonlight."

"Dying prongs," Teddy says. "I used to play it all the time."

"I died a thousand deaths," Leo says, "over that boring cobweb. So you have a drinkin' problem?"

"I said it wasn't a *problem.*"

"—How d'ya compose without writing?" Teddy asks.

"I see you do know something about music," Malcolm says. Gold-mustached Malcolm, pale yellow face, pocky, deepcreased, streaked with pink vessels, his hawknose, ultramarine eyes, and tight gold cap of wiry curls, hopelessly handsome. "Yes you *do* know something," he says softly, glassbright eyes searching the twins, his hard eyes cursed, now self-caustic, seething and pleading with the twins, a dozen moods at once rimming his eyes with self-pity. Standing water slowly spills from his lids. Foxily, he watches them watch him.

"We know a *lot* about drinkin'," Teddy says.

"Can you help me?" Malcolm gasps. "I can't stop!"

"Ya wanna stop?" Leo asks.

"I don't know!"

"If you wanna stop," Leo says, "put the cork in the bottle. That's the only way."

"I *need* my liquor!" Malcolm cries. "You don't understand. I am a *cre-a-tor!*"

"What's your booze?" Teddy asks.

"Tequila and mescaline," Malcolm says proudly. "Try it sometime!"

Tyrone shudders.

"Aw shit," Teddy says, "you don't wanna stop. You're young—you got a *lot* of hangovers left, Malcolm. What are you, forty? *Thirty!* Ya coulda fooled me. Had the deetees yet?"

"Often," Malcolm says. "You can't scare me that easily. I've learned to live with 'em, and even love 'em. They're productive of very productive insights I'd never produce otherwise. I *write* about 'em!"

"I'll bet you do," Leo says. "Creative boozing. Gibberish with halos. Slumping in your chair, year after year, plunged into yourself, a few witticisms now and then, a bit of charm, but always with the creative mind working its auroras. Religious boozing, really spiritual. I'm familiar with it."

"He don't wanna quit," Teddy tells Tyrone, "with somethin' like this goin' for him. The more bitter the thumb, the better the bottle, Malcolm. Hell, *we* wish we could drink like Auden and Stravinsky—now those guys really tank it away—and Stravinsky's in his eighties! Though Auden looks older."

"He drinks more," Leo says. "We had a brand new fifth of tequila, fell off the kitchen table. Smashed. We sponged it up into a saucepan, ran it through cheesecloth. Hardly a drop lost."

"Great margueritas," Teddy says. "Maybe a little bloody."

Malcolm shifts about, escape flickering, sits on his hands. "I wish you wouldn't mention tequila."

"Got a bottle home?" Leo asks.

"No. But I can get it *any*time I want."

"That's right," Teddy says, "you drink for Air France. No duties, huh? When'd ya have your last belt?"

"I'm getting confused. Early this morning, or more exactly very late last night."

"Feelin' the withdrawals, huh?" Leo asks.

"May I ask you something," Malcolm asks Teddy. "You won't get mad? How did you get that scar on your nose? From a knife?"

"This bastard bit me. In a fit of pique."

"I was in the deetees!" Leo insists.

"It must be very hard to live with."

"I have a *disease* that can kill me," Teddy says. "So does *he*."

Leo raises two fingers to be counted in, Tyrone raises two. Malcolm eyes Tyrone. "Is he an alcoholic?"

"My last blackout," Tyrone says, "was fourteen days. I was happily drinking in my apartment when suddenly I woke up in jail in Paris—no cash—having spent over a week in London. What did I do all that time? Business, apparently! I haven't the foggiest. Rather bad scene, though."

"I've done that," Malcolm says, nodding.

"We're just a pair of Air France alkies." Tyrone laughs, glittering.

"Tell 'im about the time you slugged me and jumped off Brooklyn Bridge," Leo says.

"That was the horrors," Teddy says. "Don't blame me for every little thing."

"You've had the deetees?" Malcolm asks Leo-Teddy.

"Petit-mal and grand-mal," Leo says. "And the roaches. We'd give each other eyedrops to try an' get rid of 'em."

"Visine helps?" Malcolm asks hopefully.

"No."

"If you wanna get rid of the miseries caused by alcohol," Teddy says, "ya gotta stop drinkin' alcohol. It's pretty damn simple. This is a simple program for complicated people."

Malcolm tears again. "You don't know what loneliness is!"

Leo-Teddy silent.

"Surrounded by my wife and children—sheer loneliness!" Malcolm cries.

Tyrone nods. Leo nods. Teddy nods.

"Oh my God, why 'm I telling you! You wouldn't understand. You have each other!"

Silence . . .

"Drinkin' only makes you more lonely, not less," Leo says quietly. "Alcohol exaggerates your feelings until every cell in your body's lonely. Don'tcha know that?"

"Don't softsoap Malcolm," Teddy says, "he doesn't wanna stop. Can'tcha see he's got fortitude?—the deetees run off him like water off a duck's ass. You can't even bear the idea of bein' sober, can ya? Sober people are such mental, emotional, and spiritual pygmies, aren't they? They lead shrivelled lives. Who could possibly wanna be like them? Has there ever been a sober artist worth a shit—aside from Bach and Mozart? You don't wanna join these fuckin' do-gooders and pygmies, do ya, Malcolm? You wanna sit on your fat hifi woofer with the purple mescaline horseshit pourin' out, with your bottle and both thumbs in your mouth, right? Wanna try somethin' new? —try a Shirley Temple record, you'll cry your ass off, it's just as good as Schoenberg—because mescaline makes everything equal, everything beautiful, right down into your guts. All your discrimination's in your intestines, where the tequila and mescaline are bein' absorbed. In a big glow, ho ho! Shirley Temple's as avantgarde as Schoenberg anyday, and *she* doesn't sing like a crosseyed violinist."

". . . I find you terribly offensive. Now—*Leo* and . . .?"

"Tyrone!" Shakes hands.

". . . and *Tyrone* I can get along with. I can tell, they understand me."

"He's all yours," Teddy tells Tyrone and Leo, and takes a call. "A.A., may I help you?"

"He's terribly rude, Leo. How long have you been sober?"

"I been in four years. But I haven't been an angel. I'm only eighteen months sober."

"Twenty months!" Tyrone grins, tobaccostained, gay. *"Ta-ta!"*

"How about *him?"*

"He's a year an' two weeks sober. He's giving his first talk tonight. Should've talked nine months ago but he stammers."

"I didn't notice. I must be far gone, Leo! I have a terrible problem! Don't you listen, Tyrone. Oh, I don't care! —I'm turning h-h-heterosexual."

"You mean homosexual?" Leo asks.

"No! It's terrible!"

"How can you tell? You feel *lust* for girls?"

"Oh God no! I just can't keep interested anymore—in bed."

"—You're impotent with men?" Tyrone asks.

"How did you know that! You should be an analyst—really, I mean that, Ty. You're fantastically insightful."

"Can't say I identify though," Tyrone says.

Leo says, "You might be impotent with anybody, Malcolm. Tried a woman?"

"Don't be disgusting. That's why I turned to men. I lost

interest in my wife. I'm divorced. I have four children in Paris."

"I can identify," Leo says. "I haven't seen my son for eleven years. I'm once and half divorced. But I can't remember booze or mescaline makin' me impotent—just the reverse, I'm Zorba the Cocksman, the inhibitions are off, I wanna go for hours. My heart can't take it anymore."

"Oh you're lucky."

"Fuck that insanity, I don't want eight hours of red pepper fuckin' anymore. I'd be happy with once a week if I could get away with it. How about stoppin' drinkin'? You *might* improve."

"I can't stop, I'd have to taper off."

"Nah ya wouldn't, you've stopped a dozen times for a day or two. You ever thought what a shitheel you are when you drink? To yourself? I mean, you feel guilt and remorse."

"Not always. Quite often I don't feel anything."

"D'ya know what you're saying? Why don'tcha feel anything? Why d'ya feel like a walkin' turd, no emotions, no nothing?"

"I don't know. Why?"

"You tell me."

"Everything's hopeless!"

Leo smiles. "That's it, go on."

"No, Cora," Teddy says on the phone, "I'm only one drink away from a drunk, just like you. Believe me, I got feet of clay."

"I have so many hangups!" Malcolm wails. "I'm afraid of syphilis, my back teeth are shot, I get rashes and wandering bruises—"

"—Vitamin deficiency, wandering bruises," Tyrone says.

"My heart, I get this funny fluttering! *Oh, Ty!*"

"Cora, just get to a meeting," Teddy says. "Your dog is dead, there's nothin' you can do about it."

"My father and three uncles all died in their forties!" Malcolm says.

"Were they drunks?" Leo asks.

"Do you mean alcoholics?"

"I mean cirrhosis, gastric bleeding, hepatitis, heart disease, schizophrenia, paranoia, blackouts, drunk tanks, automobile accidents, never payin' the rent, beating up the wife and kids, and general disorder and suffering. Hm?"

"Yes."

"Believe me, wherever he is, your dog wants you to be sober. My sponsor Nelson, sponsor-to-be, has a white German shepherd, with a pale champagne streak down his back, who throws up an' shits on the rug whenever Nelson opens a bottle of bourbon in the house. Nelson has to drink in the closet, but King *knows!* Now believe me, Mickey wants you to *stay sober*. He'll *smell* it if ya drink, Cora! You get to Butterfield this afternoon and lay your problem on the table—there'll be a lotta drunks there who've lost their dogs."

"Yes, but *I'm* hopeless!" Malcolm cries.

"Are ya dead yet?" Leo asks. "Then why project failure? I was always sayin' if I could just have one hit song—I'm a songwriter—and get some clothes an' have enough to squire some chick around and solve my poverty problem or land a rich widow or a grant or fellowship, *then* I might take care of my drinkin' problem. After all the other problems, right? After cigarettes and fat and the rent. I didn't know that if I took away the bottle problem, the others'd evaporate—if I can get over my self-defeating *yes, but's* and *poor me's*. If you take the bottle outta your life, you *won't* get canned by Air France, you will regain your sexual vigor, you may gain partial custody of your children, your constant depression and nameless anxieties will lift, *and* the deetees, and what's absolutely sure is that your composing will get a helluva rise. Alcoholic composers do their best despite their booze habit, not because of it. My best writing used to come durin' hangovers—it was the only time I was sober. So maybe it doesn't matter if you're an alcoholic—why not just stop drinkin'? Give it ninety days. See what happens. Look, your father and three uncles, poof! *Somebody* up there's tryin' t' tell you something."

"Yes, but I can't do it!" Malcolm weeps. "I've tried and tried and just can't do it."

"Yes you can," Leo says. "You can stay sober for one day, can'tcha? Don't worry about tomorrow, just stay sober today—twenty-four hours! And go to meetings. Here's a meetingbook."

"I have one. I went to some meetings on Ninth Avenue.

I couldn't wait to get out, I just wanted a drink and that's all they were talking about—drinking!"

"Recovering from drinking," Leo says.

"They were *boring!*" Malcolm cries. *"Unforgivably* BORING!"

"I never been to a boring meeting," Leo tells Teddy. "Have you?"

"Only when I wanted t' drink more than stay sober."

"Exactly," Malcolm says approvingly of Teddy. "My mind buzzes in a thousand directions at once at those meetings, I'm so bored."

"I identify completely," Teddy says. "Those meetings are much too low-key intellectually. Tryin' to shrink a giant creative talent down to the level of Don't Drink is humiliating. Malcolm needs a *complicated* program, Tyrone, with sprung rhythms and atonality, so he can spend long hours refining, diffusing, qualifying, and rationalizing it into cobwebs. It's a damned shame to chain up a genius with moronic slogans and Don't Drink—though we sat at the big table at Renewal East last weekend and twenty people admitted to bein' geniuses. An eruption of geniuses! Recovering, of course."

"Yes, but you don't understand—*I'm hopeless!*" Tears spurt again, he slumps spinelessly hanging over his chair. "Oh God, when will somebody—I *live* with the deetees! I find them interesting! They are PRODUCTIVE! I'm writing an opera about them!"

"Oh, you *write?*" Leo asks.

". . . I sing to my *friend* and he takes notation."

"He's your lover?" Tyrone asks.

"Oh my God, you have second sight!"

"And *he* drinks?" Tyrone asks.

"Oh he's much worse. He can't taper off, he's always in the hospital. I'm experienced at stopping with a complete lack of suffering, just a few gins and fruit juice. I can handle it. That's why I say I don't have a problem."

"Then what's so hopeless?" Teddy asks.

"I'm not talking with you, you're much too confused for rational conversation."

"You're not ready to stop?" Leo asks.

Malcolm digs out his wallet with ten thumbs. "Let me read you the epigraph to my opera. From *Twelfth Night,* to be precise. 'Dost thou think, because thou art virtuous, there shall be no more cakes and ale?' Frankly, I find this argument irrefutable. It's by Shakespeare."

"Tequila and mescaline aren't cakes and ale," Leo says. "You don't lose your sanity, get jailed, drive into guide rails or trees, wake up in Bellevue or Central Islip, lose your wife and kids and your Air France job over cakes and ale."

"You are talking much too fast. Well, I—I must simply be talking over your heads—all three of you. This is by *Shakespeare!*"

"I've always liked that quote," Tyrone says, guardedly.

"You don't fall on the subway tracks," Teddy adds, "get your nose bitten, break your leg, or toss up blood either, Shakespeare or no Shakespeare. We're not social drinkers, Malcolm. Neither are you. Tell me about cakes and ale when you wake up dead in your own vomit someday, or finish yourself off with an overdose."

"But don't you see," Malcolm says, "that's precisely it. A devout alcoholic does not recover. He *dies* an alcoholic death as part of his religion. Your fate is your fate, dear man. In fact, that's what I sing about."

"Man's character is his bottle," Tyrone says. "Heraclitus! *Ahem.*"

"I guess Malcolm's not an alcoholic," Teddy tells Leo.

"Of course he is, that's what he's sayin'."

"Nah, nah," Teddy says.

"Whaddaya mean!" Leo says. "He's lost his wife, his kids—"

"Nah, nah."

"—his potency, his job's next—"

"Nah, nah."

"I lost my driver's license," Malcolm says.

"Nah, nah."

"—I can't write! I'm being evicted! I've lost my back teeth!—"

"Nah, nah."

"—I have deetees regularly!—"

"Nah, nah!"

"—I'll live on a garbage heap if I can just have my tequila and hifi! And *sing!* Sitting dead drunk with my head full of mescaline in front of the hifi is paradise!"

"That proves it!" Teddy snorts. "He hasn't hit bottom yet. He can still sing! He's not *hopeless* yet, NOT REALLY HOPELESS! Go home to your gutter, Malcolm. Ya get booze anytime ya want it? TANK UP. Come back when you feel *really* sick and tired. This is a progressive disease, your bottom's *waitin'* for ya."

"Are you God," Malcolm asks, "to know where my bottom is?"

"Skip the deetees, wait until you're heaving blood, the tequila's hosing outta your ass, your liver's cooked, running sores break open, and when ya try to sing all your Schoenberg's a bunch of croaking bullshit. Try us then. We'll be waitin' for *you* with a mariachi band. But where ya gonna get your booze after Air France cans ya, I dunno, do you? I'll bet you sing like a syphilitic bullfrog. Come back when you have a *desire* to stop drinkin'. Why the hell'd ya come up here in the first place?"

"YOU PIG! YOU IMPOSSIBLE PIG!"

"Righto," Teddy says marking meetings in a meetingbook.

"I came up here for help!" Malcolm cries standing.

"Here," Teddy says, stuffing the meetingbook into Malcolm's shirtpocket. "Don't go emptyhanded."

Malcolm's rash turns scarlet with harsh, whipped agony. "This is the last straw!" he cries, weaving to the elevator.

"You've carried a bale of last straws for years. Get wise to yourself."

"Don't think I'm not getting drunk as quickly as I can get out of here."

"What else is new?"

Malcolm staggers into the elevator, the door closes.

"He may not come back," Leo says.

"Why not?" Teddy asks.

"You were pretty hard on him."

"Hell. Who else cares for the sonofabitch? All I asked him to do was stop drinkin'. He's got the message."

"What did you think about his asking if you were God?" Tyrone asks.

"If this nosebiter beside me had acted toward me the way I acted toward Malcolm, I'd've been sober years ago. *But he coddled and coddled and coddled me, year after year after year*. Got the message?"

"Hmm!"

"I hope that bastard gets evicted, loses his job, loses the rest of his teeth, and his ass drops off, all at once. The faster the better. Got the message?"

"You want him to wake up?" Tyrone asks.

"Ahh!" Teddy says, "it's a simple, simple, simple Program."

Bogus O'Shaughnessy, a tender-eyed, starey, balding dark young ex-Catholic radical writingless writing genius, stops at their desk, brimming. "Damn fine job, lads! I wasted an hour tryin' to cut through his fluff."

Leon calls, "I worked him over a half hour too!"

"His farting Harvard front had me licking his tennis shoes," Bogus says. "That wasn't piss on his sneakers, it was radical-anarchist saliva. Don't I have a sort of lemon-colored jaundice? How's my tongue?"

"Poor Bogie!" sighs Angel Selznick, a matronly Fifth Avenue divorcée. "You deserve the Long-Sufferer's Gold Medal."

"I'm just a heroic failure and always will be," Bogie says.

"And successful alcoholic!" Leon calls.

"I've got that to be grateful for," Bogie agrees.

"That's what makes you special," Leon says, lighting a chairleg cigar. "It ain't my fine clothes or this big cigar that makes you admire *me,* it's what's inside this suit that A.A. put there! Remember that when you pass my desk. And *smile*—I don't get paid for sittin' here, I need all the admiration I can get."

"I realize that, Brother Bones," Bogie says. His tense brown eyes race to match feelings with thoughts. "And perhaps someday, if I'm worthy, pious, chipper, and train on cigars, I'll inherit your desk and chair, all your telephones and hospital logs and your title: *Mr. A.A.*"

"Bogardus, you just keep waitin' one day at a time," Leon says. "And don't project! My shoes are not easily filled. We had a little rambunctiousness 'round my house this mornin'. Lady down my hall comes in cryin' FIRE! I goes upstairs with my ax, breaks down a door, and this guy's *locked* into his bedroom so I breaks down his bedroom door too, he's still on the bed. Ain't heard a thing, the room white with smoke from his mattress. *'Whut you doin' breakin' down mah doors!'* he cries when we gets him onto his feet. Man, I want to hit him with the blunt end of mah ax! An' he's *still* mad this minute. I'm goin' home and *tell him,* 'You're a drunk! You endangerin' all our lives, you drunk. I calls you that because that's whut you are!' "

"Why don't you be tactful," Angel asks, "and just mail him a meetingbook?"

"I don't care 'bout him, I cares 'bout us!"

Nelson steps out of the elevator with a bag, solemnly lays two wrapped sandwiches on Leo-Teddy's desk with two apples. Leo digs for his bills.

"Put that away," Nelson says severely.

"Thanks very much."

"Thank *you*. I listened to you guys work that hoople until I either had to go out for sustenance or strangle him. Can't ya *see* a whole ward full of empty beds just waitin' for him? Bellevue! Central Islip! Pilgrim State!"

"He'll be back," Teddy says.

"That Marjory-faggot?" Nelson says, then asks Tyrone, "Are ya gettin' the hang of it?"

"Indeed, sir. Teddy's attack reminds me of a statement by Viktor Frankl, if I may mangle a quotation. 'If architects want to strengthen a decrepit arch, they increase the load that is laid upon it, for thereby the parts are joined more firmly together.' How's that?"

"Aw shit," Nelson says. "Don't intellectualize. It's a simple Program, Ty."

"What's a Marjory-faggot?" Angel asks.

"Ya better not ask," Nelson says. "You won't find it in your damned crossword puzzle, I can tell ya."

"What's wrong with my crossword puzzle!"

"Angel," Nelson says, "we don't come down here to Intergroup to work crossword puzzles—we're here to be in the glory of A.A.! and help poor suffering alcoholics. *This* is where we get the spirit. There are men in the ranks—"

"—WHO WILL STAY IN THE RANKS—"

"—because they Just Don't Get Things Done," Nelson tells her. "If ya don't understand your spiritual opportunity in talkin' with men of real sobriety like these twins and Leon and Parker and Bogardus and Tyrone and me, and gettin' some real feeling for The Program, instead of workin' *crossword* puzzles, *agghh,* I can't tell ya."

"Well then," she says, "educate me—what's a Marjory-faggot?"

"You asked for it," Nelson says. "I got a call just now from some San Antonio cowboy who says he's *ex-President Lyndon Johnson's* fourth cousin and he's comin' up here to chew my ass out. Says he called in for help and we sent a Marjory-faggot over to speak with him. What's a Marjory-faggot? I asked him. A *hairdresser,* he says, who should have his penis tucked back between his legs, his balls cut off and his tits filled with plastic. Now ya know."

"That reminds me of my Parisian childhood," Angel says. "Daddy'd hang candycoated cognac animals on the Christmas tree—I'd prick them, sip out the cognac and give the chocolate to my sister."

"I just don't see the connection," Nelson sighs.

"My sister's name is Marjory."

Nelson sits in disgust, grabs a ringing phone for succor. *"A.A., may I help you!"*

"I had the weirdest dream of my life last night," Bogie tells Leo-Teddy, "about you two guys. I was in the Cabinet room at the White House and we were waiting for the president to show up."

"We were on the Cabinet?" Leo asks.

"Oh no! As a matter of fact, I was standing by some double doors when they opened and the president was announced by some Irish flunky, probably myself. And you lads came in on the floor."

"Drunk!" Teddy cries.

"Oh no!" Bogie wideeyed wonder. *"Worse.* Both your heads came walking in. On the floor! 'Mr. President,' I said to you, and a thrill ran through me. You seemed to be walking on your necks. Your whole bodies'd been amputated. But you were very serious and walked over to the Cabinet table and the Cabinet was seated around in a morning meeting. I remember wondering how you could possibly live in this condition—but you were standing, or resting side by side on your necks. Funny thing was, all the muscles in your faces were compensating for not having any arms or bodies. Your noses twitched to keep out dust, you seemed to *think* in flicking cheek muscles, your mouths and eyes were hyperactive—but what I remember most vividly were your eyes, so intensely serious, reflective, and focused on Cabinet problems. That's all there was to it."

"Just a pair of severed heads?" Leo asks.

"But with a kind of heavenly seriousness about you," Bogie says. "Your beards *wiggled* constantly, practically polishing the table. And despite not having any bodies, you both seemed ten times more alive than anyone else at the table. Really elevated spiritually."

"We were in heaven?" Teddy asks.

"You might say that—a kind of Arthurian heaven."

"How do *you* interpret this dream?" Leo asks.

"Oh, it was all about *me,*" Bogie says. "You were acting out my ambition—though I've given it up, of course. I'll be satisfied now to get Leon's desk when the palace revolution comes—and if my head's on straight. Or *off!* The Arthurian urge looms large in A.A., don't you think?"

"I suppress it," Leo says.

"Maybe it's my Kennedy hangover," Bogie says. "I'd rather be here than in Camelot. We're not dreamers!"

A wild grayhaired filthstreaked bum, his arm in a filthy white cast, lopes staggering from the elevator, chains on his waist, his ripped cowboy boots jangling with spurs on chains. A paring knife rests in a slot he's cut into his black chinos. "I'm the fourth cousin of ex-President Lyndon Baines Johnson and I'm *sick people!* I'm worse'n that St. Valentine's Day massacre in Chicago! I feel so bad I wanna die. Can you buy me a egg?" he asks Angel. "I'm really scared. Where shall I go—t' the back table? I'm so nervous I can't hold my coffee, will you carry it for me, ma'm? I need help, I wanna *die!"* he waves his knife. A chill runs through the office. "Please help me get inta a hospital, pretty miss. Mah name's Howard. Ya meet a lot of *good people* in A.A. I shouldna gawn on this last drunk!" he weeps. "I was sober two years! Willya gimme some money, buddy?" he asks Bogie. "Hey, miss, miss! mah angel!"

Daphne Fasma, the volunteers coordinator, rises from her desk, her hair in a taffygray ponytail, and cries, "Stop waving that fucking knife around, *Howard!* Drink your coffee and *shut up!"*

"How can ya talk t' me that way! *I'm a dyin' man!"*

"Now, now, Howard's gonna be just fine," Nelson says. "You sit here with me, Howard. Ya like Copenhagen?"

"I don't chew tobacco. Ya got a cigarette? I gotta give up these Camels, they don't taste right no more."

"Gonna change your brand?" Nelson's eyes screw up with a kind of Mongolian good will.

"I been smokin' 'em too long," Howard says. "I gotta use your phone! I gotta call my mama in San 'Tone for busfare home."

Daphne shakes her head *no* to Nelson.

"You don't want you mama to hear you whinin' like a Marjory-faggot," Nelson says. "Do ya, Howard?"

"She's heard me at my worst." Howard's chin shoots up. "And I shore don't wanna be shanghaied inta A.A. again. Nossir! Not for a cup of coffee. Ah'm a *wine-drinker!*"

"Come on, Howard, let's get honest," Nelson begins.

Leo draws up his clipboard, reads a letter he wrote ten days ago to a drunk who's been barred from Intergroup.

"Well," Angel whispers to Teddy. "I thought he'd ask me to take him home next—at knifepoint. My bones turned to jelly!"

"He's got no place to go but up," Leo says.

Angel smiles. "But not up to my house."

"Two years of meetings under his belt," Teddy says. "He's a sitting duck for the spirit side of The Program."

"But with a little Alamo fever?" Angel suggests.

"Cast the first stone!" Teddy says.

"What do you think his chances are?" she asks Leo.

"He's died a thousand deaths. He's ripe."

"Ready for an oil change," Teddy adds, lifting his receiver. "A.A., may I help you?"

Leo looks down the muttering, phoneringing, redcarpeted room, sees Cynara sitting at Angel's desk, weeping out her fears. He remembers the last bed with her, stammering to tell her of his new spirit in A.A., overblowing his message, her distant lost look as if his once-dependable souped up wild heart were being mummified in sobriety. And now, *her* bones, handground in a mortar. Niacin? The Twelve Suggested Steps? Dust hath closed Helen's eye, I am sick, I must die, *Lord have mercy on us!* Change of attitudes, only way to beat the plague.

The letter Leo reads he recovered from a shoppingbag left in his apartment by the most hopeless case he's ever met, a crippled pensioner ex-World War Two and Korean War paratrooper legs-broken-in-five places former medical student (he *says*) chef rubbing-alcohol-shaving-lotion guzzling roaring rumdum on whom Daphne calls the cops whenever he hobbles off the elevator on his cane, his Purple Heart cluster pinned to his tee-shirt, whole body awash with skinbracer and cheap antisweat lotions he drinks, his forehead dented deep and subhuman leer rocking like the sea.

Dear Perry (*Leo wrote*),

Thanks for the *inspiring* letters! Sure I'll be your sponsor. I think hopefully about your forthcoming "graduation" from Gray Moor and wonder what activities will help you conquer your drinking problem one day at a time. You'll have to 12-Step yourself hour by hour—I can't be with you 24 hours a day. Even if I were, I know you could wring booze outta your liver. So my greatest aid in sponsoring you will be you.

Your most religious act when you get out of Gray Moor will be to PHONE ME daily, but especially when that First Nip starts dancing in your mocus Italian skull. Remember *daily,* you Perry Parodi are a HOPELESS ALCOHOLIC, kicked out of A.A. and dust under the feet of those who are truly striving. Any drunk can dry out at Gray Moor, that's no big step. You are undergoing a small, in your case almost microscopic spiritual change out there, though it may seem large as heaven to you now. Forget about your past failures—22 years of unrelieved drunkenness! Put 'em out of your mind for now; just pray that the time will come when you'll be in focus at last not mocus!) and you'll be ready for your inner housecleaning, The Steps. Read The Steps *carefully* so you'll know what's in store for you as my pigeon —my hopeless pigeon! What's in store is The Program: you'll be nailed to the barn door like a catfish —no time to think of drinking. And when a shot of Old Pissbucket comes dancing into your head, you will *follow directions* (When All Else Fails, Follow Directions) and Phone Me and not sit there with a drink in your eyes and your thumb up your nether exit.

The phone call's where the real courage is: in admitting that you have a craving and telling me INSTANTLY. You are a HOPELESS ALCOHOLIC, *admit it or die*. You personally are utterly defenseless against the disease. You need help, troops, and assistance! You need a PHONE. You need 90 meetings in 90 days, more likely 180 in 90 days. Your pension (your friendly monthly drinking retainer) will go a long way when you're not blowing it in one big monthly binge. First thing first check: buy a Big Book at Intergroup. If you can walk off the elevator Cold Sober, perhaps you'll be allowed back into the big office on a comfortable basis. Then study your meetingbook like the train schedule to heaven. Don't bother thinking about going back to work—you're going to *meetings, meetings, meetings.* You couldn't possibly pack in enough meetings to give Perry Parodi the miracle of sobriety. *But you are going to try,* you hopeless alcoholic. All your morning Communion out at Gray Moor will not get Perry P. into heaven: Only A.A. can get that hopeless DRUNK upstairs, by the power of The Steps. No easy confessions and Communions and last rites for you, old heart-attack artist—don't forget Teddy and I held your hand during your last phony attack at Mt. Vernon Hospital when you got the priest in for "extreme unction" and conned an extra shot of morphine outta the docs. You are gonna be bullwhipped through The Program. And when I'm not doing the whipping, you will do it yourself. Nuff said? You can never recover by yourself, got it? As an A.A. convert, you will Speak Gratitude Constantly. Begin Now, turn to the nearest jumblie and tell him you love A.A., that it's the One Hope Left for as hopeless a rummy as you, that your greatest desire is to be worthy of the handshakes of A.A. members, that you will *Never Fear Ridicule* for being in love with A.A. Half measures will get you shit, my lad. You will embrace A.A. heart and soul. *Burn my phone number into your brain.* Remember, I was there at Queens Hospital the day you threw the sponge in, tanker—the greatest day of your life. Trust the Higher Power and get ready to clean house! See you soon, we'll be up for a visit with the razor blades and lotion you asked for.

With great heart,
Leo

Nelson sends Howard bawling with hope down the elevator. "I gave him a buck for Uncle Sam's flophouse on the Bowery. But do I really think he'll make it down there? If he *does,* he may be on his way to recovery

—if he doesn't I'm only out a buck, right? How's *your* prize pigeon?" he asks Leo.

"Sonofabitch got outta Gray Moor Monday," Leo says, "we took him to our pad, he got drunk Tuesday at his Foreign Legion post, and we poured him into St. Vincent's Wednesday. Real life's a great strain on him."

"Drank up his skinbracer for fast relief," Teddy adds. "His first swig in the bathroom, we knew it instantly. Instant mocus, beyond belief. He came outta the john singing, The moon's in the sky like a big p-p-pizza p-p-pie. *Ugh!*"

"That bottlesucker had B-A-R flashing from his forehead every time I saw him," Nelson says. "You hooples should work on drunks you can really help."

"It's a program of miracles," Leo says, "even for hooples."

"I can *see* that! But your fathead is the kind that gives A.A. a bad name. Who wants to sit listening to him sing pizza pie durin' a meeting? We threw him outta Mustard Seed five times, for Christ's sake!"

"Very powerful example in that," Teddy says. "Members see a drunk evicted even from A.A."

Leo smiles. "It could happen to you."

"*Happened* to me!" Teddy says. "An' I don't wanna forget it."

"I remember the first time I came to Renewal," Nelson says, "Teddy gettin' kicked out in his fuckin' Kraut helmet. He's improved mightily."

"That's m-m-my crash helmet for fallin' in the gutter."

Nelson sighs. "I'm too sensitive for such bullshit."

Leo starts a fresh letter to Perry Parodi:

Dear Pilgrim of the Purple Heart,

Tomorrow I'm taking all your gear to the Gun Hill VFW Post. You can call there to see if your drinking buddies have accepted the boxes, bags, and clothes the Brothers gave you at Gray Moor. Surely your fellow legionnaires of the Purple Heart, whom you blew to so many swell drinks Tuesday ($75 worth!), will look after your best interests. In one bag you'll also find the rosaries and Gray Moor medals you gave Teddy and me—they were given in a spirit bloated with gratitude but I'm afraid they disturb our serenity. I feel they won't help a bit toward not taking the first drink.

I'm afraid that your Mennen's Skin-Bracer and Polynesian Jade bottles got broken in the toilet while I was packing your gear. Also, I kept that letter I wrote you last week for your Gray Moor recovery. Since you treat its thoughts like toilet paper, I guess I'll put it to good use.

In short, I hope you'll consider our friendship, and Teddy and my endless attempts to help you, as water over the dam. Perhaps we'll see each other in a year or so when you've packed 365 days of rocksolid sobriety under your brewbelly as you fight the bottle sitting around the Gun Hill Post, singing with your cronies. Boy, I envy all those past glories you war vets sing about! Here I am, stuck in the Now with only The Steps and the Big Book while you guys have all World War Two and Korea and Vietnam to sing about— I know you'd pity me but, as you say, pity's only a word in the dictionary. I guess I'll break out my trumpet and start crying.

You've always been honest with Perry, haven't you, and admitted your respectful desire for alcohol. Excuse me, I meant sobriety. You sure taught me a lot about alcohol! I'll always remember how easy it is, when I need a drink, just to dip my hand into the basket when it's passed at a meeting and take out enough for a ball of Vitalis or Swiss Up.

You've shown me how strong I can be, old elbow-bender, how to justify my every resentment, how to blow my temper (and friendships) to get away from people who'd try to keep me from my ball. You show me how I can handle my drinking by myself, work The Program alone, how I can throw my cane (or Teddy's) away to justify myself in public, how to upset a meeting with my generous remarks, how to meet my loyal beerbellies up at Gun Hill, how to write such wonderfully sincere letters of gratitude to keep a tight grip on my con, and how to speak gratitude constantly while fastening my eye on that first drink I need so badly—when I need Mennen's before God. First things first, right? Or maybe Mennen's is God and God smells like a boxer coming out of His dressingroom. Sincerity, respect, gratitude, self-honesty—what pasta! what tomato sauce! You've taught me how to let down every A.A. friend in sight. I'll always have myself, of course, with whom I can converse with perfect honesty and perfect sincerity about my perfect desire for the first drink. Now I know what perfection is.

I hope your new hospitalization will help sweat out some of your excessive concern for others and get you concentrating on your own many problems. (Don't let those damned problems spin your eye off that first drink waiting when you get out!) *Don't phone us.* If you do, I know for a fact that you won't get through, since our line is taken up by a bunch of recovering alcoholics who want us to join 'em in their damn childish resistance to drinking. Cancel my number from your mind, you have nothing left to give us. I especially don't want to see your horrible sober face around my apartment building—I'll call the police at first sight of you in my hallways. To pack it all into one word, I *quit,* and Teddy *quits.* You're on your own, old pilgrim. Maybe you can find another sponsor up at the Gun Hill Post. Perhaps we'll run into each other if Teddy and I speak at Bellevue or Central Islip meetings—though you probably won't recognize us, old vegetable. Thanks for the wonderful feelings you fill me with, I feel gassy with gratitude for every teary, sentimental, boozey good word you've had for us. You have my sincere honest respect, somewhat bloated. Get well soon, and have a bracer for me! *GOODBYE.*

Aromatically yours,
Leo

P.S. Carry the message, not the alcoholic.

Leo shows the letter to Teddy. "How's this for a two-by-four to the skull?"

Teddy reads. "Too light—he won't even feel it through the fuzz. But if he ever gets over his medications he *may* see that someone's really concerned. You need heavy tackle for that dumdum. Mail it before ya go soft." Hands the letter to Terrible-tempered Tyrone H.

Leo-Teddy listens to the office murmur, watches the

workers in the streetmap-lined room. A cane falls, Teddy leans it against a wallmap of Queens pin-flagged with A.A. meeting places. Four new recoverers sit at the back table sealing envelopes for a big mailing, trading horror stories. Across from Leo-Teddy, Parker burns away the evasions of a sufferer on the phone, deadly serious as a bulldog: "I don't care if you are a nun, you're a drunk, Sister. *You're* telling *me* how unmanageable your life is! Your legs are numb with neuritis, you're obviously suffering from alcohol poisoning." Leo-Teddy *stiffens*. "Don't-cha think it's time you drop the baloney and get honest?" Earnest voices plugged into drunks all over the city fill Leo-Teddy with a strong sense of human life burning with angelic intensity, heavenly purpose.

Jack McFin steps off the elevator, airline bag in hand. Short orange hair graying, oceanfresh eyes quietly in touch with the room as he enters it for the first time ever. "Hey, this new office is swell!" he tells Leon.

Joy fills Leo-Teddy. *"Jack!"*

"Had to come up to the city for Teddy's first talk. It's *tonight,* isn't it?"

Leo-Teddy shows Jack around the workers' desks, gives him Leo's Perry letters to read. Jack drifts back to sit with the shaking recoverers and fresh blood at the rear table. His mild lakeblue eyes brighten even more at the table, his spirit rising like warm bread. After a while he returns Leo's letters.

"Very punchy, eh?" Tyrone asks Jack.

"This may do the bastard some good—probably won't. But don't wear yourself out. I leave rumdums and psychos to the specialists myself—I can't take 'em."

Teddy says, "You were hopeless yourself."

Leo says, "I keep hoping for the miracle."

"Boy, I sure was hopeless, and good luck to you!"

"Frankly," Tyrone says, "I'd like to rewrite The Twelve Steps myself. I find their language unnecessarily alienating—for newcomers. You think you're walking into some kind of religious organization. It's their damned salvation tone, so oldfashioned."

"Oh, I don't know," Jack says. "A newcomer might find any kind of spiritual tone nauseous. It's not the language, it's just plain resistance to getting well. Are you working them?"

"Not yet! But you may be right, sir. I'll have to think about it."

"Don't think," Jack says. "Start working."

"Hmm!"

Howard staggers off the elevator again, chains jangling at every lope. "I'm a messenger of Bill W.! I pick up vibrations from his flyin' saucer. I blacked out and I goddamn well don't like to black out. Lemme have one more a yore wop cigars, Nelson—I'm tryin' to' switch brands. I been on these tarbaby Camels too long."

"You sonofabitch—you're drunk again!" Nelson says.

"Howard, get your ass outta here!" Daphne cries. "I'm callin' the cops if you're not on that fucking elevator in five seconds!"

"I got a message from Bill W.! I been gettin' his personal vibrations all afternoon! You can't throw me outta here till I give mah message."

"Ya didn't get to Uncle Sam's, huh," Nelson asks.

Leo tells Jack, "Nelson used t' ride Brahma bulls!"

"Once swam eleven miles down the Mississippi," Teddy says.

"Why man, I was on mah way through all them Marjory-faggots—'scuse mah language, angel—in Washington Square when I found two black fellers on *mah bench*. That's mah bed! I tol' 'em with mah knife out! But they gimme a swig of Twilight Rose—jus' one swig, I swear on mah mamma's soul!—an' I *blacked out*. Woke up robbed! That's when I heard Bill W.'s vibrations from his flyin' saucer tellin' me, You can't drink no more, Howard! He tol' me so hisself, Bill W. did! Ah jus' can't drink no more, Nelson."

"So what're ya gonna do?" Nelson asks.

"I'm gonna get another dollar an' straighten mahself out at Uncle Sam's. I come chere to borrow another dollar."

"Not from me, Howard," Nelson says. "I wouldn't trust you to get there if the whole metropolitan police force took ya."

"Gee, I haven't been to Uncle Sam's in years," Jack says. "I'll walk you over, Howard."

"Not another drop, Nelson!" Howard weeps. "Ain't it a damn shame?—two years sober!"

"You better listen to Bill W.," Nelson says. "Howard, this is Jack, he's just up from Pennsylvania."

Howard waves his filthy plaster cast at Jack. "I'm just back from Mexico."

"Same booze," Jack says.

"They had two kinds of liquor down there," Howard says, "tekillya and muskillya! But it's that Twilight Rose that done me in—tastes like Pepsi-Cola. So what, Ah had a li'l slip! Ahm ready t' reform!"

Leo asks Howard, "You know that *Bill W.* says this is a spiritual program, Howard?"

"Never mind that spiritual jazz," Howard says. "Put the cork in the bottle an' stop!"

"Let's take a walk," Jack says. "See you men in an hour."

"I *luuv* A.A.," Howard says in the elevator. "A.A.'s *good people*."

Angel says, "I *think* I am about to faint with relief!"

"No, Angel," Bogie says, "you are not going to faint."

"Oh ho ho ho! You don't know how close that was. I saw green spots when he waved that stiletto."

"Merely a paring knife, Angel," Bogie says.

"And those chains! They drove every thought out of my mind. That jangle!"

"Think of that in terms of power of example," Bogie assures her. "And never wear chains."

Chinablue eyes amazed, Angel says, "Bogie, darling, there might have been *blood* shed in this room."

"And it would've been my blood before yours," Bogie says, "and Nelson's before mine."

"And Daphne's before mine," Nelson says.

"An' *mine* before Daphne's!" Leon says. "Angel has absolutely nothin' t' worry about."

"Well," she says, "that renews my sense of continuity and well-being."

"Though by the time he got down to you," Bogie says, "I dread to think what this room'd look like."

Angel looks about, terrified of the very walls. "I guess I'm just tremendously sensitive to knives. You're not that way?"

"Well," Bogie says, "I pray a lot."

"More than is good for you!" Angel warns.

"Vraiment!" Tyrone says.

When Jack returns, Leo-Teddy's shift ends and they take him off to a midtown supermarket on their way to Renewal. Spirits calm and smooth.

Leo pushes a shoppingcart. "We're the coffee brigade. Renewal has the best coffee of any A.A. meeting in the city."

"In the States!" Teddy says. "We make an espresso like caffeine fruitcake."

"Everybody gets quite a lift out of it."

"Oh?" Jack says. "What's in it?'"

"Orange extract, lemon extract, vanilla extract, cinnamon, cloves, cardamon seed, and dash of this 'n' that. The alcohol boils off, of course. None of our Antabuse people've complained."

"I'll bet they haven't," Jack says. "I'd be nervous, if I were you. Why don't you switch to real lemons and oranges?"

"Gee," Leo says"—hadn't thoughta that. *Hm!*"

"Oh, it's probably a *caffeine* lift," Jack agrees. "None for me, thank you."

"Helluva good suggestion, Jack," Teddy says. "We pour in an awful lot of extract, Leo."

"Sonofabitch," Jack says. "You mean you've got this whole meeting hooked on extract?"

"We'll switch to real fruit!" Leo cries.

"The meeting's growin' too big anyway," Teddy says.

"My God," Jack says. "How can you take the chance that it won't flip out some crutchmonger on Antabuse?"

Leo-Teddy blushing. "Slowly, Jack," Teddy says, "we strive for improvement, not perfection. W-w-we didn't even think about Antabuse."

"Everybody *loves* our espresso," Leo says.

"Boy, you guys keep me on edge," Jack says. "Even three hundred miles away!"

"Absolutely no reason for you t' feel like that," Leo says, drawing up.

"Thanks."

Wait in line, cart filled with oranges, lemons, espresso, light cream, rich cookies, lemonpuffs, Leo-Teddy's usual mouthwatering fats and pastries. They refrain from opening cookies early—Jack's along.

"An awfully sexy girl at Renewal," Teddy tells Jack. "A M-m-marilyn—m-m-mental capacity of a sex organ, b-b-but she's sober. Spent all last year on champ-p-pagne in Las Vegas. I can't even look at her, my tongue hangs out like a red necktie. Tell us what you think."

"I *try* not to think about that," Jack says. "I haven't

thought about anyone but Jill for years—and don't want to! When I was on beer and wine I was mesmerized by my obscenities and sex fixations. I like what Kafka said, talking about writing as prayer— 'When I write I feel fearless, powerful, surprising.' I had a marshmallow spine on wine and everything I wrote was evasive and gummy. Now I pray, Lord, grant me a little austerity, please."

Into great stone Central Presbyterian on Park and Sixty-fourth, take the elevator (*Cynara's breasts, dust in an urn!*) up to sixth floor, light up the meetingroom with its tremendous table surrounded by chairs, open leaded windows for crossbreezes, hit the big kitchen with its lemony walls and ceiling glaring yellowpaint—Leo-Teddy moving about inside a pound of butter.

"Old John Barleycorn plays for keeps—he don't fuck around," Jack says on the kitchen stool. "Your admirer, Rickey of Rockview, got out of stir and OD'd within eight weeks. I didn't feel so weepy about him going though—I mean *dying*, not going, why euphemize! Booze was his problem—so the sonofabitch tried heroin instead. He sure let down a lot of people—his A.A. brothers back in Rockview. Boy, those kids with dual problems out at the White Deer rehab farm really set bulldog teeth into The Program. No Shit Allowed. Most of 'em are teenagers or in their twenties. Confirmed drunkards too, their stories are born-to-lose hairraising—do they testify! They dig Reality A.A.—no substitute indulgences, and they have surprise urine tests to spot cheaters. That place's a miracle. Confrontation A.A., really rough—my sort . . . The trip up got me thinking—I was on the train about five hours with my Lawrence and didn't read a single poem—the hills were that alive. And so was I. Look at me, I'm actually here! Alcohol kept me from going where I want to go, everytime—I'd always settle for an excuse or substitute, then feel like shit because I wasn't somewhere else. Your Nelson is some punkins, isn't he? Every inch an alcoholic—that's about the nicest thing I can say about anybody. Why don't you throw the lemons right into the urn? Everyone asks about you and looks forward to your next visit. They all sing your praises—I mean your songs! Yesterday I had to go to class to spout on Tolstoy—I try not to take myself too damned seriously, I work awfully hard on Easy Does It, Live and Let Live, Let Go and Let God—simple but tough. A.A. freed me from the disease of self-analysis—and it sure could have helped Tolstoy. Well, his later power of example was a force against the vodka plague. Of course, he didn't know that Don't Drink are the most effective spiritual words a drunk can learn. Boy, I saw some glorious trout streams on the train today. Henry David Thoreau's in supershape, granite sober—he talked for half an hour at his second birthday, really strong. Then he called on Leonard, my sponsor, and Leonard strode up front—he didn't have to! —and started pacing back and forth and delivered a sublime fifteen-minute pitch on the mystery of A.A. that turned the meeting golden—and I mean memorable! 'What is lost in time is gained in power'—*wow.* Jill says he's the most profound man she's ever met. You know he started that Mill Hall meeting and went to it weekly for two years—nobody showed up but he sat there alone for two years waiting. He *wanted* sobriety. He'll be celebrating his one-thousandth Mill Hall meeting this year. If I get twenty-five years in this Program, I'll never have what he has in twelve. He doesn't pontificate, he just tells you what a rough time he had drinking and as you listen in on his disease with him, the miracle of his recovery from those grisly, freezing, heart-palsying deetees is just goddamn blinding. Mill Hall meetings are glorious, I leave 'em with my bones shaking. But Curly's gone, and so's Bill M. —boy, I'll miss 'em! When Curly gave his pitch, his bald dome used to light up like a golden bulb. What powerhouses. I never believed in the laying on of hands until one night Bill M. placed his hand on my head and dissolved me into light. If he could wake up a vegetable like me—wow, that's some gift. Faith without works is dead, don't you think?—this is a program of miracles, and all his eyes said was, You're making it, Jack, keep coming. Boy, sobriety cheers me. Even Zorba the hot dog man's back from his slip and turned holyroller—just luminous. I went to visit Bill M. in the hospital the day he died. How ya feeling, Bill? I asked him. He smiled at me and whispered, *Just great!*"

"Terrific," Teddy says, arranging lemonpuffs. "You'll never forget that."

"I don't see how—but I could. Well, shit, they're right here now, wouldn't you say, in the inspiration they give? I like what Lawrence says, 'The dead don't go away. They stay around and help.' Gosh, don't call on me tonight, I've talked myself blue, filling you in. I'll just sit back like a tourist tonight. How're you guys doing on the kid stuff? or shouldn't I ask?"

"Oh," Leo says, "we haven't had a joint since last August."

"Not that the obsession didn't rear up," Teddy says. "We just didn't smoke."

Hal Hart rushes in squinting, wet lips hectic. "I'm late, I'm late! Don't tell Nelson, he'll drum me outta the Kitchen Korps."

"Hal," Leo says, "this is Jack McFin whose power of example first brought us into the Fellowship."

"This is the pussycat from Pennsylvania!" Hal cries. "Great to meetcha! Forgive my hysteria, but just as I was walkin' outta my office, the mayor stopped me and asked for an off-the-cuff summary of the city's addiction services in five minutes or less, and I turned into a wild beast of information, a literal wild beast! I came down on him like a blizzard. And it's still pourin' outta me, facts and programs *oozin'* outta my pores, I can't stop, I'm still sweatin', it was the most intense five minutes of my fuckin' life!"

Hal lays out doilies on a rolling cart and sets up foam cups, spoons, sugar, milk, cookies, starts making pitchers of iced tea. "I'm a flack for the mayor," he tells Jack "—that's an orbiting press agent-speechwriter and full-tilt bullshit artist. I'm only four months sober, so forgive the lack of serenity. Can you imagine the grandiosity that goes with *bein'* an alcoholic bullshit artist for the mayor? I mean, for example, the mayor's opening a new playground in Harlem tomorrow and needs a two-minute spiel from me, dig? What do I do? I take down Lincoln's Second Inaugural Address and start rifling it for phrasing, for *tone,* get the picture? Here I am, silverhaired with this freaky white handlebar mustache, a schlockmeister, and I mean a secondrate human being leadin' a secondrate life among politicians of the worst sort, loudmouths eyeball-to-hiball, some of the most tasteless dudes who ever grew gray milking a desk for the city—some *pret-ty* flaky folks, —and I'm one of 'em! so bland I'm invisible—*got it?* have I made myself clear? And here I am takin' down Lincoln's Second Inaugural because I love it so, 'With malice toward none; with charity for all'—*for a black playground, no less!* My God, *where am I?* I can't possibly be sober and still workin' numbers like that on myself. I'm on the biggest fuckin' pink cloud in A.A. annals—but I'll make it. Ho ho, buddy boy, ya better believe it—I *gotta* make it!"

Paul Wildturkey arrives humming, sets up chairs for Where the Elephants Come to Die, a First-Step meeting Nelson's started.

"You're late, Wildturkey!" Hal crows.

"Look, *flack,* I don't need your bullshit—or Nelson's." Paul glowers over Hal, dark hair curly, glasses glimmering. "I arrive here *singing* and immediately you're ready to cut my balls off. I call that horseshit. I refuse to allow Inspector-General Nelson Winespear's glory in divine-right-order to upset my sobriety. Nobody can upset my sobriety but me—understand? That's *my choice."*

"Feelin' a trifle thinskinned tonight?" Hal asks.

"Be that as it may. I'm only pointing out that I walked in humming and singing and instantly I'm twisted into a net of nonexistent regulations and expected to be shining my brass. That's the kind of mentality that used to drive me into the brig after forcing me into a heavy night of rest and recreation over-the-hill. I'm not kidding. I'm serious about my sobriety and I don't need this heavy military atmosphere dragging me down. What do you guys think?" Paul asks.

Leo-Teddy shrugs.

Paul snorts. "I should've expected that from you two bluebells. And don't think I didn't hear that *thinskinned.* That's another put down."

"I'm not puttin' you down, Paul!" Hal says.

"Yes, you are. Next, you're gonna make me out to be an injustice-collector, like some folks we know, as if my gripes aren't valid. That's your next shaft, isn't it?"

"AGHH!" Hal cries. "Paul, I will go to any lengths to protect you from criticism! I'm an *expert* at protecting people from criticism! THAT'S MY JOB!"

"Now I'm being criticized. Who criticizes me? Nelson?"

"Nelson hasn't uttered *one word* of criticism about you! I'm sure he *loves* the way you handle your meeting. Everybody loves your meeting. You're a born topic-discussion leader—a magnificent, an inspired *master* of the First Step meeting."

"That's better. I don't believe you, but I accept your apology."

"I'll be more careful, Paul," Hal says. "I won't dampen your enthusiasm by one even vaguely unkind word."

"I guess I'll have to be satisfied with that," Paul says and goes out to the meeting room, humming and singing, to finish the chairs.

"Well!" Nelson cries happily, sucking a bent Italian cigar as he walks into the meeting room, "is everything in divine order?"

"NO!" Paul shouts.

"Well, why not? Paul, the chairs aren't up yet! Weren't you here on time?"

"I was *five minutes late.* Now don't push me, Nelson. Hal just got me feeling good. Don't ruin his good work, I'm warning you. I been dieting and my nerves are on edge."

"Why good for you, Paul," Nelson says, "I know just how ya feel. You look *marvelous*—partly as a result of your sobriety, I take it. But don't you recall that little talk we had, about the *meaning* of belonging to the early-bird crew at Renewal East?"

"I remember it very well—but I'm eight months sober now. The thrill is gone."

"That's the saddest thing I ever heard," Nelson sighs.

"I'm sorry. I come and I get my work done, at my own pace, and lead the meeting."

"Well, I don't know what t' say. Takes the heart outta me to hear you say you don't like to get here early and spend a few wonderful moments alone with Leo-Teddy and Hal and me."

"I notice *you're* not here early."

"And I am eternally sorry! It's my great loss. I *was* out doin' God's work, of course, but that's beside the point. Have you forgotten completely that this is *the* elite crew of all the A.A. kitchen crews in the city of Manhattan?—maybe in the whole United States! Don'tcha remember when we took you in, let ya join us, *allowed* you to take Leo-Teddy's high position in the sink? I mean *when you needed us,* Paul?"

"All *right,* Nelson! That's enough! I'll get here on time next week."

"Thank you, Paul. That shows the proper respect. We're not a bunch of snobs on this crew but we are extremely aware that we've been blessed with a quality of fellowship not easily found in a kitchen crew. Do ya need help with the ashtrays?"

"I'll manage."

"Well, bless you. We can get you an assistant if you're desperate."

"There's barely enough work for me alone. Thank you."

"Thank *you,* Paul."

Nelson comes into the kitchen, shakes Jack's hand earnestly. "Havin' you here tonight is indeed a great honor. These lads quote you at nearly every meeting! You been in these rooms like an underground spring."

"I've been embarrassed by them more than once," Jack says.

"Your sandwich is ready, Captain," Teddy says, shoving a plate at Nelson.

"Why, bless your hearts!" He inhales the sea-toast sandwich. "Oh, Lord, liederkranz and sweet onion, my favorite!"

Twins go out to the big table, letter 3×5 cards with a purple laundry pen:

No Caffeine
BRIM
The Deflowered Coffee,
You'll Sleep Like a Bride

and

Spicy, Fruity, Italian
ESPRESSO
WHAMMO!
Make This Your Last
Indulgence

Leo-Teddy tapes the cards to two steaming coffee urns on a rolling cart, surveys his snack layout of lemonpuffs, fig bars, peanut butter-oatmeal cookies, sugar biscuits and chocolate mint wafers. As Nelson observes with arms folded, Hal wheels out three sugary pitchers of iced lemon tea, his smile swelling nervously as he stares down his glasses in triumph. Nelson runs a few drops of espresso whammo into a foam cup, sips critically, then pours with light. *"Glorious!"* As new arrivals enter for Paul's

First-Step meeting, Nelson cries, "Try this espresso!" Woodsie, a beautiful bouffant-headed heavily powdered divorcée in a flowering orange explosion, her silver poodle on a rhinestone leash, sips and cries. *"Gawd!* ya couldn't get *this* in Rome! It's like Nesselrode pie."

"That's *right,"* Nelson says. "A great meeting deserves great coffee."

She kisses Leo-Teddy fast, a trace of something in her flooding perfume.

Hupton, a beatnik in denim, sits at the grand piano improvising original romances, his mouth downcast as if his throat'd been cut.

"Who were you twelve-stepping tonight," Leo asks Nelson, "when you were out doin' God's work?"

"Myself!" Nelson winks over his stogie. "You know I don't make excuses, but I do need five minutes with my dog in the park every evening or I get hungry, angry, lonely, tired, disgusted, and somewhat thirsty." His cheeks hunch Mongol good will.

About ten members sit around a set-aside area of couches and stuffed chairs for the short early meeting. Paul raps an ashtray.

"My name's Paul Wildturkey and I'm an alcoholic. I like to say that often so I don't forget it—I *have* forgotten it and the consequences were spectacular. Welcome to Where the Elephants Come to Die. This is a First-Step meeting especially designed for slippers who just can't get The Program. We accent the last drink—why we took it despite every disaster we knew was waiting for us, and what's different about our sobriety now. This meeting will be followed by our regular open discussion at the big table. Our speaker tonight is Leo."

Leo nods to mild clapping. "Thanks, Paul. My name's Leo and I am a forgetful alcoholic. Forgetful because just today I was ready to take a drink despite every effort of The Program to keep my head straight.—IDIOCY!—I got a phone call from California this morning tellin' me that an old girlfriend'd shot herself and was being cremated today. Right off, Big Baby Leo starts to howl—ready to blow his sobriety for fast relief. Actually, my emotions were pretty much under control—I'd just found an airtight alibi to drink and wanted to indulge myself in self-pity and, uh, sexual nostalgia. And I entirely forgot that my first sponsor, Jack, was comin' to visit us today for Teddy's first talk at the big table. I could really *taste* that bastardly hundred-proof piss rolling around my chops after the meeting tonight."

"Christ, don't let me stop you," Jack says.

"I've given it up! I just couldn't remember that I have a killer disease. Alcoholism is a disease that tells you ya don't have it! And then a whole sea of alcoholic thinking pours back in. Well, I've got my finger in the dike but I'm not sure which side of the dike I'm on.

"For this First Step meeting we talk about our last drink. It's hard to believe that self-pity's still my downfall —all my life I've fought depression like Atlas or Hercules. I always told myself that I drank to keep myself cheerful. I was stayin' cheerful to numb bein' a Siamese twin, somebody *overendowed* who curiously was hopeless and helpless and inadequate. My spirit bellowed, Drink up! you deserve t' be happy in any goddamn way possible. I was exempt from mental or physical damage, just standard hangovers and blackouts. A thousand defenses, a million alibis. And all insane. The liquor itself provided 'em—alcohol defending alcohol. One shot and that first drink quivered to join a second, like balls of mercury on a tabletop—drink joins drink until I'm just a big taxi for alcohol to go on consuming itself, pulling me here and there from snort to snort as the fire's building. One shot and I'm lost until I get dry again. Or at least pass out. And wake up obsessed by bountiful bottles and craving the taste and the lift. I can't possibly recognize the full insanity of my alcoholic thinking when I'm high, or the emptiness of my alibis. Once I start I finish that bottle. When I'm clever I avoid total wipeout and finish tomorrow, leaving myself a partly full bottle and an excuse to keep goin' one more day.

"Like yours, my rationalizations are infinite. Mine were that I'm seeking God. I'm tryin' t' make an artistic breakthrough. I'm givin' myself a damned well-deserved relief from pain (probably the pain of drinking!) Nobody loves me. I ain't had no sex for three-hundred-sixty-five months! Life is tragic! I'm insane anyway! People are cattle and pigs! All I wanna do is finish one perfect accomplishment, an imperishable four-line verse, and I'll be perfectly ready to die. I don't really expect to live beyond forty, SIGH—though I'm already pushin' forty-two.

"And all these rationalizations are insane—there's

nothin' I can't do better sane than insane. Why must I go on bein' the insane victim of my moods, my anxieties, my elations, and scorn real power and vitality for a souped up ego, grandiosity, and all my self-serving-addiction-continuing bullshit? My lies? My profound, worldshaking shovelsful of bullshit. Naturally I admired those ego-artists, soloists, poets, and composers who fed my self-deception with their own beautiful destruction. I thought *their* deterioration was spiritual, and mine could be too.

"My last drink!—aside from the one I won't be takin' tonight.

"A year ago last May I was invited down to the University of Florida to give a lecture. I'd written a religious cantata which had some kinda success at Judson Memorial Church in the Village. I told Nelson I'd hit some A.A. meetings in Gainesville—though I didn't look up any in the World Directory before I left. Well, I was *there* half an hour when I found a bottle of strawberry wine in the icebox at my friend's house. There was a heat wave, the wine was cold, I'd never had it before—so I blew a joint and soon had to hit the liquor store for a replacement or two and a fifth of hundred-proof bourbon. Teddy chose not to drink. After my very inflamed lecture, and an impromptu trumpet recital of no great distinction, I was given a reception for which my friend Dick'd laid out over a hundred bucks worth of booze. I hadn't the moral courage to refuse."

Teddy laughs.

"I hadn't any morals at all!—I even passed out at a nude swimming party!"

Teddy nods.

"To backtrack. I'd had the deetees the previous Thanksgiving, after four years in A.A., and had finally come to believe in the First Step. Dead people walkin' all around my bed and pleadin' with me to come in off my slip—eight hours of deetee horrors—I was at last a certified alcoholic. Beyond any arguing! Once you've had the deetees, you're susceptible for life—they're irreversible—and on less and less liquor. But even those horrors weren't enough to divert my *whim* for strawberry wine. The memory of my suffering was wiped out in a second—in fact I never even remembered that I'd had the deetees during my last drunk. I blanked 'em right out, all I could see was cold strawberry wine steamed up in the icebox. But I was about to be lionized and wanted to be properly oiled. Swept away by elephantiasis of the ego—and I *had* brought the pot with me.

"Oh shit, I knew I wanted t' drink before I even left New York—I was shipwrecked before I ever got on the plane!

"Next day Teddy and I went to visit our mother who lives down there and I drank with her for two days. And then just cut it off. Couldn't come back to Manhattan with booze on my breath. But I can't forget that last shot of bourbon. One-hundred-and-one proof, my first shot that day, and it hit my cells like deathsalts. I felt instantly etherized, even before the stuff got into my bloodstream. Every nerve died. I was numbed to the backbone by one shot. I'd hit some kind of bottom beyond the deetees.

"Back here I started hittin' ten meetings or more a week, got active, signed up here and at Yorkville, started answering phones at Intergroup, went on calls, seriously began The Steps, took my inventory with Nelson, began amends, started praying, reading the Bible, speaking on the circuit, writing stories for *The Grapevine*, getting telephone numbers, making coffee, and so on. I put my alky shoulder to the wheel—and felt like Atlas.

"I had my last joint last August and since then I feel that I've joined A.A. at last. Heart and soul. No reservations. And yet—two months ago I got stalled in my work and really obsessed by pot nostalgia. A nostalgia as strong as lust. If I could just break through my block with one evening on drugs! I forget that pot always precedes my slips. So I spent two workless months castrated by pot obsession.

"I'm sittin' home when I think maybe one ounce of orange extract, eighty-six percent alcohol, or one-hundred-seventy-two proof, will get me goin'. I drag Teddy off to the A&P, come back with the largest jar they sell, pour it into a glass, fill it with water, lift it to my mouth—when suddenly I think, *I can't drink this, I'm chairman at Yorkville!* And zap it down the sink. If this is ego, then my damned ego saved me for once. But I like to think that it was a sense of fellowship with my friends at Yorkville, and here. The Steps didn't stop me, prayer didn't stop me, The Big Book didn't stop me—fellowship stopped me. I was as active as Hercules—but I *still* got that flakey close to a glass of extract. It's insidious! But, thank God, The Program was working even though I didn't know it. A.A. is fellowship. For me, people are The Program. And I gotta love you people—or die. Thank you."

Applause, quickspirited, brief.

"My God, do I identify!" Randy—thin redblond, amazed glasses, gunslinger mustache. "You described my last drink. I spent my last ten years as an absolute waterspider. *Ginspider!* Hopping from Manhattan to Dallas to San Francisco to Chicago—you name it, I drank there. Just ridiculous, a *horrible* geographical escape from myself. Well, I detested myself, but I thought I was living the most glorious, pleasurefilled life ever known. Scintillating! I'd wake up at two-thirty in the morning in Aspen, Colorado and sit up singing. It's time to go, Randy! And I'd pack and be down at the Greyhound in a half hour. No idea where I'm going—I'm just *going*. I thought my life was absolutely, totally romantic, and it was! I loved drinking! Oh, you have to pay a little bit, don'tcha? But my last drink. I was in The Program eighty-nine days, just one short of ninety, and was overwhelmed with a sense of having become *grim* and lifeless. No pleasure at all in being sober. So dull and blah. I decided to cut my ties with The Program and pay the price for what I thought was *real life*. What better way than to get drunk and let *everyone* know. I'd QUIT this icy, depressing sobriety. What's more, I was convinced that I cannot be loved, somehow I wasn't *worth* being loved, drunk or sober, and that I could have affection *or* sex with a lover but not both at once. So I drank! I drank myself silly. And nothing happened. I didn't enjoy it at all! But what I'd forgotten until just now—on my eighty-fifth day dry I'd decided to try my first joint of marijuana ever. One joint, and my mind turned over onto the flip side. I was absolutely gripped by nostalgia for the 'romantic life' of pre-A.A. My God, how I loved to draw the drapes, set out my candelabra, put on my midnight-blue smoking jacket, stir up a pitcher of gin and sit back with Frank Sinatra singing 'Strangers in the Night,' or Billie Holiday zapped on smack—and just *soak it up!* I was a little kinky. And four days later I continued my pot high by picking up the first drink. And then getting smashed. I'd say the real basis of my decision, if it was a decision, was self-pity. But I felt so kinky, so *slippery kinky*, that God Himself couldn't straighten me out. Wherever He'd straighten me I'd get kinky again somewhere else. I was hopeless."

"So what've you done differently this time?" Leo asks.

"Well, I know I just can't drink. And that whole romantic life I wanted back so desperately had been just a lot of torment and atrocious behavior. Although I seemed to be laughing gaily all the way through it. But what's different? Well, I must be growing up emotionally. It's terrifically painful. But I've learned to *depend* on The Program. I'm on the phone at least three hours a day driving my A.A. friends mad with my symptoms. But they put up with me, thank God, and one day at a time it's getting better. And so's my self-esteem. I'm *worth* loving, goddamnit! Thanks a lot for a swell meeting, it's just what I needed tonight. And thanks to you both for spelling each other on my interminable phone calls!"

"Thank you for calling," Leo says. Teddy nods. "Diana?"

"Gee, thanks a lot, Leo," Diana says. Short happyeyed ashblonde; flat-humored, wealthy voice. "My last drink—my God, that sounds overly casual! Was a pitcher of dry martinis in an East Side airline terminal telephone booth. They'd cut *my* phone off at seven-hundred dollars. I was using the terminal phones to continue my addiction to longdistance soap opera. Although I *had* the seven hundred. But I had to choose between paying the phone bill or having the fucking *bags* removed from under my eyes, which was seven hundred. The oper*a*tion. So I'd take my pitcher of iced gin, which would get pretty wet, not just the ice melting but all over the booth, across the street into the terminal with me and make my phone calls for three or four hours until I was so smashed I'd fall out of the booth, and I resolved my problem and my brainrot telephonitis by joining *A.A.* and haven't had a drink since. And I'm much more moderate about the phone. So I *pass*."

"I identify with your pitcher," Leo says. "I could taste the extra drops of olive juice I used to pour on top my twelve-ounce mug. My big problem when I came into A.A.—people'd speak so lovingly of their booze. I'd get so high that after the meeting I'd lock in the euphoria with a dive into a double martini."

"How'dya get over that?" Diana asks. "I'd like to know!"

"I don't know! Maybe by laughing at myself. Or maybe

you people got through to me, incanting the alky wards at meetings—Bellevue! Freeport! Flower Fifth! Gracie Square! Pilgrim State! Maimonides! Beth Israel! Metropolitan! Dunc?"

"Worshipped at 'em all!" Duncan calls. "And Casa Serena, High Watch and Gray Moor! Don't leave out Gray Moor—they took me in when absolutely all the others refused. You'd think I'd learn after thirty-two hospitalizations. But I didn't. I still had to go out and try again, even after twelve years sober once. Talk about snatching defeat from the jaws of victory! Been to 'em all. How many last drinks 've I had? I remember my last martini in Mexico City," suave, silver-mustached, magnificently tailored, "where I ran an absolutely fantastic auto agency. I'd been twelve years sober and was sitting with a club soda at the Miramar Bar with its wide window overlooking a green boat basin, the clearest greenest water on earth, when a waiter walked by with the clearest greenest martini I'd ever seen in my life and I said, *Why* don't *I* have one of those? And with no more thought than that, I entered the most horrendous, howling desolation I'd ever know—until my *last* last slip in Connecticut, which left me half-dead crawling through a tomato patch with my hands bleeding out back of our house where I'd left my gin hidden. By then I'd worn out my welcome at every hospital—and bar!—in Manhattan and Connecticut, and there are quite a few. This was after I'd wound up dead, clinically dead, on an operating table and woke up with tubes comin' outta me everywhere and still not expected to survive. Things don't get much worse than dying dead, but dya think that stopped me? You're mistaken! Three months later I'm back with the breakfast club at the Plaza bar. Why'd I take my last drink? I don't know—I'd say it was the POOR ME's. *Poor widdoo Dunkie couldn't have his own friggin' way!* All I know is that I shouldn't be alive and that this room, more than any other meeting, has kept me sober over two years now—a damned miracle! And I'm employed, so to speak—another miracle. And still have my wife—still another! I still can't control my temper, especially when the bitch I work for dumps her *shit* on my desk—pardon me, ladies—but that's my job anyway, handling complaints from Fifth Avenue dowagers until I want to shout *Screw 'em!* all day long, but I keep myself in check and let off steam by phoning Nelson or these twins or my other alky friends, dear Ray, dear Betty. Let off steam, heh! PURE RAGING ANGER! I wanna *scream* and *strangle* 'em all! *Grrnnggrngrgnhh!* I don't understand me, Christ I really don't, my wife doesn't!—it takes one to know one, only you drunks understand me. *This* is my family. Now I'll shut up, I've spoken too long already, as usual, but I had to get it off my chest. When I walk through that door, it doesn't matter what goddamn anger I'm carrying with me, it vanishes. Almost. This room has more spiritual life in it than all the churches of Mexico—not that I'd know too much about churches. I only know I *killed myself* drinking and still didn't stop! so this room has *gotta have something*. Thanks for a damned fine meeting, I feel resurrected already."

"Mah name's Hupton Tugwell." Neatly ragged, shaking, ponytailed beatnik, his upper teeth missing. "And Ahm a pianist—"

"Can't hear you!" Teddy Toscanini calls.

"I'M A PIANIST and sort of entertainer and spiritual seeker from a little town outside of Atlanta, although my address right now's Uncle Sam's flophouse on the Bowery. Ah've studied yoga and religious dancing with Gurdjieff. Sought God all mah life. Wanted love and friendship. Yet nobody really *likes me* or invites me out to coffee after the meetings or accepts me for what I am, the *being I am,* except my acquaintances on the Bowery. Everybody else wants t' change me! When *I'm me!* But what Ahm interested in is your block, Leo—sometimes I can't play the piano for months on end."

"I didn't have to have that block," Leo says. "I could've asked God to take it away—and He would've. I wanted to hang onto it and nurse it and suffer with my thumb up my rectum—all to justify a coupla joints."

"I see. Well, that doesn't help me. I pray all the time—I *walk around* in prayer! And smoke pot—I'm not afraid of that. I mean I can handle it. Today I went to Central Park and it was an utterly beautiful God-given day for me. Which only made it worse, because I wanted to share it. But gettin' to my last drink. I went home to Georgia three weeks ago after bein' sober two months and my family hardly knew me. I didn't have *one drink* while I was there. It was the loveliest time I ever spent with my family. So when I was leavin' I didn't want to lose all that good feelin' and I got me a bottle of that same strawberry wine. An' I was drunk for three days."

Hupton's soft highflown voice quavers. "Ah didn't say I was an alcoholic when I gave my name. I'm not sure I am. I am a periodic drinker with tremendous recuperative powers. Or at least I used t' be. It took me a week t' recover this time, and that's what I've got to remember. My recoveries are gettin' unbelievably painful. Now the reason I say I'm not an alcoholic is that I can go for three weeks without takin' a drink. Then I feel I should reward mahself an' I have me a sip of wine, maybe a pint, an' I drink until everything's *gawn*—my money, my friends, and my health. I mean my periodic drink turns into a two-week slip. Ahm lost until I'm utterly exhausted and *have* t' stop."

"Hupton," Nelson asks, "why are you even here?"

"I don't know!"

"Well, how long ya been comin' to A.A.?"

"Four years—this time. I came for six years before, then I found I could handle it mahself and stopped comin'. I stayed sober three years on mah own! Just used regular soft drugstore drugs to get mah highs, I didn't want any of that hard stuff—just the things I could buy legally over the counter and mix up myself. I'd study the labels and drop a handful of caffeine tablets with eight or nine cold capsules and some other narcotics and *I was fine,* all legally. Of course, alcohol's legal but that isn't the point. I proved to mahself that I could *stay away* from alcohol. I stopped drinkin'!"

"But what's your problem *now?*" Nelson asks.

"I can't *recover* from mah periodic temptations."

"Drunks, you mean?"

"You can call 'em that. I don't."

"Don'tcha have any desire to stop drinking altogether?"

"Of course I do, but then after three weeks I tell myself it isn't necessary—look how *strong* I am! Ahm healthy as a horse. *Me* stop?"

"Maybe you don't feel you deserve to be sober."

"What's that mean?" Hupton asks.

"Well, you say your A.A. friends don't accept you and only your Bowery friends take you wholeheartedly for what you are. And what are you?"

"You mean—*alcoholic?*"

"That's right. And as recovering alcoholics we're your

friends. We know better'n to try and change you—that's gotta come from the man himself. *If* he wants it. The thing about bein' on the Bowery is that there's no place lower to go. You're there, you're on the bottom, right?"

"Well, I'll agree it's depressing."

"And if that's where you wanna live, that's your choice, and if that's the picture of yourself you wanna give at these meetings, after four years, *that's* your choice. But maybe we have a choice too, a legitimate choice as recovering drunks—and that is to choose our friends from those who give us some power of example—"

"But I'm a power of example!"

Nelson smiles.

"I'm a spiritual seeker. I don't know anybody in A.A. who gets more God-given beauty out of the day than I do. I can just walk and walk and walk, all day long, in communion with my inner light and my Higher Power."

"Hupton," Nelson says, "maybe all your Higher Power comes from a pill. Or pot. Or ethyl alcohol. Hm? Maybe you live where you live not because you can't get outta there but because if you keep your self-esteem low enough you won't have to stop drinking'. You don't deserve to be sober or to associate with sober people. My God, there's a whole tremendous new life waitin' for you in sobriety. We have a Program of ungodly great power! It revives the dead. And here you're still struggling with the First Step after four years and comin' to Renewal for nearly a year now. And *keep comin'*. But why don't you do us a favor and yourself a favor as well? Why don't *you* join *us* and *join A.A.?"*

"All right." Hupton's head shakes, his lips quivering. "*I am an alcoholic*. How's that?"

"Bless you," Nelson says. "That's the first step."

"Boy!" Jack sighs aloud.

"Well, time's up," Paul says. "Please stay for the next meeting."

"Fastest fifty minutes I ever spent," Jack says.

"Thank you very much," Hupton says, shaking Leo's hand. "Sorry about these tears—I guess I needed to take that step."

"Nobody wants to take away your Higher Power, Hupton," Leo says.

"Ah know they don't, they only want me to see It more clearly! May I have your telephone number?"

"Well!" Teddy asks Jack, "how'dya like the meeting?"

"Great," Jack says. "I like 'em rough."

"Nelson doesn't let any shit stick in the air, does he?" Teddy says.

"They were all good," Jack says, "especially Leo. It took real courage to admit that extract fiasco. And drinking when *you* didn't. He's asking for help, don't you think? That Hupton could use six months at White Deer though—if he's serious. Any great change of character now would be a miracle, right?"

"That's The Program!" Teddy laughs. "Boy, I feel good! Felt something pop in here when Hupton took that First Step."

"How many times has he taken it before?" Jack asks.

"I hear it takes some of us five years to give up that last reservation," Leo says.

"I'd be dead," Jack says. "My God, there must be sixty people for Teddy's talk."

"Superb!" Dunc tells Leo, shaking his hand. "I wouldn't have missed that for the world."

"Stick around," Leo says.

"Oh, I'm ready for Teddy!"

Joe Owl, a blond Wall Street broker once singlemindedly hellbent on being the world's loneliest bar drinker "without peer!" shakes the twins' hands, raises a foamcup of espresso as a grimace of spinedeep pleasure twists his eyes and mouth. *"Never better!* I'd come just for the fruit java, even if this weren't the hardest socking meeting in town. What a lift!"

"Real fruit and spices," Leo says. "It's a clean, drug-free brew.

"This caffeine hits like meth!"

Teddy shoves two more Royal Crown Flats into Charlie Parnell's shirtpocket. "You'll need these!"

Leo-Teddy, espressos in hand, takes in the room's glow of bushytailed grinning sober drunks. Nancy M., a music teacher-turned-book clerk, blueeyed in a blazing red suit, plants lipstick on Leo-Teddy.

"Who's leading the meeting tonight?" she asks, measuring Jack for availability.

"Mr. Hyde," Teddy says.

"Do I know him? What's he do?"

"He's that fast-change self-pity artist. Master of disguises, you know 'im."

"Really? I do?" She looks Jack over again. "Him?"

"Nah," Teddy says. "He's just a recovering drunk. Once got trampled by the Mexican army. Hasn't been the same since."

Leo says, "We made him our sponsor to cheer him up. Keeps his mind off his problems."

"I don't have any problems," Jack says.

Nelson bangs an ashtray, rising. Jack and Leo-Teddy sit beside him at the head of the big table. "Good evening, welcome to Renewal East. My name's Nelson Winespear and I am an alcoholic. Thank you all for bein' here tonight." Nelson's every muscle strains with sincerity, his jaw bony and deepset eyes intense as a lover's. "I'm doubly grateful t' be here myself, because of the powerful Where the Elephants Come to Die meeting led by Leo, and because Teddy's givin' his first talk tonight. I've known both these lads for two years and feel privileged to have witnessed their recovery—a recovery, one day at a time, against astounding odds. I revere this meeting, because it does bring about just such miracles. Renewal East's a meeting started *by* hardcore slippers *for* hardcore slippers—for those who've slipped and for one reason or another, shame or remorse, can't go back to their regular meetings and who especially Just Can't Get The Program. But over half our members, our regulars, haven't slipped in years, and many never slipped. Like me—and I had an ungodly difficult time gettin' sober, *insanely* difficult—they love the spirit that rises from this table when the group conscience makes us get honest with ourselves. This is usually a topic discussion but our foremost interest's in helpin' those with a recent or immediate slip. If anyone here's suffering, we hope you'll speak up after Teddy qualifies.

"Alcoholics Anonymous is a fellowship of men and women who share their experience, strength, and hope with each other that they may solve their common problem and help others to recover from alcoholism.

"The only requirement for membership is a desire to stop drinking. There are no dues or fees for A.A. membership; we are self-supporting through our own contributions. A.A. is not allied with any sect, denomination, politics, organization, or institution; does not wish to engage in any controversy, neither endorses nor opposes any causes. Our primary purpose is to stay sober and help other alcoholics to achieve sobriety.

"We have two outgoing meetings. Leo-Teddy will lead the Greenwich Village open discussion at eight-thirty Friday evening, and Dunc, Diana, and I will carry the message of Renewal to the Gotham open meeting next Tuesday at eight-thirty. I hope many of you will be at these meetings to support our speakers. On Saturday evening Hal will take Fred S., Tom H., and Joe O. down to Intergroup to man the phones from five to eight, the roughest hours of the week—and I might add that Renewal volunteered for this slot. We need three more volunteers to sign up for the following Saturday—please see Hal after the meeting—*before* he starts washin' the coffee urns. Did you have somethin' t' say, Hal?"

"By God, I do—I wanna give a thirty-minute pitch for Intergroup!—but I won't. I wanna get it across that workin' those phones is not only a privilege but a whole week's supershot of vitamins. When this team comes out of Intergroup at eight o'clock Saturday night, we come out *dancin'!* Got the picture? *Ri-ight!* And we could use more women."

"Thank you, Hal. Now, when I came into Renewal some time ago, the first night here they decided that *I* should make the coffee. I went home and moaned and groaned to my wife, D'ya know what these hooples want me t' do?—make coffee!—*kitchen work!*—like a goddamn migrant. I was so mad I drank a case of Nelson County's finest bourbon and wound up at High Watch for two months. By then I couldn't *wait* t' get back here and make that coffee. The day they let me out I came *here* before I even went home. And there was an old whitehaired guy in the kitchen makin' the coffee. I said to him, *Get out.* I'm supposed to make the coffee, he said. *I'm makin' the coffee,* I said, *get out.* D'ya know, I've never seen that poor old guy again—not at a meeting, not anywhere. I been sick about it ever since, he may never've come back to A.A. because of me! I spend nights worryin' about him. Well, I worked those urns for six months. It took a long time for anyone to show up that I thought was equal to this high responsibility. But he did—two of him—and it's with great pride and pleasure that I give you my replacement on the coffee urns, and my new sponsor—Teddy."

Clapping for Nelson and Teddy.

Jack grips his palms and whispers to Teddy. *"Shoot the drinks outta their fingers!"*

"My names's Teddy Hickman and I'm an alcoholic in search of lasting recovery. I've recovered several times in A.A. but this time I'd like it to be *lasting*. My story really doesn't matter, and it doesn't matter if I exaggerate unmercifully. Not that I will, but nothin' we say can equal the horror most of us 've lived through—if we even knew how much horror we *were* livin' through! What's really important is what happens to us after the horror stops—in these rooms. The longer we're here the less we talk about our horrors and the more we speak out for our recovery. In fact, we don't really hear the horrors. What we hear in each other is a tone of being, or spirit risen above horror. We hear hope.

"B-b-boy, I'm happy to be here. Instead of out there. And here Now. I'm not thinkin' about where I'm goin' after this meeting, or how I'm gonna buy a new trombone tomorrow—and I am—or anything else. I'm just here *now,* hoping. Trusting that my Higher Power will make me an instrument of His will. Not my will but Thy will be done. *My* will nearly killed me. I often make a little prayer before I say anything at a meeting, and ask for some of that wind I used t' find in my jug instead of in myself. This is no horror story. I'm too full of thanksgiving. Here we sit in the Now.

"Now.

"Now.

"Now."

Teddy feels a bodiless glow rise from the plain table, the whole room fills with clear amber, the faces of the members caught up in a timeless concentration of their best spirits striving for a serene deepening and grasp of the meeting's Now.

"Just so grateful! I mighta been a drunken musician for the rest of my life—they're out there dyin' like flies, on sanctified ego-trips. My idol, Louis Armstrong, drank and smoked pot sometimes—but he was moderate about nearly everything except blowin' a strong, hard horn. Somehow, I could never be moderate. I guess I thought the only way t' get what I wanted outta life was through my mouth—I sure wasn't gettin' it through my brains. Everything always had t' be souped up. I carried a shoppingbag with a gallon of wine in it for ten years. When I came to visit, I came prepared. Boy, you got a guest! One glass and the room glowed with my worldly insights. You'd be happy I was there! spreading pleasure, sophistication, ego. Including you in too. An irresistible bag of heartfelt bullshit. Sometimes I felt dishonest but I knew my heart was in the right place. I forgave myself. All day long! Had to. I was so very rarely up to the perfection I expected from myself. Except during the first glow of the booze, for maybe half an hour. Then the excuses began. Foggy and rambling, splitting some point up into so many tissues, straining at gnats. You'd be glad the strain was over when I left! I couldn't keep anything simple. Some damned synthesis was forever receding before me.

"Whenever I went outdoors I had to write down a list of places I was goin' to. The liquor store, the library, the post office, the supermarket, and itemize what I'm doin' there, and get a *Times*, a *Voice*, a *Cue*, ink, music paper, a record. Filling up my writing time with useless errands split up into sub-errands, so that when I finally get to my composing I'm shaking from frustrations such as waitin' in a queue, waitin' for traffic lights, cars to pass midblock, people to get up the stairs ahead of me, clogged doorways —a cat's cradle of self-imposed mental rendings exacerbated by wine nerves. No wonder I deserved a gallon of burgundy or sledgehammer muscatel every night, starting with a few quarts of ale so I wouldn't get too zapped too fast. I just wanted the oblivion of the Puritan work ethic, but I had a million whims to slog through before I could forget myself in work. If I don't stop myself I'll clean the stove or under the sink before I write a note. It becomes guilt about guilt!

"I saw my first shot about two years before Bill and Dr. Bob founded A.A. and 'the path that really goes somewhere.' My dad took us up to a state line bar on Lake Erie. We were about five. Sat us on the bar, ordered a double and took a kitchen match outta his pocket, dipped the flame into the whiskey. The match seemed to burn underwater, and he pulled it out still burning. That was our first sight of alcohol—*pure magic!*

"I started drinkin' at thirteen, stealin' fancy booze from my stepfather's liquor cellar. Got into it fairly heavy at fifteen. Bought a black homburg and charcoal pinstripe, grew a wisp on my lip, and was ready t' dig the bar life. The banker's night out! Unfortunately, my brother used to wear a raving yellow Woody Herman bandjacket sans lapels. On the street we kept our eyes fixed straight ahead but we gave off an embarrassing flood of raw ego—passionate waves of self-consciousness. But despite this painridden contrast, we tore the restaurant page out of our local phonebook and hit every brass rail in the city limits.

"Goin' back. One night when we were five, sittin' on the back porch we discovered the stars for the first time, particle beyond particle of light, deeper and deeper, and a sense of wonder awakened. Something about those deeps called for a word from the deeps within me. The heavens awakened something in my heart, in my breath. This is a spiritual experience we've all had—I remember the very moment it happened to me. Maybe you do too. All my life I've tried to answer a question which has no words, and surely no answer—though I sought one. I searched through adolescent atheism and bull sessions, a ten-year mental depression as black as the ruins of postwar Berlin, dismal days with Truman and Eisenhower. At last I met a genius who gave me an answer I liked, when I was twenty-six. Oscar was a genius in many fields and I asked him, Oscar, do you believe in God? His face lit up and he said, I surely do! Look at all the beauty of the universe, the gorgeous uselessness of sunrise and sunset, of flowers, and all the miracles that come in through the eye. These have no use in a purely mechanistic universe. These divine messages need a divine receiver.

"And so for ten more drunken years I lived with a religion of beauty.

"But when I was lyin' on the subway tracks in Cathedral station with Leo's legbone splintered and a train bearin' down on us, Oscar's religion of beauty was no damn use. And when we drank ourselves unconscious with our three-year-old son in my lap in the front seat, and crossed over the divider into the oncoming semis and tractor-trailers, and suddenly came to jouncing through a tomato patch at seventy miles per hour, a religion of beauty was truly useless. Not that I was beyond religion.

"I staggered into churches at midnight, and agonized to God. He didn't respond! Why should He talk to me when I only talked about myself to Him? I slumped around with terminal cancer and a hundred-thousand-dollar hospital bill which I called 'tragic recognition of God.' Meanwhile, I turned all the women I went to bed with frigid. I thought Manhattan'd been swept by a mass wave of frigidity. But how could they have ecstasy with this wine swine? I'd lie on my bed for hours unable to get over this tremendous sighing that came outta me, OOOOOOHH! OOO-OOO-OOO—OOOOOHHHH!

"Hovering in the can't sleep-can't wake up juice show deetees. Dead people walkin' around my apartment. My sheets busy with roaches that weren't there. I'd change the sheets—they always looked like leftovers from a fire sale—but the bugs were still there. Then they got under my skin. They'd go prickling down my legs in subcutaneous worm-waves, my nerves like hatching larvae. My brain softened like custard—I could feel it wobble in my head. *I could!* Pure eggcustard! I turned on the shower and roaches poured down—AGHH!—It's water! it's water! Leo tells me. I couldn't understand why he was standin' there lyin' t' me—and *smilin'!*

"So I switched drinks. I drank German beer, it was stronger than American but weaker than whiskey. But my worms came in like the tide when my circulation dropped. I began collecting material for a book on Terminal Music. This was a survey of swan songs and last notes of dyin' composers. I identified with Schubert's syphilis and teeth fallin' out, sudden baldness, illnesses and death at thirty-one. And with Schumann's madness and dictation from angels and fairly early death. And with Mahler's death-schmerz and cancer, Mozart's nephritis, Beethoven's bad teeth, deafness, syphilis, cirrhosis. And I'd play you their last gasps, pretty powerful stuff really, the last blazings as their bodies turned to manure, and I'd rub your face into genius triumphant over physical disease. Here is where his hair fell out!—the very notes, I was a specialist in the spirituality of organic decay. But my Terminal Music book deteriorated into a pile of slush, burgundy-stained notes, sugary superprose, throbbing marshmallow marginalia—no spine at all!

"One night I was talkin' with Leo when I fell right over against the baseboard. I regretted losin' my balance but was happy I didn't hurt myself. We always had fabulous balance. Next morning I find a huge abrasion on my back and kidney, a terrible scrape about two feet long. I refused to go to a doctor, not even to an emergency clinic. Those sonsabitches might tell me I'm bad off and try to hospitalize me—a serious block to my genius. I skip my more degenerate behavior. I lost the mastery of my toenail clipper. All my shorts were in rags. I began to long for a geographical escape to Bellevue as bein' really restful—my Waikiki beach where I could just float in the lovin' arms of nurses. Naturally, they wouldn't put me in the psycho ward. Nahh!

"Leo and I'd fall into long silences, days, weeks on end. One day the screw fell outta my glasses and I couldn't see well enough to drive the screw back, and he *wouldn't*. So I went to an optometrist and he put it in for free in five seconds. I was so relieved I tried to pay him a dollar and kept thankin' 'im, OH MY GOD, THANK YOU, THANK YOU! YOU'VE SAVED MY LIFE! I CAN SEE AGAIN! I wasn't only overly thankful for miniscule services, I was profoundly apologetic for my every word and deed, I'm sorry, I'm sorry. 'I'm sorry, ya won't believe me, but lemme tell ya about the terrible time I had gettin' my shoelaces tied this mornin'.' And I'd catalogue all my miseries in tyin' a shoelace. Endless Lilliputian disasters! Every other word was I'm sorry, even t' myself! I'd turn and apologize to people I brushed on the street. I was fearful of God when I stepped on a roach or swatted a fly. One day I hugged my refrigerator for five minutes, really felt it up, because it was full of ale. I'd hold my breath for thirteen floors, goin' up in an elevator—I learned to breathe in without breathin' out. We both kept a coupla squirt guns full of gin for just such tight spots where we might need a fast shot in the back of the elevator.

"Once in a while I could afford vodka, and some mornings I shook so bad that a hardened bartender had to look out the window while pouring, he was that embarrassed for himself and Leo. For several days a voice was callin' me from Brooklyn. Louder and louder. We walk over the bridge, I see a traffic cop and ask 'im, 'Somebody over here callin' me?' *'Get lost,'* he says. 'There it is again!' I say, 'sounds like a loudspeaker, officer.' I go to a precinct station to complain about this voice I can hear all the way to Manhattan. A drunken Brooklyn cop—I later met him in The Program—really *listened* with me—he'd been hearin' his own voices. We went outside and it got so hot I pulled us into the back of a parked police car. 'Seventh and B, please, Manhattan. I'm a wornout taxpayer, officer. I deserve this attention. I've paid for it through the nose.' He threw us out. Crossing Brooklyn Bridge on the way back, I tried to jump off —but nobody'd jump with me. In fact, *he* got so indignant I tried to throw him off. I wasn't too steady that day.

"My own voice was as bad as any I heard. I kept talkin' t' myself in weird Negro dialects. Punning about everything. Mashing sentences and syllables, in a circular repetition that was *so* wearying. *Hit's a fur piece, Henry, t' hebbin.* Over and over, *uhhh!*

"A friend of mine's father died and I went out on Long Island for the funeral. My friend wouldn't go to the funeral, he was absolutely without feelings, for his father or anybody, especially himself. So we sat in a bar and *I* cried and cried and cried—couldn't stop—in place of my friend who couldn't cry. I cried so hard I blacked out and came to next morning in Manhattan, in motion on Eighth Street—*poof!* there I was, diggin' a violinist out front of the Eighth Street Bookshop—he was fiddlin' *The Kreutzer Sonata.* But durin' these funerary matters I was full of urgent sex feelings, zapping up and down my spine in pink waves. Booze oversexes me, like magnolia blossoms, until even a funeral becomes sexy and I'm a tremendous electrode ready t' discharge on anything female.

"But things got worse. We got fired from our job at Metropolitan Hospital. We *deserved* to be fired. We *deserved* to be shot. Anyway, we got so melancholically deranged we committed suicide. Not for the first time either. One time Leo passed out and I decided to save him from further misery—and myself. And I dragged him from door to window, sealing up the whole apartment with newspaper, and I put our heads into the oven and turned on the gas. We woke up next morning with terrific gas hangovers—my goddamned apartment was so drafty it couldn't hold in enough gas to kill us. So next time we took pills. I took about thirty downers and he took thirty uppers. I woke up five days later in Bellevue, tubes runnin' in an' outta me, a huge bandage where Leo'd nearly bitten my nose off, tapes all over for cuts and fractures. All I could move were my eyes and all I could see was Leo's leg slung up in a traction splint. Or was it a cast? *He* hadn't slept for five days and was darkeyed and corpselidded but writing away like mad on a clipboard.

Some amphetamine song cycle about Bellevue he's since discarded. I had polyneuritis, a general name that meant anything they could think of, from alcohol poisoning to terminal vitamin deficiency, endless causes, endless complications. I'm lucky I'm not blind. I was in a half-length iron lung for six months before I could move any toes. It was another year before I could walk. They tried t' gimme crutches. Threw 'em into a corner and started out on canes instead. Didn't want crutches.

"Then things really nosedived.

"By now Leo'd been in and out of A.A. for three years, more or less impulsively. I had eighteen months dry, since *I* could handle it. Sort of. I was on a powder drunk. In the hospital they hit me with so many ups and down for hopping nerves that I c'd feel the downers droppin' me down down while the uppers pulled the floor up. I was extremely sensitive. You'd think that my fears, deetees, and paralysis would've taught me something—that I'd be reluctant to drink. But I couldn't wait to hobble outta the rehab clinic on Thirty-Fourth Street and taxi up t' The Ginger Man to burst an obsession I had for *one* superfrigid martini like some refrigerated martinis we'd had at Harry's Bar in Venice. I've left out our Mexican and European degeneracies. I was on ups and downs, and hit my dealer for some pot, hash, LSD, mescaline, and psilcybin, and stocked up on mescal and tequila—I stayed away from wine because I didn't wanna get hooked again. My time'd obviously come. I was ready for terminal music.

"Leo, meanwhile, started to go to Al-Anon, where he learned how to live with an active alcoholic in the family and I learned how to con him in new ways. I wanted a battleground but he kept castrating my every effort with peace and good will. It's totally frustrating to live within a measured drinking pattern, the kind of controlled drinking mixed with hallucinogens, that I was attempting, when your housemate only sits there with a smile like a Girl Scout cookie . . . Talk about insanity. Imagine, if you can, one alcoholic judging another! *Twitting!* I drink for the big high, I'm not a controlled drinker by nature! My emotions kept zooming, diving, snarling—but nothin' upset him. I began to feel genuinely sick, unreasonable, and insane. Sometimes I'd try to stay off the mescaline or acid—well, *acid,* it was really horse tranquillizer and strychnine. Keep off until evening. But by nine A.M., after a thirty-minute battle with myself, there'd I'd be in the icebox for a tab of acid or mescaline—and there Leo'd be, phoning his Al-Anon sponsor for support. I stayed stoned round the clock for six months on hallucinogens, drinkin' very rarely *after* my first disaster since bein' released. I'd started out one morning for an interview as an editorial assistant—well, music copyist—in a music publishing house. But I must've overconsumed on my morning drink because I came to the following night at one A.M. bein 'let out of a Volkswagen at Gray Moor by a young Al-Anon girl. It was a full moon. I looked around at this moonflooded parkinglot and instantly recognized St. Christopher's Inn and Matt Talbot Hall. 'What the hell we doin' here!' I cried. 'I'm committing you,' Leo says. 'How about askin' *me* first!' I said, bouncing one of my canes away in outrage. I was the kind of hopeless, hopheaded active alcoholic that gives Al-Anon genuine despair, sittin' there in my Nazi helmet and silvermirrored sunglasses at midnight. I'd started out to join the nine-to-five crowd in publishing, to support my habit, and here I was at Gray Moor. The girl, Vicky B., was terribly nervous, locked her doors, backed up to turn around. *'Wait, wait! there's been a mistake!'* But she didn't stop as I beat her roof with my other cane. Really took off! So there we stood on the mountain. I refused to go in. We walked down the mountain to Peekskill. It started raining. When we hit the main highway noone'd give us a ride. We walked eight miles with me on canes and not a cent for drinkin' money. But by morning I was ready to admit to a possible alcohol problem. So I sank back into soft drugs for another six months.

"I conned myself into thinkin' I'd freed myself from my booze addiction—I was the lone wolf of A.A. when I went to Leo's meetings. Well, with my sneer at topmast I liked to shoot down the speaker with a few loud whispers to my neighbors and sigh, 'Ah, I guess I'm just another Ebby T.—the guy who got Bill W. sober, then couldn't stay sober himself.' I found out I could stop but not stay stopped. After about three months I was waylaid by the 3-D image of a cold, sweating, frosty, salty marguerita, which obsessed me for another three months until I bombed out in a Mexican cafe in the Village and downed four of the bitches. Rather than get hooked on tequila again I stocked up on hundred-proof bourbon liqueur and ouzo and other juices I don't remember. By Sunday night I'd run dry and was sittin' at my livingroom desk with my legs full of pins and needles. I'd chewed up two mescaline tabs because the stuff didn't seem t' be reachin' me. Well, actually, the strychnine in the acid'd given me a terrifically overactive heart and I thought the mescaline would help bring the fake acid down to a tolerable noise in my chest. I had some rubbing alcohol for circulation in my legs and, it's the God's truth, I had no intention of drinkin' that burning piss—I just had this drug-fuzz in the throat that fooled me into thinkin' I was Superman. I wet down a dishtowel with alcohol and gave my legs a long rub at the desk, smelling the fumes through my mescaline sedation, and next thing I knew I'd sipped off an ounce like icewater. Rubbing alcohol's one-hundred-forty proof distilled lava. I couldn't believe the pain spreading down my digestive tract startin' with my lips. Couldn't move! Looked at Leo ready to tell 'im goodbye. His face was worse than the rubbing alcohol, a look of horror, of such utter moral revulsion, as if he'd opened a cupboard on a maggotty abortion, that it filtered through the dope, it got to me. I've never been seen so nakedly before or since—by either of us! I was the world's most insensitive brother, a gargoyle of alcohol, Mr. Hyde himself. My face felt overgrown with warts. And it was too late t' do anything about me. *Too late!*—that hurt. Past all reform. He was blue with revulsion! I started cryin' and couldn't stop. *And* my stomach was burning. He walked me to the icebox for some grapefruit juice. Then we sat down to work again. I was a hideous degenerate, okay, but I was happy to be alive after the holes that drink made in my stomach. I sat sniffing back tears, wondering how I could apologize for the meat-grinder I'd put him through year after year. He was no angel! but compared with me he was a howling miracle of sanity. My throat felt like an Egyptian rainpipe. I wrapped the wet towel on my legs and again not thinking lighted a cigarette. My lap turned blue. The towel was on fire. I ripped it off and threw it into the middle of the room. Then I was on fire. My legs were burning! Strangely enough, we jumped up to stomp out the towel and save the apartment before we got around to me—I wasn't feelin' anything anyway, just holdin' my breath hard.

Then my hair went up over my head like a sunrise and I got scared. We rushed as fast as I could hobble to the sink with my canes while he kept beatin' my hair out, and turned on the coldwater tap. Nothin' happened. The goddamn pipe hadn't worked for a week. The hot water came out steaming. But we doused a towel and put me out anyway. Boy, was I ungodly happy—*alive again*—and breathing!

"Well, Leo'd made quite a ruckus through all this fire, and I was ready t' go t' bed for the night, but the fire engines arrived. And firemen burst in. I insisted everything was safe, and resisted the treatment they offered. The ambulance crew wanted to take me to Bellevue but I said I was okay, all I needed was grapefruit juice. I really resisted, I thought they wanted t' lock me up, and I wasn't ready for the flight deck. Finally, I let 'em take me. When we got there the interns in Emergency started picking and digging dead flesh outta me. I had massive third degree burns over ninety-five percent of my body and should've died. They didn't know whether to separate us right then or to wait until my heart stopped. Leo told 'em to wait. The shock of surgery on top of the burn shock *would've* killed me. So Leo saved my life twice in one hour."

Teddy stops, silent, catching his breath as a sigh shudders through him. He grips Leo's shoulder.

"Thanks to him, I've lived the best year of my life. It's been my worst physically, and hard on Leo too. He's been giving skin for my grafts, they've been transplanting skin from my calves, and I'm also bein' used experimentally for a new kind of cultured skin. There's a helluva long way to go yet—"

"—before we take up tennis," Leo says—

"—but sobriety's my wonderdrug. I've listened hard to every word I've heard at this table for the past year. And I've listened with a full heart. When I came in that door, I'll admit, *God* was one word I never wanted t' hear again. But the word burned me! I got my first real sense of healing in this room, listening to you. I got the First Step here! I felt like I had a spear through my lungs the first three months I sat here. I *still* had my reservations and did not want to stop drinking! I was hopin' that someday . . ." Teddy's eyes fill ". . . that I could handle it again! I did *not* have an honest desire to stop drinking. I don't have cirrhosis or wet brain, I have a *lot* of drunks left in me! Please understand that it was not overnight—*I'm strong!*—that I came to believe in the Second Step—*I'm stronger than I've ever been in my life!*—that a Power greater than myself could restore me to sanity. It took an awful lot of talk around this table for me to see that any fond thoughts I might have about the first drink were insane. And one night I felt the Power in this room. Saw it in every face. Heard it in every word. Felt myself getting sane at last. And drew my first sober breath.

"I've put my alky shoulder to the Steps too. I feel more like Scrooge than Atlas, because I'm holdin' back on the Seventh Step. I've worked all the others but I haven't had the generosity to myself to humbly ask Him to remove all my shortcomings. I'd be left naked. My last reservation exposed. Turned at last into that damned goody-goody puritanic A.A. monster I've despised since I first heard of recovery. You know those goody-goodies who've achieved full conversion to the A.A. way of life. Despicable sobersides, like Bill W. and Dr. Bob, who were in here to save their asses, and like me may not really have had another recovery in 'em. For some of us, sitting here is bedrock survival. My next drink is an ounce of spirochetes drawn off a chancre—I better think of it that way. And get my ass into the Seventh Step. I'm no tourist, I'm not here slumming, or sightseeing. I'm here to kill that last teasing reservation that suggests I can take up social drinking, controlled drinking, gracious living, or any of those insidious illusions that insist I can handle it. *I can't handle it*. I'm insane even to consider handling it. What's more important, I don't wanna handle it—I love my sanity!

"I love your sober eyes. I love your hard handshakes. Those powerful, sober hands in mine. You give my life a vibrance I never knew. You gimme your best spirits! You've given me my brother, whose love I mislaid.

"I think bein' a monster of self-willed flopping infantilism is the easiest course life offers. It's an awful lot easier 't be an egodriven unmanageable alcoholic maniac Siamese twin than to be a human being with his feelings and abilities intact and working. For me today a good life lies in the real actions, man to man survival work with this Fellowship. A.A.'s my life, whitehot and wholehearted. I have no place for nostalgia for the bottle."

Teddy holds out his hand to Leo. "I'm quite willing to forget all the joyous drunks we've shared."

"Me too!"

"Thank you," Teddy says.

Clapping, loud, strong.

"Boy!" Jack tells Leo, "you should have *him* for a sponsor."

Leo grimaces. "He's a great brother but as an A.A. he's a goddamn Stalinist."

"I prefer that to his Nazi role."

"For our topic tonight," Teddy says, "I've chosen the Second Step, 'Came to believe that a Power greater than ourselves could restore us to sanity.' The First Step is the only step that mentions alcohol, 'Admitted we were powerless over alcohol—and that our lives had become unmanageable.' The other eleven steps are suggestions toward livin' a sober life once we admit we're hopelessly addicted, that we have a disease. The First Step's not enough to keep us sober, no matter how hard we surrender to it. We bury people every day who knew they had alcoholic cirrhosis and kept right on drinkin'. I was locked into an airtight delusion for twenty years and just sayin' I'm an alcoholic, no matter how fervently I say it, is not gonna keep me sane. I gotta scrape the crap out, get rid of my guilts, remorse, work on my character defects, make amends, strive for daily conscious contact with my Higher Power, attend meetings, meetings, meetings, and give The Program away to alcoholics still out there suffering. I gotta grow. Can't pour my new spirit into that same old alcoholic brain I been usin'. The last thing I wanted when I came in here was *change*. I wanted t' keep all my faults and self-indulgences intact, but learn how to control my drinkin'. I wanted t' go on with the same old disastrous, unmanageable life I'd always lived—my no-rent, romantically irresponsible, ripping off, conning alcoholic life. I couldn't even admit my life was unmanageable—didn't I *intend* t' pay my rent, hadn't I written seven operas—although they were unproduced? My life was perfectly manageable! The sheer regularity by which I produced gallons of burgundy outta thin air *proved* how productive and manageable my life was. It was only my body that was collapsing, not my mind or spirit. But I *have* to change. I been hangin' around this Program over four years, nursing my reservations. By

God, someday I'd hit it big, take up gracious living in Paris or Rome, with wine in a basket or iced in a bucket—no longer the compulsive gallon boozer of the Lower East Side but a sane drinker like the Parisians and Romans. But no amount of money can reverse my alcoholism, my aging metabolism, my deetees, my Zorba the Juicehead insanity after the first drink throws open the madhouse door. I gotta grow up!—this disease is progressive, irreversible, and fatal. I just can never be a gourmet drunk. For me, sobriety is sanity, and I won't be sane while carrying around my old twisted alcoholic attitudes. So for me the Second Step is: Get Sane by Asking for Help. Ronny?"

Ronny. Reclusive, nervous, former scion of a yachting empire, fallen on hard times. Clears his throat, *"Agghm! agghm! Well! The Second Step!* I believe in it! My name's Ronny and I'm an alcoholic. Thank you for your story, Teddy. I'm not a musician—or Siamese twin!—but I identify with your drinking and thoughts on recovery. I'd always hoped to hear you. I haven't got as far into The Steps as I'd like. It's taken me a long time just to get comfortable with *people,* much less The Steps. As a matter of fact, I'm constantly amazed by people who even phone Intergroup for help—I could never do that. I just drank and drank and sank and sank. I'm the world's worst procrastinator and all I can do is the best I can today. Anyway, I don't think the Second Step's anything you *take.* It's something that happens more slowly than that—you 'come to believe' and that's not an act of will. So, I haven't *taken* the Second Step. But I would say that over the past two years the Second Step has taken *me.* Thank you—your horror story was fascinating."

Beautiful Jenny, blackhaired in blackglasses. "My name is Jenny and I'm an alcoholic, but I don't want to talk about the Second Step—I want help! I'm sober two years and don't want to drink. But next week I'm going into the hospital for operations on both eyes. There's a good chance of success. But I can't help it, I walk along the street asking myself, *Why me? Why me?* It's got me so upset I'm nearly as insane as when I was drinking. And I mean it, *Why me! Why me!* Higher Power, *why me?* I just wanna cry, SCREW EVERYTHING!"

The table sits back at knifepoint.

"Don't drink," Teddy says, "and go to meetings. It's a

bitch, your operation. But everyone in this room's had a touch of the lash. You gotta allow yourself more time, one day at a time, for your pain to be lifted. Tell yourself, This too shall pass. And it will! Day by day you'll hurt less and less, if you hit those meetings."

"I go to three meetings a day!" Jenny cries.

Rhea. Middleaged, gray, one blue eye cataracted, a white patch on the other. "I'm Rhea and I'm an alcoholic. I've just gone through one cataract operation and have another coming up. They're painless! I went to sleep and woke up with a patch on my eye. The real trouble wasn't the operation but in my hanging on to past depressions and in projecting a failure in the operation. There's absolutely nothing I could do to influence the skill of my doctors, so my worrying about it was just weakening my body's spirits in bringing about the recuperation I fully expect to have. I could nurse my anger and weak helplessness—but I don't! Instead, I let my good spirits contribute to my recovery. I'm not much on slogans or asking the Higher Power's help yet—I'm pretty new, only six months—but if I could 'come to believe,' that'd be worth all I've gone through. I keep an open mind. I've never believed in anything but myself. It's very hopeful for me to know that the Higher Power might actually bloom in me someday, despite the very little I've done to attract His interest. I don't know if it'll help you—but that's what I do, Jenny. Thank you."

"Thanks, Rhea," Jenny says. "It is helpful. I just had to get some ventilation!"

Dark, brillianteyed, satanic beard, thickcurled devil's brow. "My name's Jack Perch and I'm an alcoholic, heh heh! I'm not much for that Higher Power either, Rhea. I have my own version of the Second Step and it's working for me, so that's fine. My Higher Power's this group. The way The Program works for me is not my telling you how to stop and stay stopped. I haven't had absolute success at stopping, but no one's perfect, ha ha. But I'll tell you what *I* did to get the cork into the bottle, and you draw your own profit and conclusions from my example. How's that hit ya! I gotta be damned careful I don't work *my* number on you. My number and my Higher Power may not be what you need, so why should I waste both our times shoving 'em down your throat and bein' dogmatic? Huh? My main problem isn't the Higher Power but beating my self-pity bag when I think of all my problems. And I have 'em! I talk with Leo and Teddy quite a bit—in fact, they've been over to my house twice when I needed 'em!—but that doesn't solve my case—I'm *still* stuck with my problems and gotta handle 'em on a day to day pragmatic level. But they're gettin' better, folks, they really are! I like something I heard at a meeting this week—this A.A. said, 'Me and my bottle, it was love at first sight. We went steady for awhile, then decided to marry. We were terrifically happy!—went everywhere together. But our life together finally got unmanageable. We had several trial separations. Today we're divorced and I hope it's permanent—at least, A.A. has taught me not to carry the torch.' That's how I feel about self-pity. It's carrying the torch for a whole bag of useless shit. And it's gonna get me sloshing down those double bourbons again—*cut it out, Jack!* So I get to about three meetings a week for my medicine and I hold the door closed when self-pity comes knockin'. So I guess my shoulder's my Higher Power—and meetings. Thanks, Teddy—great meeting! Glad I'm here."

"It sounds an awful lot like you're sayin', I can handle it, Jack."

"No, man, I *can't* handle it! I've proven that to myself many times over. I'm lettin' the meetings handle it now."

"Good luck," Teddy says.

"My name's Nancy and I'm an alcoholic. Teddy, you don't look a bit like Mr. Hyde. I don't have too much to say on the Second Step either, but *wow* is this a great meeting! I didn't even want to come tonight, I was too tired, but as soon as I walked in I felt the room lift me up. For me, sobriety is progressive, I get saner and saner. I can't get complacent and stay away from meetings, not if I can help it. I want more and more sanity. I want to get saner and saner! Some days are a step backward, but not many. It takes a meeting to get my head wired straight. I've heard so much incredible inspiration tonight, I can't really sort it out. I don't know what my Higher Power is, but I sure feel the voltage in this room. *Thanks a lot,* Teddy."

"My name's Manley Appledrink and I'm a sonofabitching alcoholic, or alcoholic sonofabitch—people call me everything, ha ha! Wow. I don't know where my head's at tonight but I been sober three months now and that's a madass miracle for a guy who's been trying to get this Program past the First Step for eight years and finally has the Second and is shooting for the Third and Eleventh, the Higher Power steps where the big spiritual bonanza's waiting for me if I ever make 'em. *I can't drink!* Christ, can I NOT drink. I can't pray either but I'm making big steps in that direction." Manley's a tall, craggy-handsome, wildhaired failed-entomologist turned handicapper and poet. "My father lived to be ninety-five and was still boozing and screwing the broads as if he were sixty—that's the insane power of example I gotta turn off, man, I get this insidious rationalization popping up that I'll die young if I castrate myself and stop drinking. It's *insane!* When will I get over it? I've proven to myself over and over that I may not even make it to forty if I let the bottle run up and jump into my mouth. I drink crazy, a fifth of vodka, whoosh, straight down in twenty minutes, then into a two or three-day blackout that ruins every nerve and bone in my body, I'm paralyzed, I'll never walk again! When I was thirteen I was tending bar in the Catskills and already into cathouses." *Ssssrew!* Manley whistles through his teeth, eyes rolling as he clutches his forehead. "When will I stop killing myself? Like say, today is a fucking miracle, I woke up *sober,* man, that's a miracle in itself, and the whole day was full of miracles, I saw some dying flowers in Central Park and they were miracles, I helped a little old lady through the revolving door at Schrafft's, that was a miracle, and the birds and the clouds and the—I passed a White Rose bar and it stank like shit all the way out to the curb and that was a miracle like the Red Sea jazz. Thank you, Lord! But I get a lot out of Leo and Teddy, I've heard Leo several times and thought he was the most *spiritual* cat I'd ever heard in The Program, until I heard Teddy tonight, he's a powerful mother too. 'Came to believe,' wow, man, are you running with me, Jesus? I sure hope so. I need that Big Hand on my head keeping me pointed at meetings and maybe someday this'll be a totally spiritual Program for me, not just a thousand ways to outwit my sonofabitching narcissicism when the thought of vodka runs up me like a cow's tongue and I wanna reward myself for bein' *me.* That's it from me, I'll cut it short, ha ha—I want to listen tonight! Thanks for an inspiring meeting, Ted."

A tall thin graying black shoves back his chair, *stands,*

very erect, says softly, "My name is Andrew Harvard and I am an alcoholic. This is my first A.A. meeting. I don't understand everything I'm hearing, especially about these Steps, but I'm standing so I'll be heard. One thing has confused me through both these meetings and that is how you people all seem to be putting down ego and uniqueness. It's my understanding that ego is what sets a man apart, gives him individuality, guides him to original work, boosts his determination and purpose, and is, in fact, the specific quality that not only makes him a man but a man among men. I may be wrong but what I think I'm hearing here is that ego should be flattened out, made to conform to bland thinking, and that a man should be plain and tasteless. Perhaps you could help me on this—I *want* to be unique, I was born unique and it is my destiny to be unique."

Teddy looks for a hand. *"Joe."*

"Yes, my name's Joe Owl and I'm an alcoholic—let me try to get a handle on this. What we have is a confusion of terms. Ever since A.A. began, uniqueness has meant something very special and negative. It's not the word's general usage. To an alcoholic unique means 'not fitting in with the group'—say you have a big band with a lot of soloists who are heavy drinkers, you have one big bouquet of prima donnas, right? A lot of booze-inflated egoists who think the whole band is there only to serve them personally. When I came into A.A., unique to me meant that I had more problems than anybody I heard talk in these rooms, and that if all my problems were cut down to the number of their problems, hell, I could stay sober too. As it was, I usually had my second shot at the Regency bar about ten minutes after each meeting. Again, I'm a broker and last year I was wiped out *twice* on The Street, which I thought gave me a unique right to drink. Who on Wall Street gets wiped out twice in one year? The uniqueness of the alcoholic makes him a poor social citizen, often with very exaggerated feelings of inferiority—a kind of unique 'superior inferior.' I thought my *drinking* was unique—I needed six ounces every hour and a half during the day, I needed eight to twelves ounces out of a waterglass while the coffee was perking every morning so that I could hit the office good and lathered and whip into my problems. But the booze shrank all my problems not to lifesize where I could deal with 'em—but to *Lilliput* where they weren't even important. My great goal in life was extremely unique—I thought—I wanted to make a killing that I could reinvest and draw fifty-thousand dollars interest off of annually and retire at the earliest opportunity. I'd live modestly forever on my fifty-thousand by finding the one bar in the world where I could drink absolutely alone and focus entirely upon my nest egg. I tested bars. I'd go into a fancy bar and sit at the very end. If somebody came in and sat three stools away, I left. I wanted to be alone, at the bar, the *whole* bar, dramatically alone, or at a table where I could have my ice and my fifth of scotch with a second fifth riding beside it so I could *feel* the full one whenever I felt like it, and then sit there focusing the full force of my mind on my investment and feel every warm curve and facet of that nest egg. That was my dream. I thought it was unique—and make no mistake about it, *unique means better*. But, of course, every hustling drunk on The Street has this dream!—with the desert isle or some variation—so I wasn't unique. Uniqueness of talent is something else, though, which we have every right and obligation to develop. But that's not the uniqueness we talk about in here. *Our* uniqueness is entirely negative and sets us aside so that we can suffer and suffer and suffer. Does that help?"

"Thank you, it does," Andrew says, half sitting then rising again. "Uh, it's no wonder you were wiped out twice last year, is it?"

The table bursts, laughter heaping, slithering. Joe Owl wipes tears from his cheeks, redfaced, jaw hanging in idiocy.

Laughing, Teddy points to a strangely sweating white-faced man, his high hand trembling for recognition, damp black hair fallen over his forehead, his glasses magnifying utter despair.

"I've—I've only been in A.A. six weeks," the man quavers. "This week my three children were suffocated in their room because of faulty wiring in the bedlamp and m-my wife was electrocuted when she went in to save them. It was the middle of the evening and I was called home by a neighbor from my job at the post office, and when I opened my neighbor's front door my German shepherd ran out howling and was killed by a truck. I didn't know what to do, I was so numb, and I drank a whole quart of vodka straight down. What I want to know is w-w-was this self-pity? And what should I do? I w-w-want to do what's right."

Distant sirens, car horns, silence on the table.

Teddy, shot down. *"Sandy?"*

"Thanks, Teddy. My name's Sandy Sunday and I'm an alcoholic." Sandyblond, goldrims, butteryellow turtleneck, marineblue pants, a long fresh cigar—eternal blue twinkle he tries to veil for the moment, light lilting voice deep-sounding, rich, muscular, honest as vinegar. "I know how this man—what's your name?—I know how Henry feels. My wife and six kids were taken from me by the Lord. That same weekend my partner absconded with all the funds of our tar-and-roofing business and I went bankrupt. My mother's heart failed, and the following Tuesday a blood specialist told me that my oldest remaining son only had two years to live—if he was lucky. It didn't seem possible that all this misery could fall on me in such a short space of time. And, Henry, I've left out half my disasters for that year. My son died two weeks ago. I tried to keep him cheered up with the Higher Power and what I've been gifted with in A.A., and it helped some. I think he was courageous as possible. He held on fine until the last few months. Then his energy was gone, and it wasn't up to me so much—he was on his own. But I was as numb as a man can be and still breathe. I can't tell you what to do, Henry, I can only tell you what I did—and give it to you *straight*."

Leo-Teddy's scalp prickles.

"Don't drink and go to meetings," Sandy says. "You can live through it. I did."

Bob B., a black deacon with black eyepatch, raises his hand and says, "And hold your face up to the Light, even though you don't see a damn thing there *for now*, brother!"

"Amen," Jack McFin says. "It may be a long time coming, Henry, but help is there."

"My German shepherd's just had pups," Sandy tells Henry. "If you'd like one, see me after the meeting."

"I WOULD!" Henry cries.

"Hm!" says Terrible-tempered Tyrone Hargis, shaking his graying head against the feelings washing over him. "Very moving evening indeed, sir. My name's Ty and I am an alcoholic. I noticed something very curious about myself today. All my life I've been given to sudden blind-

ing R-R-RAGES! Uncontrollable, really. That I used as alibis for my, shall we say, tippling, heh heh." He glistens ironically. *"Well!* Somehow during the past four months my reactions to the old *'stimuli'* around the house haven't been the same. Some kind of patience has been seeping into me from The Program. It's nothing *I've* done, believe me, in a conscious sense of working The Program. It's just that, since I've been participating more in the meetings—not in The Steps, mind you,—I've become *seeded* with forbearance. A tinge of new growth, you might say. I'm apparently being defused. Can't explain it rationally, it's just something curious. That's all. Thank you. Good meeting, Ted."

Nelson says, "I think we better throw this meeting open to the floor, Teddy."

"You always leave me hungry for *more!*" Fred S. cries at Tyrone. "I keep hoping you'll really *break loose.*"

"Patience, patience!" Tyrone says, operatic grin flashing warmly.

Fred, very mild schoolteacher-singer, richbrown goatee, vibrant bass, big, handsome, highdomed, eyes browncircled. "My name's Fred Sampson and I'm an alcoholic. This is—*what if I'd missed this night!"* he smacks his dome. "I almost didn't come! What can I say?—if I don't know something about the Second Step after tonight, I'll *never* know!"

"Amen," Jack says.

"I gotta calm down . . . As I sit here I keep saying to myself, I hope it doesn't end, I hope it doesn't end! This meeting's jogging the bejeezus out of me—I feel steamrollered. Does anyone realize that we've been sitting in this room one-hundred-and-thirty-five minutes now and nobody's mentioned his shrink!—not a single word about analysis—a miracle! Thanks Ted, and you Leo, for a terrific evening. These twins and I are from the same small upstate town, King James. We hadn't seen each other for twenty years when we met two years ago in the Fellowship. I'd been bouncing, bouncing, bouncing around A.A., I bounced so often I became an invincible cynic. No belief at all that I'd ever get sober for a year. Now it's eighteen months. Unbelievable—*me,* sober! I'm not too keen yet on defining my Higher Power, but I sure 'came to believe' that I could be restored to sanity. First I had to recognize that I was insane. I had no idea that everything I did was irrational, right down to the way I ate my breakfast, because *I* was irrational. And utterly self-destructive, always in a benign way, breaking my life to pieces matchstick by matchstick. Finally, I'd boxed myself in so badly I was inert. I couldn't lift a pen to correct my students' papers—a complete basket case. Not even booze could get me to do it. I'd sit all night in a rat-filled cellar surrounded by hundreds and hundreds of uncorrected assignments. At last, thank God, I met Leo-Teddy who taught me to separate my problems and my papers into manageable piles, and to accomplish just a little at a time, one day at a time, and not jump into the whole paralyzing rats' nest and try to dig myself out overnight. I 'came to believe' I could do it. *Well,* I'm an English teacher and I'd like to clear up one of our slogans I keep hearing misused. It's Easy Does It and *not* Take It Easy! There's a verb in there, damnit! Easy *Does* It. I like that verb! It means we aren't expected to get the whole Program by Friday night, Henry, or in one big gulp, but a little bit at a time. There's no reason to feel inadequate at not mastering the Twelve Steps instantly—it takes years! It's not a field of information you master and then graduate from with a Ph.D. in Sobriety. It's a Program of inner growth, like Ty's tinge, it's gotta get into your blood in daily doses before it'll ever become meaningful. I think of two pianomovers, one old, one young, moving a grand piano up five flights of narrow stairs trying not to scratch it or break a leg off—it can't be done! It's *impossible!* And the young guy's hustling and huffing, and the old guy says, Hey wait—easy *does* it. And they do it! They get up those stairs one inch at a time and get it up intact. When I really started getting The Program about a year ago I thought everything'd get better right away—I really believed that. And here I am today and here all my life problems sit, big as life—they haven't gone away! *I'm* changed, though, and I can deal with 'em infinitely better. In fact, I *can* deal with 'em and *not* ignore 'em. That's something brand new and I'm eternally grateful to The Program for the help it's given me, one day at a time, one inch at a time. My thanks to all of you for helping me move my grand piano out of the cellar. While I'm at it, let me thank Teddy for saving me from a bungling, useless slip about six months ago. I actually *used* the telephone when what I wanted to do was drink. He took me into a park and sat with me for over two hours until I came to see that what I really needed to do was not drink but get sane, *get active,* not just sit around with my small gains, filled with feeble gratitude to Renewal—but actually start answering phones at Intergroup, give The Steps my real attention, hit lots more meetings and do something about changing my depressed attitudes into a kind of responsible optimism—so that I could cope with myself. I can't say enough, I've said too much—*thanks.*"

"Amen," Jack says.

"Thank *you* for using that phone," Teddy says, feeling a current run down the table to Fred. "That took courage—I know how often I drank when I should've dialed. Just seein' you sit here week after week is one of the joys of my sobriety, especially with both of us from King James."

"That talk gained me six months in The Program!" Fred cries.

Jack asks Leo, "Where were *you* when all this was going on with Fred?"

"*Ahem!* Havin' a 'nervous breakdown.' "

"That's always helpful. When are you gonna get off the rhetoric and get real?"

Leo swallows hard, flushing, nodding.

"Well," Teddy says, "time's nearly up and I dearly want to hear a word from my first sponsor, whose power of example awakened me to spinal A.A. Jack was my Edgar Allan Poe, a great poet drinkin' himself to death and writing farewell suicide notes along the way. Boy, I wanted t' be like him! drink like him, get the alcoholic melancholy flowing in my verses. Alcohol gave such a Keatsian texture and beautiful, mothy, deathwing shine to his lines. One of his four-liners that intoxicated me was—

> After you're gone
> The dusty miller will eat
> The carpet flowers
> In my furnished room.

What melancholy! down there in the darks of alcohol. One day we hadn't seen him for a year and he came to visit us on the Lower East Side. Suddenly there he stood, hair cut, eyes bright as an ocean perch, a new suit, checked vest, tartan tie—and *shining shoes*. He'd joined A.A.—but he didn't give us one word of a pitch for The Program. He told us later that he kept quiet because he thought we were the most hopeless alcoholics he'd ever met. He didn't know anyone else who'd ever sat in one room and written seven unmountable operas about wine! That was our theme, the religion of wine, big fat Baby Dionysus rolling in the grape vats. Those operas are home in the trunk today, and each is worse than the one that went before. Work by work, you can follow the mental and spiritual deterioration. The last three are just burgundy mush and crosseyed rainbow surges. Juice joy! Jack?"

"Thanks, Teddy. My name's Jack McFin and I'm a grateful alcoholic—grateful just to be in this room and grateful that I've got enough brain cells and organs left to be a complete human being. A lot of me's burned away forever—I drank warm piss and thought I was having fun. But I get by and am happy to be productive. And am happy to be at this superb meeting. Teddy's *Now* gives me goosebumps. I attended Renewal one night about two years ago and couldn't believe anyone was really sober, there was so much god-damned analysis in the air, Fred. Well, maybe it was me—A.A. has freed me from the disease of self-analysis, thank God. Tonight I feel that the real urgency of A.A. has come alive at this table—I mean by that *getting active*. Not just sitting on our asses planning to take The Program seriously at some future date in the fog—but instead getting our feet wet *today*. That's The Program: *Now*. Like Teddy, I was in four years before I asked myself, 'Jack, what're you saving yourself for? If you'd put half the effort into staying sober that you once put into drinking, you wouldn't have any problems left.' Boy, I wanted to hang onto my problems! We *all* know about that, don't we? We avoid that Third Step like the plague—turning our will and our lives over to the care of God, as we understand Him. Well, procrastination's the thief of life. Tonight I don't have any problems. I've found what's really important for me, and that's not to postpone what I hope is my spiritual growth. Grow—or rot, Jack! Come in out of the pain or jump the goddamn hell into the river. If I take what most people consider important as unimportant, and if I take what most people consider unimportant as important, I'll start moving along in the wake of the gods.

"So here I am! I don't have anything to say tonight—I feel too good. Boy, that's a welcome change. Sobriety has given me Today. And it's also given me back that time of day I love best that alcoholism robbed me of for twenty years—my mornings. I'm one of those dawn fishermen—there's nothing greater than to feel a big pickerel hit your bait under that smooth silver glimmer just before sunrise. When I was drinking I never had Today. It was always ten years ago—or next month. Nostalgia for the future! Good God, could there be anything more hopeless? Today I have my wife, my son, my home, an acceptable teaching post I enjoy—and the Fellowship"—Jack sighs, speechless—"and, if necessary, I'd give all that up if it meant I had to go back to my shit life outside the Fellowship. This Fellowship of the Sun means more to me than life itself. My life was really never worth living until my disease drove me in here. That's where I am, this Fellowship is life-after-death for me. It took my ten thousand deaths to bring me to this life—I was *resistant!* I didn't know I was being let out of jail when I came into these rooms, that my life-sentence to narcissistic egoism had been commuted. Man, was I fogged up! I can laugh at myself now—I have to, I'd be dead without the humor of A.A. It makes commercial humor utterly bland and purposeless, doesn't it? To laugh with people whose lives are at stake—that's real living. All my humor used to be obscenities, unknowingly directed against myself, of course—I sure was obscene and curseworthy. Boy, I like that phrase Teddy quoted from Bill W. in The Big Book—that's *Alcoholics Anonymous* for those of you who might not have read it yet; it's price is the same as a pint of Jack Daniel's—Bill's phrase 'the path that really goes somewhere.' I'm encouraged to think I'm on it. And I like what he says about—when all other measures failed to lift his self-pity and his resentment toward everything that kept him from drinking—how he'd go to his old hospital in despair and talk with some shaking drunk, pitch him a few words of encouragement, and suddenly be 'amazingly lifted up and set on my feet.' That's how I feel tonight. Amazingly lifted up and set on my feet. Thanks a lot, Teddy, and good luck. I needed this meeting."

"Leo?" Teddy says.

"My name is Leo and I am an alcoholic. I like what you said about Bill's resentment, Jack, and the healing power of carrying the message. Just today I was being foxed by that first drink, and my resentments toward Teddy and Nelson got pretty hot. Kept 'em to myself, of course."

"Hell you did," Teddy says.

"Well, I didn't ventilate 'em," Leo says, "the way I should've. I gotta remember, no matter what happens, who dies or how depressed I feel, any resentment is a resentment against life. Up to a few weeks ago, I thought that if I was dying, on the street or someplace, I'd like to have a last few seconds of consciousness to give thanksgiving for my rebirth as a sane human being, and for bein' granted a good life full of real actions instead of my lifelong fantasies. I was always gonna be rich and famous, a hero like Lindbergh, so I didn't want any kids—I projected they might get kidnapped. I didn't want that vulnerability! So I projected too that when I died I'd hoped really to experience the Now in my last seconds and thank God. That was my idea of fulfillment." Leo's voice deepens; his head floats, and he is barely able to speak. He starts; catches his breath, and starts again. "Today I feel that if I'm sober at the moment of my death, forget the prayers—though I'd like 'em!—*just bein' sober* I'll have hit the ball outta the park. That's my dream today. Thank you. Teddy, you're my rock."

"All I could think of while you were talkin'," Teddy says, "was the time I lay with my cheek in my egg roll while you and Jack ate our whole dinner at the Shanghai. Well, I mentioned sitting on our back porch as kids, and the wonder we felt, and the question the stars asked. And how we pursued the answer to this question. There's no answer in words, of course, only in a feeling of something sacred, pure, and set-apart in our hearts. It's something we keep only by giving it away. This is the answer that the Fellowship has granted me, it's what Mozart felt when he joined the Masons and wrote his greatest music—it's what Louis felt with his Hot Five back in the twenties!—and it's what I feel when I hear Jack or Nelson or any of my friends sound off strong and clear for the sober life. It's like Jack says, the sense of real life you feel when your line strikes in the tide, and that blue is out there struggling, yanking like mad to get away from you, and you start reeling the bastard in, inch by inch. We didn't want our new life, did we? We didn't know we'd have to be cut up, torn to pieces and broiled in the furnace built by Bill W. and Doctor Bob. But—ego-deflation at depth, profound personality change—without these there's no lasting recovery, there's only a long lull between drinks. For me, sobriety is the kingdom, the power and the glory God offers us drunks with both hands, if we can unknot our sleep-tight ego blinders. Alcoholism is the disease that leads from deep darkness into the morning, 'the path that really goes somewhere'—that goes to this very table, *Now*, where I am renewed. God bless your sober eyes!

"Jack, will you lead us?"

"Christ, yes," Jack says, rising, the table rising, Teddy on his canes, Nelson beside him, Leo's arm gripping Teddy as Jack intones boldly with the room, the room thrumming with deep-ribbed prayer, Our Father who art in heaven, Hallowed be thy name. Thy kingdom come. Thy will be done on earth, as it is in heaven. Give us this day our daily bread. And forgive us our trespasses, as we forgive those who trespass against us. And lead us not into temptation, but deliver us from evil: For thine is the kingdom, and the power, and the glory, for ever and ever. Amen.

"Amen," Jack says. "Boy, that should hold 'em for twenty-four hours!"

October 13, 1973
Jerome-Shakespeare avenues
Bronx, New York